Judith Lennox was born in Salisbury, Wiltshire, but spent most of her chidhood in an isolated part of the Hampshire countryside, living in what had formerly been the gamekeeper's cottage of a large country house. After attending a variety of schools, she read English at Lancaster University, and has since worked as a civil servant, an abstracter of scientific reports, and as a pianist for a ballet school. She met her husband, Iain, at Lancaster, they have three sons and now live in Cambridgeshire. Her previous novel, *The Secret Years* is also published by Corgi Books.

Also by Judith Lennox

THE SECRET YEARS

and published by Corgi Books

THE WINTER HOUSE

Judith Lennox

CORGI BOOKS

THE WINTER HOUSE
A CORGI BOOK : 0 552 14332 4

First publication in Great Britain

PRINTING HISTORY
Corgi edition published 1996

Set in 10/11pt Sabon by
Phoenix Typesetting, Ilkley, West Yorkshire

Corgi Books are published by Transworld Publishers Ltd,
61–63 Uxbridge Road, London W5 5SA,
in Australia by Transworld Publishers (Australia) Pty Ltd,
15–25 Helles Avenue, Moorebank, NSW 2170,
and in New Zealand by Transworld Publishers (NZ) Ltd,
3 William Pickering Drive, Albany, Auckland

Printed and bound in Great Britain by
Cox & Wyman Ltd, Reading, Berkshire

THE WINTER HOUSE

PART ONE

–

1918–1930

Chapter One

For the rest of her life she detested the snow. It started to fall before dawn, and by eleven o'clock, when the telegrams arrived, it had blanched the familiar London landscape.

Father and mother were out for the day, so no-one opened the telegrams. They remained on the hall table: menacing, threatening. Yet Robin's routine continued just as it always did. Lessons with Miss Smith in the morning, lunch and rest and then an afternoon walk in the park. By the time she went to bed at half past eight Robin had reassured herself that everything was all right. How could life go on in its usual way if anything had happened to Stevie or to Hugh?

Afterwards, she always wondered what had woken her up. It could not have been her mother's wail of grief – the house was too big, too solid, for her cry to have reached Robin's bedroom. But, suddenly awake, she climbed out of bed and padded silently downstairs in her nightgown. The hall was deserted and dimly lit by a single electric lamp.

'Stevie – Hugh – both of them—' Robin hardly recognized her mother's voice.

'We shall leave for the hospital at dawn, dearest.'

'My sons – my beautiful sons!'

Robin's fingers slid from the handle of the drawing-room door. She walked back down the hallway, into the dining-room and out through the wide French doors that led on to the terrace. She did not stop walking: her small, bare feet tramped through the snow until she reached the bottom of the garden.

Standing amongst the rhododendrons and the remains of old bonfires, she looked back at the house. The snow had stopped falling at last, and the moon was a baleful orange-yellow in a black sky. The house that Robin had known all the seven years of her life was no longer familiar. It had changed utterly, bleached by snow, outlined by bronze light. She had a primitive realization that everything had altered, that winter had pushed its way through the bricks and tiles of the building, casting a frost over those inside.

They told her that though Stevie would never return from Flanders, Hugh would come home when he was well enough. Richard and Daisy Summerhayes left immediately for the field hospital in which Hugh fought for his life, leaving Robin in the care of Miss Smith. Later, the passing of time became marked by Hugh's slow recovery. They lurched constantly between hope and despair. The blackness of the period immediately after the telegrams; the memorial service for Steven, to Robin a muddle of flowers and hymns and tears. Nothing to do with Stevie, her bright and beloved elder brother. Optimism when Hugh took his first steps, and when he came home from hospital. A return to darkness after he suffered his breakdown. Things changed after that second homecoming: the house became tidier, because disorder frightened and disgusted Hugh. Richard Summerhayes abandoned his political ambitions, and his old aspirations for his sons were transferred to his daughter. Robin – not Steven, not Hugh – would go to Cambridge and study Classics as Richard had done. The string of visitors to the Summerhayeses' London home – for the madrigal evenings, the poetry readings, the political debates – was

curtailed, because Hugh could not bear noise. Richard
bought a motor-car in an attempt to entice his son from
the cocooning safety of home. Their noisy, happy life
diminished, becoming careful and quiet.

Yet Hugh did not really recover. His doctor emphasized to Richard and Daisy that what their son needed
above all was peace and quiet. Richard Summerhayes
began to search for another job, and was eventually
offered the position of Head of Classics in a boys' school
in Cambridge. He accepted the post even though it
meant a reduction in salary, because he had seen for
himself the silence and emptiness of the Fens.

The ploughed fields were black, featureless squares.
Grey shadows daubed the dikes and droves. Frost
lingered in the sheltered banks and ruts, and the sun, if
it had risen that day, had vanished.

The motor-car bumped and rattled along the road.
Because the countryside was so flat, Robin
Summerhayes saw the house long before they reached it.
Her resentment deepened as the squat yellow building
enlarged. By the time her father parked the motor-car,
she had to bite her lips together to stop herself speaking.

Her parents' concern was, as always, for Hugh.
Determined not to fuss him, but trying to tell whether
his shattered nerves had survived the journey. Robin
looked up at the house. It was a square box of a building,
with four windows and a front door, like a child's
drawing. Inside, the kitchen, dining-room, drawing-
room, study and lobby branched from the dark, narrow
hallway. Their furniture was already in place, but boxes
containing china, linen, clothes and books cluttered
every surface.

'Your bedroom, Robin,' Daisy Summerhayes said
brightly as she opened an upstairs door.

The room had, like the rest of Blackmere Farm, the
cold, sad look of a house that has been empty too long.

The wallpaper had faded, and none of Robin's familiar furniture seemed to fit properly.

'It needs a coat of paint, of course,' added Daisy, 'and I shall run you up some new curtains. What do you think, darling? It will be lovely, won't it?'

She wanted to shout, It's horrible! I hate it!, but she did not, because of poor Hugh. Mumbling gracelessly, 'It's all right,' Robin ran out of the room.

Blackmere Farm had neither electricity nor town gas nor running water. The scullery shelves were lined with rows of oil lamps, and the single tap in the ceramic sink was fed from the outside well. Throwing open the back door, Robin thought savagely that in saying goodbye to London, the Summerhayes family had said goodbye to civilization.

Outside, she gazed gloomily at the garden, at the wide, overgrown lawn, and at the bedraggled flower-beds. The distant horizon was low and level, the blackness of the fields merging into clouds. Robin ran towards a thin strip of silvery grey. The long grass soaked her shoes and stockings. When she reached the river she paused, looking down through the reeds into clear, dark water. A small voice in her head suggested how lovely it would be to swim here in the summer. Robin disregarded the voice, and thought of London. She had loved the noise and bustle. This house seemed to be marooned in a great, empty desert. No – not a desert, because here everything dripped, or squelched. A marsh, then. When she looked around her, she could see neither another person, nor another building.

Yet that was not quite true. A large wooden hut stood downriver. Robin began to trudge along the bank towards it.

The roofed verandah of the hut jutted over the water, where the river had gathered in a deep circular pool, studded with reeds. Robin climbed onto the verandah. Ivy wreathed around the rails, twisting and turning along the lapped wooden planks, curtaining the window. Rubbing at the dusty glass with her sleeve, she peered inside. Then she turned the handle of the door. Rather to her surprise it opened, with a creaking and tearing of ivy tendrils. Cobwebs festooned the doorway, clinging stickily to Robin's hair as she stepped inside. Something small and dark scuttled across the floor.

She had thought it a summerhouse, but she knew instantly that it was not. There was an iron stove in the centre of the room: Robin, kneeling in front of it, opened the rusty door and a runnel of ash trickled onto her lap. Summerhouses did not have coal stoves.

The wall behind the stove was lined with bookshelves. A fly-spotted mirror, framed with large, flat shells, hung on another wall. Robin, looking into it, had the fanciful notion that a different face might look back at her, the face of the person who had slept in the iron bed that stood against the wall, who had warmed herself with the wood-burning stove. But she saw only her own reflection – dark brown eyes, light brown hair, a grey smudge of cobweb along one cheekbone. Sitting on a corner of the bedstead, Robin pulled her jumper over her knees and propped her chin on her hands. She heard in the distance her father's voice, and Hugh's, and her thoughts were dragged back to that awful day in 1918. Six years ago now, but she still remembered it with perfect, awful clarity. The day they had received the telegrams. So much had grown from then: both Richard Summerhayes's and Robin's pacifism, and this exile. Her anger ebbed and, hearing footsteps outside, she rubbed her eyes on her sleeve.

'Here you are, Rob.' Hugh peered round the door. 'I say – what a frightful hole.'

Hugh was a foot taller than Robin, his wavy hair blonder, his hazel eyes deepset in a thin, high-cheekboned, eagle-nosed face.

'I'd like it to be mine.'

Hugh looked dubious. He glanced at the stove, the bed, the verandah.

'This must have been built for a consumptive. She'd have lived out here all year long, poor thing.'

Robin noticed that Hugh, like herself, assumed the former occupant of the hut to be female. The mirror, perhaps.

'It's a winter house, isn't it, Hugh? Not a summer-house.'

Hugh grinned, but he looked tired and pale. 'It should be dismantled and burnt, Robin. After all . . . tuberculosis . . .'

'I'll clean it. I'll scrub every inch of it with disinfectant!'

One of the tiny muscles beside Hugh's eye was twitching. Robin took his hand and led him back out onto the verandah.

'Look,' she said softly.

The world was laid out before them. Frost had fringed the reeds, making tiny pennants of every seed-head. Sun gleamed through the thinning grey clouds, and the dark expanse of water beyond the verandah reflected reeds, sun and sky like a looking-glass.

'In the summer,' she said, 'we shall have a boat. We shall sail for ever. We shall lose ourselves.'

Hugh looked down at his sister and smiled.

Exiled, she collected things, arranging them in the winter house. Baskets of pale shells; jam jars bristling with long tail feathers; a snake's shed skin, brittle and dry; a rabbit's skull, all papery white bone. She collected people too, her curiosity, her need to know how other people passed their lives often earning her Daisy's reprimands. It's rude to stare, Robin. Such questions! The woman who came to clean, the man who collected withies from the river and made them into eel traps, the pedlar who, shell-shocked and one-legged, ambled from village to village selling pegs and matches, she talked to them endlessly.

And Helen and Maia. Robin met Maia Read in her first term at school, and Helen Ferguson the following summer, when she was cycling in the Fens. Maia was dark, beautiful, elegant even in her dreadful school gymslip. Sharp-witted and quietly subversive, she was not remotely interested in the politics that was Robin's passion. Helen lived in the neighbouring hamlet of Thorpe Fen. When Robin first saw her, walking from the bus stop to her home, she was dressed in a white frock, white gloves and the sort of hat Robin vaguely remembered her mother wearing before the War. Helen said politely, 'You must attend St Luke's, Miss Summerhayes. It's nearer to Blackmere, I suppose.' Robin, wheeling her bicycle along the rutted drove, declared, 'We don't go to church. We're agnostics. Religion's only a means of keeping social order, you know,' just as Helen, red-faced, reached a large, yellow-bricked house and pushed open a gate lettered with the words *The Rectory*.

Somehow, against the odds, the friendship survived and prospered. Maia and Helen were absorbed into the busy fabric of the Summerhayes household. A compensation, Robin often thought, for the awfulness of the Fens.

In the warm spring of 1928 they lounged on cushions on the verandah of the winter house, and looked forward to freedom.

'Only one more school term,' said Robin. Leaning against the wall she clasped her arms round her knees and chewed a stray lock of hair. 'We'll be grown up. No more lacrosse. No more ridiculous rules and regulations.'

'I shall marry a rich man,' said Maia. 'I shall live in an enormous house with a dozen servants. My wardrobe shall be vast – Vionnet, Fortuny, Chanel . . .' Maia's light blue eyes were half-closed, her exquisite profile emphasized by the shadows and the sunlight. 'Men shall fall in love with me all the time.'

'They do already,' Robin said tartly. It was disconcerting to walk through Cambridge with Maia: heads turned, delivery boys fell off their bicycles. Shading her eyes, she squinted at the water. 'I'm going to get my bathing costume. I'm sure it's warm enough.'

She darted through the garden, and into the farm-house. In her bedroom, Robin threw off her clothes and pulled on her school bathing costume, black and baggy with 'R. Summerhayes' embroidered across its back. As she ran back across the lawn, Helen's voice floated over to her from the verandah.

'I'd like a little house of my own. Nothing grand. And children, of course.'

'I shall never have children.' Maia had unpeeled her stockings, and was letting the sun toast her bare legs. 'I can't bear them.'

'Daddy says we are to let go of Mrs Lunt. She has a habit. I think Daddy would be quite glad if she took the pledge, even though it's rather low church.' Helen's voice was subdued. Robin ran up the wooden steps, two at a time. 'Daddy says I'm old enough now to run the house. After all, I'm eighteen now.'

'But you can't just . . .' Robin, staring at her, was horrified. 'I mean . . . dusting the ornaments . . . running bazaars and all that. You couldn't, Helen. I couldn't. I'd rather die.'

'It won't be for ever. Just until we sort ourselves out. And I quite like doing the letters and things. Daddy said he might buy me a typewriter.'

'We mustn't lose touch.' Robin ducked under the wooden rail of the verandah, and stood poised for a moment above the dark, glassy water. 'We must promise to celebrate together the important milestones of a woman's life.'

She released her grip and dived into the water. The cold almost took her breath away, and when she opened her eyes she could see the dim green shimmering light above her. Breaking the surface of the water, she emerged into the sunlight and shook her head, sending out a crystal circlet of droplets.

Maia said, 'We must celebrate our first jobs . . .'

'Marriage.'

'I don't plan to marry.' Robin, treading water, tossed back her wet hair.

'Losing our virginity, then,' said Maia, grinning. She pulled her pinafore dress over her head, and draped it over the verandah rail.

'*Maia*,' whispered Helen, watching her. 'You can't—'

'Can't I?' Maia unbuttoned her blouse and, folding it neatly, placed it beside her dress. She stood on the verandah, tall and long-legged, wearing only her camiknickers.

'You do plan to lose your virginity, don't you, Robin?'

Helen looked away, pink and embarrassed. Robin began to swim backstroke across the pond.

'I expect so. If I can find a man who won't expect me to wash his shirts and sew on his buttons just because he's sweet on me.'

Maia's dive was clean and curving, hardly breaking the surface of the water. She swam towards Robin. 'I don't think any man would expect that of you, Robin, darling.' She flicked the loose button that dangled from the shoulder of Robin's complicated bathing garment.

'Well then. Losing our virginity. And finding our first job. What else?'

'Travelling abroad,' said Helen, from the verandah. 'I'd love to travel. I've never been further than Cambridge.'

Robin felt a rush of excitement mixed with frustration. The world waited for her, and yet she had to endure years more Latin and Greek.

'What about you, Robin? If you don't mean to marry?'

'Girton, I suppose.' When her father had told her that she had passed the scholarship examination, she had felt gloomy rather than elated. Robin began to swim around the perimeter of the pond. Fleeting images tumbled through her mind: the squalid cottages of the agricultural workers in the Fens; the triumphal wireless reports at the end of the General Strike; the awareness, every time she walked through Cambridge, of the many girls younger than she who worked at dreary jobs, for low wages, for long hours. Anger still often burned in her along with excitement and frustration.

'Robin means to change the world, don't you, Robin?'

Maia's voice was sarcastic. But Robin, pausing beneath the verandah, only shrugged and looked up.

'Come in, won't you, Helen? I'll teach you to swim.'

Helen shook her head. Framed by golden ringlets and a wide-brimmed straw hat, her expression mingled apprehension and longing.

'I might paddle, though.' She darted into the winter house, and came out a few minutes later, bare-footed. Cautiously, her frothy white skirts and petticoats held out of the way, Helen perched on the edge of the verandah, and dipped her feet into the water. She gasped.

'It's so cold! How do you bear it?'

Hugh was walking across the lawn towards them. Robin waved and called out. Helen, blushing, drew her toes out of the water and pulled down her skirt, but Maia, her wet camisole clinging to the slender outline of her body, swam over to him and smiled.

'Are you coming in, darling Hugh?'

He grinned, looking down at her. 'Certainly not. You are quite insane. It's only April – you will turn to ice.'

His voice drifted over to Robin, duck-diving into the deepest part of the pond. She took a deep breath and plunged again, down through water and weeds, until her cold, numbed fingers touched something half-buried in the sandy bottom.

Soaring upwards, she broke free of the water, and took a great gulp of air. Her fingers had gone white, her nails blue, but in the palm of her hand lay a freshwater mussel, just like the ones round the mirror in the winter house.

She heard Hugh say, 'I'll drive you home, shall I, Helen? And Maia – you'll stay to dinner, won't you?'

Later, in Daisy's bedroom, Robin pulled off her skirt and blouse and dropped them to the floor. The new frock slid over her head, dark brown velvet, the same colour as her eyes. She glanced reluctantly in the mirror. The dress was beautiful: drop-waisted, knee-length, trimmed at the neck and sleeves with cream-coloured lace.

'Don't you like it?'

'It's lovely.' Robin's expression was despairing. 'It's not the dress – it's me. I wish I was tall, like Maia – or I had a bosom, like Helen. *Look* at me. Short and skinny, with mousy hair.'

Daisy had a mouthful of pins. Kneeling on the floor, she began to turn up the hem.

'Have I grown, d'you think?'

Daisy shook her head. Robin sighed. Daisy mumbled, 'When you leave school, you can wear heels.'

There was the sound of a motor-car drawing up outside. Robin pulled aside the curtain, and watched Hugh limp from the car to the house, several of the weekend's house-guests following him.

'Hugh has told Richard that he'd like to do some private tutoring.'

'Oh . . .' Robin, smiling broadly, hugged Daisy.

Daisy returned to the pins. 'If only he could meet a nice girl.'

'I think he should marry Helen. They get on awfully well. And Helen's only interested in getting married and having babies.'

'You say that, my dear Robin, as though marriage and motherhood were inappropriate ambitions for a woman.'

'Marriage,' said Robin, contemptuously. 'Shopping and sewing and cooking. Losing your independence. Having your money doled out to you by your husband, as though you were a child or a servant.'

Her face reddened as she pulled the dress off over her head. Even her father, a Fabian Socialist and a staunch supporter of women's rights, gave Daisy a sum of money each week with which to run the household, and a monthly allowance to clothe herself. Daisy's back was turned; Robin was guiltily aware of tactlessness.

19

There were ten for dinner that night: the four Summerhayeses; Maia; the artist Merlin Sedburgh; Hugh's old schoolfriend, Philip Shaw; Ted and Mary Warburton, from the Cambridge Social Democratic Federation; and Persia Mortimer, who had, a long time ago, been Daisy's bridesmaid. Persia dripped beads and Indian scarves and startling head-dresses. Merlin (Robin could not remember not knowing Merlin) loathed Persia, and, being Merlin, did not trouble to hide it. It amused Robin that Persia always remained blithely ignorant of his dislike.

'Landscapes,' said Persia, over pudding, 'I hear you've turned to landscapes, Merlin darling.'

Merlin grunted and stared at Maia. He had been staring at Maia all evening.

'Landscape permits such variety, don't you agree? And one cannot exploit a landscape.'

Merlin, lighting a cigarette, blinked. He was a large man, his greying dark hair shaggily cut, his jackets often through at the elbows. Daisy patched his clothes, and fed him. Daisy was the only person he was never rude to.

'Exploit?' repeated Merlin, turning to Persia.

'Well, it's a kind of prostitution, isn't it?' Persia removed her trailing sleeve from the trifle.

The corners of Richard Summerhayes's mouth twitched. 'Perhaps Persia is referring to your latest exhibition, Merlin.'

Richard, Daisy and Robin had travelled to London to view Merlin's new work. The exhibition had been called 'Nudes in an Attic', and had featured the same model, in a variety of poses, against the background of Merlin's large but gloomy attic.

'Actually,' said Persia, 'I meant anything figurative. Portraits . . . family groups . . . nudes, of course. They are all intrusive. They all trespass upon the soul. Which is why I prefer my little abstracts.'

Persia made huge fabric collages, immensely popular with certain of the Bloomsbury set.

Maia said, 'So if I were to model for Merlin, for

instance . . . then you would consider that I was prostituting myself?'

Persia touched Maia's hand. 'Metaphorically, darling, yes.'

Merlin snorted.

'But if I *chose* to . . .'

'Aha!' interrupted Richard gleefully. 'Good point, Maia. Free will . . .'

'It would rather depend, don't you think, Richard, on whether Mr Sedburgh were to pay Miss Read for her services as a model.'

'The exchange of labour for money dignifies the relationship, of course, Ted.'

'Pay her, and she *isn't* a bloody tart, you mean?'

'Mr Sedburgh!' Philip Shaw, Hugh's friend, was shocked. 'There are ladies present!'

He was referring, Robin realized, to Maia. Maia, who, in her white blouse and navy skirt, looked serene, untouchable, pure.

'Coffee,' said Daisy firmly, and swept the pudding things away.

They smoked and drank coffee in the drawing-room. Richard Summerhayes disapproved of the customary separation of the sexes after dinner. There weren't enough armchairs to go round, so Philip Shaw crouched adoringly at Maia's feet, and Robin perched on the windowsill.

'Donald is arranging this year's programme, Richard,' said Ted Warburton. 'What date can he pencil you in to introduce the meeting?'

Richard Summerhayes frowned. 'Oh – autumn, preferably, Ted. Examinations seem to consume so much of the summer.'

'And the topic?'

'The League of Nations, perhaps . . . or . . . let me see . . . the consequences of the Russian Revolution.'

Robin touched her father's sleeve. 'The Russian Revolution, please, Pa.' She had a dim memory of the muted celebrations in the Summerhayes household at

21

the Socialist Revolution of 1917. Muted, because Hugh had just sailed with his battalion for France.

'And I believe that Mary has the date of the jumble sale.'

'The tenth of June, Daisy.'

'So soon? We shall have to be busy, won't we, Robin?'

'Perhaps Miss Summerhayes has better things to do,' said Ted Warburton archly. 'A young man . . . ?'

Robin scowled. Richard Summerhayes said, 'Robin is to start at Girton College this October, Ted. She will read Classics.' The pride in Richard's voice was clearly audible. Robin's scowl deepened, and she moved out of earshot.

Daisy, following her, whispered, 'I know Ted teases, Robin, but —'

'It's not *that*. It's just that . . .' The more she thought about it, the more she loathed the prospect of studying Classics for the next three years. She imagined Girton College as much like her school: hidebound, claustrophobic, a hotbed of intense friendships and equally overheated jealousies and resentments.

But she couldn't possibly voice the true cause of her sudden ill-humour. Instead, Robin muttered, 'It's always the same. The men go on the committees and make the speeches, and the women run the jumble sales and make the tea!'

'I should loathe public speaking, Robin dear,' said Daisy gently. 'And your father really hasn't time to go around collecting sackfuls of awful holey jumpers.'

'You've only time because you haven't a career. If you had a job, like Pa, then you wouldn't have time.'

'Then it's as well that I don't,' answered Daisy lightly. 'If we didn't hold jumble sales and suppers, then we couldn't raise the funds to pay for the hall. And then no-one would be able to speak.'

Daisy's logic was, as usual, unanswerable. Robin slammed delicate bone china cups onto a tray and stomped off into the kitchen. Then she slipped out of the scullery and ran across the moonlit lawn, towards the winter house.

Standing on the verandah, her elbows resting on the balcony, her temper began to subside. Moonlight washed the river and the pond in which they had swum that afternoon and painted the distant Fens with silver. The sound of singing issued from the open drawing-room window: *Since first I saw your face, I vowed, to honour and renown you . . .*

She heard footsteps, and turned her head to see Merlin striding across the lawn towards her. The red tip of his cigarette glowed in the darkness.

'I had to get away from that woman. And I never could tolerate madrigals. I hope you don't mind me interrupting your adolescent broodings, Robin.'

She giggled. He stood beside her on the verandah, their elbows touching.

'Cigarette?'

She had never smoked before, but she took one, hoping to make an impression of casual sophistication. Merlin lit it for her from the tip of his own; Robin inhaled, and choked.

'First one? Chuck it in the river if you don't want it.'

The song had altered. Maia was singing the madrigal that Richard had arranged for her as a solo: 'The Silver Swan', a glacial and unearthly sound, trailed through the chill night air.

Robin, catching a glimpse of Merlin's face, said crossly, 'I suppose you're in love with her too!'

He looked down at her. 'Not at all. She is made entirely of ice. Listen to her. It's inhuman. Passionless.'

There was a silence as they listened to the second verse of the song. Then he added, 'I'd like to paint Maia, of course. But I'd rather go to bed with you.'

Robin gave an embarrassed little gasp. Merlin said, amused, 'I won't, of course. I've been in love with Daisy for years, after all, and it would seem rather incestuous.

And besides, you probably think of me as a repulsive old uncle.'

She giggled again, and immediately wanted to kick herself for sounding like a schoolgirl. Then she shook her head.

'No? Ah well—'

He bent his head and kissed her. His lips were dry and hard, and his fingers threaded through her short, fine hair. Then he let her go.

'Another first? My, my, little Robin.' He studied her face. 'Do forgive me. Too much to drink. If it's any consolation, there will be others and better. I rather envy them.'

A sailor returning from his ship in Liverpool to his mother in Trumpington struck up a conversation with Maia as she travelled home by train one Sunday after visiting Robin. Mutely, she played the game she always played: one point if he spoke to her, two if he offered to carry her schoolbag, three if he bought her a cup of tea, and a resounding five if he asked her to the pictures. Ten for a kiss, and she always laughed when she thought what she should score for a proposal: her suitor on his knees in the grubby third class carriage – a triumph, surely, for any girl on a short train journey.

She'd never had a proposal; had never, in fact, scored more than two. Not because they hadn't offered, but because Maia always refused the cups of tea, the invitations to the pictures, the rendezvous in the park. In a third class carriage, Maia didn't meet the sort of man she wanted to meet.

She walked from the station to her home in Hills Road. She could hear her parents' raised voices as she fitted the key in the lock. The tenor of their voices – sometimes hysterical, sometimes sullen – once had the power to make her stomach squeeze, to make her hide in bed, her pillow over her head, her fingers in her ears. But you got used to anything in time.

Mr and Mrs Read were in the drawing-room. The

door was open, and they must have seen her walk past, but they made no acknowledgement. Angry words followed Maia as she climbed the stairs. *You don't listen to a word I say . . . it's like talking to a brick wall . . . you don't care a fig for my happiness . . .* Clichéd accusations: the quarrel was well under way, then, its specific cause long past. There remained only the insults, the tears, the sulks. It would be forgotten by dinner-time.

Maia closed her bedroom door behind her. As she took her sewing box from the cupboard she tried to ignore the knowledge that such words were never forgotten: they rankled, they wore away, they destroyed. She did not need to know the reason for the quarrel. Her parents always quarrelled over the same thing. Money, always money. Lydia Read spent, while Jordan Read's income from his investments declined. There was an air of neglect about the Read household: the upstairs rooms were no longer cleaned regularly, and dinner, unless they had guests, had become plainer and less plentiful. It alarmed Maia to witness the slow, relentless reduction in their fortunes in the cobwebs decking the ceilings of the maids' rooms in the attic (since the War the Reads had only one live-in maid), and in many small, unpleasant economies – they no longer took a daily newspaper, they ate mutton instead of beef, and only lit a drawing-room fire when there were guests. But nothing that showed, thought Maia, who had become accustomed to leading two lives. The one that showed, and the one that didn't.

Maia took off her stockings and threaded her needle. Then she began to darn: minute, careful stitches. She was darning darns, she reflected, her lovely mouth twisted in a grimace.

At tea the following afternoon, the maid, Sally, spilt the milk. When she had gone, leaving a great, dark stain on the carpet, Lydia Read said, 'We shall have to let her go, Jordan. She is a halfwit.'

'We shall have to let her go,' agreed Jordan Read, 'but not because she is a halfwit.'

Maia glanced quickly at her father.

'We shall have to let her go,' repeated Jordan, 'because we can no longer afford to pay her.'

'Don't be ridiculous. We pay the girl what – sixteen pounds a year?'

Jordan Read did not reply, but rose from his chair and left the room. Lydia poured a second cup of tea. Her lips and nostrils were white, and her eyes, the same light, sapphire blue as Maia's, had narrowed.

Returning to the drawing-room, Jordan Read dropped a sheaf of papers into Lydia's lap.

'Read them, Lydia. Then you will see, as I do, that not only can we no longer afford a maid, we also cannot afford to pay your dressmaking bills, or Maia's school fees, or even the butcher's bills.'

Maia half stood up, but her mother glared at her and hissed, 'Tea-time, Maia! Your manners!' Maia's legs wobbled, and she sank back into her chair.

One of the papers fell from Lydia's lap and skated across the floor. Maia stared at it, fascinated. It was a bank statement. The figures at the end of the columns, each marked in red, frightened her.

Lydia said furiously, 'You know I can't make head nor tail of figures.'

I can, thought Maia. Top of the class at arithmetic every term. If she had picked up the scattered papers and scanned the figures, she would have known exactly what they meant. They meant insecurity and deprivation, and an end to the sort of future she had always planned for herself.

'I'm rotten at figures myself, Lydia. That's why we're in this spot.'

Briefly, Maia almost sympathized with her mother. Jordan Read's voice was calm, almost jovial, as though he had lost a game of bridge, or been bowled out for a duck at cricket.

'Had a letter from the bank today. Explained things. We're done for. Stumped. In a spot, as I said.'

Lydia, white with fury, stared at him. 'In a *spot* . . .'

'A spot . . . a hole . . . up a gum tree. Yes, my dear. Whatever you wish to call it.'

Lydia said softly, 'And what do you propose to do about this *spot*, Jordan?'

'Dashed if I know. Camp out on Midsummer Common? Shoot m'self, perhaps?'

Maia locked her hands together so that they did not shake. Lydia had not yet poured the third cup of tea. Instead, there was genuine fear in her voice as she whispered, 'We will lose the house?'

Jordan nodded. 'There's two damned mortgages on it already, and the bank won't let me have a third.'

For the first time Maia spoke. 'But your investments, Daddy. Your stocks and shares . . . ?'

Jordan twisted the tips of his moustache. 'Bought the wrong stuff, poppet. Never had an eye for that sort of thing. The mines lost a packet during the strike . . . and who wants fancy china and glassware when you can buy much the same sort of thing from Woolworth's for a fraction of the price?'

'China? Mines? What have they to do with anything?' Lydia's voice rose in a shriek. 'Are you telling me that I will be thrown out of my own home, Jordan?'

'That's about the gist of it. I dare say we'll find a little place to rent.'

Lydia's face was twisted and ugly. 'I'd rather die!'

For a moment husband and wife stared at each other. Maia looked away, hating to see the expression in their eyes. But she could still hear.

'If you seriously think that I will leave my own home to live in some dreadful little slum—'

'It isn't your home, Lydia. It's the bank's home. Even I understand that.'

'You are a fool, Jordan, a fool.'

'I've never disputed that. But at least I'm not an adulterer.'

A gasp. 'How *dare* you—'

'I may be a fool with money, Lydia, but I am not *that* sort of fool.'

'Lionel is a *man*.'

They had, Maia knew, completely forgotten that she was there. Earlier, she had been required as an audience. Maia rose from her chair, and walked out of the room and up the stairs.

And yet, even now, that other life, the second life, persisted. Her white chiffon dress was laid out on the bed, a reminder that there would be company tonight at dinner. Though she shivered, though she felt slightly sick, Maia nevertheless washed and dressed and brushed her hair. She wondered whether tonight, at last, the façade would be broken. Whether the two lives would merge into one. She imagined herself saying to the gentleman seated next to her, 'Mother's having a love affair with the chairman of the tennis club, and Daddy's to be declared bankrupt.' Would anything change? Or would Sally merely continue to serve the charlotte russe and the guest mutter some polite response? Maia began to laugh, and then had to squeeze her fists against her eyes to stop herself crying. When she looked in the mirror she saw that her nose was only a little red; she would use some of her mother's powder.

Yet dinner, transformed when the Reads had company, was a gracious and elegant occasion. Jordan Read was courteous, and Lydia Read was charming, and Maia herself sparkled. The eyes of the two male guests, Mama's Cousin Sidney, and Mr Merchant, who owned a shop in Cambridge, followed her everywhere. If they had been on a train, Maia thought, wanting to laugh again, how many points would she have scored?

When they had gone and Maia was back in her room, her uncertain future yawned before her. She imagined herself serving in a dress shop, or teaching mathematics in some dreary girls' school. Her mother would leave, she knew that now, and her father . . . she could not think what would become of her father. Though she had known for a long time that nothing was safe, she saw that safety, like everything else, was comparative. Though school bored her, she dreaded being forced to leave it. Though this house was shabby, there were many shabbier. If her parents parted, with which one would she live?

She would have nothing, Maia thought drearily. She peeled off her dress, her stockings, her underclothes. As she hung her dress in the wardrobe, she caught sight of her reflection in the mirror. The long white limbs, the small, high breasts, the flat stomach. And her face: Cupid's bow lips, short dark hair, blue eyes.

She remembered then that she did have something. Maia stood for a while, staring at her reflection, knowing that she, unlike her father, would invest her fortune wisely.

Over the next few weeks, Lydia and Jordan Read led separate lives. They never dined together, and rarely spoke to each other. Lydia was out a great deal; Jordan kept to his study. Maia had absolutely no idea how he spent the time.

Maia left school at half term. She began to work for five mornings a week as a governess to two little girls. The girls were nice enough, but the job bored Maia, who had never been interested in children. It passed the time, though. She sensed that something awful, something unstoppable, was going to happen. She saved half her wages, and spent the rest on clothes, knowing that at all costs she must not look poor or defeated. On two evenings a week she went to an accountancy class, redis-covering her aptitude for figures. She could not quite see herself working as a bookkeeper, though. The word conjured up for Maia horn-rimmed spectacles and ill-fitting tweed suits.

She was sewing in the drawing-room when the front doorbell rang. It was a Wednesday afternoon, and her head still jangled with long division and irregular French verbs. Because of the warm August weather, Maia had partially pulled down the drawing-room blinds. Sunlight flickered on the green and cream striped walls, and on the polished wooden floor.

Sally didn't answer the door, so Maia went. Lionel Cummings, the chairman of Mama's tennis club, was waiting outside. He was fortyish, slightly overweight, moustached. He wore a striped blazer, white flannels and carried a straw boater in his hand.

Maia left him to wait in the drawing-room while she fetched her mother. Her parents were in the garden, together for once, and she saw the look on her father's face when she announced the name of their visitor. Just then, she hated her mother, an intense ache of hatred that made her run back over the grass to the terrace as quickly as possible.

Lionel Cummings stood up when Maia returned to the drawing-room.

'Mother's just powdering her nose. You'll have to put up with my company for a few minutes, Mr Cummings.'

He twirled the tips of his ridiculous moustache with his fingers. 'Delighted to, Miss Read. A pleasure.'

She hated him too, for the pitiless contempt of her father his coming here showed. She wanted to punish her mother for making her father suffer, and she wanted to humiliate this stupid, shallow man for aiding the destruction of her fragile family.

Maia smiled her best smile. 'Such a hot day, Mr Cummings! Shall I fetch you a cold drink?'

He shook his head, so she sat down and patted the sofa beside her. 'Do sit down, Mr Cummings. I watched you play at the club the other night. Such a marvellous forehand. My forehand is simply frightful.'

She had hooked him, she knew. It was so easy. You just looked them in the eye, and smiled, and made them feel big and strong and competent. Lionel Cummings was a fool.

'I could give you a few lessons, Miss Read.'

'That would be thrilling, Mr Cummings! Only I work in the mornings now, you know, and I'm too tired to walk to the club in the afternoon.'

'Poor little lady. Shouldn't fag yourself to death, y'know, pretty little thing like you.'

His thigh was touching hers, and she could smell whisky and tobacco on his breath. Hiding her disgust, Maia stood up.

'Perhaps you could show me now, Mr Cummings.'

'Lionel. You must call me Lionel.'

'Lionel,' Maia simpered.

He had one arm around her and was holding her wrist with his free hand when Lydia came into the room. A small exhalation of breath darted from Mrs Read's lips, and her eyes darkened. Lionel Cummings, embarrassed, let Maia go.

Maia felt powerful, vengeful. 'Mr Cummings was just helping me to improve my forehand, Mummy,' she explained, and sat down.

She took a perverse, contemptuous pleasure in remaining in the room, an unwanted audience to their stilted conversation. Whenever Lionel Cummings was not looking, Lydia Read glanced across to her daughter, raising her eyebrows, looking meaningfully at the door. But Maia, twitching angrily on the edge of the sofa, her fingers pressed against her mouth, obstinately remained seated.

Eventually Lydia said sweetly, 'Haven't you preparation to do, Maia? And I thought you were going to help Sally with the puddings.'

'I've all my lessons worked out for the week.' Maia crossed her long legs, letting her skirt ride up to her knees. Lionel Cummings's eyes were distended. 'And you know I'm no earthly good at cooking, Mummy.'

It was then that they all heard the sound. A short, loud report that made the ornaments on the mantelpiece and the glass in the cupboard rattle.

Lydia whispered, 'Oh my God,' and ran out of the room. Maia rose to her feet, but did not yet follow Lydia.

In the brief moment between the gunshot and her mother's scream, she was overcome by such an intense mixture of fear and dread and guilt that the green and cream striped walls darkened to black, and the bands of bright sunlight on the floor narrowed to a single small pinpoint of light. The heat, the darkness of the room, the exhilaration of youth and sex welded together with the shock of sudden death, intermingling, so that she could not afterwards tell them apart. When, at last, the darkness cleared, she was lying crumpled on the floor, and the room was empty, and her mother's screams were echoing through the house.

Everything began to crumble, then. The days lost their structure, jostling together mornings, afternoons and evenings so that Maia often lay wide awake through the night, or fell asleep suddenly and without warning during the day. Friends and relations came to the house, offering their condolences to Maia and her mother, sitting in the drawing-room. But sometimes she could not remember the names of the people that she spoke to, and always, through the hushed tactful words she could hear another voice. Her father's. *Dashed if I know what to do. Shoot m'self, perhaps?*

Yet the inquest passed a verdict of accidental death. Jordan Read had been cleaning the guns he used for shooting wildfowl, and there had been an accident. Distracted by worries about money, he had made a foolish and fatal error. Alone with her daughter for a moment on that first awful afternoon, Lydia Read had hissed to Maia, 'Don't tell anyone what he said! Don't!' Maia had known instantly to what her mother referred. She had nodded her head, hypnotized by the bright icy blueness of her mother's eyes. Yet she had never had any intention of repeating to anyone – relatives, police or coroner's court – her father's words. A muddled memory of the fate of those who had taken their own life haunted her: they were to be buried outside holy ground, or at crossroads so that their souls could not wander. She was overwhelmed by shame and desolation. That he should choose to wound his family in such a way. That he should think so little of his daughter's pain. When the coroner asked Maia, under oath, whether her father had ever given any indication that he might take his own life, she gave a calm and definite no.

Afterwards, she had little memory of the funeral. She shook hands with people; she looked through her black veil into their eyes, trying to tell whether they guessed. She wondered, hugging first Robin and then Helen, whether this too counted as a milestone in a woman's life. Whether the suicide of a parent was as significant as losing your virginity, or travelling abroad. She rather thought it was.

Robin whispered to her, 'You must come and stay with us, Maia – you must have a rest. Mother and father want you to come,' and Maia grabbed Robin's sleeve and shoved her into a corner of the room.

'I can't bear this. Escape with me, won't you?'

As Maia sneaked out of a side door and ran through the garden, she knew that both Robin and Helen were behind her. They caught up with her as she headed down Hills Road, her veil flapping and her black summer coat belling behind her with the speed of her stride.

'Maia—' Helen's voice was breathless. 'Where are we going?'

Maia hardly paused to glance at her friends. 'On the river, I thought.' Scrabbling in her pockets, she found enough change to hire a punt.

Afterwards, it touched her to recall that they had not so much as questioned her mad desire to glide along the Cam, still wearing their funereal blacks.

'Like Charon,' said Robin, punting.

'Or the three Fates.' Maia unpinned her hat and flung it out of the boat. Paused by the feathery tip of a reed, it slithered into the water, bobbing momentarily before it sank and disappeared.

Helen, sitting beside her, laid a comforting hand on

Maia's shaking sleeve. Tears of sympathy swam in her eyes. 'Poor Maia. Such an awful accident.'

Maia shook her head vigorously. 'Not an accident.' Her fingers clamped over her mouth then, as if to halt the words that had, against her better judgement, escaped.

Helen said soothingly, 'Of course it was, Maia darling,' but Maia saw that Robin, standing at the end of the boat, was staring at her.

'Maia . . . ?'

'Daddy killed himself.' The words jerked from Maia's throat, clipped and brittle. She felt sick and hot. 'I know that he did. He said he would.'

'But at the inquest—'

'I said it was an accident. Of course I did. Wouldn't you have?'

She glared first at Robin, and then at Helen. In the silence, bile rose in her throat. 'Well, wouldn't you?' Maia repeated. She knew that she sounded defensive and angry rather than upset. 'I suppose you both think that I was wicked. That I was dishonest . . .'

Her nails dug into her palms, tearing the thin black silk of her gloves. The boat lurched as Robin laid the pole along the bows and came to sit opposite her.

Helen said gently, 'We don't think badly of you, Maia dear. We only want to help you.'

'You did what you thought was best, Maia.' Robin's expression was serious. 'Neither of us have been through what you've been through. We can only begin to imagine what an awful time you've had. And Helen's right – we want to do whatever we can to help. You have to believe that.'

Maia felt her knotted hands prised apart. Helen's neatly gloved fingers curled round one; Robin's grubby paw around the other. Maia whispered, 'I don't want to talk about it ever again. Not ever,' and heard their murmured promises.

A different sort of vow to the one they had made in the spring. A darker secret that bound them, perhaps in some indissoluble way. She had needed their blessing, she realized.

And at last, Maia felt able to cry. For the first time in weeks she had recalled that she had found in her friends a small, safe haven, a haven that she could return to when she needed to. The reeds, the delicate bridges that spanned the river, and the swans that glided beside the bank, blurred as Maia began to weep.

Helen and her father always attended the annual harvest supper. It was held in the church hall, the food and drink provided by Lord Frere, the principal landowner of Thorpe Fen. The Freres lived in the Big House, which lay between Thorpe Fen and its neighbouring village; it had another, genteeler name, but to the villagers of Thorpe Fen it was always the Big House.

The harvest supper was one of the few village events that Helen looked forward to. The constraints and barriers of village life seemed to relax a little, reminding her of the evenings she occasionally spent with the Summerhayeses: evenings which to Helen often seemed chaotic, confusing and noisy, but utterly delightful, nevertheless.

Her feelings towards the Summerhayes family had for the first year or so of their acquaintance been mixed. Robin's casual dismissal of religion, the mainstay of Helen's life, had shocked her deeply. She still went hot when she recalled the day her father had discovered the truth: 'The Summerhayeses are atheists, Helen. They have no faith. One must therefore question their morals.' For a whole month afterwards she had avoided Robin and Hugh and Daisy and Richard. And yet she had been drawn back to them. Life had been – she could not think of another word for it – *dreary* without them – and Daisy had looked hurt, and Robin had been cross, and Richard had needed her to sing the new song he had arranged for her and Maia. Hugh had given Helen an enormous hug when she had visited again, and she had since not worried about either atheism or immorality.

She needed the Summerhayeses, and they (she hardly dared to believe it) also seemed to need her. She had known that in this instance she could not agree with her father. She was careful, though, rationing her visits and keeping them brief. And never, ever mentioning Richard and Daisy's more extraordinary visitors to Daddy.

After the harvest supper, the dancing began. Elijah Readman scraped away at his fiddle, and Natty Prior played the concertina. Helen, seated beside her father in a corner of the room, found that her feet were tapping. The villagers' heavy boots stamped on the wooden floor; the dancers circled and twisted, their drab clothes, enlivened by a bright scarf or a rope of cheap beads, patterned the dimly lit hall. The dance ended, and Adam Hayhoe stood up to sing. His strong, deep voice was almost overpowered by the thump of pattens on the board, and the many pairs of hands clapping to time, but Helen, from years of harvest suppers, knew the words, and her lips moved in rhythm with the song. *As I walked out one May morning, one May morning so early* . . .

She heard her father whisper in her ear, 'His lordship is arrived, Helen – will you come and greet him with me?'

She shook her head quickly. Lord Frere terrified her; and she had never forgotten one dreadful afternoon spent at Brackonbury House, supposedly playing with the Frere girls, but in fact ignored and looked down on by them.

'It is so cold outside . . .'

'Of course, my dear.' His hand rested on her shoulder. 'As soon as his lordship and I have spoken, we will go home.' Julius Ferguson's large blue-grey eyes glanced around the crowded hall. 'I will be glad when this tradition dies. I always think that there is more than a touch of the pagan to such a celebration.'

He left the hall, and Helen, shutting her eyes, let the music sink into her again.

A voice said, 'Will you dance, Miss Helen?'

Adam Hayhoe stood in front of her. Adam was tall,

dark, strong-looking, the village carpenter. She could not remember a time when she had not known Adam Hayhoe.

'That would be lovely, Adam.'

He took her hand, and led her into the ring that had formed around the perimeter of the room. The music started up again, the circle divided into two, threading in and out, weaving its ancient pattern. Faster and faster, the familiar faces of the villagers and the shabby hall altered by speed and exhilaration. Helen, too, laughed; Helen, too, felt a part of it. She found herself in Adam's arms, whirled around, making small circles within the larger one.

The dance ended, the hall alive with echoed music and laughter. The villagers quashed their thirst with tankards of beer; Helen dabbed at her hot, perspiring face with her handkerchief.

'Lemonade, Miss Helen?'

She smiled up at him. 'No thank you, Adam. I think I must have some fresh air.'

He walked with her to the side door, opening it for her to go out. The door swung shut behind them, enclosing them suddenly in silence.

'Such fun,' said Helen, still breathless. 'Such glorious fun. I do adore dancing.'

The moon was full and yellow, and stars pricked the inky sky. No wind rustled the grass and the reeds; only the quietness and the cool fresh air, touched by the first frost of winter. 'So lovely,' Helen said, looking up.

' "When the winds are breathing low, And the stars are shining bright." '

She only just caught Adam's whispered words, and she glanced at him, surprised. 'Adam. That's Shelley, isn't it? I didn't know you liked poetry.'

He did not reply, and her words echoed in her ears, her voice lacking the broad vowels of the Fens, her tone patronizing and condescending, setting her apart from Adam Hayhoe, of whom she had always been fond. She flushed, struggling for words of apology, but before she could find them she looked up and saw her father coming towards her.

'Dear me, Helen – where is your coat? You will catch a chill.'

As they walked home, Helen forgot her embarrassment, and looked again at the stars, at the sky. The most beautiful place on earth, she thought, as she threaded her arm through her father's. She recalled the remainder of the verse that Adam Hayhoe had quoted.

I arise from dreams of thee
In the first sweet sleep of night.
When the winds are breathing low,
And the stars are shining bright.

Somehow, it was almost October, and Daisy was packing the trunk that Robin would take with her to Girton. Stacks of mended and ironed skirts and blouses were piled on her chest of drawers, mute reminders of a fate she had not yet reconciled herself to. The cold wind and driving rain prematurely dragged the leaves from the willows that edged the river, and echoed Robin's mood. She shut herself in the winter house and watched the swollen droplets trail down the glass. Wrapped in jerseys and coat, Robin read uninterrupted for an hour, only putting aside her books when she heard the sound of footsteps on the damp wooden verandah outside.

Hugh pushed open the door. 'Ma says to tell you it's almost luncheon, Rob.'

Robin, uncurling, sat up.

'Special celebratory stuff. Treacle tart, your favourite—' Hugh broke off, looking at her closely. 'I say, old thing – you've been howling. What is it?' He held out his handkerchief.

'I've been reading the sad bits. Little Nell – David Copperfield's mother.' Robin evaded Hugh's eyes and blew her nose.

Hugh was unconvinced. 'I'll come and visit you as

often as I may, Rob. And I'll drive over and fetch you home every weekend. You only have to say.'

Hopelessly misunderstood, her guilt and despair only increased. 'It's not *that*—' As she shifted in her seat, books toppled to the floor.

'Then what is it?' Hugh perched on the arm of the chair, looking down at her. Ruffling Robin's tangled hair, which she had forgotten to brush that morning, he said, 'Come on, old girl, you can tell *me*.'

The words, held back for so long, tumbled out before she could stop them.

'I don't want to go to Girton!'

Hugh's eyes widened for a moment, and then he said sensibly, 'Not because you're afraid you'll be homesick?'

'*Homesick!*' Robin gestured furiously at the window. 'Look at it, Hugh! So wet and grey and empty! How could I possibly be homesick?' She shook her head. 'Girton'll be just like school, I know it will. You know how I hated school. And *Classics*.' Her voice was contemptuous.

'They'd probably let you switch. You could read history . . . or literature.' Hugh's eyes met Robin's. 'Oh.' He was silent for a moment, and then he said, 'You'll have to tell Ma and Pa.'

'I know.' Robin, sighing, ran her fingers through her hair, so that it stuck out in short feathery peaks all over her head. As she pulled on her galoshes, she heard Hugh say tentatively, 'Try and be tactful, won't you, Rob? You know how much your getting the scholarship meant to Pa,' and then she opened the door of the winter house and ran down the steps and across the soggy lawn towards the house.

She did try to be tactful, but somehow it went all wrong. She upset her father by telling him that to spend three years studying the past would be a waste of time; she upset her mother by refusing the elaborate meal that Daisy had cooked. Worst of all, she saw Hugh blench as she cried out despairingly, 'I never had a choice about

Girton, did I? Because Stevie died . . . because Hugh was ill . . . *I* have to go.' Looking round the table, she saw that she had hurt them all. Even Hugh, who had been so kind. With a howl of fury and despair, she ran out of the room, grabbed her coat from the peg, and tumbled out of the house.

She ran, her feet splashing in the puddles, until she reached Soham railway station. Miraculously, her purse was in her coat pocket. The Cambridge train was waiting at the platform; sitting in the carriage, Robin stared out at the grey, wet Fens, and tried to think clearly. The air smelt of boats burned, bridges razed to the ground. At Cambridge station, she stood among the rushing crowds, listening to the station master announce the departure of the London train. A sudden wave of nostalgia for London, for the life she had once led, almost overwhelmed her. She thought of the desolation, the silence, of Blackmere. She had to escape.

Robin began to walk towards Maia's cousin's house. Since the death of Maia's father, the Reads' house had been repossessed, Lydia Read planned to remarry, and Maia now lived with her mother's Cousin Sidney and his wife, Margery.

Helen was having a cup of tea with Maia. 'Daddy had to visit an old parishioner in Cambridge,' she explained, 'so I thought I'd do some shopping and visit Maia. How lovely to see you too, Robin.'

Maia made tea in the kitchen. Watching her, Robin saw that she had changed. She seemed older, thinner, brittle.

'You must miss your father so much.'

Pouring boiling water into the teapot, Maia shrugged. 'It's funny how you get used to things.' Her lids lowered, hiding her crystal blue eyes, shutting Robin out. 'I must get a job, though. I've finished my bookkeeping course, so I shall look around for something.' She took cups and saucers down from the dresser. 'How about you, Robin? Are you still going to be the first woman professor of Classics at Cambridge university?'

'I'm not going.' Robin's voice was bleak. 'I just told Ma and Pa. There was the most awful quarrel.'

'Ah.' Maia was never judgemental. She poured three cups of tea.

'If you don't want to go to college,' asked Helen 'then what will you do?'

'I haven't a clue.' Robin cradled her teacup and hated herself. She, who had always intended to do so much, had just abandoned the first serious venture of her adult life. Soon she must return to her family. Soon she must witness once more the disappointment in her father's eyes.

Maia said, 'What do you *want* to do?'

She was about to say again, *I haven't a clue*, when she remembered the station, and the train.

'I'd like to go back to London.'

Maia said nothing, but made a small, expressive shrug. Robin, staring at her, was seized by a wonderful, terrifying idea. She delved into her pocket, and drew out her purse.

'I've only . . . oh dear, five shillings and sevenpence.'

'I can let you have some cash, darling. Enough to get you to London. I'm supposed to pay for my board, but Margery can wait.'

Maia left the room. Helen, eyes round, said, '*London!* How exciting! Robin – you can't—'

She could, though. Though the idea both dazed and terrified her, she saw that she could.

When Maia returned, she was carrying a small holdall. 'There's a spare pair of stockings, and some soap and a flannel and a toothbrush. I didn't think you'd think of things like that. And here's two pounds.'

She handed the notes to Robin. Robin put them in her purse. Helen, too, searched through her bag and assembled a handful of small change. 'I'll tell Daisy and Richard you're all right,' she said, tipping the coins into Robin's palm, 'so that they don't worry.'

Maia perched on the edge of the table, and flicked

open a packet of cigarettes. 'Change the world, Robin darling.' Her pale eyes were narrowed, laughing. 'I'm stuck in this dump for a while – Prince Charming seems to be otherwise occupied—'

'—and the only young man I've met recently is the new curate and he has a wart on his nose—'

'—so what with accountancy classes and jumble sales and parish magazines, I'm afraid it's up to you, Robin, to be the only one of us who pursues her girlhood dreams.' Maia's voice was cynical, but she pushed the holdall towards Robin. 'Run along, won't you? You'd better hurry – the London train leaves at a quarter past.'

Robin gave both Maia and Helen a quick hug, and left the house. At Cambridge station, she bought her ticket and ran along the platform as smoke began to swirl from the funnel of the engine. Surprised faces stared at her as she pulled open a door and half fell into a carriage. The train drew away from the station, taking her back to the city, towards a new life.

Maia began to look properly for a job the day after Cousin Sidney tried to kiss her good night on the lips rather than on the cheek. Before that, she had been seized by a sort of paralysis, an extension of the waking nightmare of her father's death. At a secretarial bureau in St Andrew's Street, Maia scribbled a list of her sketchy qualifications, and was given a letter of introduction to the accounts department at Merchants.

She walked through the shop's wide double doors in a daze. She was surrounded by the sort of things she had always wanted: expensive cosmetics and perfumes, leather gloves, silk scarves, hosiery as fine as cobweb. There were often advertisements for Merchant department store in the local newspapers: 'Merchants – Cambridge's Newest and Premier Department Store, General and Fancy Drapers, Complete Home Furnishers, Ladies Millinery, Blouses and Ready to Wear Garments, and Circulating Library.'

Halfway up the stairs, she paused, looking down at

the glittering lights and gorgeous colours, breathing in the rich, warm air. She knew that she could have looked as elegant as any of the fur-clad ladies buying French perfume, and as beautiful as any of the painted faces that stared down at her from the cosmetics manufacturers' displays. It seemed to Maia that with the furs, the powder, the perfume, she could have been safe.

Walking upstairs, the letter of introduction clutched in her hand, she did not know how she would be able to bear it, stuck in a poky little office with a dozen other girls, catching only occasional glimpses of this other world. She held her head high, though, and refused to allow her bitterness and depression to show on her face. Crossing the first floor of the shop, she heard someone call out her name. Maia recognized Mr Merchant, who had dined with the Reads on that awful day when her father had told them of his imminent bankruptcy, and who had attended the funeral. She had not previously connected him with Merchants department store. He must be rich, then, said a small voice in her head.

'Miss Read. How delightful to see you.'

'Mr Merchant.' Maia smiled and held out her hand.

He was considerably older than Maia – in his early thirties, she estimated. Curly reddish-brown hair cut close to his head, and a small, thin moustache.

'Have you many purchases to make, Miss Read?'

Something made her shove the letter into her pocket, and say lightly, 'Oh – just a few odds and ends. Ribbon and thread.' She glanced around her and gave a little laugh. 'Silly me. I seem to have come to the wrong floor.'

'Let me escort you to the haberdashery department, Miss Read.'

Mr Merchant held out his arm, and Maia threaded her own gloved hand through it. He asked after her mother and murmured regrets about her father as he led her downstairs. At the haberdashery counter she sat passively as assistants ran about at his command, fetching ribbon, buttons and reels of cotton. She noticed that although he enjoyed his authority, his enjoyment did not override his efficiency and competence.

Eventually her small purchases were assembled, and she mutely thanked God that she had enough money in her purse to pay for them. Carrying her tiny parcel, he walked beside her through the perfume hall to the front doors.

She could not resist saying, 'Is this all yours, Mr Merchant?'

When he smiled, she could see his small, white, pointed teeth.

'Every bit of it. It was an ironmongers before I took it over. Don't you remember, Miss Read?'

She shook her head. 'We had most things delivered. We never shopped much.'

'Don't you think it's enjoyable, Miss Read, to be able to choose what you want? To be able to look over what's on offer and decide exactly what you'll have?'

His eyes, a sort of gingery-hazel, met hers, and she did not look away. Maia did not blush: she never blushed. He was not in the least handsome, she thought, but he possessed an aura of power and strength. She did not find his words insolent, only challenging. It seemed a very long time since she had felt even a flicker of interest in another person.

And besides, he had all this. The bright lights, the chrome-edged counters and soft carpets seemed to reach out and embrace Maia. For the first time in months she recalled her ambitions. 'I shall marry a rich man,' she had said to Robin and Helen. 'I shall live in an enormous house.'

Shaking his hand, she murmured thanks and farewells. As she walked down the street, Maia knew that he was watching her, so she waited until she had turned the corner and was out of sight before she dropped the crumpled letter into the gutter.

Because she sensed that Vernon Merchant was as clever and as calculating as she, Maia was careful. She found work in the office of a firm that specialized in installing telephones and electric lights. The office was on the outskirts of Cambridge; Maia avoided the city centre. It would have been a mistake to have visited Merchants each day, hoping to meet him. He would have despised her.

He telephoned a month after their meeting. It was six o'clock: Maia had just returned from work. The maid handed her the telephone.

'Miss Read?'

She recognized his voice instantly. She couldn't help smiling. 'Yes.'

'It's Vernon Merchant. How are you, Miss Read?'

'I'm very well, Mr Merchant.' She waited for him to continue.

'I've a pair of tickets for the theatre tonight. Will you come?'

His directness amused her. No apologies for the lateness of the invitation; no fears expressed that she might be otherwise engaged. No explanation of how he had traced where she was living.

'I'd be delighted, Mr Merchant,' Maia said, equally directly. 'You can call for me at seven o'clock.'

He telephoned her every week. He took her to the theatre, to restaurants, and to parties. He disliked the cinema, and art galleries and concerts bored him. His parents were both dead, he had never married, he had fought in the Great War and on his return to England had built up his career. He had chosen Cambridge neither for its beauty nor its history, but for its lack of a modern department store. He dressed and ate well, and owned a large and luxurious house, which Maia had not, after two months, seen.

She knew nothing more about him. He was, she suspected, as secretive as she. Or perhaps there was nothing more to know? Perhaps Vernon Merchant was just what he seemed – a successful businessman, a little lonely perhaps, but otherwise satisfied with what he had created. He did not bore her, she could not quite work out why he did not bore her. Because power fascinated her – because of the flicker of pleasure she glimpsed in his foxy, tawny eyes when he talked about his work. Had she not occasionally seen the same expression in his eyes when he kissed her, then she would have begun to doubt her own power. He had only touched her chastely closed lips, had only embraced her while they danced.

She wore an ice-blue silk sheath, the same colour as her eyes, when he collected her one Friday evening. It was February, and there was a hint of snow in the dull orangey-grey sky. Maia wore Cousin Margery's fur coat, taken from Margery's wardrobe in her absence. She could not have borne to wear her old school coat, her only coat, when she was with Vernon.

In the passenger seat of his motor-car, he drew a rug from the back, and tucked it over her knees. 'We are going to London,' he said. 'One of my business associates is having a party.'

They talked throughout the long drive. About the small events of the day, about the larger events of the world. The Belgravia house in which the party was held glittered against threatening clouds. Uniformed servants took her coat; Maia powdered her nose in a marble bathroom. They dined and danced, Vernon holding her lightly and carefully. When, at three o'clock, she reclaimed Margery's fur coat and they began the long drive home, it was snowing.

He drew up the hood of the car and closed all the windows, but flakes of snow still found their way through all the little cracks and gaps. Maia pulled the rug up to her chin, and was thankful of her furs. Driving north through rows of the new semi-detached houses that had sprung up all round London, he passed her a flask.

'Brandy,' he said. 'Drink some. It'll keep you warm.'

She didn't like brandy; she rarely drank because she had seen her mother after too many gin and its. But she swallowed obediently and found that he was right: it warmed her.

'Will we be late?'

'Perhaps.' His eyes were narrowed, trying to see the road through the endless, darting flakes. 'Will that be difficult for you?'

'Oh no. I don't have to work tomorrow.'

'Your cousin . . . ?'

'She won't care.' Only she thought of the coat and giggled a little to herself, imagining Margery's face if she searched and failed to find her precious mink.

He was silent for a moment, and then he said, 'How old are you, Maia?'

The question surprised her. It was the most personal thing he had ever asked her. 'Nineteen,' she replied truthfully.

'I am thirty-four. I was nineteen in 1914.'

She wished now that she had not drunk the brandy. She sensed that this conversation was important, and yet alcohol and exhaustion had taken the edge from her clarity of thought.

'What do you want from life, Maia?'

She said honestly, as she had once said to Robin and Helen, 'I want to marry a rich man and live in a beautiful house and have lots of wonderful clothes.'

He threw back his head and laughed, his lips peeled back to reveal his curiously pointed teeth. 'Why?'

Because then I'd feel safe, she thought. But she said instead, 'Because I like nice things. Because I do justice to beautiful clothes.'

He gave only a small nod, of acquiescence or approval. The road meandered through undulating countryside, and the snow fell more heavily. It danced in the yellow light of the headlamps like confetti.

She asked curiously, 'Why did you want to be rich?'

'Because you don't have to ask for things. The more you have, the more you are given.'

She shivered. He glanced across at her, concerned.

'Take my scarf. I'm sorry, darling – I wouldn't have dragged you out if I'd known it was going to be as bad as this.'

She shook her head and smiled because he had called her for the first time, 'darling'. 'I'm fine,' she said. 'Just a bit tired.'

'Have another swig of brandy. You might fall asleep.'

Maia did as she was told, and he was right, because she dozed off for a while, and when she awoke a coppery light in the sky told her that it was almost dawn.

'Nearly there,' he said.

He did not look tired; his driving was still fast and precise. Maia admired his skill: the flick of his wrists as he turned the wheel, his capacity to remain alert after an entire night without sleep. She respected efficiency and endurance. They were qualities that she herself possessed, and that her father had lacked.

Vernon was braking, slowing to turn into the gravelled drive of a house. The car skidded a little as it swung round, but he righted it. Laurels, their leaves weighted with snow, lined the drive. The long branches of beech trees met overhead. Maia suddenly felt wide awake. This must be his home. Vernon Merchant was taking her to his home.

The car halted outside a vast house, ornately Victorian in style, built of red brick. Baroque turrets and chimneys and pinnacles clung to its walls and roofs like barnacles on a rock.

'I had it built a few years ago,' said Vernon. 'I hope you don't mind if we stop for a moment. Only I've a few calls to make. You can warm yourself up. You look chilled, darling.'

She savoured that second 'darling'. A servant held open the car door, and Maia stepped out into the whirling snowflakes. In the hallway, Vernon picked up the telephone.

The hall was paved with marble, darkly panelled to the dado rail. Oil-paintings of bowls of fruit and of dead or dying animals lined the walls. The staircase was wide and sweeping and baronial, its finials carved eagles' heads.

Maia was shown to a large, comfortably furnished

room. A tray of hot chocolate and biscuits stood on the table, a huge fire burned in the grate. She spread out her fingers to its warmth.

She drank the chocolate, and heard footsteps and the door closing, and she turned round to see Vernon.

'A little crisis. All dealt with. A late order – incompetence, I'm afraid.'

'What did you do?'

'Fired him, of course.' He came towards her.

'Don't you ever rest?'

He smiled, but his eyes were hard and dark. 'No. That's why I have this, Maia. That's why I am a rich man, and I have a magnificent house, and I can afford to buy what I want.'

Although she was warm now, she shivered again. He had echoed the words she had spoken to him in the car. He added, 'You're still cold, Maia. Let me warm you,' and he reached out and slid Margery's mink from her shoulders. Then he began to kiss her.

Not a chaste pressing of lips, this time. His lips parted hers, his tongue tasted her mouth. His arms bound her to him, his hands discovered the shape of her body through her thin silk dress. She felt a mixture of excitement and fear. He explored her body as though it belonged to him, and not to her. And in the back of her head, standing aside, watching, a little voice whispered, *He wants to know what he is buying . . .*

Suddenly she twisted, struggling to push him away. 'No,' she said hoarsely. 'No.'

To her relief, he let her go. 'Why not?'

She could not speak, but she shook her head.

'Are you a virgin, Maia?'

She felt suddenly terribly tired and slightly tearful. It's the only thing I have, she thought. I wouldn't be worth as much without it. She nodded.

For one awful moment she thought he was laughing at her. But then he said, 'Good. Because if you hadn't been, I wouldn't have wanted to marry you,' and she was aware of a rush of triumph and relief.

Chapter Two

Joe and Francis were, as usual, late for the meeting of the Hackney branch of the ILP: Francis, because he had overslept (it was nine o'clock in the evening), and Joe because he had had to work. They squeezed into the back of the crowded hall, tripping over bags and feet and chair legs. 'Hell,' said Francis, as someone's walking-stick, hanging from the back of a chair, clattered to the ground. People turned and shushed him.

The speaker had almost finished. 'Parish boundaries,' whispered Francis, rather loudly. 'Bloody boring.'

The questions began. Francis's eyes closed, his head drooped forward. Joe, too, was tired; there had been a party last night in the basement flat that he and Francis shared. It seemed to have gone on for an awfully long time: indeed, Joe was not sure whether it was finished yet. There was no food in the flat, and he was desperate for sleep, and someone had stolen his mattress.

He began to pay attention when the discussion, by the strange alchemy common to these meetings, moved from parish boundaries via universal family allowances to equality of the sexes. A girl seated somewhere near the front of the hall, a girl whose voice Joe did not recognize, was arguing vigorously.

'Marriage and female economic dependence are inseparable, surely? Marriage is the foundation-stone of woman's dependency.'

A man's voice growled, 'The human race won't last long without it, comrade,' and there was a ripple of laughter.

'I wasn't suggesting that men and women shouldn't make love, have babies, that sort of thing.'

Joe noticed that Francis, too, was awake. Francis's eyes were gleaming.

'Free love – is that what you're recommending, miss?'

'If that's what you wish to call it – yes.' Her voice was truculent.

Joe muttered, 'I'm all for free love, myself.'

'She's probably six foot tall, weaves her own clothes, and does callisthenics before breakfast.' Francis yawned. 'Lord, I'm hungry,' he added plaintively. 'Haven't eaten for days.'

Joe rummaged in his pocket for half a crown. 'I'll wager she isn't.'

'Isn't what?'

'Six foot tall etcetera. I'll stand you dinner if she's wearing a single item of handwoven clothing.'

'Done,' said Francis, grinning.

The discussion became heated. On another occasion Joe would have joined in, just for the hell of it, but today he felt too fuddled. The remains of a rather bad headache was intensified by the raised voices.

At eleven o'clock the meeting was brought to a close. Joe and Francis both stood up and looked towards the front of the hall.

She was still arguing as she walked towards the doorway. 'The position of women within marriage may be an awkward subject, Mr Taylor, but it's surely not one that we in the Labour Party can afford to duck. And yes, I do believe that a married woman should have access to birth control, even if her husband does not want her to. I believe that all women should have access to free birth control.'

She was tiny. About five foot one, small boned, the curves of her body only just visible beneath a dress of rich dark brown stuff. Not hand-woven at all. Her eyes were the same colour as the dress, her short feathery hair many shades lighter.

'A peach,' murmured Francis. A half-crown slid into Joe's palm. 'I'll buy dinner.'

Joe shook his head. 'I'm off to Clodie's.' For the briefest of moments the girl glanced first at him, then at Francis, lounging against the wall. And then she was gone, still arguing.

Joe walked the mile and a half to Clodie's house, hoping to clear his head. A light was on in the front window of the small villa when he arrived. Clodie's face, when she opened the door to him, was sulky.

'I've only just got Lizzie off. You'll wake her with all your noise.'

He had tapped the door, softly, twice. 'I'll be quiet,' he whispered. 'Look – I've some chocolates.'

Her eyes widened greedily when he showed her the bag of chocolate creams. He bought the sweets for Lizzie, but Clodie always ate half of them. She had a child's appetite for sweets, belying the seductive curves of her body.

She let him in, but the corners of her mouth still drooped downwards. 'You'd better sit down, now that you're here,' she said ungraciously.

'Is Lizzie ill?' Lizzie was Clodie's six-year-old daughter.

'She has glands.' Clodie, biting the top off a chocolate cream, eyed Joe spitefully. 'Maybe it's mumps.'

'I've had it.' He had a distant memory of being allowed home from school early, his face hurting like hell. He added, 'We had a party. The place is impossible. Can I sleep on your sofa tonight?'

He saw that he had annoyed her again, but this time the annoyance had a slightly different source.

'Did you meet anyone nice?' she said, through a mouthful of chocolate.

He knew better than to tease her. 'Just the usual crowd. No beautiful redheads.'

At last she smiled. Clodie's hair was her greatest beauty – she had never cut it, not even when the fashion for bobbed hair was at its height. When she let it down it curled and rippled, a glorious tawny red, to her waist.

'Cup of tea, Joe?'

He followed her into the kitchen. The small room was immaculate: part of him, the part that still remembered with pain his French mother and the elegance she had somehow magically given to his huge, gloomy Yorkshire home, knew that one of the reasons he kept coming back to Clodie, putting up with her temper, coaxing her out of her sulks, was that he liked this house. Bourgeois, Francis would have labelled it. But it was pleasant to spend the night somewhere where the crockery was washed and put away, the bed-linen was laundered, and there was food in the larder.

He watched her make the tea. Her hands were deft and neat. He thought of Lizzie, of whom he had grown fond.

'Have you had the doctor for Lizzie?'

Clodie shook her head. 'I haven't the ten shillings. I don't know where the money's gone this week.' The whine had come back into her voice.

Joe fumbled in his pocket and found Francis's half-crown and his own. 'Will that help?'

She took the money, but said suspiciously, 'I hope you don't think—'

'Lord – no.' His head was pounding, and he desperately needed the tea. And sleep. 'I told you, Clodie, I'm tired.'

Satisfied, she reached up and touched his face. 'You should have shaved.'

'Sorry, love. I couldn't find my razor.'

'You'll be all scratchy.' Her fingertips threaded through his hair, and her green eyes gleamed. He covered her hand with his own, and kissed her palm, and pulled the pins from her hair so that it spilled down her back. She unbuttoned her blouse and he bent his head and kissed her breasts, taking her dark brown nipple into his mouth.

'You don't want to sleep on the couch, do you, Joe?' she whispered, and he shook his head. It didn't ache any more.

Joe Elliot had lived in London since his rather sudden departure four years earlier from one of the less illustrious northern public schools. He had shared the basement flat with both Francis and the printing press for around half that time. They only made money with the printing press when they used it for commercial brochures and flyers. The rest of the stuff – the political pamphlets and leaflets – often lost money rather than earned it. Besides, work was intermittent, dependent on Francis's ability to find new customers. Francis had a small private income, so the inevitable fluctuations in earnings affected him less severely. Joe, since the quarrel with his father, had nothing, so he supplemented his income from the press with regular bar work.

He managed, just. It had been easier to manage before Clodie. Her husband had been killed in an industrial accident two years earlier, leaving her with a small daughter and the rent to pay. She worked at home as a dressmaker, but Joe knew how difficult it was for her to make ends meet. In Joe's eyes both Clodie and Lizzie were always beautifully dressed, the house always immaculate. He admired her for that, he didn't know how she managed it. He had seen, both in the east end of London and in the north of England, how others crumbled under the burden of poverty. It had been a genuine anger at the sights he had seen that had attracted him to socialism.

That and, he had to admit, the knowledge of how much his politics infuriated his father. Since leaving home, Joe had occasionally sent his father a pamphlet – something inflammatory about capitalism or revolution, preferably. That John Elliot's son – since Johnnie's death his only son – should have abandoned his inheritance and become (in his father's eyes) a communist, had made John Elliot's roar of rage reach almost from Hawksden to London. The pamphlets had been his only communication with his father since he had turned eighteen. Joe remembered his mother with painful clarity, but his half-brother Johnnie, who had died in Flanders in 1918, had become a jumbled collection of stereotypes: captain of his House, captain of both cricket and rugby First Elevens, blond, blue-eyed, brutal, conventional. The apple of his father's eye. Johnnie had taken after his father: the only unconventional act of John Elliot's entire life had been to marry a Frenchwoman as his second wife. Sometimes Joe suspected that his father hated him because when he looked at his second son (tall, dark hair, dark eyes) he was reminded of the only time he had ever truly loved.

After the meeting, Robin went back to her digs. She was late, but smoothed her landlady over with apologies and explanations. Taking her letters from the hall table, she let herself into her room and lit the gas lamp.

The house was owned by a pair of spinster sisters. The elder Miss Turner kept an aviary of budgerigars in the back yard; the younger Miss Turner dabbled in the occult. Neither the séances at night nor the squawking of birds at dawn detracted from Robin's pleasure in renting her own room. She loved every inch of it: from the bulbous mahogany furniture to the faded floral wallpaper. She covered the garish print of 'The Light of the World' with a silk scarf, remembering to remove the scarf on Thursdays, when the younger Miss Turner cleaned.

Inside the room, she flung off her coat and collapsed on the bed. She had missed supper and was ravenous; rummaging in the bedside table she found a tin of biscuits. The first letter was from Maia. Robin choked on a currant when she read about Maia's engagement. *The diamond on my ring is large enough to be positively vulgar*, Maia wrote. *It is amusing to watch Cousin*

Margery trying to be magnanimous, while struggling to hide her envy. More about Maia's fiancé's house, his motor-car, his work. Not a word about love. Maia was no more a romantic than Robin. But Maia obviously considered marriage to be economic liberation, rather than economic slavery. 'Good luck to her,' said Robin, out loud, and tossed the letter aside.

Her smile faded as she quickly scanned her father's letter. There was no bad news, only a muted sense of disapproval. Her father's disappointment at her refusal to go to Girton had been painful, but expected, but his continued doubts about the life she had since chosen had taken Robin by surprise. She had expected understanding of her wish to be self-supporting, if nothing else – both Richard and Daisy, after all, believed that women as well as men had a right to independence and employment. 'You are wasting your talents,' her father had told her at Christmas, and she had felt hurt, angry, let down. Only Hugh, dear Hugh, seemed to understand.

Licking her finger to collect the last few biscuit crumbs, Robin recalled her arrival in London the previous autumn. She had not had the least idea where to go. The Summerhayes family had many friends in London – Merlin and Persia and all their friends and neighbours from years ago – but it would have seemed a defeat to go to them. Robin had found a small hotel in which to stay the night. The hotel had been much too expensive, so she had left it the following morning to look for lodgings and work. She had found clerical work in an insurance office – very dull, but it paid the rent. It wasn't quite what she had had in mind, but she told herself that it was only temporary. She had quickly discovered that a working knowledge of Latin and Greek were of far less use to her than typewriting or stenography.

She had met the Salters when she had fallen off her bicycle. It had been wet, and the cobbled streets were slippery with old leaves and rubbish from the flea market. The twins, Eddie and Jimmy, had roared with laughter when she had plummeted into the puddle, but Mrs Salter had invited her indoors and sponged her skirt for her and let her wash her grazed hands. That had been Robin's first glimpse inside one of the countless little terraced houses that lined her route from lodgings to work, and it had shocked her. She had seen poverty in the Fens, but somehow there the open skies and clean air had mitigated it. This was not the London that Robin remembered and loved. This was a four-roomed house with six children and countless rats and bugs. Robin could see the squashed black shapes of the bugs on the faded wallpaper. Ten people lived in the house – Mr and Mrs Salter, the children, a grandmother and an uncle. There was a bed made up on a chair in the scullery. Robin, looking at the infant that tugged at his mother's skirts, and at the swelling of Mrs Salter's stomach beneath her apron, resolved to lend her Marie Stopes's book.

Sometimes Robin's wages ran out on a Wednesday, usually she managed to make them eke out the week. Her father posted her money, which she politely returned, explaining that she wanted to manage on her own. She was, however, glad of the warm skirts and jumpers that Daisy sent on her birthday. In the evenings, when she wasn't at ILP meetings or helping out at the clinic, she taught herself touch typing on an old typewriter. She had few visitors, and so far only acquaintances rather than friends, but sometimes she felt completely happy. At night, when she lay in bed and closed her eyes and listened to the sounds of the city, she knew that she had been right to come back to London. She believed that something wonderful was about to happen: she teetered on the edge of a cliff, making ready to plunge into the teeming seas of Life.

Robin arrived early at the meeting and sat in the front row. Only a scattering of people were in the hall, one or two nodded a greeting to her. Outside it was raining; she struggled out of her damp mackintosh and propped her umbrella against her seat. She had come from the Free Clinic, where she worked in the evenings as an unpaid receptionist, nursery assistant, and general dogsbody. She wondered briefly whether she should have gone home to change: she thought she smelt of stale milk and unwashed baby.

Someone sat beside her. She glanced at him surreptitiously. Young, fair wavy hair cut close to his head, and a straight-nosed, high-browed, Greek god sort of profile. Pretending to look inside her bag, Robin managed a quick peep around the hall. It had not suddenly filled up, all the seats but three were still empty. She glanced at her neighbour again.

He looked back at her and smiled and held out his hand. 'Francis Gifford,' he said. The smile was like the sun coming out. His eyes were light grey, with a ring of darker grey around the iris.

She shook his hand. 'Robin Summerhayes.'

'What a glorious name. So . . . seasonal. Makes you think of meadows and flowers and Christmas and icicles all at once.'

It was the AGM. She said curiously, 'Are you standing for anything . . . Francis?'

He shook his fair head. 'I thought about it, but it restricts you rather, doesn't it? The party line and all that. Half the fun of these meetings are the arguments at the end of the evening.'

The hall was filling up. Francis slung his arm over the empty chair beside him. 'That's for Joe,' he said, whenever someone tried to sit down.

The chair was still empty when the meeting began. Halfway through the evening, when Robin, her mind dazed with proposals and seconders and protocols, was struggling to concentrate, the door at the back of the hall opened and Francis turned round, stood up, and waved. Someone slid into the seat beside him. They were voting again; beneath the muffled muttering and the rustle of papers, Francis murmured, 'Robin – this is Joe Elliot.'

Joe, glowering, nodded at Robin. Joe was Francis's

opposite, thought Robin – dark and thin and hungry-looking. Daisy, had she been introduced to Joe, would have sat him down at the kitchen table and made him eat a huge meal.

Francis glanced at Joe.

'Don't mind him – his lady friend's been unwelcoming.'

'Shut up, Francis.'

'He should do what I do – keep myself pure.'

Joe snorted. Robin looked ahead and tried, unsuccessfully, to concentrate on the election of a Press Officer. When the last position was filled, and the evening officially brought to a close, she stood and picked up her bag, her mackintosh, and her umbrella. The seam at the bottom of her bag, which had been fraying for weeks, chose that moment to split, spewing her uneaten lunch, her purse, hairbrush and handkerchief over the floor.

Everyone scrabbled beneath the chairs. 'Sandwiches,' said Francis, picking up a greaseproof paper parcel. He sniffed. 'Fish paste?'

An orange rolled across the floor. 'Don't you eat?' asked Francis.

Robin knew that her face was scarlet. 'I didn't have time today . . . I was behind at work . . .'

'I'll make you an omelette.'

She almost said, That's terribly kind of you, Mr Gifford, but I couldn't possibly, but she managed to stop herself. She had travelled to London to be part of Life, and Life, she suspected with a rush of excitement, was offering itself to her tonight.

'That would be lovely.'

They talked all the way back to Francis's flat. Or rather, Francis and Robin talked, and Joe walked silently beside them, his boots scuffing the pavement. It was still raining. They threw the battered remains of Robin's lunch into a litter bin, and shared her umbrella. Francis led the way down some steps and fitted a key into a basement door.

Inside, Robin heard herself make a small, surprised sound.

'We had a few people round,' said Joe. His smile mocked her stupefaction.

There was nowhere to sit down. Piles of books and leaflets, empty bottles and dirty crockery: some of the crockery was growing things. In the centre of the room was an enormous machine. Paper, smeared with black ink, trailed messily from it.

'A printing press,' said Robin.

Joe, lighting the fire, muttered, 'The damn thing's packed up again. I've just wasted the entire day trying to sort it out.'

From the adjoining kitchen, Francis peered round the door. 'There's no eggs.'

'Of course there's no bloody eggs. No-one's been bloody shopping for a week.'

The fire was lit. Joe went to the printing press.

'I'll have to take the wretched thing apart. It's clogged up with ink.' Touching the machine, his dark, angular face softened a little.

'I've found some biscuits,' called Francis, from the kitchen. 'And Vivien has sent me caviar—'

They ate caviar spread on Rich Tea biscuits, sitting on the floor because no-one could be bothered to clear the chairs. Francis explained about the printing press.

'We do pamphlets, election manifestos, and some commercial work. I bought it second hand eighteen months ago. Joe did it up, and I do the selling and design. And I'm starting up a little magazine. Poetry . . . political comment, that sort of thing. A quarterly.'

Joe poured beer into three teacups. 'We've an order for a thousand flyers for a surgical appliance manufacturer. That's why I've got to get her going again.'

Heaps of leaflets were piled on the floor beside Robin. She glanced at them: 'Fabian Democracy' by Henry Green. 'A Mother's Guide to Socialism' by Sarah Salmon. 'A Short History of the Trade Union Movement' by Ernest Hardcastle.

She picked up a leaflet. 'So these people send you their stuff, and you print it for them?'

'Sort of.' Francis passed Robin a mug. 'Well – we started off like that. Only we found out quite early on that it's much more efficient to do the whole thing yourself. Avoids ploughing through awful spelling and inadequate punctuation.'

Joe said, 'One of the benefits of a public school education.'

'Joe and I were at Dotheboys Hall together,' added Francis. 'Chucked out for unsportsmanlike behaviour.'

She stared from one to the other. Francis's light grey eyes were innocent. Joe had finished his beer, and was fiddling with the press again.

'Francis writes them all,' Joe explained kindly.

Francis smiled. 'They all have different personalities. Do drink up, Robin. Henry Green I see as a tweedy gentleman with a pipe. Likes cricket, Elgar, that sort of thing. Sarah Salmon – well, half a dozen brats, of course, used to be a mill worker. She makes some grammatical errors. And Ernest Hardcastle – cloth cap and racing pigeons, obviously. Grows leeks for a hobby.'

Robin said stiffly, 'People buy these things . . . they believe in them. You're just mocking them . . . ridiculing them. You don't care about any of it.'

Francis shook his head vigorously. 'Of course I do. I believe every word I write. I can just do it better than most people.'

Unconvinced, Robin opened a pamphlet and read a few paragraphs.

'Cigarette?' asked Francis, offering her a packet.

When the weather was fine, the Easter Bazaar was held in the rectory garden. This year the sun shone, so the stalls were set up on the wide lawn surrounded by flower-beds at the side of the house. As the widowed rector's only daughter, Helen was responsible for the organization of the Bazaar. Because she found asking favours an ordeal, she ended up doing everything herself.

For months beforehand all her days had been spent sewing little things for the haberdashery stall, baking cakes and scones, and crawling around the attics to find suitable items for the white elephant stall. Mrs Lemon, the doctor's wife, had volunteered to supply the produce and preserves, thank goodness, so at least she had not had to raid the garden as well.

Ten minutes before the bishop was due to open the fête, Helen was still anxiously scribbling price tags. The whole business, she knew from previous years, was impossible and bound to cause offence. If she priced the cakes according to their size and attractiveness, then all the bakers of the mean, plain cakes would mutter. If she charged the same price for all, then the women who had spent hours icing would be offended. 2/6d, Helen scrawled, knowing it was far too much for a Dundee cake in which all the fruit had sunk to the bottom.

One of the helpers said, 'We haven't been given our floats yet, Miss Helen.'

Helen's hand flew to her mouth. 'I meant to ask Daddy to count them out last night.' Scrabbling under the stall, she found the cash-box. 'I'll have to do it myself. I am most terribly sorry . . .'

She stared at the tin full of pennies and halfpennies and shillings. She had never had an arithmetic lesson in her life, and she found money hopelessly confusing. Her father paid all the bills.

'I'll give you a hand, Miss Ferguson, if you like.'

She looked up. A tall young man wearing a boater and a blazer was standing beside her.

'You don't remember me, do you, Miss Ferguson? I'm Geoffrey Lemon. I've missed the Bazaar for the past couple of years, so we haven't seen each other for ages.' He glanced at the jumbled coins. 'I say – won't you let me help? Ma says I'm under her feet.'

Gratefully, Helen handed Geoffrey Lemon the tin. He began to sort the change into small heaps. 'Spiffing cakes, Miss Ferguson. Frightful lot of work, a bash like this.'

'Last year I had to judge the bonny babies. All the mothers of the ones who didn't win were furious. The bishop's wife is judging it this year, but I still have to do the races and award the prizes. I'll probably give the men bags of sweets and the babies bottles of beer.'

The cakes sold out in the first half-hour, and the bishop's wife praised Helen's pot-holders and tea-cosies. The bonny babies squealed or slept, according to their natures, and Helen pacified their mothers by admiring each one. She waved to Hugh Summerhayes, bowling for the pig, and thought, once again, how much she missed Robin.

She was clearing up the tea things when Geoffrey Lemon spoke to her again.

'Won't you let me take that, Miss Ferguson?'

She handed him the heavy tray. He did not walk away, though, but stood for a moment, looking at her, blinking. It occurred to Helen suddenly that perhaps she was not the only person to feel awkward with strangers, that perhaps even young men – whom she so often found brash, unapproachable, and rather frightening – could be shy as well.

'It's been the most terrific fun, Miss Ferguson.' His words tripped over themselves a little, and he still stared at her. The tray drooped at an angle, and one of the tea-cups wobbled precariously. Geoffrey gave a snort of embarrassed laughter.

'I'd better take this over to Ma before I drop the lot.'

Helen murmured thanks and went to join Maia and Hugh, sitting under the horse-chestnut tree. Maia was lounging against the tree-trunk, her eyes covered by dark glasses.

'I didn't know you had a sweetheart, Helen.'

'I've won a pig, Helen. What on earth shall I do with a pig?'

'Daisy can give it as a prize at the next tombola.'

'No, Maia, I've decided to keep it. It can sit in the back of the car on the way home.'

Maia said again, 'He's in love with you, Helen. Madly in love with you.'

Shopping in Ely, Helen chose two lengths of cotton, one pink, one candy-striped. Her attention was caught by a display of silks. 'China silks,' said the caption, immediately conjuring to Helen's imagination pagodas and paper dragons and black-haired, tiny-footed ladies. Glorious colours: pale and deep and subtle. She stood for a long time trying to work out whether she had enough money for a length of silk as well as the cotton, or whether she must put one of the cottons back. The figures jumbled up in her head, just as they always did, and she ran out of fingers for counting. Eventually, abandoning arithmetic, she returned the striped cotton to the shelf. Stripes would emphasize her height; Helen disliked being tall. She stroked the silks with her fingertips, trying to choose a colour. After hesitating a long time, she picked out a pale mint green.

When her parcels were wrapped, Helen left the shop. Across the cathedral green she glimpsed a familiar figure. Tall, short brown hair, moustache. She stood for a moment on the edge of the pavement, uncertain what to do. Geoffrey Lemon might be in a hurry; he might not (appalling thought) remember her. Helen almost turned and ran for the bus. But then he saw her and waved.

'Miss Ferguson!' He ran across the grass towards her.

'Mr Lemon.' She couldn't shake hands because of the parcels.

There was an awkward silence. Then, inspired, he said, 'Can I treat you to a cup of tea, Miss Ferguson? Thirsty business, shopping.'

Over tea and cakes in the Copper Kettle, conversation became easier. Geoffrey was in his third year at university, and when eventually he graduated he would join his father's practice. He had four younger brothers and sisters, and lots of cousins, so his Burwell home was always busy. He told Helen a few stories about medical students' pranks that made her eyes widen. Then he asked her about herself.

'Oh – there's nothing much to say.' She poured him a second cup of tea. 'Daddy and I live very quietly. I used to have a governess, but she left ages ago. I was hopeless at lessons anyway. I like to sew and draw, that sort of thing. And I've written a few poems.' Suddenly she was blushing. She had told no-one about the poems, not even Robin and Maia.

'I say.' There was admiration in his eyes. Nice eyes, a warm toffee brown. Helen felt herself going redder.

'Just silly little things.' She stared down at her plate.

Geoffrey rubbed at his moustache. Then he blurted out, 'Do you like to cycle? I could call for you one day.'

He called one afternoon when she was weeding the garden. Helen gave a private and guilty sigh of relief that her father was out on parish business. They cycled for hours, losing themselves among the fields and dikes. Spring flowers blossomed on the verges: cowslips and ladies' smock and a few early marsh orchids. Stopping beside a river, they dropped their bicycles beneath a willow tree.

Helen told Geoffrey about Maia and Robin. 'Maia is to be married next month. And Robin is in London. I do miss her so, Geoffrey. So does Hugh.'

He was sitting against the tree-trunk, his face shadowed by the brim of his straw boater. 'It must get lonely, just you and your father.'

'Daddy is—' Helen began, but found it hard to explain how much her father needed her. How her parents' idyllic, tragic marriage had lasted only one short year, leaving Julius Ferguson a widower with a six-week-old infant to care for.

'Daddy is terribly good to me. Because Mummy died when I was a tiny baby, we are everything to each other. But the house does seem ridiculously big for the two of us sometimes.'

'Little brothers and sisters are a frightful nuisance

– you're jolly lucky, you know. I say, Helen – you must come to tea. Ma said that you must. And I'd like it frightfully.'

She blushed again, but this time with pleasure. 'That would be lovely, Geoffrey.'

'I'll fetch you in the old man's motor-car.'

They wandered down to the river to look at the tadpoles. Shells gleamed on the sandy bed of the river: big, flat shells like the ones around the mirror in Robin's winter house. 'Freshwater mussels,' said Geoffrey. Walking back to the bicycles he took Helen's hand. His fingers were soft, uncalloused and warm. Helen forgot her worries about her height, her ignorance, her awkwardness with people.

She went to tea at the Lemons' house in Burwell a week later. She already knew Mrs Lemon to be a talkative, welcoming woman. The large tribe of Geoffrey's younger brothers and sisters were at first confusing, and then entrancing. She sat with the youngest Lemon, only nine months old, on her knee. He smelt of baby powder and milk, and when she stroked his skin it was as soft as velvet. When he cried Helen comforted him, and her heart swelled with pride and pleasure when he fell asleep on her lap. Driving home, she imagined what it would be like to be the wife of a doctor. She pictured herself in a comfortable, untidy house, children always about her, kissing her husband when he arrived home at the end of a busy day. When, just outside the village, Geoffrey stopped the motor-car and the kiss became reality, her mind was a muddled torrent of pleasure and hope and confusion.

Helen lay awake for hours that night. The air was too hot, too humid, for sleep. Events of the day played out over and over again in her memory: Geoffrey's kiss, the expression in his eyes just before he had kissed her. His gangling lope as he had climbed out of the car and run round to open the passenger door for her. He had given her his hand. 'I say – mind that puddle, old thing.'

He had treated her as though she was both precious and fragile. No-one except her father had ever treated her like that before.

When she did eventually fall asleep, she was in Dr Lemon's motor-car again, speeding along the road. The car stopped, and Geoffrey leaned over and kissed her. The kiss made her feel warm and hungry inside, but then she saw that it was not Geoffrey bending over her, but her father. She could feel the papery dryness of his mouth. Helen woke suddenly, staring into the darkness, and did not sleep again.

The following afternoon she spent in the kitchen, making sponge cakes and scones. Betty did most of the cooking, but was heavy handed with cakes, so Helen baked on the maids' half-day. When the door-bell rang she heard her father's voice and Geoffrey's, but the sponge was at the critical stage so she could only call out greetings and rapidly whisk egg yolks. There was a murmur of muted voices, and then she heard the front door open and close, and the distant sound of a car engine starting up. Suddenly frozen, Helen stared at the kitchen door, the whisk motionless in her hand. Her heart began to pound; she could not believe that he had gone. The sponge mixture, balanced over its saucepan of hot water, curdled into scrambled eggs.

Her father opened the kitchen door.

'Was that Geoffrey, Daddy?'

'Is that his name? Yes.' His tone was disinterested. 'He wanted to take you to the theatre, of all things. I sent him packing, of course. Is that quite right, Chickie?'

She saw that he was referring to the sponge mixture, now an utter disaster, so she seized the bowl and plonked it on the table, burning her fingers. She said unsteadily, 'I'll have to start again.'

There was another silence. Then Julius Ferguson said, 'I told Mr Lemon, Helen, that I disapprove of friendships between girls and young men. I told him that you are too young to be anyone's sweetheart but mine.'

She looked at him, confused. 'But Mummy was only eighteen—'

'When we married?' Julius Ferguson's expression was grim. 'And my poor, darling Florence was only nineteen when I buried her.'

Helen's face burned, and she looked away. She heard her father leave the room and she stood for a moment, trembling slightly, wondering whether or not to go after him. Then she began to crack eggs, to weigh sugar. Beating the eggs, she thought that the iron stove sucked the air from the room, and that the small, square-paned windows cut her off from the light.

Robin had been mortified to discover that she found office work difficult. She had expected to find it dull, but for it to be difficult as well as dull was an unpleasant shock to her. After more than six months she was still the humblest of filing clerks; her errors were sufficiently frequent for her to be uncertain sometimes of remaining even that.

She compensated for the difficulties of the day by throwing herself wholeheartedly into her voluntary activities. On several evenings each week she helped out at the Free Clinic run by foul-tempered but utterly kind Dr Mackenzie. The clinic, supported by the council and by voluntary donations, doled out free milk and orange juice to expectant mothers and their infants, ran ante-natal and babycare classes, and gave information and practical help about birth control. Robin's tasks varied from receptionist to cleaner and baby-minder. Often, when she made mistakes, Dr Mackenzie bawled at her, but somehow she never came away from the clinic feeling as stupid and depressed as she did after a day at the insurance office.

Walking from the office back to her lodgings one day in early May, Robin read the newspaper hoardings announcing Labour's triumph in the General Election. Her whoop of delight made several passers-by turn and stare at her.

She, Joe and Francis had worked tirelessly throughout the preceding weeks. Robin had tramped numerous streets, pushing leaflets through letter boxes, and knocked on countless doors, Francis Gifford at her side. She had discovered that Francis did not lack conviction, that, listening to him, you could not doubt that he believed every word he said. His eyes, his voice, would transfix whoever opened the door, magically charming them from disinterest or churlishness to attention and then agreement.

Joe, back at the basement, printed the leaflets. Black with printer's ink, he alternately cursed and coaxed the temperamental old press into coughing out leaflets and posters. He never seemed to sleep. The basement walls and ceiling resounded day and night to the clatter of the press.

After she had eaten her supper, Robin walked to Francis's flat. Halfway down the street, she could hear the noise from the basement, drowning the sounds of delivery vans and children's games. Robin hammered loudly on the door.

The woman who opened it had finely plucked eyebrows, emerald-green eyelids, and a helmet of smooth black hair.

'Can I help you, darling?'

Inside, the basement heaved with people: dancing, singing and drinking. 'Is Francis in?'

The door opened a little wider. 'In the bath, darling,' said the woman, and disappeared.

There seemed to be a hundred people crammed into the four small rooms. Robin recognized some from ILP meetings. The printing press was draped with red flags, and a piano had appeared in the kitchen. Someone had daubed in scarlet paint on the wall, 'Workers of the world, unite!'

Robin ducked through the crowd, heading for the back room. She found Francis, fully dressed, sitting in the empty bath.

'Robin, darling.' He blew a kiss and waved a bottle at

her. 'Find yourself a glass. Celebrating the election . . .'

She picked up a glass from the floor, and wiped the rim with the sleeve of her blouse. 'Isn't it wonderful?'

'The dawn of a new age.' Inaccurately, Francis poured beer into Robin's glass and his own. 'We are witnessing the death throes of capitalism.'

She looked around. 'Who are all these people, Francis?'

'Oh . . .' he said vaguely. 'Comrades . . . contacts . . . and some of them are friends of Vivien's. Joe's here somewhere. Come and sit with me, dear Robin, and drink beer.'

She climbed in and sat opposite him in the tin bath. Her bent knees touched his. The beer went quickly to her head.

'It's bloody terrific,' said Francis dreamily. 'Ramsay MacDonald for PM again. Everything's going to change, Robin. No more pompous asses in top hats and tails . . . everyone'll have their say . . . I tell you, when I put my cross on that little bit of paper, well . . . it made me feel bloody good. Thought I was changing things. Didn't you?'

She shook her head. 'I couldn't vote, Francis. I'm not old enough.'

The woman with the green eyelids knelt down beside the bath. 'Robin's only nineteen,' explained Francis. His voice was slightly slurred and his hair looked rumpled.

'Such a baby. I can hardly remember being nineteen. It seems so long ago.'

'That's because you're an old hag, Diana.' Francis stared at his empty glass. 'Hell – I've nothing to drink.'

'Would you, darling?' said Diana to Robin. 'I've no shoes.'

Diana's feet were, Robin saw, bare. There was black nail polish on each of her toenails.

By the time she returned with Francis's glass, Diana was in the bath, sitting on Francis's knee. Robin dumped the glass on the floor, and wandered off, looking for Joe. She found him sitting in the back yard with a woman and a child, making paper aeroplanes out of leftover election leaflets.

Joe looked up when Robin appeared. 'Meet Clodie and Lizzie. This is Robin Summerhayes, Clo. A comrade.'

'Charmed, I'm sure,' said Clodie. The little girl giggled and covered her face with her fingers. 'Mind your manners,' said her mother sharply, and Lizzie extended an ink-stained paw.

As she shook the child's hand, long green eyes inspected Robin, discounting her as unimportant. Clodie was, Robin guessed, a few years older than Joe. And she was as beautiful as Maia, but in an entirely different way. Francis had told her weeks ago that Clodie was Joe's lover. Terribly Burne-Jones, he had added, and Robin now understood what he had meant. Clodie's skin was milk-white, her hair an extravagant cloud of dark red. Beneath her green sweater and tweed skirt, her body curved voluptuously. Beside her, Joe looked more of a scarecrow than ever. The child, Lizzie, appeared to have inherited little of her mother's shapely good looks, and was mousy-haired and slight.

'One of my aeroplanes flew into next door's yard,' confided Lizzie to Robin.

She had a sudden sharp memory of herself, perched on the sofa beside Stevie, watching him crease a sheet of paper into the form of an aeroplane. He had been wearing his school uniform; she could have been no older than the child who now sat next to her.

'Mine all fall on the floor,' said Clodie complacently.

Joe aimed another paper dart, and it soared up into the sky, circling and dancing before it landed nose-first in the gutter.

'Story of my life,' said Joe, cushioning his head on his threaded hands, and leaning back onto the scrubby grass.

Later that evening – or perhaps it was the night – she danced. She knew the names of none of her partners, and remembered none of their faces. Then, somehow, she was playing the piano, the pianist having passed out in a corner of the room. She managed to remember most of the notes, and to thump the keys loud enough for the melody to be heard.

She saw Joe kissing Clodie good night and, stumbling into the kitchen, came upon Francis and Diana, locked in a passionate embrace. She knew that she was drunk for the first time in her life because instead of just tactfully disappearing, she staggered out of the room towards Joe, and seized his elbow, turning him towards her.

'Who is that awful woman with the green eyelids?'

'Jealous?'

'Not in the least! Only she wasn't tramping through the streets in all weathers . . . getting barked at by awful dogs . . .' She heard her voice getting louder, more indignant.

'One of the unfairnesses of life, dear Robin.' Bending his head, he kissed her on the mouth. 'There. A consolation prize.'

In her muddled state she couldn't decide whether to be furious with him, or to laugh. Instead, she said curiously, 'What are you doing?'

'Printing a celebratory pamphlet to send to my father.'

The press shuddered into noisy life, groaning and spitting paper to the floor. Robin stooped and picked one up. 'Labour Victory,' she read. 'Socialist triumph marks an end to private ownership.'

'Your father . . . ?'

'His worst nightmare.' Joe's dark eyes were narrowed, glittering. 'Elliot's Mill turned into a cooperative. I'd sell my soul for that.'

Robin glanced back to the kitchen. Diana was pulling a fur coat over her black dress. Her green eyelids were a little smudged. The remainder of the room was emptying. A few stragglers were grouped by the door, and when someone suggested a nightclub, there was a ragged cheer.

'I suppose I should go home . . . What time is it, Joe?'

72

'Almost four,' he said, and she shrieked.

'My landladies—'

'In my experience, it's better to stay out for a whole night than half a night. Then you can make up some terribly impressive excuse about having to go home to mummy suddenly to help with the church social. Or something like that.'

She giggled. She was not sure whether she was able to walk home.

'Besides, Francis is making coffee.'

The flat had miraculously cleared. There was only Joe and Francis and herself, and the printing press, heaving and churning away. Francis made thick, sweet Turkish coffee, and they drank it sitting on the floor amid a muddle of streamers and paper aeroplanes and cigarette ends. Then they played bezique and poker, for bottle tops. And then Robin found herself in bed, Joe to one side of her, Francis to the other, Joe snoring slightly because he was sleeping on his back, Francis's arm flung carelessly around her shoulders.

Chapter Three

Maia and Vernon married in June. The ceremony was small and quiet: Maia wore a wedding-dress of cream shantung silk with a white gauze overskirt; defying the fashions of the decade the hem of the dress reached her ankles. She carried a sheaf of white lilies and wore a coronet of the same flowers in her hair. Helen and Robin were her only attendants, and of the thirty guests at the wedding-breakfast Maia knew only a handful.

They set off for Scotland later that day, travelling in Vernon's motor-car. Scotland in June was wet and cold. Mountains, black and wreathed in mist, circled the hunting-lodge in which they honeymooned. Vernon rowed her on a loch of black glass.

After a fortnight, they drove back to Cambridge. Vernon carried her over the threshold of his house. The servants lined up in the hallway, applauding politely. Looking round at the smiling faces, the sparkling glass and gleaming woodwork, all the glittering possessions that seemed to divide her from the past, Maia felt triumphant.

She wrote to Robin, in London. *Obviously I have passed one of the milestones in a woman's life.* She wrote to Helen also, arranging a date. On a warm August afternoon she waited for her friends in the conservatory at the back of the house. She wore a long-sleeved blue linen dress, the same colour as her sapphire earrings, the same colour as her eyes. The dress was beautifully cut, the linen not of the sort that creased as soon as you wore it.

Maia gave a squeak of pleasure when the butler showed Helen and Robin in. 'Darlings! How lovely to see you! You look so well, Helen – and so brown, Robin. I have to hide from the sun or I burn so.'

She kissed both Helen and Robin on the cheek. 'I thought I'd show you round the house first.'

It took her over an hour to parade all the splendours of her house. The Rennie Mackintosh chairs, the Marion Dorn carpets, and Vernon's collection of Lalique glass. Helen was admiring, but Robin was not.

'Don't you get lost?' The expression on Robin's face began to annoy Maia.

Maia glanced at her sharply. 'Of course not.'

'I suppose you have an army of servants to look after this stuff.'

'Half a dozen, actually, though they don't all live in.'

'It's a bit much, isn't it, for two people?'

'It's a beautiful house, Maia,' interrupted Helen soothingly. 'How proud you must be.'

They had tea on the lawn beneath the beech tree. The garden was, like the house, perfectly manicured, bursting with gazebos, trellis-work and fountains. Maia poured the tea. A shadow fell over the white damask tablecloth, and when she looked up, there was Vernon.

She put the teapot aside. 'You're early, darling.'

He bent to kiss her. 'I had to collect some papers from my study. Winterton told me you were out here.'

Winterton was the butler. Maia was terribly proud of having a butler.

'Vernon – this is Helen – and Robin—'

He shook hands with both women.

'You'll have tea with us, won't you, darling?'

Glancing at his watch, Vernon said, 'I have to dash. Meetings all afternoon. You must excuse me, ladies.'

He walked back across the lawn, leaving Maia with a mixture of resentment and relief. Robin, her gaze following his distant figure, said, 'We should drink a toast. "Milestones passed" . . . or something like that.'

Maia felt herself flush. 'I take it, Robin, that you're still—'

'Virgo intacta? 'Fraid so. Any useful hints or advice would be kindly received, wouldn't they, Helen?'

Maia glared at Robin. Robin glared back. Then Maia, settling back into her chair, a little smile on her face, beckoned the maidservant and ordered her to bring a bottle of champagne.

Maia opened the bottle herself. Champagne gushed over the wrought-iron table, dripping onto the lawn.

'To losing one's virginity . . .' Maia raised her glass. 'It was simply divine. You can't imagine. It's not easy to describe to . . . to . . .'

'Virgins?' said Robin smoothly.

Maia shrugged. 'We were in a hotel en route to Scotland. I wore the most gorgeous satin nightgown. Vernon was fearfully gentle and considerate. He's thirty-four, you know,' she added, looking at Robin. 'Frightfully experienced. I can't think what it would be like with a younger man. Rather horrible, perhaps.'

After Robin and Helen had gone, Maia went up to her room to change for dinner. Her bedroom was particularly luxurious: the wide windows that looked out onto the back garden were swathed in filmy white fabric, and the carpets were a deeply embossed cream. Wardrobes covered the length of one wall, and there was an adjoining bathroom, with a marble bath and gold taps. Maia had insisted on the marble bath and gold taps.

Her maid had already run the bath. Maia let her unbutton the linen dress, and then she dismissed her.

In the privacy of the bathroom she peeled off the blue linen, letting it drop to the floor. It had been a hot day to wear a long-sleeved dress. But she had had no choice: ringed around each slender arm was a bracelet of blue bruises. Like sapphires, thought Maia, as she sank into the scented bathwater.

Clodie opened the door to Joe. There were curlers in her hair, and her bottom lip stuck out just as Lizzie's did when she was about to have a tantrum.

'The sitter's only just come, and I haven't a thing to wear.'

'You look lovely in that.' She was wearing a green checked cotton dress and white stockings.

'This?' Clodie's mouth curled scornfully. 'I've had this old rag for years. I can't remember when I last had anything new. The doctor's put Lizzie on a special diet – how I'm going to afford it, I really don't know.'

Joe followed her upstairs to her bedroom and sat on the bed as she tried on dress after dress. Today had already gone badly wrong, and he had a suspicion that it could only get worse. There had been a fight in the pub in which he worked at lunch-time. Someone had cracked him on the head with a bottle; gingerly, sitting on Clodie's pillow, he fingered the bruise.

Clodie was standing in front of him in her camisole and stockings. Joe patted the bed beside him.

'Let's not bother going out, Clo. I'm sure we can find something better to do. And you wouldn't have to find a dress.'

Her eyes filled with contempt. 'I haven't been out all week, Joe Elliot. And when your friend's so nice as to offer to treat me . . . I can't believe that you should want to spoil my evening. You know I hardly ever get out . . . It's not easy for a widow with a little one . . .'

The scorn had degenerated into a series of whines. Joe rubbed his eyes and made an effort.

'You looked stunning in that thing with the flowers, Clo. Francis'll say you look like a Pre-Raphaelite painting.'

Now she looked suspicious. 'A what?'

'You remember – I showed you in the National Gallery.'

To his relief, she began to pull the floral dress back on.

'All cream-coloured skin and big eyes and enormous breasts,' added Joe, closing his eyes, wishing he could fall asleep.

On the Tube, they quarrelled intermittently. The train was crowded, and Clodie snagged her stocking on someone's umbrella. Francis had chosen a restaurant in Knightsbridge. Another bad idea, Joe realized as soon as he walked through the door. Most of the other diners were wearing evening clothes. The head waiter glanced contemptuously at Joe's well-worn jacket and frayed cuffs, but Francis muttered to him – some rubbish about his wealthy relations, Joe guessed – and another waiter cringed and fawned and they were shown to a reasonable table.

Robin, of course, passed in this sort of place. She wore the brown velvet dress in which he had first seen her, perfectly fitting, presumably made for her by some underpaid dressmaker. Someone like Clodie. Joe reached across the table for Clodie's hand, but she touched his fingertips only briefly, and then withdrew, accepting a cigarette from Francis. Francis ordered champagne.

'Ever so nice,' said Clodie. 'Are we celebrating?'

'It's my anniversary.' Francis poured her a glass of champagne. 'Lost my virginity to the captain of rugger ten years ago.'

Clodie looked shocked.

Joe said irritably, 'Don't talk rubbish, Francis.' He turned to Clodie. 'Gifford Press has just won a big contract. Well – big for us.'

'And I've put together the first issue of my magazine.' Proudly, Francis drew a folded journal from his pocket and placed it on the table.

The title, 'Havoc', was lettered in black, angular type. The poems and articles, by Francis and various of his acquaintances, were listed on the title page.

Clodie leaned across so that Francis could light her cigarette from his own. 'You are clever, Francis.'

Francis said cheerfully, 'And you're looking especially

gorgeous tonight, Clodie. You're wasted nowadays, of course. You should have lived thirty years ago and been a painter's model.'

Clodie giggled. Robin glanced first at Joe, then at the menu. 'What shall we have? The Dover sole sounds lovely, doesn't it, Joe? I haven't eaten Dover sole since I came to London.'

Joe drank a glass of champagne rather quickly, and tried to concentrate. That damned waiter was hovering, looking supercilious.

'Joe's used to plain northern food, aren't you, Joe?' Francis blew a smoke ring. 'You don't do boiled tripe or pig's trotters, do you, waiter?'

Clodie giggled again, tossing back her long loose red hair. Francis filled up the champagne glasses.

Robin said quickly, 'I think we'll all have the Dover sole please, waiter,' and Joe didn't know which of the three of them he disliked more. Francis was being an annoying bastard because Francis enjoyed being an annoying bastard; Clodie was flirting with Francis because it was instinctive to her to flirt. And Robin was being polite and socially adept and organizing them all.

Francis told Robin and Clodie about the printing contract. 'Wedding stationery, would you believe? Ghastly bridal lists and invitations. Hideously bourgeois, but then, needs must. It'll help finance "Havoc".'

'I love a good wedding. I can still remember my mum taking me up town to see Lady Diana Manners' wedding. Such a lovely dress . . .' Clodie looked wistful.

'What about you, Robin? Are you besotted by orange blossom and confetti?'

Robin made a face. 'Not at all. I'll never marry.'

Clodie stared at her. 'You mustn't give up, Miss Summerhayes. With a nice perm and some pretty frocks you wouldn't be wanting for sweethearts, I'm sure.'

Joe said, 'I don't think Robin *wants* to get married, Clodie.'

Clodie looked even more confused. 'But if Mr Right came along . . . ?'

Francis shook his head. 'I absolutely agree with you, Robin. Dreadful institution, marriage.'

'Marriage makes a woman her husband's chattel.'

'But if you fell in love, Miss Summerhayes?'

'Marriage is to do with possession, not love.'

'I was happily married for five years, that's all I can say.' Obstinately, Clodie stubbed out her cigarette. 'I had the most gorgeous wedding-dress – I made it myself, of course – and Trevor was a wonderful husband. He worshipped me.'

'It must be awfully hard for you, Mrs Bryant,' said Robin, 'bringing up a child on your own.'

Clodie looked martyred. 'It's ever so hard. Every week's a struggle. If it wasn't for Lizzie I think I'd have put my head in the gas oven long ago. I know that's a wicked thing to say but, well, it's how I feel.'

Joe snorted into his second glass of champagne. Clodie had come into his life at the beginning of the year, like a whirlwind, dragging him along in her wake. It was impossible to imagine anyone more alive – more attached to life – than Clodie.

'Lizzie's all the reward I need. I do a bit of dress-making to keep us both going. What do you do, Miss Summerhayes?'

'Oh – I work for an insurance firm. Very dull – filing and things like that. I'm teaching myself typewriting.'

Robin looked, Joe noticed, rather glum. Mentally he gave her a year at the job, at reality. A little middle-class girl like Robin Summerhayes would run home to mummy and daddy as soon as things got difficult.

The waiter arrived with the Dover sole. Francis said, 'And you help at a nursery, don't you, Robin?'

'A clinic.' Robin stared at her plate.

'Practical socialism, you see, Clodie.'

Robin had gone very quiet. She usually enthused for hours about the Free Clinic, about the babies and the mothers and, her pet subject, modern birth control.

The waiter fussed between them, serving vegetables with a spoon and fork.

'Ever so nice,' said Clodie again. 'Such a treat for me. Ever so nice of you, Francis.' Her long, white hands hesitated over the cutlery.

'Fish knife, darling,' said Francis, pointing. 'Though I always find it's like trying to eat your dinner with a palette knife.'

Clodie giggled, a high-pitched sound that made the other diners in the restaurant look round. The champagne had gone to her head; she was, Joe knew, trying to punish him by flirting with Francis. Francis, generally easy-going by nature, neither encouraged her nor was embarrassed by her. But Joe felt a mixture of pain and anger: only he knew the Clodie who could take his breath away in bed, leaving him satiated and desirous again both at the same time. Only he knew the Clodie who genuinely loved her plain little daughter, and who would fight like a tiger to get the best for her. As Clodie became sillier, Joe became increasingly monosyllabic and sullen. Robin, to his fury, tried to distract him with the sort of conversation that people like her found so easy – and people like Clodie found so impossible. Books and music and ideas and places that she had seen. The common currency of middle-class life. Bourgeois life. The things that made day-to-day existence tolerable, that marked out the educated, that left out people like Clodie. The knowledge that he, too, could have talked for hours about these things only made him angrier.

They had reached the dessert course, a horrid concoction of cream and meringue and sponge. Francis was regaling Clodie and Robin with stories about school.

'I only got away with it so long because the housemaster was a foul old pervert. He had a penchant for pretty blond youths, so poor Joe hadn't a hope. I was teacher's pet. He even made me a prefect.'

'I was blackboard monitress at my elementary school,' said Clodie dreamily. Her normally pale face was pink, and her fingers rested on Francis's forearm.

'How about you, Robin? Prefect?'

'Robin must have been head girl,' said Joe nastily.

'She organizes everyone at the ILP, and at the clinic too, no doubt. She's only failed with Francis and me.'

All the colour seemed to go out of Robin's face, and she stood up, her spoon clattering to the floor. Then she ran out of the restaurant.

Even Clodie was silenced. Then, looking at Robin's empty place, she said, 'Well! She hasn't even eaten her pudding!'

Joe ran after her. He had meant to hurt, but not so much.

Calling her name, he caught up with her before she reached the Tube station, and when she failed to stop, he grabbed her sleeve.

She spun round. 'Just leave me *alone*!'

He was out of breath. She pulled away from him again. He was aware that he had been unfair to her, that he had taken out on Robin his irritation and frustration with Clodie. He felt slightly ashamed of himself.

'Robin – for heaven's sake – I'm sorry.'

She folded her arms defensively in front of her, and said proudly, 'It isn't your fault.'

Joe didn't believe her. 'I was in a foul mood,' he explained. 'A bad day . . . and Clodie . . .'

'It isn't your fault,' she repeated. 'It's my fault.'

He stared at her. There was something so horribly young, so horribly innocent about her. He made a real effort to pacify her.

'What I said about you organizing everyone—'

'Bossing everyone, you meant, Joe.'

He started to speak, but she stopped him.

'You were right, of course. I do organize people. I am bossy. I didn't realize—' She broke off and he thought she was going to run away again. Then she said, the words all in a rush, 'I met this lovely woman a few months ago, Joe. She's called Nan Salter, and she lives in a little house in Stepney and she was terribly kind to me when I fell off my bicycle. Anyway, she has seven children, and I thought . . . I persuaded her to go to the Free Clinic. So she wouldn't have eight children. It took

82

ages to persuade her, but I managed it. I'm quite good at persuading people, Joe – not as good as Francis, but quite good. She came with me a few weeks ago, and the nurse was awfully kind and fitted her with a diaphragm and told her how to use it. And I hadn't seen her for a little while, so I went along today, after work . . .'

'And . . . ?' prompted Joe curiously.

Her voice, when she spoke, was flat. 'And she had a black eye and bruises all over her face because her husband had found the diaphragm and said it was interfering with nature and meant she could be unfaithful to him. Only he didn't put it quite like that. Nan says I shouldn't visit any more. And it's all my fault.'

Her face had become closed and pale. She added fiercely, 'Go on – say it. I was interfering. Meddling in other people's lives.'

He shrugged. 'You couldn't have known.' But he thought privately that she had tried to apply the rules of one England to another, very different England.

He heard her mutter, 'I should have listened. I just charge in, don't I? And I'm in such trouble at work, Joe! I lost a file . . .'

She started to walk towards the Tube station again. He followed alongside her, enjoying the sharpness of the October air after the stuffy restaurant.

'I'm beginning to think that I'm not much good at anything.'

He said, 'Will you go home, then? I mean – to your parents?' and she stopped and turned, and stared at him in amazement.

'Go home? Of course not. Why on earth should I do that?'

'Because it's what a girl like you would do.'

Momentarily, he thought she was going to hit him. Instead, glaring at him, she dug her hands into her pockets and hissed, 'You are the most unbearably arrogant and offensive man I have ever met.'

He began to walk away from her. He heard her say, 'And what about you, Joe? If Clodie starts looking elsewhere . . . if you run out of work for the press . . . or if you get tired of pulling pints . . . will you go home?'

He flushed with anger. 'Of course not.'

'So why should it be any different for me?'

He shook his head. 'No reason.'

'Because I'm a girl – is that it, Joe?'

She left him then, disappearing into the black archway of Knightsbridge Underground station, and this time he did not follow her. He perched in a shop doorway, lighting himself a cigarette, listening to the noises of the street, and the newsvendors shouting out the late headlines. Something about the New York stock-market: he did not bother to listen. He knew that he was right, that Robin wouldn't stick it out much longer. There had been a lot of things, he thought a little regretfully, that he should have said to her. A mixture of clichés like, *Everyone makes mistakes,* and things she wouldn't listen to like, *Don't fall in love with Francis.* But he had said none of them, having learned long ago that people only hear what they want to hear. And besides, at twenty-two, without a proper job or a home or a family and in love with a woman who half the time shut the door in his face, he was hardly the person to offer advice.

For the first few months of her marriage, Maia's delight in her possessions occupied her – showing her new home to her friends and relations and enjoying their envy, or just wandering around the rooms and gardens, trailing her fingers on the moiré silk upholstery or breathing in the scent of a rose. Most of all, walking through the glass doors of Merchants department store. 'Won't you sit down, Mrs Merchant? Shall I fetch Mr Merchant for you?' She had thought her pleasure in her wealth would last for ever. She still adored and needed these things, but somehow they were not quite enough. And it wasn't *her* wealth, of course, it was Vernon's.

She was allowed to arrange the flowers, but not to redecorate a room. She was allowed to choose the menu for dinner, but not to select the guests. She was allowed little trips to her dressmaker or hairdresser, but not to go away for a weekend by herself. Vernon made the rules plain without raising his voice, and without, usually, violence. Maia had learnt to recognize a particular expression in her husband's foxy red-brown eyes: an expression which reminded her clearly of the penalty of insisting on her own way. That expression both excited and taunted her: she was clever, she was beautiful, and she was used to men giving her what she wanted. Her agile mind demanded something more than choosing between the blue silk and the cream, or between vichyssoise and iced cucumber soup.

She tried to take an interest in Vernon's business. She had read somewhere, in some awful magazine of Margery's, perhaps, that a wife should take an interest in her husband's work. And besides, the shop fascinated her, it always had. She noticed that when she commented on Merchants' women's wear department, or the perfumery, then Vernon listened to her. She suggested placing sofas and rugs and lamps like miniature drawing-rooms within the home furnishing department, and when next she called at the shop, the sofas were no longer ranked in lines, the lampshades no longer banished to the electrical department. Vernon congratulated her. Sales were up.

But if she tried to talk to him about profits and losses, about advertising campaigns and rival stores, then he did not respond. Those were things that men talked about. He even checked her household accounts.

Bored, she began to push against the bounds he set her. That he had hurt her once or twice angered her, but did not yet frighten her. She was used to getting her own way; her parents might have neglected her, but they had rarely thwarted her. So she wore a frock that Vernon disapproved of, and she arrived home late after a visit to Helen. And then, fatally, she flirted.

It had rained all day, and she had not even been able to go out into the garden. She had asked Vernon to buy her a motor-car – it was ridiculous that she hadn't a motor-car of her own – and he had refused. Maia resented his refusal. That evening they gave a dinner party, and one of the young men was really rather attractive. It was only a very mild flirtation – the sort of game she had played with Lionel Cummings, once Mummy's tennis partner, now Mummy's second husband. A smile, a touch of the hand, a flattering response to his conversation. She sensed that Vernon was annoyed, and enjoyed his annoyance, feeling that she was paying him back for his meanness that morning. It pleased her to know that because of their guests, he could not criticize her behaviour. By the end of the evening she had begun to feel a little less stifled, a little less afraid that, with marriage, she had instantly become frumpy and housewifely. Vernon might be angry later – well, then, she would be sweet to him and eventually he would promise to buy her a car.

When the last guest had gone, the butler offered to serve brandy in the drawing-room, but Vernon refused, dismissing him, and instead poured himself a generous measure of brandy. He had drunk steadily all evening: gin and its, red wine, white wine, liqueurs. Maia picked up her silk shawl.

'I think I'll walk in the garden for a while. It's stopped raining at last.'

Vernon's fingers enfolded her wrist. 'It's bedtime, Maia.'

She wanted to argue but, noticing his expression, managed to stop herself. She started up the stairs beside him.

Inside the bedroom, he slipped off his jacket and said, 'Do you know who that young man was, Maia?'

'Which young man?'

'The young man you were making up to, of course.'

'"Making up to",' she repeated irritably. 'Such a vulgar expression.'

'Making eyes at, then. Leading on. Whatever you wish to call it. I said, do you know who he is?'

'Leonard . . . Leonard something . . .'

'Not his name. I mean – *what* he is.'

They entertained a tableful of Vernon's business colleagues each week. Maia could rarely tell one from the other. 'A bank manager . . . someone at the golf club . . .'

'He is one of my managers. Bright chap – I promoted him only a fortnight ago. Now I shall have to find a reason to sack him.'

She frowned. 'Why?'

'Oh Maia. You do see that I can't possibly have one of my junior managers gossiping about my wife? Telling other members of my staff that my wife tried to seduce him?'

'I'm sorry, Vernon – I didn't realize. I wasn't trying to seduce him, though.' She gave him her sweetest smile, and fondled his arm. 'I was only flirting, darling. I was bored.'

'Flirting . . . seduction . . . they're just different labels for the same thing.'

She tried to explain. 'Flirtation's just . . . playing, Vernon. It's just fun.'

And yet that was not quite true. When she flirted with men like Leonard, like Lionel, she felt powerful. Nothing else in her life, she realized suddenly, gave her that feeling of power.

'I'd never be unfaithful to you, Vernon.'

'I'd kill you if you were, Maia.'

She did not doubt him. His voice was calm, but his eyes had a cold intensity that Maia found much more threatening than anger. She began for the first time to feel frightened. There was an expression almost of pleasure in his eyes. As though he was looking forward to what was about to happen.

He said suddenly, 'You're awfully good at it, you know, Maia. Flirting – seduction – whatever you call it. As good as the professionals.'

'What do you mean?'

'As good as the whores.' He sat down in one of the basketweave chairs, his legs slung out before him, and unknotted his bow tie. 'There were whores in France, in the War, y'know. I lost my virginity to one of 'em. After four years, when I came home, I thought the so-called nice English girls my mother found for me would be different. But they weren't.'

Maia was still wearing her black sleeveless cocktail frock. She did not dare begin to undress. Usually he liked to watch her, but tonight she wanted to run into the bathroom and bolt the door and feel safe and alone among the gold taps and the marble tiles.

'Some of the whores were even younger than you, Maia. Damned pretty girls, too, until they lost their looks to the pox.'

She said stiffly, 'I don't want to hear about women like that, Vernon.'

''Course you do. You're no different from them. You'd make a very competent whore.'

She hissed angrily, 'Of course I'm different—'

'No. You're just like the rest of them. You'd sell yourself for a few jewels and a wardrobe of clothes. Come, Maia – did you marry me for *love*?'

She recognized the cynicism in his eyes then, and felt an ice-cold shiver of fear run along her spine. He knew her, he understood her.

He smiled, and drawled, 'There's not the slightest difference between the sluts in the Pigalle and the little girls behind the counters in Merchants . . . or the hard-faced bitches who shop there. They're all the same. It's just a question of luck . . . of chance. They'd all sell themselves . . . whether it's for a ten bob note, or for marriage lines and a semi in the suburbs. All women are potentially, if not actually, tarts.'

'Vernon.' Maia tried to laugh. 'You don't really believe that, do you?'

'Of course I do. There are no exceptions. My mother . . . your mother. Hard as hell, the pair of them.'

She stared at him blankly. She did not dare even glance at the bathroom door.

'But you are my wife now, Maia, and if you play the harlot to my employees, you must be punished.'

His tone had altered. As a child, the shouting of her parents had frightened her. Vernon did not raise his voice, but Maia was just as frightened now. She ran for the bathroom door, but as she turned the handle he grabbed her, forcing her fingers apart.

'Bitch,' he said. 'Whore.' His breath was hot against her neck, and his hands pinioned her arms behind her back as he shook her. 'The whores in France didn't have to tout for business, Maia. We'd just line up, all of us soldier boys, and the sergeant would shout our numbers. Ten minutes for each of us. Of course, when I was an officer, it was different. We had high-class whores then. That's what you are, isn't it, Maia? A high-class whore.'

She couldn't speak, and there were tears in her eyes. Before, he had only slapped her and pushed her about a bit, but now the pain was so severe that her vision began to blur, and she had to fight for her breath. She managed to gasp, 'Let me go, Vernon. You're hurting me. You'll dislocate my shoulder—'

'Mustn't do that. We'd have to call the doctor then, and that would never do.' He released her so suddenly that she collapsed to the floor. She thought, with a flood of relief, that it was over. Then he said, 'Take off your jewellery, Maia.'

She looked up at him. He had sat down in the chair again. 'Hurry up, Maia,' he said softly and, somehow, she obeyed. Her hands were clumsy, her earring caught in her lobe, and she wanted to snap the chain of her necklace.

'That's better. Of course, the clothes are wrong. Too expensive.' Standing up, pulling her to her feet, he began to unbutton her dress. It slid to the floor, a pool of black silk. Then he unlaced her camisole, tearing the delicate ribbons and lace. 'I shall buy you some street-walker's clothes. And you haven't enough lipstick. Put on some more – and some of that black stuff round your eyes.'

Naked, she sat at her dressing-table. Her hand shook, spoiling the outline of her lipstick so that the face that looked back at her from the looking-glass was not hers, but had been made ugly and cheap.

'Get on the bed, Maia.'

'Vernon. *Please.*'

He smiled again, showing his small, white, pointed teeth.

'This is what I bought you for.' She had seen the expression in his eyes before. He had worn that greedy, hungry, pleasured look just before he had hit her the first time.

'Get on the bed, Maia,' repeated Vernon, and she did as she was told.

After the disastrous evening at the restaurant, Robin avoided both Francis and Joe. Joe's assumption that she would run back to her parents as soon as things became difficult annoyed her intensely, and as for Francis . . . When she thought of Francis she felt muddled. She had not enjoyed watching Clodie flirt with him. Neither had she enjoyed comparing herself to Clodie. She thought crossly that both Francis and Joe often treated her as though she was twelve, rather than nineteen. It bothered her that after almost a year away from home she had found neither an interesting job, nor travelled abroad, nor lost her virginity. She longed to be able to write to Maia and Helen, inviting them to celebrate with her the passing of at least one of the milestones in a woman's life. Particularly Maia, who, with her enormous house and wealthy husband, had become quite smug and awful.

She missed the ILP meetings and the impromptu evenings in the Hackney basement. Determined not to brood, she began to scan the newspapers for other work, looking for something more interesting. She joined a touch-typing class, and by the end of a fortnight could type 'The quick brown fox jumps over the lazy dog' with her eyes shut. Dr Mackenzie asked her to help out on another evening at the clinic, and she did so, reorganizing the notes and files he was gathering for his research project on poverty in the East End. Because the work interested her, she was quick and efficient.

Returning to her lodgings one evening, Robin heard voices from the parlour. The younger Miss Turner's voice, and a man's voice.

Francis. Robin picked up the letter waiting for her on the hall table, stuffed it into her pocket, and opened the parlour door.

'Robin, darling!'

The room was in almost complete darkness, the only light a small oil lamp in the centre of the table. Francis, standing, kissed her on both cheeks.

'Emmeline has been showing me her simply marvellous ouija board. I have been quite terrified, expecting all sorts of ghosts from my dubious past to come and reclaim me.' He took Robin's hand. 'I have been explaining to Emmeline about my mother's house party this weekend. You must have forgotten, darling.' A meaningful squeeze of the fingers. 'The motor's outside,' added Francis. 'Have you packed?'

She hesitated only for a moment. She could continue, worthily and drearily, doing voluntary work or sitting alone in her room, or she could begin again to take part in the exotic and unpredictable world that Francis Gifford inhabited.

Robin smiled. 'Give me five minutes, won't you, Francis?'

A quarter of an hour later, they were parked outside the Navigator in Duckett Street, waiting for Joe to finish his shift. Robin's overnight bag was stuffed with crumpled dresses, stockings and jumpers. She had never seen the motor-car before – a friend's, Francis explained. It was old and open-topped, and one of the mudguards was loose, battering against the wheel-arch as Francis drove. Outside the pub, Francis leaned on the horn. Joe appeared out of the gloom, slinging a bag into the boot of the car, and squeezing himself into the narrow back seat.

'Stop that bloody racket and drive, won't you?'

They drove at breakneck speed through London. It wasn't until they were out in the suburbs that Robin was able to make herself heard over the noise of the car and the traffic.

'Are we really going to your mother's house, Francis?'

He nodded. 'Vivien sent me a telegram this morning. We haven't seen each other for ages.' His light grey eyes were bright and exhilarated.

'But is it all right . . . I mean . . . about Joe and me?'

He glanced at her and smiled. 'Of course. Vivien simply adores Joe, and she'll adore you too. The more the merrier. She loves the old place to be crowded.'

They drove on through the countryside. Crouched sideways in the back seat, Joe slept. Soon the glow of the street-lamps was replaced by stars glittering in a frosty sky.

'Where are we?'

'Suffolk,' said Francis. 'Nearly there.'

A pale and perfect half-moon had risen. Robin first saw the house as a silver silhouette picked out by moonlight, all the chimneys and crenellations and gargoyles and belvederes like white lace against the black sky. She read the house's name as they drove through the gates: Long Ferry Hall.

Climbing out of the car, looking up at the house, she felt nervous. 'Are you sure Mrs Gifford won't mind?' she whispered to Joe. She imagined a terrifying old dragon with a monocle.

Joe shook his head. 'Not in the least. But Francis's mother isn't Mrs Gifford any more. She was Mrs Collins, and now she's something else, but I can't remember what. You'd better call her Vivien – I do. So much easier than having to keep track of all the husbands.'

Francis led the way across the courtyard to the front door. The stones were weathered, crumbling in places, and weeds sprouted from the gutters. Francis rang the doorbell, and they were shown into the hall: a high ceiling, ornamented with faded escutcheons and shields, walls panelled with dark wood.

A woman appeared from out of the gloom. She wasn't an old dragon at all, but was tall and slim and blue-eyed, and her hair was as fair as Francis's.

'Francis! Darling!' she cried, and embraced her son.

Attempting to iron her one decent evening dress with an ancient flatiron, Robin tried to picture Francis, as a small boy, living in this house. None of the floors or ceilings were level, narrow staircases loomed in unexpected places, and the windows were dark, dusty and mullioned. What a glorious place, she thought, for hide-and-seek.

The dress, a tawny brown embroidered with terracotta and gold, and made for her by Persia, was as free of creases as it ever would be. Robin pulled it over her head, and hoped that the ladder in her stocking didn't show. There was no mirror in the small, angular bedroom, most of which was taken up by a high and uncomfortable four-poster bed. In the distance a gong chimed; Robin hastily dragged a comb through her hair, and rummaged in her bag for a lipstick. Then she ran off in search of the dining-room.

Everybody was sitting down to their soup when Robin arrived. She offered her apologies to Vivien.

'You mustn't worry in the slightest, darling. Angus – pour this poor girl a glass of wine. Francis says that I should provide all my guests with a map.'

Vivien introduced her to the other diners. Angus had been a colonel in the Royal Scots Guards, someone else owned a chain of garages. There was a racing-driver and a man with cold eyes and spidery hands, who owned a vast farm in Kenya, and an American gentleman who had just lost all his money on the New York Stock Exchange. All the women were rather plain.

'Made it in '28 and lost it in '29,' the American gentleman was saying. 'Damned shame.'

'Frightful bore for you, sweetie.' Vivien patted his hand sympathetically.

The soup was tepid and had a rather peculiar taste. There didn't seem to be any servants; Vivien just chose a guest to pour the wine or serve the soup.

'Francis – be an angel and collect up the bowls, won't you? And Joe – you shall come to the kitchen with me and see whether our roast pheasant is ready.'

Francis stacked soup bowls; Joe, wearing an ancient and crackling dinner jacket, disappeared into the maze of passages beyond the dining-room.

'They'll be gone for hours,' Angus confided to Robin gloomily. 'Kitchen's miles away.'

'Cook's a dipsomaniac, I hear,' said the man with the cold eyes. 'God knows what was in that soup.'

'So hard to get good servants these days. Poor Vivi puts such a brave face on things.'

Francis, searching in the huge sideboard for plates, said, 'The pheasant will be superb. Vivien shot them a week ago.'

The pheasants, six of them, ornamented with their splendid tail feathers and trimmed with bacon and shallots, were delicious. Robin discovered that she was ravenous: the Misses Turner's evening meals relied rather a lot on boiled cabbage and potatoes.

Francis was talking to Vivien.

'We've been terribly busy for the last couple of months – I've published the first issue of the magazine, and we've had plenty of work for the press.'

The American gave a dry laugh. 'Make the most of it, Mr Gifford. The good times won't last.'

Francis, disregarding him, turned back to his mother. 'Joe has taken the entire press apart three times, Vivien. I'm never convinced that he'll be able to put it together again.'

'So clever – you must mend my stove for me, Joe. Cook says it isn't drawing properly.'

'I've had some good reactions to "Havoc". A chap

94

who works for the *Listener* told me he thought it had promise.'

The American gentleman's mouth had curled in a mocking smile. 'I should forget the magazine, Mr Gifford. Find yourself a steady job while there's still time.'

'A steady job . . .' repeated Francis slowly. 'Such a deadly ring to that phrase, don't you think? So much more worthwhile to do just one great thing . . . something to be remembered by. I'd die happy if I could manage that.'

'*Darling*.' Vivien touched Francis's hand. '*Death*. Such a dreary subject for the dinner table.'

'But becoming horribly popular in New York just now, ma'am. The wealthy men of yesterday are throwing themselves out of the windows of skyscrapers because they know that tomorrow they will not be able to feed their families. It will happen here, Mr Gifford. Britain's economy is tied to that of the United States of America.'

There was a short silence. Robin shivered. Despite the log fire, cold draughts blew from the wide chimney mouth.

Vivien said, 'We shall have to go on a long holiday together, Francis darling. Somewhere abroad. Somewhere hot.'

Francis kissed his mother's hand. 'Italy. All those palazzos and gondolas.'

'And fascists.' Robin was unable to stop herself. 'You couldn't, Francis.'

'Of course not. Spain, then. Crumbling monarchy, decent weather, and marvellous beaches.'

The pheasant was finished. Vivien rose to her feet again; Francis and two other gentlemen began to rush about, collecting plates and cutlery.

Robin's neighbour said, 'You don't admire Fascism, then, Miss Summerhayes?'

Had it not been for his eyes, then she supposed he would have been handsome.

95

'Not at all.'

'You don't admire order – and decency – and patriotism?'

'Of course I do. But I also admire tolerance and liberty, Mr . . . ?'

'Farr. Denzil Farr. "Tolerance and liberty" – such mushy words, Miss Summerhayes. In my experience, tolerance and liberty can so easily become degeneracy and effeminacy.'

'Do you think so?' She found herself loathing him. 'I believe that the world would be uncivilized without them.'

Denzil Farr had lit a cigar, even though dessert had not yet been served. He leaned back in his chair, and blew smoke through his narrow lips.

'I wonder if you will be so convinced of that, Miss Summerhayes, when you cannot walk down the street for fear of being molested by some beggar or scoundrel. When your livelihood and future are held in jeopardy by a Jewish usurer to whom you owe money. When even the breeding stock of your country is weakened by the blood of degenerates.'

She was searching furiously for a reply when Vivien said, 'Don't tease Miss Summerhayes, Denzil. Soufflé, everyone?'

When, in the early hours of the morning, only a handful of guests were still awake, Francis whispered to Robin, 'Let me show you round the house, darling. A Grand Tour. So much better by candlelight.'

She rose and followed Francis out of the room. The candle that he held cast weird shadows on the walls and floor.

'The main staircase.' He had paused in the Great Hall. Carved dragons on the finials of the balustrade. Black shadows crouched in corners. Francis led the way up the staircase. 'Are you cold, Robin? Have my jacket.'

Standing on the landing, peering through the window,

Francis wrapped his dinner jacket around her shoulders. 'It might snow,' he said. 'Look – the stars have gone.'

She rubbed a clear patch in the dusty pane.

'From the belvedere you can see the sea.'

'The sea . . . ?'

'We're only a mile from the coast. I used to have a boat.'

Robin's hand slipped through the crook of his elbow. She said, remembering her earlier thoughts, 'What a wonderful place to have been brought up in. So . . . magical.'

Francis's answer surprised her. 'I've never really lived here. Vivien didn't acquire the place till I was twelve, and by then I was at school, of course.'

'But the holidays—'

'Sometimes. Though never for long. Vivien likes to travel. I stayed with Joe a few times, enduring his utterly grim parent.'

'Oh.' They hurried through rooms and passageways, Francis every now and then flinging open doors for Robin to gaze into panelled rooms.

'Joe doesn't get on with his father, does he?'

Francis chuckled. 'The understatement of the decade, my dear Robin. They simply loathe each other. Elliot père is the blunt northern type – you know, strangles ferrets for fun, and thinks anyone who reads a book is a cissy. Pots of money, though. Look, Robin – here's our priest hole.'

She stared into the gloom. A panel creaked open, and a run of small stone stairs led down into inky darkness.

'Ghastly, isn't it? Entire families used to hide in here. Personally, I'd recant.' He slid the panel back, and they walked on.

They reached another set of stairs, narrow and crooked, winding upwards. Gingerly, Francis tested the bottom tread.

'Long Ferry has dry rot and wet rot and beetle. One has to be careful. I think it's all right, Robin. You take the candle and I'll follow after you. I'll catch you before you begin to plummet to your doom.'

She laughed, and climbed up the stairs, the candle clutched in one hand, her skirt held out of the way with the other. The darkness grew more intense with each step that she took; the candle flame was small and insignificant against the immense blackness. She felt as though the walls were pressing in on her, as though the cold must grow intolerable and ice begin to flower on the old stone.

And then, suddenly, she smelt the open air, and saw the wide sky above her.

They were on the roof, encircled by the walls and balustrades of a small stone building. A stone table stood in the centre of the circular room, and the wide windows were unglassed, curtained only by the night.

'Oh *Francis*.'

She remembered how she had felt when she had first found the winter house, when she had discovered somewhere that was private and separate and particularly her own.

'Splendid, isn't it? I adore it.'

He was leaning against the balustrade, his profile outlined by the light of the candle.

'People used to eat their dessert here. Can you imagine? Trooping all the way up to the roof with the blancmange and jelly and apple pie.'

Robin laughed.

'We tried it once. I made a syllabub, and Joe and I carried it up to the belvedere, like Elizabethan gentlemen. Unfortunately we'd both drunk too much and we dropped the lot going up the stairs.'

'It's glorious, Francis.' She stood beside him, resting her arms on the balustrade, and gazing out to the darkness. She narrowed her eyes. 'I can't see the sea.'

'Too cloudy. I'm sure there are snow flakes.'

They stood in silence for a while, and then Francis said, 'Where were you, Robin? You haven't been to any of the damned meetings, and you haven't visited the flat.'

His tone was curious rather than complaining.

She said evasively, 'I've been busy.'

'You're so . . . elusive. We've missed you, you know. *I've* missed you.'

'I missed you too, Francis. Awfully.'

He touched her face with the palm of his hand. 'How silly of us both, then.' And he bent his head and kissed her lightly on the mouth.

'Gorgeous dress. Gorgeous scent.'

There had been a bottle of L'Aimant in the bathroom, and she had stolen a few splashes. She wanted him to kiss her again.

'Dear Robin – could you love me a little, d'you think?'

She glanced at him, startled. She said, rather shakily, 'I really have no idea, Francis.'

He blinked, and then he laughed. 'My dear girl, you can be quite painfully honest.'

She saw that it had begun to snow. Tiny crystalline flakes floated in the dark air like thistledown. Francis's arms were around her, but she felt suddenly cold, and as he drew her closer to him, she pressed herself against him while he covered her face with kisses.

At three o'clock in the morning, Joe was in the kitchen, trying to repair the stove. Long Ferry's kitchen was inconvenient and cavernous, its stove a vast, coal-burning affair, littered with dials and knobs and little drawers and hot-plates. Vivien stood behind Joe, encouraging him.

'It's still warm, that's the problem.' Joe opened one of the doors, and peered inside. 'These things take days to cool down.'

'You mustn't burn yourself, darling.'

He lifted out a drawer that was clogged with ash, and emptied it into a bucket.

'Does anyone ever clean it?'

'Cook won't, since she did her back. And I did try, darling, but I'm not terribly good at that sort of thing.'

Vivien was still wearing her evening dress, a clinging

affair of sea-green satin and feathers. Joe imagined her placing coal in the stove with sugar-tongs, one lump at a time.

'No . . . I'll have a go, Vivien. I think it's just clogged up.'

'You see, if we can't eat . . . I do so adore this house, but it really would become too intolerable.'

He said comfortingly, 'These stoves never really break down. They just need a bit of care and attention.'

'We all do, darling.'

'Hell.' He had burnt his finger on a piece of hot metal. Joe shook his hand to take away the pain, and then sucked the blister.

'Let me.' Vivien pressed her own small, reddened mouth against his finger. She looked up at him.

'Better, darling?'

Her small, cool hands still held him. Slowly, deliberately, she drew his hand closer to her, until it rested against her breast. His heart began to pound. Since the evening in the restaurant, Clodie had made herself maddeningly unavailable. His body had grown used to her, it ached for her.

'We haven't seen each other for simply years, have we, Joe?' Vivien whispered. 'You used to be Francis's little friend . . . You were terribly sweet even then, of course. But you do seem to have grown most awfully . . .'

He stood up, and she released his hand. Her fingers ran down his chest, towards his thigh. She pulled him to her, and when she kissed him, he felt her tongue flick inside his mouth. He could not help responding to her.

'Do you know, I think that you bring out the mother in me, Joe darling. I'm not the most terribly maternal woman, but one wants to feed you and cosset you and do all sorts of nice things with you . . .' Her body rubbed against his. She felt different to Clodie, so small and lithe and sinuous.

Then, suddenly, she pulled away from him. 'So sweet of you, Joe,' she said loudly, 'to repair the stove,' and, turning, he saw Denzil Farr at the kitchen door.

'But you should run along now,' added Vivien. 'It's late, and we all want to go to bed, don't we, darling?'

When she woke the following morning and ran to the window, Robin saw that a thin coating of snow had fallen overnight. For once, the snow did not remind her of the night she had learned of Stevie's death, but instead recalled to her the previous evening, and herself and Francis, embracing in the belvedere. Leaning against the window, her eiderdown wrapped around her, she felt the sort of undiluted happiness she associated with being a small child, at Christmas and birthdays.

After she had dressed, she ran downstairs, looking for Francis. The dining-room was empty, still strewn with the remains of the previous night's meal. Running back through passageways and anterooms, she heard a noise from the kitchen.

'Joe?'

He was crouched in front of the kitchen range, still dressed in the black trousers and white shirt he had worn the night before. The shirt was no longer white, but streaked with coal dust.

'What on earth are you doing?'

'Fixing this blasted thing.' He gestured to the stove. 'I'm just about done.'

'Haven't you been to bed?'

He shook his head. 'Couldn't sleep.'

'I was looking for Francis.'

'Haven't seen him yet.'

'Oh . . . is there breakfast?'

They made toast and tea, eating it perched at the huge wooden kitchen table. None of the other house-guests appeared, and neither was there any sign of the cook. Washing-up from the previous night's dinner was piled in the sink.

Joe yawned and stretched. 'We could go out for a drive, if you like, Robin.'

She glanced at the clock. It was not yet nine. 'To the coast?'

He nodded. 'Give me five minutes – I'd better change.'

Vivien was awakened at eleven o'clock by someone knocking at her door. She slept alone; Denzil Farr had shared her bed the previous night, but she never allowed them to sleep with her until morning. It made them proprietorial, and besides, men took up so much room. And she could not have worn the flannelette nightgowns and knitted bedsocks, so necessary to survive the winter nights at Long Ferry Hall.

She called out, 'Who is it?' and Francis answered:

'It's me, Vivien.'

'A moment, darling.' She pulled on a dressing-gown, and checked her face in a looking-glass. Then she let him in.

He was carrying a tray. 'I thought we could breakfast together.'

'How simply gorgeous.' There was coffee and toast and oranges. Francis began to squeeze the oranges, Vivien poured coffee.

'I know it's unreasonably early, Vivi, but I thought unless we talked now, you'd be surrounded by all these ghastly people the entire weekend.'

She sighed. 'They are dull, aren't they, darling? People seem to get duller as one grows older.'

'Why bother with them, then?'

She ruffled his fair curls. So lucky, she had always thought, that her only child should be both charming and beautiful. She shuddered to think of the offspring some of her lovers might have sired.

'One needs friends,' she said. 'You know that, Francis.'

His eyes met hers, but she only shrugged.

'Angus and Thomas are frightful bores,' said Francis, 'and Denzil whatever-he's-called is a pig.'

Vivien sipped her coffee, and did not reply. It was not that she disagreed with Francis, it was just that Denzil Farr was terribly rich, which went a great deal towards making up for his other deficiencies, both in bed and out of it.

Francis said hesitantly, 'I'm a bit short of funds just now, actually, Vivien. I was wondering if you . . .' His voice trailed off as he chucked the empty orange skins into the wastepaper bin.

She gave a little laugh. 'But I thought you were doing so well just now, darling.'

'So we are. But I have such enormous expenses. London rents . . . and it's cost a huge amount to get the magazine off the ground.'

'Expenses!' exclaimed Vivien. Her head ached, and she had only a rather dim recollection of the events of the previous night. 'This place simply eats money! The surveyor tells me that the entire roof should be replaced . . . and the mould in the kitchen cupboards . . . like cabbages!'

'Still . . . if you could see your way to lending me a bob or two. Not for long. Just to tide me over . . .'

Vivien had a talent for spending money, and a talent for acquiring it. Recently, though, when she took off her make-up and looked long and hard at her reflection in the mirror, she knew that she must try harder to hold on to what she had got.

So she squeezed his knee and said, 'Frightfully sorry, darling, but I haven't a bean. Such a bore.'

Francis shrugged, and then smiled at her. 'No matter. I'll get by. But we'll go to Spain, won't we?'

Vivien stared at him, bewildered.

'For a holiday . . . just the two of us. You said . . .'

She couldn't think what he was talking about. 'Spain? I don't think so. Whatever gave you that idea?'

She recognized the flicker of hurt and anger in his eyes. Francis had inherited the sudden mood-changes of his father, a wealthy but tiresome man. Vivien herself was never moody.

'Squeeze me out another drop of coffee, won't you, darling?' She smiled brightly. She couldn't bear grumpy people. Often, it seemed to Vivien that she spent an unreasonable amount of time and effort trying to coax her friends and relations into a more pleasant frame of mind.

Joe and Robin walked for miles on a grey, stony beach. The wind whipped up foamy white peaks on the waves, and seagulls dipped and swooped overhead. Joe threw pebbles into the surf, and Robin gathered shells from the sea-strand.

When, at midday, they drove back to Vivien's house, the sky had cleared. There was still a thin layer of snow on the manes of the old stone lions that guarded the gateway of Long Ferry Hall, but the lawns were patchily green. 'There's Francis,' said Joe, and hooted the horn.

Francis was standing in the doorway. Joe brought the car to a halt in front of the house.

'Where've you been?' asked Francis. He looked cold and tired. 'I've been waiting for hours.'

'Robin wanted to see the sea.' Francis's overnight bag stood in the doorway. 'Are we leaving?'

Francis nodded. 'Too bloody cold. And there's no food.'

Robin said, 'But your mother, Francis . . . ?'

He turned and looked at her. His eyes were bleak. 'Vivien's off to Scotland with that Farr chap. The fascist.'

'Oh.' The day, so promising at first, seemed to Robin to be slipping away, melting like the snow. 'I'd better pack, then.'

Francis drove back to London, Joe sitting in the passenger seat beside him. Robin curled up in the back, wrapped in the rug. Nobody spoke much.

Halfway home, shoving her frozen hands deeper into her pockets for warmth, she discovered, amongst the shells and sand, Helen's letter. It was oddly comforting to read about the harvest festival and the Michaelmas Bazaar. Then, conscious of a confused heart and too few hours' sleep, Robin stuffed the letter back into her pocket, and closed her eyes.

Chapter Four

Maia felt that she was living in a nightmare. A different nightmare from the one she had inhabited after her father's death, but a nightmare none the less. Some days – for as much as a week or a fortnight, perhaps – the nightmare would retreat and everything would become normal, and she would live again the life she had thought she had chosen. Mrs Vernon Merchant, with the rich husband, and the big house, and the servants. But then it would all dissolve, and she would be back in the nightmare, and the house would seem like a prison, and the jewels and gowns and furs the prison's bars.

Usually she was careful to be, on the surface at least, the docile, obedient wife that she still sometimes thought Vernon wanted. She was afraid of physical pain, but most of all she was afraid of Vernon's usurpation of her soul. It was as though she had unleashed something in him, something terrible that grew stronger rather than weaker. She was never sure whether what he did to her hurt her more than what he said to her. Gathering the fragments, piecing together the things he told her about his past in those awful private moments that they spent enclosed with each other, she began to realize that this was the true Vernon, that the man she thought she had married had never really existed. Slowly, she understood that he needed to hurt and to humiliate her. That he despised not just her, but every woman. That his contempt for her was a fundamental, unchangeable part of him.

Every time he hurt her, she felt a little bit less Maia Merchant, a beautiful, clever and sophisticated woman, and a little bit more some broken, slavish thing of his creation. When, once, he made her kneel and beg his forgiveness for a trivial misdemeanour, then she almost ran from the house, aware that if she stayed he might shatter her spirit into little fragments. But she did stay, because she knew that all the security that Vernon's wealth gave her was in some way essential to her: she simply could not live without it. A divorce would ruin her reputation, her future. So much better, Maia often found herself thinking, to be widowed.

As he turned the corner of the road into Butler Street, Joe saw a man leave Clodie's house, and disappear into the fog. Joe tapped on the front door. Lizzie opened it, and he gathered her into his arms, picking her up and kissing her on the top of her head. 'Look in my pocket.'

Lizzie reached inside his jacket pocket and drew out a sherbet dab. She squealed with delight. Joe glanced across at Clodie, seated behind her sewing-machine.

'Who was that?'

'Who was who?' She was trying to thread the needle.

'The man I saw coming out of here.'

'Oh. Him.' Her tone was uninterested. 'Some salesman. He was trying to sell me a washing-machine. I couldn't afford it, of course.'

'Let me.' Clodie was long-sighted. Joe took the cotton from her and threaded it through the needle's eye.

'You should get yourself some spectacles.'

'What? And look a fright? Not likely.' But she did not, just now, sound cross.

As she turned the wheel of the sewing-machine and caught the thread up from the bobbin, he muttered, 'I've missed you so much, Clo.'

Her gaze flicked to Lizzie, sucking up sherbet. 'Didn't

Mrs Clark say you could go and play with Edith this afternoon, lovey?'

Lizzie ran off out of the door. Clodie stood up.

'I've missed you too, Joe.' She began to unbutton his shirt.

They made love on the hearth in front of the fireplace, hot and hurried, unable to wait. And then slowly, savouring it, making the pleasure last as long as possible. Afterwards, Joe filled the zinc tub with water from the copper, and they bathed together. Soaping her white, heavy breasts that were veined with blue like marble, Joe wanted her all over again. But Clodie, glancing at the clock, pushed him away, and said, 'I can't ask you to stay for supper, I'm afraid – there's only two kippers.'

Drying and dressing, he wished he had money enough to take her out. But money had been horribly short lately – nothing from the press, and the Navigator only ever provided him with enough to pay his share of the rent and to eat.

Outside, walking home, the fog had thickened to a soupy yellowish grey. When he reached the basement, he almost tripped over Robin, sitting on the steps.

'Robin! What on earth are you doing here?'

'Waiting for you.' She was all wrapped up in a green velvet coat, but there were beads of moisture on the ends of her eyelashes, like tiny pearls.

'You must be frozen. Come in.'

He unlocked the door, and led the way inside. The basement was little warmer than outdoors. Damp seemed to be seeping up through the floor, and the fire hadn't been lit that day. Joe started crumpling up old newspapers and laying kindling.

'Where's Francis?'

'Off touting for business. Damned annoying,' he added. 'We're running out of work. It's usually not too bad at this time of year – Christmas, and all that.'

Joe was going to voice his fear that the downturn was permanent, that it was to do with the fall of the

American stock-market at the end of October, but when he looked at Robin, he saw that she wasn't listening.

'I came to tell you that I'm going home, Joe,' she said. 'My brother's ill.'

'I'm sorry. Is he bad?'

She shook her head. 'Hugh has bronchitis. He has it every winter. Mother's always afraid that it will turn into pneumonia. I just thought I'd let you know . . . in case you wondered where I was . . .'

Her voice trailed away as she went to the front door.

'But I'm only going away for a week or so,' she added suddenly, defiantly. 'You needn't think I won't be back.'

She shut the door behind her, and he found, as he arranged pieces of coal in the fire, that he was smiling.

The dreariness of the Fens in mid-December was unequalled, Robin thought. Rain dripping from every twig and leaf, the land a uniform greyish-brown colour.

From London, she brought Hugh two of the newest records. They had cost most of a week's wages, but it was worth it to see the pleasure on his face. In the winter house, she wrapped him in blankets and stoked up the stove and then danced alone to 'You're the Cream in my Coffee' and 'Tiptoe through the Tulips'. At the end of it, having tripped over her feet three times, she collapsed to the floor, laughing.

'It's the galoshes.' Robin kicked off her boots, and spread her toes to the fire. Hugh, she saw to her delight, was smiling too.

'Ma was terribly worried about you, Hugh. She wrote me a letter.'

He grimaced. 'I know. I wish she wouldn't fuss. Still' – he grinned – 'at least I've been spared the little horrors for a few weeks.' For the past year Hugh had been teaching at the same school as Richard Summerhayes.

'Are you fed up with teaching?'

He shook his head. 'They're good kids, actually – I enjoy it. How about you, Rob? How's the job? How's big, bad London?'

It was her turn to scowl. 'The job's awful, Hugh. I've been thinking of chucking it, but it isn't easy to find anything else just now. Don't tell mother and father, though, or they'll say I told you so. But London . . . London is *wonderful*.'

And then, hesitantly, she told him about Francis.

'He's such good fun,' she explained. 'And his mother lives in an extraordinary house with priest's holes and belvederes and things. It's so . . . so *magical*, Hugh. So different to dismal old Cambridgeshire.' Her voice was scathing. 'And Vivien is terribly beautiful and never fusses about Francis and just lets him get on with his life. And he's so . . . so unexpected. Only he goes away for weeks at a time, and I haven't a clue where he is or whether he's forgotten all about me.'

'Are you in love with him, Rob?'

She stared at Hugh, and then she laughed. 'Of course not – you know I don't believe in that sort of thing.' Yet Francis's voice whispered in her ear, *Could you love me a little, Robin?*

'Love isn't something you believe in . . . like ghosts . . . or faith healing,' said Hugh gently. 'It's just . . . there.'

Restlessly, she stood up, staring out of the window to the river. 'What about you, Hugh? Have you ever been in love?'

He said lightly, 'Now what would I fall in love with, Robin? The ducks . . . the eels . . . the fish in the river . . . ?'

She laughed again and, resting her chin on her elbows, stared out into the gloom. Slowly, out of the mists and dankness, a figure appeared.

'Helen!' cried Robin.

Helen was welcomed with hugs and kisses. 'Daisy told me you were coming home, Robin, so I borrowed Daddy's old bicycle and cycled over.' Helen's honey-blond hair was wet with mist, and crowned by a tam o'shanter. 'It's so lovely to see you – just like old times.'

'You haven't visited us for weeks, Helen,' complained Hugh.

Helen looked guilty. 'Daddy wasn't well, and I've been doing a lot of dressmaking. I've taken a few little jobs to keep me busy. I thought . . . as I like sewing . . . and as we are all so far from the shops . . . I thought some of the ladies . . .'

'You'll be setting up in Paris soon.'

Helen blushed. 'Wouldn't that be splendid? Only I was a bit down, you see, and I told Daddy that I thought I'd look for a job in one of the dressmaking shops in Cambridge or Ely, but Daddy said that wouldn't do at all, as our sort of people don't work in places like that. So then I had an idea – why not be a private dressmaker, working from home? And Daddy thought that would be much more suitable.'

Robin started to say something, but Hugh interrupted, 'I think that's terrific. Absolutely splendid. I'm sure you'll be a tremendous success.'

Helen beamed. 'Have you visited Maia, Robin . . . Hugh . . . ?'

'Ma invited her to tea before I fell ill, but she couldn't make it.'

'Only I thought she was rather unhappy.'

Robin stared at Helen. 'Unhappy? *Maia?* In that ghastly house, with her awful husband? Helen – Maia is in *heaven.*'

Helen looked uneasy. 'Well . . . maybe. Only I called on her when Daddy and I were in Cambridge a few weeks ago, and I thought she looked . . . different. You know how she can look. Hard . . . and glittery.'

Hugh said, 'Maia can't help but look glittery, Helen dearest. It's just the way she's made.'

Robin recalled the last time she had seen Maia. That huge, ugly, fake baronial house. Her smug, foxy-looking husband who had made it quite plain that his wife's friends were just too unimportant for him to bother talking to. Maia's boastful pleasure in her new status.

Hugh was winding up the gramophone again. Robin, forgetting Maia, seized Helen and began to whirl her round the winter house.

'You really are the most hopeless dancer, Rob,' groaned Hugh, watching. 'Poor Helen. Here – may I have the pleasure?'

He took Helen in his arms and began to dance. The music filled the small hut, and the light that shone through the windows illuminated the dark, reedy pond beyond. But halfway through the song, Hugh, his face red and perspiring, began to cough. At that moment the door of the winter house opened, and Daisy came in.

She took one look at her son, and told him to go back to the house. Then she whispered to Robin, 'How could you? Taking him out in the damp and the cold – making him dance – when you know he has been so unwell—'

Hugh tried to speak, but started to cough again. Helen just looked terribly upset. Robin, furious, glared at her mother and, slamming the door behind her, ran outside and across the darkened lawns.

If they had always rubbed each other up the wrong way, then it seemed to Robin that she and Daisy had recently become quite expert at it. Disapproval just brought out the worst in Robin, so that she found herself increasingly trying to provoke. Later, alone at night, she hated herself, and made innumerable resolutions to be more patient, less tiresome. But the resolutions rarely lasted beyond breakfast.

Matters came to a head one lunch-time, when Daisy suggested that Robin train to be a teacher, like Hugh. Somehow the discussion degenerated into argument, just as it always did, and Robin stormed out of the house. Even the long walk to the railway station was not enough to cool her down. She had just enough money to buy herself a return ticket to Cambridge. There, she wandered around rather aimlessly and, finding that she hadn't the twopence for a cup of tea and that she did not yet want to go home, she walked towards Maia's house. Recalling the ups and downs of Maia's life, she had begun to feel slightly guilty that she had been so long out of touch with her. If she had had to endure the upheavals that Maia had had to endure, mightn't she covet the sort of things Maia coveted?

Robin, ringing the Merchants' doorbell, resolved to grit her teeth and admire all Maia's possessions. She still thought, looking up, that the house was hideous. Dark and heavy and gloomy – north-facing, so that the windows did not seem to reflect any light.

The superior manservant who opened the door to her told her that Mrs Merchant was unavailable. Robin, with a mixture of relief and disappointment, began to wander back to the road. And then, hearing a scuffling in the laurel bushes at the far side of the drive, she looked back.

A small black-and-white dog was darting about in the dry leaves beneath the laurels. A familiar voice called, 'Teddy? Teddy – where are you?'

Maia was shadowed by the heavy darkness of the shrubbery. Robin watched her stoop and pick up the little dog.

'Teddy – you naughty thing.'

Robin said, 'Maia?' and Maia glanced up, startled.

'Your servant told me you weren't in.' It was too dark to make out the expression on Maia's face. Robin walked forward. 'I know it's a bit of a cheek, barging in like this, but I'm not often—'

She stopped. She simply could not help staring. The whole of one side of Maia's face was covered in a bruise: it flowered, blue and purple and yellow, across her cheekbone, around her eye.

Maia said defensively, 'I tripped over and hit my face on the banister. Silly, wasn't it?'

Some of the women at the clinic said things like that. I hit my head on the stove, doctor. Walked into the door, didn't I, nurse? Other women were long past dissembling, and just admitted, The old man always lays into me after a pint or two. They can't help it, can they?

'No, you didn't,' said Robin. Her voice, even to her own ears, sounded odd.

'What do you mean?'

She took a deep breath. 'Maia – I can see the marks of his fingers.'

It was true: if she looked carefully, the bruise was like a five-pointed star.

'Nonsense.' Maia stepped back into the shadows. 'Don't talk such nonsense, Robin.' She sounded furious.

'Was it Vernon?'

Maia just clasped the dog tighter to her. 'I told you, Robin – stop it!'

The twilight washed over the house and garden, and the windows stared back at them, blank dark eyes in an ornate façade. Robin chose her words very carefully.

'I won't say anything about it if you don't want me to, Maia. But, really – do you think I would judge you for something like this? Do you think I would think less of you?'

Something in Maia seemed to crumble and almost collapse. Her shoulders drooped, and she closed her eyes. Then she said, very softly, 'I despise myself, you see, Robin. That's the worst of it. That's what he's done to me.' She began to walk back to the house.

In the kitchen, Maia made tea. It was the cook's half-day holiday, she explained, and neither of the kitchen-maids were full-time. The dog ate biscuits from a bowl as the kettle boiled. The kitchen was big and warm and well-lit, but Maia's hands shook as she spooned tea into the pot. Watching her, Robin's heart ached. Maia wore a pearl-grey two-piece, exquisitely cut, clinging to her slender figure. Her stockings were undoubtedly of silk, her shoes of matching grey kid. And yet her face, her lovely face, had been made grotesque.

Robin realized that she had been staring when Maia said, 'He doesn't usually hit my face. It was the first time.'

In spite of the warmth of the kitchen, Robin felt cold inside. 'Has Vernon hit you before, Maia?'

'Oh yes.' Maia poured boiling water into the teapot.

She added fiercely, 'Don't look at me like that, Robin. I can't bear it.'

Robin blinked and turned away. Maia began to pour the tea. Vernon Merchant didn't hit his wife's face because he didn't want people asking awkward questions. You could explain one black eye as an accident, but not a series of black eyes. Robin found that sort of cold, calculating cruelty sickening.

'Why don't you leave him?'

'Leave him?'

'Yes – get a divorce. Grounds of cruelty—'

Maia snorted scornfully. 'And have everything that has happened to me written all over the newspapers? Have all the girls who were at school with me laughing about me? Have my mother – and Cousin Margery – look down on me? Never.'

'Then just leave him. You don't have to go to court.'

'And where would I go?' asked Maia bitterly. 'There would be nowhere for me to go. I'd end up on the streets.'

'You've got me, Maia – you've got Helen.' But she thought, even as she said it, that Helen's father might not offer Maia shelter. 'You could stay with me, Maia, till you get yourself back on your feet again.'

'I can just imagine it – the two of us sharing some dreadful poky little room in a ghastly boarding house.' Maia's laughter was hollow. 'I haven't a penny of my own, you know. It's all his.'

Robin stared at her, bewildered. 'But you can't choose to stay with him.'

'Oh, I can.' Suddenly Maia's face was calm. Sitting down at the table opposite Robin, she said, 'Don't you understand, Robin? I may not want *him*, but I do want his money.'

She was silenced, then, her gaze meeting Maia's. There was an implacability about Maia's expression that Robin had rarely encountered before. Those light blue eyes, the one beautiful, the other made swollen and ugly, were both amoral and cold.

'No-one shall take this away from me.' Maia's glance took in the large room, its sparkling furnishings and modern machinery.

Robin shivered. Just then she longed to be home with Hugh and Daisy and Richard. Quarrelling, even. Just to be somewhere that was normal and reasonable and comprehensible. She thought, disturbed, that there was something in Maia's eyes that was not quite rational.

She tried again. 'Maia.' Her voice was gentle. 'He has hurt you already. He may do worse. What if—'

Maia silenced her, shaking her head. 'No. You don't understand. Vernon needs me. He needs me to be his wife and to host his dinner parties and entertain the people he's trying to impress. That's why he married me. And he needs me to share a bed with him. I'm cheaper than going up to London to buy some tart.' Maia's smile was a ghastly travesty of her customary beauty.

'Vernon may not be able to control himself, Maia.'

'Vernon is always controlled. He always knows exactly what he is doing. I told you – he's never hurt my face before. I moved, you see. He was terribly sorry afterwards. He sent me flowers.'

Robin, appalled, followed the direction of Maia's gaze to the huge bunch of hothouse roses in the sink.

'So you see, there's no need to worry.' Maia lit herself a cigarette, and offered the packet to Robin. 'You should go soon, darling – Vernon will be home from work. I don't think it would be an awfully good idea if you two met.'

She sounded almost amused. Slightly unsteadily, Robin rose to her feet.

'Run out the back, darling – I think I hear his car.'

For a moment she hesitated. 'Can't I . . . ?'

Maia's mouth twisted mockingly. 'How chivalrous of you, Robin. No. I don't think so.'

Robin flung her arms round Maia's neck, and hugged her. She heard Maia take one great sobbing indrawn breath, and then felt her pull away.

'If you should ever need me . . . Just write, Maia. You know where I live.'

As she turned to go, Maia grasped her elbow, stopping her.

'You're not to tell anyone about Vernon and me, Robin. No-one at all. D'you swear?'

Held by those great, pale, damaged eyes she nodded. 'I swear.'

Walking home from the bus stop, Helen's parcels scattered in the bitter wind. Adam Hayhoe broke off from hoeing his winter vegetables, and helped her retrieve them.

When she had thrust the lengths of fabric, the thread and the lining material back into her basket, she said breathlessly, 'So kind of you, Adam. Such a wind!'

'Perishing, ain't it, Miss Helen.'

The vicious breeze tugged at her hat. Helen gave a little shriek, grabbed ineffectively at the brim, and dropped the basket again.

Her hat was caught by the rose bush that grew round the door of the Hayhoes' cottage. Adam disentangled it from the thorns, while Helen exclaimed, 'Look! You've a rose, Adam. In December!'

He broke off the single yellow bloom, and tucked it beneath the ribbon that bound the brim of her hat. 'There. Looks better now, don't it?'

She smiled at him, and he picked up her basket and walked beside her along the drove towards the rectory.

'How is business, Adam?'

'I've been working up at the Big House for the last month or so, repairing window frames and kitchen cupboards.' Adam glanced down at Helen's basket. 'I hear you're busy yourself now, Miss Helen.'

In a place as small as Thorpe Fen, secrets were impossible. Helen blushed.

'I've been doing a bit of dressmaking. That's what all this' – she gestured to the parcels of fabric and thread – 'is for.'

They had reached the rectory gates. Adam returned the basket to Helen.

'Better than all this shop bought stuff, ain't it, Miss Helen?' he said, and touched his cap, and walked away.

She let herself into the rectory. It was mid-afternoon, but as it was the first Thursday of the month, Julius Ferguson was in Ely with the bishop. Helen went to the kitchen first, where Betty was cutting vegetables and meat to make a stew, and Ivy, the scullery-maid, was turning out the larder. Then she sat at the dining-room table and answered her father's correspondence. The Reverend Ferguson pencilled notes at the foot of each letter; Helen wrote the replies out in full in her laborious longhand. On the sideboard stood a large sepia photograph of Florence Ferguson, framed with a border of pressed snowdrops, and the phrase 'The white flower of a blameless life' written in italics beneath the photograph. Helen sat with her shoulders covered with a rug (Betty never lit the dining-room fire before seven o'clock), and Percy, her cat, curled on her lap. When she had finished, Helen cut out all three of the blouses that the archdeacon's wife had ordered from her. She had promised them by the end of the week, and was anxious to finish them in time. She had been delayed in going to Ely to buy the material – the Christmas Fair, the minutes of the parish meeting, and, of course, the running of the household, had all interceded.

When she had finished, Helen folded the pieces carefully and placed them in her sewing-basket. The dining-room seemed very big and dark and quiet. Both Betty and Ivy had gone home to their families in the village. None of the Ferguson servants lived in. Helen lit two oil lamps, but their light cast only small pools in the darkness. She wished they owned a wireless, but her father disapproved of wirelesses. The cat, bored, had wandered outside. She took the little book from the bottom of her sewing-basket, and wrote down the costs of the material she had bought in Ely. This was the worst part of it. She liked the sewing, but she couldn't make sense of the money. Adding the columns of figures, she seemed to have spent more money than she had taken to Ely. That could not be right, surely. She tried again, and the entire total came to two shillings and sevenpence, which seemed awfully little. Tired, her head aching, Helen closed the book and rested her head on her arms. The money worried her. She didn't like to ask her father, who would only say that she had taken on too much. Suddenly, she thought of Hugh Summerhayes. Hugh was terribly clever and patient, and wouldn't be in the least bit cross with her. She recalled herself and Hugh, dancing in the winter house – the warmth of his arms as he held her, the steady, easy grace of his tall frame. Hugh would sort everything out. Helen smiled, and fell asleep.

When she awoke, she was no longer alone. Opening her eyes, she saw her father sitting in a chair across the table from her, watching her. She had no idea how long he had been there.

A week before Christmas, the under-manager of the insurance office called Robin aside and spoke to her. Because he mumbled and refused to look her in the eye, it took her a while to work out what he was saying. Something about modernizing and cut-backs and economies. Eventually she cried, outraged, 'You're giving me the sack!'

'It is regrettable, Miss Summerhayes, but in the current situation—'

'But you can't just—'

It appeared that he could. Times were hard, she had only been with the company for a year, and her contribution had been uneven, to put it politely. Robin found herself walking through the front door of the office with her coat and hat and a week's pay in lieu of notice.

To her great delight, Francis was at home. She had seen him intermittently since she had returned from the Fens, falling back comfortably into their earlier acquaintance of political meetings and the occasional party. Any fleeting thoughts that Francis might become more to her than a friend, she had put aside. When he had kissed her at Long Ferry they had both, after all, been rather drunk.

Francis opened a bottle of beer. 'One should celebrate the first time one is sacked.' He raised his glass. 'To failure and ignominy.'

She giggled, and began to feel better. 'But what shall I live on, Francis? I've my rent paid until the end of December, and . . . let me see . . .' she peered inside her purse '. . . six pounds, twelve shillings and tuppence.'

'You should come to France. Much cheaper to live in France.'

There was the sound of a key in the lock as Joe let himself into the basement. It was still raining, and his dark hair was plastered wetly to his scalp.

'I was telling Robin,' said Francis, pouring a third glass of beer, 'that she should come to France with us.'

'Why not?' Joe shrugged off his wet jacket, and slung it on the back of a chair.

'Angus has a place in Deauville – Vivien has given me the key. You surely can't intend to stay in England for Christmas, Robin. Too dreary. Ghastly turkey and pudding and sprouts. Dreadful parlour games . . . consequences . . .'

'Sardines.'

'Mah-jong.'

'Perhaps,' said Joe meaningfully, 'Robin intends to go home for Christmas.'

'To the bosom of her family . . .'

The idea appalled her. To the grey, wet Fens, to family arguments and family ritual. The idea was unbearable.

'France!' she whispered. She had always longed to travel. 'Oh Joe . . . Francis! It would be wonderful!'

Two days later she was on the cross-Channel ferry. Neither she nor Joe was ill on the choppy sea-crossing, but Francis lay on a bench on deck, groaning, wrapped in his greatcoat. He would only remain well, he said, if Robin read to him. Something very dull. She read the sports page of the *Daily Express* out loud, column after

119

column about football and horse-racing and greyhounds.

'Ghastly,' muttered Francis. 'So wonderfully tedious.' Then he fell asleep.

She had her first sight of the Continent standing beside Joe, her forearms resting on the rail, staring out through the mist and darkness. France emerged out of the gloom, a dark ribbon of land to begin with, and then, slowly, a coastline with cliffs and beaches and ports and harbours.

'Your first time?' asked Joe.

Robin nodded. 'I've never been out of England. Well – we went to Scotland once for a holiday. What about you, Joe?'

'I came here as a child with my mother.'

She looked up at him, surprised.

'My mother was French. We stayed with her family in Paris . . . oh, two or three times. But after she died, we lost touch.'

'Do your relatives still live there?'

'I've no idea. No idea at all.'

He had always, she thought, an air of rootlessness about him. She said curiously, 'Will you look them up?'

'Perhaps. Francis intends to stay in Deauville – he thinks that Vivien may drop in. But I might go to Paris.'

She wanted to ask more, but there was a groan from the deck behind her. The boat docked at four o'clock in the afternoon, amid a great cawing of gulls and squalls of rain. On the train journey from Dieppe to Deauville, Francis cheered up, producing champagne and a bar of chocolate from his knapsack. The only cure for seasickness, he said, breaking off pieces of chocolate and sharing them amongst the occupants of the third class carriage – infants, severe looking grandmothers swathed in black, and a dog.

Angus's apartment faced out to the sea. There were two bedrooms, one for Francis and one for Robin. Joe would sleep on the sofa. There was a shelf full of dubious books, and nothing to eat except a very old tin of salmon. The storm rose up out of the Channel, drowning the tinny cracklings of Angus's crystal radio. They ate salmon and chocolate, and drank the bottle of very cheap Calvados that Joe had bought from a farmer on the train from Dieppe.

Three days before Christmas, Joe hitchhiked to Paris, thumbing lifts in dogcarts and lorries.

The storm had subsided and the wind was still, the air clear and blue and cold. Paris, which to Joe as a child had seemed a fairytale city, seemed every bit as magical as he recalled it. The wide boulevards, the treelined avenues and the cobbled squares were iced with a thin skim of frost. Paris, the City of Light, made the industrial cities of northern England seem like incarnations of darkness.

It took him a while to get his bearings. To be surrounded by people speaking a different language disturbed him in a way he had not anticipated, transporting him suddenly and abruptly back to the past. Whenever they had been alone, his mother had spoken French to him. His father had loathed the language, protesting that no decent Englishman could get his tongue round it. Joe had gone to public school with perfect French, to have it mangled by a master who had never set foot out of England. The language now hovered uneasily on his lips, just out of his reach.

He found the street at last, counting along the houses until he was outside number fifty – an elegant, four-storeyed building with a curly wrought-iron banister running alongside steps rising to an imposing front door. A Christmas tree, complete with candles, was framed by one of the windows. He stood outside for a while, remembering. A young woman wearing a maid's white, frilly cap stared suspiciously through the panes at him. Blowing her a kiss, Joe disappeared into the café opposite.

The café was all crimson plush and opulent art

nouveau mirrors and lamps. The waiter looked at Joe disdainfully and began to lead him to a seat at the back, but Joe insisted on sitting beside the window. There was only one vacant window table, the others were crowded with students, talking very loudly and drinking a lot. Joe ordered a coffee and a marc. Then he lit a cigarette, and stared out of the window.

The front door of the house opened, and a woman walked down the steps. He could not see her face; she was swathed in furs and a tight-fitting cloche hat. A tiny apricot poodle skittered at her heels. She did not correspond to his recollections of grandmère, a daunting and dignified figure. He watched the woman disappear down the street. He knew, after a while, that he would not walk up those steps and knock on that door. If he did, then whatever uniformed servant answered him would look at him as the waiter had looked at him, taking in his old corduroy trousers, his jacket that was out at the elbows, and his boots that needed soling. If he said, I am Thérèse Elliot's son, then they would laugh in his face. Even if he succeeded in convincing them of his identity, then they would still stare, they would still wonder. He would climb those steps, knock at that door, when he had done something with his life.

The trouble was, he thought, that he hadn't the least idea what to do with it. His father had expected him to work at the mill, and they had come to blows over that. Joe had wanted to go to university, but his father had thought college for nancy-boys and the idle rich. So he had left home, drifting through the last five years. He had met up again with Francis, and he had fallen in love with Clodie. He had joined the Labour Party, finding something in it that reflected his convictions; he had survived, keeping himself housed, clothed and fed, but that was all. When so many others seemed to be finding a cause, he had none.

Joe inhaled his cigarette and drank his brandy. Some of the students sitting next to him wore blue raincoats and berets, the uniform of the Jeunesses Patriotes, a

Fascist organization. There was a copy of 'L'Ami du peuple', a dreadful right-wing rag, on the table in front of them. Joe threw all the coins in his pocket onto the table and left the café. Then he began to walk back down the avenue, looking for an alleyway that would lead to the back of the house. There was more than one way of storming a citadel.

Robin had woken at six that morning, when Joe had left for Paris. Since then, she had made a desultory attempt to tidy the apartment, had bought croissants and baguettes for breakfast, and had tried, and failed, to write a Christmas card to her parents.

Francis rose at nine, ambling round the kitchen in Angus's rakish maroon dressing-gown, grinding beans and making coffee. His coffee bowl clutched between his fingers, he came to stand beside Robin, staring out at the beach.

'Shall we go for a walk?'

She put on her coat, and they left the flat and strolled to the sea-front. The boardwalk, in the wind and showers, was sludgy and deserted. At the sea's edge, waves lashed the pulpy sand. Francis made a huge sand-castle, all baroque turrets and shells and extravagant ribbons of seaweed. The tide, surging in, sucked it back into the sea.

'How utterly metaphorical,' said Francis. He glanced at his watch. 'One o'clock. Shall we eat? I know a lovely little restaurant.'

Tucking Robin's hand through his arm, he walked with her through the town. Grey clouds were piling on the horizon, and the showers were becoming more insistent.

The restaurant was small, only half a dozen tables. Fishermen huddled around the bar – short, thickset, black-haired men, smoking and drinking. Paint was peeling from the windowsills, and a faded advertisement for Pernod was the café's only decoration.

'Vivien and I holidayed in Deauville once – oh,

donkey's years ago. She was between husbands. We came here every day. The food is utterly divine.' Francis pulled out a chair for Robin and she sat down. 'Especially the *fruits de mer*.'

'I've never eaten it before.'

'The first time's always the best.' Francis beckoned the waiter.

Robin thought, sitting in the scruffy little restaurant, that life could not be more perfect. Smoking a cigarette as they waited for their meal, she felt sophisticated and grown-up. The smell of garlic and Gauloises was wonderful, and it seemed almost wickedly decadent to drink red wine at lunch-time. She congratulated herself on having escaped the dreary boredom of Blackmere Farm, on having broken away from the dreadful tedium of a family Christmas – and her father's expectations of her, and her mother's effortless efficiency.

Their food arrived, a single plate heaped with a cornucopia of seafood, the opalescent shells garnished with wedges of lemon and strands of glistening seaweed.

'Just dive in,' said Francis, brandishing a spoon.

When, failing to extract a whelk, she sent the shell whirling halfway across the restaurant and collapsed in giggles, he fed her fragments of langoustine and mussel, pulled cleanly from their shells, tasting of the sea.

'Like salty rubber,' she said.

Francis shook his head in mock despair. 'Try this.' He speared a morsel of crabmeat and held it out to her. She met his gaze, and felt herself blush. Men didn't look at her like that – with such a mixture of longing and admiration and . . . desire. Men only looked like that at women like Maia.

She turned away, suddenly unable to eat. But he had laid his hand on hers, the ball of his thumb gently stroking her knuckles.

'Just a little bit,' said Francis, pleadingly. 'For me.'

She took the crab from the fork, and ate. It tasted delicious. Francis refilled their glasses.

'Tolerably good, isn't it?'

'Oh Francis – it's *wonderful*!' She glanced round the little bar. 'All of it – so perfect!'

He raised her hand to his mouth, and kissed it, his lips lingering on her skin. 'Just like you. Small and perfect and delicious.'

Pulling her hand away, she stared at her plate. She heard him say:

'Sorry, Robin. I thought—' He sounded bewildered.

'What, Francis?'

'I thought you felt the same way as I do.'

She couldn't speak. There seemed to be a lump in her throat.

'Obviously not. Stupid of me. Forget it. Please forgive me.'

Looking up, she could see the hurt in his eyes. Reaching across the table, she touched his sleeve.

'Francis . . . it's just that—' She struggled for the right words. 'It's just that I'm not used to any of this.'

He frowned. 'Do you mean the food . . . or France . . . or men wanting to make love to you?'

'Any of it! The food and France are simply marvellous, of course.' She paused. Her heart was thudding in her chest.

He prompted gently, 'And men?'

She tried to explain. 'Men generally seem to think of me as a friend . . . or a sort of sister . . . or a good sport!' Her voice was despairing.

'How ghastly.' He was looking at her intently. 'And how idiotic of them.' Francis shook his head. 'Whereas I have thought of you for simply ages as a woman I would absolutely adore to go to bed with.' His fingers threaded through Robin's. 'Shall we?'

Staring at him, overcome by a mixture of fear and longing, she nodded, speechless again. Francis paid the waiter, and they left the café.

Outside, it was raining hard, windblown squalls driven horizontally from the sea. Under the tattered striped awning of the restaurant, Francis took her in his arms and kissed her. Rain beat against her face and trickled down the back of her neck, but she did not notice. The warmth of his body against hers, and the taste of his lips, was delightful.

But he drew away from her after a while, and said, 'You're soaking, you poor little thing. I'm so sorry. We'd better dash.'

He took her hand and they ran back through the deserted town to the apartment. There, he helped her take off her wet coat. Then her sweater, and then he began to unbutton her blouse. He paused only once, to say, 'Are you sure, Robin?', and she smiled and said, 'Absolutely sure.' The touch of his hand and his mouth against her neck was wonderful. His lips nuzzled the corner of her mouth, and the hollows of her chin. She threaded her fingers through his hair, finding utter delight in touching him. When her blouse slipped from her shoulders she felt momentarily ashamed of the safety pin that held together the strap of her camisole. But Francis seemed unbothered, and when he stroked and kissed her stomach and her breasts she, too, ceased to care.

She had read books about this, but the books hadn't told her how she would feel. How great was the pleasure it was possible to find in another person. She wanted the rain to go on for ever, cutting them off from the rest of the world. His mouth nuzzled her belly, her breasts. His body, shadowed by the firelight, was firm and muscular. When, at last, he kissed the hot, aching place between her thighs, she moaned with pleasure and gave herself to him. She could not have done otherwise.

Joe, arriving back at Deauville just before midnight, guessed what had happened as soon as he saw them. It knocked the wind out of his sails slightly: he had always thought of Robin as someone they shared. There was a sort of transparent happiness about her face that made him groan inwardly. She bustled around, telling him to take off his wet things and dry them in front of the fire, and she even made him a cup of lumpy cocoa. She couldn't cook at all. Even Joe could cook better than Robin could.

Curled against Francis on the sofa, she asked him about his day. Joe told them all he had discovered, which was very little. The pretty maid in the elegant house had told him that his grandparents were dead, and that the house was now lived in by a different family.

'Oh Joe – I'm sorry.'

He shrugged. 'I hardly knew them. And they were rather terrifying, actually.'

'Do you have any other relatives?' asked Robin. 'Aunts . . . cousins . . . ?'

'I had an aunt.'

Tante Claire had been a younger, shorter, plumper version of his mother. She and Joe had spent rainy days playing bezique, for centimes. He would look her up sometime.

Joe, rising to his feet, glanced at Robin and Francis.

'I take it I won't have to sleep on the sofa tonight?'

Vernon gave Maia her Christmas present two days early. Something special, he said, handing the parcel to her late one evening. I'll give you the other stuff on Christmas Eve.

Sitting on the end of the bed, her hands trembled as she opened the parcel. It was a basque, a tawdry thing of black satin and red ribbon, and a pair of awful fishnet stockings. She wanted to throw them in his face, but she didn't dare. Instead Maia did as she was told, and put them on. When she made up her face how he liked it, and glanced at her reflection in her dressing-table mirror, she felt tears prick at the back of her eyes. She refused to let them fall, though.

After it was over and she lay in the darkness again, she knew that Robin had been right. She could not endure this. She could endure it when he hit her, but she could not endure this. Slowly, inexorably, he was making her into something else. Not someone else, some*thing*. Something he despised, yet needed. She feared that one day she would begin not to notice, not to care. That when he raped her she would lie there, staring at the ceiling, and thinking of the clothes she intended to buy, or the parties she intended to go to. Then he would have made a whore of her.

The next morning, fighting the nausea that seemed her increasingly frequent reaction to the events of the night before, Maia did not dare take even an overnight case with her when she left the house. She took what jewellery she could find, which wasn't much as Vernon always locked her jewellery away in the safe, to which only he had the key. She told the butler she was going shopping for the day, but asked the taxi driver to take her to the railway station. On the journey to London, she thought of all that she was throwing away, and wondered how she would bear it. She could think of no honest way that she, a woman, could earn the sort of living that Vernon earned. Vernon had built up his own fortune, but even Vernon had begun with a small inheritance from his mother. Maia would have nothing. She'd probably be able to make a decent living as a whore, thought Maia, and giggled hysterically, and all the other occupants of the first class carriage stared at her.

She took a taxi from Liverpool Street station to the lodging house where Robin lived. Shown inside by a pasty-faced maid of all work, Maia waited in the narrow hallway. The house smelt of boiled cabbage and something indefinable and musty. The stair carpet was worn, and the net curtains were yellowed with age.

A woman appeared out of the gloom and introduced herself as Miss Turner, Miss Summerhayes's landlady. Miss Turner's hair was escaping out of its net, and she wore an extraordinary and shapeless ensemble of dark purple crushed velvet and lace. Miss Turner explained that Miss Summerhayes had gone abroad for Christmas. Did Mrs Merchant wish to leave a message? Did Mrs Merchant – a hopeful glance, a step forward – wish to Make Contact in another way? The Astral Planes were very active at this time of year . . .

Maia, refusing politely, escaped and found herself back in the street again. Looking in her purse, she discovered that she had spent almost all her cash on the taxi fare. She stood for a moment on the pavement, uncertain what to do, knowing that she was on the brink of breaking down in tears. She and Vernon had been to London simply dozens of times, of course, but she could not have called any of the people she had met there a friend. She realized that she had only two friends in the world, Robin and Helen. Robin was abroad, and she could not go to Helen, because Helen's father would certainly tell her that her duty was to return to her husband. Standing there in the chill December afternoon a small tear escaped from Maia's eye, and rolled slowly down her cheek. Dashing it away, she began to walk down the street.

Lacking money, she had to take the Underground back to Liverpool Street station. People stared at her furs and her jewellery; a couple of factory girls mimicked her. She knew that she had no alternative but to return to Vernon, because she had nowhere else to go. She got lost on the Tube twice as, tired and upset, her usually agile brain failed to understand the maps. She had not eaten that day; nauseous and depressed, she had refused everything but tea that morning. When, eventually, Maia reached Liverpool Street, she made herself sit down and eat a bun and drink a cup of tea, because she was afraid that she might faint. Sitting in the tea-room, forcing down small fragments of bun, she heard the Salvation Army band start to play outside. 'Joy to the World' . . . She had forgotten that it was Christmas Eve.

She did not arrive back at the house until seven o'clock. Walking up the drive, Maia saw that all the lights in the house glittered. For a moment she could not think why, and then she remembered. They were having a party. She and Vernon were hosting the Christmas Eve party for the staff of Merchants.

She stood there for a moment, transfixed with horror, her hands clasped over her mouth. Music was filtering through the windows. The house that to Maia had once seemed so glorious, so grand, now seemed huge and dark and threatening. She heard footsteps on the gravel, and she jumped.

It was only her maid, though, not Vernon. 'Mr Merchant said I was to look out for you, madam. He says you're to come in through the back, and get changed as quick as possible. He's told the guests you've a migraine and had to lie down for a while.'

Maia followed her maid through the kitchen and up the servants' stairs. In her bedroom she quickly bathed, changing into a dress of midnight blue lace. Downstairs, she kissed Vernon on the cheek, and greeted all the shop girls and clerks and managers. She knew that they envied her, but she herself, Maia thought, envied them far more. She had a debt to pay. She knew that she would be punished. When she glanced at Vernon, he smiled at her, courteous and loving, the good husband. But he drank steadily, and she became, as the evening wore on, more and more nervous.

The last of the guests left at one o'clock in the morning. Maia remained in the drawing-room, listening to the final clatterings of the servants as they cleared up the kitchen. She felt, unusually, physically fragile, as well as mentally exhausted. She, who had always prided herself on her good health.

She heard Vernon murmur to her, as she had known he must, 'You were late, Maia. Why were you late?'

'I went to see Helen,' she lied. 'I missed my train.' She added, with a fleeting return of her old spirit, 'If you bought me a motor- car . . . It's ridiculous that I have not my own car.'

'If you had your own motor-car, Maia, then how would I know where you were?'

For the second time that day, tears oozed from between her eyelids. She nodded, silently, understanding him. She was his possession, just as this house, the shop, her jewellery were his possessions.

He said softly, 'How do you think I felt, when all our guests arrived and I did not know where you were?'

She said sarcastically, 'Did you miss me, Vernon?'

'I resent . . . yes, that's the word, *resent* . . . having to lie to my employees.'

'Then you should have told them the truth,' she hissed, 'that I went out for the day, and could hardly bear to return to you!'

She ran out of the drawing-room and into the hall. Something was breaking inside her, and she had forgotten to be careful. She felt trapped and hopeless.

He caught up with her before she was halfway up the stairs. She knew that he was very drunk because his reddish-brown eyes glittered, and he stumbled slightly as he began his ascent. When he clutched at her, she stopped, chilled by his touch. She had, she thought, disgusted at herself, fallen into the habit of obeying him.

He said, 'I bought you, Maia.'

Somehow she gathered up the scattered remains of her courage. She had to make him understand what he did to her. She had to make him understand that she teetered at the edge of a precipice, and that beyond that precipice lay an abyss she could not dare contemplate.

'You're not to hurt me again, Vernon.' Her voice was hoarse. 'You're not to make me do those things.'

She started to climb the stairs again, gripping the banister as though she was an invalid, her high-heeled shoes clicking unsteadily on the polished wooden margins.

'You'll do what I tell you to do, Maia.'

As she gripped the newel post at the top of the stair-case, she felt a wave of hatred so intense that she had to close her eyes for a moment, fighting dizziness. She felt him push past her. In their brief moment of contact, she was aware again of the strength of his body, the weakness of her own. Once more she loathed herself for her own craven impotence, for the mesmerized paralysis he reduced her to.

'Not any more, Vernon,' she whispered. 'I won't—'

He lunged at her then, taking her by surprise, but she ducked instinctively, crouching against the newel post, and it registered with her that he must be drunker than usual. A tiny spark of hope was born inside her. Recognizing the fury in his eyes, she began to step backwards down the stairs as quickly as she dared, one tread at a time, not daring to stop watching him, held by the intensity of his expression. Stumbling down after her, Vernon grabbed at her again, seizing a handful of dark blue lace. As she twisted away from him, Maia glimpsed the long, sweeping length of the stairs beneath them, and suddenly hope flowered, offering her for the first time a possibility of freedom.

At New Year, Francis stayed behind on the Continent with Vivien, and Robin and Joe travelled home together. Robin couldn't help but feel pleased with herself. She had, within the space of a few days, passed two of the important milestones in a woman's life. She had travelled abroad, and she had lost her virginity. She had enjoyed both immensely. She had celebrated the coming of the 1930s in a tiny bar in Deauville, crushed in the gloom with a great many rather drunk Frenchmen, Francis to one side of her, Joe to the other. They had drunk toasts to World Peace.

Joe saw her to her lodgings. As she fitted her key in the lock, the younger Miss Turner appeared, fluttering anxiously, a flimsy scrap of paper in her hand.

'Miss Summerhayes. Too dreadful that you have been away . . . This arrived a week ago . . . Such a black aura . . .'

Robin's knees shook when she saw the telegram, and she had to sit down at the foot of the stairs. She thought of Stevie and Hugh, all those years ago. The telegrams that had sat on the hall table for the entire day . . .

'I can't,' she whispered to Joe. 'Please. Could you . . . ?'

As he ripped the telegram open and folded it out, she

said, 'Hugh . . . ?' and he looked up, and shook his head immediately.

'No. It's from your mother, though. About someone called Merchant.'

Robin took the telegram from Joe, and read it herself. *Vernon Merchant dead STOP Inquest January fifth STOP Mother STOP* She had to re-read it several times before the disjointed words sunk in. Then her earlier fear for Hugh was replaced almost at once with an entirely different sort of dread. Maia's voice echoed inside her head. *I may not want him, but I do want his money . . .*

She became aware that Joe was speaking to her. She managed to say, 'Maia Merchant is an old friend of mine. She and Vernon were married only last year.'

Miss Turner tutted, Joe scowled. 'I'm sorry, Robin. Were you fond of him?'

She stared at him, surprised, and said, 'No. He was loathsome,' and only then remembered what else Maia had said to her.

You're not to tell anyone about Vernon and me, Robin. D'you swear?

And she had sworn. She had promised poor, bruised, broken Maia that she would keep the secret of her disastrous marriage. She said hastily, flustered, 'I mean – marriage and all that. You know I disapprove of it, Joe.'

'A Mrs Merchant came to see you just before Christmas, Miss Summerhayes,' said Miss Turner timidly. 'I told her that you were abroad.'

She felt winded. She wanted to be alone, she must have time to think. Saying goodbye to Joe, she ran out of the house towards the post office. When she had sent a telegram to her mother telling her that she would come home the following day, Robin walked slowly back to her lodgings, thinking. Her conclusions were black and alarming. Glancing at her watch, she saw that it was almost five o'clock, and remembered that it was Thursday night, her night to help in the clinic.

The queues of sniffling children and tired-looking

women seemed longer than usual. The last patient did not leave until after nine o'clock. Dr Mackenzie yelled at Robin for losing his prescription pad, but Robin, instead of yelling back as she usually did, put on the kettle and made a large pot of tea. Assembling cups and sugar and milk, she placed it all on a tray and carried it in to him.

He was sitting at his desk behind a mountain of files and medical equipment. Dr Mackenzie was in his mid-forties, a big, kind, noisy bear of a man. He looked up when Robin came in.

'Found it.' He waved the prescription pad at her. 'Under the telephone directory.'

She grinned at him, and began to pour out the tea.

'You've hardly said a word all night, Robin. You're usually nattering away nonstop. What's wrong?'

'I'm fine. Just a couple of things on my mind.'

'Tell me. I can't afford for you to go into a decline. You're the best assistant I've had in years.'

She glowed at the rare compliment. 'Well – I've lost my job.'

'Ah. Bad luck. A new recruit to the ranks of the unemployed?'

She nodded. 'If I can't find anything else, I'll have to go home, I suppose.' An awful prospect.

He stirred sugar in his tea, looking closely at her. 'Don't want that, do you?'

She shook her head vigorously.

'Could you bear to work for me?'

Robin stared at him. 'What – full-time, you mean?'

'Very much so – though I could only pay you a pittance, I'm afraid.'

Cradling her tea, she said softly, 'Go on.'

'You know that I'm interested in the diseases of poverty in this area – TB, rickets, diphtheria and so on. I've been trying to write a paper for one of the medical journals, but I've run into a problem. It's easy enough for me to collate material about disease – I see it every day. But there's things I don't know – I don't know about my patients' diet, for instance, and I don't know enough about how they are housed. I don't always know whether the family's in employment or out of it. There's a tremendous need for some sort of study, Robin, that really explores the link between poverty and disease. Politicians so often try to deny that there is any link. Papers must be written – a book or two, perhaps – something the general public could get to grips with. But I need an assistant. I haven't the time to do it all myself.'

She couldn't help smiling. 'Me?'

'What do you think?'

'I'd love to do it. I really would, Neil.'

'That's what I hoped. And you have a good, methodical mind, Robin, when you can be bothered to use it. What about it, then? Shall we go into partnership?'

For the first time in her life, she felt as though she was being offered work that mattered to her. Useful work, something that might in the end make a difference. 'Yes,' she said. 'Oh yes.'

'It'll be hard work,' he warned her. 'I can give you a corner of the dispensary for your records, but most of the time you'll have to manage on your own. There'll be a lot of travelling around, and you'll see some sights you'll wish you hadn't. Things are going to get worse, Robin – I know it. The ripples from the collapse of the American economy have only just begun to touch us.'

He began to hurl files into drawers, to put away his stethoscope and thermometers. Then, seeing she was still sitting there, he said, 'You said there were two things bothering you. Well, that's one dealt with. What was the other?'

Robin willed herself not to blush. 'I have a lover, Dr Mackenzie,' she said proudly. 'And I don't wish to marry him, and I certainly don't want a baby just now. So do you think that someone could fit me with a diaphragm?'

Attending the inquest in Cambridge, Robin was glad of Daisy, sitting beside her. Both Richard and Daisy had been shocked by what had happened to Maia, whom they regarded with great affection. Yet the gulf between her and her parents had, Robin thought, widened. Richard and Daisy's sympathy for Maia was unmixed. Robin's was not.

The inquest told, coldly and factually, how Vernon Merchant had fallen downstairs, fracturing his skull on the marble floor of the hallway. His wife had been the only person with him at the time of his death, his servants all having gone either to their homes, or to their beds in the attic of the house. Mr Merchant, who had hosted his staff's Christmas party on the night of his death, had been drinking heavily.

Robin's heart sank as the procession of doctors, policemen and servants from the Merchant household gave their evidence. From where she was sitting, she could see Maia, seated in the front row of the court. When, eventually, Maia took the witness stand, and folded back her veil, Robin could see that her face was pale, and that there were dark shadows around her great, blue eyes. Maia told the coroner the date of her marriage, and the length of time she had known her husband before they had married. When the coroner asked Maia whether the marriage had been happy, Robin gripped her hands together and bit her lip.

'We were very happy, your honour. Very happy.'

Robin, watching Maia, recalled that other inquest. The one into Jordan Read's death. Maia had lied then, too.

Now, Maia's face had the still, carved look of a Renaissance pietà as she described to the court the events of the day of her husband's death. How she had travelled to London to visit her friend, Miss Summerhayes, only to find that Miss Summerhayes had gone abroad. She had missed her train, and returned home late. She and Vernon had hosted the party, and then, tired, she had started up to bed. Vernon had run to catch up with her, and he had stumbled on the stairs. Maia's voice trembled when she described how she had flung out a hand to help him, but had been unable to reach him. The coroner, ordering an usher to give Maia a glass of water, dismissed her from the stand. Robin found that she had been holding her breath, and that she had bitten her lip until it bled.

It was all over then. The coroner announced a verdict of accidental death, and Robin knew that it was only she who saw the glint in Maia's eyes before the verdict was announced. A glint of hope, perhaps, or of fear? Not sorrow, thought Robin, as the veil was flicked back over Maia's white face. Certainly not sorrow.

'Thank goodness that's over,' whispered Daisy, and squeezed Robin's hand. 'Poor Maia. Such a dreadful thing to happen.'

She couldn't think of anything to say. Without answering her mother, she pushed her way out of the courtroom. The atmosphere seemed suddenly hot and stifling, and she could not bear yet to go to Maia and join the crowd around her that offered their condolences. She had passed three of the great milestones in a woman's life, thought Robin, as she took a lungful of cold, fresh air. She had a job that she would enjoy, she had travelled, she had a lover. But somehow she could not imagine going to that pale, still figure and sharing these things with her. That promise belonged to childhood. They were not children now.

She wondered whether, if the worst of her fears were true, she would have wanted the verdict to be different. Whether, had she been called to the witness stand, she too would not have perjured herself. Whether, if Maia had been responsible for her husband's death, she, Robin, would not have felt there was a sort of justice in it. She simply did not know.

It was all hers. The money, the house, the business. Either Vernon had not been able to conceive that he might die young, or it was his last payment to her, Maia the whore.

Somehow, she had survived. There was remaining one small, nagging problem, but she felt certain she would find a way round that. She glanced at the maps spread out on the bed. She would travel for at least six months, and by the time she returned to Cambridge what gossip there was would have died away. Only Robin, after all, knew even part of the truth, and she had never doubted Robin's loyalty. When she came home, all this would be hers. She would never share anything with a man again.

Maia, aware that she had narrowly avoided disaster, pressed the clasps of her suitcase shut.

PART TWO

–

1930–1931

Chapter Five

Working for Dr Mackenzie, Robin discovered a different London, and what she witnessed made her alternate between anger and despair. Her scribbled notes bore testament to the endless struggle of other people's lives. 'Two bedrooms, parlour and scullery. Rent 6/-. Man aged 31, wife 28, and five children aged 10, 9, 7, 3 and 4 months. Man is off work. Family are in arrears with rent and paying heavy doctor's bill for youngest son, who is asthmatic.' And then, and somehow worse, a pathetic description of the family's inadequate meals, composed largely of bread and margarine and condensed milk.

Sometimes, knocking on the doors of strangers, she was sent packing with a proud shake of the head from those who suspected charity. Sometimes she was cursed for an interfering busybody, and just once she was sent sprawling in the mud by a man who accused her of working for the Public Assistance Committee. Often she was met by the sort of apathy that she began to realize was the most usual and perhaps the most dreadful result of months or years of unemployment, but mostly she was greeted warmly by people who welcomed any sort of diversion in a long, purposeless day.

With Francis, she discovered yet another London. A city of dingy cafés, nightclubs and restaurants. A city of dark, damp streets made magical by the first hazy light of dawn. A city of unexpected, secret places, of people who flitted in and out of her life like exotic butterflies.

In the September of 1930, Robin waited in a smoky basement nightclub. At almost eleven o'clock she looked up and saw Francis weaving in and out of the crowd towards her. He bent and kissed her, and then he signalled to the waiter and ordered drinks.

'Guy and Charis should be here soon. And I bumped into Angus in Fortnums.'

'Where's Joe?'

Francis looked vague. 'With Clodie, I think.' He lit himself a cigarette. 'I think that Joe's afraid that she's cheating on him. Which she is, of course. So he's keeping an eye on her.'

'Joe is spying on Clodie? Oh, Francis. He wouldn't. Surely not.'

'Joe is in love. People do strange things when they're in love.'

She thought, for no particular reason, of Maia and Vernon. Maia had never loved Vernon, but had Vernon, in his twisted way, loved Maia?

'*Love*,' said Robin, exasperated. 'People just muddle up sex and possession. It's utterly ridiculous.'

'Quite. Terribly bourgeois.' Francis leaned back in his chair, his eyes narrowed. 'All the same, I feel a certain amount of sympathy for the poor sod.'

Other people began to drift around their table: Guy Fortune, who wrote poetry, and his sister Charis, and a communist who occasionally had pamphlets printed by Gifford Press. Angus, whom Robin had met at Long Ferry Hall, appeared with a bottle blonde draped over his arm. Selena Harcourt, an artist, had most of a jazz band in tow. Those who had money bought drinks for everyone else, the toasts becoming increasingly extravagant each time glasses were raised.

At midnight, they left the nightclub. Fog yellowed the night, dampening the roads and pavements. They meandered along the street, a noisy and motley band. After a while, they bundled Angus and his girlfriend into a taxi, and left Guy and Charis painting revolutionary rhyming couplets in red paint on the walls of a disused factory. Back in Francis's basement, which was dark and cold and quiet, they made love, shutting out everything else.

Often in the gathering darkness Clodie's house would remain silent. On those nights Joe, watching from across the street, hated himself for not trusting her. But sometimes a motor-car or a taxi would draw up outside her house, and he would move quietly forward in the darkness, trying to identify a face or to overhear whispered words before the green door shut. Sometimes the door opened again after ten minutes; at other times Clodie's visitor did not leave until an hour or two had passed. The visitors were always male.

Joe knew that he was behaving irrationally; he knew that he should simply ask Clodie whether she saw other men. But he was afraid of offending her; afraid, too, of the answer she might give him. His temper grew short as he lurched between hope, despair and self-disgust. He concocted all sorts of explanations for Clodie's frequent visitors, explanations that in the day seemed perfectly reasonable. Clodie had called a doctor for Lizzie, or her landlord was collecting the monthly rent. When Clodie told him that she had started doing men's tailoring, Joe felt a great weight slip from his shoulders as he stared at the half-finished jackets and waistcoats slung carefully over the backs of her dining chairs. He almost laughed and shared his suspicions with her, but managed to stop himself just in time, knowing that his jealousy could halt their affair just as effectively as her faithlessness.

Yet he could not stop watching. He followed one of her visitors home one night, leaving the Underground train at the same stop as his quarry. Clodie's visitor lived in a large villa in a leafy part of Hampstead. Somehow Joe couldn't quite convince himself that the sort of man who lived in that sort of house would have his suits made by a little dressmaker living in Hackney.

*   *   *

Returning to Cambridge after nine months' absence, Maia felt apprehension grow in her. Sunlight touched the spires and colleges as she drove over the Gog Magog hills, and a hard ball of fear gathered in her stomach. Her hands slipped damply on the steering wheel as hill and wood gave way to the broad roads that made up the outskirts of the city. The long, curling drive, the dense thickets of laurel, and Vernon's house, huge and shadowed, made her throat tighten until she could hardly swallow. She knew, parking her car outside the front door, that her life had, since the beginning of the year, irrevocably split into two, and that the dark undercurrent must always remain hidden beneath the glittering, smooth outer surface. Just for a moment, as she opened the car door, she wondered whether she could maintain the façade.

But after the ordeal of greeting the servants was over, after she had seen curiosity flower and die in their eyes, Maia found that she had regained her confidence. It had been a difficult year, but she had come through. Walking through the rooms, climbing those great, winding stairs, she realized that it was different. *He* was not there. The absence of him changed the place utterly, making it hers, and imbuing it with a glorious sense of freedom.

She spent the morning closeted with her accountant and lawyer, and in the afternoon headed out to the Fens to visit Helen. Leaving Thorpe Fen, she drove towards the long, straight bank of the Hundred Foot Drain. There, Maia parked the car and took a flask of tea from the glove compartment.

Helen touched the dashboard admiringly. 'Is it yours?'

Maia nodded. 'Isn't she beautiful? I drove her all through France and Italy.'

'Weren't you afraid?'

'I'm never afraid of those sort of things.' Maia poured out two cups of tea.

Helen cradled the cup between her fingers. 'You must

144

still feel awful, Maia. About Vernon, I mean. Such a tragic thing to happen.'

There were tears of sympathy in Helen's eyes. Maia said firmly, 'I don't want to talk about it.'

'Of course not. I didn't meant to upset you—'

'Darling Helen, you haven't upset me in the least.' She touched Helen's gloved hand.

'We should drink a toast, then. You've travelled abroad, Maia – that's another of the milestones in a woman's life.'

Maia blinked. 'I'd forgotten all that. How long ago it seems.' She was about to add, *how childish*, when, noticing Helen's expression, she smiled instead, and raised her cup.

'To you too, then, Helen. To your dressmaking business.'

Helen looked miserable. 'Oh – that. I don't do it any more, actually. I got in such a muddle about the money, and though Hugh Summerhayes was perfectly sweet and helped me, I didn't like to ask him too often. And people don't seem to be able to afford new clothes just now.'

'The ones who can are buying them ready-made, I suppose,' said Maia thoughtfully. Then she made herself ask, 'And Robin? Have you seen her?'

'She came home for a week in the summer. She has a new job that keeps her terribly busy.'

Maia half listened to Helen telling her about Robin's work. She thought, privately, that Robin was still trying to change the world, which was completely pointless. Maia knew that the world was unchangeable, and that those who were rich or clever or beautiful would always scramble to the top, using the backs of the poor and the stupid as stepping-stones. She was aware, too, of her shudder of relief as she silently thanked the God she had never believed in for Robin's continuing loyalty.

Maia felt not apprehension but anticipation as she drove to Merchants the following morning. She enjoyed the small stir she made as she walked through Merchants' wide double doors, and when she glimpsed herself fleet-ingly in the chrome and mirrors of the perfumery she knew that they saw what she saw: a slim, elegant woman, her pale skin only slightly tanned by her summer on the Continent, her clothes understated and exquisite.

By the time she reached the first floor, her arrival at the store must, by some sort of jungle telegraph, have been conveyed to the store manager, Liam Kavanagh. A short, muscular, blue-eyed Irishman, he greeted her as she walked through the ladies' outfitting department, heading for the offices.

'Mrs Merchant. How pleasant of you to call in. May I get you a chair . . . tea . . . ?'

'Nothing, thank you, Mr Kavanagh. Oh—' Maia's brow creased in the smallest of frowns '—there is some-thing. Would you fetch Mr Twentyman and Mr Underwood? I would like to speak to them both. And to you, of course.'

Mr Twentyman was the head buyer, Mr Underwood the chief accountant. Maia smiled prettily at Liam Kavanagh.

'Of course, Mrs Merchant. Would you like to wait in the staff sitting-room?'

'I don't think so, Mr Kavanagh. My late husband's office would be a much more suitable place for what I have to say.'

She noticed the flicker of irritation, quickly disguised, that crossed his face. In Vernon's office, she realized why. Liam Kavanagh's files and pens were spread across the desk; Liam Kavanagh's overcoat and hat hung on the stand. She did not feel angry. In his position she would have done the same.

When all three men were present Maia shook hands with each, and sat down on the chair behind Vernon's desk.

'First of all, gentlemen, I wanted to express my thanks to you for your hard work during this difficult time. I'm sure that you have done your utmost to keep Merchants running as Vernon would have wanted it.'

Mr Twentyman uttered smooth and respectful condolences; Mr Underwood coughed and looked bored. In Liam Kavanagh's limpid blue eyes there was an expression of . . . Maia was not quite sure what.

He said, 'I think you will find that your investments have been satisfactorily protected, Mrs Merchant.'

'I don't doubt it, Mr Kavanagh.'

'And I think you'll also find that Merchants has been and will continue to be in safe hands.'

She beamed at him. 'We appear to be in complete agreement, Mr Kavanagh.'

'Mr Underwood will keep in touch with your accountant as usual, Mrs Merchant.'

Fleetingly, Maia touched the files on the desk. 'Oh, I don't think there'll be any need for that, Mr Kavanagh. After all, it will be so much easier for Mr Underwood just to knock on the door of my office.'

Three pairs of eyes stared at her. Only in Liam Kavanagh's did she detect comprehension, mixed with fury.

'One can hardly run a store from home, can one?' she added lightly. 'One would miss so much.'

The chief accountant, the truth dawning at last, said, '*Run* the store, madam? You cannot mean to . . .' His voice trailed away.

'But I do mean to, Mr Underwood,' said Maia sweetly. 'Merchants is mine now, and I intend to see that it thrives. Each of you will report to me, just as you reported to Vernon when he was alive. Now, I would like to speak next to the managers and to the buyers. You will arrange that, perhaps, Mr Twentyman? And send Miss Dawkins to me, if you please, Mr Underwood.'

Maia glanced at her watch. 'I should be through with the preliminary business by midday. Will that give you long enough, Mr Kavanagh, to remove your belongings from my office?'

That autumn Robin knocked on the doors of the worst houses in Stepney. There was a fine drizzle, and she had left her umbrella on the bus, but she forgot the weather as she worked methodically down the dingy little street. The terraced houses were privately owned, none had water, all twelve shared two taps and two drains in the back yard. Two dreadful lavatories huddled in the rain at the back of the houses.

The door of the last house in the row was opened by a barefoot child in a grubby cut-down shirt. Robin could smell dirty linen and unwashed baby and damp. A woman shuffled into view.

Robin explained about her survey. 'It's just a few simple questions. I won't take up too much of your time.'

Invited into the house, she looked around the room. There were orange boxes for tables, sacks stuffed with straw for seats. Both the baby and the infant who had opened the door were hollow-eyed and listless. The walls were encrusted with mould, and the windows let in rainwater. Though a small coal fire flickered feebly in the grate, the room was cold.

Robin ran quickly through her list of questions. The woman's name was Mrs Lewis, and her husband was an unemployed docker, who had been out of work for six months following an injury to his back. Mr Lewis was thirty-one, his wife was twenty-nine. Only nine years older than herself, thought Robin, horrified, as she glanced at the thin, pale creature holding the baby. Mr Lewis received twenty-five shillings a week from the Public Assistance Committee, and the rent for the house was ten shillings and sixpence.

'We're in arrears,' said Mrs Lewis. 'Landlord's given us till Friday.' Her voice was flat and apathetic, showing neither fear nor distress.

Robin had to remind herself of Dr Mackenzie's warnings, months ago. Don't get too involved. Be objective.

'How many children have you, Mrs Lewis?'

'There's Lily and Larry, and the two at school. And the baby. And Mary, in there.'

She thought at first that Mrs Lewis meant that her daughter was playing out in the back yard. But then she heard the whimpering noises from the room beyond, and she followed Mrs Lewis into the scullery. It took a few moments for Robin's eyes to accustom themselves to the poor light. When she saw the child she almost retched. Mary huddled in a large basket cluttered with filthy scraps of blanket. Like a dog, thought Robin. Her mouth was open and drooling, her eyes unfocused, her hair matted.

'She's not all there,' explained Mrs Lewis. 'Been like that since she was born. Hush now, Mary.'

'How old is she?'

'Ten last April. She's my eldest.'

Robin knelt down beside the basket, and gently stroked the child's dirty face. 'Hello, Mary.' Mary seized Robin's fingers, and rocked backwards and forwards on her haunches.

Mrs Lewis added, 'My Jack's ever so good with her, but since he hurt his back he can't carry her upstairs, see. So she sleeps down here.'

Somehow, Robin managed to finish the interview. Her hand shook as she listed the bread and margarine and cheese that made up the family's diet, and when she had finished, she scrabbled in her bag and brought out a handful of boiled sweets.

'For the children. And could you tell me the name of your landlord, Mrs Lewis?'

Mrs Lewis's landlord lived half a mile away in a house that was bigger and better equipped, though not tidier, than his tenants'. Robin hammered on the door for five minutes before it was opened. Eddie Harris was tall, broad-chested and accompanied by a large dog.

Showing Robin into a front room littered with greasy chip wrappings and empty beer bottles, Mr Harris eyed her suspiciously. Robin explained about her survey.

'I met some of your tenants this morning, Mr Harris. The Lewises, of Walnut Street. They told me that they're behind with their rent.'

He pulled a battered notebook from a drawer, and thumbed through it. 'Five weeks behind.'

'Mrs Lewis tells me that you're going to evict them if they haven't paid up by the end of the week.'

'Six weeks is the usual time.'

'Couldn't you give them a little longer, Mr Harris?'

He belched. 'Six weeks is usual. Good business practice.'

She thought of the awful little house, with its mould and damp and lack of any facilities. 'Perhaps you could reduce the rent, Mr Harris, and then the family might find it easier to pay.'

He stared at her and then laughed, displaying a mouthful of blackened teeth. 'Reduce the rent? Now why would I want to do that, miss?'

'Because it isn't worth what you charge for it.'

The amusement died from his small sharp eyes. 'I've half a dozen families wanting a nice little house like that.'

Robin forced herself to remain polite. 'Mr Harris – I'm sure that you know that the rent is high for a property as derelict as those in Walnut Street. Perhaps you don't know that Mr Lewis is unemployed, and that they have six children, including a daughter who has been chronically ill from birth. Where are they to go if you evict them?'

'None of my business, is it?' The small weasel eyes examined her closely. 'And none of yours neither, miss.'

He stared at her in a way that she found disturbing. She wore, as usual, a knee-length skirt and her green velvet coat, and high heels. She adored the high heels because they made her look taller, but now she almost wished that she had worn an ankle-length sack and galoshes.

He grinned. 'Is that all you've come to say, sweetheart? Or is there something more I can do for you?' His hand rested on her shoulder: involuntarily, she recoiled at his touch. The dog crouched by the door, panting.

'You won't reconsider, then?'

He said softly, 'Depends what you're offering,

darlin',' and his short, stubby fingers moved slowly from her shoulder to fondle her breast. Without thinking, she twisted her head and sank her teeth into his wrist.

His howl of pain made the dog rise to its feet, snarling. Robin saw her chance, though, and as Eddie Harris snatched his hand away from her, she ducked round the dog and the door, and ran out into the street.

She was taken aback by Dr Mackenzie's reaction when she described the incident to him at the clinic that evening.

'You went to see the landlord? Eddie Harris? You went alone to try to persuade that brainless oaf to reduce his tenants' rent?'

Robin said defensively, 'What else could I do? Someone had to try.'

He thumped the table with his fist. 'Not you, Robin! Not alone!'

Suddenly she too was angry. 'I'm not a child, Neil. I have a job to do.'

'You are in my employ,' he said coldly. 'If you ever do anything so stupid again, you will no longer be in my employ. Do you understand?'

She glared at him furiously.

He added, exasperated, 'The man's an animal – I've had to repair the damage he's done more than once. Don't you see, Robin – anything could have happened—'

'But that poor child—' she wailed, recalling the girl in the scullery. 'Couldn't you do something for her, Neil?'

'Not if the bairn was damaged at birth. It happens, and it's a tragedy, but there's some things that cannae be repaired.'

'If you'd seen how she was living!'

'Where would you rather she lived, Robin? In the workhouse? In an orphanage? There's nowhere else for her. The poor wee thing is probably best off where she is. She may be living in squalor, but at least she's with her family. The mentally defective offspring of the rich are often sent away to so-called homes, and never thought of again – some people think these conditions are hereditary, you see, so they're ashamed of the poor bairns. I've been to some of those places, Robin, and they're worse than what you saw this morning.'

Dr Mackenzie began to throw files haphazardly into a cabinet. 'Now, run off, won't you? And remember what I said. Be objective. Don't meddle in what cannae be changed.'

It seemed easy enough at first, sitting in Vernon's office and dictating letters to Vernon's gaunt and severe secretary, Miss Dawkins, or emerging twice a day to prowl round the store, terrifying the shopgirls, running her finger along counters to check for specks of dust.

Too easy. After a few weeks, Maia realized that she had been sidelined, shut out by Merchants' old triumvirate as effectively as Vernon had once shut her out from all this power and influence. While she sat, bored, in her office, the managers and the buyers continued to take their problems to Liam Kavanagh, just across the hall. Her Monday morning meetings with her accountant, her store manager and head buyer were a sham, a piece of playacting connived at to keep her quiet. The letters that she signed were only a fraction of the letters that Miss Dawkins typed: the work that took up most of Maia's secretary's day was dictated by Liam Kavanagh.

When she remonstrated with Mr Underwood and Mr Twentyman they placated her for a day or two. The littleness of the problems they brought to her, the unimportance of the issues they pretended to discuss with her made a fierce rage burn inside her. Silently, Maia concluded that Mr Twentyman was vain, that Mr Underwood was unintelligent, and that she must confront Liam Kavanagh, who was neither. Mr Kavanagh was clever and hardworking and attractive. Most of the shopgirls were in love with him, and those who were not were afraid of him. A smile from him reduced Miss Dawkins, a stalwart churchgoer in her late fifties, to girlish giggles. The men respected Liam Kavanagh for his undoubted ability, and were wary of him for his cutting tongue and cold temper.

Maia waited until late one Friday, and when the clerks and shop assistants and buyers had all gone home she asked Liam Kavanagh into her office.

'A cigarette, Mr Kavanagh?' As she offered her cigarette case, she saw the derision in his eyes.

'A pleasure, Mrs Merchant.'

'Sit down, won't you.' There were two comfortable leather armchairs. Maia sat in one. 'I know nothing about you, Mr Kavanagh. Are you married?'

His lip curled slightly. 'No, I am not, Mrs Merchant.'

'Why not?'

His eyes widened. 'That's my affair, don't you think?'

She shrugged. 'I am interested in the well-being of all my staff.'

'Really? In that case . . . I have never married because I haven't had the time.'

'You are wholly dedicated to your work, then.'

'I'm almost forty, Mrs Merchant, and it has taken me since I was fifteen to achieve the position I have today. I haven't married, but then I haven't done badly for a lad from the back streets of Dublin, have I?'

His gaze met hers, challenging her. She said calmly, 'Whereas I am a spoilt little girl who's been given it all on a plate?'

He looked away. 'I didn't say that.'

'Oh . . . you've been saying just that for some time, I think. Silently, though.'

His fair skin reddened slightly, but he said nothing. Maia continued, 'Let me tell you a little about myself. I was brought up in a nice house in Cambridge, and I was privately educated. A silver spoon, yes. But my parents quarrelled from the day I was born, and most of the time they simply didn't notice whether I was there or not. My father lost all his money, and died when I was eighteen. I was married to Vernon for six months, as you know, and widowed before I turned twenty-one. It may seem

hard for you to believe, but I have never, ever had anyone to depend on but myself.'

Except my friends, Maia thought. Yet the events of the
last year had driven a small but perceptible wedge
between herself and Robin. And often, comparing herself to Helen, she felt cynical and used.

Liam Kavanagh said, 'All this is very affecting, Mrs
Merchant, but it doesn't alter the fact that you have just
walked into what took me twenty years to learn.'

'I'm a quick learner.'

'And—' he began, and stopped.

Maia almost smiled. 'And I'm a woman?'

'Yes.' The cornflower-blue eyes met hers, defying her.

'We may have had to fight different prejudices, but the
struggle is the same, isn't it? I would have thought a boy
from the bogs who'd fought his way up the ladder would
have some sympathy for my predicament.'

A flicker of anger crossed his face, quickly quelled.

'Obviously,' added Maia smoothly, 'I was mistaken.
And since you cannot argue with the undoubted fact of
my ownership of Merchants, you seek to undermine me
in other ways.'

'I don't know what you mean.'

'Come now, Mr Kavanagh. Neither of us are fools. In
fact, I think we have quite a lot in common.'

His gaze ran over her then, from the top of her gleaming dark head to the tips of her small high-heeled shoes.
She felt for the first time uncomfortable and unsure of
herself.

He drawled, 'D'you think so, Mrs Merchant?'

Maia felt her face grow hot. 'Do *you* think, perhaps,
that a woman cannot do the job?' Though she tried to
control it, she could hear her anger. 'That I cannot add
up – or understand sales figures – or calculate profits?'

'Not many women can.'

'Only because they haven't learnt. And I can – I've
made sure of it.'

'Running a place like Merchants isn't just about
adding up pennies.' Liam Kavanagh's words were slow,

patronizing. 'It's about hiring and firing . . . about knowing what to buy and what not to buy . . . You have to be ruthless.'

She thought, if only you knew. Memories flickered; memories that she usually managed to avoid. The sound of a gunshot, and the image of a body tumbling over and over again down a flight of stairs. The four blank white walls of a convent . . . Maia had to drop her gaze.

'And who will you marry, Mrs Merchant? No – I make no apologies for asking the question – you've pried into my private life already. That's the worst of it – what asset-stripper – what incompetent – will you marry?' His voice was bitter.

So that's it, she thought. 'You're afraid that I'll remarry and give Merchants to someone else?'

'Of course.' Again he looked at her; again she had to force herself not to pull down the hem of her skirt, to clutch together the open halves of her jacket.

'A young woman like you isn't going to stay a widow for the rest of her life.' His gaze had settled on the deep V of her blouse.

'I will never marry again.' Maia's tone was vehement. 'I can promise you that. Never, ever.'

He looked at her disbelievingly. 'You say that now—'

'And I will say it in five, in ten, in twenty years' time.'

'Grief fades.'

'Does it?' She knew privately that she would never forget the nightmarish months of her marriage. Never forget what an obsessive, cruel person like Vernon had almost made of her. The greatest legacy of the first twenty-one years of her life was an utter contempt for men.

'So they say.' Liam Kavanagh stubbed out his cigarette; he glanced at his watch. 'This is all very interesting, Mrs Merchant, but I've things to do.'

He was dismissing her as if she was an inefficient shopgirl, or some colleen that he had rolled with in the hills of Donegal. This time, Maia could not control her fury.

'You'll stay and listen to me, Mr Kavanagh, if you wish to keep your job!'

She saw the flare of anger in his blue eyes, and then he said, his voice taut, 'What was it you wished to say to me, Mrs Merchant? Are you unhappy with my work?'

She hissed, 'You know what I am unhappy with, Liam Kavanagh! I am unhappy that you take me for a fool – I am unhappy that I am treated as though I am a puppet, with you pulling my strings!'

She thought he smiled. If she had been certain, she would have dismissed him there and then. But he said, 'Just trying to help, Mrs Merchant. To make things easier for you.' The mockery was scarcely disguised.

'When I want your help, Mr Kavanagh, then I shall ask for it. In the meantime, you will make sure that any problems, any decisions concerning Merchants are to be brought to me. This department store belongs to me, and not to you. Do you understand?'

He rose to his feet. 'Perfectly, Mrs Merchant.'

'Then you may go.'

After he had left the room, Maia sat for a few moments. The muscles in her legs were shaking, and her fingers were knotted together. She thought that her victory had been hollow, that she had in fact lost. He had made a fool of her, and that left a sour taste in her mouth.

Rising, Maia went to the filing cabinet and took from the bottom drawer the half-bottle of Scotch that someone had left there. Unstoppering it, she drank deeply.

When Joe reached Clodie's house, he saw, as he had seen on the last four Friday evenings, the car parked outside. He swore under his breath, then sank back into a doorway, leaning against the jamb while he lit himself a cigarette.

The cigarette failed this time to calm him. He thought of the things that had recently appeared in Clodie's house: the new sewing-machine, the toys for Lizzie, the perfume that she had begun to wear. Worst of all, the clothes and the jewellery. The green velvet frock that superbly skimmed the lines of her voluptuous body; the pearls that nestled on the lobes of her ears. The new coat, the silk stockings, the jaunty little hat. She had said carelessly, 'I've had a lot of work recently, Joe. You can earn five pounds for a man's jacket,' and her complacent acceptance of his own naivety had further fuelled his jealousy. He had to know. He could not wait any longer. Dropping his cigarette and grinding it into the pavement with his heel, he crossed the road and knocked loudly on the green-painted door.

It took a full five minutes for Clodie to answer the door. When she did, she was wearing a flowery kimono, and her hair was down. Her eyes widened when she saw him.

'It's late, Joe – nearly one o'clock—'

'You weren't asleep, though, were you, Clo?'

Her eyes evaded his. "Course I was. I'm ever so tired. You can't come in, love—'

Pushing past her, he glanced quickly round the front room. The fire was only just dying, and there were two empty wine-glasses on the table.

'I gave Lizzie a mouthful,' said Clodie quickly. 'Doctor said a little wine's good for her stomach.'

He spun round, staring at her. 'The worst thing is – the worst thing is that you must think I'm so bloody stupid—'

Anger briefly flickered in her eyes. But she went to him, gently stroking his face. 'I don't think you're stupid at all, Joe. I think you're perfectly sweet.'

He pushed her away. 'Where is he, Clodie?'

'Who?'

'Hell . . .' He started up the stairs. He heard her cry out, 'You're not to go up there, Joe – you'll wake up Lizzie!' but he ignored her, and, reaching the landing, flung open her bedroom door.

He was in bed, of course. Middle-aged and balding, grabbing his discarded trousers from the floor as soon as he saw Joe. Like some awful French farce, Joe thought, and almost wanted to laugh. But then, recalling the lifetime that he and Clodie had spent in this bed, not wanting to laugh at all.

'Get out of here—' He lunged at the man on the bed.

'There's no need for that.' Clodie seized Joe's arm, trying to pull him back. 'Kenneth's just going, aren't you, Kenneth?'

The scene disintegrated into farce again as Kenneth hopped around, hastily gathering shirt and socks and shoes, and then ran out of the room and down the stairs. Joe heard the front door slam shut.

He turned to face Clodie. 'Are there others?'

She shook her head. 'Of course not, Joe. Ken's just an old friend.'

'You're lying!' he yelled. 'I've seen them, Clodie . . . I've watched outside your damned door for months, and I've seen them!'

She stopped attempting to placate him. Anger flamed in her green eyes.

'What of it?' she hissed. 'What's it to you?'

There was a fur coat slung over the back of one of the chairs. He grabbed at it, holding it out to her. 'Was it for *this*?'

She said scornfully, 'Could you give me anything like that? Could you, Joe?'

The coat slipped from his hands to the floor. Clodie picked it up, lovingly stroking it, arranging it on a hanger. 'Kenny bought me the coat,' she said. 'And the earrings. And Eric bought all those lovely toys for Lizzie, and he's paid for the doctor since the beginning of the year. Albert just buys us lovely dinners and takes us out in his motor-car.'

He said, 'You've sold yourself, Clodie. Will you sell Lizzie when she's old enough?' and she struck him hard across the face with the flat of her hand.

'Get out!' she hissed. 'Get out!'

Outside, Joe tasted blood in his mouth from where her rings had caught his lip. He walked back to the basement, but the cold night air failed to cool his anger. Reaching the flat, he kicked the door shut after him, and struggled with shaking hands to light the gas lamp.

'Joe?' Turning, he saw Robin behind him. She was wearing one of Francis's shirts, and her eyes were heavy with sleep. She stared at his face. 'You're hurt—'

'I'm fine,' he said impatiently. 'Go back to bed.'

She remained where she was, though. 'Was there a fight at the pub?'

'I haven't been to the pub.'

'Then what . . . ?'

Her insatiable curiosity was one of her worst faults. 'Clodie was . . . entertaining . . . this complete ass. Some fat, balding, pompous—'

'Clodie has been seeing another man?'

He laughed bitterly. 'Clodie's been seeing *three* other men. So we're finished.'

'Why?'

He couldn't believe she could be so obtuse. Interfering, yes – naive, even, but generally reasonably intelligent. Joe struggled for patience.

'Isn't it obvious?'

'Not really, no.'

He flung his jacket onto the sofa. 'I wasn't aware that I was part of a four-way co-operative. That I had bought shares.'

'Because you and Clodie were lovers, you *owned* her?' She was twisting his words. 'Of course not. I just thought we had something – that we loved each other—'

Robin sat down on the sofa, pulling his jacket around her shoulders to keep herself warm. 'You desired each other, Joe, that's all. Does it really make any difference to you if Clodie desired other men as well?'

He knew suddenly that she was wrong, utterly wrong. And knew also that the anger he was feeling only temporarily masked the pain that was soon going to begin, and last for a long time.

'People confuse desire with love,' she said, lecturing him. 'And they think they have to possess the people they love. You're just behaving like any bourgeois husband, Joe.'

159

'She was taking *money,* for God's sake!' he hissed at her. 'Clothes – jewellery—'

He turned away, not wanting her to see his distress. He heard her add, her voice kinder, 'Widows are the poorest of the poor, Joe – especially if they've a child tying them to the house, like Clodie.'

He mumbled, 'I know,' aware that the worst thing was his complete failure to provide for them. Aware that he would miss Lizzie as well as Clodie.

There was a silence, and then he said, 'I couldn't share her, Robin. I just couldn't. You couldn't share Francis, could you?'

'What has Francis to do with it? We're friends and we sleep together, that's all. I'm not in love with Francis.'

He looked back at her, small and curled up in Francis's shirt and his own jacket, and he said wearily, 'Of course you are, Robin.'

Rubbing his eyes, he sat down on the sofa beside her. 'You are in love with Francis, and have been for over a year, and it's time you stopped fooling yourself.'

He heard her start to argue, but he closed his eyes, then, and cut himself off. He couldn't be bothered going to bed. As he drifted off to sleep, the scene with Clodie replayed itself through his head, and he felt an intense misery, mixed with regret.

You will make sure that any problems, any decisions concerning Merchants are to be brought to me, Maia had said, and she realized within a week or two that Liam Kavanagh had followed her instruction to the letter. To the full stop, to the swirling, atypically flamboyant flourish beneath his signature.

Every problem, large and small, landed on Maia's desk. The late orders in the household goods department; the stray cat in the garages. The steady, unstoppable decline in profits in the last two quarters; the lumps in the rice pudding in the canteen. Arriving at Merchants at a quarter to nine in the morning, she would find her desk, cleared the previous night, heaped with memos, letters to sign, accounting books. She knew that he was testing her; she knew that to complain again would confirm her as a weak, incompetent, whining female both in his eyes, and in the eyes of his allies.

She began to arrive at Merchants at half past seven each morning, and she rarely left before ten o'clock at night. A silent contest between herself and Liam Kavanagh, who also worked long hours, had begun. But in her case, almost swamped both by petty complaints and by real anxieties for the future, the long hours were a necessity. When Maia slept, she dreamed of order books and credit ratings; dining alone she had a memo pad constantly to hand to scrawl herself notes and reminders. It was not a bad thing, she told herself, that Liam Kavanagh had forced her to become involved in every ridiculous little squabble that a great enterprise like Merchants threw up. She must get to know the place intimately, like a lover. There was so much she didn't know.

She understood the dangers. That in this mire of trivia she would lose sight of the essentials, and the slide in Merchants' profits, visible in the half-yearly figures, would gather momentum. That she would make some huge, noticeable blunder, and they, the men, would smile to themselves, and mutter *I told you so*. When she felt them watching her, waiting for her to make a mistake, she worked even harder, consigning to her excellent memory all the information she had acquired during her first months at Merchants. She was exhausted, she had lost weight, she had not seen any of her friends for weeks, but she was beginning to understand this place. A plan formulated in her head, a battle campaign.

She began with Miss Dawkins. She knew that if she could win Miss Dawkins round, she would have a substantial advantage. Miss Dawkins's adoration of Liam Kavanagh (subtly fostered, of course, by Mr Kavanagh himself), and the secretary's old-fashioned notions of female inferiority made Maia's task doubly difficult. Most of Merchants' immense quantity of paperwork passed through Miss Dawkins's bony, capable hands at some time or another. Liam Kavanagh's campaign of swamping Maia in trivia could not have succeeded without Miss Dawkins's co-operation.

Maia asked Miss Dawkins to tea one Sunday afternoon. 'Just a little plain cake,' she explained, pre-empting any Puritan protests about the Sabbath Day. Maia dressed, as she did at work, in black, and had the tea things set out in the drawing-room. The large photograph of herself and Vernon on their wedding-day, that had lain in the bottom of a drawer for a year, was dusted off and placed prominently on the mantelpiece. 'I am working at Merchants for Vernon,' she explained, blinking back the tears as she stirred sugar into Miss Dawkins's tea. 'Such a struggle for a woman on her own, but he would have wanted me to keep his name alive. It would have meant so much to him. No matter how difficult, how *distasteful*, I find it sometimes, I feel that I must go on for poor Vernon's sake.' Maia glanced at the older woman through lashes that were beaded with tears. 'You do understand, don't you, Miss Dawkins?' On Monday morning, the huge, formless heap of paperwork on Maia's desk was pared down, subdivided into neat little sections by virtue of its urgency and subject matter.

Which left the men. The head buyer, Maia discovered, could be won round by flattering his vanity and by employing, when it suited her, an appealing if nauseating sort of helplessness. Her chief accountant, Mr Underwood, infuriated her with his lack of imagination and his hidebound sense of tradition. She concluded that Vernon must have endured him only for his nitpicking thoroughness, a necessity in his trade. Thoroughness was no longer enough, though: Maia, reading the financial pages of the newspaper, and talking to owners of other retail outlets, had begun to fear for the future. Staying awake one entire night, running her finger down columns of numbers, some of her old dread began to return. That she would lose it all, that it would slip through her fingers, that she would not be safe. She began to make notes, to plan again. The following morning, prowling round the store, checking stock cupboards and warehousing, she cornered Mr Twentyman in his office.

She said, 'You are buying in too large quantities, Mr Twentyman. You are to cut down your orders.'

He looked at her, incomprehension on his bland, handsome face, his raised eyebrows almost disappearing into his hairline.

'We have far too much warehousing, Mr Twentyman.' Maia spread out invoices on his desk. 'Linen . . . floor coverings . . . furniture. We are buying too much at a time. If we bought in smaller bulk then we could cut down on warehousing.'

He smiled. 'Let me explain, Mrs Merchant. The supplier offers a bigger discount for a bigger order. That is how it works.'

Her head aching from her sleepless night, Maia had no patience with patronage. Resting her palms on his desk, she leaned forward and said, 'And have you compared the discount with the interest lost from our investment accounts? Have you realized that, even excluding the cost of the warehousing, Merchants loses more money buying in such quantities?'

His smile diminished only slightly. 'That is Mr Underwood's concern, Mrs Merchant.'

'That is *my* concern, Mr Twentyman. And it is therefore your concern.'

There was a small silence. Then Maia said, 'You will cut your orders by at least twenty-five per cent. And you will put them out to tender.'

Now she had his attention. 'Madam—'

'Competition, Mr Twentyman.' The corners of her mouth curled slightly. 'That is how it works.'

He drew himself up stiffly. 'We have always worked this way, madam.'

'And now you are going to work my way,' said Maia sweetly. 'Bring me your order book at the end of the week, Mr Twentyman, so that I may check the figures.'

She saw the expression of outrage on his face, and felt not triumph, but exasperation, directed largely at herself. She had made another enemy. And as she turned and glimpsed Liam Kavanagh standing in the corridor behind them, watching, listening, she was aware of an utter weariness, mixed with a premonition of encroaching failure.

'Mr Kavanagh.' Her head held high, Maia forced herself to meet his eyes.

'Mrs Merchant.'

As she walked down the corridor, she realized how tired she must be. In Liam Kavanagh's bright blue eyes she had thought she had seen not anger, but admiration. Maia told herself that she must be mistaken.

Chapter Six

The shopping took Helen longer than she had expected, and the bus did not reach the outskirts of Thorpe Fen before dusk began to daub the fields and ditches with dark purplish-grey shadows. She tripped jumping down from the platform, snagging her stocking and catching her string bag on a stone, and when, walking home, she looked back, Helen saw that a trail of onions and turnips marked her route, falling through the hole in the bag onto the muddy drove.

It was the maids' afternoon off. As she let herself into the rectory, Helen saw the lace curtain that covered the front parlour window twitch.

'Helen?' Her father's voice. 'You are late.'

'I missed the bus, Daddy. I had to wait an hour.'

The Reverend Ferguson emerged out of the gloomy linoed corridor. The darkness shadowed the hollows of his eye-sockets, and emphasized the full, curving red lips and long, slightly tip-tilted nose, features that he had in common with his daughter.

'Mrs Lemon is here. She called to collect the subscriptions to the Parish Fund.'

Helen's hand slammed guiltily against her mouth. 'I haven't finished the collection yet, Daddy. Oh dear.'

The truth was that she hadn't even started. She loathed knocking on the doors of people she did not know well, and the money, as always, confused her.

'Dear me, Helen, you really must not be so remiss

with your responsibilities. And we have been waiting half an hour for our tea.' The Reverend Ferguson retreated back into the darkness. As he opened the door of the parlour, Helen heard him say, 'I'm afraid you will have to be patient, Mrs Lemon. Helen has not yet completed her task,' and, answering him, Mrs Lemon's 'No matter. There is no hurry.'

Helen picked up the letter that waited for her on the hall table. Her father's voice echoed along the corridor, following her to the kitchen.

'Helen can be backward in her duties, but I cannot help feeling glad that she is such a home girl. These modern girls who drive motor-cars and work in offices are hardly a credit to their sex.'

In the kitchen, Helen put away the shopping and sponged the mud from her knee. Then, sitting down at the table, she opened Maia's letter. It was short, only half a page.

Darling Helen – I'm afraid I shall have to cancel our lunch. Robin can't make it, and I have simply oodles of work. I'll rearrange as soon as poss. Lots of love, Maia.

The kettle was boiling. Helen rose, and began to spoon tea into the pot, and to cut cake. She could not think why she felt so low. Because of the damp spring weather perhaps, or because she saw, suddenly and painfully, how her friends had run ahead of her, leaving her trailing behind. She could not imagine ever being too busy to have lunch with Maia and Robin. She could not imagine running her own business, like Maia, or living alone in London, like Robin. She was not one jot nearer to her humble, reasonable ambition of marriage and motherhood than she had been three years ago, when they had sat on the verandah of Robin's winter house and talked about the future.

After Mrs Lemon had gone, her father beckoned her to him. His mood, always unpredictable, had altered. 'I was so worried when you were late, Helen,' he whispered. 'So worried. If something dreadful were to happen to you, as it happened to my beloved Florence

. . . I could not bear it.' His long, thin fingers touched
Helen's swathe of honey-coloured hair. 'Such lovely
hair, Chickie. So like your dear mama's.' Bending his
head, he kissed her cheek, then her mouth. His lips were
rough and dry.

Each day in the *Financial Times*, Maia read about businesses that had failed – businesses that had once been
viable, like hers. Though the open hostilities of Maia's
first months at Merchants had eased to a sort of truce,
she and Liam Kavanagh still circled each other, old
enemies, confined to their quarters, exercising power in
their own carefully demarcated spheres. Friction had
declined to civility, or perhaps to a certain guarded
respect. She thought that he was biding his time, hanging
fire. She needed him though. She needed Liam Kavanagh
so much.

She invited him to dine at her house. Issuing her invitation, Maia saw derision flicker again in Mr
Kavanagh's eyes, and she smiled a little to herself. Yet
he rang her doorbell promptly at seven o'clock on
Saturday evening, resplendent in a dinner suit and stiff
boiled shirt.

Over oeufs mornay they talked about trivia. He was
fidgeting, restless; Maia saw him glance at his watch.

She said, 'When I invited you here to dine with me,
Mr Kavanagh, what did you think?'

His eyes opened wide.

'You'll do me the courtesy of answering honestly, I
hope.'

He sat back in his chair and looked at her. 'If you wish
. . . I thought that you meant to soften me up . . . to win
my approval.'

'To seduce you?'

She saw his hand tighten around his glass. She added,
meeting his eyes, 'Metaphorically, of course.'

'Of course.'

Maia the whore, she thought cynically, had not yet
needed to employ the full range of her talents.

The maid cleared away the hors d'oeuvre and served the fish course. When she had gone, Maia said, 'You are an attractive man, Liam – I may call you Liam, mayn't I? – but I have no intention of seducing you. It wouldn't be useful to me.' She smiled, and saw to her delight that she had shocked him. 'I regard my appearance as being a weapon in my armoury, you see – just as you do. It's a valuable weapon, and I'd be a fool not to use it. But not with you. You'd only despise me, wouldn't you?'

For the first time, he looked uncomfortable. 'I apologize if I have given the impression that—'

She interrupted him. 'Oh, Liam, please – there really is no need. I brought you here not to seduce you, but to discuss cost cutting and advertising. Getting rid of surplus stock . . . reducing our overheads. Don't you think that sounds far more interesting than seduction?'

She thought that he might rise and walk out of the room, leaving the Dover sole to grow cold on his plate. But then some of the pride and defensiveness seemed to slide almost visibly from his shoulders, and he smiled and said, 'An impossible question, Mrs Merchant. If I agree with you then I insult you as a woman, and if I disagree I insult you as my boss.'

Looking at him, she felt her entire body relax and heard her own crack of laughter. For the first time it occurred to her that Liam Kavanagh could be a friend, someone who could share the immense burden she had taken on. She said softly, 'I need you, Liam. I need your intelligence and your loyalty and your experience. And I need you because you are a man. I need you because there are places that I will always be shut out from, where you must go in as my representative.'

His eyes narrowed. 'Go on.'

She came straight to the point. 'Our profits have declined over the last three quarters.'

'Not a great falling off, Mrs Merchant. Compared to others, we've held up reasonably well.'

'I don't compare Merchants to other businesses. You know that. I have my own standards for judging

Merchants. And I'm sure that you also suspect, as I do, that things will get worse before they begin to get better.'

He inclined his head in a small nod of agreement.

'I have a few proposals, Liam.' She put aside her knife and fork, all pretence of eating abandoned. 'I intend to close the lending library, which will allow me to enlarge the electrical goods department. And I am going to set in motion a major advertising campaign. We'll use a new agency.'

'Not Naylors?' Naylors had been responsible for the past ten years for Merchants' advertising.

'Too staid, don't you agree? I want something new and exciting and sophisticated. Something that will make people sit up and take notice.'

'Had you another agency in mind?'

'No.' Frowning, Maia shook her head. 'I thought you might have some suggestions. The golf club . . . the Town and Gown . . . all the little restaurants and pubs and clubs that men go to – you must hear people talking about such things.'

Often she realized how much more difficult the simple fact of her femaleness made her task. If she had been a man, then she would have gathered to herself all the complex and informal contacts that would have smoothed her way. A woman, she was excluded from those routes.

'You are so good at all that, I imagine, Liam. A man's man, when it suits you.'

Again, he was not offended. Drumming his fingers on a corner of the table, he said slowly, 'Closing the lending library is sensible – it makes a small enough profit. It'll mean putting half a dozen clerks out of work, though.'

Maia nodded. Working late these past few weeks, she had been seized by the horrible suspicion that the dismissal of a mere half dozen staff would not be enough. She did not yet trust Liam Kavanagh enough to share her more radical ideas with him. She still expected mockery and condescension. And besides, a part of her shrank from what she guessed she might have to do. Wage costs were high, a great yawning maw that swallowed up their shrinking profits. Neither did Maia share with Liam the fact that she had begun to take note of those who arrived late to work, and to list the names of those staff members who took a longer lunch break than the prescribed three quarters of an hour. Merchants employed over one hundred people. Maia intended to make sure than every one of those hundred people was, like herself, wholly devoted to the continuing success of Merchants' department store.

'And as for advertising . . .' Liam Kavanagh ran his fingers through his thick, curly fair hair '. . . you should go to London, Mrs Merchant. There's nowhere in Cambridge that'll give you the sort of thing you're looking for.'

Hot and flustered, Robin arrived late at the ILP meeting. As she slid into the seat between Francis and Joe, boiled sweets escaped through the hole in her pocket, and Francis whispered, 'You're all blue.'

Her fountain pen had leaked over her jacket. 'Damn,' muttered Robin. 'Damn and blast.'

She mopped up the ink with Francis's handkerchief. Joe seemed to be asleep; Francis ate one of the blue boiled sweets. Argument raged around her, but tonight she could not concentrate on it.

She had visited the Lewises, the family with the handicapped child, late that afternoon. Though Dr Mackenzie had lectured her for interfering, he had nevertheless contacted a local charity on the Lewises' behalf, and the family had somehow managed to remain in their dreadful little house. Mr Lewis had found work, and Robin had called on the family once a month or so to give sweets to the children and to help Mrs Lewis bathe poor Mary.

That afternoon she had learned that the pickle factory which employed Mr Lewis had closed, putting fifty men out of work. Chaos had returned to the terraced house in Walnut Street; the Lewises were once again four weeks in arrears with their rent.

After the meeting closed, they ambled along the pavement to the pub, still arguing.

'Collectivization,' called Guy as he stood at the bar, a ten shilling note in his hand. 'It's the only way forward. Pool the fruits of labour and distribute them amongst the workers. Stalin's got it right.'

'You should join the Communist Party, Guy.'

'I intend to. The trouble with socialism is that it's so wishy-washy.'

'Communism is inhuman – doesn't give a damn about workers' rights, that sort of thing.'

'It can't do, Joe. Once you start giving concessions to the unions, or handing out dole to the poor, then you only put off the day of the revolution.'

Robin looked up from her beer. 'What are you saying, Guy? That you should let people starve?'

'If necessary. It's a means to an end.'

Robin recalled the Lewises' house, with its orange box furniture and mouldy walls. 'And the end justifies the means, I suppose?'

'Guy has a point, Robin.' Francis, leaning back in his chair, lit himself a cigarette. 'All these little measures – Poor Relief, family allowances, whatever – are just putting sticking-plaster over a gaping wound, aren't they?'

'They don't work, anyway,' said Joe. 'The bourgeoisie have had their charitable works for centuries, yet the poor are still with us. The fat cats with their top hats and Bentleys still run the country.'

Robin was enraged. 'So we should do *nothing*?'

Joe scowled. 'Making things a little bit better just makes the workers a little bit less angry. And then nothing changes. Don't you agree, Guy?'

'Absolutely.' Guy fumbled in his pocket. 'Damn. Almost out of cash. My allowance isn't through for another week. Your round, Francis.'

Searching through his jacket, Francis drew out an

empty packet of Craven As, a battered copy of *Crome Yellow* and a handful of loose change.

'It's all right,' said Selena, rising from her seat. 'I'll go. I've done a few little woodcuts for a book of fairytales, so I'm in funds. I must introduce you to my cousin Theo, Francis. I showed him a copy of "Havoc", and he was frightfully impressed. He has simply pots of money, and is terribly interested in the arts.'

Robin's fury had not yet subsided. She glared at Joe and Francis as Selena bought more drinks. 'So you think that we should do nothing – that we should just let things get worse and worse—'

Francis frowned. 'What can one do, when all's said and done? Capitalism's obviously on the way out – there are banks collapsing all over Europe. The system's got to change.'

'And until we change the system?'

'What do you suggest, Robin? Jumble sales and fork suppers in aid of the deserving poor?' Joe's voice was sarcastic.

'Of course not! You know I detest that sort of thing.'

'Private charities, then, that'll pick and choose those they'll help—'

'*No*—'

'Or we could all do as you do, Robin,' said Joe. 'Give our packed lunch to some docker's kid whose dad's out of work. That'll change the world.'

She stared at him, momentarily speechless. He looked pale, angry, bitter.

'I just meant,' she said at last, almost breathless with fury, 'that we should all do what we could. I don't do much, but at least I *try*. At least I know that I have a responsibility. You two – you're just playing at politics, aren't you? Playing at *life*. Standing on the sidelines – not getting involved. Enjoying yourself arguing about non-Marxist socialism and Trotskyism and all the other isms, while you stand aside and watch people struggle.'

There was a small silence. Then Joe rose to his feet and walked out of the pub.

As the door banged behind him, Francis said slowly, 'I think that for the first and probably the last time in his life, Joe's regretting having passed up on the family fortune,' and Robin turned to him and asked:

'What on earth do you mean, Francis?'

Francis stubbed out his cigarette. 'The poor sod found out today that Clodie's hitched herself to some idiot with a Morris Minor and a villa in Brompton.'

She stared at him, appalled. 'Clodie has *married*?'

He nodded. 'Joe ran into her in town this morning, and he's been like a bear with a sore head ever since.'

'Oh *Francis*.' Robin's anger evaporated, leaving her overcome with guilt. 'And I said . . .' Her voice trailed away.

'Shouldn't worry. He'll drown his sorrows in drink and won't remember a thing tomorrow morning.'

'Poor Joe. We must go and find him.' Robin stood up.

Francis, eyeing her, sighed. 'I suppose it would be futile for me to point out just how many pubs there are within a five mile radius? And that Joe could be in any one of them – or all of them?' He groaned, but rose to his feet.

They found Joe eventually in a dark little inn near the river, propped up precariously at the bar, arguing with a very large stevedore. Robin steered him away from the bar, Francis bought the stevedore a pint of beer. Joining them, Francis said, 'We've decided to keep you company, Joe.'

'Shove off, Francis.' Joe, elbowing his way out of the pub, began to walk unsteadily down the street. They followed behind him.

They drifted around the docklands, calling in at every pub they passed. Moonlight gleamed on the black, oily water of the Thames, and small waves slapped rotting wooden piers. By closing time they had composed a new socialist manifesto, had drunk a large amount of beer, and had made Joe laugh. Walking back to Hackney, they passed the Lewises' house.

Robin whispered to Joe, 'You didn't mean what you said in the pub, did you?'

Pausing, he looked down at her. ''Course not.' Joe bent down and kissed her on the cheek.

Francis's eyes were bright with laughter. 'We'll prove our good socialist credentials to you, Robin. To each according to his need, etcetera. Which house d'you visit?'

She pointed to the Lewises' home. She saw Francis go to Joe and say something to him, and heard Joe mumble in return and rifle through his pockets. Then she watched, her knuckles pressed against her mouth to silence her laughter, as Francis posted all their loose change through the Lewises' door. The florins, sixpences and pennies chimed as they tumbled onto the tiles.

Robin met Maia in the Lyons Corner House in Oxford Street. 'You look wonderful, Maia. Marvellously elegant.' She hugged her, and kissed her on the cheek.

'You look peaky. I shall order you an enormous lunch.'

'Too many late nights.'

Late nights and tiring, dispiriting days. She had, Robin often thought, achieved most things Neil Mackenzie had asked of her. She had collected and analysed information, and her work had contributed to an article co-written with Dr Mackenzie, published in a scientific journal the previous month. Now, they were planning a book. In only one respect had she failed utterly. She could not stand back, an objective witness to the deprivation she saw. She always became involved.

They found a table and sat down. 'I've been consulting our advertising agency,' said Maia. 'The most lovely man is managing Merchants' account. He's called Charles Maddox, and he's tall and dark and handsome.'

There was a silence as they studied the menu. They

had never, Robin thought, regained the easy intimacy of their earlier years. Maia's complicated, troubled past had come between them, so that Robin found herself questioning whether she had ever really known Maia all, or whether she had seen only what Maia wanted her to see.

'Maia . . .' began Robin hesitantly.

She saw the small crease form between Maia's brows, and guessed that Maia too felt uneasy. She and Maia, both strong-willed and opinionated, had often quarrelled in the past – it had been Helen who had held the three of them together. But now Robin thought she detected in Maia something else – a resentment, the beginnings of a faint dislike. People – especially deeply private people like Maia – rarely felt comfortable with those who knew their worst secrets.

But Maia only looked up, smiled, and said, 'Yes, darling?'

The nippie was hovering, notebook and pencil in hand. The moment passed. She could not ask Maia about Vernon; she would never, Robin realized, ask Maia about Vernon. She had learned discretion, and besides, there were perhaps some things that it was better not to know.

'Maia . . . I need a new evening dress.'

She thought she saw a glimmer of relief in Maia's pale, unrevealing eyes. Maia ordered salad for herself and steak and kidney pie for Robin.

'A new evening dress?'

'Something glamorous. I really don't know what. Mother or Persia have always made all my dresses, and you know I never think much about that sort of thing.'

Robin saw Maia glance at her knitted jumper with a hole in the elbow, and her old black pleated skirt.

'No . . .' said Maia slowly. 'Your hair looks as though it's been hacked off with a breadknife, darling. You really must get a decent cut. I shall give you the name of a simply marvellous man.'

'I seem to be going to masses of parties and dances,

and I can't keep wearing the same dress each time. Perhaps I should buy one of those satin things.'

'Cross cut on the bias, with shoe-string straps?' Maia shook her head. 'You're not tall enough.'

Their food arrived. Maia said, 'I'll find you something, or I dare say you'll buy the first hideous old rag you see. I'll send you something beautiful, Robin.' Maia sprinkled French dressing on her salad, and changed the subject.

'Tell me about the boyfriend, darling. Francis. Has he simply masses of sex appeal?'

The Thorpe Fen Feast, in September, was for Helen an annual ordeal. All the villagers attended, churchgoers and non-churchgoers alike; the families from the most squalid cottages and from the furthest outlying farms. Huge quantities of buns and sandwiches and jellies and cakes were eaten. Helen had each year to decide whether to set up the trestle tables inside the rectory, or in the garden. Faced with grey skies and lowering clouds that morning, Helen had dithered. It was preferable to hold the Feast outside rather than in the rectory's gloomy, echoing rooms, because then the children could run around and the birds would collect the crumbs. Crossing her fingers for luck, she had instructed the gardener and his boy to set up the trestle tables on the lawn. By mid-afternoon, however, Helen knew that she had made the wrong decision. The clouds thickened, and the wind blew across the Fens, carrying with it an intermittent and depressing drizzle. The paths became slick with a layer of black mud, and the rectory lawn, trodden by many pairs of hob-nailed boots, was a soup of grass and water.

Helen and a bevy of female helpers bustled around, refilling plates with cakes and sandwiches, pouring tea into cups. It was lucky, Helen reflected, that the sandwiches were seized from the plates and crammed into mouths before the rain had time to dampen them.

One of the Dockerill children asked for more lemonade. Helen, returning with a heavy pewter jug from the kitchen, lost her footing on a slippery clump of grass. The jug flew out of her hands, soaking two small children, and Helen herself plummeted into the lap of a pig farmer. Extricating herself, she heard him say, 'Best Feast I've 'ad in years!' and saw that he was staring at her bosom. The top button of her blouse had come undone. Scarlet-faced, Helen was ready to die of mortification. Adam Hayhoe muttered, 'Shut your dirty mouth, Elijah Readman,' as she scrabbled beneath the table, looking for the jug. When she tried to do up her blouse, the button came off in her hand, and she just wanted to stay under the table and never come out. The two wet children were howling, and the tablecloth was soaked. Her father, seated at the top of the table, murmured, 'Oh dear, Helen. Dear oh dear.'

Somehow, Helen forced herself to emerge from under the table, the jug clutched in one hand, the two straining halves of her blouse held together by the other. Adam had removed the wet tablecloth; Helen, promising lemon drops and licorice, managed to shepherd the bawling children into the rectory kitchen. As she cleaned them up at the huge ceramic sink, they stopped howling, and she began to feel slightly less harassed.

'Can I help, dear?'

Mrs Lemon was standing in the doorway. Helen shook her head. 'I think they are almost dry.'

Mrs Lemon searched in her capacious handbag, and produced a safety pin. 'This should do the trick, Helen dear.'

The children, their mouths full of sweets, ran back to the garden. Helen's hands trembled as she pinned her blouse together.

'I remember,' said Mrs Lemon, 'when I was introduced to Alfred's mother – my future mother-in-law, a terrifying woman – that I noticed she was looking at my feet. When I looked down I saw that I was wearing black woollen stockings with my pink silk dress and kid button shoes. We never wore silk stockings at home, you see, the house was too cold, and I had forgotten to change. Imagine, Helen – a pink silk dress with black holey woollen stockings knitted by my old nanny!'

Helen managed a watery grin.

'I am quite hopeless with clothes, of course. Whereas you are so clever.' Mrs Lemon had put the kettle on the stove, and was spooning tea into the pot. 'A little bird told me that you did some dressmaking for Mrs Longman.'

Mrs Longman was the bishop's wife. 'A few little things,' said Helen, adding hastily, 'I thought I might become a dressmaker, but it didn't work out.'

Mrs Lemon poured boiling water into the teapot, and looked enquiringly at Helen.

'The money,' she explained. 'I am so hopeless at arithmetic.'

The memory of her father's voice saying, *Helen's just a home girl*, echoed. She was horribly near to tears.

Mrs Lemon took two cups from the dresser. 'It must be terribly dull for you here. Just the two of you, shut up in this great draughty old place. And doing private dressmaking at home isn't the answer, you know. A young girl like you needs company – something that gets her out of the house.'

Helen was speechless. Mrs Lemon patted her hand, and said without a note of apology in her voice, 'Don't mind me, dear. Alfred always tells me that I have the tact of an elephant. Still – I'm right, aren't I?'

Helen whispered, 'I can't think what else I could do. I can't type, and I haven't my school certificate. I'm not very good at anything.'

She was handed a cup of tea. 'Nonsense. You are terribly good with children, Helen. I remember that when you came to tea with us, you had Edward to sleep within a few minutes. And he was a very tiresome baby. You must train to become a nanny, or a nursery nurse. I could teach you First Aid and mothercraft. I've had half a dozen of my own, after all.'

'I couldn't impose on you—'

'It wouldn't be an imposition. I should enjoy it. What do you say, Helen?'

She stared down at her tea. It was true, she had always adored children. She pictured herself working in a nursery, pushing a pram in the park, or rocking a dear little baby to sleep . . .

Her fantasies crumbled. 'I couldn't leave Daddy.'

'You wouldn't have to,' said Mrs Lemon briskly. 'You could find a post where you weren't expected to live in – in Ely, perhaps, or in Cambridge. And I'll have a word with your father, so that he understands it's a respectable profession, and I'll help you find a post with a refined family. After all, it would be excellent training for when you are married and have children of your own.'

Mrs Lemon finished her tea and began to rinse out the cups. 'I shall expect you on Wednesday morning, Helen, at ten o'clock,' she called, as she left the kitchen.

Helen cycled to Burwell on Wednesday morning. The worry that had haunted her since the Feast – that Geoffrey would be at home – was disposed of when Mrs Lemon, in the course of welcoming her to the house and taking her hat and gloves, explained that her two eldest children, Geoffrey and Hilary, were holidaying in France with their cousins. Helen gave a quiet sigh of relief.

'Now where shall we begin?' said Mrs Lemon briskly. 'Of course – the feeds. I told Violet to leave Anthony's bottles for us. Come with me into the kitchen, dear. Put that apron over your dress, Helen, and I will show you how to measure the formula. Six scoops, dear – that's right. The most important thing is to sterilize the bottles and teats beforehand. Everything must be thoroughly boiled.'

Maia sent Robin a dress of olive-coloured raw silk, with shoes and a bag to match. Maia's note explained that the dress had a tiny little fault, so she could not sell it. Robin sent a postal order for the shoes and the bag. She saw the admiration in Francis's eyes when she first wore the dress. 'Stunning,' he said, running a finger down her silk-covered spine, and she felt almost faint with desire for him. Then he began to kiss the back of her neck, and they forgot the party they were supposed to be going to, and the dress was discarded, a little pool of dark green silk, on the floor of Francis's bedroom.

She was out every night of the week, at the clinic, or at meetings, or with Francis. She preferred the scruffy basement clubs, or the noisy nights in the pub to the smart parties. She preferred Joe and Guy and even Angus to Selena Harcourt's cousin Theo and his acolytes. Desperately short of finance for 'Havoc', Francis was courting the wealthy Theo Harcourt. Robin thought guiltily that she neglected her old friends: she hadn't taken part in one of Miss Turner's séances for months, and she had only managed a very hurried visit to Maia and Helen.

Francis travelled with her to Wales for a week to see the condition of the mining towns in the Rhondda Valley. His presence in the silent, grimy streets comforted her. Back in London, while Robin worked long into the night trying to calculate the average protein and carbohydrate content of an unemployed miner's diet, Francis wrote a furious and passionate article describing what he had seen. Theo Harcourt, quickly scanning the new edition of 'Havoc', was languidly complimentary. Francis was invited to more parties, more dinners. More friends gathered in the Hackney basement; Robin rarely slept before the early hours of the morning.

When the Conservative-dominated National Government won the general election in October, Francis, furious and disillusioned, travelled with Angus to join Vivien in Tangiers. Without Francis, London seemed cold, dull and grey. The following evening, Robin caught the Ely train from Liverpool Street. She dozed on the train and, after Hugh met her at Soham station, fell asleep again in the motor-car. Blackmere Farm rose like a mirage out of the marshy fields, but this time the tedium she generally felt on returning to her home was replaced with something like relief. Hugging her parents, she ate the enormous dinner that Daisy had cooked, went to bed, and slept until ten the next morning. When she talked about her work to her father, Robin recognized, to her surprise, the pride in his eyes. Pride she had not seen since her refusal to take up her scholarship to Girton.

Returning to London after a week, she realized that she had fallen behind with her work. Stacks of notes – some scribbled on the backs of envelopes and shopping lists – littered the small table in her bedroom. Robin shut herself in her room, emerging only to eat, and by the end of a month had converted the notes into neatly typed sheets of paper. Congratulating herself, she pulled a comb through her hair, and tried to find her lipstick. There was a knock at the door as she discovered it under the bed.

Robin opened the door. The younger Miss Turner whispered, 'Mr Gifford is here, Robin dear.'

Both the Miss Turners adored Francis. Robin's heart lurched, and she ran downstairs. Francis was waiting for her in the parlour, his skin tanned, his hair bleached by the African sun. She ran into his arms, and hugged him. The day, which until then had been merely ordinary, had become delightful.

'How was Tangiers?'

'Hot. I've had to wear three sweaters ever since I got home. Angus had prickly heat, and the food was awful.' Francis sounded restless, edgy. 'Get your glad rags on, won't you, sweetheart, and I'll take you out.'

She shook her head. 'I can't.'

'Please, darling. I've missed you.'

'I've missed you too, Francis, but I've a meeting tonight.'

'Your dreary pacifist thing? Come on, Rob – you can miss that for once. All those ancient suffragists and Christians with beards.'

His casual dismissal of the cause closest to her heart

angered her. 'I'm on the committee, Francis. I have to introduce the speaker. I really can't miss it.'

He stared at her for a moment, and then he said, 'As you wish,' and turned on his heel and left the room, and the house.

She wanted to run after him, but she managed to stop herself. She endured the rest of that day, and then the next two days, alternating between cursing herself for her pride, and reminding herself that it had been Francis who had been at fault. After three days, convinced that she had lost him, her nails were bitten to the quick and she snapped at anyone who spoke to her. She replayed the scene of his departure constantly in her mind, until her head ached. She had been unsympathetic, or he had been unreasonable, she was never sure which. Then, walking back to her lodgings in the evening, she caught sight of him sitting on the wall outside the Misses Turner's house, most of the upper part of his body hidden by a huge bunch of flowers. She ran towards him.

'I'm so sorry – I was a pig.' Francis handed her the flowers, a great pink and white mass of lilies and stephanotis. 'Tangiers was awful. So bloody hot, and that snake Denzil Farr was there the whole time. I caught some awful stomach bug and spent most of the time puking my guts up.'

When Robin looked carefully at Francis she saw that beneath the suntan, the fine lines around his eyes were white. He said, 'Forgive me?' and threw his arms round her, crushing the flowers so that their heavy scent perfumed the grimy London air. At the weekend, he drove her to Long Ferry. They spent two days alone in the old house, making love, feeding each other tinned sardines and peaches in the belvedere, curtained by frost and stars.

After that, her life returned to what it had been before he had gone away. She was out every night of the week, and most of the weekends as well. The Hackney basement was always full of people; getting up in the morning to bring in the milk, she had to step over snoring bodies in the living-room. Once, in the middle of the night, she came across a stray poet in the kitchen, searching through the cupboards for food. The elder Miss Turner began to mutter disapprovingly, and Robin was forced to invent increasingly improbable excuses to explain her absences.

In the middle of December they went to a photographic exhibition. Joe prowled round, peering at the dark, grainy prints, his gaze intense. Francis explained, 'Ages ago, in the school holidays, Joe used to drag me onto freezing cold moorlands to take photographs of *stones*.'

Joe, overhearing, said, 'Crags, Francis, they were bloody crags. You know the sort of thing, Robin. Moody prints of reeds in ponds, bleak hillsides. I imagined my stuff in a chi-chi little gallery in Hampstead.' He was grinning, but Robin could see the passion in his dark eyes.

Early one morning, she stood beside Francis on Waterloo Bridge, watching the sunrise. The mist over the Thames was turned to pink and gold by the weak rays of the winter sun. She remembered that she had not written home for weeks when she received a postcard from Hugh, demanding to know whether she was dead or alive. Scribbling a hasty and deceitful note, Robin shoved it in the post box immediately.

She realized, working one afternoon, that she was only a few streets away from the Lewises' house. It was snowing intermittently, and the gutters and the pavements were grey and sloshy with mingled mud and ice.

A few well-aimed snowballs struck her as she neared Walnut Street. She waved to Eddie and Larry, playing in the gutter, and searched in her coat pockets for sweets.

'Ma's bad.' Eddie accepted Robin's offering of a few fluffy bits of licorice. 'She was having a baby but it wasn't ready.'

Larry nodded, his eyes huge. Robin pushed open the Lewises' front door.

Mrs Lewis was curled up on the bed in the front room. Her face was skin and bone, and there were purple shadows around her eyes.

Robin knelt beside the bed. 'You should have sent for me . . .'

'I just had a miss.' The older woman's voice was weak and hopeless. 'I've been bad this time, though . . . worse than with the others. Miss Summerhayes—' Mrs Lewis struggled to sit up. Robin helped her arrange the pile of grey, lumpy pillows. 'Would you have a look at Lil? I think she's got croup. She wouldn't take her dinner.'

She made Mrs Lewis a cup of tea, and then she went upstairs to the room where the girls slept. The three-year-old, Lily, and the baby, Rose, shared a cot. The baby slept deeply, but Robin, looking down at Lily's hot red face and badly swollen neck, was worried. Lily's breathing was noisy and uneven. Very gently, Robin lifted the child out of the cot, opened her mouth, and peered into her throat.

A thick, white membrane stretched across the back of the child's throat, almost blocking the airway. Just for a moment Robin was paralysed, unable to think. Then she seized a blanket from the bed and wrapped the little girl in it, and carried her down the stairs.

'I'm taking Lily to the clinic, Mrs Lewis. Don't worry about the cost – Dr Mackenzie won't charge.'

She always afterwards remembered the half-mile journey from the Lewises' house to the clinic as something out of a nightmare. The light was fading and the snow had begun again. Her shoes slipped constantly in the slush. She half ran, half walked, goaded by the terrible sounds the child made as she clawed for breath. There were no cabs, and none of the buses were going in the right direction. A stranger cursed her when, confused by the darkness and the falling snow, she collided with him. Her arms and back ached with the weight of the child. She could see only the blond hair, peeping from the cocooning blanket, hear only the groaning struggle for breath.

When she reached the clinic, she hurled herself through the heavy front door, and ran down the corridor. She did not knock on the door of Dr Mackenzie's consulting room, but pushed it open with her shoulder. The patient on the examination couch, his foot half-bandaged, stared at her open-mouthed as Dr Mackenzie said furiously, 'Robin – for heaven's sake—'

'Neil – I think she has diphtheria. You must look at her – please—'

His expression altered. He said, 'If you'd be so kind as to step outside for a few moments, Mr Simpson,' and his patient limped outside.

'Sit down, Robin, and let me have a look at her.'

She sat down with Lily on her lap. Lily's breathing seemed louder, more troubled. The dreadful noise filled the room as, very gently, Neil Mackenzie opened the little girl's mouth and shone his small flashlight into her throat.

'Dear God,' he said softly. 'The poor wee mite.'

She stared at him mutely, willing him to tell her that the child would recover, that she was not too late. But instead he rose, and went to the telephone.

'I'll get her admitted to the fever hospital immediately.'

He was dialling the operator when it happened. The silence: a small shiver running through the child's body, the sudden absence of the awful sound of the fight for breath. Just for a moment Robin thought that the dreadful choking membrane had cleared, allowing Lily to breathe naturally. Then, looking down at the little girl's still face, she whispered, 'Neil . . . Oh, Neil.'

He was at her side already, taking Lily from her arms, and laying her on the couch. It seemed an age before he said, 'The poor bairn's gone, I'm afraid. Her heart must have given out. It happens like that sometimes.'

She stood up, walking shakily to the couch, staring down at Lily's face, rapidly paling above her grotesquely swollen neck.

'I wasn't quick enough.'

'Robin – she was beyond our help.' His voice was gentle as he drew up the blanket. 'Even if we'd got her to the hospital, it would have made no difference. You must believe me.'

She found herself in the kitchen with a mug of hot, sweet tea in her hands. Looking up suddenly at Neil Mackenzie, she said, 'I'll have to tell Mrs Lewis.'

'The mother? She's had a miscarriage, you said? I'll go round myself. You're to go home, Robin, and to burn every stitch that you're wearing, and to scrub yourself with disinfectant. And that's an order.'

She did not go home, though. She knew that she could bear neither the Misses Turner's concern, nor the four confining walls of her room. She wandered through the streets, letting the flurries of snow blow sharply against her face. When she reached the Hackney basement and the only reply to her knock was darkness and silence, she wanted to lean her head against the door-jamb and weep. But she began to walk again, down a long road of houses and pubs and shops. She remembered that other snowstorm, that other death. But Stevie's death had been invisible, something that had happened in a far-off country, and had not seemed, to the child she had then been, real. Tonight she had glimpsed the frail partition between life and death.

She reached a familiar landmark. As she opened the door of the Navigator and walked in, the noise of the pub was jangling and shocking. The barroom was crowded: men in cloth caps stared at her, calling to her, offering to buy her drinks. She could not see another woman. Pushing through the crowds of sweaty, jostling bodies, she reached the bar, and stood there patiently until Joe saw her.

'Robin . . . ?'

'I was looking for Francis.'

'He had to see someone about an article for "Havoc". Said he'd be a day or two.'

Her legs shook. If she hadn't been so hemmed in by people, she would have fallen to the floor. Hazily, she saw Joe seize a brandy bottle and a glass, and duck under the bar. Putting his arm round her he steered her to a table at the side of the room.

'Here. Drink this.'

The brandy was awful, cheap and rough, and her teeth clattered on the edge of the glass.

She heard Joe say, 'Robin – what is it? What's happened?'

Haltingly, she told him about Lily.

'My God. Poor kid.'

'She was only three, Joe! Such a pretty little thing—' She rubbed her fingers against her wet eyelids. 'I feel so *useless . . .*'

'You're not useless. Think of your work – think of all that you've done—'

She interrupted him savagely, 'I don't *do* anything, Joe. None of us *does* anything. We go to meetings and we sign petitions and we write pamphlets, but we don't *do* anything, do we?'

His gaze met hers, and she saw the truth, bitter and bleak, mirrored in his dark eyes. Then he said, 'You're almost right, Robin. Both Francis and I are useless bums, of course. We just talk. Endless talk.' Joe shook his head, fumbling in his pocket for cigarettes. 'I can't seem to find anything worth fighting for, and though Francis has great ambitions, I doubt if he'll stick at anything much for long enough.' He lit two cigarettes, and passed one to Robin. 'But you're doing something. You're going to make people sit up and take notice.'

She tried to make him understand. 'It's my fault, Joe, you see. I hadn't visited the Lewises for weeks. Too busy going to parties and things.' Her voice was harsh.

Studying her, he inhaled his cigarette. 'Then it rather depends—' he began, and then stopped.

'What, Joe?'

'It depends on whether you want Francis.'

She no longer had to ask herself. She had come to know herself within the course of the past year; her emotions had been laid bare, flayed raw for anyone to

187

see. She knew now that she had never wanted anyone as she wanted Francis.

'Ah. No contest.' The expression in Joe's eyes was unreadable. 'Then you have to run with him, Robin. He simply isn't interested in anything else.'

Chapter Seven

Her maid helped Maia into her evening dress: satin, cut on the cross, fitting fluidly around her perfect contours. Maia, smoothing the cool, snaking fabric over her hips, glanced at the mirror. The dress was cobalt blue in colour, a deeper shade of blue than her eyes. She had grown her hair, and brushed it back into a dark, sleek chignon.

'Yes,' said Maia, satisfied, and dismissed her maid.

It was almost seven o'clock. Checking her face once more in the looking-glass, Maia went downstairs to the drawing-room.

'Charles,' she said, and allowed Charles Maddox to kiss her cheek.

Charles Maddox worked for the advertising agency that had taken over Merchants' account. Maia had allowed her relationship with him to progress quickly from that of colleague to friend. If she would never be admitted to the men's networks of clubs and pubs, then she knew that she must begin to take her place again in society, because business was done and contacts were made at the dances and dinners that she, a widow, was not invited to. She needed an escort, and Charles Maddox was a handsome and admiring escort.

Through Charles she had been invited to this cock-tail party – her first since Vernon's death. Speeding along the Backs, Charles explained to Maia about his former tutor.

'Old Henderson was a bit miffed, I think, about me going into advertising. But I couldn't have stood the academic life. Cambridge can be a bit of a monastery, you know.'

He grinned at her, a glimpse of white teeth and blue eyes and dark curls clustering around a smooth, unlined forehead. She thought, yet again, what a good-looking boy he was. Charles Maddox was twenty-five, three years older than she, but years, years younger in experience.

'Has he forgiven you?' asked Maia lazily.

'My tutor?' Charles braked, parking the car outside a large, well-lit house. 'I think so. He lectures me every now and then on wasting my First, but I think he's resigned to it.'

She smiled, but she was hardly listening to him. When he opened the passenger door and walked with her up the steps to the front door, Maia felt again a thrill of apprehension.

Inside, introduced to the other guests, Maia recognized a few of the faces. Some had dined at her table when Vernon had been alive. Not the academics – but she recalled a bank manager, and one or two men that Vernon had known from his golf club. Maia, smiling demurely, saw the recognition in their eyes.

And the desire. She knew immediately, running a practised eye over the room, that she was easily the best-dressed woman there. It was not conceit that told Maia that she was also the most beautiful, but a cool, objective appraisal of her own assets. The men smiled at her, brought her drinks, made sure that Maia, in her backless, shoulderless gown, was not standing in a draught. Their wives, most of them twice Maia's age, their corseted figures thickened by childbearing, looked at her with envy, or with disapproval, or disinterest. Maia was untroubled: the men had power and influence, their wives did not.

'Maia?'

Looking up at Charles, she smiled. His gaze met hers,

and she saw the small jolt in his expression and knew that he was in love with her.

'Oh Maia . . .' he whispered.

'Oh Charles,' she said drily. And then, taking pity on him, she followed him out of the crowded drawing-room and into the garden-room. Beyond, the garden was crisp and cold and bathed in moonlight, and the shrubs and trees were a multitude of shades of grey.

She said, 'I was thinking how clever you are, Charles.'

'I was thinking how beautiful you are, Maia.'

As he faced her, his fingertips rested lightly on her hip-bones, and she had to force herself not to pull away from him. If she let him realize that his touch disgusted and frightened her, then she would lose him.

Instead, she said lightly, 'Have you a cigarette, darling? I've a bit of a head.'

Concerned, he took a cigarette from his case and lit it for her. 'Shall I get you a glass of water, Maia?'

She was horribly afraid that he wanted to kiss her.

'Another G and T would do the trick.'

When he returned with her drink, she said, 'Rather a tiresome day, darling – enough to give anyone a headache.'

'You should let up a bit.'

She smiled absently, swallowing the last of her gin, and rubbing the small crease between her eyes with her fingertips. *Let up* . . . even if she had been able to let up, she would not have wanted to. The small adjustments she had made to Merchants' huge, unwieldy hierarchy – even the stunning series of advertisements that the Maddox agency had brought out – had not staunched Merchants' decline. Extreme measures were necessary, and she had called a meeting of her triumvirate for nine o'clock the following morning.

They left soon afterwards. Maia drove Charles's flashy little MG – rather drunk, she drove fast, exorcising some of the strains and frustrations of the day. As she parked the car, Charles said hopefully, 'Saturday . . . ?', but Maia shook her head.

'I have to go away this weekend.'

Then she pleaded the lateness of the hour and the heaviness of her head and, kissing him briefly good night, breathed a huge sigh of relief as she shut the door behind her and was alone once more.

They assembled in the meeting-room: Maia, Liam Kavanagh, Mr Underwood and Mr Twentyman, and Miss Dawkins, shorthand notebook and pencil in front of her. Maia had not slept well the previous night, but had made up her face carefully, disguising any small signs of weariness.

She said, without any preamble, 'If our profits continue to fall as they have been doing, then we will be in the red within a few months. I cannot allow that. I have called you here, gentlemen, to discuss the measures that I intend to take.'

Her mouth dry, Maia poured herself a glass of water. 'First of all, I intend to extend the competitive buying policies that I have already introduced. You must look for new sources, Mr Twentyman, for as much of our stock as possible.'

He began to protest, as she had known he would. 'But we have favourable arrangements with many of our old suppliers, Mrs Merchant. Relationships that have been built up over the years . . . that exist for our mutual benefit.'

'*Merchants*' benefit?' enquired Maia, who had heard rumours of a gift of a case of Scotch, and Giles Twentyman's name recommended for the golf club. She saw the head buyer's smooth face redden.

'Mrs Merchant—'

'I expect you to reduce costs by at least fifteen per cent. More, preferably.'

He seemed to puff himself up, crimson-faced, stony-eyed. 'I have gentlemen's agreements with many of our larger suppliers – do you seriously expect me to renege on such agreements?'

'I expect you to do your utmost to keep Merchants

afloat, Mr Twentyman. All our futures – *your* future – depend on that.'

There was a silence, interrupted only by the furious scribbling of Miss Dawkins's pencil.

Maia added, 'You may call upon Mr Kavanagh or myself for assistance if you feel too *gentlemanly* to undertake hard bargaining, Mr Twentyman.'

The head buyer's face was still flushed dull red, but he said nothing. Maia's unspoken threat had been clear: that he would lose his authority, and perhaps even his job if he did not co-operate. She suspected that Mr Twentyman's sense of self-preservation was well-developed. Maia glanced at her notes.

'Very well. Now, because we have successfully cut down on our levels of stocking, I intend to sell the warehouse in Histon Road.' She looked round the table. 'I was fortunate enough to find a buyer – a gentleman who intends to build a garage there.'

Mutters of approval from Mr Underwood, a nod from Liam Kavanagh. Mr Twentyman was still sulking.

'Thirdly . . . credit. We are giving too much credit, for too long. At present, we pay our bills promptly, while our customers prevaricate over theirs. This is entirely the wrong way round. I will require you to delay all our payments until the second red reminder, Mr Underwood—'

'Mrs Merchant!' Aroused out of his usual torpor, the chief accountant looked, thought Maia, like an outraged turkey-cock. 'Mrs Merchant – that is hardly—'

'Gentlemanly, Mr Underwood?' Maia did not smile. 'I suppose not. As well as delaying our settlements, you will send out letters requiring payment of our debts after the first month is up. Except to our very best customers, of course.' Maia, looking through her portfolio, drew out a list. 'Liam and I shall deal with these.' She glanced at the chief accountant. 'Is there a problem, Mr Underwood? No? Good.'

Maia swallowed another mouthful of water. Then she said, 'I also intend to cut wages across the board by ten per cent. Your wages, gentlemen . . . and yours, I am afraid, Miss Dawkins. The wages of the buyers, managers, clerks and assistants. Cleaners and drivers and storemen as well. Those unhappy with their reduction in earnings may exercise their privilege to look for work elsewhere.' She took advantage of the shocked silence that followed to add, 'At the same time as the cuts are made, I will institute a commission system for junior members of staff as well as a bonus scheme for the managers and buyers and for yourselves, gentlemen. So that if . . . *when* we emerge from this difficult time, you will be suitably rewarded for your hard work.'

The silence ended.

'Look for work elsewhere? There is no work elsewhere—'

'There'll be a lot of resentment, Mrs Merchant.'

'A difficult scheme to administrate—'

'I'm sure you'll find a way, Mr Underwood.' Maia cut through the clamour, and took a deep breath. She made sure her voice remained steady.

'And we must lose some staff, I'm afraid. About thirty people.'

Mr Twentyman's mouth dropped open. In Mr Underwood's greyish-brown eyes she saw a flicker of fear. Liam Kavanagh said, 'Sack them, you mean?'

She inclined her head. 'I'm afraid so. We are overstaffed. And there are people who are not pulling their weight. We cannot afford that.'

She glared at him, defying him to argue with her as she passed him the list of names. But Liam's expression altered as he read, and his washed-out blue eyes narrowed.

'I've been thinking along the same lines for some time, Mrs Merchant. With one or two exceptions.'

She would not allow for exceptions. She suspected that once she permitted them, the men, to chip away at her design, then her independence too would be worn away, and all that she had worked for would slide from her control. She said briskly, 'You agree that the slump is deepening. You agree that people have less money to spend. That matters are going to get worse rather than better. I intend that we shall survive.'

Liam Kavanagh's strong square fingers indicated her memo.

'That *some* of us shall survive, Mrs Merchant.'

'Most of us, Liam. I've chosen carefully. No-one who works hard and conscientiously need fear for their job. Some of those girls are engaged and are more concerned with planning their weddings than making sure that our customers have the best possible service. They would leave us soon anyway. We shall simply not replace them. And some of the older men are on the verge of retirement.'

Liam said, as she had known he would, 'But Mr Pamphilon . . . He has worked for Merchants for years.'

Edmund Pamphilon was the short, round, genial manager of the gentlemen's tailoring department. Some of the younger male assistants imitated his bouncing gait, his slight stutter, his beaming smile. Maia, unbeguiled by his old-worldly courtesy, had noticed that he was careless with his timekeeping, and frequently late in handing in reports of the day's takings.

'I cannot afford to employ a manager who arrives late for work, and who seems to take an extra half day whenever it suits him.'

Liam Kavanagh looked across the table at Maia. 'There are family problems, I believe. Pamphilon's a proud man, so he doesn't discuss them, but—'

She interrupted him sharply, afraid, just then, that she would breach even the fragile alliance she had achieved with Liam.

'Mr Pamphilon's personal affairs are no business of mine, Liam,' she said. Her voice was cold.

'The man's over fifty,' said Liam bluntly. 'He won't find another job. Not now.'

She felt no sympathy for inefficiency, or for the sort of messy, blundering life that she suspected that Edmund Pamphilon led.

'Then we shall have to hope that Mr Pamphilon has

made sensible provision for his retirement, won't we?' Maia glanced at her watch. 'I think that's all for now, gentlemen. Miss Dawkins will issue you with an account of the minutes of the meeting as soon as possible. And you will bear in mind, of course, that what was said in this meeting must be kept absolutely confidential.'

She watched them leave the room. Gathering up her notes, Maia went to her office. There, opening her filing cabinet, she watched her fingers shake as they curled round the stopper of the whisky bottle.

A voice said, 'Awful early in the morning for that, isn't it, Mrs Merchant?' and she spun round. Liam Kavanagh had come into the room.

'I suppose it is.'

'Mind you, I was thinking just the same thing.'

She smiled, cold and shaking with relief, and held out the tumbler to him. 'I've only the one glass. You don't mind sharing, do you, Liam?'

After her first week in her new job was over, Helen realized that she was happy. To begin with, she had dreaded that she would not come up to scratch. But she had soon realized that her employers, the Sewells, were just as nice as Mrs Lemon had told her they were. Mr Sewell lectured at the university; his wife, Letty, was a vague, kind, generous creature. There were only two children: Augusta, a little moppet of three, and Thomas, a plump baby of six months. The nursery was large, well-equipped and hopelessly untidy. Mrs Sewell, showing Helen round, apologized constantly for the untidiness.

'I tried to manage without a nanny, dear – plenty of people do nowadays. I had a girl, but she married six weeks ago – a very pleasant girl, and her young man too, and I'm glad to say that they are *so* happy . . . Gussie adored her . . . Such a pretty room, don't you think, and it overlooks the garden, of course. You must use the garden whenever you want, Helen dear . . . so nice, don't you think, after lunch . . .'

Mrs Sewell fluttered after Helen for the first day or

two, uttering a stream of inconsequences. Then her other interests – her husband, her numerous friends and acquaintances – reclaimed her, and Helen was left alone to get to know her two charges.

Gussie, at three, was fair-haired, serious and organized. Thomas had two teeth in the middle of his upper jaw, and a smile that made Helen fall in love with him the minute she set eyes on him. Gussie was adorable, but there was something about Thomas that utterly melted Helen's heart. By the end of the week, Helen and Gussie had tidied the nursery, arranging the books in one corner, the toys in another, and clearing a little area where they could have their elevenses and their tea. Helen worked from Monday to Friday, returning home each evening.

By the time she had been with the Sewells for six weeks, she found it oddly difficult to remember a life without them. The last few years had telescoped, so that she could recall, scattered over the months, only a few events. Now her days seemed crammed with incident. At first, the Sewells' family life shocked her: Mr Sewell, clad only in his pyjamas and dressing-gown, roaring for hot water to shave with in the mornings; Mrs Sewell, remonstrating mildly with her husband for having forgotten that they were engaged to dine with Mrs Sewell's mother. These things Helen found confusing and faintly disturbing. The careless chaos of the place – the children's toys scattered on the stairs, the jumble of newspapers and journals and magazines in the drawing-room – worried her, so that she spent much of her first fortnight feeling somehow responsible for the untidiness of the Sewell household. The cheerful informality of a house where the cook-general told Mr Sewell off for using the best china in the garden, and where Mrs Sewell and Helen frequently shared a cup of tea in the kitchen, at first made her tense, expecting retribution. Then, quite suddenly, she realized that this was how the Sewells liked to live. Since then, returning to the rectory each evening, she found the old house frighteningly silent, and saw how isolated Thorpe Fen was, how lonely her last few years had been.

Buying new boots for Gussie in Merchants one day, Helen caught sight of Maia in the distance, and waved madly. Maia, elegant in black and cream, crossed the store to greet her. Helen introduced Gussie; Maia looked at the child, gave a small, stiff smile, and then stood, her entire body expressing fidgety, angry boredom, while Helen launched into a long anecdote about the little girl. Halfway through, Helen stopped, daunted by those cold, pale blue eyes, and had to quell her hurt by reminding herself that Maia did not like children. Shortly afterwards, Maia took her leave.

Once, when Mrs Sewell had taken the children for tea with a friend, Helen met Hugh Summerhayes in the Botanic Gardens. It was Founder's Day at the school where Hugh taught, and he had the afternoon off. The April weather alternated between sunshine and cloud as they walked through the water garden. When it began to rain, Hugh put up his umbrella and took Helen's hand in his as they ran towards the glasshouses.

'*Soaked*,' said Hugh, as he flung open the door for Helen to go inside.

'I must look a sight.' Helen had not tied back her long hair that day; it fronded, wet and heavy like seaweed, around her face.

'Not at all. You look as beautiful as always, Helen.'

She had to turn away then, pretending to look at the pelargoniums so that he would not see her blush. She thought he might be going to kiss her. But then a trio of small boys ran through the glasshouse, their mother calling to them distractedly, and the moment was gone.

'How are the brats?' enquired Hugh, offering her his arm.

'Not at all brattish. Thomas is so clever, Hugh – he can sit up all by himself.'

The chill air of the alpine house, with its pots of delicate, miniature plants, was followed by the heavy dampness of the tropical house. Succulents hung from the glass ceilings, their leaves fleshy and pendulous, their flowers brightly coloured, rank-smelling. A palm tree cast its shadow over them. Helen, her hand curled around Hugh's elbow, imagined herself in India, or Africa. Hugh could teach at a mission, and she . . .

His voice broke through her fantasies. 'Is it working out all right, old thing? Your father must miss you awfully.'

With a jolt she returned to England, and Cambridge, and the fleeting exotic pretence of the Botanic Gardens. Helen smiled up at Hugh. 'Daddy is being quite splendid. There are the servants, of course, to look after him, and I catch up on the parish work on my half day.'

Hugh gave her a quick hug. Helen thought it impossible that any girl could be happier. Hugh began to talk to her about Maia: Helen, smiling up at him, chattered back.

She often took the children to the Botanic Gardens for their afternoon walk. Pushing Thomas's pram along the wide gravelled paths, Helen looked at the lawns and recalled Hugh holding her hand as they had run through the rain. Frequently she imagined different turnings to their conversation: she could almost hear his pleasant, familiar voice saying to her, *I say, Helen, old thing – I am most awfully fond of you, you know*. Hugh's lips pressed against hers, his strong, warm arms encircled her, holding her to him. Once she dreamt about Hugh, and woke hot and happy but suffused with guilt.

It was summer now, a dry, bright summer, and it had not rained for weeks. Helen parked the pram by the pond and sat down on the grass with Thomas on her lap. Unable to sit still for long, he wriggled into a standing position, his hands in hers, smiling widely. He had three teeth now: Helen thought she could see the beginnings of a fourth. He smelt deliciously of talcum powder and baby soap. Helen held him to her, loving the feel of his warm, velvety skin against hers. Gussie threw more bread to the ducks, Helen watching her carefully to make sure she did not go too near the water's edge. 'Is it like the sea?' the little girl asked Helen. 'The sea is much, much bigger,' Helen answered, and smiled. She, who had never seen the sea, was to go on holiday with the Sewells in two weeks' time, to Hunstanton, on the east coast. Helen suspected that she was even more excited than Gussie. A few days ago, she had plucked up courage to ask her father's permission to accompany the Sewell family on holiday. It's just for one week, Daddy, she had said. I'll write every day. He had not forbidden her to go, and a glorious anticipation was welling up in her, as she imagined warm seas and blue skies and golden sand. She had begun to make herself a bathing costume.

It was four o'clock. Helen settled Thomas back into his pram, and began to walk back to the house. As soon as she turned the corner of the street, she knew that something was wrong. Mrs Sewell was standing at the gatepost, her faded, pretty face creased with anxiety. Helen, pushing the heavy pram faster along the pavement, felt hot.

Mrs Sewell ran out to meet her. 'Oh, Helen – you must go home immediately . . . I'm afraid we have had a telephone call . . . Your father . . .'

Helen's hands clenched around the pram-handle, and she stared at Mrs Sewell.

'Is Daddy ill?' Her voice wasn't much more than a whisper.

'An accident, they said. A nurse telephoned . . . she wouldn't tell me any more . . . Mr Ferguson is in a nursing home in Ely, dear. I would ask Ronald to drive you to the hospital, but he has a lecture and I really am so hopeless with the motor-car . . . such temperamental things, you see, Helen, and one has to do different things with one's hands and one's feet. But there is a train in half an hour . . .'

She had plenty of time, on the train journey from Cambridge to Ely, to imagine what had happened. Her father had scalded himself trying to make a cup of tea, or Betty had given him fish, which always made him unwell. Or his summer cold had turned to pneumonia, or Percy had darted out in front of him, and he had fallen downstairs.

At the nursing home, anxiety made her stomach ache and her heart pound as she walked through the echoing, polished corridors. A starched, severe-looking sister barked information over her shoulder as Helen scuttled after her to her father's room.

'Your father had a little fall, I'm afraid, Miss Ferguson. He has broken his leg. He is rather chilled, and suffering from shock.'

Her heart squeezed and wrenched in her breast when she saw the cage over her father's leg. His skin had a greyish tinge, and he lay back, cushioned by pillows. She had never before seen him so defenceless, so . . . old. A single tear spilled over her lid and ran down her cheek.

'*Daddy* . . .' Helen whispered, and took his hand.

'Tripped over the garden broom . . . someone had left it on the path . . .' croaked Julius Ferguson. His full lips curved into a rueful smile. 'Such a silly old fool.'

She stared at him, horrified. Late the previous evening, she had tidied the garden. She could not remember, no matter how hard she tried, whether she had put the broom away.

'Old Shelton's as deaf as a post,' explained the Reverend Ferguson. Shelton was the gardener. 'And the boy wasn't with him today. Lay there for an hour. The maids couldn't hear from the house, I suppose. Almost shouted myself hoarse. Luckily, a fellow came round to sharpen the knives, and he found me.'

The nurse fussed around, straightening blankets. 'We shall have to keep Mr Ferguson here for a few weeks, Miss Ferguson, but there is no reason why he should not make a complete recovery.'

'Oh no,' said Julius Ferguson. 'I can't bear hospitals. Ever since my poor dear wife . . .' His eyes met Helen's. 'I shall go home. Helen can look after me, can't you, Chickie?'

*　　　*　　　*

Helen spent the night in the rectory alone, unable to sleep, picturing her father lying on the garden path for hours, cold and in pain. At five o'clock in the morning, she got up and began to clean the house. She saw the results of her months of absence: the dust that lined every shelf, the little balls of fluff gathering in the corners of the stairs, and the cobwebs strung across the high ceilings.

When she had finished cleaning, she wrote her letter to Mrs Sewell. She started to cry when she realized that she had not said goodbye properly to Gussie and Thomas, and she crossed her arms over her breast, rocking a little, longing to hold the baby again. She felt a surge of resentment against her father, and then, recalling him pale and helpless in his hospital bed, was overwhelmed with guilt. Suddenly, she had to get out of the house: the bare, gloomy rooms, the cold corridors, even the ticking of the clocks filled her with a nameless fear. Splashing cold water from the sink onto her face, Helen took her letter and walked out to the post box.

The wind had got up, whipping the dry, fine black soil from the fields and Fens. By the time she reached the letter box at the end of the drove, fragments of dust stung her eyes and dirtied her hair. Shading her eyes, she could see dust devils racing along the runnels of the ploughed fields, crushing the new stalks of wheat. A Fen blow could mean disaster for farmers and smallholders; Helen, staring up at the blackening sky, felt the great weight of her fear intensify. The land seemed to be closing in around her, cutting her off from the rest of the world. The wind blew more violently, whisking her skirt into the air, pelting her legs with a thousand tiny sharp grains of earth. Dust clouds billowed into the sky, obliterating the dawning sun. The sky was dark and ominous, all greenness rubbed away by the wind and the dust. *He swalloweth the ground with fierceness and rage*, thought Helen, as she stood there alone, watching the unnatural night take hold of the Fens.

*   *   *

Because so many small firms were going out of business, there was little money coming in from the press. Joe looked for other work, enquiring in garages, in builders' yards, and at the docks, still irked by the lack of focus in his life. But a hundred young men like him were chasing work, and many of the builders' yards were closed, and the same families tended to work in the docks for generation after generation. At nights, he worked at the pub, knowing that he was lucky to have work at all. During the days he became increasingly involved with the activities of the National Unemployed Workers' Movement – supporting the NUWM's marches and taking part in their demonstrations outside labour exchanges. As the NUWM was Communist-backed, the Labour Party had no official links with the organization, but many Labour Party members helped covertly, sympathizing with the plight of the unemployed, providing food and bedding for the hunger-marchers, and allowing their premises to be used for meetings.

In June, Vivien returned to England, and Francis planned a party to celebrate her homecoming. A fancy-dress party, Francis explained, and Joe, who had worked endless dull evenings pulling pints for endless dull people, looked forward to getting very drunk for one long, glorious night. Francis borrowed a motor-car from one of his rich new friends, and they drove down to Long Ferry one Saturday morning. Selena and Guy were travelling to Suffolk by train. Robin sat in the front passenger seat next to Francis, and Joe, as usual, fell asleep in the back.

He woke up as they swung through the gates of Long Ferry Hall. The car skidded to a halt in front of the house, throwing up a cloud of dust. The air smelt of sea-salt; Joe rubbed his eyes.

Francis climbed out of the car and stared at the house, Robin's hand hooked around his arm. 'Heavens – look at the *weeds*,' he said. Joe stared at the ragwort and dock that had pushed through the flagged courtyard. Ferns sprouted in the gutters, and the rose that tangled around the great front door had become thorny and flowerless. The sun glittered on the ancient lacework of crenellations and gargoyles that decorated the roof, and the dusty mullioned windows caught the light and reflected it dully. Long Ferry Hall was like an ageing beauty, still proud and elegant in the years of her neglect.

The fancy-dress party was to have a theme of Gothic Romance, Francis explained. Long Ferry Hall was to be shrouded in cobwebs and mystery – not difficult, thought Joe, glancing round the Hall. The atmosphere was chill and damp, and some small creature – a mouse, Joe hoped – scuttled back into the kitchen as Francis opened the heavy curtains.

They raided coffers and chests, wardrobes and clothes presses. Selena surveyed the house with her artist's eye and made suggestions and gave orders, and Francis and Joe teetered on step-ladders and banisters, hanging tapestries and draping furniture with black muslin that Selena had brought with her from London. Robin cut cobwebs out of tissue paper, and Guy, mournfully quoting Byron and Shelley, hacked thick sandwiches from the loaves of bread in the kitchen.

At five o'clock, Angus's Rolls drew up in the courtyard. Angus unloaded wine while Vivien, shrieking with delight, hugged them all in turn. 'I've booked caterers,' Angus said. 'Should be here any moment.'

The caterers arrived at seven, having become lost in the wilds of Suffolk. Francis searched through the cupboards again, flinging at Joe, Robin, Selena and Guy mouldering, moth-eaten garments of black silk and crimson velvet. Robin, changing into a long black clinging gown, had to take up the hem with safety pins. The gown had a half-cloak of a gauzy greyish material. She looked like a bat, she decided, a small, gloomy black bat. Powdering her face so that it was suitably pale and interesting, outlining her lips with the darkest red she had been able to find, she looked forward to spending an entire evening with Francis. Francis's increasingly urgent struggle to find a financial backer for 'Havoc' had taken up much of the last few weeks. And life seemed recently to have become a bit tangled – a constantly turning wheel of work, her voluntary activities and social life. It seemed to Robin sometimes that she was performing a complicated circus act, and that unless she concentrated very hard all the fragile glass balls would fall tumbling to the ground.

The door opened, and Francis came into the room. He laid the palms of his hands on her shoulders, and she looked at his reflection in the mirror of the dressing-table. His hair, in the dim light of the small-windowed room, was silvery fair, and his face was pale and shadowed. Tilting her head, she rested her cheek against the back of his hand and closed her eyes, breathing in the scent of his skin. His lips touched the crown of her head, and his hand caressed her breasts. She was aware of his other hand flicking open the hooks and eyes she had only just done up.

'The party—'

'The party can wait, don't you think?' Francis kicked the door shut. They made love in the four-poster bed, hungry and urgent, unable to wait long enough to undress properly. Motor-cars drew up in the courtyard outside, and guests ran through the passageways, calling to each other. But for Robin there was only the bed, and Francis, and a desire that seemed mutually insatiable.

Dinner was a disorganized buffet: sixty guests milling round the great hall, maids bearing trays of drying canapés and flabby vol-au-vents. Francis was talking to Vivien and Angus about 'Havoc'. Vivien smiled gratefully as Angus filled her wine-glass.

'*Such* hard work, darling. I am so hopeless at spelling and punctuation and things like that.'

Angus patted Vivien's hand. 'You can't have brains as well as beauty, Vivi darling.'

'I've always had to live on my wits.'

Francis's eyebrows rose slightly. 'I'm afraid the

magazine might fold, though. I am hideously short of funds.' He sounded gloomy.

'So how,' Angus asked, wiping his plate clean with a bread roll, 'will you keep the wolf from the door, old boy, if you don't mind me asking?'

'Guy has written a play. It has the most marvellous role in it. We're looking for someone to stage it. It could raise me some cash.'

'You must speak to Freddy.' Vivien touched Francis's hand. 'He does something with theatres. He's a dreadful old sourpuss, but he has simply *pots* of money. Denzil introduced me to him.'

Covertly, Robin glanced around the hall. She could not see Denzil Farr.

'Left him in Tangiers, did you, mother?' There was a touch of malice in Francis's voice.

'The poor darling had business to attend to.'

'Pretty boys and the odd ounce of hashish.'

'*No*, darling. Denzil is a sweetie. I do wish you two would try and get on better.'

Vivien's voice was only mildly petulant. She was dressed tonight with no concessions whatsoever to Francis's theme of the Gothic, in a fashionably clinging cream silk dress which enhanced her fair skin and hair. Diamonds sparkled at her ears and at her throat. Compared to Vivien, Robin felt short and dowdy.

After dinner, they danced. Candles gleamed in the wall-sconces; one of Robin's paper cobwebs caught fire, and had to be doused with champagne. Wine flowed like summer rain. It occurred to Robin when, late in the evening, she tripped over the long, trailing hem of her black dress, that she was more than a little drunk. Stumbling, she found herself in Joe's arms.

'You look . . .' he said, trying to focus on her '. . . you look *vampirish*.'

'You look very drunk, Joe.'

'That's because I am very drunk.' His dark, hollow eyes glittered. 'Bloody ridiculous outfits, don't you think?'

Robin smiled. 'Black suits you, Joe. It goes with your lean and hungry look.'

Yet as they circled the room, she did not look at Joe, but searched round the ballroom, examining each couple and every group of chattering people huddled around the perimeter.

'He's in the drawing-room,' said Joe, watching her.

He had stopped dancing. She looked up at him. His hands still rested on her waist. She said, 'Francis?'

'Of course.'

In his eyes there was a mixture of pity and mockery. He said, 'You were looking for Francis, weren't you?'

She nodded, mutely. Months ago, Joe had said to her, *Then you have to run with him, Robin.* And, my God, she had run until her breath was tight in her chest.

Joe lit himself a cigarette. 'Don't worry. He's seducing some bastard with an over-full wallet. Go and see for yourself.'

Vivien asked Joe to dance, and at the end of the foxtrot she raised herself on her tiptoes, and kissed him. Her lips lingered against his mouth.

'I simply must have some fresh air, Joe.'

Her small, slim hand gripped his, so he followed her out of the ballroom, and through the tangle of small rooms at the back of the house. In what he concluded vaguely must once have been a gun room, and was now full of galoshes and old mackintoshes and broken umbrellas, she paused, turning to him, and began very purposefully to unbutton his shirt.

'You look so utterly divine I could *eat* you, Joe. So gaunt and beautifully Byronic. I have always preferred dark men. Francis's father was an exception, of course.'

She punctuated her sentences with kisses. He kissed her back: he was far too drunk to have made, even if he had wanted to, any protestations about the nature of their relationship, the unsuitability of this coupling. He pressed her against the rickety old chest of drawers, and she moaned with pleasure when he caressed her breasts, her stomach and buttocks. The chest of drawers rattled, and an old blunderbuss, balanced precariously on top of it, clattered to the floor. Vivien's eyes were gleaming, and her lips parted. He could hear from the ballroom distant sounds of music and laughter. Her small fingers expertly undid the fastenings of his clothes; Joe wrestled futilely with her close-fitting dress, her complicated undergarments.

'Let me, darling,' she whispered, and as he sank into her, his overriding thought was an utter relief that he had not, after all, drunk too much.

'— a simply stunning production, Freddy,' Francis was saying. 'The lighting – the staging – everything. So original.'

Robin had paused in the drawing-room doorway. Francis was walking the bounds of the room with a middle-aged, lanky, tow-haired man. The man – Freddy – was dressed in the same flowing, nineteenth-century clothing that Francis wore. Yet he looked ridiculous, not romantic.

'That was my second production,' said Freddy. 'I financed a little revue in the mid-Twenties – you wouldn't remember that.'

They had paused beside one of the pictures on the wall. 'My grandfather,' said Francis, gesturing to the portrait.

Freddy looked up. 'You have a bit of the look of him . . . it's the eyes, I think . . .'

'He was a hellraiser.' Francis grinned boyishly. 'All sorts of sordid habits.' Briefly, he laid his hand on the other man's arm.

She turned away then, but his voice followed her.

'You simply must read Guy's play, Freddy. I know that you'd love it. It has the most marvellous leading role . . . I haven't much acting experience, of course – only school and the odd am. dram. thing since, but I'm sure I could handle it . . .'

*   *   *

Vivien sat at the huge scrubbed kitchen table, a mug of cocoa in front of her, an old duffle coat around her shoulders. When she looked up at Francis, he noticed that her make-up, usually perfect, was slightly blurred, her blond hair a little untidy, and he noticed also, perhaps for the first time, that she was not young any more. He felt a wave of pity for her.

'You look tired, Vivi.' He planted a kiss on the crown of her head.

'It's almost two o'clock.' Vivien yawned. 'But it is the most marvellous party, Francis. Thank you so much.'

He sat down next to her. He said, 'I think your friend will help me out with the play.'

'Oh, *good*.' She beamed at him. 'I knew darling Freddy would come up trumps.'

'Have you seen Joe and Robin?'

She shook her head. 'I thought Robin was with you, darling. And I bumped into Joe in the gun room a while ago, but I don't know where he is now.' She shivered, and pulled the duffle coat closely around her. 'This place really is becoming quite impossible. Cold even in *June*, and it took me half an hour to make a cup of cocoa on that wretched stove. I shall have to do something.'

Francis lit cigarettes for them both. 'Will you sell?'

'Who would buy?' Vivien raised her fragile shoulders in a gesture of resignation as she inhaled her cigarette. 'This dreadful Depression, darling . . . My estate agent told me that you can't give away places like this. Besides – I'm rather fond of the old house. It gives me somewhere to come back to. It just needs a bit of cash spent on it.'

'If this play comes off – and I think it will – then it'll lead to other things. I'll be able to send you something, I'm sure. That'll help, won't it?'

'Sweet of you, Francis.' She patted his hand. 'Only I shall have to find some funds awfully soon. There is a dreary problem with the drains.'

Vivien only ever had one way of raising money.

Francis said uneasily, 'You won't marry again, will you, Vivien?'

'I might. I could hardly get a *job*, could I, darling?'

Stubbing his cigarette out in a saucer, Francis moved restlessly around the room. 'Not Denzil Farr, for heaven's sake, mother.'

He thought, suddenly depressed, that the patterns of his childhood merely continued. Vivien had appeared at school at random intervals, entrancing and beautiful, accompanied always by one man or the other, lading him with presents and kisses. His fleeting certainty of her love and attention had been invariably followed by a long, fallow period in which she would neither write nor visit. Sometimes he thought that only Joe had got it right, by detaching himself permanently from his family.

He said carefully, knowing that if he showed his anger she would only evade him, 'I can't stand the chap, that's all. He's not good enough for you. Marry someone else – marry Angus, if you must – marry anyone but Denzil Farr.' He bent and kissed the back of her neck. 'Promise me,' he whispered.

'I promise,' said Vivien, looking up at him. Francis could see the sincerity in her blue eyes.

Later that night, the party spilled out onto the courtyard. The great stone wings of Long Ferry Hall surrounded them. 'Like a theatre,' whispered Francis and then, running to the wall, began to shin up a rickety drainpipe. Though they had taken outside candles and oil lamps, his face and body were lost in shadows, and only his pale hair was flagged by the moonlight. Reaching the roof, he began to tread along the crumbling crenellations, a champagne bottle in one hand, his other arm flung out for balance. When he reached the topmost corner of the wing, and was lit only by a backdrop of the stars and the sky, he began to speak. His voice was clear in the echoing silence of the courtyard.

'"O what a rogue and peasant slave am I . . ."'

He recited the entire soliloquy perched on the

battlements, his clothes, blurred by the night, passing quite acceptably for Hamlet's suit of solemn black. At the end of it he bowed precariously, and Vivien applauded, and others cheered and clapped. But Robin, her knuckles pressed against her mouth, thought that he looked so fragile, so lost, so easily toppled.

Afterwards, they danced on the rooftop, a great snaking line threading in and out of the belvederes and the chimneys. The dance dissolved, and someone suggested hide-and-seek, and they fanned through the house, haunting the priest hole, the chests and cupboards and alcoves like drunken ghosts. Selena twisted her ankle tumbling down the winding stone stairs, and Angus collapsed in the pantry, snoring, scattered with spilt flour and currants. Francis, with a demonic light in his eye, orchestrated everything.

Towards dawn, Robin left the house to sit on a stone bench in the courtyard. She had lost her grey cloak, and the early morning air was cool and soothing on her bare arms. Her head cleared, watching the slow coming of the day. A crumbling griffin, a waterspout protruding from its grinning mouth, jutted from the wall above her. 'It's all very well for *you*,' said Robin, out loud, glaring at it.

'First sign of madness,' whispered Francis, sliding onto the bench to sit beside her.

She had not heard his approach. She had lost track of both Francis and Joe hours ago. She acknowledged, sitting in the darkness, that the times she spent with Francis were always like this: she invariably had to share him.

'I've missed you,' said Francis.

She saw that his defences were down, and that she could glimpse the unhappiness that occasionally showed through the attractive exterior.

'I looked through every room in the house for you, Robin. Took me *hours*.'

'I wanted some fresh air. There were too many people.'

He said bleakly, 'There always are, aren't there? Too

many people – too much noise – too much talk. You can't think sometimes, can you?'

Dumbly, she shook her head.

'You will put up with me, Robin, won't you?'

She could hear the fear in his voice.

'I know I've been busy, Robin. I know I drag you along to things you'd rather not go to. But you will put up with me, won't you?'

Moving closer to him, she laid her head against his chest, and he put his arm around her. His kisses now were different from the passionate love-making of the earlier evening. Gentle and undemanding, tokens of friendship rather than desire.

She whispered, 'Of course I will, Francis. You know that I will.'

Maia had been away for the weekend, leaving Cambridge on Friday afternoon, returning late on Saturday. She had fallen into the habit of going away for the first weekend of every month. No-one – not Liam Kavanagh, nor her housekeeper, nor Robin or Helen – knew where she went. The long drive had exhausted her, at least she told herself that was why she was tired and upset. Sitting alone in her drawing-room, a gin and it cradled between her hands, she tried not to think about Friday. Yet the memory would keep intruding: Edmund Pamphilon's last day at Merchants. He had insisted on speaking to her alone. All he had said was, *Won't you reconsider, Mrs Merchant?*, but she had understood the expression in his eyes. The vague joviality that had always irritated her had gone, replaced by desperation and fear. She had uttered conventional phrases of sympathy and regret, and he had nodded his head in a vestige of an old-fashioned bow, and left Merchants for the last time. She could not understand why such a trivial incident haunted her. She told herself that it was all right, that the worst was over, that she had done what she had to do. Yet the unease remained, forcing her to question her certainties. She knew that she drank because otherwise she would look at herself, and perhaps not much like what she saw.

Francis, spurred by his own and Vivien's need for money, met Theo Harcourt at his club in Mayfair. Theo ordered whiskies as Francis sank into one of the deep leather armchairs.

Francis swallowed a large mouthful of Scotch. Then he said, 'I wondered if you'd had the chance to think any more about "Havoc", Theo. Whether you feel like putting any cash into it.'

Theo looked gently enquiring, but said nothing.

Francis felt himself floundering. 'The thing is . . . I'm not sure how much longer I'll be able to keep going if I can't find a backer.'

Theo Harcourt always made Francis think of a snake. A python, or a cobra, arching ready to spit. Theo's eyes were hooded, a gleaming grey-brown. Francis, forcing himself to meet them, always expected to see golden pupils, vertical, lizard-like.

Meeting those eyes, he made himself smile. He could feel his charm, which he had always known to be his greatest asset, deserting him under that cold gaze.

Theo spoke at last. 'The thing is, dear boy – there are so many little magazines. I really cannot summon the enthusiasm to back yet another.'

Francis felt a stab of disappointment and anger. Disappointment that 'Havoc', which he had nursed from a baby, was about to perish for lack of funds, and anger that Theo, who had made encouraging noises for simply *years*, should fail him now. Just then, Francis hated Theo Harcourt. He hated his power, his affluence, his cold crushing of his own hopes. He rose to his feet.

'I'll go, then. So sorry to have troubled you, Theo.'

Theo, moving quickly, caught Francis's sleeve as he reached the door. He said softly, 'You really must learn to control your temper, Francis.'

He stood quite still for a moment, unsure whether to listen to Theo, or whether to hit him.

Theo said, 'I don't want to back "Havoc". I would like to *buy* it, though.'

Francis, overcome by a mixture of emotions, stared at him.

'It's a crude little thing as it is, but I'm sure that, with money, something could be made of it. I can find the facilities for colour plates – reproduction of photographs – that sort of thing. It would look a little less amateurish.' Theo glanced at Francis. 'I'd give you a fair price, dear boy.'

Francis, quelling his anger at Theo's criticism, managed to speak. 'And I'd keep editorial control?'

'I'm sure that all such details could be worked out to our mutual satisfaction. Let us complete the financial transactions first. Then all the technicalities can be settled between us, as gentlemen.'

Three days later, Francis received in the post a cheque. Signing it on the back, he stuffed it in an envelope, and scribbled a note to Vivien. *Thought this might help with the drains, etcetera. Now you won't have to marry Dreadful Denzil. Lots of love, Francis.*

It was Hugh's birthday at the end of June, so Robin went home for the weekend. On Sunday, Maia drove over from Cambridge. The sky was a deep forget-me-not blue, the warm air heavy and hazy. Dragonflies – blue and green and gold – darted around the reeds. Hugh took the boat from the shed, and rowed them along the river, following the gentle meanders until both the winter house and Blackmere Farm were out of sight. Leaning back in the boat, trailing her hand in the peaty water, Robin began to feel slightly less prickly, slightly less edgy.

Maia said, 'Did you ask Helen, Hugh?'

He nodded. 'She couldn't come.'

'Why not? Even Helen,' said Robin lazily, 'doesn't go to church in the afternoon. And she doesn't go to work on Sundays.'

'She doesn't go to work at all now.' Maia adjusted the

brim of her hat so that the sun did not catch her face. 'Didn't she write to you, Robin?'

She vaguely remembered skimming through one of Helen's more garbled letters.

'Daddy had a little fall,' explained Maia. 'Broke his leg. So Helen's safely back at home again.'

Maia's eyes were a light, pure blue, the same as the sky. Her voice, though, was coolly sarcastic.

Hugh murmured mildly, 'When the Reverend Ferguson's better . . .'

'Oh – I don't think so, do you, Hugh? I can't see Helen escaping again.'

Robin stared at Maia. Maia added, 'If he hadn't managed to trip over the hoe or whatever, then he'd have sat in the cold until he caught pneumonia, or eaten toadstools and poisoned himself. Anything to keep poor old Helen on the leash.'

'She really should stand up to him.'

'Don't be silly, Robin. How can she?'

Hugh was edging the boat to the bank. Robin said impatiently, 'Helen is twenty-two. An adult. She should just walk out. *I* did.'

She was aware that she sounded pompous, yet Helen's spinelessness irritated her. Once, years ago, they had shared their ambitions. Helen had wanted to travel, for goodness sake, and yet she was still immured in that huge, grim rectory.

Hugh helped both girls out of the rowing-boat, and lugged the picnic hamper onto the grass. Opening the wicker basket, he said, 'It's not the same for Helen as it was for you, Rob. When you left home, you knew that Ma and Pa had each other. Helen's father is completely dependent on her.'

'But she's wasting her life! Just throwing it away!' Robin made a wild, sweeping gesture.

'You don't understand, do you, Robin?' Maia began to butter the bread rolls. 'Helen's father wants to possess her. He believes that he has a *right* to possess her.'

'She's all he has, Maia.' Hugh tied the painter of the

215

rowing-boat around an old tree stump. 'One chick in the nest, and all that.'

'I sometimes think that he's more like a husband than a father towards her . . .' murmured Maia. 'I wish I could visit Helen more often, but the shop keeps me so busy . . . Do you think, Hugh . . . ?'

'I'll drive over as often as I can.'

'You are a darling, Hugh. A darling.'

Hugh was standing the wine bottle in the river to cool, his back to Robin and Maia. When he turned back, his face was flushed. He delved into the hamper, and brought out a cake. 'My God – pink icing,' he said, with a sort of amused despair. 'Ma still thinks I'm in short trousers.'

Maia rummaged in her bag. 'I've brought you candles.' Her pale eyes glinted maliciously. 'Thirty-three of them. You must blow them all out, and then you can make a wish.'

Neatly, she stuck the tiny candles into the pink icing, and lit them. Hugh closed his eyes and blew. In the merciless brightness of the sunlight, Robin noticed the threads of grey running through his dark gold hair, and the fine lines that clustered around the corners of his eyes. The candles shivered, and went out.

Struggling with graphs, Robin carted her books round to the Hackney basement one morning, to ask Joe's advice. After a long night's work at the Navigator, he was prowling round the flat, unshaven, clad only in trousers and a loosely flapping shirt.

'I'll buy you breakfast if you'll help me with these wretched things,' she said, looking critically at his lean, undernourished frame.

She made black coffee; he lit a cigarette, and thumbed through her notes. Robin knew that Joe had the sort of practical, level-headed mind that could understand things as diverse as car engines and mathematics. After lecturing her on the illegibility of her handwriting, he gave a brief, clear explanation of x and y axes, and then said, 'But you don't need any of that, Robin. Just some nice, chunky columns to catch the eye. Most people won't be able to follow anything more complicated.'

He did a quick sketch on the back of her notes to illustrate, and she suddenly felt immensely relieved. The awful feeling of juggling her responsibilities was still with her, but at least if her work was under control, she felt slightly less harassed.

'Dear Joe,' she said, and kissed him on the crown of his head. 'Breakfast?'

'I have to be outside the labour exchange at ten o'clock.' He glanced at his watch. 'There's a demonstration against the means test. Do you want to come, Robin?' Looking up, he grinned at her. 'Just think of the fresh air and exercise . . . much more fun than being stuck at a desk, adding figures.'

'You must promise—'

He held up his hands, palms facing out. 'No violence. It won't be a big affair.'

Yet when they reached Hackney labour exchange, there were already two hundred or so people milling around the outer doors of the building. Banners and placards protested against the injustices of the means test. The strong summer sun blazed down on the heads of the men in their cloth caps, the women with their berets or cheap straw hats. Groups of unemployed men huddled around the street corners, scuffing their battered boots on the dusty pavement, watching the protesters with apathetic eyes.

Then, 'Damn,' whispered Joe, and Robin glanced up at him.

'What?'

'There's Wal Hannington. Look, Robin.'

Someone had dragged an orange box onto the pavement outside the doors of the labour exchange; a man was threading through the crowd towards it. Robin looked with interest at the leader of the NUWM.

'You'd better go, Robin.'

She was outraged. 'Go? Certainly not. I want to hear him speak.'

Joe, looking down at her, explained impatiently, 'If Hannington's here, the police won't be far behind. He's a communist and a firebrand, and he's been in and out of jail for the past year. There'll be trouble – do go.'

She glared at him. The crowd surged behind her, as people struggled to hear Wal Hannington speak. She made the decision not to leave, and then it was too late to leave anyway. As Hannington's first, blistering cry of '*Comrades!*' pierced the air people pressed suddenly forward, and she felt Joe's fingertips briefly touch hers as he tried to grab her hand. Then, struggling to look round, she could no longer see him.

Robin was never quite sure what happened next. Hannington began to speak, but the cheers that greeted him changed almost immediately to murmurs of anger. When, with difficulty, she managed to peer back over the heads of the crowd, she saw the gleam of sunlight on a polished buckle, a domed helmet, a wooden baton. The police were mounted, the great, muscular bodies of their horses towering over the throng.

She never knew who started it. A baton swung through the rays of sunlight; a bottle was hurled through the air to smash in glittering fragments on the pavement. Bricks, pieces of paving-stone, tin cans gathered from a dustbin soared towards the policemen. The lines of battle had been drawn up; buffeted by larger, heavier bodies, Robin slipped to the ground, landing heavily on her knees. Someone – not Joe – yanked her to her feet. 'Go home, lass – you shouldn't be here.' She knew that her rescuer was right, and that she, who rarely felt fear, was aware of a cold, tight feeling in her chest, and a panicking dislike of the sudden explosion of mob violence. She began to work back through the crowd, towards the alleyway by which she and Joe had arrived. A policeman, struck by a brick on the jaw, fell against her; a man in a cloth cap, blood streaming from his nose, pushed past her, running for safety. When the crowd shoved against her she could hardly breathe. The noise – the shouting, and the crashing of sticks and batons on bodies and buildings – echoed in her ears.

Someone pushed between them, and though Joe grabbed at Robin's hand, her fingers slipped through his. He yelled her name, knowing she could not hear him. Something jarred his shoulder, and Joe fell back into the crowd, and when he looked again, she was gone.

Caught up in the movement of the crowd, he was pushed back against the wall of the labour exchange. In moments, the most intense fighting was centred around Wal Hannington: the police would try, yet again, to gaol Hannington. Hannington's supporters, of course, wanted him free. Sticks and batons thwacked in the air; at Joe's side a man was yelling the same profanity over and over again. A fist thumped Joe in the ribs and he lashed out. There was a loud crash as a brick went through a window and fragments of glass showered his back and shoulders, glinting like diamonds. Joe caught a brief glimpse of a head of light brown hair on the far side of the road, and then the ranks of seething bodies closed over her, and she was gone. Pushing through the crowd, fists clenched, he struck out at anyone in his way. The force of the crowd, which had become a single angry body, threatened to crush him back against the wall. Kicking and shoving, he pushed forward.

He was at the thinning edge of the riot, but still he could not see Robin. From behind him, a hand seized his shoulder, and a voice said, 'Not going anywhere, are you, son?' His response was instinctive. With a twist and a sharp backward jab of the elbow into someone's soft protruding stomach, he was free, running along the far side of the road.

Only momentarily, though. He had a brief swirling glimpse of hooves and mane and whitened eyes, before the blow that struck the back of his head felled him and he heard, as he drifted into unconsciousness, 'Got you, you little bastard.'

At the opening of the alleyway, Robin stopped and looked back, straining to see Joe. The mêlée of heaving bodies hid him, and when she screamed his name her voice was lost in the clamour. Only a few feet away from her, she saw a policeman raise his baton to strike a protester.

The baton swung up, then plunged down with nauseating force. Robin heard the crack of wood on bone. The man's knees buckled, and he slid to the pavement, his lips parted in a gasp of agony. And then, as she watched, frozen with fear and revulsion, the policeman raised his baton to strike again.

Outrage suddenly overcame her fear. It took only two paces to put herself between them. '*No*,' she said. To her own ears her voice sounded odd. 'Can't you see that you've hurt him?' The policeman stared down at her open-mouthed and, momentarily, she almost wanted to laugh at the expression on his face. Yet if her hands had not been clasped together they would have shaken like quaking grass.

She stooped to look at the injured protester, and when she glanced back over her shoulder, the policeman had gone. The man on the ground – middle-aged, thin-faced, cloth-capped – was pale beneath the fingers of blood that covered the side of his face. She took her handkerchief from her pocket, and pressed it against the wound, as she had seen Dr Mackenzie do. 'There's a doctor near by who'll look after you. You'll have to walk, I'm afraid, but you can lean on me.'

She managed to help him to his feet. Supporting him as best she could, they began to shuffle slowly down the alleyway. He muttered, as they left the noise and the rain of missiles behind, 'The Public Assistance Committee took half my furniture away last week. I just wanted to shout a bit about it.'

'I know.' She had her arm round him; he leaned heavily against her. 'It's not far. Don't talk.'

Somehow they struggled to the clinic. She thought

she detected an expression of weary resignation in Neil Mackenzie's face when she turned up with yet another unannounced patient. She watched him examine and stitch the deep cut. She always loved to watch him work. When he had finished, and the injured man had been despatched home in someone's motor-car, he looked at her, waiting silently for an explanation.

She said defensively, 'There was a demonstration outside Hackney labour exchange. A fight broke out.'

'I heard. Joining in, were you, Robin?'

'Of course not. You know I'm a pacifist, Neil.'

Washing his hands at the sink, his back was turned to her. 'I suppose it would be futile to suggest that you confine yourself to writing about the effects of unemployment instead of taking part in the brawling?'

Furious, she managed a stiff goodbye, and ran outside into the street. When she walked cautiously back down the alleyway, she saw that the pavement outside the labour exchange was now empty of all except the debris of the engagement. She began to run to Francis's basement flat.

When she hammered on the door, Francis opened it. Robin just gasped, '*Joe . . . ?*' and he stared at her dishevelled clothing and shook his head.

When she could explain what had happened, he grabbed his jacket, and told her to wait in the flat. Too exhausted to protest, she sank into a chair, and heard the door slam behind him, and then the sound of his feet running up the basement steps. She sat for a while, biting her nails, and then began to wander restlessly round the untidy rooms, making herself a cup of tea and forgetting to drink it.

Francis returned in the late afternoon. She knew from the grimness of his expression that his news was bad. Mutely, she waited for him to speak.

'Joe's in Bow Street police station.'

Robin's hand went to her mouth. '*Why?*'

'Apparently he hit a policeman. They wouldn't let me

see him. I'll try again tomorrow. They're putting him up before the magistrates on Monday.'

'Francis – we must do something—'

'They could give him six months, you know, Robin. I'll make some enquiries – there must be someone to speak up for him. Tell them about his unblemished character, and all that.'

The worst thing was neither the headache nor the bruises nor the confinement, but the not knowing. Joe came round briefly in the Black Maria, but sank back into a stupor as they manhandled him out of the van and into the cells. Later, an officer took his name and address before sending him back into the crowded, foul-smelling cell. After an hour or so, when his head had cleared a little, he stood and yelled at the cell door until someone came and told him to shut up. Politely, he asked the policeman about Robin, and was told that no women had been arrested. A number of people had been injured though: the officer had no details of their names, and would not have shared them with Joe if he had. Then the small window in the cell door slammed shut.

The following morning, he was taken upstairs to a room, where they made him write a statement. His memory of the latter part of the riot was blurred, and all Joe could recall was his overriding fear that Robin had been hurt. When he had signed his name, the officer said to him, 'There's someone to see you, Elliot.'

Francis was shown in. Joe thought that he had never in his entire life been so glad to see him. He said only, '*Robin . . . ?*'

'Is fine, you daft bastard. Well – worried sick about you.'

Momentarily, he closed his eyes with relief. Suddenly things did not seem quite so black.

'They want to charge you with assaulting a police-man,' said Francis. 'I've found you a lawyer – he's going to try and get it reduced to disorderly conduct. They'll fine you for that, if you're lucky – the assault charge would almost certainly carry a prison sentence.'

'It makes no difference – I couldn't pay a fine.'

'I can. Thank God it's the beginning of the month – my allowance is just in.'

He said furiously, 'Francis – I couldn't possibly—'

'Of course you could.' Francis rose, and placed a brown paper parcel on the table. 'That's my suit – wear it on Monday. And there's a clean shirt and I found my old school tie, so wear that as well. You never know – it might help.'

He was going to protest again, but Francis interrupted him.

'If you go to gaol, Joe, you'll lose your job, and God knows when you'd find another one. Robin spent hours ironing your shirt and cleaning the tie, and I've toadied to some simply hideous old bores to get you a good lawyer. We'll see you in court.'

Hating it, Joe did as he was told, and wore the suit and the tie and a penitent expression. The lawyer, an oleaginous type, explained in cultured and patronizing phrases that Joe, the only son of a prominent northern gentleman, was a virtuous but hotheaded young man. He had been caught up in the mêlée accidentally and, concerned for the well-being of the young lady he had been with, had in the heat of the moment mistaken a policeman for a rioter. Joe submitted to a lecture on behaving appropriately to his station in life, was fined twenty pounds and bound over to keep the peace for six months.

Afterwards, they celebrated. The party, growing from nothing in the basement flat, spontaneously took life until a hundred people crowded into the four small rooms, and the noise could be heard the length of the street. It was only in the early hours of the following morning that Joe, retiring to a quiet corner with a bottle of beer, a packet of cigarettes, and an appalling headache, recalled the memory that had preoccupied him during his three nights in the cell.

A kiss. Cool lips briefly touching the crown of his head.

Chapter Eight

The world, which had briefly welcomed her, had shut
Helen out again. After a week in hospital Julius
Ferguson had returned to the rectory, carried upstairs
to the front bedroom that, years ago, he had shared
with his wife. Mementoes of Florence filled the room:
an oil-painting on the wall opposite the bedhead; the
teddy bear and collection of china dolls – all Florence's
– on the chest of drawers, along with the photograph
taken shortly after her marriage. In the photograph,
Florence wore a frilly white dress and her hair was in
ringlets. She played on a swing, cuddling a puppy on
her lap.

The room was north-facing, dark and sombre. The
windows were small-paned, the walls washed in ochre
emulsion, and the linoleum, laid to welcome Florence
Ferguson to her new home as a bride, had since become
cracked and blistered. Helen brought in fresh flowers
each day but somehow, in the large, echoing space, they
looked dull and lost. Tired and in pain, the Reverend
Ferguson's moods were capricious, his approval, so
necessary to Helen's peace of mind, frequently withdrawn. He picked at the egg custards, the junkets and
the soups she spent so much time preparing. No matter
how often she adjusted his pillows or rearranged his
bedclothes he was never comfortable. His voice, queru-
lous and demanding, followed Helen downstairs with
her trays and hot-water bottles, and drew her back up

to him as soon as she curled up to read in the drawing-room.

As the weeks slowly passed, her patience ebbed away, leaving her increasingly short-tempered. One morning her father complained about the temperature of his shaving-water, and she turned aside and left the room, hiding her face so that he would not see her sudden anger. If thick, vertical stair-rods of rain had not pulverized the paths and grass, if she had not feared the curious gaze of the servants, then she would have run outside.

Instead, she climbed the attic stairs, oddly unfrightened of their narrowness and ricketiness. She had always loathed the attics, venturing up there only once or twice a year to find things for jumble sales or fêtes. Stepping carefully through the trunks and boxes and old chests of drawers, she saw a harp, festooned with cobwebs, its strings gaping like an old man's teeth, and an umbrella stand made from an elephant's foot, and boxes of books, their spines cracked and fraying, mould blossoming on their pages. And a pram – her own, presumably – and a cradle. Helen touched the cradle, which rocked creakingly, and her fingertips left a trail through the thick felting of dust. Spiders, surprised by movement in their still kingdom, scuttled across the floor. Helen walked on, ducking under beams, feeling her way when the light from the trapdoor no longer illuminated the darkness. The attics covered the entire area of the house, and were partitioned into a series of rooms. Soon she had passed all familiar objects, and it occurred to her that it was as though she had gone back in time, stepping through the old, decaying possessions of her father's predecessors. Candlesticks and a Victrola, and a top hat. Crumbling sheets of music: sentimental Victorian songs about hearts and tears and dying children. Then she opened the door in the last partition.

Light flooded over her, as she stared around the small, empty room. The square-paned window looked out onto the garden, and when she cleared aside the dust with her fingertips, she could see down to where Adam Hayhoe was tending the vegetable garden. It touched her that, unasked, knowing that their gardener was unwell, he had come twice a week since her father's illness to work in the garden. Helen's anger left her suddenly, and she sat down on the dusty floor, her eyes closed, and tried to pray.

Hugh drove to Thorpe Fen at least twice a week, staying perhaps for an hour or so, helping to fold sheets or peel potatoes if Helen was working in the kitchen. In the desert of time between his calls, she thought about his last visit, or looked forward to his next one. She replayed their conversation in her mind, picturing Hugh as he had sat in the kitchen or garden or drawing-room, recalling the sunlight on his wavy gold-brown hair, or the way that his long, bony white fingers had gripped the handle of his teacup. At night, before she slept, she would imagine herself and Hugh, driving round the Continent, perhaps, or sailing a boat. The boat would be tossed by a tempest, and she would plunge into the sea, and Hugh would save her. *I could not bear it if I lost you, Helen,* he said, before he kissed her . . .

When Hugh did not call, the days seemed long and bleak. Taking her afternoon walk, she felt eyes watching her from the small, mean houses that made up the village; and the countryside around her, with its endless plain of field and ditch and marsh, produced in her an unreasonable terror. She was not sure what she feared: old shadows of the Fens, perhaps – the pagan bogles and boggarts that still, for many of the villagers, haunted the loneliest paths and marshes. The words of even the most familiar prayers failed to give her comfort, and the darkening countryside seemed ancient, pre-Christian, unsanctified.

The weather changed suddenly from summer to autumn. A greyish cloud hung low in the sky, yet it did not rain. There was no wind, and when Helen, after checking that her father was comfortable for his afternoon nap, looked through the drawing-room window, everything seemed gripped by an unnatural stillness. Not a leaf, not a bird nor a beetle moved in the garden. Bars of love and duty imprisoned her.

She was unable to shake off the blackness of her mood. Hugh had not called for over a week; she had ticked off the days in her diary with mounting anxiety. When she thought of Gussie and Thomas, she wanted to cry. She tried to play the piano, but her fingers were clumsy, and she forgot the words of her favourite songs. She opened a book, but could not lose herself in it. It was two o'clock, and there were letters to post. She pulled on her hat and buttoned her coat, clutching the letters in her gloved hands as she let herself out of the house. The door shut behind her, and she stood quite still as tears blurred the grey, silent landscape. Then, suddenly, she ran to the shed and pulled her father's bicycle from the spidery tangle of gardening tools and flower-pots. The letters fell unheeded to the path. Helen's skirt caught inelegantly on the crossbar as she began to pedal the five miles to Blackmere Farm.

Only Hugh was at home. He had bronchitis, he explained, and had been off work for a week. Because he had lost weight, he looked taller and thinner than ever, and his spasms of coughing distracted Helen from her own miseries, replacing them with concern for him.

'This is my first day up. Ma's orders. I'm supposed to be sorting jumble.'

The kitchen table was covered with a vast heap of old clothing. Hugh stared at it gloomily. 'I've been feeling so damn useless – sorry, Helen, I do beg your pardon – but I thought perhaps if I could *do* something, instead of having everyone run around after me . . . Only now, just to look at it makes me feel fagged out.'

'I'll help, if you like, Hugh.'

'Would you, old thing? That would be so kind of you. But what about your father?'

Helen began to sift through the pile of clothes. 'Daddy always sleeps in the afternoon. And the curate said he'd call.'

'Decent stuff here, things for the rag and bone man in the wicker basket, and anything really repulsive I'll just put in the stove.' Hugh grimaced as he picked up a pair of discoloured long johns. His back to Helen as he opened the kitchen stove, he said, 'The last few months must have been pretty frightful for you. Do you have many visitors?'

'The curate.' Helen checked through a child's dress for holes. 'And the doctor, of course.'

'But to see *you*, Helen—'

'Only you, Hugh,' she said, folding the dress. 'And Maia, when she can. But she's terribly busy.'

'Maia loves to be busy. One cannot imagine Maia doing anything as mundane as reading a trashy novel, or simply sitting dreaming in an armchair.'

When he smiled, the skin around Hugh's clear, hazel eyes crinkled. Helen wanted to smooth away those tiny lines with her fingertips, to kiss the small hollow at the base of his throat. Instead, she continued to sort through the jumble.

After they had finished, they sat in the drawing-room, toasting crumpets on the fire. Hugh's face was flushed scarlet, his cough worse, his restlessness, Helen suspected, due to the remains of a fever. She helped him begin to make the huge jigsaw that Daisy had found among the jumble: sitting still, sorting through the pieces, drinking the tea that she had made, Helen saw his colour slowly become more normal, his eyes less bright. Later, after Daisy had come home, Helen played the piano, and Hugh fell asleep in the armchair. Daisy, seeing Helen out of the house, whispered, 'Thank you, dear Helen. I have been dreadfully worried about him. You are so good with him,' and Helen, cycling home, forgot her fears and enjoyed the cold air against her face, and the exhilaration of the long, straight flat roads across the Fens.

There were three sorts of houses in Thorpe Fen. There was the rectory, which was much the same size as all the other dwellings put together; there were the craftsmen's houses, like Adam Hayhoe's cottage; and there were the farm labourers' homes: small, thatched, one-storey shacks that huddled together on the lowest-lying ground. These were tied cottages, owned by the family who lived in the Big House. Their crooked front doors, because of the sinking land, stood several feet above the surface of the drove; their windows leaned drunkenly, and the last cottage, a zig-zagging fissure snaking up its brickwork, was uninhabitable. They shared a communal well, which dried up in hot summers and overflowed in wet winters. The drove outside alternated between dust and mud.

Helen found Percy, her cat, who had been absent from the rectory for two days, skulking beneath the water-butt belonging to the cottages. Great lumps of fur were missing from around his neck, and his whiskers were bent at odd angles. 'You've been fighting again, haven't you, darling?' said Helen, tenderly, disregarding the cat's spitting and snarling as she lifted him from his hiding place and cradled him against her bosom.

On her way home, Helen whispered to Percy about Hugh. She knew that she was in love with Hugh: what she had felt for Geoffrey Lemon had been nothing compared to what she felt for Hugh. She had known Hugh for years; he was, she realized, one of the few men she had never found intimidating. Hugh never raised his voice in anger and, most important, he was always the same. His friendship was constant, never unpredictably withdrawn. She did not mind being alone with Hugh, with him she felt perfectly at ease. Helen thought that Hugh was fond of her, truly fond. He sought her company, he had told her that she was beautiful. Why, then, she wondered, did he not propose to her? Helen recognized that there were enormous hurdles to their engagement: Hugh's atheism, and even the age gap of ten years between them were problems enough. She thought it possible that Hugh's atheism was not so deeply ingrained as Robin's. Through finding a wife,

Hugh might also find God. And Helen knew that she needed Hugh. She had only a rather hazy idea of the physical duties of marriage, her father having told her nothing, of course. Robin would, given half the chance, have no doubt explained everything in scientific detail, but Helen, whose nature was a mixture of the prudish and the romantic, had always halted Robin's attempts at enlightenment. The novels she borrowed from the lending library led Helen to imagine a simply glorious sort of melting into each other. Like kissing, only more so. She spent a large part of the day imagining Hugh kissing her.

But the greatest obstacle to their marriage was her father. It must be as obvious to Hugh as it was now to Helen that she could never leave her father. He needed her. The possibility that she might spend the rest of her life an old maid crept up slowly upon Helen, horrifying her.

Through Charles Maddox, Maia had acquired a social circle. Dinner invitations fluttered through her letter box; well-connected people telephoned her, requesting her presence at cocktail parties. Maia realized that, young, wealthy and widowed, she was a valuable commodity. She played a careful game with her admirers, knowing that they must be kept interested, but their hopes must not be raised too high.

Tonight Charles was to take her out again. She neither looked forward to nor dreaded the evening: it was, simply, something she had to do. The owner of Merchants must attend the first charity ball of the season. It was an event that she and Vernon had attended in the past. At the recollection Maia put her glass to her lips and drank steadily.

The autumn weather was cold and frosty, and Charles, helping her on with her fur coat and into the car, was protective. 'Don't fuss, Charles,' said Maia, mildly, as he carefully tucked the rug around her. His blue eyes, meeting hers, were soft with the adoration that she had lately begun to find just a little bit irritating. At the ball, she managed to lose him; bright, beautiful and witty, she flitted from admirer to admirer. He caught up with her eventually, plying her with champagne and canapés, resting a possessive hand on her waist, threading his arm around her shoulder as though he was warding off the rest of the world. When he bent and touched her bare neck with his lips, her irritation changed to disgust, and she excused herself.

A dozen other women were in the ladies' room, prinking themselves in front of the looking-glass. They were talking about childbirth, the sort of conversation Maia always tried strenuously to avoid. But she did not yet wish to return to the ballroom and Charles, so she took her lipstick and powder compact from her small, beaded bag, and began very carefully to outline her lips, trying not to hear the chatter. It was not yet midnight, far too early to go home. Studying her reflection in the mirror, she knew that it was perfect. Curious glances from the other ladies punctured their conversation.

'Twenty-three hours in labour . . .'

'My dear, it was simply *weeks* before I could even walk properly . . .'

'The doctor had to use forceps. Poor little Roger's head was such a funny shape . . .'

Maia returned to the ballroom. The band was playing; men clustered round her, demanding dances. She danced with one after the other, favouring none, allowing them to bring her drinks, to light her cigarettes. And then a hand curled round her shoulder, detaching her from her partner, and a familiar voice said, 'Got you.'

Charles steered her into the centre of the room. 'Now I'm not going to let you go,' he murmured. 'You're mine, now, Maia, and I don't intend to let anyone else have you.' He looked down at her, and his tone of voice altered. 'Maia? Are you all right?'

She felt rather sick and rather faint. She said, 'I'm tired, Charles, that's all,' and allowed him to escort her to one of the balconies that led off the ballroom. There she sat down, threading her hands together so that they did not shake.

'You poor darling – you look all in.'

'I'm fine, I said, Charles.'

The drive home cleared her head a little. Charles insisted on coming into the house, and she simply did not have the energy to refuse him. As he helped her out of her coat and poured drinks for both of them, she wondered why she was not attracted to him. Other women were attracted to Charles Maddox – she had often seen the desire in their eyes as they looked at him. He was young, tall, dark-haired, blue-eyed – surely any woman must find him attractive? It occurred to her that Vernon had extinguished from her all that sort of desire. The thought depressed her. The only men she felt at ease with were Liam and Hugh. Liam and she had come to an understanding; Hugh was Robin's brother, and thus her friend. She thought that something of Vernon remained, that he still attempted to control her life.

'Maia?'

She realized that Charles was speaking to her. She smiled at him. 'I'm so sorry, Charles – I was dreaming. What did you say?'

'That you'll knock yourself out, working so hard. It isn't right that a pretty girl like you should have to slog away like that.'

She tried to make him understand. 'But I love it. And I'm good at it.'

'Oh – you'll get by, I'm sure. And you've good people to help you out. Liam Kavanagh knows his job.'

She said sweetly, 'Don't you think that's a little patronizing, Charles?'

He stared at her, surprised. 'I say – no offence meant. I'm sure you keep them all on their toes.'

Restless, she stood up, and went to draw the curtains. She heard him say, 'I'm just trying to tell you, Maia, that I'll always be here. And that if you want a hand with anything, you only have to say the word.'

'Sweet of you, darling,' she said absently.

Then he said, 'You know I'm mad about you, don't you?' and she paused at the window, the long tassels of the curtain cords in her hands, pleating and unpleating their strands over and over again.

'I adore you, Maia.'

That she felt only a mixture of fear and boredom at his declaration both angered and frightened her. There was something wrong with her. What Vernon had done to her had marked her permanently. Or perhaps she simply wasn't trying hard enough. She had not properly kissed a man since Vernon, she had not permitted a man even to begin to make love to her. And Charles Maddox was good-looking, personable, charming.

She turned to him. 'Really, Charles?'

His eyes were hot and dark. He crossed the room to her, taking her in his arms. Bending his head, he kissed great handfuls of her dark hair, and the curve of her neck. Then his lips touched hers.

She wanted to gag. She stood motionless, her eyes open but unseeing. She smelt the male salty scent of his skin, and the dressing on his hair, and his cologne. Vernon had worn cologne, Vernon had dressed his hair. Charles's moustache scratched her face, as Vernon's had done; Charles's fingertips dug into her back, as Vernon's had done. His breath was Vernon's, the hard force of his body pressing into hers was Vernon's . . . When he let her go, and stood back a little, she expected him to say, *Now take your clothes off, Maia. Lie on the bed.*

But he did not. Instead, when she looked at him, she saw that the desire in his eyes had changed to shock. She moved at last, adjusting her dress, tidying her hair with her hands, scrubbing her mouth with her handkerchief, trying to remove all trace of him from her body. He was still staring at her when she finished, but she knew that he did not desire her any more.

Instead he said, 'My God – you're not remotely interested, are you?' and his voice shook a little. 'You're only interested in profit margins . . . and accounts . . . in *money* . . .'

She did not attempt to explain. She knew that it would have been futile.

'You'd better go, Charles.'

'You bitch. You cold bitch.'

'Go. Please.'

'You're not capable of normal human emotions, are you, Maia? You're not capable of *love*.'

Seizing his overcoat from where he had flung it on a chair, he walked out of the room. Maia heard the front door slam as Charles Maddox left the house, and then the roar of his car hurtling up the drive.

She poured herself another drink. She was cold, and her head ached. She curled herself up in a chair, her fur coat snug around her shoulders, and sipped her gin. Maia wondered, as she drank, whether he was right. Whether she had ever possessed the capacity for love and, if she had, whether Vernon had taken that from her along with her virginity and her self-respect.

Guy's play, which was called *Left at the Crossing*, began its six-week run. The theatre in which it was performed did not, in the end, match up to Francis's expectations. Instead of a glittering first night in a West End theatre, they shivered in a draughty church hall in Islington. The hall was packed, though – Guy had already published two volumes of poetry to some acclaim, and Francis had friends enough to fill the place three times over. If the national newspapers did not attend, then many of the small left-wing journals and magazines did. 'A searing indictment,' wrote one, 'of the failures of the capitalist system.' The play, entirely in blank verse and breaking away from the traditional three-act structure, employed a masked chorus and half a dozen other characters. All the action took place at a crossroads, represented on an almost bare stage by bands of coloured light. At the end of the play, the lights moved slowly upwards until the cross, by then red in colour, was reflected against the backdrop, and the principal character, played by Francis, exited stage left. 'Clever,' said Merlin approvingly, applauding furiously, and nudging Robin. 'Socialism as the new Christianity.'

She and Francis spent the weekend together, driving to Suffolk on Saturday night, hiring a boat the following morning and ambling gently along the coast. Robin took the helm, Francis did all the complicated things with sails and rudders. The sea was green and opaque, like glass washed by waves, and the coming winter sharpened the cold breeze.

A few days later, Robin took a train north. Neil Mackenzie had arranged for her to stay with friends of his in Leeds, so that she could include a chapter on poverty in the industrial north in their book. It seemed to Robin that she had tramped down a thousand grimy streets, that she had been welcomed into a thousand dark, cramped houses. The interiors of the houses were depressingly familiar; poverty had much the same face whether it was in Leeds or in London. The grubby rag rugs on the cracked linoleum floors, the overcoats blanketing the stained mattresses, the bugs and vermin infesting the fabric of the houses: all these she had seen in the east end of London. There just seemed to be more of them in Yorkshire – and more poorly dressed men standing at street corners, more white-faced women, old before their time.

It was colder, too. The wind blew down from the moors, funnelling along the rows of terraced houses, kicking the old newspapers, the discarded Players packets and the bottle-tops into the gutters. In the early morning, when the sound of the mill girls clattering in their clogs to work was like the cavalry of an invading army, ice edged the puddles on the road, and frost rimed the trees in the park. Despite her thick skirt and jumper, her gloves and her beret and her coat, Robin never felt warm. The cold seemed to have seeped into her bones, making its home there, refusing to quit.

She lodged in a stone-built villa in one of the better

parts of Leeds. She travelled to Keighley, to Barnsley and within Leeds itself, writing up her notes in the evening, trying not to dream each night of the things that she had seen. Trying not to feel hopeless, trying to retain the optimism that had always before been a part of her. Yet the misery that she witnessed seemed so huge, so intractable. So many men out of work, so much slum housing, so much apathy, so much indifference. Whereas once she had believed that all these problems would one day be resolved, she now felt that confidence slipping away. Poverty seemed as much a part of the landscape as the huge mill chimneys towering over the back-to-backs, as the coal dust ingrained on the walls of the buildings.

On the day before she was due to return to London, Robin caught a bus and went out onto the moors. She had not slept well the previous night, and she could not bear another day in the city. The moorland air was cool and scented with peat and heather; the wind had dropped at last. The pale blue sky was feathered with high white clouds, and the sun lit the hilltops with gold. She was reminded of the silent vastness of the Fens, though the two landscapes were so different. Walking for miles, she began to feel free again, less chained to the earth. In the mid-afternoon she left the hills and took the bus, stopping at a village along the river valley for tea and cakes. The village was called Hawksden, and the settlement was dominated by its mill. A single huge, round chimney soared into the sky, and the vast frontage of the factory building, with the name 'Elliot's Mill' painted in great square letters on the brick, took up almost an entire street. Rows of stone-built terraced cottages clustered around it. When the whistle blew for the end of the shift, the streets swarmed with mill workers, the older women with their shawls pulled up over their heads, the younger girls wearing cheap, pretty hats. The sound of their clogs echoed on the cobbles.

She was eating a piece of Yorkshire curd tart when she stared for a second time at the lettering on the wall, and blinked. *Elliot's Mill.* Joe's father, Francis had said, owned a mill in Yorkshire. It occurred to Robin that whoever owned this mill owned the village as well. She thought of Joe, a dark scarecrow, taciturn, permanently hungry, his jackets always out at the elbows, and she felt confusion mixed with a flicker of curiosity.

Paying her bill, it was easy enough to answer her curiosity. Elliots, said the girl who gave Robin her change, had built the mill fifty years ago, and had owned it ever since. The master's name was John Elliot, and yes, he had had two sons. But he had been unlucky, because the elder son had died in the War, and he had quarrelled with his younger son. And he had outlived both his wives – the plain one from Buxton, who had died giving birth to Johnnie, and the pretty one, the Frenchwoman.

The light was dying as, leaving the teashop, Robin walked around Hawksden. It had begun to rain again, and the yellow sulphur lamps gleamed amber on the wet pavements. It was easy enough to find John Elliot's house – the house in which Joe, presumably, had grown up. There was, simply, no other house of that size in Hawksden. The house was vast, ugly, three-storeyed, an octagonal tower clinging clumsily to one wall, hideously encrusted with garlands and curlicues of stone, and it spoke to Robin of wealth, and of the power that always went with wealth. It lay a little back from the rest of the village, surrounded by a high wall and an area of blackened grass with pretensions to parkland. A motor-car was parked outside the front door, yet only a few of the many windows were lit. Robin, standing at the gates and looking in, tried and failed to imagine the child Joe playing with a ball in that front garden, or walking with his French mama among the flower-beds.

In October, Joe skirted round Trafalgar Square as the first Fascist rally took place. The ranks of Blackshirts, the soaring, hypnotic voice of Sir Oswald Mosley and the uniform braying of the crowd, all angered him, inspiring him to stay and heckle. But he resisted the temptation: bound over to keep the peace for six months, he could not afford to get into trouble again. Besides, he would be late for work, and the landlord of the Navigator would dock his pay. He had almost paid back the twenty pounds that Francis had lent him for his fine. He seemed to have lived on bread and margarine and the odd pint of beer cadged from the pub these last few months, but in doing so the debt was nearly cancelled. Not that Francis was pressing him for money: Francis, carelessly generous, had forgotten the sum as soon as he had lent it. But Joe did not want to be indebted to anyone – even, or especially, to Francis. Recently he had found himself increasingly short-tempered with Francis. The play had fizzled out two weeks before its official closing date, an event which seemed to Joe entirely predictable, and Francis was once more filling the flat day and night with his friends. And Joe, working overtime, was tired. Two nights ago, at around three in the morning, he had seized bodily a particularly loud and discordant jazz pianist and deposited him in the area steps beyond the lobby, along with all the other rubbish.

Back in London, Robin looked for Francis. She found him in the Fitzroy Tavern with a dozen friends. 'We are to go to my rooms later,' whispered Selena to Robin, as she squeezed onto a seat. 'Francis and I have arranged a séance.'

The séance was superbly orchestrated: all flickering lights and ghostly creakings. Robin, unimpressed by the spirit world, watched Francis. He stood a little back from everything, stage-managing it all. He was neither fearful nor amused; what enjoyment he had lay, she thought, in controlling the drama. His eyes were pale pebbles washed by the sea, and there was a small twist to his mouth as he watched Selena, swathed in scarves and beads, crouching over her ouija board. When one of the men, startled by a voice that seemed to come from nowhere, upended a glass of whisky over himself, Robin saw Francis's quick, fleeting smile. And when Charis Fortune fainted, it was Robin who helped her into the kitchen and put her head between her knees and gave her water. Francis remained on the windowseat, watching. Robin went to him and whispered, 'Francis. You know that Charis has a weak heart.'

He turned slowly to look at her. She did not think that he had drunk much, though his eyes were glazed.

He said, 'But it's all nonsense. Isn't it?' Then he whispered, 'I've had enough. Let's go.'

They walked the mile and a half back to the flat. She had thought that she would tell him so much – about her work, and about Hawksden – but he strode fast along the pavement, her hand tucked around his sleeve, the noise of the traffic and the wind robbing her of the desire to speak.

In the flat, they took off their wet things and she climbed into bed. Before he touched her, he said, 'You're free tomorrow, aren't you, Robin?'

His face was shadowed; she could not read his expression.

'Yes. Why?'

'Because we have to go to Long Ferry. Vivien is getting married.'

He was standing naked beside the gas lamp. Now she saw that his eyes were emotionless, blank, absent. His body, with its firm musculature and athletic grace, looked as though it was made of stone.

She whispered, 'To whom?'

She guessed the answer before he spoke. 'Denzil Farr,' said Francis and, extinguishing the light, kissed her.

He had never made love to her like this before. His body used hers, exploring every inch of her flesh, forcing her to an intensity of feeling she had not previously experienced. His lips bruised hers, his teeth marked her breasts. In the darkness, she could no longer distinguish between her flesh and his. Her skin seemed joined to his skin, her body consumed by his. He possessed her in a way that an incubus might possess the object of its desires: sucking her dry, branding her soul, annealing her to him, until they were no longer man and woman, but were united in their ecstasy.

Yet as they travelled to Suffolk the following day, her joy ebbed steadily away, to be replaced by a sort of dread. They overslept, and Robin had to run back to her lodgings to find a suitable dress. Then they missed their train, and the next train was so crowded they were not able to sit together. Arriving at Ipswich, Francis glanced at his watch.

'We're too late for the ceremony. We'll just go to the reception.'

Their connection crawled along the branch line; by the time they reached the end of the line, the bus had already left. They walked the last two miles to Long Ferry. The sky overhead was leaden, grey clouds rolling in from the sea. Francis's face was pale, the wind seemed to be bowing him, crushing him. They hardly spoke. Eventually, unable to bear it any longer, she stood in front of him, grabbing his arms with her hands, stopping him.

'We don't have to go.' Her voice seemed lost in the wind.

He stared at her coldly. 'Of course we do. It's my mother's wedding. People would think—'

'You've never worried what people thought before. Let's go home, Francis.'

'Home?' The pale grey eyes focused on her only momentarily. 'Long Ferry is my home, Robin.'

He started to walk again. They were following the path beside the sea: its surface was dull, broken up by waves. The delicate structures of Long Ferry Hall came into view.

'I can't think,' said Francis suddenly, 'why you are making such a fuss. After all, it's only a *wedding*.'

Her eyes stung. Because of the salty air, because of the wind, she thought. They walked the last half-mile through the salt-marshes in silence. She could see, long

241

before they reached the house, the rows of motor-cars parked in the courtyard and on the drive. Music issued through the mullioned windows, and seeped through the old stone. Francis lit himself a cigarette as they went inside the house. Robin thought she heard someone call her name, and in the moment of glancing away the crowds shifted, hiding him.

She felt, as she had never previously felt, a stranger at Long Ferry. There was no Joe, no Selena, no Guy . . . not even Angus. The furniture was differently arranged, the old rooms had been cleaned and polished. When she sat down to dinner, she found herself between two strangers, both of whom were engaged in absorbing conversations with the people seated to the other side of them. The food – a complicated French menu – was served by uniformed waiters. The talk was of hunting and shooting and property and the servant problem. It was like one of those fairytales, thought Robin, where you believed you had only been away for a few months, and you returned to find things altered beyond recognition.

By the time the savoury was served, her head ached and she no longer even attempted to join in the conversation. She sat through the speeches in silence: the best man was dull, Denzil Farr was competent and slick. Francis, seated at the far end of the table, whispered constantly to his neighbour throughout Denzil Farr's speech. The girl's giggles interrupted the smooth monologue, and Farr's toast to the bride was punctuated by an unforgivable series of muttered phrases and stifled laughter. Francis had not, Robin noticed, so much as spoken to Vivien. There was a bottle of champagne in front of him, from which he refilled his glass constantly.

After the speeches, they left the great hall for the ballroom. Francis was surrounded by people; Robin could hear his low familiar voice, hear also the ripple of amusement from the circle that surrounded him. When she joined the circle for a while, he did not pick her out, or move closer to her, or distinguish her in any way. She found his neglect unbearably painful. Part of her wanted to shout and scream and remind him of what had taken place between them the previous night, but the greater part wanted to withdraw, her pride intact. His cold, glittering grey eyes passed her over with the same studied insouciance with which they passed over Vivien. She saw how his acolytes applauded and encouraged him in every further push against the boundaries of acceptable behaviour. She watched Vivien approach him and speak to him, and the slow, pleasured shake of Francis's head as he refused whatever she had asked him. She almost felt sorry for Vivien then. It occurred to her that there was an innocence about Vivien, a helpless inability to understand the consequences of her actions. Francis had succeeded in making himself, and not Vivien, the centre of attention. What vengeance, thought Robin, unable to watch any longer.

Moving away, she went from room to room, unwelcomed by the small clusters of unfamiliar people, an outsider in every clique. She knew, looking down at herself, that she had dressed all wrong. She should have worn the silk dress that Maia had sent to her, instead of her beloved embroidered terracotta smock. These people judged you by your appearance, and they had decided, glancing dismissively at Robin, that she was not worth talking to. I should go home, thought Robin, suddenly. She had not brought night things, and the prospect of remaining for another twelve hours in this house, that had become so strange, so unwelcoming to her, was intolerable. When she looked out into the courtyard, she saw that it was dark. Great pale bands of light spread out from the windows, igniting the weeds that poked through the flags with a fiery glitter. Long Ferry itself – beautiful, crumbling Long Ferry – was somehow entangled with her falling in love with Francis. He could not just throw all that away. She would not let him.

She went back to the ballroom, where she saw that he

had made a high narrowing pinnacle of champagne glasses. As she watched, he uncorked a bottle of champagne, and began to pour wine into the topmost glass so that it waterfalled down the sloping sides of the pyramid. But his hand shook, toppling the glass, and the whole fragile structure trembled, and one by one the glasses shivered and crashed to the floor. Shards of crystal skidded across the polished wood, making the ballroom look as though it had been scattered with diamonds. There was a great roar of laughter and a surge of applause from Francis's audience, but Robin briefly glimpsed the shock and distress in his eyes. She went to him, treading through the broken glass and champagne.

She laid her hand on his arm, and whispered, 'Francis – we should go.'

'Go?' He attempted to focus on her. 'Certainly not. I'm having a terrific time.'

'We can walk to the station together.' She heard the urgency in her voice. 'There's still time to catch the last train.'

'I don't want to catch the last train. I told you – I'm having a terrific time. These—' his arm made a wide, sweeping gesture '—these are my friends.'

'And what am I, Francis?' As soon as she said it, she wanted to draw the words back, dreading his reply.

'You?' He seemed to see her for the first time. His expression altered from glazed bewilderment to malicious amusement. He was leaning against the wall of the ballroom, one shoulder resting against the plasterwork. He said clearly, 'You're on the list, Robin. You don't need to worry.'

Without thinking, she raised her hand, palm flat to strike that attractive, insulting, drunken face. And when her hand froze in mid-air, a few inches from his cheekbone, he glanced at it and then at her expression, and began to laugh. He did not stop laughing, even when he slid slowly down the wall, until he was crouched in a pool of champagne and glass fragments.

Robin ran out of the house, pausing only to grab her

coat from the cloakroom. It was only when she was halfway along the windswept sea-path to the station that she looked down and saw the blood that oozed from the sole of her foot, where a shard of glass had pierced the thin velvet sole of her slipper.

At the weekend, Maia turned down all other invitations, and drove out into the Fens. She collected Helen from Thorpe Fen, using all her charm on the rancid old rector (Mr Ferguson, Maia had noticed a long time ago, never refused anything asked him by a prettily dressed young woman), and then continued at full pelt to Blackmere Farm, and Hugh.

They spent the afternoon in Ely, giggling over an awful film in the Electric Cinema, and then eating sandwiches and cream cakes in a little teashop. Maia entertained them both with anecdotes about Merchants, giving her outrageously accurate imitation of Madame Wilton, the doyenne of the ladies' wear department. By the time she drove out of Ely she felt better, able to face her own company again, able to deny the accusations that still echoed in her ears. *You're not capable of normal human emotions, are you, Maia? You're not capable of* love. She drove very fast to Blackmere, making Helen shriek and grab at her hat as they swung round bends in the road. When, at the end of the evening, she took her leave of Helen and Hugh, she hugged them hard, almost reassuring herself that it was not true, what Charles Maddox had said to her.

Hugh drove Helen back to Thorpe Fen. The night was mild, all the stars hidden behind a thick covering of cloud. When they reached the rectory and Hugh braked and drew up outside the gates, he did not immediately climb out of the car to let her out. Instead, he touched her hand, halting her in the middle of picking up her bag and tucking her windswept hair beneath her hat.

'Wait a moment, won't you, Helen?'

She was glad that he could not, in the darkness, see

the blush that crept across her face. His hand still lay on hers, electrifying her even through the thin covering of her glove.

'How did you think she was?'

She could not at first think who Hugh was talking about. Her blankness must have registered, because he added, 'Maia – I thought she seemed upset.'

With an effort of will, she thought of Maia. Helen frowned, and nodded. 'She was glittery. That's Maia's way of being upset.'

'*Glittery?* Ha.' He seemed amused at her choice of word.

'I expect it's because it's nearly Christmas. You know, Hugh. Because of Vernon. He died on Christmas Day.'

'Of course.' Briefly, Hugh squeezed her fingers, then let her go. 'How stupid of me not to realize.'

Helen thought how nice it was, how companionable, that they could sit here like this, having a conversation about an old friend. He climbed out of the car, walking round to the passenger door to open it for her. She put her hand on his shoulder and, standing on tiptoe, kissed him on the cheek. With Hugh, who was well over six foot tall, she never felt big and gawky.

He said, looking up at the rectory, 'What a huge place it is, Helen. You and your father must rattle around in there. You could lose half a dozen families in that house.'

It was when she was walking down the rectory path that she realized that Hugh himself had found the answer to their problem.

Over the last month or so, Joe had seen little of Francis. Although they shared the same flat, Francis had recently been largely nocturnal, sleeping much of the day and going out at night, while Joe rose early, dividing his time between the pub and his political activities. Joe knew that Vivien had remarried (he had been invited to her wedding, but had declined the invitation with the excuse of his work), and he had witnessed Francis's return to the Hackney basement, three days later, in the shivering,

246

sick stage of too long a binge. In the fortnight since then, they had hardly spoken to each other. Both their interests and their friends had diverged.

Neither had he seen much of Robin recently. Robin was always busy, of course, rushing round London like some small, preoccupied whirlwind, furiously involving herself in other people's problems. Joe would have assumed that Francis was seeing Robin in the evenings, except that recently Diana Howarth and Selena Harcourt and Charis Fortune, all old flames of Francis's, had called. Joe, telling himself that what went on between Robin and Francis was none of his business, nevertheless felt uneasy.

He was serving in the pub one evening when Francis came in. It was a Friday night, ten o'clock, and the Navigator heaved with men trying to spend their week's wages in the shortest possible time. Fights often broke out on a Friday. Just now the landlord hovered beside the bar, sleeves rolled up, watchful for trouble.

Joe poured Francis a Scotch, and passed him the jug of water. Francis lit himself a cigarette while Joe turned aside to serve another customer. When he was free again, Joe said casually, 'Where's Robin? Only I haven't seen her for a while.'

'Nor I.' Francis swallowed a mouthful of whisky.

'Is she away?'

'I haven't a clue,' said Francis, uninterested. 'Probably not.' He returned to the cigarette and the whisky, not looking at Joe, gazing unfocused at the ranks of bottles behind the bar.

Men were calling for their tankards to be filled. After Joe had served a few of them, he persevered.

'Have you quarrelled?'

'Has who quarrelled?'

He knew that Francis was being deliberately obtuse. He said evenly, 'You and Robin.'

'A little tiff.'

'When?'

'At the wedding. I . . . um . . . had a few too many.'

247

Francis smiled, and glanced up at Joe. 'Don't look so outraged. It doesn't matter. She'll come running as soon as I click my fingers. Like a puppy.'

He didn't even think about it. His clenched fist struck Francis on the jaw, throwing him back, knocking over the glass of whisky. Then he jumped over the bar, and dragged Francis up from the floor, and hit him again. The expression of blank amazement on Francis's face delighted him, but Francis did not yet fight back. And Joe wanted him to fight back.

A small space cleared around them in the packed barroom. Joe, hauling Francis to his feet, whispered something in Francis's ear. Francis's pale face suffused with fury, and his fist struck Joe in the stomach. Joe, pushing him back into the crowd, hit him again. Seized with a mixture of violence and pleasure, Joe knew that Francis was very drunk. His blows rarely found their mark, whereas his own fell with a telling force. Others had begun to join in the fight: bottles, glasses and barstools flew through the air. Joe did not stop hitting Francis until the landlord, a huge man with meaty forearms, forced his way between them, holding them apart.

He said softly to Joe, 'I don't know what your quarrel is, son, but I hope it was worth losing your job for,' and Joe, suddenly sober, let his fists drop to his sides.

Besides, Francis wasn't capable of fighting any more. He leant against the bar, choking, blood streaming from a cut above his eye. The pub had suddenly emptied, leaving just a few old soaks huddled round their pints in the corners. The floor was littered with broken glass.

Back at the flat, Joe stuffed his meagre belongings into a bag, and left, chucking his keys onto the kitchen table. The cold winter air washed the last of his anger away. He felt tired and bruised and, walking quickly down the pavement away from the house in which he had spent the last five years of his life, he began to realize the implications of what he had done.

He had thrown away his job – his only source of

income – at a time when jobs were becoming harder and harder to come by. He had nowhere to live at the coldest season of the year. He had – Joe delved into his pocket – a total of two pounds three shillings and sevenpence. He knew better than to ask the Navigator's landlord for his last week's wages – they would have to pay for the breakages. As a part-time employee he was not entitled to unemployment benefit, and besides, he had been sacked, rather than made redundant. He did not think that the Public Assistance Committee would look kindly on any claim that he made.

But what puzzled him most of all was *why* he had hit Francis – he, who had little difficulty controlling his temper. And why, when Francis was disinclined to fight back, had he told him the one thing that would be bound to make the rift between them permanent?

Shivering, pulling up the collar of his jacket around his ears, Joe recalled their conversation. They had been talking about Robin. *She'll come running as soon as I click my fingers*, Francis had said. *Like a puppy.* His jaw clenched again.

He had hit Francis because he had not been able to stand aside and listen to him insult Robin. Elliot, you fool, Joe muttered to himself, you've been in love with Robin Summerhayes for ages. He could kid himself that he and Robin were just friends, that he was fond of her, that he felt elder brotherly towards her, but he knew that he would be lying. He could not pinpoint the moment at which friendship had turned to love, but he could see, looking back over the years, when the slightly patronizing scorn he had first felt towards her had changed to respect. When he had realized that she, alone amongst the three of them, had a direction, a purpose in life. He had witnessed how deeply she had felt for the child who had died of diphtheria, and how steadfastly she persevered with work that must often be disillusioning and depressing. Even now, when he thought of her small dogged figure, wrapped in her familiar green velvet coat, plodding down London's more dismal streets, his heart squeezed and he wanted to put his arm around her, to protect her, to give her somewhere that was warm and sheltered and good to come home to.

But Robin was in love with Francis. And he had had little, and after his work this night, had nothing.

Chapter Nine

Hugh's term had finished, so he took Helen Christmas shopping in Ely. She bought knitting wool to make presents for the maids and the gardener, and glass eyes for the cuddly toys she had made for the small girls in the village. She had made Hugh's present – a warm muffler – already, and she always knitted her father new gloves and socks each Christmas. Peering in the window of a toyshop, she tried to decide what she could afford for the village boys. Surreptitiously, she glanced in her purse, and laboriously counted the half-crowns, florins and sixpences. The balloons were a penny each, which was easy, but the tin cars, which she knew all the boys would love, were tuppence three-farthings. There were five little boys in Thorpe Fen. It was the sort of sum she found impossible.

'Helen?'

She looked up at Hugh. The expression in his eyes made her feel weak-kneed.

'Can I help?'

She went scarlet, but she wasn't sure whether it was because of her shame at her stupidity, or because he was looking at her like that. She blurted out, 'I don't know how much money I have left, Hugh. Could you count it for me?'

She emptied the contents of her purse into his cupped hands, and within a few seconds he said, 'You've ten shillings and fivepence, Helen. How many toys do you have to buy?'

They bought the small gifts together, she choosing, Hugh adding up and paying. When they had left the shop, she said, still flustered, 'You must think me a complete idiot.'

He caught her elbow, stopping her in the middle of the pavement. 'Never, Helen,' he said. 'Never.'

They walked back to the car. She felt a sort of panicking excitement. She had promised herself that she would talk to Hugh today, but she had put it off and off, until there was only the drive home left for her to do so. They drove for a while in silence. A flock of geese, in a great V-shaped formation, flew overhead; the reeds and the ice that skimmed the ditches were grey with frost. It had rained heavily the previous week, and the fields were streaked with frozen tongues of water.

Hugh broke the silence. 'Is your father well, Helen?'

'Daddy is holding all the services now. Dr Lemon says that his heart is weak, though.'

'You won't go back to work, then?'

She shook her head slowly. When, a few weeks ago, she had broached with her father the possibility of returning to work, he had gone bluish-white, and had to rest the remainder of the day. Hugh smiled at her sympathetically.

'Bad luck, old thing.'

She knew that she must speak. Touching his arm she said, 'Stop the car a moment, won't you, Hugh?'

He braked, and they came to a halt at the edge of the drove. Just then, Helen was filled with a rare confidence, a certainty that what she was about to commit herself to was utterly right. She climbed out of the car, and Hugh followed her, coming to stand at the edge of a ditch crowded with frozen reeds.

She said, 'I just wanted to tell you that it'll be all right about Daddy. It's not my marriage that he worries about, it's my leaving home.'

He looked confused, and she realized that she had not explained things very well.

'I mean – the rectory is so big. And you could drive to school, couldn't you? I wouldn't have to go away.'

She and Hugh could have the guest bedroom with its adjoining drawing-room. Helen's bedroom could eventually be the nursery. Perhaps Daddy would even enjoy the company of another man in the house.

Hugh whispered, 'Helen . . . ?', and she smiled and said, 'Yes. Dear Hugh.'

Then she looked up at his face. She knew instantly that she had got it all wrong. There was in his familiar beloved hazel eyes neither love, nor happiness, but pity. The ground seemed to fall away beneath her, and in that long, awful moment she simply wanted to cease being.

He said, 'Helen . . . Helen, I am very fond of you, but—'

'But you don't love me.' It took more courage than she had known she possessed to say that.

'Oh, I do.' His voice was very gentle. 'But not in that way.'

She stood there, looking out at the frozen marshes, and knew with dreadful certainty that this was a turning point in her life, and that she would never be the same again.

'I should love you, Helen. You are my dear friend, and you are sweet and kind and beautiful, and you will make some lucky man very happy. But not me. I am so sorry if I have given the impression that . . .'

His words trailed away, but not before they had twisted a knife into her. '*Why?*'

A silence. Then, 'Because I love someone else.' A brief phrase, almost lost on the wind, that destroyed the last tatters of her hope. She just stared at him, her question written in her eyes. But suddenly things fell into place, and she whispered:

'*Maia.*'

His head bowed. 'I've loved her for . . . oh, years. Since the first time I saw her. I know that it's hopeless.'

Just for a moment, she almost forgot her own misery and shame in witnessing his. Then, knowing that this was intolerable, and wanting at all costs to keep what remained of her dignity, she said, 'Take me home, won't you, Hugh?'

They hardly spoke during the remainder of the drive back to Thorpe Fen. When they reached the rectory he did not insult her by begging that they might still be friends, but waited while she took her bags from the car, and walked down the path to the house. Inside the house, she hung up her coat and hat with shaking hands. She heard Betty call from the kitchen, 'Luncheon's almost ready, Miss Helen!', but did not answer her. Instead she ran up flights of stairs, along corridors, through the dark cobwebby gloom of the loft until she was alone in the small bare attic room.

She did not cry. Curled up in a corner, her head on her knees, her fists against her face, she knew that the memory of her conversation with Hugh would taunt her for the rest of her life. That the shame would increase rather than diminish over the next days, weeks, months. Helen shivered, rocking herself, letting the back of her head strike repeatedly against the wall of the attic.

Francis had said to her, *You're on the list.* Robin kept away from him, knowing that those few words had reduced her to a brittle, fragile state. She had not realized that he was capable of such unkindness. In the painful aftermath of Vivien's wedding, she was forced to recognize that there were two sides to Francis: the side that was witty, intelligent and tender, and that she loved without reservation, and the other side, the dark side, that was both changeable and malicious. She realized that she too had changed. She, who had always believed that the central core of herself would remain inviolate, untouched by any man. Trying futilely to submerge her misery in work, Robin immersed herself in her book again. The completed manuscript must be sent to the publisher by the end of March.

Her entire day, the busyness that she enforced upon herself, was nothing but an attempt to avoid thinking about Francis. Without Francis, she had more time to read the newspaper and listen to the wireless. She read about events in Germany, and was forced to conclude that the unthinkable could happen again, that there could be another war in Europe. She wanted to do what most people did, to pretend it couldn't happen, but she made herself write letters, attend meetings, make speeches, aware all the time of a cold, numbing dread. Not many people listened to her; some heckled. She caught a cold and lost her voice, but persisted with dogged perseverance, hoarsely croaking out a message that few wanted to hear.

Her days broke down into messy chaos. She lurched from one small crisis to another. She left her notes on the bus, and spent a day calling at lost property offices. All the Lewis children caught measles; for three exhausting nights she helped Mrs Lewis nurse them. The Misses Turner's mother died: foreseen in a séance, the house was draped in black before the telegram arrived. Her landladies disappeared into the depths of Essex to arrange the funeral, leaving complicated instructions to Peggy, the maid of all work, about the budgerigars, and to Robin about the geyser, the geyser being thought beyond the competence of the maid.

She was wrestling with the geyser when there was a knock at the door. Peggy opened it, and Robin, hearing Francis's voice, began to cough again, and the flame that she had been nursing for the last ten minutes flickered and went out. The door opened, and he stood there, looking at her. The girl hovered beside him, her mouth half-open as she gazed at him, her nose running, her eyes stupid with adoration. Robin, when she had managed to stop coughing, said, 'You run home, Peggy. I'll sort this thing out.'

Peggy shuffled off.

'If you want me to go away,' said Francis, when they were alone, 'I will do.'

She shrugged, unable to trust herself to speak. Because the geyser wasn't working, and because the house was cold, Robin was wearing two thick jumpers, a scarf and boots. She knew that her nose was red and her eyes watery. She resented that he should appear when she was looking like this. It seemed to advertise her unhappiness.

'I came to say . . . oh, hell . . .' Francis grimaced. 'I came to say that I was sorry.'

She stared at him. '*Sorry?*' Her hands knotted together with fury.

'I know.' Without his usual props of cigarettes, drink and company, he seemed oddly defenceless. 'Feeble, isn't it? Words are so inadequate.'

Suddenly very tired, she sat down at the table, her head in her hands.

'I wanted to hurt someone,' he said. 'Only it was Vivien I should have hurt, not you.'

'All very Freudian, Francis.' Her voice was sarcastic, and she saw him wince.

'I behaved abominably, I know that. If it's any consolation, I don't much like myself either.'

She thought that he was telling the truth. His voice was flat, his movements economical. The layers of deception, the excuses, the glittering exterior had peeled away. He muttered, 'I just couldn't believe that she'd marry that swine. I still can't. I sent her some cash, so she wouldn't have to. He won't even make her happy.'

At that moment, she did not care a jot for Vivien's happiness. Robin said savagely, 'I won't be a part of it, Francis. Do you understand? I won't be *used*.'

He bowed his head. In the silence that followed a few tears gathered on the edges of her lids.

Then he said, 'The day before the wedding, I went to see Theo Harcourt. You know that he bought "Havoc". He told me that he was giving the editorship of the magazine to someone else – not to me. I haven't enough of a *name*, apparently.' Francis's voice was bitter.

Robin stared at him, appalled. She knew how much

'Havoc' had meant to Francis. Shivering, she said shakily, 'This wretched cold . . .'

'It's bloody freezing in here. How do you bear it?'

'Peggy had one of her turns and forgot to light the fires, and I've let the geyser go out. It's terribly temperamental. I need Joe, I suppose.' She realized that she hadn't seen Joe since before Vivien's wedding.

'I'll have a go.'

She noticed for the first time how well dressed Francis was: a suit, a clean shirt and tie, an overcoat. His fair, curling hair was short and tidy; the unhealthy pallor of the previous month had gone.

'You'll spoil your clothes.'

His eyes widened. Striking a match, he looked down at himself. 'I've a job, Robin. Gentleman secretary to a friend of Theo's who's broken his wrist.'

'But I thought . . . I thought you and Theo had fallen out.'

His expression was bleak. 'I need work, Robin. There's not much about these days. Especially for people like me. I can write a bit, act a bit, talk a lot. I've the right accent, but not quite the right background. Theo *knows* people, you see. That's what counts.'

She said nothing. He added, 'It's only for a couple of months, but I have to dress the part.' There was a mixture of pride and mockery in his voice. He held the match to the gas, and waited a few moments. 'I think that's caught.'

She scrubbed at her eyes with her sleeve. Francis said, turning back to her, 'I do need you, Robin. It wasn't true, what I said. You're not like the others, you're straight with me. Life doesn't seem so much of a mess when you're around. I adore you – you know that.'

He still had not said what she wanted to hear. She despised herself for needing it, those three little pennynovelettish words. Yet she guessed how much it had cost him to say as much as he had, to admit a need for anyone. And she knew that she must be equally honest in return.

'I'm not your mother, Francis. And I'm not your sister. And I'm not sure that I can go back to being just your friend again.' *I am in too deep*, she thought. Even now, hating him for his carelessness with her feelings, she was aware of his physical presence. It appalled her that she still wanted him. It humiliated her to know that when she thought of him dancing with another woman, she felt not only jealousy, but also desire.

He said, 'I wanted to tell you that I'm going to America for a couple of months. The chap I'm working for likes to winter in Florida. It should be rather jolly – ocean cruises and glorious beaches.'

When he looked up at her she could see the mingling of optimism and anxiety in his eyes. 'I got the job because of you, Robin. I wanted to show you that I could make something of myself. I know that you're worth a dozen of me, but I promise you that I'm going to change – I'm going to be different. When I get back, I'll come and see you again. You said once that you'd put up with me – do you remember? Think about it, please. I promise that I'll change. I promise that things'll be different. I'll never hurt you again. Please – can't we try again?'

Robin looked away, unable to speak. She heard Francis leave the room, and the front door close as he let himself out of the house.

For the first few nights, Joe slept on a friend's couch or floor, whichever was available. But his friends tended to be Francis's friends, and consequently asked too many awkward questions; and as his small supply of money dwindled, he knew that he was in danger of becoming what he most despised: a sponger. So for three shillings and sixpence a week, he found a room in a lodging house, a dreadful place with rickety fire escapes and shuffling, defeated inmates. His room, one of the cheapest in the house, was on the ground floor. At night, slugs slithered across the low ceilings, leaving a silvery trail on the cracked plaster. The chimney didn't draw properly, and besides, he had no money for coal.

To begin with, he tramped the streets with enthusiasm and some confidence, looking for work. The enthusiasm withered, along with the money in his pocket, as he suffered rejection after rejection. After the first few weeks, he knew that he looked poor and cold and hungry: he could see prospective employers sizing up his worn, dirty clothes, his boots that had begun to gape at the toes, concluding that he was a loser. He was inclined to agree with them. In the three weeks before Christmas he managed only a single day's work – selling enyclopedias to downtrodden housewives who neither wanted them nor could afford them. When he found himself agreeing with his prospective customers that the books were an overpriced waste of money, he realized that he was a hopeless salesman, and, dumping his samples in a rubbish bin, knocked on no more doors.

The hunger was the worst thing. He survived on bread and margarine and tea, which kept him alive, but that was all. He hoped he would get used to it, but he didn't. He thought about food constantly; when he slept, he dreamt about food. He would stand for minutes at a time outside bakeries, gazing at the piles of buns and cakes and pies, watching them as avidly as if he were watching a particularly good film at the cinema. The scents of roast beef or ham or steak and kidney puddings from restaurants and inns almost drove him insane.

He was also, he realized, terribly bored and terribly lonely. The boredom came as a surprise to him, it was not something he had previously experienced. People like Francis, who had bright but not tenacious minds, became bored, not people like Joe. But though he had taken his books from the Hackney basement, he was too distracted by hunger and cold to read. And though his room was full of things that didn't work properly, it seemed futile to repair them. He never slept well at night, but dozed frequently during the long, dull workless hours of daylight. He missed the company of other people, but knew, looking at himself, that he was not fit for company. He was out of the habit of proper conversation, and his clothes were grubby. He could not recall when he had last had a bath. The lodging house had no running water; he could have borrowed the unpleasantly communal tin bath and filled it with water from the tap in the yard, but it all seemed too much trouble. When he thought of Robin, which he often did, it seemed to Joe that she lived in another world, a world in which he was no longer permitted. He wanted to visit her, but he knew that to do so would only cause him pain.

One day the shops were shut, and there was a peculiar sort of stillness in the streets. He couldn't make it out at first, but then he realized that it was Christmas Day. He walked for miles into one of the better parts of London, and he watched the people coming out of the churches after morning service. A lady came up to him and pressed something into his hand, and when he looked down, he saw that she had given him a sixpence. He stared at the coin, torn between laughter and fury. He found himself imagining Francis's amusement as he recounted to him the incident, and then he remembered that his long friendship with Francis was over, finished quite deliberately by him with one muttered phrase. He went home and spent the rest of the day in bed, unable even to spend his sixpence because the shops were shut. In the late evening, seized by a terrible hunger, he ate everything in his cupboard that was edible. Then, because his hands had gone white with cold, he smashed both the spindly chair and the table, threw the pieces into the fireplace, lit them, and felt warm for the first time in a month.

He left the lodging house a few days later, creeping out when the landlord wasn't looking. He no longer had the three and sixpence for the rent. He slept for a couple of nights on park benches, but the temperature plummeted, and he realized that he would not survive a week of that. So he went to the doss-house, where you could get a bed of sorts for eightpence. The night he spent in the doss-house was, he thought, the worst of his entire life. It was dry and, because of the number of men in the dormitory, reasonably warm, but the terrible aggression and futility and hopelessness of the lives of those with him filled him with despair. A fight broke out over the ownership of a snaggle-toothed comb: horrified, Joe watched them, two men whose age he could not even attempt to guess, balding, their muscles wasted by years and hardship, wrestling on the dirty lino floor. At night, in the darkness, he woke after haunted sleep to feel a hand caressing his body. He smelt hot, foul breath, and he moved so fast and swore so loud that most of the other men in the dormitory woke. His would-be seducer slunk back to his bed. Joe never saw his face.

The following day, he stole a pie from a stall in a market-place. Eating it, he caught sight of his reflection in a shop window. Snarled hair, white face, ragged clothes.

He knew then that he had no alternative. Almost eight years ago he had defied his father and left home, intending to make a new life for himself. He had failed; he had made nothing of himself. He did not know whether his father would welcome him, the prodigal son, but he did recognize the intense shame he felt at that reflection in the glass. Joe slung his rucksack onto his back and headed for the Great North Road.

Over the Christmas season, Maia was deluged with invitations to parties and dinners. She had become, at the age of twenty-three, one of Cambridge's jeunesse dorée. One's soirée, one's cocktail party, was only considered a success if Maia Merchant attended. She had succeeded in making her disadvantages – her widowhood, her career – into a source of fascination. Sometimes she even appeared without an escort, creating an excited ripple of disapproval and admiration.

On New Year's Eve she was invited to a party at Brackonbury House, which lay north of Cambridge, not far from Thorpe Fen, where Helen lived. Driving

261

through the moonlit Fens, Maia realized that she hadn't seen Helen for ages. She had written to her once a week, as she always did, but had received only brief, uninformative replies. On Boxing Day, when she and Robin and Helen usually gathered in Robin's winter house, Helen had been absent, confined to her bed by a cold. Maia, looking out of the car window at the black, featureless landscape, felt a faint flicker of guilt. She must visit Helen soon. Not this coming weekend, because it was the first weekend of the month, and therefore her weekend away, and not the weekend after because it was the first day of the January sales. But soon.

It was a fancy-dress party. Maia was dressed as Columbine, in a wide striped skirt and black bodice, with flowers in her hair. The lights of Brackonbury House, built on one of the many small, land-locked islands that pocked the Fens, shone over the fields and marshes like the lights of a ship in a calm, dark sea. Maia had accepted this invitation rather than any of the others because Brackonbury House was owned by Lord and Lady Frere, who were landed gentry. It delighted Maia to think that she, whose silk stockings had once been made almost entirely of darns, would tonight be dining with landed gentry.

Inside, she rid herself of her escort, a genial but dull man, and proceeded to enjoy herself. Within half an hour of arriving, her dance card was complete, and she moved everywhere surrounded by an adoring circle of admirers. The most attractive, the most witty, the most wealthy men all at some time that evening spoke to Maia. She danced the tango with a ridiculously handsome man dressed as a pirate, and was proposed to by a teddy bear with a scarlet bow around his neck. Lord Frere's nineteen-year-old son, Wilfred, pursued her with the sort of slavish worship she was accustomed to receiving from her pet spaniel.

At dinner, she sat between a captain of the Guards dressed as Harlequin, and an Honourable got up as a Charlie Chaplin tramp. There were endless supplies of champagne, and Maia's glass was always full. A brawl broke out between a few of the young men, and ended with half a dozen dunked in the icy fountain in the courtyard. The main lights in the ballroom were extinguished, so that the large room was lit only by the wall-sconces. The dim lighting shadowed the dancers' faces, and exaggerated their garish make-up. Maia felt a tremendous surge of triumph when Lord Frere himself asked her to dance, but when they paused at the end of the tango and his fingers traced the entire length of her spine, she quickly made her excuses, and ran for the powder-room. Climbing the stairs, she stepped carefully around a young woman slumped against the banister, sobbing. She had to drink two glasses of champagne rather quickly in order to find courage enough to return to the ballroom, but by then it was midnight, and they all hugged and kissed and sang Auld Lang Syne. Her mind was sufficiently numb with alcohol to accept with enthusiasm the embraces of her admirers. Suddenly she felt elated and strong. She was an independent woman with money in the bank, a large house, and a wardrobe full of beautiful clothes. Her business was surviving the worst recession this century. She had successfully gained readmission to society.

Then a voice from behind her said politely, 'Mrs Merchant?', and she turned round to see a uniformed maid.

'There's a gentleman to see you, Mrs Merchant.'

She followed the maid out of the ballroom, and into the drawing-room. Liam Kavanagh stood beside the window. Her immediate pleasure at seeing him was cancelled by the grimness of his expression. She was suddenly afraid: thoughts of a fire, or theft, flashed through her mind.

'Liam? What is it?'

He shut the door so that they were in private. Then he drew a newspaper out of his overcoat pocket.

'I thought I should show you this before anyone else

does.' He held the newspaper out to her, its front page uppermost.

It was a copy of the *Cambridge Daily News*. The headline screamed at her, 'Sacked Man Drowns Himself.'

She took the paper from him, and began to read. Edmund Pamphilon . . . dismissed from the post at Merchants department store that he had held for the past twenty years . . . his chronically sick wife . . . an accumulation of expensive doctor's bills . . . There was a photograph of Mr Pamphilon, smiling his eternal, benevolent smile, and a photograph of the section of the Cam in which his body had been found. The water looked very black, very cold.

'But they don't know . . .' she whispered, staring at Liam. 'Suicide . . . they can't know . . . how could they ever be sure?'

She managed to stop herself. He said, and she thought she saw a trace of sympathy in his eyes, 'They don't know, of course. The reporter's jumped the gun rather – the body was only found today. But I've made some enquiries – telephoned a few people – and there doesn't seem to be much doubt.'

I couldn't have known, she started to say, but the recollection of her own words echoed in her ears, silencing her.

Mr Pamphilon's personal affairs are no business of mine, Liam.

She left without saying goodbye to her hosts. As she waited for the maid to collect her coat she saw how tawdry and ridiculous the fancy-dress costumes were. The pirate was pot-bellied, and the clown's make-up had begun to smear. The house was huge and ancient, but there were square shadows on the walls where paintings had been sold to pay taxes.

On the long drive home, Maia managed almost to silence the clamorous voices. The phrase *three of them now* did not rebound like a drumbeat in her skull. She had instructed the two servants who lived in not to wait up for her. Tossing her fur coat onto the sofa, she poured herself a large drink and ran herself a bath, immersing herself in the scented water. Columbine's crushed rags lay in a crumpled heap on the tiles. Afterwards, she dried herself and put on her nightgown, and went to bed.

She fell asleep easily, but in the early hours of the morning the nightmares came. A great weight pressed on her chest, and she tried to scream. There were eyes staring at her: small, tawny, foxy eyes. Vernon's eyes. Even when she at last managed to drag herself awake, Maia could still see those eyes. Familiar, reproachful, edged with a white rime as though in the years since his death he had been frozen in frost.

It took Joe two days to hitchhike to North Yorkshire. He had to walk the last eight miles from the main road to Hawksden. It was dark and he had no torch, but the sky was clear and cold and a full moon lit the narrow, winding, unsurfaced road. He heard the church clock chime midnight as he entered the village.

He knew, as he wrestled with the icy iron clasp of the gates, that he could not have gone on much longer. He could not remember when he had last eaten a proper meal or slept soundly at night. Everything seemed slightly unreal. The steep cobbled streets of Hawksden itself, glazed with such theatrical moonlight; the vast black mill; the great looming backdrop of the hills all seemed to shift subtly in and out of reality. He realized that he had dozed, standing at the gate of his home, his fingers still gripping the latch. He did not know how long he had slept – a few minutes, presumably, but he could not be sure. He began to walk up the path, his frozen hands dug deep into his jacket pockets, his collar pulled up round his neck. He was shivering violently, but whether that was because of the cold or because he was apprehensive, he did not wish to consider. He climbed the front steps, leaned against the door jamb, and pulled the bell-rope.

He drifted off to sleep again, standing at the door, his head cushioned on the cold stone. When, with a clattering of chains and bolts and latches, the door was opened, it almost took him by surprise. There was a great flood of light, and the housekeeper stood there, a shawl wrapped around her voluminous nightgown. He watched the expression in her eyes alter as she focused on him. From irritation at having been woken, to disgust at the sight of him, and then, slowly, as she recognized him, to amazement. Her outraged *Be off with you* froze on her lips, and she whispered uncertainly, 'Master Joe . . . ?'

He nodded. He said, 'I've woken you up, haven't I, Annie?', yet though she stepped back, allowing him into the house, he could not just then move. His limbs would not obey him. He said uncertainly, 'So bloody cold . . .', and he heard her automatically tut at the profanity.

Then another voice said, 'Well, come in, why don't tha, lad, and shut that ruddy door,' and he looked up and saw his father.

Somehow, he managed to shuffle inside. The light in the hall – electric lights, John Elliot's pride and joy – almost blinded him, so that he could not quite read the expression on his father's face. A mixture of shock and disapproval . . . and something else, quickly hidden.

'Ran out of brass then, did tha, son?'

John Elliot's tone was a familiar mixture of sarcasm and triumph. Joe discovered that he hadn't the strength to defend himself. Or the will. He moved past his father and the housekeeper and sat at the foot of the stairs, his head in his hands. He had not realized how it would overwhelm him: the memory of his mother. How he would still expect her to walk down these stairs and take him in her arms and kiss him. How he would recall her perfume, her gentleness, her softly accented voice.

His father was staring at him. Joe, looking up at last, saw how much John Elliot had aged. His father had always been short, stout, heavy-boned, Joe's opposite, but now there were threads of white in the fair hair, and

266

deep lines furrowed his rough-hewn face. He had become an old man. Joe heard him whisper, 'Dear God, the state you are in . . .' and then say to the housekeeper, 'Heat up some soup, woman. Don't stand there like Patience on a monument.'

Joe ate in the kitchen. He was surprised at how little he could swallow. Half a bowl, and he began to feel nauseated, bloated. Silently, his father placed a tumblerful of whisky in front of him.

'Drink that, lad, and then tha'd best go t'bed. Tha could do with a bath, by the look of thee, but that'd best wait till tomorrow.'

His father walked with him up the stairs. Once or twice it seemed to Joe that he almost offered his arm – for support, or for something else. But they did not touch, and Joe, falling on the bed fully dressed and drifting off almost immediately into a deep and dreamless sleep, thought that he must have been mistaken.

When he woke the next morning, someone – Annie, he guessed – had pulled off his boots and his jacket and tucked a blanket and thick quilt around him. He lay there for a few moments, still disorientated, dazed with sleep and tiredness. He had no idea what time it was, but the sun streamed brightly though the window. The room was familiar, yet unfamiliar: all his things – his books, his sheet music, the battered model trains of his childhood – were still here, yet he could not quite believe that they had ever belonged to him.

He dragged himself out of bed and down the corridor to the bathroom. He ran a deep, boiling bath, and began to peel off his filthy clothes. His feet were a mass of blisters and sores. There were scarlet patches on his torso that he suspected were flea bites. He sank into the water, immersing his head completely, letting the heat seep into his bones.

He dressed in a mixture of his own old clothes and Johnnie's. He could find no boots or shoes that fit him, but his feet hurt too much for shoes anyway. Tutting again, Annie applied disinfectant and lint. One of the maids cooked him an enormous breakfast of bacon and sausages and black pudding and eggs. After he had eaten, he limped around the house for a while. Nothing much had changed. Elliot Hall had always been unnecessarily big and unnecessarily ugly, and full of hideous, useless things like cocktail cabinets and epergnes. He tried to read the newspapers but, suddenly tired, fell asleep again. He was woken by the smell of crumpets and cake. The maid – a new girl whom he did not recognize – placed a pot of tea beside the plates and left the room. Joe ate ravenously.

Later he played the small grand piano that had once belonged to his mother. He was out of practice, his hands clumsy, often fumbling for notes, but he persevered, surprised at how much he remembered. He was halfway through a Chopin nocturne, a favourite of his mother's, when he realized that he was no longer alone. His hands paused, frozen over the notes, and he looked round and saw his father.

John Elliot said, 'Aye – tha always had the knack of that sort of thing.' He managed, thought Joe, to make playing the piano sound like one of the seamier vices.

Standing up, he closed the lid of the piano. 'You're back early, father.'

'Aye, well . . . business is poor. Very poor. We're only working the one shift.'

The news took Joe by surprise. Foolish of him, he realized, to imagine that Elliot's Mill would be immune to the effects of the Depression. Looking up, he saw that John Elliot was staring at him, his gaze coming to rest on his son's bare, bandaged feet. 'At least I manage to keep myself in shoe leather,' he muttered. 'I need a smoke. Tha'll come to the parlour, Joe. She never liked tobacco in here.'

They left the small, pretty drawing-room, and went to the parlour. The room was vast, pillared, masculine, utterly unsuited to the small, cottagey description of 'parlour'. The name was a leftover, Joe assumed, from his father's younger, poorer days.

John Elliot lit his pipe, a huge, wheezing affair. When it was belching out blue clouds, he said, 'There's a cigar, lad. Or I've t'other pipe.'

'Have you any cigarettes?'

The expression of disapproval returned. 'Silly little things. Never liked them meself. A lassie's smoke . . . still, there's no accounting for taste. I'll send the boy out for some.'

Joe muttered furiously, 'I haven't the cash, Dad . . .' and his father, eyeing him again, said:

'Aye, I thought not. But I settle up with Thwaites at end of t'month, if tha remember. And I reckon I can stand thee a packet of cigarettes. Now, pour us a drink, Joe, and stop fidgeting.'

They drank Scotch and smoked together in a silence that would, in another family, have been companionable. For Joe, though, it was merely tense with all that remained unsaid. It was later, over Yorkshire pudding followed by roast beef and horseradish sauce, that the inevitable questions came.

'So what've tha been doing with thaself, then, lad? Nigh on eight years, i'n't it, since we've seen hide nor hair of thee?'

Joe shut out the recollection of the furious argument that had provoked his leaving Hawksden. It wasn't much easier, though, to think of London. When he thought of London, he thought of Robin. Robin, who needed only Francis, and who did not need him.

'I helped run a printing press – just a small one, Dad. We printed pamphlets and flyers, that sort of thing.'

John Elliot snorted. 'Communist claptrap, by the look of what tha sent home. Much brass in it, was there?'

He shook his head. 'Not really. I worked at a pub, as well, to keep going.'

'A son of mine, pulling pints . . . and after all that education . . .'

He couldn't defend himself. Years of independence, and he had ended up sleeping in a doss-house, without money enough to buy his own cigarettes.

'That fancy school were a waste of money . . . Johnnie would ha' made summat of himself, but you, Joe . . . it just taught you to talk proper and to think you were better than the rest of us . . .'

His father's voice had sunk to a low mutter. Joe had to bite back his anger.

'I never thought I was better than you, Dad.'

'Didn't you?' John Elliot's eyes, a faded blue-grey, met Joe's. 'I thought the place might knock some sense into you. Your mother didn't want to send you there. Mebbe she were right.'

His parents had never argued; but they had managed to live, within the same house, almost entirely separate lives. Separate bedrooms, separate drawing-rooms, different interests and different acquaintances. John Elliot had had the mill, Thérèse had lived for music and letters and her only child.

'And what now, then, Joe? Now that you're back?'

It took an enormous effort to swallow his pride. But he managed it, and said, 'I made a mess of things in London. Have you any use for me here?'

His father had risen from the table. His back to Joe, he stared into the fireplace.

'Aye . . . well . . . about bloody time. You've fooled about for long enough. You'll have to get yourself a haircut, though, and some decent clothes. And put some weight on your ribs. I won't have a son of mine looking like a half-starved tramp.'

In the New Year the fogs returned, dousing London with a yellowish-grey gloom. The fog made Robin's cough worse, and reflected her state of mind. She felt that she had become befouled in a fog of her own making: her work, her interests, her friends and, most disastrously of all, her love life, were all chaotic and difficult. Although she had compiled most of the information for her book, the last few chapters were unexpectedly difficult to write. Her room was littered with heaps of paper, box-files, books and scribbled notes. The younger Miss

Turner rearranged some of the piles during her Thursday dusting; Robin, returning to her room after a morning in the library, found herself shouting at her. It will take me *weeks* to get it right again, she cried, staring horrified at the disarranged papers. When Miss Turner, almost in tears, backed out of the room, shame overtook Robin, and she wanted to sit on the bed and howl too. But instead she ran down to the drawing-room and blurted out her apologies, pecking Miss Emmeline on the cheek whilst the elder Miss Turner and the budgerigars looked on disapprovingly. Upstairs, her head aching and her throat hurting, she started to organize things again. The trouble was, she concluded as she clipped papers back into files and leafed through notebooks, that she had never been an organized person. She needed someone like Joe to look at all this and tell her how to sort it out. But she hadn't seen Joe for simply ages. She did not know where he was. Knowing that Francis was in America, she had walked round to the basement flat several times, and knocked at the door. But the window had been unlit, and there had been no reply.

She missed Joe, she missed Francis. She missed the sort of life they had led when she had first arrived in London, when things had been fun. Things didn't seem to be fun any more. She didn't know what to do about Francis. No-one else had the same capacity to transform her life, and no-one else had the same capacity to hurt her. Though he had made it clear that he wanted to see her again, a part of her wanted to withdraw, to avoid the pain that she feared he might still give her.

Her work had become a formless monster, tripping her up, confusing her. When Dr Mackenzie asked how it was going she snapped at him. When he suggested that she was tired and that she take a few days off, she stormed out of his office. Furious with him, fearful of condescension, she avoided him, appearing only intermittently at the clinic. Though she still attended Labour Party meetings, she always half expected Francis and Joe to appear, sliding noisily and cheerfully into the seats beside her. She continued to act as secretary to the No More War group but knew that her speeches were uninspired and pessimistic. The news from Germany alarmed her; she could hardly bear to read the newspapers.

Returning from Mrs Lewis's, Robin missed the bus and, unable to face the Underground at rush hour, began to walk home. The drizzle started as she reached Hackney, a fine, misty haze that seeped through her clothes, chilling her. It was dark, and she lost her way, but eventually she found herself in Duckett Street, outside the Navigator. When she went inside, the familiar chorus of jeers and whistles from the men who entirely populated the public room greeted her. Ignoring them, she pushed through the crowds.

She looked the length of the bar, but could not see Joe. A barmaid approached her. Robin said quickly, 'I was looking for Joe Elliot. He works here.'

The woman shrugged. 'Stanley—' she yelled to a large man on the far side of the bar '—does someone called Elliot work here?'

'Used to,' said the man. 'Not any more.'

Robin felt confused. 'Joe's left?'

'Gave 'im the sack.'

She stared at him. 'When? *Why?*'

'Six weeks or so back. For fighting.'

'Fighting? *Joe?*'

'That's right, ducks. Laid into some pal of his – had to pull them apart meself. Can't have my staff brawling in my own pub.'

She thought of the empty, silent flat. She said hesitantly, 'This friend . . . was he fair-haired . . . much the same age as Joe . . . ?' and she saw the landlord nod.

Outside in the street, it was still raining. She felt suddenly terribly tired and rather hopeless. She began to walk the remaining mile to her lodgings, trying to make sense of what the landlord had told her.

Back at the Misses Turner's, there were letters for her from her parents, from Maia and from Helen. She read them all, but nothing much seemed to sink in. She ate what she could face of her tea, and then went back to her room. Huddled over her desk, Robin began to make notes for the conclusion of the book, but she could not concentrate, her mind seemed paralysed, and as her pencil stumbled on the paper, she began to cough.

If they did not at first quarrel, then that was only because Joe bit his tongue in an effort to remain silent. There was, as there always had been, an acre of difference between himself and his father. Everything that Joe held most dear – music, books, socialism – his father despised. John Elliot criticized the way he dressed, the way he spoke, the way he spent his time. They had not one thing in common. If Joe no longer retreated to the adolescent sullenness of his earlier years, then that was only because he was older and wiser, and because he had begun to respect his father's unlimited capacity for hard work.

He had accepted that in returning to Yorkshire he must also return to the role he had earlier rejected. He was his father's sole heir: after John Elliot's death he would inherit the mill, the house, and much of the village as well. Joe toured the mill and saw again the ranks of great, thundering looms; working in the office, helping with the paperwork, he was aware of the unending effort that went into keeping Elliot's Mill afloat in the middle of a depression.

His father owned most of the rows of terraced houses that made up Hawksden. He had built the school; his patronage kept the three small shops going. Village men raised their caps to the Elliots; village girls bobbed curtseys. John Elliot saw himself as a sort of benevolent squire, but Joe saw it all rather differently. He was aware that the tiny back-to-back houses had neither electricity nor running water, that the children of the mill workers played barefoot on the cobbles, and that patronage was a poor substitute for independence.

He saw, and pitied, his father's constant struggle between the roots that would keep claiming him, and the aristocratic way of life that he aped. The voice that would keep sliding back into broadest Yorkshire, the constant veering between the 'you' of BBC announcers and royalty, and the 'thee' of his childhood. In sending Joe to public school, John Elliot had made his own son into the sort of man he both envied and despised.

Their quarrels were now only a faded and feeble echo of their old conflicts. It was as though neither of them had the heart any more. At every meal they bickered or ate in silence; they did not seem capable of anything else. Other families managed to talk to each other, but not the Elliots. In one of their clumsy, fragmented conversations, Joe discovered that his Aunt Claire, his mother's sister, had written to Hawksden years ago, asking for Joe's address. *Told her I hadn't a bloody idea as you hadn't seen fit to tell me*, said John Elliot scathingly, as he stuffed tobacco into his pipe. The letter, with any clue it had once held to Claire's whereabouts, was long since lost.

The silences brought back vividly to Joe the similar silences of his childhood: the huge, ugly, empty house; the dinners punctuated by his father's dull and lengthy descriptions of little events at the mill; his mother's polite, indifferent response. Then, he had pitied his mother's boredom; now, himself loving without return, he recalled his father's blundering attempts at conversation, and winced.

A fortnight passed. He tried not to think of Robin, but he did, all the time. He had not contacted her for almost two months. He could not telephone her, there was no telephone in her lodging house. He could have written to her, but was uncertain what to say. Playing the piano in his mother's room, he remembered clearly the aridity of his parents' marriage, and wondered whether that sort of hopelessness could be transmitted from generation to generation, like blue eyes, or a hunchback. Ploughing through one of Beethoven's more turbulent sonatas, he tried to distract himself. His father's voice broke into his thoughts.

'Have tha cloth ears, lad? T'dinner gong went near ten minutes ago.'

Joe raised his hands from the keys. His father looked at the piano disparagingly.

'Bloody waste of time, that thing.'

'It made her happy.' Joe, swinging round on the piano stool, was surprised at the vehemence in his voice.

'I meant, for a lad. It's different for a lassie. Besides, Thérèse were always happy. She had everything she wanted.'

'Oh, for pity's sake . . .' Rising, Joe shut the lid of the instrument so hard that the strings shivered and sang. Then he went to the window. 'Look at it, Dad. Just look at it.'

It was a grey, gloomy January day. All the buildings in the village were blackened by years of coal fires, all the paths and cobbles and stunted trees sheened by the satiny gleam of rain.

'There isn't another house even half the size of this one, is there? Who did she talk to? Where did she go? She was brought up in *Paris*, for heaven's sake. You've been there, haven't you?'

There was a silence. 'Once,' said John Elliot, eventually.

Joe wondered, for the hundredth time, how such an unlikely coupling had ever come about. Why his mother had chosen to exile herself in cold loneliness, cut off from her family and from the country she had loved.

'I gave her this house, and a pony and trap of her own, and all the dresses and fancy jewellery she wanted.'

Joe heard the short, angry exhalation of his own breath. Then he said, 'She died here. She withered and died, and I saw it.'

At once, he wished he could take the words back. But then the glimpse of pain in his father's eyes was overlaid by bitterness as John Elliot said, 'And you think that you're the same, don't you, Joe? What I can give you isn't good enough for you.'

'It isn't that,' he said wearily. 'It's just that I don't fit. Don't you see?'

There was a long silence. Then his father said, 'And the mill?' and Joe shrugged, searching for words.

His conviction that he must make something of himself before he could slip into the shoes that his father had made for him, would, he knew, be met with scornful incomprehension. And his reluctance to cut himself off completely from Robin by remaining in his birthplace made him despise himself.

'I'm not ready for it yet, Dad. Just . . . not yet.'

His father, staring at him, said eventually, 'Well, *I* don't believe in wasting a good dinner,' and went to the door. In the doorway, he stopped, and turned back to Joe.

'I suppose you'll be gone again, then?'

He could hardly bear to meet his father's eyes. Such a mingling of contempt and bewilderment and grief. Joe said gently, 'Just for a while. I'll be back, Dad. And I'll write.' He began to rise from the seat, to add, *I'm sorry*, but John Elliot had already turned his back, was already leaving the room. He heard his father's retreating footsteps. Joe stood quite still, his fists clenched, his mouth drawn in a narrow line. Then he went back to his room and began to pack.

He found his photographs, stark shots of moorland and crag and stream, tied with a ribbon, neatly filed in his mother's writing-desk. And his mother's address book: flicking through the pages he glimpsed the names of long-forgotten French cousins. He studied the photographs on the mantelpiece – his mother, sepia-shaded and parasoled; Johnnie, ebullient and moustached, his medals prominent on his army uniform; a baby, himself presumably, glowering in a pram. Tucking the photograph of his mother into his jacket pocket, he looked round the room for the last time, and knew why here his memories of his mother were so startlingly clear. This room was unchanged, unaltered by the years since her death. It waited, breathless, for the door

276

to open and Thérèse Elliot to return: to play her piano, to write her letters, to breathe in the scent of the hothouse flowers on the side table. Joe, with a sudden shiver, realized that his father had made a shrine to her. Such love, he thought: such unrewarded, humiliated love.

Joe picked up his rucksack and slung on his greatcoat. Speaking first to the housekeeper and then to the overseer at the mill, he discovered that his father had left for Bradford half an hour earlier. Joe, seized by a mixture of exasperation and pity and regret, began to walk away from the village. He did not stop talking until he was two miles out of Hawksden, and the hills hid the high thin silhouette of the mill chimney. Then he leaned against the dry stone wall, and searched in his pocket for his cigarettes. The packet was half-full, and there was something tucked between the cigarettes and the silver lining paper. Joe unfolded three new twenty pound notes. He stared at them for a moment before putting them in his inside pocket, lighting his cigarette, and starting to walk again.

Robin couldn't sleep at night because of her cough. Miss Emmeline made her hot lemon and honey, but it didn't seem to do any good. The elder Miss Turner fell ill, and was taken to hospital with pleurisy. Two of the budgerigars died, Peggy had a bad turn, and Miss Emmeline's fiancé, who had been killed in the War, appeared at a séance. The small lodging house slipped into chaos and confusion.

The book just wouldn't come right. Robin kept pulling it apart and trying to put it together again, but things seemed to get worse and worse. She worked until midnight, her head aching, overcome with feverish anxiety. There was an epidemic of scarlet fever in the East End: Neil Mackenzie was far too busy for Robin to bother him with either her health or with her worries about her work. When she turned up to help at the clinic, the sister sent her away, scolding her for coughing over the mothers and babies.

She had letters from Helen and Maia and Richard and Daisy, all complaining of her not writing, and a postcard from Francis, in America. Standing in the hallway, Robin looked at the picture of blue skies and white beaches. She touched with her fingernail the cresting wave that touched the sand, the gleaming sun in the cloudless sky, and could hardly believe that such places existed. She put the postcard into her pocket; she already knew the words written on it by heart. *Home March. Missing you dreadfully. All love, Francis.* Opening the front door, she stepped out onto the pavement. The rain streamed down in thick cold bands and, though it was the early afternoon, the street-lamps were already lit. Her hat pulled down, her collar up, Robin walked to the library.

In the library, she read about childhood disease and maternal nutrition, and understood not a word of it. Though she could see from the window that the rain was chilling to sleet, and though most of the other readers wore coats and hats, she felt uncomfortably hot. Peeling off her coat and scarf and gloves, bundling her hat into a ball and shoving it in her bag, her face burned and her palms were damp with sweat. She made notes, but when she read them back to herself they did not make much sense. Her head ached unbearably, so she left the library briefly for a cup of tea in the next door café. It didn't make her feel any better; she went back to her desk, gathered up her things, and returned home.

Her lodgings were empty. There was a note on the hall table from Miss Emmeline, explaining that she was visiting her sister in hospital and that she had left a stew on the stove for Robin's supper. The smell of the cooked meat made Robin feel sick; she walked slowly up to her room and lay, fully dressed, on the bed.

She knew that she was ill, but could not think what to do about it. She wanted Francis, she wanted her friends. She wanted her mother. She kicked off her shoes and curled up on the bed, pulling the covers over her, and took the postcard from her pocket and stared at it, at the sapphire-blue waves, at the fine, pale sand. When she closed her eyes and fell asleep, she was lying on that beach, and dreadful creatures were emerging from the water, slithering silently up the strand towards her. She awoke, hot and startled, and then suddenly cold again. The room looked dark and unfamiliar. Helen was with her, and they were walking through a huge, empty house. There was a sense of menace about the house – the long, ill-lit corridors, the curtained windows and closed doors only half hid the threat of something hiding, waiting. Helen was wearing her white dress, white gloves and straw hat, and white button shoes. They reached a staircase: at the top of the staircase Robin could see Maia and Vernon. They were talking, quarrelling. Helen seemed to have gone, and Robin felt very alone as she watched Maia slowly turn and push Vernon, so that he tumbled head over heels down the stairs. She had not thought Maia capable of such strength, such anger. Vernon lay at the foot of the stairs, but when Robin looked again, she saw that she had been mistaken, that it was not Vernon who lay there, motionless, but Hugh. She began to scream, but then the whole house started to tremble, so that she was shaking, shaking . . .

When she opened her eyes and recognized Joe, she wanted almost to weep with relief. But instead she began to cough, unable to catch her breath even to speak to him. He helped her sit up.

'Have you seen a doctor?'

She shook her head.

'Why the hell not?' He sounded angry.

'Didn't want to bother him.' She was so glad to see him – competent, efficient Joe would sort out the mess that she had got into. 'Where have you been, Joe?'

'Home . . . Yorkshire, I mean. I got back this after-noon. I knocked, but there was no reply. I saw your coat in the hall, so I went round the back. That doctor chap you work for – where does he live?'

When she had given him Dr Mackenzie's address, she closed her eyes again, and dozed. She lost track of time, but heard, interrupting her sleep, Miss Emmeline's return to the house and, later, Dr Mackenzie's motor-car drawing up outside. When he appeared at her bedside, she expected to be told off, but instead Dr Mackenzie was kind and gentle and diagnosed bronchitis, and prescribed medicines and a long rest. 'I want to speak to Joe,' she croaked, knowing suddenly what she must do.

She heard Joe running up the stairs two at a time. Reaching out, she took his hand and whispered, 'Take me home, Joe, won't you? Please take me home. *Now*.'

He stole a flashy little sports car from one of Francis's rich friends, hotwiring it in the moonlight, pinning a ten pound note to a piece of paper on which he had scribbled a few words, and shoving it through the letter box. They left for Cambridgeshire just after midnight.

He wrapped her in blankets, and dosed her with tea and aspirins. The sleet turned to snow as they travelled north. There was a map in the glove compartment of the car: balancing it on the dashboard, Joe drove up through Essex and into East Anglia and then out into the icy fastness of the Fens. He could not believe the silence of the place, the absence of hills, the empty landscape of sky and horizon. It was dawn when he drove beyond Cambridge, yet the coming of day was only a low, heavy, gleaming light. Snow blurred the skyline, and darkened the sun.

Robin slept through most of the journey. Joe glanced at her every few minutes, checking her colour and breathing. Eventually he saw that her eyes were open.

'Look, Joe,' she croaked. 'There it is. There's Blackmere Farm.'

He struggled to make anything out of the swirling whiteness. Then he saw the foursquare little building, the stunted trees and level meadows threaded with ditches marking its boundaries. Frost glittered on the roofline, both house and countryside were enchanted, shimmering white and silver. Joe slowed the car, parked in front of the house, and climbed out.

After he had pounded on the door for a few minutes, it opened. He could have picked Robin's father from out of a crowd. He had his daughter's dark brown eyes, the same carefully sculpted cheekbones and high forehead.

'I'm a friend of Robin's. She's not well. I've brought her home.'

He carried Robin into the house. When her mother and brother appeared, he knew that it was going to be all right. Mrs Summerhayes was small and blonde and efficient. No-one made a fuss, they just quietly and calmly did all the right things. The brother – *Hugh*, thought Joe, with an effort of memory – came to stand beside Joe, and said, 'Come and sit by the fire, old chap. You must be dead beat.'

He was taken to a drawing-room filled with books and plants and richly coloured Indian rugs. The piano in the corner of the room was heaped with music. A large fire burned in the grate. The room was beautiful, colourful and friendly. Hugh disappeared into the kitchen to make tea and toast, but Joe, who had not slept for the two nights since he had left Hawksden, fell asleep in the armchair before he returned.

Waking, stiff and disorientated, Joe searched round the lower storey of the house until he found Robin's father in his study.

'Aha. You're awake.' Robin's father smiled and held out his hand. 'I'm afraid that introductions were over-looked. I'm Richard Summerhayes.'

'Joe Elliot.' They shook hands. Joe said, 'Is Robin . . . ?'

'She's asleep just now. Daisy is sitting with her, and Hugh has driven to Burwell to fetch Dr Lemon.' He glanced at Joe. 'I don't know how to thank you. We were worried about her at Christmas, Daisy and I – she seemed so tired and upset. And she didn't write after she returned to London. Hugh wanted to drive down to see her, but Daisy and I both felt . . . well, if you are a friend of Robin's, you will know how jealously she guards her independence.'

Joe couldn't help grinning. 'Like a wildcat.'

'Exactly.' Richard Summerhayes's expression altered. 'Yet we were wrong. Sometimes one should interfere.'

There was a small silence. Then Richard Summerhayes said, 'How remiss of me. You must be hungry, Joe. Come to the kitchen, and let's see what I can find you to eat.'

The kitchen-maid, a vague, disorganized creature, managed to cook a plate of bacon and eggs and make a pot of tea. Joe, suddenly ravenously hungry, ate at the huge kitchen table. While he ate, Richard Summerhayes talked. Though it felt nothing like an interrogation, by the time he had finished eating it seemed that there wasn't much about the first twenty-five years of Joe's life that Richard didn't know. Joe, who was not accustomed to making easy confidences, even found himself telling Richard about the doss-house.

'I had *fleas*. You can't imagine the self-disgust. You just want to burn all your clothes and bathe in disinfectant.' Joe ran a hand over his unshaven chin. 'I do apologize. I must look a mess . . .'

'Don't apologize.' Richard's hand touched Joe's shoulder. 'Daisy and I have been raising money for a men's hostel in Cambridge. The sights we have seen . . . young men, like yourself, without money or hope.' There was genuine feeling in Richard's voice. 'At least you have family, Joe.'

Joe rose from the table. 'Thank you for the breakfast. I should go . . .'

'Go?' Richard looked surprised. 'Not at all. You must stay with us. You are our guest.'

Joe stood for a moment, his unlit cigarette between his fingers, uncertain.

Richard said gently, 'But perhaps I'm being selfish.

No doubt you have reasons to return to London . . . work . . . or a girl . . .'

Joe shook his head. In London, he still had no home, no work. And the only girl he wanted – the only girl he would ever want – was asleep upstairs in this house.

'No, nothing,' he said. 'If you'll have me, I'll be delighted to stay.'

And was surprised to realize just how much he meant that.

For almost a week Robin was confined to her bed, ordered to remain there by both Dr Lemon and her mother. Gradually the cough lessened, her temperature went down, and she began to be able to eat and sleep properly again. Some of the peace of mind that had almost entirely deserted her over the past six months began to return. The snow continued to fall, and she was content when she was awake to lie watching the great soft heavy flakes drift through the sky. From her bedroom window she could see the river and the winter house; a thick blanket of snow covered the roof of the little hut, and icicles clung to its eaves.

When she grew bored, Richard read to her and Hugh played snap with her and Joe talked to her. One afternoon, Joe was lounging in the armchair beside her bed, his long legs flung out before him. She said, refusing to let him evade her eyes, 'You've quarrelled with Francis.'

'We both have. Haven't we?'

She looked at him closely. 'But you'll make it up, won't you, Joe?'

'I don't think so.'

Bearing a grudge was not one of Francis's vices. She hated to think that the rift between them might be permanent.

'Joe – whatever it was, Francis will forget. He always does.'

He shook his head.

She said, exasperated, 'But you've known each other

for years! You surely don't intend to fall out permanently with him? *Joe.* For heaven's sake . . .'

He scowled. 'It isn't what Francis has done, Robin. It's what *I've* done.' He stopped, gazing at the ceiling. Then he said, 'I told Francis that I made love to Vivien.'

For a moment she was speechless, staring at him.

'Then I'm not surprised that Francis . . . But you'll tell him the truth, won't you, Joe?'

He didn't say anything, but just looked at her.

'Oh,' she said faintly, eventually.

'So you see, it's not just a question of shaking hands and forgetting about it.'

'No.' Her head had begun to ache again. She felt stupid, naive and rather depressed. She should have noticed that Joe was attracted to Vivien, and she could imagine all too clearly how Francis had felt about Joe making love to his mother. She heard Joe say, 'You look tired. I'll go,' and then he stooped and kissed her on the forehead, and left the room. She knew, staring out at the snow, that what Joe had done marked the end of an era. That it had finally torn the three of them apart, and that what she and Joe and Francis had once shared was over, gone for ever.

He had not meant to tell her, but he had had, in the end, no alternative. He walked out of the house and through the garden, down to the river. The whiteness of the snow-covered fields melted into a bleached sky, so that the horizon was invisible. He thought what a mess it all was. That Robin loved Francis, that he himself loved Robin, that he had hurt Francis, who perhaps loved no-one except Vivien, in the worst possible way.

He heard footsteps crunching the snow, and he turned to see Hugh Summerhayes. In his week in the Fens, he had come to like Hugh.

'Glorious, isn't it?' said Hugh. His hazel eyes focused on the snowy fields, the ice-encrusted river.

Joe nodded.

'One wants to build snowmen and make the first foot-prints, that sort of thing.'

Joe realized that Hugh was watching him carefully, searching for words, perhaps. Eventually Hugh said, 'This chap that Robin's seeing. Francis. Do you know him?'

Again, he nodded. 'I've known Francis for years. We were at school together.'

Hugh said bluntly, 'Is he good enough for her?'

He didn't think anyone was good enough for Robin. Not Francis, certainly not himself. But he tried to be fair. 'Francis is . . . you only meet one or two people like him in a lifetime. He has everything – looks, talent, charm, brains. I don't think I could have endured school if it hadn't been for Francis.'

Hugh Summerhayes, no fool, noticed what Joe had evaded saying. 'But will he be kind to her?'

Joe began to trudge along the river-bank towards the small hut that jettied out over the water. 'Sometimes.' The single word was flung back by the wind to Hugh.

'*Hell.*' It was the first time he had heard anything like a curse escape Hugh Summerhayes's lips. 'Unrequited love is so *wearing*. And Robin is madly in love with him, isn't she?'

Joe did not answer. When he swung up onto the verandah of the hut, he could see through the window a stove, a table and chairs.

'It's Robin's,' explained Hugh. 'I'm sure she'll show it you when she's well enough. She'll need someone to keep an eye on her. I would myself, but I'm useless in London. Haven't the nerve for it any more. So would you . . . ?'

The question hung on the bitter wind. Joe, meeting Hugh Summerhayes's eyes, knew that Hugh understood him. He said softly, 'Is it so obvious?', and Hugh said, 'Only to me. I'm quite good at unrequited love.'

Joe stood for a moment on the verandah, his arms resting on the thin wooden rail. He recognized just what it would cost him to do what Hugh asked; he could guess at the pain that returning to London with Robin would inevitably involve. Having to stand aside and watch Francis hurt her, over and over again, picking up the pieces afterwards.

Yet he had, in the end, no choice. 'I'll make sure she's all right,' he said.

There was a silence. Then Hugh Summerhayes, grinning, said, 'Snowmen, then? If we make them close to the river, Robin will be able to see them from her bedroom.'

They made a snowman and a snowbear, and an igloo, and something that was supposed to be a penguin. By that time it was dark, and they had to light the garden with flares and throw snowballs at Robin's window until she looked out and applauded and Daisy told them all off for making so much noise.

Joe went for long walks in the frozen Fens each morning, often alone, sometimes with Hugh or Richard. Richard, who had wormed his passion for photography out of him in his first week's stay, insisted first on seeing the photographs that he had brought back from Yorkshire, and then on lending him his old box camera. Joe spent hours crouched in icy reed-beds, the heavy camera balanced on a tripod, trying to capture the bleak, haunted land. He had fallen in love with the place, and something in its isolation, its fragility, enraptured him. He drove into Cambridge and bought developing and printing equipment, and then worked for hours in Blackmere Farm's freezing outhouse, the small window blanketed to keep out the light, feeling the beginnings of an almost forgotten satisfaction when he bathed the prints in developing fluid, and saw pictures slowly emerge from nothing. Richard Summerhayes, scanning the images of drove and marsh, cajoled him gently and scribbled the name of a photographer friend in London on the back of an envelope. Joe mumbled embarrassed protests, but began, for the first time in years, to see a way forward.

On the day that he learned that Adolf Hitler, the

leader of the Nazi party, had become the Chancellor of Germany, Joe walked alone for miles and miles. He felt that here nothing could touch them, they were safe. It was impossible to believe that the cruelties of Fascism should ever interrupt this ancient silence; impossible also to believe that this land, stolen from the sea, would ever be touched by the threat of war.

A day later, they celebrated Robin's first full day up. Daisy made an enormous lunch, and Richard opened a bottle of wine. The conversation ranged wildly from politics to music to literature. After they had had coffee, and after Richard had played the piano and Daisy had sung, Robin crouched down beside Joe, and said, 'Come and see my winter house, Joe.'

'You must borrow my rabbit, Robin,' called Daisy, 'and, Joe, you are to bring her back after half an hour.'

Robin wore Daisy's moth-eaten fur coat as they walked together across the snow-covered lawn to the small hut.

'Light the fire please, Joe, and the oil lamp.'

He did so. The stove was already laid; the lamp swung from a hook on the ceiling. The wooden hut gleamed like a treasure cave in the golden light.

'Those are my collections, and those are the twigs Maia brought me, and this is the drawing that Helen did of the three of us.'

He studied the pencil sketch that was pinned to the wooden wall. Three girls: one dark haired, one fair, and Robin's familiar beloved face.

'Your friends?'

'Mmm. Though we seem to have grown apart.' Her voice sounded sad.

'It's a good likeness of you.'

She smiled. 'Isn't it?' She knelt by the stove, warming her hands.

He said, 'I should go . . .' He had begun to feel restless again, knowing that this was an interlude, a temporary haven, no more.

'Will you go back to Yorkshire?'

He shook his head. 'No. It was . . . unsettling.' Joe leaned against the window, where the frost had made flower shapes. 'What about you, Robin? Will you stay here for a while?'

She rose, coming to stand beside him. The little hut had become quite warm. 'I thought I'd go back to London soon,' she said. 'It's been lovely here – it's funny, I always hated this place, but it's been so peaceful. I've things to do though.' She laid her hand on his arm. 'Come back to London with me, won't you, Joe?'

Just for a moment his heart leapt, and he allowed himself to hope. But he knew that he must ask.

'And Francis?'

Her face was shadowed in the dim light. She gave a small gasp. 'I've thought and thought about it, but I don't really have a choice. I tried to see whether I could do without him, but I can't. And Francis'll change, Joe. I know he will. He promised. It's like the song my mother was singing. My heart's entangled, Joe. Hopelessly entangled. It always will be.'

He drew her to him, his arms around her, his chin resting on the top of her head. He acknowledged that his own heart was every bit as entangled as hers. He acknowledged what it would cost him to see her loving someone else.

The words of Daisy's song echoed through his head as he stared outside at the black water that reflected the starlit sky.

> Since first I saw your face, I vowed,
> To honour and renown ye.
> If now I be disdained, I wish
> My heart had never known ye.
> What? I that loved, and you that liked,
> Shall we begin to wrangle?
> No, no, no, my heart is fast,
> And cannot disentangle.

PART THREE

–

1933–1935

Chapter Ten

Maia, after studying the weekly accounts, looked up at Liam Kavanagh.

'We are in profit again, Liam. We have been in profit since June.'

'Six consecutive months.' Liam, too, smiled.

'I shall increase the Christmas bonus. Everyone has worked so hard.'

'Especially you, Mrs Merchant. Congratulations.'

She said nothing, but she knew that he was right. She had reversed Merchants' downward decline, she had placated the bankers and kept her staff in employment through the worst years of the Depression. She had had to make difficult choices, but she had made the correct choices.

Maia's pale eyes gleamed. 'We'll go ahead with the plans for the new cafeteria. The builders can start work in the New Year.'

It was Saturday evening, and through the window of her office Maia could see rain battering the rooftops. She said suddenly:

'We should celebrate, Liam. There's a ballet at the theatre . . . do you like ballet?'

He looked embarrassed. 'I'm sorry, Mrs Merchant . . . it would be great, but . . . well, the thing is . . . I'm otherwise engaged.'

She thought at first that he meant the Irish Society, or the golf club. Then, looking at him, she knew that he did not, and she had to disguise her small jolt of pain.

'Liam . . . have you met a young lady?'

'Not so young. My landlady. Eileen's a widow – she's always been good company. We've been friends for years, but recently . . .' His face had flushed brick red.

'Recently you have been more than friends?' Maia rose, and kissed him on the cheek. 'I shall expect an invitation to the wedding.'

After he had gone, she stood for a while, motionless, listening to the hammering of the rain. Then, seeing that it was almost eight o'clock, she packed her briefcase, and put on her coat and hat, and left her office. Passing through the dimly lit department store, she felt, as she always did, that familiar surge of pride. She remembered walking through Merchants years ago, mesmerized by the colourful, glittering displays, the shining chrome and glass, and the soft, pastel décor. Now all this was hers, and no-one could take it away from her.

She drove home, bathed, and dined alone. It was while she was eating, waited on by a uniformed housemaid, that her feeling of elation began to crumble and dissolve. She dismissed the maid once the girl had served coffee, and sat, staring at the dark liquid in the neat little Clarice Cliff cup, dipping the spoon in and out.

She tried to work after dinner, spreading her graphs and charts out on the carpet in front of the drawing-room fire, turning on the wireless so that the house was not so quiet. She heard the footsteps of the cook and the kitchen-maid on the gravel drive, and knew that she was alone. Eventually, unable to concentrate, she went to the cabinet and found a glass and the bottle of gin. The music rippled in the background, failing to lift her spirits. She should be happy, Maia told herself – why was she not happy? Not because of what Liam had told her – never that. She had never wanted Liam to be anything more than a colleague. *You are incapable of love*, Charles Maddox had said, and she had been unable to deny his accusation. If she was not attracted to men, did she still need men to be attracted to her? Or was it just that to be in, alone, on a Saturday night when you were only twenty-four years old, seemed to Maia suddenly to be a terrible thing. Nowadays, she found herself longing for the first weekend of the month, her regular weekend away. What had begun as a duty had become a pleasure. She felt tears pricking at the back of her eyes and, brushing them angrily away, poured herself another drink.

Only a year ago she could have been out every night. But then Edmund Pamphilon had died, and the inquest had decided that he had taken his own life, and since that time, people had still looked at her, but in a different way. Once they had looked at her with admiration and desire; now they looked at her with dislike and with . . . fear. So ironic, Maia often thought, that the deaths of those close to her – the deaths of her father and of her husband – should not have reflected on her. Yet the death of a man whom she had thought unimportant, an inefficient employee, no more, should have made people judge her so harshly.

Sitting there, Maia could not avoid her memories of her interview with Mrs Pamphilon. She had not shirked her duty visit; she had done what she had to do as Edmund Pamphilon's recent employer, and had called on his invalid widow to offer her condolences. She had expected polite thanks for her flowers and her fruit and her offer of a pension, or at the worst a veiled and tearful resentment. She had found instead anger and hatred and a sort of spitting, feline loathing. *Do you think I would accept a penny from the woman who murdered my husband?* Maia, wide-eyed and remembering, swallowed the contents of her glass and stared into the fire.

Vernon had come to her that night. His visits were occasional, confined to her dreams. He had knelt at the end of her bed, and he had laughed at her. It had taken her a while to work out why he had laughed, and then she had realized that it was because she had become like him. She had learned his ruthlessness, his lack of care for the welfare of another human being. She had shouted, '*I only wanted to feel safe!*', but still he had laughed.

Helen waited until her father had left the house, and then went quietly upstairs. Betty was working in the kitchen; Helen could see, looking out of the landing window, Ivy unpegging the washing on the line. Helen walked through the rectory's twisting corridors until she reached the attic stairs. Climbing the stairs, she pushed aside the trapdoor, and entered the gloomy, spidery rooms beneath the roof.

She had become, in the past year, familiar with the grey, cobwebbed objects that cluttered the eaves. The elephant's foot, the Victrola, the perambulator, the hat box. More than familiar. Helen felt a flutter of excitement well up in her as she pushed open the door that led into the little room at the far end of the attic.

Her room. She thought of it as her room in a way that she had never thought of her bedroom as her room. The maids did not sweep out this room, her father did not enter unannounced as she was brushing her hair or buttoning her shoes. She had let the dust stay clinging to the one small window, afraid that someone might notice if she cleaned it. Besides, she liked the grey cloudiness between herself and the world outside. She liked to feel shut in.

She had begun to explore, afraid at first to shift boxes and delve through trunks, worried that her movements would be heard in the bedrooms below. The dust and the spiders had added to her reluctance; once she had seen a mouse, perched on top of an old tallboy, little black eyes glinting, and she had had to clamp her hands over her mouth to stop herself screaming. But a few days ago she had found the trunk under the eaves. Helen had opened it, breaking the padlock with an ingenuity and strength that surprised her, kneeling in the darkness, a candle balanced on the trunk's riveted corner as she sorted through the ribbons and withered nosegays, uncertain at first what she had found. Then, suddenly, she had known. 'Florence Stevens', the old dance card had said. Her mother's maiden name. The letters and the photographs had been buried beneath lace gloves and whalebone stays and moth-eaten fur stoles. As though someone had thrown them in higgledy-piggledy, slamming the trunk shut, shoving it beneath the eaves, not expecting it ever to be opened again.

Now, seated on the floor beside the window, Helen struggled to untie the string that held the papers together. The knot was hard, and she had eventually to bite it, so that all the yellowing, crumbling fragments of paper slipped from her grasp and danced across the floor. Holding the candle closer to a fragment of paper, she read the unfamiliar round hand. *Shoelaces . . . three pairs of kid gloves . . . speak to grocer about raisins.* A shopping list. Helen put it aside, and picked up an envelope. Glancing at it, she recognized the handwriting. Her face suffused with red as she drew out of the envelope the letter that her father had written, many years ago.

Yet this, too, was disappointing. '*My dear Miss Stevens,*' Julius Ferguson had written, '*I am writing to thank you for the enjoyable evening that you graciously permitted me to spend with you. Your presence happily ameliorated my discomfort at an activity some would deem inappropriate to my calling. I trust you were not too fatigued by the dancing.*' And then something about the weather, and his best wishes to Florence's guardian, and a final '*Yours respectfully, Julius Ferguson*'.

Helen placed the letter on the windowsill, and spread out on the floor a handful of photographs. A very young Florence with her parents, stiff and serious-looking; Florence in her Girl Guide uniform, the wide-brimmed hat casting shadows on her thin, big-eyed face. Florence on her swing in the rectory garden; Florence standing beneath the horse-chestnut on the front lawn. A dozen photographs of Florence, all taken in the rectory garden. In every picture she wore a pale, frilled dress, buttoned shoes and wrist-length gloves. Though she must have been married when the photographs were taken, her ringleted hair was still loose to her shoulders. Yet marriage had changed Florence, Helen thought, glancing back at the earlier photographs. Her eyes had altered, they had become secretive and evasive, and her mouth no longer curled in that shy, tenuous smile.

Her father had a cold throughout the next week, so she brought him hot lemon and honey and wrapped him up in rugs next to the parlour fire. Helen sat at his feet, reading aloud the letters she had written for the Parish Appeal. December brought more rain and a gusting wind that howled around the rectory's many chimneys, sending rooftiles crashing to the terrace. In the village, the drove turned to black mud, reaching over the tops of Helen's galoshes when she walked to the letter box. Adam Hayhoe, helping to lash sodden, collapsing reeds to the roof of one particularly dilapidated cottage, caught sight of her and flung his oilskin over the deepest puddles. Calling her thanks, she took his hand as, Queen Elizabeth-like, she stepped from the worst of the mire onto comparatively dry land.

Maia called one Saturday. 'I thought I'd give myself an afternoon off,' she explained breezily, before whisking Helen away in her motor-car.

They drove to Ely, wandering around the cobbled streets, sheltered by Helen's umbrella. The wind got up, blowing the umbrella inside out, so they ran inside the nearest shop. It was a clothes shop – ready-made clothes, rail after rail. Maia rubbed the material between her fingers, and said, 'They skimp on the cutting, of course,' but Helen was entranced.

'I've never had . . . I've always made my own . . .' The cheap dresses, with their gilt buttons and artificial silk collars, suddenly seemed to Helen unbearably desirable.

'Try one on. What size are you? You should try this . . . and this.'

Bundled into the changing room with three dresses and a haughty assistant, Helen's temporary elation left her. She did not know how much money she had in her purse, but she was sure that it was not enough to buy a dress. But, trapped and embarrassed, she had no choice but to allow the assistant to help the dress over her head, and to button up the back while she smoothed the cheap, clinging fabric over her hips.

She tried on all three: the cherry red, the navy blue, the black. Her reflection in the looking-glass startled her, she hardly recognized herself. Maia, her eyes narrowed, made her twirl round like a mannequin.

'The black is too old. The navy is smart, Helen.'

'I adore the red.' Then, remembering that she could afford neither, Helen caught Maia's eye. Maia, smiling, whispered in her ear.

'I shall buy it for your Christmas present. Don't argue.'

Helen insisted on wearing the dress while they had tea and scones in a little place in the high street. In the ladies' room, Maia twisted Helen's golden hair up into a knot, securing it with hairpins, and offered Helen her lipstick. She had never worn lipstick before. When she went back into the tearoom, a voice called, 'Fancy the pictures, tonight, do you, love?' as they passed one of the tables. Maia walked haughtily on, but Helen, looking a second time at the table and the three men sitting there, realized that the man with the moustache had spoken to her, and not to Maia. She stared at him for a moment, uncertain whether a reply was expected, and then, scarlet-faced, joined Maia.

Maia dropped her at the rectory, made her farewells, and drove back to Cambridge. As Helen opened the front door, the dinner gong chimed. Walking to the dining-room, she caught sight of her reflection in the dull glass of the framed prints, and in the dark, highly polished furniture. She had scrubbed off the lipstick in the car, but she still wore the dress, and her hair was still up. She kissed her father and slid into her place as Ivy finished serving the soup and left the room.

Julius Ferguson spoke. 'That is a new dress, isn't it, Helen?'

'Maia bought it for me.' Helen knew that she sounded defensive. 'It's my Christmas present.'

'Really?' He was staring at her, his full red lips pursed into an expression of disapproval. 'Yet Maia always looks so elegant.'

Helen said nothing, but was aware of a growing anger in her as Ivy reappeared to serve the main course. When they were alone again, she heard herself say, 'You don't like my new dress, then, Daddy?'

He said dismissively, 'I'm not sure that is suitable attire for a young girl.'

'But I'm not a young girl. I'm twenty-four. Almost an old maid.' Her voice was savage. She tried not to think of Hugh. Although it had happened a year ago, she still could not bear to think of Hugh, or to remember what she and he had said.

Julius Ferguson continued to sprinkle salt on his mutton, then to dab at the corners of his mouth with his napkin, a habit that Helen had recently come to find unbearably irritating.

'What nonsense,' he said mildly. 'You'll always be my little girl.'

She couldn't eat. She was aware of the stillness of the room, of the low tick-tock of the clock, of the empty countryside beyond. They had sat together like this a thousand times before, and would sit together like this a thousand times more. For the rest of her life, perhaps. Until she, or he, died. Just as he and Florence had, twenty-five years ago, also sat here, listening to the silence, surrounded by emptiness.

He said, 'And it really does not become you to wear your hair like that, Helen. It makes you look older. And rather cheap, I'm afraid.'

Merlin's latest exhibition was held in a disused factory in Whitechapel. Robin, arriving with Joe, saw that some of the machinery was still in place: portraits were propped against lathes, and a huge triptych painted with a particularly gory representation of the

Crucifixion looked down from the summit of a furnace.

Charis Fortune grabbed Joe and dragged him away to dance; Robin searched for Merlin. She found him eventually, curled up on a spiral staircase, his head resting in a redhead's lap, his hands clutching a bottle of Scotch. The redhead was asleep.

'Merlin.' Stooping, she kissed him on both cheeks. 'It's marvellous. Simply marvellous.'

'Do you think so?' Gloomily, he surveyed the crowds. 'Do you think they come to see the paintings, or for the free booze?'

She said honestly, 'Both, I suppose. Have you sold any?'

'*Four*.' He looked disgusted. 'I've painted Maia's portrait. Would you like to see it?' Merlin disentangled himself from the redhead and struggled to his feet. 'It's over there.'

Robin took his arm as they threaded through the dancers. She saw a dozen familiar faces – Diana Howarth and Angus and Freddy and a huddle of Persia's Bloomsbury acquaintances. But when they reached the portrait, the chatter and dancing faded into the background as Robin looked at it. Maia was in white. There was a suggestion of feathers and waves and the open Fenland skies.

'I've called it "The Silver Swan", ' said Merlin. 'Do you remember?'

Of course she remembered. Her first kiss. Herself and Merlin standing on the terrace of the winter house, looking out over the water while Maia sang.

Merlin laughed. 'Did I tell you, Robin – I'm afraid I tried to seduce her. Once the painting was finished, of course. I was curious.'

'And . . . ?'

'She almost froze my balls off. I pity the poor devil who falls in love with her.'

She had seen little of Maia during the past year. She had heard, of course, about the Merchants' employee who had killed himself after Maia had dismissed him, but when she had tried to talk about it to Maia, Maia had responded with such icy arrogance that even Robin had been silenced. It had deepened the rift that had lain between them since Vernon's death, a rift that Robin now suspected was unbridgeable.

Merlin said, 'Where's what's his name? Vivien's son? She was here earlier, with Denzil. I'm trying to persuade him to buy my Crucifixion.'

'Francis is at a meeting. Joe's here somewhere. He's coming to Blackmere for Christmas.'

'So'm I.' Merlin's voice was slurred. 'I'll give you both a lift. Now, darling Robin, I am going to get completely and utterly plastered. *Only four bloody sales . . .*'

Merlin returned to the redhead and the whisky bottle. Someone pushed a glass of beer into Robin's hand; someone else asked her to dance. The music of the jazz band echoed in the huge warehouse. Encircling the room, she thought through the events of the past year. Francis's return from America, the glorious holiday they had taken on the Continent in the summer, and Francis's decision to try and carve out a political career. The publication of the book that she and Neil Mackenzie had written in October: it had been received kindly, if quietly, but although she had felt a thrill of pride when she had opened her advance copy of the finished book, she had no wish to write any more. She earned her living now by working part-time at the clinic, and by a succession of short-term researcher's jobs. Some of her old restlessness had begun to return, unsettling her.

She danced with Guy and with Joe and then with Selena, who had broken her ankle and hobbled one-footedly around, leaning on Robin's shoulder, drunk with beer and laughter. Someone had flung open the huge double doors at the end of the warehouse, so that they could see the silhouette of churches and offices against the blurred, orangey-black London skyline. A clock struck midnight, and Robin, collapsing against the doors, trying to recover her breath, felt a hand briefly touch her elbow.

'Fräulein Summerhayes?'

'Yes?' She looked up. A man stood beside her, dark-haired, shabbily dressed, thin-faced. Robin smiled. 'Herr Wenzel. How lovely to see you again.'

Earlier in the year, Germany's Chancellor, Adolf Hitler, had assumed the power of a dictator, and the subsequent persecution of racial and political minorities had led to a steady stream of refugees from Germany – Jews, communists, socialists, artists and intellectuals – many of whom wished to be allowed to remain in Britain. Robin, fundraising for the International Solidarity Fund of the Labour Party and Trades Union Council in her spare time, had met Niklaus Wenzel, a political refugee from Munich, a few months ago.

'Have you any news of your brother, Herr Wenzel?'

'Hans is still in Dachau camp. I have heard nothing of him for three months.'

His voice was quiet and courteous, but she could see the despair in his eyes. She was leaning against the door jamb, half in, half out of the warehouse. To one side of her was the warmth, the music, her friends, to the other a chill, fog-laden air that brushed against her face and seeped damply into her skin.

Robin left the exhibition shortly afterwards, walking alone to the club where she was to meet Francis. He was waiting there when she arrived, sitting in the corner, a glass cradled in his hands. She studied him for a moment unseen, finding a deep and familiar pleasure in looking at him. The fair, slightly curling hair, just touching the collar of his black jacket; the half-closed, sleepy grey eyes; the spare, graceful body that she adored to make love to. Since his return from America in the spring Francis had lived within his income, and had given serious thought to a career in politics. In turn, she had accepted that he needed his friends and other interests. She still disapproved, after all, of possessiveness.

He looked up, and then crossed the room and kissed her.

'How was the meeting?'

Francis grinned. 'Deadly dull. You wouldn't believe it, Robin – they spent an hour deciding whether the next fundraiser should be a fork supper or a bring-and-buy sale. Hardly the cutting edge of democracy.'

She kissed him again. 'But you'll stick it out, won't you, Francis?'

'Of course I will. I'm doing it for you.'

He took her hand, raising it to his mouth, pressing his lips against her palm. Then he said, 'There's a bottle party at a nightclub in Soho. Everyone's going. Shall we?'

On Boxing Day, Helen, having written a polite refusal to Daisy Summerhayes's suggestion that she join them for lunch, waited until her father had fallen asleep after dinner before going into the attic. She took an oil lamp with her, and curled up on the floor of her room, a thick cardigan round her shoulders to keep out the cold. She had saved the best of her discoveries until last. Her mother's diary, a leather-bound journal. Now, with the frost crystallizing on the windowpanes, she opened it and began to read.

There were two or three entries each week. Sometimes the entry was just a single paragraph ('Miss Cooper' – Florence's governess, Helen guessed – 'left today. I cried for simply ages. She has gone to the Bowmans, in Aylesbury. I worked her a bookmark and a hair-tidy as goodbye presents.') At other times Florence's round, schoolgirlish handwriting covered as much as two pages – a lengthy description of her first dance, where she had worn a white tussore silk gown with a bustle, and had drunk 'gallons of scrummy lemonade', and another two and a half pages describing the awfulness of a house party. Helen scanned pages, flicking through them quickly. When she found the first reference to her father ('8 May 1908, Benton House'), she began to read more carefully.

'Stella introduced me to the Reverend Ferguson, who has a living in East Anglia.' That was all. Helen had expected something more – love at first sight, perhaps, some indication that Florence had felt the same way about Julius as Julius himself had felt about her.

'26 May 1908, Benton House. We played doubles. Teddy was Stella's partner, and the Reverend Ferguson was mine. It felt rather odd to be playing tennis with a vicar. He is very old, almost thirty. Stella and I had a midnight feast. We raided the pantry after the cook had gone to bed. Just like school!'

Helen turned a few more pages. Another ball . . . the play that Florence and Stella and another schoolfriend, Hilary, had put on. A game of French cricket on the back lawn with Stella's brothers ('Teddy is very sweet and quiet. Not like a boy at all'), and a cycle ride in the countryside.

'18 June 1908, Benton House. It was so hot that we swam in the millpond at the bottom of the garden. I hadn't a costume, so I took off my dress and tucked my petticoat into my knickers. It was glorious – so cool and weedy and there were little fishes and sticklebacks in the water. But we did not hear the tea bell, and the Reverend Ferguson came to find us. I was so embarrassed that he should see me dressed like that, but Stella said that clergymen have to see much worse things – dead bodies and ill people and all sorts of dreadful things.'

Helen imagined the pond to be like the one outside Robin's winter house. She thought of the many summer days that she had sat on the verandah watching as Robin and Maia had swum, and felt a flicker of regret that she had never joined them. Florence would have done so. Helen looked down at the diary, and continued to read.

'19 June 1908!!! I can hardly write! I have just received my first proposal!!!

'20 June 1908, Benton House. I am an engaged

woman. Stella's father, who is my guardian, of course, said that I should accept the Reverend Ferguson's offer. *Julius* Ferguson, I should call him now. Julius (Julius!) has an independent income as well as his stipend, and no dependants, so he is a Good Catch (a vulgar expression, Stella says). Mrs Radcliffe says that we could marry at the beginning of September, though I must not expect a large wedding. I wish I could talk about it to someone. I tried with Stella, but I think she is rather miffed that I was proposed to first, and was quite catty. I do so miss Mama.'

Helen buttoned up her cardigan. Her fingers, turning the pages of the diary, were ice-cold. She read on – Florence's wedding-dress, the menu planned for the wedding-breakfast, her trousseau. Endless lists of under-garments and sheets and linen and china.

'9 September 1908, Benton House. An awful day. Mrs Radcliffe took me aside, and started to speak to me about men's appetites. I suppose she meant to make sure that I plan big enough dinners – men do eat more than women. But I burst into tears and tried to talk to her about the wedding tomorrow, and all the things that have been worrying me, and she became quite cross. She said that the wedding couldn't possibly be postponed, and that she was expecting Mr Lindrick to make an offer for Stella any day now, and that it really was too bad of me to make a fuss at such a time. Stella saw that I had been crying, and asked me if it was because of the birds and the bees. I did not know what she meant, but she told me that babies are born through a woman's navel, and that it hurts a lot. I don't believe her. It is all too horrible.'

Helen turned the page. It was empty. Turning another page, and then another, she found that there were only seven more words written in the entire diary.

Dear God, what women have to bear.

Robin went home for a week at Christmas. Blackmere Farm was almost bursting at the seams: Richard and

Daisy and Hugh, Persia, Merlin, Joe, Maia and a string quartet from Bavaria whom Richard Summerhayes had met through the International Student Service, all squashed into the house. Merlin slept on Hugh's floor, Persia and Maia squeezed into the little guest bedroom. Joe endured the winter house, three quilts and his overcoat slung over him to keep out the cold. The Bavarians spoke little English, and had never before celebrated Christmas, but their music was beguiling and magical. But the absence of Helen – quiet, unobtrusive Helen – was to Robin increasingly noticeable.

When she tried to work it out, she could not remember when she had last seen Helen. Six months ago, surely. Helen had written every week, just as she always did, but her letters had become small catalogues of even smaller events. 'People grow apart,' said Daisy, when Robin questioned her. But Robin, uneasy, cycled to Thorpe Fen alone the day after Boxing Day.

She found Helen in a dark little room at the back of the rectory, sewing. Helen glanced up at her, and then returned to her work. 'I have to finish these.' She gestured to the lengths of chintz she was making into cushions.

'They can wait, can't they?' Robin felt a flicker of annoyance. 'I haven't seen you for ages.'

There was no response; Helen's white, tapered fingers threaded needles, smoothed out fabric. *People grow apart*, Daisy had said, and Robin began to think that she might be right, that Helen had, without her noticing, grown into this dull, distant woman. That the passivity in Helen that had always irritated her had deepened to apathy.

She tried one last time. 'Is it your father?'

Helen's head was bowed. Robin said impatiently, 'You must stand up for yourself, Helen. You are entitled to a life of your own. It's ridiculous that you are still stuck at home, looking after your father.'

Helen looked up at last, eyes wide. Then she shook her head. But Robin glimpsed in that brief, upward glance the expression in her red-rimmed eyes. Some of the refugees looked at her like that – not the confident, wealthy, talented ones, but those bewildered and frightened by their sudden displacement.

'*Helen,*' she whispered.

The length of thread in Helen's hands snapped. 'It's not because of *Daddy*. It's because of Hugh.'

Robin stared at her, confused. Helen had taken up the broken piece of thread, and was winding it round her fingers.

'I told Hugh that I loved him.'

She could see where the thread cut into Helen's smooth, white fingers. There was a hollow, sinking feeling in Robin's stomach.

'I told Hugh that I loved him. And I asked him to marry me.' A small sound escaped her lips, a sound that Robin did not immediately recognize as laughter, as Helen looked up at her. 'Me! Asking a man to marry me! Can you imagine it, Robin? Helen Ferguson, who doesn't even have the nerve to tell the maids to sweep the stairs properly, asking a man to marry her! He refused, of course.' There was an audible weight of bitterness in her voice.

'Perhaps Hugh doesn't approve of marriage . . . I know that he is fond of you—'

'Hugh loves Maia.'

'Nonsense,' Robin said. She almost laughed, to think Helen should make such a ridiculous mistake. Then the laughter faded as she glimpsed the anger in Helen's eyes.

'Hugh loves Maia,' said Helen coldly. 'He told me so himself.'

Small incidents of the past gathered together, making a certainty that Robin did not want to believe. Hugh's birthday, and the expression on his face when Maia had called him *a darling* . . . The many times Hugh had watched Helen and Maia sing, pain and delight mingling in his eyes.

'He said that he had always loved Maia. So there never was any hope for me.' Helen had returned to her sewing and was ripping out a row of tacking, the movements of her hands savage and wild. 'Maia has everything she ever wanted, doesn't she? She is beautiful and rich and has a lovely home. And all the men fall in love with her, don't they?'

Hugh was in love with Maia. Hugh, her gentle, damaged brother, loved Maia Merchant. Robin, recalling Maia at the inquest into Vernon's death, shuddered.

'Does Maia know?'

Helen shook her head. Then, at last, the wild light faded from her eyes, and she said, 'I have almost hated her. But I couldn't, somehow. After all, it isn't even her fault, is it? It's just the way she is.'

Maia had married Vernon Merchant for his money and property. But Hugh was penniless, so Hugh had nothing that Maia wanted. Hugh had loved Maia for ten years, perhaps, and Maia had remained indifferent. Nothing would come of it. Nothing must come of it.

'You do see, Robin, why I don't visit any more?' said Helen as she threaded her needle and began to sew another seam.

Throughout the past year, Joe had kept his promise to Hugh. He had taken Robin to cafés and filled her up with chocolate éclairs and tea when she looked thin; he had accompanied her to concerts in the winter and hiking in the summer when Francis had been away. He had listened to her worries about Francis while struggling to disguise his jealousy, and, more recently, her worries about Hugh. He had guessed months ago, when he had first met Maia Merchant, that Hugh Summerhayes was in love with her, but he did not tell Robin that. He had known, seeing her, that Maia had the sort of flawless beauty that could inspire men to irrational acts. He had managed, just, to convince Robin that she should leave Hugh to his hopeless love, that to interfere would be fatal.

Joe's feelings for Robin – equally hopeless, equally

unvoiced – had not altered. He found the ambiguity of his position intolerable. When she was not there he longed to see her; when she was with him the knowledge that he could look, but not touch, was unbearably frustrating. Sometimes he resented the promise that Hugh Summerhayes had extracted from him; often, when he thought of Francis and Robin, he was almost overwhelmed with an uncivilized sort of jealousy that he despised himself for feeling. Pretending to be a friend, when he longed to be a lover, he had daily to confront the invidiousness of his position.

Yet he had come a long way in a year. Joe worked for Oscar Prideaux, Richard Summerhayes's friend, for twenty years the proprietor of a successful photography business that was run with the help of a series of underpaid assistants. For Oscar, Joe took flattering photographs of debutantes (blurred lenses and soft lights), and attended countless weddings. It was an invaluable apprenticeship, but Joe's ambitions lay in different directions. He had already sold a set of photographs to a left-wing journal. The Rothermere-owned newspapers had reported hunger-marchers rioting against the police, but Joe's pictures had told a different story, one of mounted police charging unarmed men. He planned to visit Paris shortly, both to witness for himself the smouldering unrest that had begun to haunt the city and to attempt to trace his Tante Claire.

He left for France in the first week of February, throwing a few clothes into his rucksack, but packing his camera, his most precious possession, with much greater care. He caught the boat train from Victoria. The crossing was long and stormy, the train from Calais cold and crowded. He arrived in Paris at midday to a tension that he sensed the moment he stepped off the train at the Gare du Nord. The streets were unusually busy for a Parisian lunch-time, and there seemed to Joe to be an ugliness and aggression in the air that was ill-suited to the city's cool elegance.

He dined on baguettes and red wine in a small café.

He realized that many of the people in the streets belonged to the Jeunesses Patriotes and the Croix de Feu, both right-wing organizations. Small scuffles erupted at street corners and were savagely broken up by the police. The waiter, when Joe questioned him, said:

'They intend to stage a coup. The *fascistes* and the anti-republicans are assembling in the Place de la Concorde, and from there they will march on the Chamber of Deputies. The *patron* tells me that the police are waiting on all the routes of access to the Chamber of Deputies.' The waiter shrugged. 'There will be a blood-bath, monsieur.'

It was late afternoon and the sky was darkening already, yet the street-lamps, shimmering in the rain, showed the excited, vengeful faces of the people seething on the roads and pavements. Joe followed the general direction of the crowds towards the Place de la Concorde. Ducking into a doorway, he loaded film into his camera, and then he vaulted up onto the parapet of a wall, and focused the lens. The vast expanse of the Place de la Concorde was filled with people – tens of thousands of them, an incalculable number. Joe slipped the exposed plates carefully into his rucksack.

Fragments of speeches, blared through megaphones at the Place de la Concorde, assaulted his ears. The decadence of the Third Republic . . . the Jewish bankers' plot to destroy France . . . He realized that if he continued to press forward he would become caught up in the mob, so, taking one last photograph of the surging crowds in the Place de la Concorde, he turned back, fighting his way through side roads and through the Jardin des Tuileries to the Seine. In the garden, despite the ugly roar in the background, he found himself caught up once more in the beauty of Paris: its elegance, its mystery. He had a vague, fleeting recollection of walking with his mother in these gardens. Leaving the Jardin des Tuileries, he reached the banks of the Seine and looked up towards the bridge that led to the Chamber of Deputies.

As Joe watched, the violence seemed to spring up spontaneously in several places at once, like fragments of broken glass igniting a hayfield on a hot, dry summer's day. Beneath the yellow light of the gas lamps, he saw a man knocked to the ground by a policeman and then trampled on by a hundred of his fellow fascists. The great wall of policemen stood fast against the wave of anti-republicans, so that a shudder seemed to go through the city of Paris itself. Joe, worming his way nearer and nearer to the fighting, cradled his camera against his body, and cursed the darkening night.

The following day, French newspaper headlines shouted reports of the unsuccessful coup, and counted the dead. Joe, waking in a small hotel room after a few hours of broken sleep, fished his mother's address book out of his rucksack and searched for a name.

He could remember Cousine Marie-Ange only vaguely. His mother's family, the Brancourts, had been, like the Elliots, unprolific. There had been Grandpère and Grandmère and Tante Claire and Cousine Marie-Ange and a scattering of great-nephews and great-nieces, none of whom appeared to be listed in the address book. A child, he had classed Cousine Marie-Ange as one of the daunting, distant adults. Tante Claire, who had played ball with him in the park, and who had crept with him into the kitchen to steal biscuits and bonbons, had been an ally, a friend.

Paris was littered with the debris of the previous night's riots as Joe walked through the streets towards Cousine Marie-Ange's house. It was early, and a cold, watery sunshine reflected from the roofs and pavements. Policemen, in small, hostile groups on every street corner, eyed him suspiciously. Joe walked fast, clearing his head, until he found a small, greyish building on the outskirts of the town. The shutters were closed, the brass door-fittings impeccably polished. Joe knocked at the door.

A grey-haired elderly maid peered out at him.

'Madame is attending Mass,' she said disdainfully, in answer to Joe's query. The door closed, leaving him standing alone on the pavement. He retreated to a wall opposite, kicking his heels until a small, middle-aged woman dressed entirely in black walked around the corner, and then he sprang off the wall and crossed the street.

'Madame Brancourt?'

A glance, followed by a nod of the head.

'Excuse me, madame – I'm Joe Elliot, Thérèse Brancourt's son.'

At the door, she paused and looked at him. 'Thérèse's son?'

'I'm looking for my Tante Claire. I wondered if you had her address. My mother died some years ago, you see, and—'

'I am aware of that, young man.' Madame Brancourt rapped smartly on the door. 'You had better come in, I suppose. I do not believe in discussing family affairs in the street.'

The maid opened the door, and Joe followed Madame Brancourt into the parlour. There were crucifixes and religious pictures on the walls, and on the sideboard a vast collection of family photographs. He could not resist glancing at the photographs.

The small, acid voice said, 'If you are looking for your mother or your aunt, monsieur, you will not find either. Thérèse and I never got on, and I had no wish to look at Claire's foolish face again after she left my house.'

'She lived here?'

'For a few months. After her parents died.'

'Where has she gone?'

'To Munich. Claire married a German. A musician, would you believe.'

She made the profession, Joe thought, sound almost criminal. 'Do you have her address?'

Another small shrug. Then Madame Brancourt rang the bell for the maid.

'Fetch me my portfolio, Violette.'

When the maid returned, carrying a leather folder, Madame Brancourt began to search through its contents.

'After Claire married, she wrote several letters to me. I did not reply, of course, so she stopped writing soon enough. Claire was almost forty, you understand, monsieur. To marry at that age is undignified – to claim that you are marrying for love is degrading.'

It was as much as Joe could do to stand there, mutely witnessing her contempt. He forced himself to remain silent, guessing that if he offended her, she would take pleasure in keeping from him what he wanted to know.

She drew a piece of notepaper from an envelope. 'Here you are, monsieur. You may keep it, it means nothing to me.'

He took the paper from her, glanced at it and folded it and put it in his pocket. 'Thank you, Madame Brancourt. You have been most helpful.'

But he did not yet go. Her earlier words returned to him, provoking his curiosity.

'Why didn't you like my mother, Madame Brancourt?'

'She was a coquette.'

Prim and self-satisfied, the lines of disapproval etched permanently into her face were distorted as she smiled at his anger.

'You don't believe me, monsieur? It is true. Thérèse was always fickle.'

Her judgement was damning, and he saw that she took pleasure in it. Her eyes narrowed as she looked at Joe. 'You have the look of her. I have always thanked God for giving me a plain face. One is less exposed to temptation.'

He took his leave soon afterwards, glad to escape the oppressive atmosphere of the house. He told himself that he had discovered what he had come here to find: that Claire Brancourt had married a German musician called Paul Lindlar, and was living in Munich. If he had found out other things as well, if that envenomed description of inconstancy lingered with horrible possibility when he recalled his mother's utter indifference to his father, then he tried to put that out of his mind.

When Lord Frere telephoned Maia to ask her to dine, she felt overwhelming relief. It was not that she particularly liked Harold Frere, it was just that this must mark the end of her isolation. He was rich, influential, well-bred, a leader of society. To be taken up by the Freres could only mean that she had become socially acceptable again.

They dined in one of Cambridge's best-known restaurants, talking about his estate and her business and the places they had visited on the Continent. While they were dining, several other people in the restaurant – people who had snubbed Maia since Edmund Pamphilon's death – crossed the room to speak to them. Maia felt a rush of satisfaction and triumph, and slept that night better than she had for an entire year.

A few weeks later, when she received an invitation to dine at Brackonbury House, she knew that the difficult months were almost over. The invitation was hand-written, the signature 'Frere' scrawled across the bottom of the note. Gleefully, Maia wrote her acceptance and thought carefully about what to wear.

She drove alone out into the Fens. The sky was clear and a full moon lit the ditches, swollen with rain, and shimmered on the fragile sails of the disused windmills. Brackonbury House, raised by its own small island of clay, was visible miles before she reached it. A chauffeur parked her motor-car for her, a butler welcomed her indoors, and a maid took her coat. There were no other cars visible and she could see no other guests. She thought that she must be early. She was shown into the drawing-room.

Lord Frere was standing by the fire. Maia, greeting him as the butler poured drinks, glanced at the clock on the mantelpiece. Ten minutes past eight. The invitation had been for eight o'clock. The horrible idea occurred to her that she had confused the day.

'I am so sorry – have I mistaken the time?'

Lord Frere smiled. He was a tall, well-built man, his face smooth but florid, his thinning hair brushed straight back from his forehead.

'Not at all, dear lady.'

'But the other guests—' She glanced around her.

'Didn't I explain in my note? How remiss of me. This is just a quiet little dinner à deux. I thought you might appreciate a change from the bustle of your daily life, Mrs Merchant.'

She smiled and said all the right things, but she had begun to feel uneasy. Her unease deepened when, entering the dining-room, she saw that the table was laid only for two.

'Lady Frere . . . ?' she began, hesitantly.

'Primrose is indisposed, I'm afraid. Can you bear to put up with my company for an evening?'

·The dinner passed pleasantly enough. The food was plentiful, the wines were excellent. Nervous, she drank more than she had intended to. By the end of the meal Lord Frere had begged her to call him Harold, and she had begun to relax a little, to tell herself that there could be nothing questionable in a widow dining with an elderly man.

It was after dinner that she realized how mistaken she was. They had returned to the drawing-room, where the butler had poured brandies and left. Maia said, 'I must go soon. Such a long drive home.'

She was sitting beside the fire, her hands cradling her brandy glass. Lord Frere looked at her in a way that made all her former unease return.

'My dear Mrs Merchant. Always so proper.'

There was something about his last three words that made her pause and look up at him. He was smiling slightly; she could see his discoloured teeth, and there was in his eyes a sort of amused contempt.

'What do you mean?'

He took her empty brandy glass from her and placed it on the mantelpiece. He said, 'I mean that I admire the way you always appear to preserve the proprieties.'

'*Appear* to?' Her voice was stiff.

'Now, you mustn't be offended. I admire your demeanour almost as much as I desire your person.'

That time, there was no possibility of mistaking his meaning. She felt an utter disgust, that this man – this old, married man – should think that she should even consider him as a lover. She said coldly, 'Would you please ring for the maid to fetch my coat, Lord Frere. I think I should go.'

His hand did not reach for the bell. 'My dear Maia – you cannot leave so soon. We have business to discuss.'

'Business? What business?' She was confused.

'You have not considered what I can offer you, Maia. What I can do for you.'

She thought for a moment that he was referring to the shop. Half-formed ideas of loans or partnerships flashed through her mind. Then she heard him say, 'The past year hasn't been easy for you, has it, Mrs Merchant?', and she looked up at him, her question written in her eyes.

'Since the death of your employee,' he added, very softly.

At first she couldn't speak. She was mesmerized by him, by the complacency that she recognized in his eyes, by the way his scalp gleamed through the patchy, oily covering of his hair, by his unquestioning assumption that his wealth and position entitled him to whatever – whoever – he wanted.

She said feebly, 'I don't know what you mean.'

'Come, come. Let us be frank with each other. We both know that since the scandal concerning your employee's suicide, you have been persona non grata within polite society. You have been shunned, Mrs Merchant. You are not the sort of person that the wealthy ladies of Cambridge – or even the gentlemen – would wish to sit next to at a dinner table.'

She stood quite still, ice-cold despite the heat of the fire. She could not deny what he said, but no-one had voiced it to her in such blunt, brutal terms before.

'It must be rather trying for you. Very dull and rather trying. People can be so narrow-minded.'

She whispered, 'My business is successful. That is all I need.'

'Is it? I could not help but notice how pleased you were to dine with me the other month. To be ostracized is so humiliating, is it not?'

She felt herself nod. His eyes, a protuberant, watery bluish-grey, were glazed as they studied her.

'So I thought I should put a little proposal to you.' He took a cigar from a box, and clipped the end of it, his gaze not leaving her. 'You don't object if I smoke, do you, Maia?'

She shook her head.

'I can give you an entrée back into society, you see. Breeding still tells, even in these egalitarian times. I can get you invitations for the right places. Your little faux pas will soon be forgotten.'

'And the price?' she said harshly. There was always a price.

He smiled. His lips were wet and slightly parted; she could see the desire in his eyes. 'You are a business-woman, Maia. I'm sure you can calculate the price.'

He cupped the palm of his hand around her face, and let his forefinger trace her profile from her forehead to her jaw, coming to rest on her mouth. His breathing was fast and audible. His touch nauseated her, and she swung her head away.

Her voice, though, was calm and cold. 'You are saying, Lord Frere, that if I become your mistress you will in return help me regain my position in society?'

'I have tried to avoid putting it as crudely as that, but – yes. An equitable arrangement – I would be very discreet.'

'And your wife? Does she approve of this . . . arrangement?'

316

'Primrose and I have an understanding.'

She stood quite still for a moment, staring at him. Then she said softly, 'My Lord – you must understand that if all the doors of all the houses in the land were closed to me, then I still would not willingly go to your bed. You disgust me.'

She wanted to say more, but managed to stop herself. She saw the sudden chill in his eyes, and it frightened her.

Yet he did not respond with the physical violence she dreaded. Instead he said coldly, 'Mrs Merchant. You have just made a very serious error. Perhaps the worst error you have ever made.'

She grabbed her evening bag from a nearby chair, and headed towards the door. His smooth voice halted her as she grasped the door-handle.

'Rumour is, of course, that you bed your store manager. The Irishman. There are other rumours, much more damaging ones. I shall do my best to encourage them.'

Maia ran out of the room and through the hallway, almost tumbling down the steps that led from the front door to the driveway. She found her motor-car in the stable block. Her hand was shaking too much to press the self-starter, so she took her flask from the glove compartment and drank deeply, until the whisky had run through her veins and warmed her. Then she wrestled to engage gear, jamming her foot on the accelerator as she drove away from Brackonbury House in a great skirling of dust and gravel. A skilful driver, she screeched round corners, crashed gears, and brought up the clutch too quickly. She knew that she was driving too fast, but did not let up. Taking a wrong turning at a crossroad, she became confused and drove even faster, desperate to get away from the unfamiliar, threatening land that the Fens had become. As she drove, she drank.

Then she saw him. She was speeding along a straight, narrow road. There were no houses beside the raised drove, only the dark, empty fields and marshes. Out of the night, picked out by her car's headlights and the moon, came the solitary figure standing at the roadside. A man – medium height; brown, foxy eyes; a smiling mouth with rows of small, pointed white teeth.

Vernon.

Maia, ramming her foot hard on the accelerator, screamed as the car skidded out of control and veered over the edge of the drove into the ditch.

The cold water, lapping at her feet, woke her.

Maia opened her eyes, and saw that the world was at a crazy angle. Reeds and bulrushes pressed against the shattered windscreen, and the roof of the Bentley sloped up above her. She had slid into the well between the seat and the dashboard. Because it was dark she could not see the water, but she could hear the small hiss as it trickled through gaps in the motor-car's body-work. Terrified, she wanted to curl up and cry, but instead she forced herself to grasp the sides of the dri-ver's seat and pull herself upright – or what counted for upright in a vehicle wedged nose-first in a ditch. As she moved, the car wobbled precariously, and tears of fright escaped from her eyes. She did not know how deep the water was. She was afraid that the Bentley might roll, tail over nose, until it was upside-down, drowning her.

She could hear the quick, panicking sound of her own breathing as she leaned sideways and seized the handle of the driver's door. At first it would not open, and she gave a sob of terror, but somehow fear lent her strength, the handle turned, and as she crawled out, the dented metal scraped at her bare arms, and the grass and reeds that grew on the bank scratched her face. Rushes dug into her as she slipped and slithered back up the bank to the drove. When she had almost reached the summit she paused, frozen, crouched in the long grass, certain that when she looked over the parapet, *he* would still be there. Yet when finally she forced herself to stand up, she saw that there was no-one – only the long, narrow road, the empty fields, and a scrubby tree, bent towards the clay by the wind. Maia gave a sob of relief as she climbed over the summit of the bank and collapsed on the verge.

Eventually she was able to sit up and look around her. She did not seem to be hurt, and she realized that she was not lost at all. She and Helen and Robin had cycled along this road, Hugh had rowed the three of them on the river that ran through the field. Maia, hugging herself, felt a sudden intense longing for the simpler days of childhood. It all seemed so long ago.

She began to walk the mile to Blackmere Farm. She was desperately cold, and she had left her coat in that awful house, and her sleeveless dress was soaked. Her steps were unsteady, but she was not sure whether that was due to shock, or because she was still rather drunk. When she saw the farmhouse, pale and square and welcoming in the moonlight, she began to run.

It was almost one o'clock, and though Hugh had tried to sleep, he had been unable to. So he pulled on his battered old dressing-gown and took his book and his pipe and went down to the kitchen, the only reliably warm room in Blackmere Farm. The night was still and quiet, the silence unbroken until he heard the footsteps crunching on the gravel path at the side of the house, followed by an urgent tap-tap on the window-pane.

Putting his book aside, Hugh opened the kitchen door.

'*Hugh*,' cried Maia, and ran towards him.

He cradled her against him, stroking her hair. He could not afterwards remember what he had murmured to her, but he did recall how privileged he had felt, holding her. Then he realized how cold she was, and that her dress was wet, and he helped her into the kitchen. She was in a dreadful state, her clothes torn, her face bruised and scratched. A terrible fear for her seized him. He sat her in a chair by the fire and put his jacket around her shoulders, and said, 'I'll wake Ma and then I'll drive to Burwell for the doctor.'

She stopped him. 'No, Hugh. I'm not hurt – I don't need a doctor.'

He looked closely at her. 'Maia – what happened?'

'I crashed the car.' She tried to smile. 'So silly. It's in a ditch, by Jackson's Corner.'

His heart was pounding. 'You might have been killed—'

'But I wasn't.' She was still shaking despite the jacket and the heat of the stove.

'I'll get you a drink.'

Maia shook her head. 'I've had too much already tonight.'

It was true, he could smell the whisky on her clothes.

'Cocoa, then,' said Hugh calmly.

He set the milk to boil on the range while he looked for lint and arnica for her cuts and bruises. 'Did you skid?' he asked, his back to her.

'Yes.' Her voice was small and frightened, not at all like Maia. 'I saw him—'

Hugh said sharply, 'Who?'

'Vernon.' Her voice was only a whisper.

The milk had begun to boil. Hugh poured it into the cup and took it to Maia. 'Drink this.' He enfolded her cold hands around the cup. Then he said very gently, 'You know that Vernon is dead, Maia.'

'I know.' There were tears in her eyes. 'But I saw him, Hugh.'

Once, ten years ago now, he had seen in the London crowds friends who had died in Flanders, and he had heard mortar-round and cannon-shot mingled with the noise of traffic.

'When you have been attached to someone – when you miss someone very much and their death has been untimely – then sometimes you *think* that you see them.'

She had stopped shaking at last, but Hugh was not reassured.

'I've seen him before,' she said. 'But only in dreams.'

He sat beside her, but he did not touch her again. He had sensed long ago Maia's dislike of human contact.

The embrace that she, frightened and distressed, had allowed him would probably never be repeated.

He tried to explain. 'It's because you loved him.'

She looked up at him. He saw in her lovely blue eyes at first bewilderment, then pain.

'You don't understand, Hugh,' she said. 'I never loved Vernon. Never, ever.'

Chapter Eleven

Thorpe Fen flooded badly in the spring of 1934, a black glaze on the fields one day, on the next two feet of water in the lowest-lying farms and cottages. Adam Hayhoe helped the cottagers bale out, a dispiriting task as the water only seeped up again through the peat to gleam, dark and complacent, beneath the floor-bricks.

He was filling a last bucket of muddy water, when he heard a tap at the door. Turning around, he saw Helen. Adam, straightening, smiled, and touched his cap.

''Morning, Miss Helen.'

'Good morning, Adam. I thought I should see whether there was anything I could do.'

'If you could make a cup of tea, Miss Helen. Poor old Jack hasn't had a drop yet today.'

He watched her fill the kettle and place it on the range that he had earlier lit. She said, 'How is Jack?' and he lost the patience that was natural to him, and gave vent to his anger.

'Jack Titchmarsh is seventy, he has rheumatics because of the damp, and can't straighten his back because of the years he's worked as a turf-cutter. And he has to live in a place like this.'

She turned towards him. She had the look of a frightened hare, all big eyes and high forehead and soft, curving cheeks.

He said more gently, 'I'm sorry for the poor soul – he won't last another winter here.'

The cottage was tied to the Big House. Jack Titchmarsh, who had worked for the Freres for almost sixty years, had only been allowed to remain in it because of its dilapidated state. Built on turf that was steadily sinking, the whole building stood out of true. The shabby curtains had to be pinned to the wall or they hung, ridiculously, almost a foot out from the sill. The bitter east wind blew through the crack between door and jamb. Once, in the summer, Adam had seen a couple driving through the village laugh and exclaim at the tiny, crooked house.

Adam lifted aside the scrap of dirty curtain that divided the front room from the back, so that Helen could carry through the cup of tea. She moved with a gawky grace that he found entrancing. He wondered for the hundredth time how they lived up there in that vast, ugly house, she and the old rector. Were they a small, close family, content with each other's company? Adam, thinking of the unhappiness he had glimpsed recently in Helen's eyes, was doubtful. Disturbed, wishing he could reach out to her and knowing that he must not, he began to sweep the mud from the floor with the besom.

The Hayhoes had lived in Thorpe Fen for countless centuries. Hayhoes had always been carpenters; generations of skill and craftsmanship had been passed down to Adam. Until recently, Thorpe Fen had always needed a carpenter.

Now, though, times were changing. Those who could afford it bought cheap ready-made furniture from the new department stores, and those who could not paid the new man in Soham to knock things up for them. Adam knew that the ready-made stuff would not last five years, and he despised the Soham carpenter's shoddy workmanship. The pieces Adam made would last a lifetime. He would have been ashamed to do otherwise.

Twenty years ago there had been work enough to keep Thorpe Fen's craftsmen – the blacksmith, the basket-maker, and the carpenter – comfortably off. Their lives had been more secure and in many ways easier than the lives of the farm labourers, the turf-cutters, the domestic servants who made up the rest of the village. Then the War had intervened, and neither the blacksmith nor the basket-maker had come back from Flanders. Adam, returning to his village at the end of 1918, had found that change had begun to touch even Thorpe Fen. The girls no longer automatically went into service at the Big House at the age of fourteen, but looked instead for shop work in Ely or Soham, and the young men – what remained of them – moved their families from the land as soon as they found work in the town. Thorpe Fen's population had dwindled since the end of the War. Adam, himself struggling to survive, wondered if soon the village would be no more than a church, a rectory, and a collection of tumbledown cottages peopled only by ghosts.

After she had read the diary, Helen had kept away from the attic. Recalling the photographs, recalling that short, smudged final sentence – *Dear God, what women have to bear* – she had felt ashamed of herself. It was as though she had peered through a keyhole, watching the most intimate moments of another person's life.

Worse than the shame, though, was the fear. Those photographs, that diary, threatened her life in a fundamental way. She had always been told that her parents' marriage had been idyllic, that Florence's early death had broken a small but happy family. Now she was forced to question whether she had been told the truth. When she thought about the photographs of Florence with her ringlets and frills, Helen thought she remembered misery, not delight, in those wide, shadowed eyes. Her readings of the diary could not be reconciled with her father's description of love at first sight and nuptial bliss. She began to ask herself whether her father had been deluded, or whether he had instead tried to force the young Florence into a form she had been unable to fit. Whether Florence, too, had felt trapped, frightened, in this bleak, inhospitable land.

When the rain finally let up Helen made herself carry out the duties that she knew, guiltily, she had recently skimped. The preparations for the Easter Bazaar, the necessary calls on the sick and the old. Walking down the drove, away from the little huddle of houses around the church, she was aware once more of the emptiness of the countryside. The flat fields stretching for miles, the wastes of marshland and the long, silver lines of ditch and dike. It dwarfed her, diminishing her. She went into Ely, hoping that an afternoon out would cheer her up, but it did not: the streets, the shops, the cinema reminded her of happier times that she had spent there with Hugh and Robin and Maia. Her shopping took longer than she had expected, and she missed her bus and had to wait an hour for the next. When it finally arrived and she asked for her fare, she was horrified to discover that she had not enough money in her purse to take her all the way to Thorpe Fen. The conductor watched unsympathetically as, red-faced, Helen laboriously counted out the coppers and found herself tuppence short. She had to alight from the bus two miles short of Thorpe Fen. The countryside was bleak and open, with only a single farmhouse and a couple of cottages within sight of the bus stop. The light was fading, the clouds casting streaking black shadows over the Fen. Helen walked fast, her collar up, her scarf wrapped tightly around her neck. There was not another soul in sight, only a flock of wild geese flying overhead. But she imagined eyes watching her as she almost ran along the road, and when she looked up and saw the lights flickering in the marsh, she stopped for a moment, transfixed and horrified. Hearing a small sound behind her, she screamed and dropped her bag.

'Miss Helen? Are you all right?'

With a great rush of relief, she recognized Adam Hayhoe's voice. He brought his bicycle to a halt behind her. She pointed at the marsh.

'I saw lights . . . down there . . .' Common sense returned. 'Marsh gas, of course . . . how silly of me . . .'

Adam picked Helen's bag up from where she had dropped it on the verge, and slung it over the handlebars of his bicycle. They began to walk along the roadside.

'Will o'the wisps, the old folk in the village call 'em. Or corpse candles. I reckon a lot of the fairy stories must have come about because of the will o'the wisps, see. It must have been a fearful thing, to walk through the fens a few years ago. Always afraid you'd end up in a bog or a ditch . . . scared stiff by lights where there shouldn't be no lights. But,' he glanced back over his shoulder, 'I've always thought they were beautiful.'

The lights were dancing again, drawing a fleeting pattern of phosphorescence in the darkness.

'I suppose they are.'

Adam glanced at her. 'We could cut through the fields, if you like, Miss Helen. It's quicker that way.'

They left the road, and took the narrow muddy path between the fields. The light on Adam's bicycle lit the reeds that crowded the ditches. If she had been alone, Helen knew she would never have walked here. With Adam, though, fear drifted away, returning her to the other thoughts that had preoccupied her in the months since she had read her mother's diary. She said suddenly, 'Do you remember my mother, Adam?'

She saw him glance at her. He had a nice face, brown hair and eyes, and the sort of features more suited to smiling than frowning.

'Yes,' he said. 'Just about.'

'Was she pretty?'

'Yellow hair like yours, but thinner-faced. Tall . . .' She saw his mouth curl into a grin. 'All hands and feet.'

'Clumsy, like me?'

'Oh no, my love . . .' He had gone ahead of her, crossing the narrow plank bridge that spanned the ditch, and the wind had picked up, rustling the reeds and grasses, so she thought she must have misheard the endearment. Adam dropped his bicycle down on the far bank of the ditch and offered his hand to help her across the plank.

'I meant . . . just very young. She played cricket once with us lads. We were having a game on the green, and Ted Jackson sent the ball wide and she caught it. Then she took the bat and hit the ball and hoiked up her skirts and ran like a boy. Half a dozen runs Mrs Ferguson scored before Rector saw her and told her to go home.'

They began to walk again. The sun, that had almost dipped below the horizon, put out a last pink and amber flare of light. The colours lit the entire Fen, so that it seemed to Helen just for a moment to be beautiful, not threatening.

There was one more thing she had to know. Lately she had even found herself questioning her father's love for her. If he had moulded Florence into something that had suited him, had he distorted his daughter's life in the same way? Had he selfishly set out to deny her the husband, home and children she longed for?

'Was my mother happy here, Adam?'

He turned to look at her. She thought she saw pity in his eyes.

'I don't know, Miss Helen. I was only a boy, see. And she was with us such a short time. Only a year.'

Adam Hayhoe took Helen to meet his friends, the Randalls, who farmed the land that lay between the river and Thorpe Fen. They were Methodists, attending the small, squat little chapel not far from Blackmere Farm.

The Randalls had three children: eight-year-old Elizabeth, six-year-old Molly and the toddler, Noah. Noah, plump, dimpled and good-natured, scrambled onto Helen's lap; his older sisters, staring at Helen's long golden hair and flowered, starched cotton dress, hung back, clutching their dolls. Cuddling Noah in her arms, Helen admired the dolls and asked their names. Elizabeth, forgetting her shyness, led Helen to the low-ceilinged little room at the back of the house where she slept, and showed her the tiny wooden dolls' cradles that Adam Hayhoe had given the sisters for their birthdays.

Walking back to the village through the fields, Adam

explained that the Randalls had recently bought their farm.

'Samuel Randall was a tenant of the Big House. Only his lordship decided to sell, so Sam had to find the money or get out.' Adam held out his hand to help Helen over the stile. 'They're finding it hard,' he added. 'Still – who isn't, these days?'

Something in his tone made Helen glance at him, surprised. '*You're* all right, aren't you, Adam?'

He did not immediately answer. As they walked through the lush meadow, with its ranks of nodding buttercups and clover, it occurred to Helen that Thorpe Fen had changed in the past few years. She had believed it unchangeable, paralysed by time, but now suddenly she recalled the cottages that stood empty because their tenants had drifted to the towns, and the land that was no longer farmed, but sown only with teasels and thistles. When she had been a child there had been a shop in Thorpe Fen. She could not remember when it had closed.

'Adam,' she repeated timidly, touching his shirt sleeve. 'You're all right, aren't you?'

''Course I am.' He looked down at her and smiled, and the vague, unformed fear evaporated. 'Only,' he added, 'there's not much call for my sort of work these days.'

She remembered the two dolls' cradles with their exquisite workmanship, and she exclaimed, 'But people will always need a good carpenter!'

There was no stile at the far end of the field, so he gave her a hand to climb over the fence. When she reached the topmost bar, he said, 'Look at it. Look at it, Miss Helen.'

Sitting on top of the fence, she looked at the fields and marshes that spread out to either side of them like a vast patchwork quilt. At the dikes and river and ditches, silvery in the sunlight, criss-crossing the pattern of green and black. Overhead arched the sky, blue and empty of clouds.

Adam said, 'My grandfather never travelled more than five miles away from Thorpe Fen. He had no need to, see. My father went to Ely once or twice a year, but he thought it a cold, unfriendly place. When I came back from Flanders in 1918, I promised myself I'd never leave home again.'

'I've always wanted to travel.' Helen voiced an ambition she had almost forgotten. Sitting on the fence, looking down at Adam's curly head, tears pricked at her eyes. 'But I've never been further than Cambridge.'

'There's plenty of time,' he said gently.

She thought that there was not. She was twenty-four, and she had somehow allowed herself to settle into an old maid's sort of existence, looking after her father, helping the poor of the parish, knitting shawls for other women's babies. The restlessness that she felt was unfocused, doomed to wither and dissipate. She wanted to run through the flowery meadow, or to swim in the distant river, or to touch Adam Hayhoe's brown, muscular forearm, resting only a foot or so away from her on the fence. But she knew that she would do none of these things.

On 7 June, Robin and Joe travelled to Olympia. On the Tube they argued, he exasperated, she indignant. Climbing the stairs, when he tried, one last time, to dissuade her from attending the meeting that Sir Oswald Mosley had called, she swung round and said:

'I don't know why you're making such a fuss, Joe. But I'm going, and no-one's going to stop me, and that's that.'

She heard him swear under his breath. 'Then stick with me, and get out if this affair turns into a riot. Promise?'

Unwillingly, she promised. At Olympia, sneaking through a side entrance, Joe's camera was hidden beneath the folds of his coat as they passed a phalanx of fascists in uniforms of black shirts, black trousers, and black jackboots. The chanted slogans of the anti-fascists outside faded into the distance. Inside the auditorium, every tier was crowded, every row flanked by a self-important, blackshirted steward, hands on hips, gaze flicking casually and menacingly along the ranks of seats.

Under the folds of his coat, Joe loaded film into his camera as a trumpet fanfare announced the entrance of Sir Oswald Mosley, attended by four blond young men and a troop of Blackshirts bearing flags. As the formation marched slowly into the limelight, the applause swelled into a triumphal, uncontrollable roar. All around Robin, arms were raised in the Fascist salute. At last Mosley's arm rose, quietening the crowd. And then, from somewhere towards the back of the hall, interrupting the sudden silence, voices chanted, ragged at first, then gathering confidence:

Hitler and Mosley mean hunger and war!
Hitler and Mosley mean hunger and war!

A spotlight searched for the protesters, picking them out from the crowd. Stewards moved through the rows, dragging the dissidents from their seats, manhandling them out of the hall. Then Sir Oswald Mosley began to speak.

Afterwards, Robin knew that Mosley had said nothing of substance. That his promises had been vague, his accusations unsubstantiated, and that those he accused were no more than popular scapegoats. *We shall prepare to meet the anarchy of Communism with the organized force of Fascism . . . Fascism combines the dynamic urge to change and progress, with the authority, the discipline and the order without which nothing great can be achieved.* Meaningless, empty words, but spoken with such fire, such passion, that they possessed an almost hypnotic force. Every now and then Robin's repulsion was overcome by a fleeting understanding of the attraction this man had for his audience. An almost sexual power, a force that touched a more primitive need than intellect. The heckling was continuous, though, and the violence that greeted the demonstrators' shouted questions was sickening. The spotlight searched once more, settling on a man only a few rows in front of them. Joe rose to his feet; there was a short, blinding flash as he took his photograph. Mosley began to speak again, but the heckling intensified. The howl of the crowd almost drowned his words – something about international finance and Jewish bankers and the Soviet threat. Several Blackshirts seized a heckler, dragging him from his seat, punching and pummelling him before ejecting him from the hall. The camera flashed again and, just for an instant, Robin's eyes met those of the steward as he looked along their row of seats towards Joe.

'He's seen you!' she hissed, pulling at Joe's sleeve.

Joe was loading the camera again. 'I'm going out,' he said. For a moment Robin thought that he had seen enough, had photographed enough. Then she saw where he was heading, and she began to follow him, battling through the crowds. The almost tangible aura of tension and violence surrounded her, trapping her. Mosley's voice, colourful and hectoring, rose over both the howl of the mob and the attempts of the opposition to obstruct the meeting. The Union Jacks flaring from wall and stage, and the black-uniformed stewards seemed omnipresent. Holding on to the tail of Joe's jacket, Robin wormed her way out of the hall. When she glanced back, she saw that the Blackshirt who had seen the camera was lost in the crowd. In the corridor beyond the auditorium, six men kicked a single protester as he lay on the ground. Nausea rose in Robin's throat as their booted feet struck his head, his face. Flat against the wall, hidden in the shadows, Robin saw Joe's camera flash again and again as he quickly loaded another plate and slid the exposed one into his coat pocket. The man on the ground lay motionless. Robin wanted to run forward and help him, but she could not; she was literally paralysed by fear. Unable to move, hating herself for doing nothing, she saw Joe take a last photograph as one of the Blackshirts tipped the prone body with his boot so that it tumbled slowly down the stairs. Then another steward looked up, searching for the source of the flash.

Joe muttered, 'Take this—' he bundled his overcoat into Robin's arms '—and *go*.'

This time she did not argue. Joe darted for the front door. Robin, clutching his coat, ran along the passageway, down another set of stairs, and slipped out of a side door. Running along the street, heading for the Tube station, she looked back, and saw not Joe, but two Blackshirts, a hundred yards or so behind her. Her forehead, and the palms of her hands, were damp with sweat. She could hear her anxious, laboured breathing. Glancing backwards a second time, she saw that the Blackshirts were nearer, and her footsteps quickened, stumbling slightly on the dusty pavement. Desperately she searched for a policeman, but the ranks of mounted police that she had earlier seen were nowhere in sight. They were only fifty yards or so away now – tall, muscular young men, thick-jawed, heavyset. Robin saw her chance when she turned a corner. Temporarily out of her pursuers' sight, she glimpsed the gate that led from an alleyway into the back yard of a house. Darting through it, she looked round for a place to hide. The yard was empty except for a dustbin, a scrubby, leafless tree and a coal bunker. Ducking inside the narrow opening of the coal bunker, she froze, pressed against the wall, hardly daring to breathe. The small concrete structure was blackened and thick with dust. Voices echoed in the alleyway. Robin's knuckles, gripping the overcoat, were white. Then she heard the diminishing footsteps as the Blackshirts left the alley and walked away, and she began to shake, huddled there in the dark among the glistening nuggets of coal.

She waited for Joe back at his lodgings. One of his neighbours let her wash off the coal dust at his sink, and gave her a cup of tea. At eleven o'clock she went out to the street and called the hospitals from a public telephone box, but found out nothing. So she sat at the top of the stairs, Joe's coat over her knees, waiting. Every now and then she drifted off to sleep before waking with a jerk a few moments later, her eyes staring into the darkness.

It was past midnight when his footsteps, slow and laborious, woke her. She stood up.

'Joe?' *Are you all right?*, she was about to ask, but when he turned the corner of the stairs and was illuminated by the single lightbulb hanging from the stairwell, the words froze on her lips. Had he not spoken, she did not think she would have recognized him. His face was a bloodied mass of cuts and bruises, his clothes were torn and dirty.

'Bastards smashed my camera,' Joe mumbled, halfway up the final flight of stairs. 'The key's in my pocket, Robin. Could you . . . ?'

She took the key from his jacket pocket, and opened the door. 'Sit down. You should see a doctor, but I'll do what I can.' Her voice was unsteady. She pulled out a chair, and he sat down. She could tell by the untypical slowness of his movements that he was in pain. His skin, where it was not bloody and torn, was pallid.

She searched around his flat for disinfectant and bandages. The rooms were bare, spartan. There was no lint, so she took a clean pillowcase from where it dried by the gas fire, and tore it into strips. She set to work, trying not to hurt him, but she saw his fists clench when she touched the raw edges of the wounds. Trying to take his mind off the pain, she talked. About anything and everything, about school and home and her friends. His mouth was set in a thin, hard line; the eye that was not closed with bruises was dark and clouded. 'They had knuckledusters,' he explained when she commented on the ragged cuts. When she had finished, he looked up at her.

'You'd make a good nurse.'

'I'd make a good *doctor*,' she said tartly as she began to clear up the mess. 'Neil Mackenzie has been teaching me First Aid.' She glanced at him more closely, and saw

333

how shocked, how brittle he was. 'Have you any Scotch, Joe? It's not recommended in the books, but . . .'

'In the bedroom.'

Like the rest of Joe's flat, the bedroom was sparsely furnished. Only a bed and a chest of drawers – no fire, no rug, no pictures except for a small framed photograph. Robin picked up the photograph and looked at it. A woman, her black hair piled up on top of her head in fin-de-siècle style, her eyes dark and deepset. Her features were fragile and patrician. She took the Scotch and, returning to the other room, held out the photograph to Joe.

'Your mother?'

He glanced up and nodded. Robin poured an inch of whisky into a cup and passed it to him. He swallowed the whisky in a couple of mouthfuls.

'I'm going to Munich later in the year, Robin, to look for my aunt. As soon as I've the cash – as soon as I've replaced the camera.'

'Joe. *Munich*. Do you speak German?'

'Not a word. Do you?'

'Mmm. My father taught me. Perhaps I should . . .' But she thought of Francis, and her voice trailed away.

Joe looked at her sharply. 'Hell – I forgot. My photos—'

Robin retrieved his overcoat from where she had dropped it on the landing, and patted the pocket with the exposed films.

'All safe.'

'Thank you.' She heard Joe's sigh of relief. 'I knew I could count on you, Robin.' He drooped forward in the chair, his head in his hands.

'You should go to bed.' She glanced around the room. 'I'll sleep in a chair.' It was almost one o'clock, too late to return to her lodgings.

'You must have the bed.'

'Oh – don't be ridiculous, Joe. You're almost dead on your feet.'

'Then we'll share it,' he said. 'For pity's sake, Robin—'

For a moment, they glared at each other, old adversaries. Then she laughed, and followed him into the bedroom.

She borrowed one of his shirts, and curled up on the left side of the single bed. She had thought she would go to sleep immediately, but she did not. The white light of the full moon and the amber glow of the street-lamp illuminated both the bedroom and the living-room beyond. It occurred to her that the flat's emptiness gave it an air of transience, as though Joe used it as a staging-post, somewhere to go to ground before he moved on. Her thoughts drifted, inevitably, to Francis. Recently, she had sensed his increased restlessness and, at the parties and nightclubs they attended, had glimpsed in him the beginnings of a need for adulation rather than appreciation. There was nothing she could put her finger on, no return to the calculated malice of Vivien's wedding-day, but still, lying awake in the darkness, she felt a mixture of sadness and unease.

Her isolation became, for Maia, an almost tangible thing. Her house seemed to echo with the lack of words, and when she caught sight of her reflection in a mirror, she started, shocked by the movement. She became a different person at home and at work, remaining at Merchants later and later each night, putting off the moment when she must quit the place where she was something, and return to the house where she was nothing. The nights were the worst. She would put on all the electric lights, but there was still the hollow sound of her heels clacking on the floors, the small creaks and rustles of furniture and drapery. And the nightmares, when Vernon came to her in death, just as he had in life. She dreaded to fall asleep, could only allow herself to do so if alcohol had taken the edge from her fear. Her nights were interrupted, broken by her terrible attempts to claw herself awake, to escape him. The lack of sleep and her drinking gave a glaze of unreality to her days. Figures danced in front of her eyes when she gazed at ledgers; she forgot the names of people she had known for years. Driving through the countryside on her weekend away, she became lost in the familar tangle of narrow lanes and woodland that enclosed her secret destination. Once, walking downstairs, she stumbled and would have fallen had she not gripped the banister. Sitting on the stairs, looking at their wide sweep that tumbled precariously beneath her, and at the hard marble floor of the hallway, she began to laugh, her fist pressed against her mouth, knowing that he had almost had his revenge.

She struggled to pull herself together. She would go to a concert, and if no-one wished to accompany her, well then, she would go by herself. She wore a gown she had picked up in Paris in spring (black and silver, with a little bolero jacket), and she did her hair in a new way, and made up her face carefully. In the concert hall, listening to the orchestra tuning up, she felt fine. She was the old Maia Merchant again, who did not care what other people thought of her.

Then, when the auditorium was almost full, she saw Vernon. He was on the other side of the hall, moving between the lines of seats. He wore a dinner suit, and his hair was cut close to his head, just as he liked it, and his eyes searched the audience, looking for her. But the lights dimmed, and in the jumble of people looking for their seats, she lost him. She searched for him all through the first half of the concert, but did not see him again. At the interval, she collected her coat and left the hall. At home, Maia took the gin bottle from the cupboard and curled up in bed, Teddy on her lap. Hugh's voice echoed. *You know that Vernon is dead, Maia.* Of course she knew: she, and no-one else, had seen him die. So what she saw was a ghost, or she was mad. Rational to the point of cynicism, she had never believed in ghosts. Sitting up, her knees hunched up under her chin, she remembered hearing that madness could run in

336

families, like red hair, or left-handedness. It could take different forms in different generations. Suicide or delusion or imbecility . . . Maia, shuddering, filled her glass, and drank deeply. When alcohol had taken the edge from her terror, she went to her bureau and scribbled a note to Hugh. The writing was not as neat as usual, but she thought it would do. Then she flung a coat over her satin pyjamas and went out to the post box. It was midnight, and the dark, leathery leaves of the laurels rustled at her as she ran down the drive.

Hugh called at three o'clock the following afternoon. They went for a walk together, watching Teddy chase squirrels in the park, and then they had tea in the conservatory. He drove away just before eight o'clock, leaving Maia able to face the week ahead. He came the next Sunday, and the next. Then it was her weekend away, and then the awful thing happened.

There was only one letter waiting for her when she came home. She often worked late on Saturdays: there were always figures to be checked, ledgers to be inspected. Maia was usually the last person to leave Merchants. By the time she had dined and taken the letter from the tray it was ten o'clock, and she was alone in the house.

She poured herself a drink as she slit open the cheap brown envelope. Teddy danced around her feet, desperate for her attention. There was only one folded sheet of paper inside the envelope. Maia raised her glass as she opened it out.

Bitch.

The glass slid from her suddenly nerveless fingers, shattering on the floor. The single word, printed in large black capitals, loomed out of the page at Maia. She heard herself moan.

She did not know afterwards how long she stood there. She could only remember tearing the letter into tiny pieces and scattering it in the grate, and then running to fetch the dustpan and brush from the scullery, scrabbling round the drawing-room floor on her hands and knees as she swept up shards of broken glass. She found Teddy cowering in the hallway, and took him to bed with her, drinking gin until she fell back on the pillows unconscious, and did not dream.

She woke with an appalling headache at midday on Sunday. Her maid brought her black coffee, and when she eventually rose and bathed, a hammer pounded against her skull. She pulled on the first clothes she could find – an old pair of slacks and a jumper that Helen had knitted for her. When the doorbell rang and the maid announced that Mr Summerhayes had called, she felt a mixture of relief and dismay. Glancing at her reflection in the drawing-room mirror, Maia knew that she looked awful, but had no time to do anything more than quickly tidy her hair with her hands.

'Hugh! Darling – how lovely to see you!'

She acted the old Maia for a bit, dragging him upstairs to see the lacquer screen that she had bought, taking him out to the garden to admire the herbaceous border. Then she saw the bewildered, hurt expression on his face, and she stopped laughing and talking and stood beside the flower-bed, drooping like one of the ranks of scarlet-lipped begonias.

'Maia,' he said. 'Should I go?'

She saw that he meant it. She could not just then bear that he should go and she should be left alone again. 'No,' she whispered. 'Hugh. *Please.*' A tear trickled down her face, and she turned away from him so that he could not see.

He said, 'If you don't want to tell me what's wrong, then why did you write to me?'

She heard herself gasp. 'I just needed company—'

'Then write to one of the dozens of young men who I'm sure are desperate to spend a half hour with you.' His voice was harsh; he had never spoken to her like this before. 'Or write to Helen or to Robin.'

'Helen wouldn't understand, and Robin hardly speaks to me nowadays.' Defiantly, she turned to face him. 'You must have realized, Hugh, that Robin disapproves of my business methods. Perhaps you feel the same? Perhaps all the virtuously socialist Summerhayeses disapprove of my nasty capitalist habits.' She could hear the sarcasm lacing her words.

Just for a moment the anger in his eyes matched that in hers. Then his mouth twisted into a smile, and he said, 'Oh, Maia. You could clap them all in irons and I'd still adore you.'

She managed to smile. 'Sweet of you, Hugh.' Then she threaded her arm through his. As they wandered through the rose garden, he talked.

'Helen once said to me that when you were upset, you were "glittery". She meant . . . oh, hard and amusing and cynical and fast. Like a candle that's burning too brightly. You've been glittery for weeks, Maia, and you still haven't told me why. And I resent that – it means that you too think that I'm poor old Hugh, who mustn't be worried, mustn't be upset.'

His bitterness surprised her. She stopped beneath an archway of roses, and looked up at him.

'It isn't that, Hugh. It isn't that at all.'

'Isn't it? Then tell me what it is, Maia.'

'It's . . .' She thought of the letter again, and her fist went to her mouth, as though she wanted to prevent herself from speaking about it. But she knew that she could not afford to lose another friend.

'I had a letter yesterday. I won't tell you what it said, but it was horrible.'

'A poison pen letter?'

'Mmm. And I thought—' Yet she stopped, unable to voice the terrible fear that had seized her the previous night.

'What, Maia? *Maia.*'

She said hopelessly, 'I thought it was from Vernon.'

Bitch, Vernon had said to her before he raped her. *Whore.*

She began to walk again. 'I know what you are going to say, Hugh. That he is dead, that it's only because I'm upset and tired and frightened that I imagine I see him.

339

I've said all those things to myself, you see, over and over again. But there's a little bit of myself that I can't quite convince. That's the trouble.'

' "I fled Him, down the labyrinthine ways of my own mind . . ." ' muttered Hugh.

'Quite. Only I'm fleeing a ghost, not a god.' Her knuckles pressed against her mouth once more. 'Though I've even thought of turning to religion, Hugh.' She tried to laugh. 'But I'm too much of a sinner, aren't I? Much too much of a sinner.'

Their account customers were deserting Merchants: one or two a month, at first, but then more, too many to ignore, too many to regard as coincidence. Maia called Liam Kavanagh to her office.

'I had a letter from Mrs Huntly-Page, Liam.' She slid the sheet of paper across her desk towards him. 'She's had an account with us for almost ten years, but she writes to say that she has decided to close it.'

'*Hell.*' She just caught the soft, muttered word.

Maia added, 'That's half a dozen closures this week. Thirty-five within the last three months.'

He shrugged. 'Only a small proportion of our customers are account-holders.'

'They are our better-off customers. We cannot afford to lose them.'

'They'll come back to us when they realize that they can't get as good service elsewhere. You mustn't worry, Mrs Merchant.'

'You are very kind, Liam. But it is possible, is it not, that they are motivated by considerations other than profit?'

His cornflower-blue eyes met hers, and she sighed and said, 'You go to the clubs, the pubs, the restaurants, Liam. What are they saying about me?'

He stood up, walking restlessly round the room. 'Nothing,' he lied.

She took the envelope out of her desk. When she had opened it that morning she had been physically sick.

'It's the third one. I burnt the others.'

She watched him take out the scrap of cheap paper and read the single angry, insulting word. It was always the same word. He began to speak, but she motioned him to be silent.

'So – what are they saying about me?'

There was a short silence, and then he said, 'There is a rumour going around that Mr Merchant's death was not . . . that you, um, contributed to it.'

Her heart lurched. Wordlessly, she stared at him.

'I mean – that you flirted, so he drank, and so on.'

'Is that all?' Maia's voice was like ice.

'That you were happy to see him dead.' Liam scowled. 'I'm sorry, Mrs Merchant. I thumped the fellow who passed on to me that little gem, of course.'

She saw how foolish she had been in believing that she could ever be safe. You made decisions that perhaps did not seem so significant at the time, and they caught up with you. Everything left its snail-trail of silvery deceit and guilt.

It had been a misjudgement to believe that she could keep the two strands of her life apart. They existed, so close together, the darkness now and then showing, baleful and opaque, beneath the bright glitter. She heard Liam, behind her, speak.

'When I first met you, I thought you were a stuck-up cow who didn't believe in getting her hands dirty. Then, when Mr Merchant died and you took over, I wagered you'd last a couple of months – six at the outside. I've worked with you for four years now, and I've discovered that though you might look like a china doll, you're as good at the job as any man. You'll forgive my nerve, Mrs Merchant, in speaking like this, but you must understand that you've admirers as well as detractors.'

She turned to face him. She knew that she owed Liam Kavanagh a degree of honesty, at least.

'You may change your mind about that, Liam. I didn't want to tell you this, but I think I have to. There are other rumours, I'm afraid, that affect you as well as me.

341

That link our names in an unpleasant way. I would understand if you should wish to go . . . if you should wish to give in your notice . . .' Her voice faltered. She was afraid that he would detect her desperation.

He crossed the room to stand beside her. 'Do you want me to leave, Mrs Merchant?'

'No.' Maia shook her head violently. 'Of course not.'

'Then I stay.' He took a cigarette lighter from his pocket, and ignited a corner of the letter. 'Have you any idea who's writing you these charming billets doux?' Liam dropped the burning paper into the ashtray, where it greyed and curled.

'I think so. I'm not sure. But I can guess who started the rumours.'

'I know some fellows, Mrs Merchant . . .' he said casually. 'Fellows who'll sort out other people's problems.'

She stared at him. Then, smiling, she shook her head. 'No, no. Nothing like that, Liam.'

That evening, after dinner, Maia talked to Hugh about Merchants. She told him about Edmund Pamphilon, and then about Lord Frere. How she had turned him down and insulted him, and how she suspected that he was using his influence to damage her name further. She did not tell him how the loneliness that was the result of her ostracism had begun to gnaw into her, so that she was only a blackened, hollowed husk. But she thought that he guessed.

'People are envious, Maia,' said Hugh. 'Other women envy your freedom, and plenty of men resent working for a woman. Especially a young, beautiful woman.'

'They are saying such dreadful things . . .'

'Tell me.'

Her back to Hugh as she poured him a drink, she said, 'People are saying that I wanted Vernon to die, so that I could inherit Merchants.'

It was the first time she had ever put it into words. It made it more real, more relentless. Often, now, she dreamt of the expression on Vernon's face as he had begun his long, backward fall. Terror, and disbelief. Her dreams haunted her, and she wondered how long she would be able to keep up the façade. When would the two halves of her life merge together, trapping her in a nightmare?

Maia heard Hugh's 'Dear God', as she turned and handed him his glass of Scotch. Then she poured out a large gin for herself, and sat down in the chair opposite him.

'After all you have been through,' he muttered. 'How could people even think such a thing of you?'

The whisky blurred his words, her fear. She said more lightly, 'I don't care what people think, Hugh – you know that. The problem is that we are losing our most valuable customers – friends of Harold Frere's, I suppose. If it goes on, then it will affect Merchants.' She paused, draining her glass. 'There is a solution, of course.'

He frowned. 'Go on.'

'That I leave. No, Hugh – hear me out. The rumours concern me – our customers are leaving because they disapprove of *me*, not because they disapprove of Merchants. It would be the simplest answer – we are in good shape, there'd be buyers, I'm sure. And I could start again somewhere else.'

'You don't *want* to sell, do you?'

'Of course not.' Her tone was vehement. She tried to explain. 'I was always bored before I owned Merchants – always unsatisfied. I thought I wanted a rich husband and a beautiful house, all that, and then I found that I didn't. Or I did – I still need lovely things – but they weren't enough. But I may have to sell, Hugh. I don't want to, but I may have to.'

She did not tell him that she feared, sometimes, for her sanity. That she was afraid of disintegrating, falling apart. That the fragile structure she had created with her own hands seemed threatened, and that she could not bear to have her enemies watch her fail.

She could hear her weariness in her voice. She felt as though she had battled for years, and was losing the will to fight. Standing in front of the fireplace, her hands twisted together as she added bitterly, 'Everything I touch seems to turn to dust.'

'You have to stick it out, Maia. If you leave Merchants, then you'll give credence to these lies.'

Frowning, rubbing at her aching forehead with her fingertips, she wondered whether he was right. Whether she cared.

'I'm afraid there are those who'll assume resignation to be a tacit admission of guilt,' he said bluntly. 'It would reflect on you, Maia – and on your family.'

Her hands clenched around her glass. She did not care a jot about her mother or Cousin Margery or Cousin Sidney, but she realized for the first time that there was someone she wanted to protect. Someone whose future she – and only she – could safeguard. She might not care what other people thought of her, but she could see that Hugh was right: her reputation, her security, might affect others. Whatever she had done – whatever she had become – must not jeopardize the struggles and secrets of the last few years.

Hugh – peaceful, gentle Hugh – said, 'I'd like to kill the lying swines.'

She looked up at him, startled. Then she smiled. 'Liam Kavanagh offered to find me some thugs to deal with the rumourmongers. Can you imagine, Hugh – a few burly heavies cornering Harold Frere in a dark alleyway?'

Hugh, too, smiled. 'Shillelaghs at the ready—'

Maia began to giggle, the laughter almost sliding out of control.

'Do you know the trouble with us, Maia?' Hugh, putting his glass aside, looked at her. Getting a hold of herself, she shook her head.

'We were never young. I went into uniform as soon as I left school, and you were married and widowed and running a business by the time you were twenty-one. We never had any fun. Not like Robin, who seems to have had years sowing her wild oats.'

Rising from his seat, he fiddled with the dial of the wireless until dance music filled the drawing-room.

'Perhaps we should complete our education.' Tall and graceful, he stood over her and held out his hand to her. 'What do you think, Maia? Shall we dance? Shall we learn to have fun?'

Chapter Twelve

To get anywhere in politics you had, Francis had realized, to start at the bottom and work your way up. Particularly in the Labour Party, where vaguely upper class connections, an education at a less than illustrious public school and a decent accent were of dubious value. It would have been easier, Francis had often reflected, if he had chucked his convictions to the wind and thrown in his lot with the Conservatives. Then no doubt some second cousin with a handle to his name might have arranged introductions and soon he would have found himself put up for a nice safe, dozy seat in the Shires.

As it was he had to attend endless boring meetings, to speak in little halls the length and breadth of London, and always, always, be nice to the old duffers with influence. It was all too slow, and he could feel himself becoming impatient. More and more he had to fight back the urge to say what he really thought when they droned on interminably about part ten of some dreary protocol of yet another bloody resolution.

The difficulty was that he couldn't afford things to be slow. For some time now he had got through his allowance in the first fortnight of the month, which meant that the rest of the time he was living off others or getting deeper and deeper into debt. People like Guy and Selena and Diana never had any money, and the ones with money – the ones he had believed to be his friends – weren't inclined to lend it. He had borrowed from

Robin once or twice recently, loathing himself, vowing each time it would be the last time. But the letters from the bank kept coming, letters that Francis no longer dared open. And you had to eat, and you had to look right as well, or certain doors were closed to you. It all cost a hellish amount of cash.

He had begun to think recently that some sort of extreme measures might be necessary to remedy his situation. He thought through the options. You could either inherit money, or earn money, or marry money. He had failed to be born with money and he knew himself well enough to acknowledge that he had no particular talent for earning it. His ambition to do something great, something stunning, something to be remembered by, seemed constantly thwarted by the business of day to day survival. Which left only marriage. Even the idea of it depressed him. Some of Vivien's marriages had ended in divorce and some in widowhood, but none had brought her much more than a crumbling house, a couple of years of comparative affluence, and a few jewels to sell at the next lean time. Somehow, he could never imagine himself making much more of a success of marriage than his mother had.

Readmitted to Theo Harcourt's circle, Francis drifted from nightclub to cocktail party, from cocktail party to house party. Because for some time he had avoided Theo, he was on probation. One night, after he had led them all in dancing in the fountain in someone's ornate gardens, and he had staggered inside alone, cold, dripping, and extremely drunk, he heard a cool voice say, 'You'll catch your death, you know.'

Francis squinted in the darkness. The only light in the room was the gleam of her cigarette in its holder.

She added, 'I bet you don't even know where you are. The name of this house, I mean.'

'Haven't a clue,' Francis said cheerfully.

'It's mine, darling. We are in Surrey, and this is my house.'

She moved closer. Francis, rubbing his eyelids dry

with the back of his hand, saw her long, oval face, her slanted eyes, her long, thin nose and small crimson mouth. A remarkable face: lean and lovely and voracious.

'My name's Evelyn Lake,' she said. 'We've met before, Francis. I don't suppose you remember, because you were drunk that time as well.'

'Sorry.'

'It doesn't matter.' Her head to one side, she inspected him. 'You do look silly. You'd better get out of those wet things.'

Momentarily he was not sure what she was saying to him. Then, when she said, 'Do hurry up, Francis. Or the others will be in,' he shook himself, and followed her upstairs.

In a gold and turquoise bedroom, he made love to her. Or rather, she made love to him. She told him what to do, and he did it. Momentarily he felt as though he was seventeen again, out of his depth, no longer in control. 'No, not *that*,' she said, disgusted, when he displeased her. '*Dull*, Francis – don't disappoint me. You must use your imagination.' So he used his imagination, and hers, which was freakish and uninhibited and edged with a dry, impatient boredom. And some time in the early hours of the morning, when she turned aside and lit two cigarettes, passing one to him, he said:

'Did I disappoint you?'

She inhaled her cigarette. 'Not too much.' Then she said, 'You let us use you, don't you, Francis?'

He glanced at her sharply. Evelyn sat up in bed, the satin sheets kicked off, shadows gathering beneath her breasts, at her groin.

'I suppose so.'

'And you use us in return. What for, Francis?'

He was honest. 'Theo knows the right people. I'm hoping that he'll introduce me to some of them.'

'Short of cash, are you, darling?'

It occurred to him that she must be very, very rich. And that there was no wedding band on her left hand.

348

'Horribly,' he said.

'The question is,' she said 'whether you've the staying power. Theo demands a lot of entertainment for his money, you see.'

He saw that she was smiling, laughing at him a little, perhaps. He thought of Robin, and felt a wave of intense guilt and, rising and dressing, promised himself in future to avoid Evelyn Lake.

But they met again only a few weeks later. He had taken Robin to a little nightclub in Soho, and some time in the early hours of the morning a hand tapped Francis's shoulder as he was dancing, and a voice said, 'It has all become predictably dreary. A few of us are escaping to Theo's house. We need you, Francis.'

He knew her voice immediately. It sent a shiver along his spine, a phenomenon he had only previously encountered in cheap fiction. Francis had borrowed a friend's MG. He drove, Robin in the front seat beside him, Evelyn Lake in the back. He found her presence disturbing. When Evelyn said, her voice bored and dry, 'Do hurry, Francis – so dull,' he pressed his foot hard on the accelerator and hurtled through the dark London streets, swerving round corners, darting through narrow alleyways with only an inch or two to spare.

Theo Harcourt's house in Richmond was crowded, but empty of servants. A gramophone played in the drawing-room, where the French doors had been opened so that music and dancers spilled out into the walled garden. Young men lounged in the basement kitchen, raiding the larder and the refrigerator until every surface was a litter of discarded bottles and dirty plates. Robin searched for clean cups and saucers to make tea. People drifted in and out of the room, arguing.

'Yes . . . but if someone threatened your *sister*—'

'Don't be ridiculous, Leo—'

"S not ridiculous. If some bastard with a gun threatened your *sister* . . . wanted to, you know—'

349

'My sister would tell me to bugger off and let her have some fun. She's a face like the back of a bus.'

A roar of laughter. Leo said plaintively, 'C'mon, Bertie, you know what I mean. You'd have to kill the bugger, wouldn't you?'

'He's right, though it grieves me to say it. It's where pacifism falls apart.'

'See,' repeated Leo, his finger stabbing the other man's chest, 'if some filthy foreigner was after your *sister*—'

'Does your sister have any say in all this?'

Francis, leaning against a dresser and lighting himself a cigarette, glanced at Robin. So did the young men. Francis knew that Robin was furious.

'You're talking as if women can't look after themselves. As though we can't even *think* for ourselves.'

'Come on, sweetheart.' Bertie's inebriated gaze rested fleetingly on Robin. 'There's a limit to how far you can take emancipation. If there's a war and we're invaded, it would be every man for himself. The strongest would win, and the weakest would go to the wall.'

'That's hardly the basis, is it, for a civilized society?'

Leo, wagging a finger at her, mumbled again, 'If he was after your shishter . . .' and slid slowly down the wall to lie still, a crumpled heap, on the tiled floor.

'Never could hold his drink.' Bertie and his friend dragged Leo out of the kitchen.

'Such asses,' said Francis mildly, when they had gone. 'Still, they have a point.'

He saw Robin turn and stare at him.

'What on earth do you mean?'

He shrugged. 'Most of Theo's admiring undergrads believe the tripe they read in *The Times*. That Adolf Hitler's an unimportant little lower-middle-class foreigner who couldn't possibly threaten the great British Empire. At least that lot seem to have grasped a little of what's going on.'

'But they were wrong.' Her voice was vehement. 'Utterly wrong. There can't be another war.' Her face had gone paper white.

He said, 'Of course there will be.'

'How can you say that, Francis—'

'Oh, come on, Robin. You know that it's true.'

'Thousands of people are pacifists nowadays. Simply thousands.'

She had put the tea caddy down. The kettle screamed disregarded on the hob. 'And how can you sound so *complacent*—'

'I'm not complacent. Just realistic.'

'And I'm not, I suppose?'

He did not answer her directly. He said instead what he had known for some time to be true. It was not a truth he wanted or welcomed, just one he had become accustomed to.

'There's going to be another war, Robin. This time we'll all be caught up in it. You – me – everyone. Not just the young men, like the last time. All of us.'

'And all the work I do . . . all the petitions—'

He interrupted her. 'Will not in the end make the least difference. Germany has left both the League of Nations and the Disarmament Conference. Doesn't augur well, does it? If people want a war, then all the talk in the world won't stop it.'

She stared at him for a moment, and then she walked quickly out of the room. He knew that he had upset her, that he should go after her, and yet he also knew that he was right. He had spoken the truth because he was drunk, yes, but he believed every word that he had said. On reflection, he could have framed it less brutally perhaps, but that was all.

There was half a bottle of Scotch on the kitchen table. Francis unstoppered it and drank deeply. Then he wandered through the house, trying to take his mind off things. He saw Evelyn and Robin and avoided them both. He could not look at Evelyn without a complicated mixture of humiliation and desire; and he knew, watching Robin standing alone in a corner of the drawing-room, that he should not have brought her here. The part of him that found peace and delight in Robin's company was not the part of him that Theo Harcourt appreciated. More than ever now, he needed Theo's money and the doors that Theo could open. Guiltily, Francis supposed that Robin would soon call a taxi and go home alone. Couples were leaving, drifting off into the night. It was – and Francis squinted at a clock, making an effort of concentration – almost four in the morning. The music still played, though, and Theo still prowled the house, refilling glasses, igniting conversations, goading them when they became dull or sleepy. That suited Francis; he did not want to be alone long enough to think.

He was in the dining-room, searching at the back of a cupboard for another bottle of whisky, when he heard the shot. He found Theo and half a dozen of the others at the foot of the stairs. One of the chaps had a pistol in his hand and was aiming up towards the large portrait on the landing. 'My grandmother,' said Theo. 'Ghastly old witch.' The trigger was pulled, two shots rang out, and everyone looked upwards. Two small holes pitted the plaster by the portrait.

'My turn,' said Bertie Forbes, and aimed and fired.

'You've hit her hat, Bertie,' said a girl. 'Not exactly lethal.' There was a ripple of amusement.

'Francis?' said Theo, handing him the pistol.

He had always been a good shot. It was one of his odd, useless talents, none of which added up to anything. Despising the Officers' Training Corps in which he had been forced to take part at school, he had nevertheless, when he had put his mind to it, won every shooting trophy. Yet another of life's little ironies, he had always thought.

Francis aimed carefully, concentrating so that his hand did not shake. The bullet went through the portrait's painted forehead, between the eyebrows. One or two people applauded.

'The trouble,' drawled Theo, 'with sickeningly brilliant people, is that they do crush one so. I mean—' he gestured to the painting '—what point is there in continuing?'

Francis smiled. 'There's other games,' he said, and spun the barrel of the gun, and put its muzzle to his forehead. A girl screamed as he pulled the trigger.

Robin traced the sounds of the shots. When she reached the hallway, the first person she saw was Francis. He was smiling, and he had put a pistol to his head. Robin heard her own small, stifled crow of terror, and then he pulled the trigger.

Just a small click. Her knees shook, and she fell back against the wall. When she opened her eyes, Robin realized that Francis had seen her, so she turned and ran along the hallway, throwing open the front door and hurling herself down the steps. The open-topped MG was parked at the roadside. Half falling into the driver's seat, she pressed the self-starter and the engine fluttered into life. As she struggled to release the handbrake she heard a voice call out her name.

'Robin!'

'Go away. Go away, Francis.' Just now she hated him.

'For heaven's sake—' He leaned over the door, grabbing her arm just as she managed to release the handbrake. Her foot stabbed at the accelerator, and her hand, gripping the steering-wheel, was forced wildly to the right by the impact of his body. The MG lurched forward, and there was a crunch as its bumper collided with the rear wing of the Rolls Royce parked in front. Then the engine stalled and died.

'Now look what you've done!' She could hear herself screaming like a fishwife. 'Now look what you've bloody done!' Kneeling up on the seat she seized the sleeves of his jacket, trying to push him away.

'Just get out, Francis – go away – leave me alone—' Her clenched fists pummelled his chest.

She was vaguely aware that they had an audience. A small, interested crowd of spectators perched on the front steps of Theo's house; and curtains in the neighbouring house had begun to open, lights to flicker in bedroom windows.

She heard Bertie say, 'God. My poor bloody car—' and then she managed to restart the engine. Francis had fallen back onto the pavement. Forcing the gears into reverse, Robin drove, a tangle of collapsing bumpers and shattered headlights, away from Theo Harcourt's house.

She did not stop until she had reached the street in which Joe lived. There, she braked at the side of the road, and sat still for a few minutes, shaking. Eventually she managed to scribble a few words on a scrap of paper, to fold it over and write Joe's name on the front. Tears blotted her writing. Then she drove to the tenement block in which Joe lived, and shoved the note through the letter box.

Joe – I'm coming to Germany with you. Don't argue, you need an interpreter. Love, Robin.

They left for Germany three weeks later. The researcher's job that Robin had undertaken for a university lecturer friend of her father had slithered to a halt, complete yet utterly unsatisfying. She had had tentative offers of work but had not yet followed any of them up. She needed a change, she thought. She needed to get away from smug, safe little England.

She needed to be away from Francis for a while. To think. On the long train journey across Europe, she looked unseeing out of the window at the endless succession of field and village, and thought about Francis. Whenever she closed her eyes and tried to go to sleep, she recalled that small click as the hammer had struck the empty chamber. When she looked out to the fields and saw the harvest scenes that might have existed in Brueghel's time – the scythes cutting the corn, the hay stacked and golden – she knew that Francis had been wrong, that these things were unchanging, unchangeable.

Arriving in Munich late in the afternoon, they made

their way to the address that Niklaus Wenzel had given them. *Käthe and Rolf Lehmann are dear friends of mine. You will be able to trust them*, Herr Wenzel had said. The recollection of that last phrase made Robin, hurtling through Munich's wide streets on a tram, feel uneasy.

But they were welcomed warmly by Käthe Lehmann, and shown into a large drawing-room in an attractive apartment. Käthe Lehmann was a tall, big-boned woman, her greying hair cut in a short bob. She took Robin's hand, and kissed her cheek.

'Fräulein Summerhayes – how good to meet you. And Herr Elliot.' Frau Lehmann greeted Joe in English. 'You must both be so tired. Such a long journey.'

The maid, Lotte, a stolid girl with blond hair wound in a coronet of plaits around her forehead, took their coats and hats. Frau Lehmann's sons, Dieter and Karl, were introduced. Her husband, Frau Lehmann explained, was working at the hospital and would not be home until late at night.

They dined at seven, after the boys had been put to bed. The food was good, the chatter light and inconsequential. Whenever Robin tried to steer the topic of conversation to something more interesting than the pleasantness of the weather or different methods of cooking cabbage, Käthe steered the talk back, politely but firmly, to the dull, the trivial. Robin soon lapsed into bored silence, leaving Joe to fill in the gaps.

After coffee, Käthe said to the maid, 'You can go now, if you wish, Lotte. I know your mother will be waiting for you.'

Lotte left the room. There was the sound of her putting on her coat and hat in the hallway, and then the slamming of the door and the diminishing echo of her heavy feet plodding down the stairs. Käthe sighed and sank back into her chair, her eyes half-closed.

'You wouldn't happen to have a cigarette, would you, Herr Elliot? An *English* cigarette?'

Joe took a packet from his pocket and offered it to her. 'I dare not smoke in front of Lotte.' Käthe exhaled and glanced at Robin. 'Remember, won't you, Fräulein, when you travel in Munich, that it is not thought appropriate for a young woman to smoke in public – or to wear lipstick or powder. I have seen a girl assaulted on a tram because she was wearing make-up. Now – you'll help me clear up the dinner things, won't you, Fräulein Summerhayes? A small price to pay, I hope you'll both agree, for the chance to talk freely.'

Robin followed her into the kitchen.

'You don't like to talk in front of Lotte?'

Käthe, piling up dirty plates and turning on the hot tap, nodded. Her voice was dry. 'Lotte is a leading light in the Bund deutscher Mädchen – the league of German girls. Her Heil Hitlers put my embarrassed mumbles to shame. I suspect she has a votive photograph of the Führer on her dressing-table at home.'

She could hardly believe what Käthe was saying. 'You are *afraid* of Lotte?'

Käthe Lehmann turned to look at her, her expression a mixture of defiance and resignation. 'Yes. Yes, I suppose I am.' She stubbed out her cigarette in an ashtray. 'At the moment we live unmolested, Fräulein Summerhayes. Rolf can continue his work, if I cannot, and if we are careful we can read the books we wish to read, and listen to the music we choose to listen to. A few words from Lotte into the wrong ears could change all that.'

'Then why don't you dismiss her?'

The sink was full. Käthe turned off the taps. Then she said patiently, 'Because, Fräulein, she would then certainly betray us. Her work here is well-paid and congenial.'

Robin plunged her hands into the hot water and began to scrub the plates. 'But it's intolerable . . . in your own home . . .'

'It's not so bad. I have not yet had to grow my hair into Gretchen plaits.' Käthe's mouth twisted into the shadow of a smile. 'You are scrubbing that plate so hard the pattern will wash off it, Fräulein.'

'Robin, please.' Lifting the clean plate out of the sink she passed it to Käthe to dry. 'You said that you can't work any more. What did you do?'

'I was a doctor, like Rolf. We both graduated at the same time, and worked at the same hospital. I loved the work.'

'But you left when Dieter was born?'

Käthe Lehmann shook her head. 'Oh no, Robin. I had a nanny to look after Dieter and Karl. I left last year, after the Nazis seized power in Germany. All women doctors were dismissed from their posts, you see. *Kinde, Kirche und Küche* . . . that is all we are fit for.'

Sleeping fitfully, Joe woke early the following morning. From the window of the guest bedroom he could see down to the broad avenue below. Sunlight flickered on the lime trees, and the sky was a wash of pale blue. Looking out, he saw, among the people hurrying to work, men kneeling on the asphalt. Bewildered, he could not for a moment work out what they were doing. Then he realized that they were cleaning the road: scrubbing it with brushes and soap to remove – and Joe squinted, struggling to see – the painted slogans daubed on the tarmac. Brownshirted guards stood to either side of them. The surreal scene was heightened by the presence of the passers-by. They ran for trams, or scurried to work with briefcases tucked under their arms, not even glancing at the prisoners kneeling on the road. As though half a dozen grown men wielding scrubbing-brushes on a Munich highway was an everyday affair. As though they were invisible.

Dressing and breakfasting and leaving the Lehmanns' apartment, the image of those invisible men remained with him. Out in the street, which was empty now of buckets and scrubbing-brushes, Joe wondered for a short, almost hysterical moment whether he had dreamt it all. The juxtaposition of pleasurable normality and irrational horror persisted as he and Robin took the tram across Munich. It was a sheer delight to be alone in the sunshine of a foreign city with Robin, and the desire to take her hand, to kiss her, was almost overwhelming. He had not questioned her sudden offer to come to Germany with him, but he strongly suspected that Francis had something to do with it. She had been unusually quiet during the long journey to Munich, and she had not mentioned Francis once throughout the last few days. Here, alone with her in the sunlight and warmth, Joe remembered the night they had spent together in his flat – the feel of her soft, warm body, the scent of her hair against his face – and allowed hope, suppressed for so long, to bubble to the surface again.

They passed the Marienplatz, complete with cupola-crowned cathedral and bulky, ornate Rathaus. The tram was crowded, Joe's face squashed up against a Stormtrooper plastered with swastikas and badges, Robin squeezed uncomfortably on a seat between two large matrons. Rolf Lehmann had shown him the location of Claire Lindlar's apartment on a map. Joe had written twice to the Munich address that Cousine Marie-Ange had given him, but had received no reply.

At last the tram disgorged them into a suburb of Munich, where tenement blocks stood on either side of the street. Joe looked up at the four-storeyed block.

'Joe?' Robin's hand touched his arm. 'What is it?'

He shook his head, unable to find the right words. Her fingers threaded through his, briefly clasping them.

She smiled. 'It'll be all right, Joe. Come on.' She began to walk towards the front door. He followed after her.

The janitor was absent from his desk. The stairs and corridors of the tenement block were high-walled and ill-lit, their windows shuttered to keep out the sunlight. Dust motes floated in the narrow bands of light streaming from the shutters. Robin walked ahead. Joe felt dazed by her presence, dazed by her proximity. He wondered whether he was permitted to hope. Whether her heart was still quite so inextricably entangled with Francis Gifford's . . .

'Joe . . . ?' she said again. She was standing outside a green-painted door.

He shook himself. Concentrate, Elliot, he told himself. Stop behaving like a fool. He knocked, and waited. The wait seemed endless. Then he heard voices and shuffling, and a clinking of chain as the door was unbolted. It opened, and he stared, bewildered, at the woman who stood in the doorway.

'Excuse me, madame, but I am looking for a lady called Claire Lindlar. I was told that she lives here.'

Foolishly, he spoke in French. The woman stared at him with a mixture of incomprehension and suspicion. He guessed her to be in her forties, her plaited hair a mixture of ash-blond and grey, her face worn, her body sprawling at the hips and bust. He heard Robin, beside him, speak in German. A brief conversation followed, nothing of which Joe understood. As they talked, half a dozen children clustered round the doorway of the apartment, staring curiously at Joe and Robin. The older boys wore the uniform of the Hitler Youth, and the girl cradling the baby was dressed in the dirndl skirt and white blouse of the Bund deutscher Mädchen.

Robin stooped and offered a sweet from her pocket to the smallest blond-haired girl. The woman stepped back into the apartment. After a few moments she returned, and held out her open palm to show them the medal that lay on it.

Robin smiled and muttered farewells and, grasping Joe's sleeve, steered him back to the stairs. She did not speak until they were out in the street again.

'She's not there, I'm afraid, Joe. That woman hadn't heard of your Aunt Claire. I told her both names – Brancourt and Lindlar – but she didn't recognize either.'

He dug his hands into his pocket, and began to walk fast along the pavement. Some of the brightness of the earlier part of the day seemed to have faded. Now, travelling on foot, he saw everywhere the oppressive evidence of a totalitarian regime. The great numbers of people in uniform, the martial music played by the brass bands, the loudspeakers mounted on pillars on the street corners and the wirelesses inside the restaurants. The quiet, attentive crowds who gathered around the loudspeakers, who applauded the message of the wirelesses. The marching columns of uniformed guards that paraded along the roads. The enthusiastic 'Heil Hitler!'s that automatically greeted the standards carried by the soldiers. Joe realized, after the first hostile glances, that it was unsafe not to join in the Nazi salute. So they ducked inside shops, examining goods they had no wish to buy, waiting until the columns had passed. The bellow of the loudspeakers, the clash of drum and brass, sickened him. Or perhaps it was not that which sickened him, but something deeper. A growing sense of the evil that was here, rooted in Munich, flowering like some foul, distorted growth over Germany, and then perhaps, over Europe itself. Walking, cold with disappointment, his mouth set, Joe could imagine all too easily how it happened. You let yourself conform in small ways – the salute, the rapt attention to the Nuremberg Rally speeches relayed over the ubiquitous loudspeakers – because those things were only outward signs, not worth fighting about. But then the insidious contagion grew into other parts of your life, entering your home, controlling what you wore, what you spoke about, how you brought up your children. And last of all, of course, how you thought.

Robin pulled at the sleeve of his jacket. 'Joe? Can we stop? I'm hungry.' She was scurrying along beside him, darting through the crowds on the pavement.

He stopped so suddenly that passers-by cursed as they cannoned into him. 'Of course. So sorry.' He glanced around. 'Not a restaurant . . . there's a park over there – we could buy some sandwiches.' He delved in his pocket and drew out a handful of marks.

They bought sandwiches and bottled beer and found a small, quiet area under a beech tree. He flung his jacket on the grass for Robin to sit on. She said, looking up at him, 'Poor Joe. You must be so disappointed.'

He grimaced. Then he said, 'I didn't think family mattered. Thought I was glad to be free of the lot of them. But now . . .' His voice trailed away.

She passed him the beer bottles, and he flicked the tops off with his penknife. He could see the pity in her eyes. He tried to explain.

'It isn't that, anyway. It's this city. Don't you think?'

He saw her shiver and look around her.

'There's two layers to it . . . the bright, shiny one on top . . . and the awful one just beneath.' Robin swallowed a mouthful of beer. 'It keeps showing through. Just listen to us, Joe. We don't even dare to speak out loud.'

It was true, he realized. Their voices were low and muted, even though they were alone in the small, shady dell.

'Even in the *houses*,' she added. 'The Lehmanns . . . They can never say what they really feel. They have to pretend all the time. It's loathsome, don't you think?'

The leaves on the tree painted her face and head with dappled shadows. Joe thought that he, too, had pretended for a long, long time. For how much longer could he keep up the pretence? He was beginning to despise himself for the falseness of his position. He knew that he must speak.

'Loathsome,' he repeated. 'Robin—'

'Francis once said to me that hypocrisy was the thing he most despised. Saying one thing and doing another. I know he's not perfect, Joe, but he never says things he doesn't mean. He's never *false*.'

He saw, shocked, that there were tears in her eyes. He allowed the hope that he had briefly treasured to drift away, forgotten, almost unmourned. She blinked, and looked away from him. The sandwiches had curled up in the heat.

'Robin.'

'I don't want to talk about it.' Her voice was a sort of gasp. 'It'll be all right.'

He thought that could be their motto, his and Robin's

– and Francis's too, perhaps. *It'll be all right.* If they said it often enough, then perhaps it would be true. Only lately he heard echoes of desperation in the repeated phrase.

He searched wildly for a change of subject, and at last recalled the medal that the German woman had shown them.

'She seemed very proud of it. Was it her husband's?'

Robin shook her head. She had recovered herself, her eyes were no longer reddened. 'It was hers. She has nine children, Joe, so she has been awarded the Gold Honour Cross of the German Mother. Hitler himself gave it her last August.'

They dined together that night: Käthe and Rolf Lehmann, Joe and Robin. Again, Robin felt the relaxation of tension as soon as the maid left the house. Rolf opened a bottle of hock; Joe, seated at the Lehmanns' piano, began to play. Later, Rolf left for his shift at the hospital, and Joe, pleading tiredness, went to his room. Käthe's eyes followed him as he left the drawing-room, and then she glanced back at Robin.

'You are just friends, you and Joe?'

Robin nodded. 'Just friends.'

'He is very fond of you, I think.'

'We've known each other for simply ages.' She frowned, counting back through the years. 'Almost six years.'

'Joe tells me that he is a photographer. And you, Robin – what are you?'

'I'm nothing much, just now.' Restless, irritated with herself, she rose and went to the window. 'I've done lots of things, I suppose, but none of them for very long. I did some office work for a while, but that was very dull, and I've written a book. But since then I've just done . . . bits. Odds and ends.'

Käthe lit herself another cigarette. 'Nothing to occupy the heart?'

She echoed sadly, 'Nothing to occupy the heart.'

She glanced out of the window: the sun was setting and the quiet streets were painted with streaks of pink and gold and red. Just for a moment Munich seemed peaceful, serene.

'What do your family do?'

'My father and brother are teachers. And all the Summerhayeses except me are terribly good at music and art and things like that.'

Käthe's voice was gently mocking. 'And are you so talentless, Robin? Is there nothing you are good at?'

She thought of the clinic. Of the hours she had spent there – unpaid, many of them. Of how, when she was there, she was never bored, and never wanted to be somewhere else. She said, 'I want to do something useful. Something that makes a difference. I thought—' and then she stopped.

'You thought . . . ?'

'I thought maybe I could train to be a doctor.' The words all came out in a rush: it was the first time she had voiced such a huge, terrifying ambition to anyone. 'Only I've left it rather late, and the medical schools don't take many women anyway, so . . .' The words trailed away.

Käthe rose from her seat, and refilled both wineglasses. Then she sat down beside Robin on the sofa.

'Listen to me, Robin. Many of our friends have already left Germany – it is possible, if you are a professional person and you have money. Rolf and I, too, could emigrate. You see how we live, always thinking before we speak, always afraid to show what we really think. And I miss my work terribly. But I hope that things will change.' Käthe placed a clenched fist on her heart. 'I have to believe – *here* – that things will change. Robin – if you really want to be a doctor, then you must do it. It would grieve me to think that fear, or lack of resolution, should stop you.' She smiled and raised her glass in a salute.

'Do it for me, Robin. Even things up a little.'

*   *   *

They left Germany a week later. By then, Joe had found out that Paul Lindlar had died only three years after he had married Claire Brancourt, and that Claire had since returned to France.

He knew nothing more. No address, a trail as cold as ashes. They took the train from Munich station on a chill autumn morning, and did not look back.

Autumn in the Fens was wet, cold and blustery. Another family left for the town, their shabby linen and battered furniture piled on a cart, their abandoned garden soon tangled by the wind. Tiles tumbled from Thorpe Fen rectory's roof, and beanpoles scattered over the garden like ninepins.

'I'll ask Adam if he can do a day or two's work for us, shall I, Daddy?' said Helen, over pudding at lunch-time. 'Eddie Shelton really is too doddery now to clamber over the roof.'

There was a silence as her father helped himself to custard. Then he said, 'I trust you never forget, Helen, that you are and always will be Adam Hayhoe's superior.'

She looked up at him. 'What do you mean, Daddy?'

He continued to pour custard onto his stewed prunes. A small, patient smile hovered round the corners of his mouth.

'Merely that you have been seen together frequently. People talk, I'm afraid, Helen. And there is nothing as distasteful as an unequal alliance.'

His blue-grey, protuberant eyes focused on her, and he dabbed at his full lips with the corner of his napkin. She felt, as always, as though he saw through to her soul. The friendship that she and Adam had enjoyed over the summer months became, with her father's glance, something dirty, something to be ashamed of. She remembered how she had wanted to touch Adam, to let her hand rest on his strong, brown one. She remembered how once she had thought he had called her *my love*.

'There is nothing unsuitable between you, is there, Helen?'

She shook her head vigorously. 'No, Daddy. Of course not.' She knew that she was blushing, and when she picked up her glass, her hand trembled and water spilled onto the polished table top.

'You will write to Hayhoe, and tell him that we have some labouring work for him.' The Reverend Ferguson ate the last of his prunes, and placed his spoon in the centre of his bowl, for Betty to clear away.

After he said grace and rose from his seat, Helen followed him into the study. He dictated, and as she wrote the beginnings of a terrible anger burned in her. *Never forget that you are Adam Hayhoe's superior,* her father had said, but now she wondered whether he was right. She could not see that she, Helen Ferguson, was in any way superior. Adam had fought for his country, had supported his widowed mother until she died, and had made countless beautiful and useful things. Helen drew a deep, shuddering breath. She had done nothing with her life. The future frightened her, and she saw with horrible clarity how her father had thwarted her every small break for freedom, and how her own weakness had contributed to her confinement. Her mother had escaped that stifling love only through death.

She was not in love with Adam Hayhoe, though. Adam was older than she, his features unremarkable, nothing like the portraits of the heroes on the covers of the novels that she borrowed from the lending library. But he was her oldest friend.

When her father told her to sign her name at the foot of the letter, Helen wanted to break the pen, or to run from the room. But she did neither, because her occasional glimpses of liberty had been insufficient to break her habitual obedience. Biting her lip, she scrawled her signature.

A lack of regular work had driven Adam Hayhoe to take casual employment as a beater for the Freres. The work was loathsome and humiliating. Standing in the driving rain in woodland on the edge of the Brackonbury estate, flushing the pheasants from the coverts and watching them soar up into the sky, he found himself wishing that they would go free, that the gunshot would not reach them. As the brightly plumed birds struck the ground, the sound echoed against the trees.

He had a week's work. A week of rising before dawn, dressing in whichever clothes were not soaked from the previous day, and cycling the six miles to Brackonbury House. Then, eight hours of standing beneath dripping trees, mud seeping into his boots, every layer of clothing soaking. Lord Frere's party dined under awnings erected by servants; Adam and the other beaters ate their dockey crouched under bushes or leaning against tree-trunks.

It was not, though, the weather that he disliked most. He had seen worse than this; in Flanders (and the comparison made him smile a little) he had eaten, slept and worked in mud. And there they had been shooting at him, rather than at pheasants. *Your country needs you*, the poster had said, all those years ago, and he, loving his country, had joined up and done his duty. Now, though, his country did not need him. The years of slump that had hit East Anglia, dependent on agriculture, so hard, had taken away from him his craft. People who could hardly afford to eat or clothe themselves did not buy new furniture. Adam's soul rebelled against going into service or taking the pittance that went with farm-labouring. So he was reduced to this.

He realized, watching it all, that the beaters were treated worse than the dogs. The dogs were given food and water and kind words when they did well; Adam and his fellow beaters were cursed at, shouted at, patronized. Some of the beaters were young lads, a few were old men. One of the lads slipped in the mud, frightening the birds from the coverts before the shooting party was ready. Lord Frere bellowed angrily, 'Get out of the way, you stupid little sod,' and Adam stared at him for a moment, and then at the white-faced lad. Then, knowing that this was unendurable, he began to walk away, out of the wood, his boots clumping the soggy ground, not caring how many pheasants he startled, wings whirring, into the air.

Outraged voices followed him. 'I say . . . what do you think you're doing? . . . Stop that fellow, won't you – he'll ruin the whole bloody day.' But he just kept walking, enjoying the rain on his face, taking great lungfuls of fresh air.

When he reached his cottage, Adam found the note pushed beneath his door. Water streamed from his clothes onto the brick floor as he picked it up and read it.

It asked him – no, *commanded* him – to come to the rectory the following morning to do some odd jobs for the Fergusons. It was signed, 'H. Ferguson'. That was all. Adam, putting the note on the dresser, took the kettle, filled it from the hand-pump in the garden and placed it on the range. Then he began to cook his tea.

Working, he saw the cottage clearly. The brick floor, the low plaster walls with their faded paper, the earth closet outside. Though it would always be beautiful to him, he knew that it could never be enough for Helen, who was used to something better. He knew now that he had been foolish, that he had for a while believed that the barrier that lay between himself and Helen Ferguson could be lifted. He had been deluding himself. He did not resent her, he could not dislike her, but he knew that the love he might have offered her – might have offered her, indeed, years and years ago – could never be acceptable to her. The rigid social striations of village life ensured that.

Helen was in the garden, deadheading the roses, when a small boy delivered the note. She sent him away with a penny from her pocket, and then unfolded the scrap of paper. It said, *Regret cannot do work, Yrs, A. Hayhoe.*

She stared at it for a moment, and then she flung down the secateurs and the basket, and ran out of the gate and down the drove. When she reached Adam's cottage, she saw that the door was open. Calling his name, peering round the jamb, she went inside.

The cottage was cold, because the stove had not been lit. Adam, dressed in his old army greatcoat and boots, was standing in a corner of the room, struggling to do up a rucksack. Looking up at her, he said, 'Too many books. Can't choose which to leave behind, see.'

She said stupidly, 'Are you going away, Adam?'

He had managed to do up the buckle. 'There's no work to be had here, Miss Helen. Well – not proper work.'

His words stung. She looked around the cottage, whose small, cluttered cosiness she had always loved, and blinked. Emptied of his things, it had begun to change. She noticed for the first time the patches of damp on the walls, the paper that always peeled around the windows.

Helen gathered up all her courage. 'Are you leaving the village because of my letter?'

Adam shook his head, but he did not look at her. 'Jem Dockerill will do your roof. I've had a word with him. He's getting on a bit, but he's still a good worker.'

She almost said, *My father made me write it*, but she knew that would sound both weak and disloyal. Instead, she said, 'But you'll come back, won't you, Adam?'

For the first time, he smiled. 'Thorpe Fen's my home. 'Course I'll come back, Miss Helen.'

'*Helen*,' she corrected him angrily. Her eyes ached. 'Just Helen.'

Adam's hands, securing the rucksack's last strap, paused. Then, turning, he crossed the room to her. There was a quiet confidence in his dark brown eyes. She thought for a moment that he would touch her, that he would take her hand, but he did not. She heard him say, 'I'm going to make summat of myself, Helen. Then I'll come back.'

Hugh and Maia learned to have fun. Nothing serious, nothing that needed thinking about, said Hugh, rejecting Maia's suggestions of a concert or a Shakespeare play. So they went to the fair on Midsummer Common and ate candyfloss and toffee-apples and rode in swing-boats. Hugh won a teddy-bear at the shooting-range, and Maia carried it cradled in her arms, a lop-eared creature with a red bow around its neck.

They went dancing at the Dorothy Café, taking the floor with the shop girls and typists and the clerks with Brylcreemed hair and boils on their necks. They hired a boat and punted on the Cam when it was fine, and played Ludo and Snakes and Ladders and roasted chestnuts in the fire when it was not. They cycled to Grantchester, and ate cream teas at the tea-garden. Hugh taught Maia to fish, and Maia, rather drunk one evening, chalked on the terrace and taught Hugh hopscotch.

In December, they drove to the seaside. Aldeburgh was ice-cold and windless, the sea glassy and grey. Walking together along the beach, they played ducks and drakes. They had brought a picnic. Maia spread out the rug on the pebbles, Hugh put down the hamper. Fishermen stared at them and gulls soared overhead, waiting for scraps.

'They think we are mad.' Maia nodded to the fishermen.

Hugh smiled. 'Potted shrimps?' He offered the jar to Maia.

'We've done awfully well, Hugh, don't you think?'

'We have worked terribly hard at having fun.' His voice was only slightly mocking. 'If we keep going – oh, for another four or five years, perhaps – we should attain the status of being giddy young things.'

Maia giggled. 'The business would go to pot.'

'Maia.' Hugh was stern. 'You are becoming serious.'

After they had dined, they followed the coastline north, their feet crunching on the pebbles. Maia collected shells, seaweed, and the tiny transparent skeletons of crabs. She realized that this was the first time she had done such things. Her childhood had not been made up of days like this. It had been Robin who had made vast untidy collections, Helen who had scrawled sentimental poems about Days in the Countryside or Picnics on the River. She did not realize she had sighed until Hugh said, 'What is it, old girl? You look quite down. Are you cold?'

'A little.' Then, because she had grown used to being more honest with Hugh than with anyone else, she added, 'I was just thinking – I've never really done this sort of thing before.'

'I know.' He looked down at her. 'We should turn back now. I'll buy you a cup of tea in that funny little teashop we saw, and you can warm yourself up.'

He put his arm round her shoulders, and drew her to him as they walked towards the village. It was while they were walking that Maia realized several things. One was that she had neither dreamed of Vernon nor seen him for a long time. Hugh seemed to protect her from all that. And it had been weeks – months – since she had received one of those dreadful letters. The writer had, perhaps, grown bored with his single-minded, self-imposed task. Because of these things – because of Hugh – she had even managed to control her drinking. She – and Merchants – had passed through the worst of the crisis.

She knew also that Hugh loved her, had always loved her. She expected men to love her, but she was beginning to understand that Hugh's love had a different quality. She wondered whether she could endure his love; and whether he was strong enough to love her. She had, after all, a habit of destroying those who loved her.

The other thing she realized was that she did not mind him touching her. His arm rested along her shoulders in a way that was pleasant, warm and protective. Hugh was one of her oldest friends; she liked his graceful, rangy body to be next to hers. He made her feel safe. She began to think, walking with Hugh, that she could change. She had changed in other ways recently: she had begun (the thought astonished her) to *feel*. If she had learned, at last, to love, then could she – cold, hard Maia Merchant – *express* love? The idea frightened her, so that her heart began to pound, and her hands, encased in their soft leather gloves, became clammy.

Yet, when they reached the café, she regained her courage. And when Hugh's arm slid from her shoulders, she turned to him, and let her lips touch his.

Sometimes Francis realized that the precarious control he had once had was slipping away from him. That the intelligence and perception that had formerly enabled him to stand back from people like Theo Harcourt and Evelyn Lake had, in a blur of alcohol and late nights and nicotine, almost deserted him. He knew that they permitted him to join their gilded circle only because he made them laugh, only because he would do things they hadn't the nerve to do. Sometimes he felt like a circus animal, turning somersaults for the carrot of a lucrative job or an advantageous friendship. He performed for them partially because, he acknowledged, he had always liked an audience, but also because he knew that his financial situation was now not merely dire, but desperate. His monthly allowance no longer restored his bank account to a positive balance.

He spent Christmas at Long Ferry with Denzil and Vivien. The marriage was already on the rocks, Vivien's eyes straying to pretty boys, and Long Ferry, Francis knew, was the sort of bottomless pit that would swallow up any fortune. But he still nerved himself (half a bottle of Scotch whipped from the drawing-room, hidden in his room) to ask Denzil for a loan. He had to.

Denzil was cutting, crushing. Francis, persisting in self-abasement, asked about a job in Kenya, or whatever overheated country it was in which Denzil farmed. I don't think so, Francis, Denzil drawled. Have you looked at yourself recently? Back in his room, Francis finished the rest of the Scotch and glanced in the mirror. He looked, he had to admit, bloody awful. He spent the afternoon searching the kitchen for several particularly large cockroaches to put in his stepfather's bed, and then left for London.

At New Year he and Robin travelled to the Cotswolds, where they walked through the hills and stayed in youth hostels at night. He realized, for the hundredth time, that when he was with Robin he didn't want to be anywhere else, or be with anyone else. His health improved, his cough cleared up, and he drank nothing stronger than tea for a fortnight. Borrowing some money from Robin, he repaid the worst of his debts, and resolved to avoid Theo and Evelyn and all the rest of that crowd. Theo was abroad, so that was easy, and Evelyn wasn't the sort of woman who ran after you. Returning to London, he kept to his resolve for a couple of months. He found part-time work tutoring a boy who was recovering from rheumatic fever, and paid off some more of his debts. Then it all started to go wrong again.

He and Robin were dining in their favourite restaurant one night, when she told him that she was planning to become a doctor. She rattled on for ages about how she was saving up to pay the fees, and how she was going to evening classes to buck up her science. Francis listened, stunned. He knew what she was telling him, though she did not say it in so many words. That she would leave him, that he had been a stage in her life, something temporary, and that she would move on. He had not realized until then how much he had come to depend on her. He saw his affection for her suddenly as something dangerous, something that would only expose him to pain. They parted on reasonably civil terms, but Francis was aware of his slow-burning anger.

The next evening, he had to attend a meeting of the general executive committee of the local Labour Party. Unable to face it sober, he had a few drinks beforehand. They were choosing candidates to stand for the local elections, and Francis was supposed to be on his best behaviour. Bored and infuriated, he listened to stolid speeches about irrelevant issues. *There's a war waiting to start out there!*, he wanted to shout, but instead, when it was his turn to speak, he heard himself adopt the broad Lancashire accent of the chairman, Ted Malham. He even rubbed his forehead with his handkerchief in the way that Ted did, even shuffled his feet in imitation of Ted's working class diffidence. He simply couldn't stop himself. It was the sort of mimicry that had always gone down well in the pub, that had had Selena and Guy and Diana in stitches.

This time, no-one laughed. The secretary interrupted, very coldly, 'I think we've heard enough, Mr Gifford,' and the chairman, his face scarlet, said, 'Some of us haven't had the advantage of an education, lad,' in such a humble, wounded way that Francis wanted to shoot either Ted or himself, he was not sure which.

Outside, in the fog, he walked to the nearest public telephone box and asked the operator for Evelyn Lake's number.

In Adam's absence, Helen continued to visit the Randalls. Mrs Randall's new baby, a boy, was born in late spring; Helen, arriving at the farmhouse on the afternoon of his birth, was seized by Elizabeth and taken to see him.

'He's called Michael. Isn't he *tiny*?'

Helen arranged the flowers she had brought in a vase at Susan Randall's bedside, and then knelt and looked into the cradle. She drew back the blanket and very gently stroked with her finger the baby's small, downy curved cheek. He was stirring, his mouth pursing, a frown wrinkling his forehead.

'Can I pick him up?'

'Of course, Helen.' Mrs Randall tried to smile, but she looked exhausted.

Very carefully, Helen lifted the baby out of the cradle and held him against her. His head, supported by the palm of her hand, nestled against her shoulder. His tiny body was warm against her breast. She could feel the small, fast motion of his breathing, and the pattering of his heart. She could not speak, and when she looked down at him, there were tears in her eyes. When he began to whimper and to open and close his mouth, searching for food, she did not want to relinquish him.

She walked to the Randalls' house each day that week. Mrs Randall had a fever and could not nurse the baby; Helen helped Elizabeth prepare feeding bottles. Feeding Michael, changing him, bathing him, she was completely happy. Sometimes, sitting in the rocking chair, the baby cradled on her lap, she allowed herself to imagine that he was hers. That no-one could take him away from her, that she had something of her own at last.

At tea one day, her father brought up the subject of the Randalls.

'They are chapel, of course, not church.'

Helen said nothing.

'You must not allow one family to take up too much of your time, Helen. You have written the letters for the Parish Appeal, I trust. And I hope that the preparations for the Jubilee celebrations are well under way. Lady Frere has graciously consented to attend.'

Still she was silent. She knew what he was trying to do, though. He was trying to separate her from Michael in the way that he had separated her from Adam, and from Geoffrey. From Hugh, too, perhaps. Had Hugh loved Maia because Maia, unlike Helen, was independent, strong, a woman instead of a little girl? Each night, now, lying awake, Helen recalled the chances that she had allowed her father to steal from her; each night her anger grew as she saw how her life had telescoped into a barren existence.

Helen poured herself another cup of tea. Then she said coldly, 'There is a cake crumb on your chin, Daddy,' and began to drink.

Francis, wearing an overcoat, dark glasses and a wide-brimmed hat, went to see Joe's photographic exhibition.

Robin had told him about it. He, listening to her

effusions with a mixture of jealousy and curiosity, had said, 'I suppose you slept with him while you were in Munich, darling? Sex among the Stormtroopers. Terribly erotic.' She had looked hurt (Robin was awfully easy to hurt), and then she had risen from the sofa and walked out of his door. He had not seen her since.

In retrospect, he hated himself for teasing her. He knew that soon he would go to her, patch things up, promise to start again, yet he was uncomfortably aware that for him events were sliding irretrievably out of control.

He could not remember much of the last few weeks. There had been a rather unpleasant little incident – two thugs in an alleyway, something about gambling debts, terribly clichéd – and he had been forced to part with the gold watch that had once belonged to his father. There had been Theo, dangling the vague possibility of a job at the BBC in front of him. And there had been Evelyn. In retrospect, some of the things he had done with Evelyn revolted him.

He walked to the grimy little Soho studio where Joe worked. There was a busker singing outside in the street. Francis gave him the remaining coins in his pocket. When he entered the gallery, he saw that neither Joe nor Robin was there, so he shrugged off the overcoat – much too warm in May – and began to look at the photographs.

Mosley's mob, laying into some poor sod outside Olympia. Riot police and demonstrators in – Francis, squinting, recognized the Place de la Concorde – Paris. SA men, the swastikas on their armbands clearly visible, kicking a man curled up on the pavement. There was a depressing similarity about the photographs that told their own story. Francis moved on to the next display. 'Munich', the caption said. These pictures were different – at first glance they portrayed something chillingly like normality, but the darker underside became visible when you looked and thought. A street scene, where Francis had to peer carefully to see the line of

375

Brownshirts threading through the housewives and schoolchildren. The maid, a coronet of blond plaits encircling her plump, well-scrubbed face. Something about her eyes made Francis shudder. Oddest and most disturbing of all, the men kneeling in the road, scrubbing the tarmac. Around them, people hurried to work, to school, to the shops. Not one of them was looking at the stooped figures on the road. *Clever sod*, muttered Francis, under his breath. And at that moment, if Joe had been there, he would have forgotten the past and gone to him and thumped him on the back and congratulated him.

But Joe was not there. Francis left the gallery and went out in the street again, seeing the glittering sunshine, the strolling crowds through rather different eyes.

Chapter Thirteen

Robin waited for Francis in a café in Oxford Street. She had arrived at six o'clock; they were to go to the cinema and then to dine with Guy and Charis. Once more, she looked out of the window and along the pavement. No sign of Francis, only the girls in their summer dresses, and the businessmen in lightweight suits, hurrying to catch their trains.

The waitress was glaring at her, so Robin ordered tea and glanced up at the clock. A quarter to seven. The film began at half past seven. Her stomach felt hollow, but she could not have eaten. She took her diary from her bag and checked the date, the time. The crowds in the street had begun to thin out as the commuters left for the suburbs, but the queue for the cinema opposite was now curling along the pavement. The girls standing in the queue were hatless, their dresses short-sleeved. The men wore open-necked shirts and corduroy trousers. The heat lingered on into the evening, making London airless and oppressive. There was an unnatural, apprehensive feeling about the summer of 1935. As though they were waiting for a storm to break.

She thought she saw him then: a fair-haired young man in cricket whites and open-necked shirt, walking out of the mouth of the Underground. He had Francis's springy, confident step, but she realized almost immediately that he was a stranger. Turning away from the window, Robin began to drink her tea. If she did not look for him, then he would come. The small café, decorated with pseudo-Viennese swags of tasselled velvet, was crowded. Voices echoed on the polished wooden floor. A man slid into the seat opposite Robin. She almost said, *I'm sorry, that seat's taken*, but the words withered and died on her lips, a small, polite smile substituting for them. Twenty past seven. The long snake of people outside the cinema had grown shorter. The flower-seller opposite was wheeling her handcart away from the entrance of the Tube, her flowers wilted and ragged in the heat.

She thought now that he would not come, but still she waited. Throughout the years they had known each other, they had quarrelled and raged and made up with a passion that had almost consumed her. She had never thought that it could end like this: waiting, watching, a slow dying of something that had once burned like fire.

Her tea had grown cold. Prompted by the waitress ('We don't allow just drinks after eight o'clock, miss'), she ordered a sandwich and sat, shredding it with her fingers. She still stared out of the window, but she no longer expected to see him. The queue was long gone, swallowed by the cinema. Couples ambled along the pavement, arm in arm in the comfortable, easy way that she and Francis had lost. She knew that he was seeing someone else. She faced that thought here, now, in the crimson, plush, stifling little café, faced it for the first time, and found it unbearable. The rumours had reached her, along with other rumours: salacious, whispered descriptions of Francis's more unedifying ways of passing the time. What had once been amusing had become merely sordid; what had once enchanted her had begun to disgust her.

She did not know who Francis's lover was. Not Selena, not Diana, not Charis, though she knew that all three had at some time shared his bed. Someone more dangerous, she thought. Someone whom Francis wanted as much as Robin still wanted him. Someone with whom even Francis, who liked to lead, not to follow, became lost and directionless. His absences were of mind as well as body; and when he returned to her he was changed, burnt out, frail.

She knew that they should part. That she should not answer his notes, that when he called at her lodgings she should send him away. That whatever had once been between them was almost done with, exhausted, and that to continue to force it into life was making something ugly and destructive out of it. Yet she could not end it. She still sometimes saw the need in his eyes. As Robin rose from her seat and walked out of the café, she saw that the gaudy sun had begun to fade a little. She, who had always prided herself on her courage, now found that she despised her cowardice. Once she had boasted of her lack of possessiveness; now, aware that she was losing Francis utterly, she did not know to what depths she would abase herself in order that she could continue to lay claim to some part of him. *No, no, no, my heart is fast, and cannot disentangle.*

There was a motor-car parked on the lane outside the rectory when Helen returned from her visit to the Randalls. The driver of the car stepped out into the street as she passed by, and raised his hat. He was in his mid-thirties, with short brown hair, a small moustache and blue eyes. A cigarette dangled from his fingers.

'Afternoon, madam.'

'Good afternoon,' said Helen politely, opening the gate.

Leaning against his motor car, he looked at her in a way that she found unsettling. She began to walk down the path. From behind her she heard him say, 'Stunning old place.' His eyes were still focused on Helen, though, and not on the rectory. 'Got a refrigerator, have you, madam?'

Helen looked back, confused. 'No. We have a larder and a meatsafe.'

He exhaled a plume of smoke, and shook his head. 'Well, I call that a shame. A lovely young lady like you

379

having to manage without a nice, modern refrigerator to help you out. Look.'

Taking a book out of the car, he flicked through the pages. 'I sell refrigerators, you see, madam. This is my most compact model—' he pointed to a large, oblong white box '—but for a house like this you'd need something bigger. The "Supreme", or the "Princess". What do you think?'

She looked at the photograph of an enormous refrigerator, its shelves crammed with cold chicken and jellies and hams. A young woman stood beside it, short-skirted, pencil-waisted, eternally smiling.

'It's very nice,' she said timidly, 'but . . .'

'Just think how pleased your husband would be, on a hot day like this, if you could serve him with a cold drink whenever he wanted.'

Helen felt her face go scarlet. 'I'm not married.'

'Not married!' She could hear the disbelief in his voice.

'I live with my father, you see. He's the rector of St Michael's.'

'Then I must apologize.' The salesman shook his head, and tilted the brim of the hat back from his face. 'But . . . a pretty girl like you . . .'

He was rather handsome, Helen thought. He reminded her of the illustration of the hero in the novel she had recently borrowed from Ely Public Library, *Her Constant Heart*. Short dark hair, blue eyes, broad shoulders.

The salesman let fall his cigarette stub, and ground it into the dirt with his heel. His eyes were dismissive as he glanced around the huddle of cottages, church and rectory that made up Thorpe Fen. 'You're out in the sticks here, aren't you? Not much in the way of picture houses or dance halls, is there?'

'And I'm afraid we haven't electricity,' she said, looking regretfully at the glossy brochure.

'No *electricity*! Then I'm wasting my time, aren't I?'

But he did not yet go. Instead, watching her, he smiled.

'I suppose so.' Helen took hold of the gate again.

'Have you ever been to a roadhouse?'

She paused, the latch in her hand, and shook her head.

'Great fun. You can have a dance, a drink, something to eat. I know a lovely place near Baldock.'

Her heart was beating so loudly she thought he would hear it.

'How about it? Tomorrow night?'

Helen shook her head. 'Oh – I couldn't possibly—'

'You can't get a lot of fun, living in a dump like this. You deserve it.'

She almost shook her head again, but stopped herself just in time. She had missed too many chances: she thought first of Geoffrey Lemon, and then of Adam Hayhoe. She had neither seen nor heard from Adam for almost a year. It had occurred to Helen that, in spite of his promise, Adam might never return to Thorpe Fen. The thought filled her with a sudden, unexpected despair.

If she dismissed this opportunity out of hand, then what right had she to hold her father responsible for the narrowness of her life? Helen told herself that here was a chance, at last, to grow up a little. To do the sort of thing other girls took for granted. To spend an evening with a good-looking man; to escape for a few hours from the prison that Thorpe Fen sometimes seemed to be.

She heard him say, 'Hey – no harm meant and all that. Just thought you might like a bit of fun,' and she nodded and whispered, 'All right.'

He smiled. 'That's the ticket. I'll call for you at six, shall I?'

Thinking rapidly, her heart pounding, Helen said, 'Half past six.' Her father would be safely at evensong. 'And don't knock. I'll be out here.'

'Right-oh.' The salesman put away his book, and slid

back into the car. Then, leaning out, grinning, he said, 'My name's Maurice Page, by the way, Miss . . . ?'

'Ferguson.' Helen, flustered, held out her hand to him. 'Helen Ferguson.'

Helen caught the bus to Ely the following morning and, praying that no-one she knew would see her, bought herself lipstick and powder in the chemist. While the maids had their lunch hour, she ironed the cherry-red dress that Maia had bought her. It would be rather warm for such sultry weather, but it was the only sophisticated dress she had.

She told her father that Maia had invited her to tea, and at six o'clock watched him leave the house for church, her heart full of guilt and excitement. In her room, she changed into the red dress and applied lipstick and powder. Brushing out her hair, Helen twisted the long blond rope into a knot at the nape of her neck, copying an illustration from Betty's *Woman's Own*. The reflection that stared back at her from the looking-glass shocked her. The lipstick emphasized the fullness of her mouth, the drawn-back hairstyle showed off her high cheekbones and her tip-tilted, wide-nostrilled nose. Frightened, she wanted to scrub off the paint, to become the old Helen again, Daddy's little girl.

But it was already twenty-five past six. She had time only to throw her purse, comb and handkerchief into a handbag, to button her shoes and run out of the door. When she reached the gate she could see Maurice Page's car in the distance, a cloud of dust on the drove. He drew up beside her, his eyes widening when he stepped out of the car and saw her.

'I say. Stunning dress.' He opened the passenger door for her. Ducking her head, Helen climbed in. She had put on weight, she realized, since Maia had bought her the dress, it pulled a little across the bust and hips and rode up as she sat down. Surreptitiously, she tugged down her skirt as he restarted the engine.

As they drove south, Maurice told her about himself.

'I had a small engineering business, but the whole caboodle went down the tubes in the Slump, leaving yours truly without a dime.'

Helen made sympathetic noises.

'I'd a bad couple of years, but then things began to look up, and I landed this job. Terrific business – people are queuing up to buy electrical goods. Then I bought this little baby—' he patted the dashboard '—Austin Seven – four years old, sound as a bell.'

'It's lovely.' The car rattled and bumped along the unmade roads of the Fens. 'You must have to travel an awful lot.'

'A fair bit. But I'm my own boss and I meet all sorts of people.' He smiled at her, and his hand briefly touched her thigh. Helen froze, suddenly frightened, all her doubts returning in double measure. She knew nothing about this man: she had been safe with Adam, whom she had known since she was a baby; and she had felt safe with Geoffrey, whose father was their family doctor. Maurice Page's hand returned to the steering-wheel, and Helen tried to reassure herself. She reminded herself that she was only doing the sort of thing that Maia and Robin had done years ago. Maurice Page was well-spoken, and wore a suit and tie. He looked like a gentleman, and would behave like a gentleman.

The flatness of the Fens gave way to the gently undulating countryside of south Cambridgeshire. Helen realized, as they drove beyond Cambridge, that she had never travelled so far. She said hesitantly, 'Is Baldock in London?'

Maurice laughed, throwing back his head. 'You have led a sheltered life, haven't you?'

She blushed furiously. 'I've forgotten, that's all. I've been there lots of times.'

'Here's a nice straight bit of road,' he said. 'Shall I show you what she can do?'

The car gathered speed, hurtling along the leafy road. He drove as fast as Maia, but the motor-car, which was, Helen guessed, not as expensive as Maia's, rattled and lurched until she began to feel rather ill. She was relieved when Maurice braked.

'There it is. Car park's almost full. You'll love it – it's a lively little place.'

The roadhouse was a new, red-brick building, built alongside the main road. Maurice squeezed the little Austin between two larger cars, and opened the passenger door for Helen. It seemed even hotter here than in the Fens. The tight, long-sleeved dress was uncomfortably warm.

It was slightly cooler in the bar. Helen looked around, trying not to stare. She had never been inside a pub before. The rows of bottles, the chinking of glasses and the faint, beery smell seemed both repellent and enticing.

'What'll it be?'

She realized that he was asking her what she wanted to drink. She blurted out, 'Oh – a lemonade,' but he grimaced and shook his head.

'You must think I'm a cheapskate. How about a G and T?'

She hadn't a clue what a G and T was, but she nodded her head.

'There's a nice little corner table over there. You go and sit down, Helen, and I'll bring it to you.'

There were chunks of ice and a slice of lemon in her drink. It looked like cheap bottled lemonade. Helen, thirsty, swallowed a large mouthful, and then choked. Her hand over her mouth, she felt Maurice pat her on the back.

'Take it easy, love. Slow and steady, that's my motto.'

She made herself drink the awful stuff because she was too embarrassed to do otherwise. When she looked around, she saw that though most of the people in the bar were men, there were a few women seated at the tables dotted round the perimeter of the room. The women drank and smoked, just like the men. One woman did not wear gloves, but had bright scarlet nails, just as Maia sometimes had, though she was not as pretty as Maia.

'Gasper?' said Maurice, holding out a packet of cigarettes.

Helen took one, and he lit it for her. Forcing herself not to cough, she sat up straight, toying with her glass like the scarlet-nailed woman opposite. Although the gin tasted awful, it made her feel more relaxed. She could hear music from the adjoining room. Helen's feet began to tap.

Maurice bought her a plate of sandwiches and another gin, and told her some more about himself. A childhood with his parents in a little seaside town, followed by several years at a boarding school in Hampshire. He had left school when his father had died, had joined the army, but been invalided out. Flat feet, would you believe, said Maurice, and guffawed. Helen found it difficult to concentrate; her head felt blurry. When he paused, waiting for her to laugh at some joke she hadn't quite understood, her shriek of amusement seemed unfamiliar and overloud. He never asked her about herself.

She ate the sandwiches and smoked another cigarette. If you blew the smoke quickly out of your mouth it did not taste so bad. 'Another drink?' asked Maurice, and Helen nodded. The drink quelled the vague unease that had been with her since he had touched her in the car. Helen saw Maurice walk into the hall and speak to the lady at the reception desk. When he pocketed the key that the receptionist gave him, Helen concluded that Maurice must be staying in the roadhouse overnight.

She drank her third gin, and then he led her onto the dance floor. There was a small band, playing the sort of slinky, lazy music that her father disapproved of. *Swing*, Maurice called it. She thought that it was delightful – it seemed to go right through her body, so that even she – big, ungainly Helen – could dance. Maia had taught her to dance, years ago, in Robin's winter house. She felt terribly tired: when she closed her eyes, Helen could imagine herself there, the small wooden hut smoky and comfortable, the lazy river and Fen beyond.

He murmured, 'Hey, don't go to sleep, darling,' and she looked up at him and shook her head and laughed that peculiar laugh. She tried to explain, 'I'm just very happy,' but the words tripped over themselves. 'Sure you are, sweetheart,' he muttered, drawing her towards him. His body was pressed against hers, and she felt his mouth nuzzle her neck. His breath smelt unpleasantly sour. Helen stumbled, and then stopped, swaying, in the centre of the dance floor.

'A bit dizzy . . .' she said.

'Poor little thing. Here – let's go somewhere nice and quiet, shall we?'

She thought that he was leading her out into the garden that she could glimpse through the windows. But instead she found herself almost pushed up the stairs, his hand against her bottom, his face suffused with an urgency that she did not understand. Then they were standing outside a door with a brass numberplate fixed on it, and Maurice had taken out from his pocket the key that the woman had given him.

'This is nice, isn't it?' he said, unlocking the door, and nudging her in. She heard the door close behind her.

There was a chair, a small table, a washstand and a bed. Helen's heart began to pound. She knew suddenly that she had got it all wrong, that she had given him the wrong impression. That he thought she was cheap.

'Maurice – perhaps I should go – it must be awfully late—' She could hear herself gabbling nervously.

'Don't be silly. Don't be a silly little thing.' He kissed her, his lips pressing hard against hers, his chin scratching her face. 'That was nice, wasn't it?'

Then, before she could push him away, he began to unbutton the fastenings of her dress. His hands went around her waist, sliding across her stomach, searching for her breasts. She heard him whisper, 'Oh God,' and then he pulled her dress down off her shoulders. Bending his head, he pressed his mouth against her breasts, kneading them with his hands.

The pain shook her out of her frozen immobility, and

she pulled away from him. 'Don't – you mustn't—' She thought he was letting her go, then, as with a final painful squeeze he drew his hand out from inside her dress. But instead he leaned against her, so that she stumbled and fell onto the bed. His hands clawed at her skirt, pushing up the tight material past her thighs, her stocking-tops, her knickers.

'No – don't—' she heard herself shout.

'Shut up. Shut up. I didn't buy all those bloody drinks for you to turn all virginal now.'

His eyes were glazed, and he was breathing heavily. He was trying to prise her legs apart. Helen kicked out wildly. She heard him shriek and then suddenly he let her go. He was bent in half, his face contorted in agony. He muttered, 'Bitch, you bitch,' and she saw her chance and ran out of the room. Somehow she remembered, as she half fell downstairs, to do up her dress, to pull down her skirt. As she ran through the barroom, she saw the people staring at her open-mouthed, and heard a ripple of laughter.

She found herself in the car park at the front of the roadhouse. At the verge she looked wildly to left and right, but could see no other buildings. Fearing pursuit, she began to run along the road, her feet stumbling on the tarmac. When she reached a gap in the hedge and ducked inside the field, she collapsed to the grass and was violently sick.

Retreating to a corner of the field, she sat for a long time, shaking and crying. She had left her bag in that awful room, she had neither money nor transport home. She had no idea where she was. Her head ached terribly and she was afraid that she might be sick again.

Eventually she went back to the road, and began to walk. Every time a car passed, she was terrified that it might be his. At last she reached a village where there were a few houses and a pub. Inside the pub, she asked to use the telephone, and made a reverse charge call to Maia. The landlady stood watching her suspiciously while she made the phone call, so she couldn't tell Maia what had happened. Tears trailed constantly down her face, dripping from the end of her nose.

When she went to the ladies' room she realized why the landlady had stared at her. Her stockings were laddered, her dress was askew. Her lipstick had smeared, giving her a clownish look, and her hair had pulled out of its chignon to stand in wild disarray around her head. Her eyes were unfocused, and the scarlet of her lipstick clashed with the red of her dress. She looked, thought Helen, as cheap as Maurice Page had believed her to be.

Maia was in the house alone when Helen telephoned. Driving fast, she reached her in less than an hour. In the ladies' room of the pub, she soaked her handkerchief in cold water and gently sponged Helen's red, swollen face, and combed out her tangled hair. Helen, trembling, hardly spoke. Concerned, Maia offered her a brandy, but Helen shook her head violently.

In the car, driving back to Cambridge, Helen began to speak. The words jerked out of her in muddled phrases, but Maia eventually managed to make sense of it. Helen had gone out for a date with some dreadful little travelling salesman, and he had made a heavy pass at her. When Helen described the roadhouse, Maia sympathized, but was privately appalled. But that's what those places are *for*, she almost said. Instead, she asked carefully, 'You didn't let him go all the way, did you, darling?'

Helen stared at Maia, her eyes huge and reddened. It occurred to Maia that Helen did not really understand what she was asking.

'I mean . . . what did he do, Helen?'

Helen's face crumpled up. 'He kissed me. It wasn't like I thought it would be. It was *horrible*. And he . . . he *touched* me. So I kicked him.' Tears spilled over Helen's eyelids.

Maia, relieved, squeezed her hand. 'At least you got rid of the swine. And it sounds like you've ruined his love life for a few days.'

Helen did not smile. Maia thought quickly. The important thing was to get Helen back to the rectory as though nothing had happened. She could imagine all too clearly the Reverend Ferguson's reaction if he found out about Maurice Page. Maia felt a wave of intense anger. Girls like Helen, on whom society imposed an extended artificial innocence, were the least able to protect themselves, and the most blamed when their ignorance landed them in a situation they couldn't handle.

'I'll drive you home,' said Maia, 'and I'll tell your father that you've a headache and must go to bed immediately.'

Still Helen said nothing. When Maia glanced across at her, she saw that she had begun to shiver again, and that her eyes, glazed and wide, stared unblinking ahead. Maia said gently, 'It was a horrid thing to happen to you, darling – men are such beasts,' but there was no response. Maia pressed her foot on the accelerator, and drove faster.

In Thorpe Fen, she helped Helen out of the car, and into the rectory. It was late and the house was dark and gloomy, as usual, so the Reverend Ferguson, appearing in the corridor like some gaunt black bat, could not see the wreck of Helen's face. Maia said breezily, 'She's a frightful head, I'm afraid, Mr Ferguson. I'll see her to her room,' and gave him her best smile before going upstairs with Helen to her bedroom. Inside, she helped Helen out of the red dress and into her nightie. 'Climb into bed, darling, and have a good long sleep and you'll feel much better in the morning.' Helen obediently got into bed.

Maia caught a glimpse of her eyes then, in the dim golden light of the oil lamp. What she saw alarmed her: a sort of deadness, a loss of hope. She knew that she was no good at this sort of thing, that just as she locked away her own deepest feelings, so for years had she barricaded herself against the pain of others. Robin or Daisy or Hugh could have dealt with this, she, Maia Merchant, could not. Maia stood for a moment, shuffling from one foot to the other, trying to think what to say, and then she stooped and pecked Helen on the forehead, and left the room.

Aware that she had neglected Helen because of her friendship with Hugh, she drove over to Thorpe Fen the following Sunday afternoon. It was a bright summer day, but Helen was not in the garden as Maia had expected her to be. The Reverend Ferguson was out, and at first Maia could find only the under-maid, a flustered, feeble-minded creature. After a few moments Helen appeared, rather out of breath.

'I saw your car.'

'What have you been doing, Helen? There's something in your hair.' Maia grimaced. 'Ugh. A cobweb.'

Helen ran her fingers impatiently through her hair. Then she grabbed Maia's arm. 'Come with me.'

Maia followed Helen up the stairs, along corridors, and up another flight of stairs. 'My *shoes*.' Maia wore pointy little high-heeled slippers.

'Take them off.'

They climbed into the attic. Vast and sloping-walled, strangely shaped objects loomed at Maia through the darkness. Helen carried an oil lamp, and its pinpoint of light bobbed ahead of Maia as she stumbled through the trunks and boxes, her shoes in her hand.

Helen opened a little door set into the dividing wall. She turned to look at Maia.

'See? Isn't it splendid?'

Maia followed Helen into the room. She heard Helen say, 'It's my secret – no-one else knows about it. You are the only person I've shown it to,' and Maia looked around her.

Because there was a window, and because the walls were whitewashed, the room was much lighter than the rest of the attic. Maia blinked. There was a chair and a table and a small bookcase filled with – Maia ran her finger down the spines of the books – cheap romantic novels. There were pictures on the walls – Helen's water-colours, and pages cut from magazines – and a rug on the floor. There was a little oil stove, and a cup and a plate and a knife and fork. There was a washstand, with a jug and a bowl on top of it.

And there was a cradle. Carved and wooden, standing in a corner of the room. When Helen sat down, Maia noticed that the movement of the loose boards made the cradle rock.

Increasingly, the days passed for Francis in a haze. Often he did not recognize the bed in which he woke; sometimes he had no memory whatsoever of the events of the previous night. Once he lost an entire twenty-four hours.

Throughout the muddle of his days ran two clear threads. The bright thread was Robin, the dark one was Evelyn. Neither, just now, brought him any happiness. Robin made him feel guilty, when he resented that any woman should make him feel guilty; and Evelyn produced in him (after the event) a raw self-disgust. He realized that Evelyn was incapable of feeling either guilt or self-disgust, that she had the sort of insouciance he had always pretended to, yet was forced now to acknowledge he did not in fact possess. Sometimes he hated them both for the self-knowledge they inflicted on him, for the sham that he realized himself to be. He knew that for Robin's sake he should come to a decision. That, sooner or later, he must choose between Evelyn and Robin. It was not a choice he felt able to make, but he despised himself for allowing things to drift, for sparing himself the misery of confessing to Robin the truth, face to face, and for lacking the courage and self-respect to resist Evelyn.

When he was with Robin, he promised himself that he would never see Evelyn again. His other problems – his lack of money, his lack of anything one could properly call a career – seemed to become less significant when he was with Robin. He could believe, when he was with her, that he could still sort things out. Yet, making love to Evelyn, who reflected his dark side, he forgot about Robin. Only once, when he had unexpectedly run into Evelyn in the foyer of a theatre, and she had said, glancing at Robin, 'So this is your little friend, Francis,' had he looked at her with intense dislike. He was only usually capable of dislike when she was not there.

Occasionally, Evelyn talked about marriage in a vague, general way that nevertheless gave Francis hope. *So convenient – one always needs an escort.* Away from her, his emotions were mixed. Marriage to Evelyn Lake would restore his finances to an even keel, yet the idea horrified him. If he had married anyone, he would have preferred it to be Robin. Robin did not demand things of him. But Robin, of course, was penniless.

Sometimes he thought that his only answer was to abandon the pair of them. Leave the country, join the Foreign Legion. Then Robin would marry Guy, who had been in love with her for years, and Evelyn would find another slave. And he, Francis, would remember what he had intended to be and would be able at last to do the one great thing that would negate the mess he'd made of the rest of his life.

Maia and Hugh had fallen into the habit of seeing each other on three Sundays out of four; she still always went away for the first weekend of the month. To Hugh's one, tactful enquiry about those solitary journeys, Maia was unforthcoming. Hugh, as always, respected her privacy, and asked nothing more.

With Hugh, Maia learned to ride a horse, to sail a boat, to make sandcastles, and to recognize the flowers that bloomed at the margins of the rivers. The hot weather continued, gathering into a sultry, restless heat as the end of August approached. They drove out into the Fens, picnicking at the edge of a field. After they had eaten, Maia sat against the trunk of a tree, and Hugh lay with his head cushioned on her lap. When he closed his eyes she looked down at him, and saw the fine lines that converged around the corners of his eyes, and the silver threads among his dark gold hair.

'Hugh – you are going grey.' Maia seized a single white hair and plucked it out, for evidence.

He groaned, looking at it. 'I'll lose my teeth next.'

'Poor darling. I can imagine you, silver-haired, with your cottage and your vegetable garden . . .' She smiled. Looking up, she saw that clouds had begun to gather on the horizon, blemishing the blue sky.

'I shall be a crusty old bachelor, with my dogs and my pipe. And you?' He squinted at her, golden-eyed in the dappled light.

She never thought of the future. She had taught herself to live only in the present, knowing that if you could not confront your past, you could not depend on your future.

Maia shrugged. 'I don't know.'

'You are unchangeable, Maia. "Age cannot wither her, nor custom stale her infinite variety."' Hugh sat up, rubbing his stiff neck.

'Rheumatism, darling,' Maia said mockingly, and began to pack the picnic basket.

The clouds were swirling upwards into a huge anvil shape. Maia folded the rug, Hugh put the hamper into the back of the car. The shadow cast by the clouds painted the land with darker tints. She thought, *It is the end of summer*, and felt suddenly despondent. He must have seen the look on her face because he came to her and put his arm round her, and held her to him for a moment or two. 'There'll be plenty more summers,' he said, and then the rain began to fall in round, heavy droplets to the dusty ground, and they drew apart.

'We'll outrun it.' Hugh started up the engine.

She thought at first that they could. Turning the car in a great skirl of dust, Hugh began to speed back along the drove. They reached the sunlight again, leaving the shadows behind them. Maia laughed. 'You've done it – you've done it!' When she looked across at Hugh, she saw her own laughter reflected in his eyes.

But the rain caught up with them as they drove through the Fens. Swathes of icy water, edged with tiny

393

hailstones, lashed the open-topped car. In the distance Maia heard a rumble of thunder, and shrieked as the rain pelted against her skin. The drumroll of rain and thunder almost drowned the noise of the engine. 'I'd better put up the hood,' shouted Hugh, and pulled in at the side of the road.

She ran out of the car to help him. But her fingers fumbled and the clips were stiff and wet. He came to help her, his body brushing against hers as she tried to release the hood from its moorings. And then, and she was never afterwards quite sure how it happened, she was in his arms, and they were kissing, no longer aware of the rain, the thunder.

Aware only of his warm body against hers. His arms, pulling her to him, his lips, touching her forehead, her eyes, her neck. And, dear God, her mouth. She had not realized how much she had wanted him to do that. Her hunger for him was thoughtless and instinctive, driven by a primitive need Maia had believed herself immune to. And only a very small part of her stood aside and watched her begin to break the self-imposed chastity of the past five years.

When, eventually, he let her go, she realized that every stitch of clothing she wore was soaked. Dye seeped onto her skin, and her silk dress was ruined. The dust had turned to mud, and the rain still battered down, hard rods of it, bruising her arms. He raised her head with his hands, and when she saw the expression in his eyes, she knew that for the first time in her life she had made someone completely happy. It was not something she had ever experienced before, and the realization jolted her. 'Dear Hugh,' she whispered, and though the rain robbed her words of sound, she knew that he had understood her.

They went back to the car and began to drive again, hardly speaking. Cambridge seemed too busy, bustling with people after the privacy of the Fens. She hated that there were servants in her house; she hated, for the first time, the cold formality of the place – the marble floors,

394

the dark polished wood, the dull little prints of huntsmen and horses. Changing, bathing, Maia thought that she would make it all different. She would have flowers and books and clutter as the Summerhayeses had, and then it would be a home, not a house.

Hugh had lit a fire in the drawing-room and was drying himself in front of it when Maia came down. They dined together, unable to eat, drinking only a mouthful or two. Afterwards, the wireless filled in the silences as they sat in the conservatory, the large French windows folded back as they looked out to the rain-soaked garden. It was still hot, steam rising from the warm earth. Rose-petals tumbled to the ground, beaten from their branches by the violence of the rain. The lawn had become a multicoloured carpet: pink, apricot, white and red. The wind picked up the petals in a whirling dance, scattering them beneath trees and beside walls.

The servants had gone; they were alone again.

Maia said, 'We can go to bed if you like, Hugh.'

She waited, dry-mouthed, her heart battering against her ribcage, for his reply. She did not look at him.

He said, at last, 'That's not what I want,' and she was unsure whether she was disappointed or relieved. She almost smiled to think how many men she had refused over the years, to find that the one man she could bear to bed did not want her.

Then he spoke again. 'I mean – of course I want it. I want you more than anything else in the world, Maia. But you know that I'm a conventional sort of chap. I don't want a clandestine affair. I want to marry you.'

He was standing at the edge of the terrace. Water dripped from the tangles of wisteria, darkening his hair. She said, 'Hugh – do come in. You'll catch your death,' and her voice trembled.

Her hands placed palm against palm, she sat, trying to sort out the confusion of her thoughts. He crossed the terrace to her, and knelt in front of her. She said shakily, 'I thought we were *friends*.'

'We were. I didn't mean this to happen, Maia, but it

has, and we can't go back. I can't pretend to be just your friend now. I can't deceive you about something like that. I couldn't deceive you at all.'

She turned away from him, unable to bear that his eyes should meet hers. She had seen such a mingling of delight and anguish in his expression. 'Nothing's changed,' she whispered. 'We can go on just the same.'

He stood up, hands in pockets, walking out to look at the rain again. She could hear it drumming on the glass roof, like gunshot.

'Don't you see, Maia – what there is between us can either grow or it can die – but it can't remain the same. We've reached a turning point. We can't unsay things or undo things.'

She remembered his mouth against hers, and the salty scent of his skin.

'If you don't want me, then just say so. I won't make a scene. I'll just go back to being Hugh Summerhayes, old crock, schoolteacher. Only maybe I'll go and teach in the Outer Hebrides, or somewhere like that. But I would never make things difficult for you.'

Maia, biting her lip, remembered how lonely she had felt before there had been Hugh. How big, how empty, this house had seemed. How her dreams had haunted her, how she had affixed her dead lover's face to the features of the living. She shuddered to think that she might return to that.

The music from the wireless mingled with the patter of the rain as she heard him say, 'I cannot go back to what I was, because being with you has changed me. Loving you – being loved, a little, perhaps, by you, has changed me. If I thought that you loved me a bit . . . you are so beautiful, so strong, Maia. When I'm with you, *I* am strong.'

She thought that she, too, had changed. Could she become the person he believed her to be? Yet a voice still echoed in her head. Her own voice, speaking to Liam Kavanagh.

I will never marry again. Never.

'Marriage . . .' She gave an unsteady laugh. 'I'm not much good at it, Hugh. I wasn't much of a wife to Vernon. I told you that I hated him, and it's true. A wife shouldn't hate her husband, should she? I was afraid of him, and I'd never really been afraid of anyone before. He hurt me, you see.'

He said, 'I guessed,' and she looked up at him, surprised.

'You don't like to be touched by people,' he explained. 'It's as though you expect pain rather than comfort from human contact.'

'I married Vernon for his money, and he married me because I was very young and very naive. We were both disappointed in each other. The money wasn't enough for me – and I—' Maia's voice faltered '—I was not *compliant* enough for him.'

She could not look at him, but she heard him say very gently, 'You don't have to tell me about this, Maia.'

'Oh, I do. You have to understand.' The words came out in a gasp. 'He used to hit me, you see. Worse. I can't say it. I felt . . . dirty. I still do.'

She looked up at him, dreading to see disgust or rejection in his eyes, but saw only pity.

'I was glad when he died. So some of what they say about me is true. I was wicked, wasn't I?'

'Never. You could never be wicked, Maia. You're just not capable of it.'

She could not look at him. She closed her eyes, wishing she could wipe the past away, and heard him add, 'What Vernon did to you does not shame you, Maia. It shames only Vernon.'

She wondered whether he was right. She had many other reasons for shame – things that she could never, ever tell Hugh about – but tonight one of the burdens that had weighed so heavily on her shoulders for so many years rolled silently away, leaving her lighter, freer.

'I am not Vernon,' he said. 'If you marry me it won't

be as it was with Vernon. I could never hurt you, Maia. I have loved you since the first day I saw you.'

She thought that Vernon too had loved her, in his own distorted way, but she did not yet speak.

'Marry me, won't you, Maia?'

'I don't know, Hugh . . . maybe . . .' Her fist was against her mouth, but she saw the expression on his face alter. As though he had readied himself for certain despair, and had just discovered hope. Such happiness. Such transparent happiness. She, Maia Merchant, had the power to make someone happy. The old spell had ended, perhaps, she did not only destroy. And she owed him so much. Without Hugh, she might return again to the lonely, haunted creature she had once been. She could not bear that.

She whispered, 'But I am afraid . . .' and he held out his hands to her, raising her out of the chair. He said, very gently, 'You mustn't be afraid. There is nothing to be afraid of. Will you marry me, Maia?'

Slowly, she inclined her head. And was scarcely aware that she shivered.

'We'll go to the seaside for the weekend,' Francis had suggested. It was only when he drew up outside her lodgings and Robin saw the two other people sitting in the car with him – Guy Fortune and Evelyn Lake – that she realized that they were not to go alone.

As they drove to Bournemouth, the weather alternated between feeble autumnal sunshine and brief, spiteful rainshowers. Because of the rain, they had to keep the hood of the MG up. Evelyn Lake sat in the front, next to Francis. She wore silk stockings and patent-leather shoes and a pale yellow crêpe coat. Robin, looking at her, acknowledged that Evelyn Lake could not possibly have squeezed in the back with Guy.

They reached Bournemouth in the mid-afternoon. 'Delightfully slummy,' said Evelyn, looking around her at the resort where the Summerhayes family had many years ago spent several summer holidays.

'We won't stay in an hotel, Francis. You must find a dreadful little B and B. Flowery wallpaper and winceyette sheets and pebbledash. We must have pebbledash.'

Francis grinned, and began to drive again. Rows of bed and breakfast houses clustered in the back streets. The MG crawled from one house to the next as Evelyn inspected them. 'No, Francis – too smart. All the curtains match. And no – not that one. There are salmon coloured lisle stockings on the washing-line. I could not eat my breakfast if it was served to me by a woman wearing salmon-coloured lisle stockings. *Darling!*' Evelyn peered out of the window. 'That one is quite perfect. *Mauve* pebbledash.' Briefly, her hand covered Francis's, still holding the steering-wheel.

She knew then. Sitting in the back of the car, Robin knew, witnessing the brief intimacy of that gesture, that Evelyn Lake was Francis's lover. It surprised her that she did not move, did not cry out, did not reach forward and pull from its roots every gleaming dark hair. Instead, she remained still, watching the older woman as a mouse might watch a snake. The narrow, almond-shaped eyes, the long oval face, the long slender nose and small pursed mouth. Like a Modigliani portrait, thought Robin. A very expensive Modigliani portrait.

Francis and Guy carried their luggage into the guest-house. The three adjacent bedrooms were cramped and garish, looking out over a back yard crammed with dust-bins and sacks of coal. There were two patterns of wallpaper in the room that Francis and Robin were to share, and the cerise candlewick bedspread matched neither of them. The bathroom was at the far end of the corridor, a nightmare jumble of pipes and lino and a spitting geyser.

They left the car outside the guesthouse, and walked back to the esplanade. Sullen waves lashed at the yellow sand. Gulls called, and the air was filled with the bitter scents of salt and sea and tar. Conversations welled up and died, incomplete, dissipating with spent force like the breaking waves. Occupations seized them and then were abandoned with a bored gesture from Evelyn, or Francis's fidgety discontent. They carried out a mime of enjoying themselves, Robin thought, but could not maintain the façade; it crumbled, leaving them disunited and adrift. They dined in a seafront café on fried fish and chips and thick wedges of white bread, and drank tea served in chipped mugs. The tables were covered with oilcloth, and the windows of the café looked out to where the sun sank into the sea, briefly painting it with glory. 'Frightfully amusing,' said Evelyn, fitting a cigarette into her holder, and looking around. 'Don't you agree, Miss Summerhayes?' Francis lit Evelyn's cigarette.

'Frightfully,' said Robin, but she was aware of an utter melancholy, a sadness that matched the town's end-of-season air.

They watched a show at the theatre at the end of the pier. There were only a dozen or so people in the audience. Sitting in the front row, Robin could see that the juvenile lead was forty, not eighteen, and that the chorus girls' tights were patched with darns. She was sitting at the end of the row, next to Guy. Evelyn was between Guy and Francis. At the interval, Evelyn whispered to Francis, 'This is pretty frightful. Do let's go, or we shall have to endure another hour.'

They walked back to the guesthouse. No-one spoke, and it had begun to rain more steadily. The headlamps of the passing cars reflected on the rain-sheened road. When they reached the guesthouse, Francis rang the bell, and the landlady opened the door.

'You go on up, Robin. I'll be a couple of minutes.'

She went upstairs. Inside the room, she took off her raincoat and stood at the window, her hands on the sill, looking out. There was a knock at the door.

'Robin? May I come in?'

'It's unlocked, Guy.'

Guy shut the door behind him. 'I managed to smuggle these past the old dragon.' He opened his coat and showed Robin the two beer bottles hidden in his inner pockets.

'Francis . . . ?' she asked.

'In the garden, having a smoke. There's a tooth mug on the washstand.'

He had forgotten an opener, so he had to prise off the cap with his teeth. Beer bubbled up into the tooth mug. Guy clutched his jaw as he passed the mug to Robin.

'I've probably broken a tooth, and this stuff will give me indigestion. Stout always does.'

She drank, all the time listening for Francis. Guy told her about the epic poem he was writing. 'It's set in a factory making parts for cars. Gaskets or widgets or whatnot. The rhythm of the words is supposed to echo the rhythm of the machinery.' Guy sat on the bed and pulled off his shoes. 'Hell . . . I knew I had a blister. A sort of dah dah-de-dah dah rhythm. I say, Robin, have you anything for this?'

He had a tiny blister on his ankle. She rummaged around in her sponge bag. She could not hear Francis.

'Witch hazel. Will that do?'

'Rather. Would you do it for me, Rob? I am most frightfully squeamish.'

She dabbed his foot with witch hazel, and stuck a piece of plaster over the blister.

'Francis must be smoking an entire packet of cigarettes.'

Guy was sitting against the bedhead, beer bottle in hand. Because there was only an uncomfortable and rickety wooden chair, Robin sat beside him.

'I'm trying to finish it by Christmas, because I don't know how long I've got.'

It occurred to Robin that Evelyn Lake, too, remained downstairs. She realized that Guy was looking at her, expecting some sort of response.

'Finish what?'

'My poem.'

'Oh.' She was guiltily aware that she was only giving him half her attention. 'Have you a deadline, Guy?'

He shook his head, and put aside the beer bottle. 'I'm trying to finish it because of my cough. There's tuberculosis in my family, you know.'

She looked at him, and saw that there was genuine anxiety in his eyes, so she said kindly, 'Guy – you haven't got TB. You cough because you smoke too much.'

'D'you think so?'

She heard the footsteps on the stairs then: two sets, and felt a great wave of relief. The low, murmured voices became louder as Francis and Evelyn walked down the corridor. But the door-handle did not yet turn. Instead, Robin heard the door of the adjacent room open, and then close.

She knelt up on the bed, her heart pounding. He was saying good night, that was all. In another moment or two he would be here, with her.

'D'you think so?' said Guy again.

She could not for a moment think what he was talking about. She made a great effort, and said firmly, 'Guy – you know that I work at a clinic. Well, I've seen quite a few people with TB, and I've heard them cough. You have a smoker's cough, not a tubercular cough. Honestly.'

He smiled. 'You are very sweet, you know, Robin,' he said, and took her hand. 'I have always been immensely fond of you.'

And for the first time the awful possibility that this was not accidental, that Francis would not at any moment open the bedroom door, occurred to her. She pushed the thought away. It was not possible. He could not be so cruel.

Yet Guy was still holding her hand, running his thumb along the back of her fingers. And she could hear voices from the adjacent room. The partition wall was flimsy, made only of plasterboard. If she could not make out the words, she could interpret the intonation. A low murmur from Francis, a brief response from Evelyn. A few coaxing phrases, followed by a ripple of laughter. Then silence.

She realized that Guy was speaking. 'You know, things have been terribly difficult for me lately, Robin. Pa's on at me to go and work for the family firm – can you imagine it? – and he won't give me a bean. He is such a ghastly capitalist. Mummy sends me food and stuff and the odd cheque, or I simply couldn't survive. I get so frightfully tired. My eyelashes are falling out, you know.'

She said absently, 'Poor Guy,' and he bent and kissed her hand. Then her wrist, and then small butterfly kisses along her arm to the crook of her elbow.

'Guy. Don't be silly.'

In the adjacent room, no-one had spoken for several minutes. She could hear the bedsprings creaking. Half of her wanted to bury her head under the pillow, the other half wanted to run out into the corridor, and hammer on Evelyn's door.

Guy slid down to the end of the bed.

'Such lovely little feet.' He rubbed his chin against the arch of her foot.

She realized that he was trying to seduce her. Schoolboyish, inept and neurotic, Guy Fortune was nevertheless trying to seduce her. She heard, through the partition, Evelyn's moan of pleasure, and knew also that she had no need to ask Guy whether Francis had permitted or suggested this seduction. It was all too neat, too pat. *Guy, old chap – Robin is frightfully keen on you, you know.* She could almost hear Francis's lazy drawl. She sat motionless on the bed, as Guy ran his tongue along the sole of her foot. The depth of this betrayal was such that it was impossible for her immediately to comprehend it. Her humiliation was so complete that it seemed to her quite feasible that she should lie here, allowing her body to be used by someone she did not love, while she listened to Francis and Evelyn making love in the room next door.

But somehow she managed to scrape together the remains of her pride. She rose from the bed, and put on her shoes and her raincoat. She heard Guy say, 'Robin – where are you going?', and she answered, 'To the railway station. You're not to follow me, Guy.' Then she picked up her bag and walked quietly down the stairs and let herself out of the house.

In the early hours of the morning, the town was deserted. She did not cry; she felt still that blank, uncomprehending shock. With sick certainty, she knew that what Francis had done this time was unforgivable. He had engineered her humiliation with a thoroughness she had believed alien to him. Whether he did or did not love Evelyn Lake was irrelevant. Trust, she had learned over the past few years, was a necessary part of love, and she knew that she could never trust him again. In the past she had mistaken trust for possessiveness, and had judged others naively. Now she knew that though possessiveness might destroy love, trust was an essential part of it.

She reached the railway station at last. The ticket office was closed, of course, and she stood for what seemed like hours trying to make sense of the London timetable. Then she sat on a bench, her bag beside her, watching the rain sweep the leaves from the trees in the street outside. She could not sleep; a cat yowled at the moon, and the hands of the clock moved only very slowly round, and she did not even try to make sense of it all. She thought that if anyone touched her she would break like glass, shattering into tiny fragments over the lino floor.

But no-one came except a policeman, shining his torch into the waiting-room, so that she had to shield her eyes from the light. Inventing a respectable reason for being alone in a station waiting-room in the middle of the night, she was surprised that he did not immediately see that she was a false, hollow creature, someone for whom the familiar world was now imbued with a deep sense of wrongness, as though the earth had shifted slightly on its axis and become strange and unrecognizable. But he touched his helmet and walked on, leaving her alone again with the clock and the cat and the rain.

At half past six she bought her ticket and climbed onto the train. As it pulled away from the station, she thought she saw a pattern in things. That as their love affair had begun in one seaside town, so had it ended in another. That just as she had once, when very young and very hopeful, tumbled onto a train to begin a new life in the city, so was she now returning to that same city. Only she was old now, so very old, and she did not understand the maps any more.

Enquiring at Robin's lodgings on Saturday morning, Joe was told by Miss Turner that Miss Summerhayes had gone away for the weekend with Mr Gifford. Walking away from the house, he kicked at the heaps of dead leaves in the gutters with a violence that sent them scattering halfway across the street.

Back in his flat, Joe recognized that the frustrations of the past two years had built up to an almost intolerable level. He had kept his promise to Hugh Summerhayes, a promise which, he thought, was no longer relevant. Robin had changed, had become stronger, more independent. Hugh had been wrong, Robin didn't need anyone to look after her. Joe had no doubt that she would ultimately achieve her ambition of becoming a doctor. The small role that he had once fulfilled was now redundant. Her love for Francis had not wavered, while his own position had become increasingly untenable and distasteful. He must make the decision to break away from her, to begin again.

The realization gave him no pleasure. Knowing that he must get away from London, if only for a few days, he flung a few belongings into his rucksack, left the flat and walked to the Tube station. There was a train to Leeds from King's Cross in half an hour. Since his last visit to Hawksden, he had kept in touch with his father by letter. Every so often he received in return a postcard from his father. The postcards always seemed to Joe wildly unsuitable – two kittens in a sock on a washing-line, a row of bathing beauties on Scarborough beach – and on the reverse John Elliot would have written something about the weather, or the mill, or the price of coal.

When he arrived at Elliot Hall, his father's critical eyes inspected him. 'Aye – you don't look quite so much of a scarecrow, lad.' Joe showed him the cutting about his exhibition, and was rewarded by a grunt that might have indicated approval. On Monday morning, John Elliot showed him round the mill. Joe admired the new looms ('Cost me a bloody fortune, they did'), and took photographs while his father watched with a scathing foot-tapping impatience that Joe had come to suspect was his only way of showing pride. As they left the huge, noisy building, his father said, 'A couple of days every three years or so isn't enough to learn a business, Joe.'

They walked home up the steep, cobbled street. After a while John Elliot paused, meeting Joe's eyes. 'You took her photograph. It were always one of my favourites.'

'I'm sorry, Dad,' Joe muttered. 'I'll make some prints, and send you one.'

'Aye. I should bloody hope so.' John Elliot began to walk again, breathing heavily as they climbed the steep slope.

'You should let up a bit, Dad. You're looking tired.'

John Elliot snorted. 'Let up? And let the place go to rack and ruin? You'd inherit nowt but an empty mill and a few rusty machines if I let up.'

He wondered whether he would one day take over the mill. He could alter things a bit; surely even Hawksden could change with the times. Perhaps Elliot's Mill could shake off its nineteenth century paternalism and this small, hidebound little village could be dragged kicking and screaming into the 1930s . . .

Not yet, though, not yet. The newspapers that morning had headlined the invasion of Abyssinia by Mussolini's Italy, the first openly aggressive act of a Fascist government. A far away war in a far away country, or a first fatal step in a much more dangerous game? If it was the latter, then Joe knew that he could not stand aside much longer. At Munich he had stood aside, and at Olympia. But he thought that it was not enough just to watch, to speak, to bear witness. That soon they would all have to choose, and that the small, private battles of home and family would be swamped by greater struggles.

Joe slowed his steps to match his father's. Since his last visit John Elliot had grown old. His father's hair was now completely grey, and the flesh had begun to dissolve from his bones, creating hollows around his eyes and beneath the wide planes of his cheekbones. He was no longer the strong, virile man whose touch and tongue Joe had once feared. Joe put a hand under his father's elbow, helping him up the slippery wet steps to the gate of the house, and was not pushed away.

In the week following her return from Bournemouth, Robin went through the motions of normal life, but felt as though she was an unwilling actor in a rather confusing play. She worked at the British Library, completing the piece of research she was carrying out for a friend of her father's, and spent several mornings at the clinic. The days passed, slow and joyless, something to be lived through, and she was aware of a great hollowness inside, an incapacity to feel much about anything. If she had been capable of anger, then she would have felt angry that Francis had stripped her of her passion and her ambition as well as her pride.

She received three letters from her various committees, enquiring about her absences during the week. She dropped them into the waste-paper bin, unable to face writing and explaining. For the first time in her life she just didn't care. The fire that she had once possessed seemed both futile and slightly ludicrous. Francis had been right: there would be another war, and there was nothing she could do to stop it.

A letter from Daisy arrived at her lodgings. She had

to read the first paragraph twice for it to make sense, and then she sat down suddenly on the bed, as breathless as though someone had struck her. When she looked up from the page, she felt as though the walls of the room were squeezing together. 'The Light of the World' looked down at her mockingly as she seized her raincoat and pulled it on. Then she dashed out of her room and out of the house.

There was only one person she could go to, one person who might begin to understand. Running through the streets, the anger that she had suppressed throughout the week bubbled to the surface, finding a focus other than Francis. Joe's front door was, as usual, swinging ajar, so she ran up the three flights of stairs, and pounded on his door.

He opened it, bare-chested, shaving, his chin still soapy.

'*Joe.*' She almost fell into his room. 'Joe – I must talk to you.'

'Fine. I've something I wanted to say to you.'

'Not here.' She had never liked his flat, it had never lost that impression of transience. 'In the park, perhaps.'

'May I dress?'

'Of course.' She tried to smile. 'Sorry.'

Within five minutes he had found a shirt and jacket, and they were walking in the small park across the road. Robin took the letter out of her pocket.

'It's Hugh, Joe. He and Maia are engaged!'

She looked at him, expecting to see reflected in his face the shock and anger she felt. 'I don't know what to do – I could catch the train tonight – I'd have to walk from Soham to Blackmere, but it's not too far . . . Oh – I wish they had a telephone!'

'*Do?*' repeated Joe. 'I would have thought a letter of congratulation was all that was necessary.'

She held Daisy's letter out to him. 'Joe – this can't happen. Hugh can't marry *Maia*. It's quite out of the question.'

He scanned Daisy's note quickly. They were standing on the perimeter of a small circular pond: leaves, tan and russet, fallen from the surrounding beech trees, floated on its surface.

'Robin,' Joe said gently, 'I know that you are very fond of Hugh and that you have become used to the idea that he'll stay a bachelor, but you really have to accept that Hugh and Maia are engaged, and that they will marry.'

'But she killed her husband!' she almost shouted. A woman and a little boy on the far side of the pond looked up.

'Robin – for God's sake—' She could see the shock in his dark eyes.

'I know it, Joe. Oh – she's never admitted it, and the inquest found that Vernon had died accidentally, but I know it!'

He said reasonably, 'If she's never admitted it – and you weren't even there, Robin, you were in France at the time – then how can you possibly know?'

'I know *Maia*. I know that she's capable of perjury. And I know that Vernon was a swine and a brute and that he beat her and humiliated her . . . Maia wouldn't just put up with that. She wouldn't, Joe.'

'Plenty of women do – they have little alternative.'

She shook her head. 'Not Maia.' She began to walk again, kicking up the dead leaves with her shoes. 'She can't marry Hugh. I have to stop it, Joe.'

'You can't just wade in, fists up—'

'I have to.' She had realized that for the first time in her life she must chose between her family and her friends. The choice sickened her. She must break her promise to Maia, or Hugh would marry a woman capable of destroying him. She took a deep breath. 'I'll have to tell Hugh about Vernon.'

Joe took hold of her shoulders, turning her to face him. 'And do you think that he'd believe you? Do you think that he'd even *listen* to you? My God, Robin –

haven't you understood that Hugh's been in love with Maia for *decades*?'

She stared at him for a moment, and then she said shakily, 'I don't think I've ever known a man who wasn't in love with Maia. I expect you are as well, Joe.'

He said angrily, 'No. Actually,' and he fumbled in his pocket for his cigarettes. Robin shook her head as he offered the packet to her.

'If you dash home to tell Hugh that the woman he's madly in love with is a murderer, then Hugh will reject you, not Maia.'

She knew, looking at him, that he was right. People believed what they wanted to believe about the people they loved.

'Then I'll speak to Maia.'

'And what? Have you thought it through, Robin? Suppose you persuade Maia to break off the engagement. Do you think Hugh will thank you for that?'

'I can't do *nothing*!'

'You have to, Robin.' His tone was flat, final.

She clenched her fists, and pressed them against her eyes. 'I can't bear it, Joe.' Her voice wobbled. 'I can't.'

He steered her to a bench beneath a beech tree. 'You don't really know about Vernon Merchant, Robin – you admit that yourself. And Hugh is an adult. He may know Maia better than you think he does. You must leave him to make his own decisions.'

'You don't know what it was like when Steven died, when Hugh was ill.' Her voice was calmer, and her gaze fixed on the pond as she recalled that awful day in 1918. 'I was just a little girl – I can remember hearing my parents talking about Stevie and Hugh, and I can remember running out into the garden and looking back at the house, which was all covered in snow, and thinking that everything had changed. And I was right. Everything had changed. Stevie never came back, and Hugh was never the same again. He was almost destroyed. I couldn't bear to watch him go through that again.'

She saw Joe frown, and rub his forehead with the back of his hand. She thought, fleetingly, how much she had come to depend on him.

'If they are both damaged,' he said, 'if they have both been hurt, then perhaps they will heal each other.'

The woman and the little boy had gone, and a small gust of wind was blowing the leaves, so that they tumbled like dark confetti from the branches.

'Maia has never loved anyone in her entire life. So how could she love Hugh?'

Her voice was bleak. She felt, at that moment, terribly sad. She heard Joe say, 'It's not just Hugh, is it, Robin?' and she shook her head. She had not told him about Francis, but it did not surprise her that he had guessed. The cruelty and humiliation that Francis had inflicted on her must be etched on her face. In the six days that had passed since her flight from Bournemouth early on Sunday morning, she had passed from shock, to the desire to see him again at any price, to a soul-destroying acceptance that it was finished.

She said, 'It's Francis,' and the paved edges of the pond blurred as the tears began to slide down her face. 'Five years,' she whispered 'and he just threw it away as though it didn't matter at all. How could he, Joe? How could he?'

They sat for a long time, her head resting in the crook of Joe's shoulder, his arm around her. Tears dripped constantly onto the lapels of her raincoat. Her head ached, and her eyes were sore.

It had begun to grow dark. She said, mopping her eyes, 'Dear Joe – you are so comfortable. What was it you wanted to say to me? I've talked about myself for hours.'

He looked down at her. 'I can't remember. Nothing important.' It was too dark for her to see the expression on his face.

She stood up. 'I'm finished with love. Never again, Joe – I promise you.'

She heard him say, 'Then let's drink to that. Let's go to the Six Bells, and drink to an end to love,' and she walked with him out of the park and into the street.

Part Four

–

1936–1938

Chapter Fourteen

The wind blew the droves to black powder, and bruised the silky scarlet petals of the poppies. When she walked back from the Randalls' house, the memory of Michael still heavy in her arms, high stalks of ripening corn scratched Helen's legs. She had walked this same path through the autumn, when the mud had sucked at her galoshes, and the thorns on the brambles had tugged at her skirt. In October, Maia had told her about her engagement to Hugh. Helen did not mind about Hugh any more, but she did not, somehow, think that they would be happy. In winter, the frost had glazed the marshlands, and the well from which the rectory took its water had frozen over. They had boiled the water from the butt, pouring it into the cavernous brick mouth until the ice thawed.

Now, it was summer. Helen reached the rectory as the dinner gong chimed, pausing only to change out of her dusty dress. The house was hot and airless. Sweat sheened her arms, gathering beneath her breasts and down the shallow hollow of her spine. She put on the green silk dress that she had made years ago, and went to the dining-room. Tomato soup and roast mutton and suet pudding. The roast mutton was almost cold, fat coagulating around the rim of the plate. Betty had left Thorpe Fen at Christmas to work in a shop in Cambridge. They had not been able to replace her, and Ivy struggled to do the work on her own.

She could not eat her pudding: the custard was lumpy, the suet pale and gelatinous. Staring at her plate, Helen pushed damp tendrils of hair out of her eyes.

The Reverend Ferguson said, 'Are you well, Helen? You have not eaten.' The harsh winter had aged him, repeated bouts of bronchitis and heart trouble had subtracted the flesh from his gaunt, grey frame.

'I'm perfectly well. Don't fuss, Daddy.'

She pushed aside her bowl, staring out of the window at the still, dusty garden. She would not have spoken to him like that a year ago, and neither would he have meekly accepted her insolence. Where he had once demanded, he now pleaded. The balance of power had shifted, Helen thought, too late.

He rose from the table, and came to stand behind her. She hated that he should be so close to her. When he touched her fingers and murmured, 'You are rather warm, Chickie . . .' she snatched her hand away, cradling it. His touch reminded her of Maurice Page. Through Maurice Page, she had come to understand what Florence Ferguson had written in her diary. *Dear God, what women have to bear.*

The following day, Sunday, was still hot and oppressive. In church, Helen watched a bumblebee batter against a window, clumsy, whining, circling round the chips of jewel-coloured glass, trying to find an outlet. The words of her father's sermon echoed against the stone walls and arches. She had forgotten to do the flowers this week, and last week's arrangements had browned and wilted in the vases. She felt ashamed, until she looked round and saw the empty pews. Startled, she could not work out what had happened. But then she remembered that both the Lovells and the Carters had gone, and that Jack Titchmarsh and old Alice Dockerill had died last winter. The church had always been too big for the village, and now Helen, counting slowly, realized that her father preached to a congregation of less than two dozen people.

416

The bee, trapped in a cobweb, buzzed angrily, and then dropped to the stone flags, tangled in gossamer. Helen slid along to the end of the pew and stooped, gathering it up between her gloved hands. Then she walked out of the church.

Blessed are the meek for they . . . She knew her father had seen her because he paused, losing the familiar words. He was wrong anyway: the meek did not inherit the earth, they watched, abandoned, as the strong and the brave and the beautiful took everything. When Helen opened her cupped palms, the bee took flight, weaving its dance across the dog roses and honeysuckle.

As she walked away from the church, she saw the desolation that had overtaken Thorpe Fen. The tumbledown cottages, with their sad, grimy windows and sagging roofs; the great hollows in the unsurfaced roads where puddles would gather in the autumn. Helen realized that it was not only she who had been abandoned, but the village. No electricity pylons marched across the fields towards Thorpe Fen; the new roads avoided it, linking other villages to the towns. The familiar was dissolving, and nothing was taking its place. The old festivals that had once marked the passing of time were dying. Christianity had struggled to replace an older religion, but now Christianity itself was failing. Standing there, looking at the clogged ditches and overgrown fields, Helen wondered whether Robin had been right all along. *There is no God.* The words pounded in her head like the church bells.

Reaching the Randalls' farm, holding Michael in her arms, she felt better. The bleak vision of a formless, meaningless universe subsided as he welcomed her with crows of laughter and great wet kisses. Helen helped Mrs Randall give Michael his lunch and put him to bed for his afternoon nap.

It was only when she was putting on her hat, making ready to leave, that she noticed the expression on Susan Randall's face. Mrs Randall closed the door of the cloakroom behind her, so that they were alone.

'Helen . . . is everything all right?'

'Of course.' Helen smiled brightly.

'Only you don't usually call on a Sunday.'

'No.' Helen buttoned her gloves and frowned. She hadn't realized how odd it must look. 'I felt a bit unwell in church,' she lied. 'I was too hot. And I do love to see Michael.'

'Of course. I know how fond of him you are, dear.' Yet there was still anxiety – and bewilderment – in Mrs Randall's eyes. Helen, walking back to the rectory, realized that she must be more careful. If she occasionally felt unwell – ill, confused, adrift, the times that she privately called her Black Days, when it seemed as though she was kneeling on the edge of a dark pit, about to tumble in – then she must hide it. Mrs Randall might not trust her with Michael if she thought that she was ill. And that she would be unable to bear.

Maia had realized almost immediately the impossibility of her engagement to Hugh Summerhayes. The very first night, the night that he had proposed to her, she had lain awake, eyes wide open, staring at the ceiling, mentally composing the letter that would break off their engagement even before it became public. And yet, rising in the morning, she had not written. It would have been too cruel, and when Hugh had called, the marks of his own sleepless, euphoric night written in dark thumbprints of exhaustion beneath his eyes, she had not spoken either.

So she had allowed things to drift. Hugh never bullied, he never coerced, yet his happy persistence wore away at her. In October she agreed that he could tell his family of their engagement. At Christmas she allowed him to buy her a ring. In April they fixed their wedding-day for December.

And now she was in London, to be fitted for wedding-clothes. A widow, she would be married in a silver-grey costume, and would go away in a crimson one. The great bales of material waterfalled in shimmering lengths to the floor of the dressmaker's shop. Maia thought that the grey looked dusty, cobwebbed, and as for the crimson . . . Crimson had been a mistake, it did not suit her, she was too pale. Besides, crimson was the colour of blood.

How ironic, she thought, as the dressmaker pinned and measured, that Hugh, alone among his family, should be a conventional sort of chap, and should want marriage. The sort of liaison that would, with Charles Maddox or Harold Frere, have disgusted her, she would have welcomed with Hugh. Yet Hugh, when she had tentatively suggested a less formal arrangement, had been adamant. He wanted marriage, nothing less. He did not even want to share her bed before the wedding-night. She wondered, thinking back over the years, just how much experience he had of women. The brief igniting of passion of the day of the thunderstorm had not recurred; she thought it possible that Hugh was as uncertain as she was about sex. It was their only similarity. In every other respect, in the most important respect, they were utterly different. For he was good, and she was not.

His goodness, his patience, made her feeble attempts to break off the engagement die stillborn. When she was touchy, he was understanding; if she was gloomy, he made her laugh. If she could have married anyone, then that person would have been Hugh Summerhayes. If she was not good herself, then she was still able to recognize goodness in other people. She did not, like some of the fast, sophisticated set she had once been a part of, despise goodness. She knew what Hugh was; the difficulty was that Hugh did not yet understand what she was. He was never flippant or cynical, weapons that she had since a child protected herself with. Beside him, she sometimes felt cheap and second-rate, and resented that she should feel like this, she, who had achieved so much. Merchants thrived: Maia, smiling, pictured the gleaming new chrome and glass cafeteria, completed just this week. It was to be officially opened in July, with a band and a tea-dance and balloons and streamers. If she was still socially ostracized, then she no longer cared, because she had created her own successful world that no-one could take from her. The fashion shows that the dress department held each month, the prize draw, the tea-dances, all her ideas, all a success. She would use this afternoon, she thought, to visit Selfridges and Marshall and Snelgrove, picking inspiration from Merchants' larger cousins.

'All done, madam,' said the seamstress, helping Maia out of the pinned jacket and into her day-dress.

Outside, Hugh waited for her. She had forgotten him, and she had to disguise a small flicker of irritation that she should have to share her afternoon with someone else. 'Darling Hugh,' said Maia, and kissed him.

Yet, walking round London with him, she remembered why she had said, in that small moment of weakness, *yes*. When he looked at her she saw herself as a whole person, no longer split in two by the events of the past. If Vernon's violent possessiveness had been a distorted reflection of love, then Hugh's feelings for her were clear glass, untarnished by the darker aspects of desire.

'Tea?' asked Hugh eventually.

Maia glanced at her watch, and shook her head. 'I must get back to Cambridge. I have a meeting.'

She drove, the hood of the car open, enjoying the cool air after the hot stuffiness of London. Hugh looked across at her.

'How are the glad rags coming on, darling?'

She scowled. 'Well enough. I loathe fittings, though. I wish I could buy them off the peg, like the girls at Merchants.'

He laughed. 'I'll marry you in overalls and a turban if you wish, Maia.'

Perhaps it was possible, after all. She could keep her secrets: Hugh was incurious and unjudgemental, there were things he need not know.

Maia swung the car around a tight corner. 'Thank God it's a registry office. I should loathe all that fuss.'

He had offered to marry her in church, and she had refused. To marry in a church would make it seem more real. She could not imagine herself and Hugh as man and wife. This way, it still seemed a sort of game, a leftover from the picnics and cycle rides of earlier years.

He said hesitantly, 'There's something we should talk about, Maia,' and she glanced at him quickly.

'Yes, darling?'

'I thought we should discuss where we will live.'

The hedgerows and fields whirled by, a smudge of bright midsummer colours. 'Where we'll live?' she repeated, her voice sharp.

'I feel bad about it – not being able to provide for you as well as I'd like to. I've my salary from the school, of course, and a small legacy from an uncle who died in the War, but that's it, I'm afraid.'

A herd of cows straggled the road ahead; Maia slowed and changed gear. 'Hugh – don't be silly and old-fashioned.'

He grimaced. 'It's just that . . . I feel I have no right to say it, but, well, I can't imagine living in Vernon's house.'

She almost said, *Why on earth should you do that?* but, of course, when they married they must live together. Eating her breakfast with Hugh, sharing a bedroom with Hugh.

'No,' she said faintly. The cows had passed, she started up the car again.

'What do you think? Are you fond of the place, or would you like to look for somewhere else?'

She thought of Vernon's house, and wondered why she had remained in it so long. Even now, climbing the stairs, she still remembered. 'Somewhere else, I suppose. Where, Hugh?'

'The country, perhaps. I'm not much good in towns. And the country is so much better for children, isn't it?'

Maia's hands gripped the steering-wheel. She stared at the road ahead, reminding herself to steer, to press her foot down on the accelerator. A bubble of laughter rose up in her throat, but she bit her lip, suppressing it. 'We shall have such beautiful children,' said Hugh, and she wanted to scream.

Through the winter of 1935–6, Robin had at first mourned Francis, and had then become angry, bitter at the wasted years. Years spent waiting for him, years of planning her life around his. The anger took months to fade, and was succeeded by a sort of relief, an exhausted realization that she had, at last, sloughed off a yearning that had in the end brought her more pain than pleasure.

It was as though she had turned a page and could begin to read the rest of the book. Her sense of judgement and purpose returned. She began to work full-time as a clerk-receptionist at the clinic; she asked Dr Mackenzie to help her compose a letter of application to the London medical schools. She left the Miss Turners' house, bidding a tearful farewell to the sisters and the budgerigars, promising to return for séances, and moved into a single room in Whitechapel: a living-room with a gas ring and a sink and a piece of furniture optimistically described as a day-bed, and a shared bathroom. She kept the place wonderfully tidy for a fortnight, and then let it deteriorate into a comfortable mess. She decorated the walls with cheap, bright posters and piled her books on shelves made of planks and bricks. On her birthday, she invited Joe to dinner, following the recipes in Daisy's old cookbook with the sort of attention to detail she had once given to science experiments at school. When he arrived, there were pots and pans and basins of peel scattered all over the living-room.

'Happy birthday.' He waved a bunch of daffodils at her. And then, 'Dear God,' he added, dazed, looking around.

'Isn't it awful? Pile everything on the cupboard, Joe, and throw something over it. Lovely flowers – they remind me of home. I'll find a vase.'

The small table was beside the window, so that they

could see out to the square while they dined. Joe poured each of them a glass of cider, and Robin served the food.

'Happy birthday,' he said again. Their raised glasses clinked. 'I've forgotten how old you are, Robin.'

'Twenty-six.' She pulled a face, and thought back eight years, remembering the winter house, and bathing in the pool and promising to celebrate with Maia and Helen the great milestones of a woman's life. The years had taken away the significance of those milestones.

'Just think, Joe – if I hadn't been to that meeting years ago, then I'd never have met you.'

He said, 'Or Francis.'

Or Francis. She stared at him, and then she looked down at her plate, confused, her mind momentarily blank. She heard him say, 'Are you all right, Robin?'

'Of course. The rissoles taste a bit funny, don't you think? I'd run out of tomatoes, so I used beetroot.' She gulped her cider.

Joe said, 'I had a letter from my father this morning. You remember that I was looking for my Aunt Claire in Munich?'

He seemed to expect a response. She nodded, but was not able to speak.

'Well – Claire has written to my father again – she wrote to him years ago, asking for my address, but Dad didn't know where I was living then. Anyway, he's forwarded her note to me.'

She managed to say something at last. 'That's marvellous, Joe.' Her voice sounded curiously hollow.

'I've written back to her, and given the address of the flat. She's living in a nunnery, Robin – no wonder I couldn't find her.'

Her lips twitched in a failed attempt at a smile. Robin watched her hand raise her glass to her lips, and then pick up her fork. Even the simplest, most familiar things seemed suddenly altered. The view from the window – the pavements, the road and the lime trees just coming into leaf – had changed, bathed in a different sort of light. Sharper, more closely defined, translucent. Her room, which she had thought she had known so well, had become unfamiliar; she examined each object, the chairs, the table, the lampstand, and found them strange.

If I'd not been to that meeting, I'd never have met you. Or Francis.

Yet it had not been Francis whom she had remembered; when she had thought back through the years she had seen only Joe arriving late at the meeting, scowling as he walked along the aisle to the seat that had been kept for him. And later, Joe stooping to pick up the sandwiches and coins that had spilled out of her bag, and walking back to the Hackney basement, sharing caviar and biscuits, sitting on the floor.

Through the years, there had been Joe. Parties with Joe, evenings at Long Ferry with Joe. That awful dinner with Clodie and Francis, she remembered how hurt and cross she had felt that Joe should believe her to be a lightweight, uncommitted sort of person. The trip to France, the riot outside Hackney labour exchange, her awful, panicking fear for his safety. Later, when she had been ill, she had wanted only Joe, and he had come to her and taken her home.

She remembered sitting on the stairs at his lodgings, waiting for him after Mosley's Olympia rally. Her shock when she had seen his injuries. Sharing a bed with him. She had always loved Joe, of course, but, bewitched by Francis, she had thought it second-rate, something less than love was supposed to be.

Oh Joe, she thought. Dear Joe.

It was not that Francis had been unimportant, it was just that he seemed to have faded, to have become insubstantial, a thistledown memory she could no longer quite grasp. When she tried to picture Francis, she could hardly recall him. Fair hair, grey eyes, straight nose, she reminded herself, but they seemed like pieces from different jigsaws, no longer fitting together. Whereas Joe – Joe was all of a piece: strong and loyal and dependable. She looked up at him and he smiled, but she found that she could not meet his eyes, and she seized the plates and left the table, hurling the leftovers into the bin. He was asking her about her day at the clinic. Her replies were monosyllabic and awkward. She wanted him to stay and she wanted him to go, both at the same time. She wanted him to stay because his presence made ordinary things – eating dinner, watching a film, taking a walk – special. She wanted him to go because she needed time to think. When, after they had washed up, he picked up his jacket and suggested a walk in the park, she shook her head, aware that her face was hot and scarlet, muttering that she had letters to write. Alone, she sat on the bed, her fingers knotted together, her chin jammed on her knees. She did not know what he thought about her. She knew that he was her friend, but she could not decide whether she meant any more than that to him. When she thought through the past few years she veered between hope and despair. Some of his actions seemed those of a lover, but if he loved her, why did he not say so? She remembered with startling, daunting clarity, standing in the winter house and telling Joe how much she loved Francis. If Joe had ever loved her, then surely those words had destroyed his love.

She began to watch him surreptitiously, looking for signs. Hope rose and died in an exhausting, repetitive cycle. A note from him, pushed through her door, made her heart flutter. At the foot of the note, the endearment, *Love, Joe*, and she was light-hearted, certain. Yet when she saw him her certainty vanished as he made no move to touch her or kiss her. To be with him was torture, a constant seesawing of emotion. She began, brittle and tired, to avoid him. She lost her old ease with him, and saw by the bewilderment in his eyes that he sensed her unease. All her worst faults recurred in a horrible parody of the adolescence she had thought herself long finished with: she became tongue-tied, clumsy and tactless, and it seemed to her that he called on her less often, that he did not greet her at meetings and rallies with quite such blithe cheerfulness as once he had done.

* * *

They took the train to the South Downs and walked for the day in the humid July sunshine. Everything went wrong: Robin fell in a puddle, climbing over a stile, a bull charged at them as they walked through a field. Once they would have laughed about these things, but they had become awkward, formal, even their conversation chopped and rusted and unnatural. Returning to London, they dined together. Long silences interrupted the meal, the restaurant seemed permeated with their mutual nervousness. The food was awful, delayed and ill-cooked. Joe, who rarely lost his temper, twitched on the edge of doing so as he spoke to the waiter.

When they had finished, he said, 'Come back to my flat, won't you, Robin? There's something I want to say to you.'

Her heart lurched, making her breathless as they walked back to his rooms. Joe carried the half-finished bottle of wine they had taken to the unlicensed restaurant. It was dark and late; they hardly spoke.

He showed her into the flat. She shrugged off her cardigan, the room was hot and close. He took two glasses from the cupboard and filled them and passed one to her.

He said, 'I think we should see less of each other, don't you?'

She looked at him. His face was grim, his eyes dark and cold. She just said, 'Oh,' but felt inside a deep and awful sadness. She made a habit of it, she supposed. If she thought about it, not many of her friendships lasted for more than a few years. She found it easy to get to know people, but eventually, it seemed, they grew bored with her.

He added, 'I mean – it's not working, is it?', and she heard herself blurt out:

'You're sick of me?'

'*No.*' His brows contracted, he sounded angry. 'It's the other way round, isn't it? Come on, Robin – you've changed. You must know that you have.'

'I suppose so.' Her voice was a cry of anguish. 'But I thought we could still be friends.'

He went to the window, his glass cradled in his hands. His back was turned to her, his body silhouetted by the dusky sky. She heard him say very softly, 'That's what I thought. But now I'm not so sure. I've had enough, I think. I find myself – burnt out.'

His words stabbed her. She said wildly, 'I suppose I'm not as pretty as Clodie – and Vivien is so sophisticated—'

He swung back. She could see the confusion in his eyes. 'Clodie? Vivien? What have they to do with it?'

'I should have thought that was obvious.' He was playing games with her, she thought, angrily.

'Not to me.' His face had become cold and blank again, dark runnels of shadow trailing from his eyes, and around his set mouth.

She had begun to feel a terrible hurt, that he should choose to leave her. 'They were your lovers.'

He blinked. 'As Francis was yours.'

She said bitterly, 'I suppose you only like – *love* – women who are older than you.' There were tears in her eyes, she forced them back. 'I suppose you are at least . . . *consistent*, Joe.'

Violence flared in his eyes. A small movement of his hands, and the glass he held shattered between his palms in a small, shocking explosion of sound, and crimson liquid splashed the floor.

'Like you?' he whispered. His lip curled. '"No, no, no, my heart is fast, and cannot disentangle".'

The familiar, beautiful words taunted her. She stared at him, appalled. The red that trailed from his hands was not just wine, blood oozed from a cut the length of his palm. Her heart ached that she should lose him now, that she had understood everything too late.

She said, very carefully, 'Yes. I loved Francis . . . once.'

There were beads of sweat on his forehead. He did not move at all. '*Once?*'

She nodded, unable to speak. They were separated by

only a few feet, but she could not cross that short distance. How did you begin to explain to someone like Joe, who was capable of a deep and easily wounded love, that you had been so wrong? How did you convince a passionate, possessive man that you had made such a fundamental mistake?

When he spoke, she could hear the exhaustion in his voice. 'What – *exactly* – are you saying, Robin?'

And then, suddenly, it was simple. 'That I love you, Joe.'

Still he did not move. Blood trailed down his forearm, staining the cuff of his rolled-up shirt sleeve.

'I've loved you for ages, Joe, but I was too stupid to see it. I loved Francis, too, but that was different. It wasn't the sort of thing that lasts, and I was wrong to try and make it so. And it's done with – I don't want him any more.'

'Love is . . . such an inexact term.'

Yet she saw the hope in his eyes. And knew that even if she was mistaken, even if she humiliated herself again, she must tell the truth.

'I love you, Joe. I want to be with you when you get up in the morning, and I want to be with you when you come home from work at night. I want to spend the rest of my life with you. I want your children.'

She was walking towards him now, the soles of her sandals crushing the thin slivers of broken glass.

'I want to go to bed with you, Joe. Now. Please.'

She took hold of his cut hand and lifted it, and kissed the thin red line that was drawn across his palm. Then his neck, then his mouth. She heard him whisper, 'Are you sure?' but knew that his question needed only the answer of her body, pressing against his. When his lips touched hers, when she felt his body, taut and hungry for her, all her uncertainty dissolved.

He was steering her away from the fragments of broken glass and the wine that pooled the floor. His kisses covered her face and her hair; her lips pressed against his skin, intoxicating her. The ceramic edge of the sink dug into Robin's back. Pots and pans clattered to the floor, their clothes, quickly torn off, tumbled on top of saucepans and jugs, scattering among the debris like rags. Her knees buckled as his mouth tasted hers, as his tongue traced the curve of her neck, her breast, her stomach. They fell to the floor, and then he was inside her, and she was moving in rhythm with him. Her pleasure was quick, overwhelming and almost painful in its intensity, and she heard herself cry out, and felt him shudder as she gripped him. Her head fell against his chest, she did not move to separate herself from him. At first, only the tight, exhausted sound of their breathing broke the silence.

Then: 'Hell,' said Joe. 'I've stabbed my elbow on a fork,' and, still clutching him, she began to laugh.

Sometime in the night, they managed to reach the bedroom, making love again before they fell back on the pillows. Early in the morning, when she woke after a short sleep, his arm was still curled round her, the sheets and blankets in a tangled heap on the floor.

They went away for a week to Northumberland, walking along wild, windswept moors, and following the long, snaking line of Hadrian's Wall. At night, in the tent, they lay together, curled against each other. They made love beside a deserted waterfall, bathing naked afterwards in the ice-cold, peaty water. Robin wrapped a blanket around herself, and tucked pieces of heather into her hair. The Spirit of the Woodland, she said, dancing Isadora Duncan-like among the mossy tree-stumps and clusters of honey-coloured fungi, before collapsing giggling to the ground. Sitting against a tree-trunk, Joe took photograph after photograph of her, shadowed by beech-leaves, her face framed by heather.

On the last day of their holiday they went to Dunstanburgh, walking from the fishing village of Craster to where the broken remains of the castle stood on its black basalt crag. Cormorants gathered on the rocks, and the springy grass was embroidered with sea pinks and wild thyme. In Craster you must eat kippers, said Joe, so they dined in a tiny pub near the harbour, picking translucent bones from the brown flesh of the fish.

They took a train from Alnwick the following day, spreading themselves and their rucksacks in the compartment, trying to keep for just a little longer the solitude they treasured. Someone had left a copy of *The Times* on one of the seats. Joe, opening it, scanned the columns. Robin asked, looking at him, 'Anything?'

'Something about an attempted army coup in Spain. An "absurd plot", the reporter calls it. Um . . . the plot has been suppressed in Morocco, and hasn't spread to mainland Spain. So they say.' Joe, frowning, folded the newspaper. The clear blue air of Northumbria clouded as they drew nearer to the industrial cities of Tyneside. The train rattled along, belching smoke from its funnel, drawing them back to the city.

It began like a peat fire, smouldering, hardly visible, yet gathering heat and energy until its fierceness was inescapable. *Spain.* Robin thought she heard the muttered word in every pub and nightclub, in every Bohemian drinking den, at every unruly, impromptu party. By the time she understood the significance of the flames they had encircled her, and she and her kind were trapped by their brightness and beauty.

Spain. Working out what had happened was like assembling a jigsaw puzzle with some of the pieces missing. Fragments from one newspaper or another, a letter from someone's grandmother in Madrid, a conversation with a friend who had been hiking along the Spanish coast when the uprising began. The report in *The Times* had been misinformed, or was a misrepresentation. On 18 July a group of right-wing army officers, supported by monarchists and fascists, had risen against the elected Republican government, provoking rebellions in Spanish Morocco and mainland Spain. Morocco fell almost immediately; fighting broke out in many mainland towns and villages. Spain, which had only just emerged from a bitterly divided society of impoverished peasants and immensely wealthy landowners, seemed about to lose its first taste of democracy and retreat into darkness again.

Joe bought the French and American newspapers that reported the Spanish Civil War more extensively – and, he suspected, more honestly – than the British editions. The newspapers described the aeroplanes that Hitler and Mussolini had sent to the Spanish generals to help the pro-Fascist Nationalists. Planes that both transported soldiers from Morocco, and bombed towns and villages in southern Spain. Small groups of volunteers – many of whom had in recent years escaped from Europe's Fascist regimes – began to cross the Spanish border, to help fight the Republican cause. A chance for the individual to fight back, to regain self-respect, to defeat Fascism before it engulfed them all.

Spain was the cause they had all been waiting for. Soon there was no other topic of conversation at dinner, in the pub, at political meetings. If Spain fell to the fascists, they argued, then all Europe, Britain included, must eventually fall. Mosley's Blackshirts would be not a small, extremist splinter group, but a harbinger of horrors to come. The battles that had been lost in Germany, in Abyssinia, in Italy and the Rhineland must be won in Spain. As they watched, hoping that this time it would be different, that this time the democracies would stand firm against Fascism, the great powers dithered.

Joe and Robin went to a party in Whitechapel, sharing quarts of beer with artists and sculptors and their models.

'Britain will appease Franco, just as she is appeasing Hitler,' said a painter, downing a one and sixpenny quart bottle of beer in one swallow.

'Appeasement?' said someone bitterly. 'Baldwin *adores* the Spanish generals. The British government would love to outlaw the unions and throw all their leaders into gaol.'

The studio's walls were plastered with posters of sunlit tractors and heroic workers, lettered beneath in the Cyrillic alphabet. Brightly coloured pamphlets, battered hardbacks from the Marx-Engels-Lenin Institute, and well-thumbed copies of the latest offerings from the Left Book Club were scattered around the room.

'The English bourgeoisie has always been far more afraid of Communism than Fascism. I'm taking the ferry to Boulogne tomorrow. Then I'll hitchhike to Marseilles and find a ship to take me to Barcelona.'

The speaker, a slight and red-bearded watercolourist, was drunk with beer and optimism. Robin, glancing across at Joe, saw the glint in his eyes, and the narrowing of his lids.

Though she still rented her room, Robin spent more and more time at Joe's flat. The two attic rooms were more spacious, more private, the building populated by a raffish assembly of musicians and artists and failed poets. She pinned posters to Joe's walls, and cluttered the place so that the small flat lost its transient air, and began to look like a home. They spent the evenings and weekends together, taking turns to cook, or dining in cheap little restaurants with friends.

In September, the Russian Comintern approved the setting up of International Brigades to fight for the Spanish Republican government, using Communist headquarters in countries around the world as recruiting stations. The unemployed, factory workers, students, academics, artists and poets, men who had never held a gun in their lives, set out on the long journey to Spain.

Rumours of the bombing of Madrid reached them, paragraphs in the newspapers hinted at the destruction. Photographs of Madrid: bricks splintered to powder, shellholes pocking the roads, and men, women and children sheltering from the bombardments in Underground stations. Guy Fortune was going to Spain, his convictions triumphing over his ailments and anxieties;

Niklaus Wenzel, the German refugee, had crossed the Channel the previous week. They went to Guy's send-off at the Fitzroy Tavern; Joe shook Guy's hand, Robin kissed him on the cheek. Dear Guy, she said, seeing behind the bravado, fear and uncertainty. Write a wonderful poem. Tell the truth.

They did not yet go home, but walked around London, hardly speaking. The soft light of the gas lamps smudged the harsh angles of the buildings. Leaves scratched at the gutters, funnelled along by the wind.

Robin said, 'Guy says it's terribly cold in Madrid in the winter, Joe. I'd knit you a scarf and balaclava, but you know I'm not terribly good at that sort of thing.' Her voice only shook a little.

He stopped beneath a street lamp, looking at her, not speaking.

She smiled. 'Of course you must go, Joe. I know that you must.'

'Robin . . .' His fingers brushed a stray lock of hair from her face as he struggled for words. 'I can't just stand aside and watch any more, you see. In Munich . . . at Olympia . . . I hated myself half the time. Oh, I knew that taking photos was all that I *could* do – but still . . . standing and watching begins to feel like complicity, doesn't it?'

He put his arm round her shoulders as they began to walk again. She heard him say, 'I've been wanting to do something for such a long time. I've felt so useless. Now I've a chance to fight back.'

'I know,' she said softly. 'I know.' Yet, walking in silence back to Joe's flat, she wondered where this left her. In England, alone, but she could bear that. Just. But unanswerable questions haunted her: she, as much as Joe, loathed Fascism and everything it stood for; she, unlike Joe, was a pacifist. Did there come a point when pacifism failed, when she must disregard all her memories of what war had done to her own family, to so many other people's families? Must she, too, accept that violence could only be answered with violence?

'When will you go?'

They had reached the tenement block. Joe opened the door.

'Next week, I hope, if I can arrange things with Oscar.'

All her reasonableness suddenly dissolved, and she wanted to shout out her anguish and physically hold him back, preventing him from leaving her. Instead she turned away, so that he should not see her face, knowing that she must not let him see how much this hurt. They began to walk up the stairs.

'I've Thursday off work. I'll go into King Street, and find out what the form is.' Joe added, 'At least all those years of bloody Officers' Training Corps at school might come in handy at last.'

Joe felt as though all the different parts of his life had joined together, making sense at last. Once, he had wanted a cause: now, in Spain, he had found one worthy of all his energy and ideals. And he had found Robin, too; often, waking, seeing her beside him, he could not believe his luck. He wanted nothing more. At work, he smiled at the bashful debutantes, whose portraits he was photographing, and annoyed Oscar by singing in the developing room. When he was with Robin, only the knowledge that they soon must part, and only the shadow of Francis that still, sometimes, he glimpsed standing between them, subtracted from his contentment.

When he made his way to the Communist Party headquarters at King Street, off Covent Garden, a few other men were there, waiting, cloth-capped and Sunday-suited – unemployed men, hungry, like Joe, to make a difference.

Afterwards, he remembered only a handful of questions that they had asked him. His age, his state of health (there was no medical), his political affiliations. Someone had barked at him, 'Why do you want to go to Spain?', and he had said, simply, 'To fight the fascists,' and had realized to his relief that he had answered correctly. He was given twenty-four hours to make his arrangements, and ordered to return to the King Street office the following morning.

On the way home, he bought a few things for his journey to Spain – soap and a new toothbrush and a pair of gloves. He wanted to give something to Robin, but could not think what. He stared in jewellers' windows at the ranks of bracelets and earrings and necklaces and did not know what to buy. Robin hardly ever wore jewellery. His eye lingered on a tray of rings: antique settings, pearls and garnets and other semi-precious stones, clasped in delicate twists of gleaming metal. He opened the door of the shop.

When he returned to his flat, a woman was waiting on the outside steps. Small and dumpy, all bundled up in medieval-looking grey and black. A nun. Joe smiled to himself; she seemed incongruous.

He nodded a polite, passing greeting, not really looking at her face. Then she said, 'Joseph?', and his hand froze in the act of turning the door-handle, and he looked back, very slowly.

He couldn't see her hair because it was hidden beneath her head-dress, but he knew that it had once been black. Her eyes were the same brown-black as his own. The same colour as his mother's. 'Claire . . . ?' he whispered, uncertainly, 'Tante Claire . . . ?' and she smiled and flung her arms round him and hugged him.

He took her up to his rooms and settled her on the battered couch. Then he perched on the arm of the couch as she said, 'I hope you don't mind, Joe. I should have written first, but I was so pleased to hear from you. And besides, I was running out of time.'

'Mind?' he said. 'How could I possibly mind? I've been looking for you for *years*.'

'You said in your letter that you'd been to Paris and Munich, chéri. I left Munich after Paul died. And I did not wish to go back to Marie-Ange – we did not get on.'

Joe recalled the grim, censorious woman who had told him about Claire's marriage. 'No. I suppose not.'

He lit the fire to take the cold edge from the room, and made tea as she told him about the years since they had last met. The death of her parents, his grandparents, within six months of each other; her discovery that there had been debts to pay rather than an inheritance. Her months with Cousine Marie-Ange; her meeting with Paul Lindlar, whom she had heard play in a small concert hall in Paris. Their marriage, six weeks later, followed by three years of happiness. Her husband had been twenty years older than she, and had died of a heart attack just before Hitler had come to power. Claire had returned to France, wandering from town to town, unable to settle anywhere, earning her living by teaching the piano. Joe, who had just found happiness himself, sensed the continuing intensity of her grief. And then, one day, she had remembered her great-niece in the convent at Caen, and had visited her, and had somehow remained. She had loved once, she told Joe, and had known that she would not love again.

'So now you're a fully fledged nun?' He placed the cup of tea and the packet of biscuits in front of her.

She laughed. 'Not yet. I am a postulant, Joseph. I take my vows next month, which is why I came to see you now. I will soon have less freedom to travel, you understand. And it always troubled me that I lost touch with you.' She smiled. 'So we have both been searching for each other, my dear.'

He knew that he must ask now, or he never would. Part of him did not want to, because he feared her reply. Yet the questions that had haunted him for years could not be shut away any longer. He said, 'I wanted to ask you about my parents. I wanted to ask you why they married.' Joe thought of the room his father had kept for Thérèse: the piano, with music still propped on the stand; the flowers and photographs and notepaper. 'He loved her. But she only tolerated him. She didn't hate him, but most of the time she pretended he wasn't there.'

She whispered, 'Pauvre Thérèse.'

He had had plenty of time to work it out. He said angrily, 'She was in love with someone else, wasn't she?'

'Don't you think, petit,' her voice was careful, 'that some things are best laid to rest?'

He had moved to the window; his hands suddenly gripped the sill as he understood how the events of the past might reflect on the present. He almost wanted to agree with her, to change the subject, to talk about the weather, or about how one became a nun. Anything.

But if he did not ask, then he would always wonder. Ghosts and shadows – Thérèse and Francis – would flicker darkly, tainting the present. So he shook his head, and said, 'No. I don't. Please tell me what happened.'

When she spoke, her tone was reluctant. 'Thérèse was in love with another man – you are right, Joe. She was very young, you must remember – only twenty – and Etienne was . . . oh, everything a girl would want. He was handsome and clever and charming – I was almost in love with him myself. For a year they saw each other at balls and at parties, and then, suddenly, he became affianced to someone else. Etienne had no money, you see, my dear, and Thérèse had none either. He was one of a large family – his father's estate would be split up when he died, divided between the children. So he had to marry money.'

There was a silence. Handsome and clever and charming, Claire had said. Joe imagined his mother's faithless suitor as fair-haired, grey-eyed, raffishly dissolute. Women went for that sort of thing.

He hardly listened to the rest of what she said: he could have filled in the gaps himself. John Elliot had turned up in Paris, sampling the delights of foreign travel for the one and only time in his life. Somewhere – in the park, at a concert or a dance – he had met and fallen in love with Thérèse Brancourt. He had married before, but he had not loved before. Widowed, John Elliot had not expected to fall in love with a tall, thin, dark-haired Frenchwoman, but he had, and his life had altered. He had married Thérèse because without her all the getting and spending that sustained him would have seemed pointless. And she had married him because she could not bear to remain in Paris, which daily echoed with reminders of the man she had loved and lost.

Yet it seemed to Joe that through all the cold, gloomy years Thérèse had spent in Yorkshire she had kept a part of her heart for her first love. When she looked at her husband, her eyes had been disinterested, her smile polite rather than affectionate. When his wife had given all her love to her son instead of to her husband, John Elliot must have felt time and again the cold arrow of disappointment.

Joe felt a hand gently touch his shoulder, and a voice say, 'It was a long time ago. It does not matter now.'

But it did matter. It mattered that a first love could not be forgotten; it mattered that that soaring, intoxicating passion could not be replaced by loyalty, constancy and devotion. It mattered horribly.

He forced himself to talk to her about other things for another half-hour, to check that she was staying somewhere decent, to take down her address. But all the while the shadows hovered, darkening the corners of his mind.

When he helped her into her coat and saw her out of the house, he saw that it had begun to rain. He watched Tante Claire's small retreating body diminishing as she disappeared up the pavement, and then he flung on his coat and began to walk, in no particular direction.

When she left the clinic, Robin saw the figure standing across the road, hunched in the drizzle.

Though she had not seen Francis since that awful trip to Bournemouth, almost a year ago now, she recognized him immediately, of course. She had at first avoided his friends, his haunts, and when, angry at such strategies, she had begun to go again to the familiar pubs and cafés, he had not been there.

She crossed the street and touched his shoulder, and he turned to her, and smiled.

'Robin. I was waiting for you.'

She saw what the past year had done to him. Time, and the way that he lived, had almost robbed him of his beauty, so that the colour of his hair and eyes seemed to have faded. Small lines had gathered round his eyes, and his face was taut and hollowed. His hair had begun to thin at his temples.

He seemed to read her thoughts. 'I know. I look pretty bloody awful, don't I? Made rather a pig's ear of things recently.'

He took a packet of cigarettes from his pocket, and offered it to her. She shook her head.

'I've given them up. They make me cough.'

'I'm trying to chuck the booze. The bloody quack's told me my liver will pack up otherwise – can't give these up as well.' He flicked his lighter, and lit the cigarette. 'That would be just too abstemious.'

She said warily, 'What do you want, Francis?'

'Just to see how you are.'

'I'm fine. Terrific, actually.'

He ambled towards the bench beside the bus stop. She wondered what he wanted this time: forgiveness or absolution? Or – she took in his shabby raincoat, his scuffed shoes – the loan of a five pound note?

'How is Evelyn?'

He sat down on the bench beside her, and said slowly, 'Ah, Evelyn,' and exhaled a thin plume of blue smoke. 'We almost married, actually.'

'Congratulations,' she said sarcastically.

'Fortunately she ducked out at the last minute.'

'Leaving you at the altar?'

Francis blinked. 'At the pub with a very large whisky in my hand. And a few chasers. I lost three days, Robin. Damned confusing. Then Theo got me a job at the BBC – reporting on the arts, concerts and stuff. I thought everything was going to be all right then, but I blew it. Absolutely blew it.'

439

His hand shook slightly as he raised the cigarette to his lips. Robin said softly, 'You drank?', and Francis nodded, and said:

'Came to work under the influence once too often. They're very proper about things like that at the BBC. Don't want their wireless announcers slurring their consonants.'

She almost laughed with him but, looking at the wreck he had made of himself, could not. 'And then?' she prompted.

Francis shut his eyes for a moment, and ran his fingers through his hair. He said, 'And then I went on a blinder.' His voice was flat, all trace of flippancy suddenly erased. 'The blinder to end all blinders. Lost a few dozen friends, crashed the car, ended up weeping on Vivien's doorstep at three o'clock in the morning. She paid for me to go to a clinic.'

She thought, *Dear God*, but said nothing. She realized dully that he could still cause her pain. Turning away from him she saw where the rain had made the road like satin, and tiny rivulets of water had begun to gather in the gutters.

She heard him say, 'I know I've been a bloody idiot. Of course, the most bloody idiotic thing I ever did was to finish with you. When I was in that ghastly clinic, I had plenty of time to think. I thought about you a lot, Robin. I know it's taken me a hell of a long time to work it out, but I wanted to tell you that I love you.'

Some of her bitterness returned when she thought how such a declaration would once have made her feel. He was too late. Far too late.

He asked, as he had asked her before, a long time ago, 'Could you love me a little, d'you think?'

It seemed a long time before she could reply. 'Oh yes, Francis.'

A flick of the eyelids, masking his eyes. 'But . . . ?'

'Francis – Joe and I have been lovers since the summer.'

A small pause. Then, 'Good. I'm delighted.'

440

She would have believed him had there not been that brief blanking out of emotion.

He smiled and added, 'I always thought that you and Joe were made for each other. It seems only right that the two people I'm fondest of in the entire world – apart from Vivien, of course – should get together.'

'Joe's going to Spain,' she said.

'Is he? Good for him. Though it's a lost cause, you know.'

And he bent and kissed her, a small peck on the cheek. She knew in that kiss that she was free, that she did not desire him any more, that it was over. If she still loved him a little, would always love him a little, then it was not the sort of love that she was able to give to Joe.

Joe walked and walked, letting it all sink in, trying to shake off the black mood that had settled on him since he had said goodbye to Claire Lindlar. Her story haunted him: first love, the most intense, enduring love, never forgotten, never entirely abandoned. He reminded himself that Robin loved him, that she had said so, that she had finished for ever with Francis, that he had nothing to fear in going to Spain and leaving her in England. He realized that he was within a few streets of the clinic; his need to see her, to hold her, was overwhelming.

He turned the corner and they were there, Robin and Francis, seated on a bench on the far side of the road. As though his jealous imagination had conjured them out of aether. Joe leaned against a wall, trying to recover his breath. The rain sheened down, they had not noticed him. When he saw Francis lean across and kiss her, Joe's fists clenched, his nails digging red, perfect half-moons in his palms. He dug his fists into his pockets, and the knuckles of his right hand touched something cold, hard, metallic. *No, no, no, my heart is fast, and cannot disentangle.*

Robin's voice, condemning the bourgeois institution of marriage, rang in his ears. The independence that he had learned to admire in her taunted him. His father had made the mistake of marrying a woman whose heart was inextricably bound with someone else's, he could not allow the past to repeat itself. He could not cast himself in the humiliating, beggarly role his father had endured, and neither would he use his going away to Spain to persuade Robin to live the rest of her life a lie.

When he reached the flat Joe took from his pocket the ring that he had bought, with its tiny chips of amethyst and lapis lazuli, and stuffed it in the bottom of his rucksack.

Chapter Fifteen

Maia met Monsieur Cornu, the owner of a lingerie manufacturing business, at a restaurant in the Strand. Léon Cornu was, Maia estimated, in his early fifties: well-dressed, good-looking, cultured and sophisticated in a way common to Continental men, but rare in Englishmen. Monsieur Cornu had a wife and four children in Paris and, it was rumoured, a mistress of twenty years. Maia's lunch with him was a yearly pleasure; they never discussed personal things, but talked about Merchants, and about Monsieur Cornu's exclusive little shop in the Avenue Montaigne. About the cost of raw materials and labour, about the difficulties in obtaining a particular size of ivory button or a special shade of satin ribbon.

'My accountant will get in touch with you,' said Maia, over coffee, 'and I shall look forward to dining with you next year, Léon.'

Glancing at the clock, she saw that three hours had passed since they had met: three hours in which she had successfully put out of her mind her other reason for coming to London that day.

Léon smiled. 'Let us hope our little lunches may continue, ma chère Maia.'

Something in the tone of his voice made her glance at him sharply.

He shrugged. 'I'm sure you wonder, as I do, madame,

how much longer there will be a market in Europe for luxury goods.'

'Women will always want pretty things . . . for their trousseaux . . . for birthdays . . .'

Monsieur Cornu signalled to the waiter for more coffee. When their cups were refilled, and they were alone again, he said, 'I suppose you feel safe here, on your little island.' His gaze drifted round the crowded restaurant, at the tables of diners, the men in their dark three-piece suits, the women in their fitted costumes, their heads crowned with jaunty little hats. Surprised, Maia thought she could see derision in his eyes.

'Léon. What are you talking about?'

He turned back to her. 'Don't you read the newspapers, Maia?'

'Of course I do. Though to be honest, I spend more time on the markets, stocks and shares, that sort of thing. The political news is so depressing.'

'Yet the one may affect the other. And war in Europe, my dear madame? Even England cannot ignore that.' His voice was dry, almost amused. Opening his cigarette case, he offered it to Maia.

'Oh, *Spain*, you mean.' Hugh had talked to her about Spain, and Daisy and Richard and their friends had discussed Spain at length with a passion alien to Maia as, bored, she had struggled to stifle her yawns.

'Spain, of course,' said Léon. He lit their cigarettes.

'It's a civil war, darling. Nothing to do with us.'

He raised his eyebrows slightly. 'The Spanish war could drag in the great powers – which is what Great Britain and France fear, of course, and why they stand on the sidelines.'

'Do you disapprove of that, Léon?'

'I suspect one cannot stand aside for ever. That is why I am seeking to protect myself, and my family. I am buying an outlet in New York.'

'In case there is a war in Europe?'

Again, that small, amused smile. He said, 'If there is

a war, my family and I will leave France for America. I am Jewish, Maia.'

She almost said, *But what does that matter?*, but managed to stop herself in time. Though she was aware that anti-Semitism existed both in England and on the Continent, she herself rarely thought about things like that. Religion, appearance, the colour of a person's skin had never been very important to her.

Maia left shortly afterwards, kissing Léon on both cheeks, making him promise to keep in touch. She thought that he was wrong, that he was being unnecessarily cautious, but all the same the conversation troubled her.

Outside, she took a deep breath and set about the more difficult business of the day. Maia hailed a taxi.

'Harley Street,' she said to the driver as she climbed in.

Maia felt edgy and tired as she drove from London to Thorpe Fen that evening. The maid showed her into the rectory; Helen and her father were just finishing dinner. The Fergusons always dined early: Maia imagined Brown Windsor soup and badly cooked mutton and no fire or candles lit until it was dark. Maia shivered in the parlour, her furs clutched around her face, her hands still cold.

'Maia?'

Helen peered round the door. 'Helen darling.' Maia rose from her seat, and pecked Helen on her cheek.

'So dark. I shall fetch more lamps.'

Helen returned with two oil lamps, lighting both so that they cast pools of light on the brown linoleum and dark wainscoting. Then she stooped and lit the fire. It drew badly, smoke funnelled back into the room.

'Tea, Maia?'

Maia thought, watching Helen, that she had changed. The uncertainty, the timorousness had gone. It was Maia who was uncertain now, Maia who was almost torn apart by the choice she must make.

She glanced at her watch. 'I'll be late at the Summerhayeses' – but yes, please, Helen – I'd love some.'

The smoke and the hot, heavy scent of the oil made her feel slightly sick. She waited, her hands threaded together, while Helen left the room and returned in a few minutes with the tray.

Helen had changed in other ways too. Her face had fined down, and there were bluish shadows around her eyes. Her hair, once so carefully curled, now lay long and heavy and lank, flat against her shoulders. The white cuffs of her dress were slightly grey, and there was a ladder in her stocking.

Helen handed Maia a cup of tea. Then she said, 'You mustn't marry Hugh if you don't want to, Maia.'

Maia almost dropped the cup. Some of the tea sloshed into the saucer as she placed it on the table. She heard herself laugh.

'Of course I want to marry Hugh.'

Yet she could not even convince herself. She tried again.

'If I wanted to marry any man then that man would be Hugh.'

Helen said, 'That's not quite the same.'

Angrily, Maia looked away.

'I'm not saying you shouldn't marry Hugh. I know that he's been in love with you for ages, and I'm not even saying that you have to feel like that about him. But you mustn't marry him and regret it. It would be kinder to finish with him now than to do that.'

Yet she had tried, time and time again, to release herself from the promise that she had made. Prevarications and half sentences (Perhaps we should talk, Hugh . . . There is something I must tell you . . .) had all foundered on the twin rocks of her guilt and his patient devotion. She had begun to believe that to break this engagement she must make him hate her. And she was not brave enough to do that.

'Do you want to talk about it, Maia?'

Knowing that in a few short weeks everything might come to a crisis, she said sharply, 'To you? I don't think so.'

Immediately, Maia wanted to draw her words back. What she had wanted to say, yet could not, was that Helen was her only friend, and that to tell Helen the reason she could not marry Hugh would destroy that friendship. Of all people, Helen could not sympathize. She could not bear to lose Helen as well.

As she fumbled for words, she saw Helen's face become pale and closed.

'I suppose old maids can't really understand about marriage.'

'Helen. I didn't mean that. And you're not an old maid—'

'Of course I am. I am twenty-seven and I shall never marry, I shall never have children of my own.' Helen's voice was dignified, unemotional. 'If it wasn't for Michael, I think I would rather be dead.'

For a moment Maia couldn't think who Michael was. Then she remembered: he was the baby son of some yeoman farmer that Helen visited. Maia stared at her.

'You don't mean that, darling.'

Slowly, Helen turned to look at Maia. 'Oh, I do. This house . . . this village . . . they have trapped me. Other people escape, but not me. I used to think that life would open out as I became older. But mine has shrunk, it has become almost nothing. Sometimes I think that I am invisible. That no-one can see me. That no-one would notice if I wasn't here.'

Maia shivered. 'You've the people at church . . . and in the village . . .' She hesitated. 'And your father . . .'

Helen laughed. 'Daddy doesn't see *me* when he looks at me – he sees *Mummy*. Don't you know that, Maia?'

Maia, shocked, watched Helen rise and place more coal on the fire.

'And there's hardly anyone left in the village.'

'But there's *me*. *I'd* notice if you weren't here.' Maia felt oddly near to tears; she, who never cried. The long day, she thought, and the consultation she had had in the afternoon. Helen, her back to her, jabbing the fire with the poker, did not reply.

Robin had a card from Joe with a Paris postmark (*'Vous aviez mon coeur, Moi, j'avais le votre'*), and then nothing. Weeks passed. She told herself that the absence of news did not signify, that you could not expect an efficient postal service from a country at war. Each day she read the newspapers, studying every word, every photograph, a map of Spain spread out on her table. In November, reading about the fighting in Madrid, she felt cold inside. She made a parcel for Joe: a tin of biscuits, a hipflask of brandy, chocolates, cigarettes and one of the latest Penguin paperbacks.

She worked at the clinic, she wrote her letters of application for medical school, and received the letters of rejection by return of post with a mixture of bloody-mindedness and fortitude. Neil Mackenzie had become involved in the Spanish Medical Aid Committee; Robin listened, a mixture of emotions burning inside her, as he talked about the ambulances and medical aid units that had begun to set out for Spain. She acted as secretary to a Spanish Aid Committee, collecting money for food and medicine, holding rallies to explain the Republican cause. The generosity of the people who attended the rallies and the sight of the small food parcels – tiny tins of cocoa and condensed milk – donated by miners' families, touched her immeasurably.

Joe had sublet his flat during his absence to a friend, an impoverished writer of detective novels. Robin visited the flat once before the writer moved in, claiming Joe's post, and wiping the dust that had begun to gather on the shelves. Everything in the flat reminded her of Joe's absence: the gas ring that needed mending, his summer jacket on the peg on the door, the old razor on the bathroom shelf that she had not the heart to throw away.

*   *   *

Merlin drove Robin home for Richard Summerhayes's sixty-fifth birthday at the end of November. He drove at great speed and with little precision, hurling his ancient car around frost-glazed corners, ramming his foot down on the accelerator when they reached the long, flat roads of the Fens, narrowly avoiding plunging into ditches and drains.

'Richard must be retiring soon,' bawled Merlin, as they lurched across a narrow bridge. 'Sixty-five. Gold watch and all that.'

'At the end of term,' Robin yelled back. 'Hugh's to be Head of Classics.'

They had almost reached Blackmere Farm. Merlin jerked at the steering-wheel and the car skidded into the forecourt, its tyres sending up a snowstorm of gravel. Maia's car was parked by the side gate, and cars and bicycles and a motorcycle were scattered round the paths and lawn. Robin's breath made small clouds in the icy air, and frost flowers had already begun to form on the windowpanes of the house.

Inside, guests spilled from the drawing-room into the hallway. Richard called, 'There are only seven matching teaspoons, Daisy!' and hugged Robin and shook Merlin's hand. Daisy, small and pretty in cornflower-blue silk and a beaded shawl, said, 'The best spoons are in the scullery, Richard darling. The maid put them there. She thought she was being helpful.'

'That is because she is mad.' Hugh came out of the drawing-room, Maia beside him. Hugh's arm crept around Maia's waist: Robin noticed her small pulling away. 'Hester is uncommonly mad even for a Summerhayes maid.'

'Hugh – won't you ask everyone to go into the dining-room. I think we are ready.'

Great ranks of candles stood on the long, scuffed table. The velvet curtains, in rich faded shades of terracotta and ochre, were drawn across to reveal only a narrow sliver of the chill black countryside beyond. Two walls were lined with books from floor to ceiling, and the heaped logs in the fire glowed rose pink at their heart. Fragments of conversation filled the room as the maid served the consommé.

'Shall you miss school, Richard?'

'Undoubtedly. I shall keep in touch, though.'

'Ghastly job, teaching. I tried it once, just after I left art college. Lasted a week.'

'I have put some things aside for the Christmas Bazaar, Daisy. I thought perhaps all the proceeds should go to Spain, this year.'

'Butter . . . Ma, there doesn't seem to be any butter . . .'

'I'll go.'

'How kind of you, Philip. In the larder, on the shelf at the top. Maia, what a perfectly beautiful dress.'

'— the most marvellous little gallery, Merlin. I've sold half a dozen pieces – I'll put in a word for you.'

An awful absence, hovering at the edge of what was comfortable and familiar. If something happened to Joe, then would she, somehow, know? Or would they talk and eat and laugh and squabble just the same?

Cold salmon, glazed with cucumber and tomato. Persia said, 'I'm sure there is snow,' and when Robin looked towards the window, she glimpsed the tiny flakes, amber-coloured as they reflected the candlelight.

'Just a stray cloud,' said Ted Warburton. 'It's too cold to snow.'

Roast beef and Yorkshire pudding. Potatoes Dauphinois and mixed vegetables, and Daisy's speciality, a very hot horseradish sauce. The maid dropped the gravy boat, making a great dark puddle on the hall tiles. Richard gave the hiccupping, hysterical girl a glass of Madeira to calm her, and sent her upstairs to her room to lie down. Daisy fetched a mop and bucket and cleaned up the mess as Robin gathered the fragments of broken china. Daisy's silk dress was unmarked; Robin's had a rim of gravy browning around the hem. Daisy, returning to the dining-room, whispered, 'Poor Hester is not at all the thing. She still misses her baby.'

Persia raised her eyebrows. '*Oh*. Another unmarried mother, Daisy darling?'

'It has been six weeks now, but she just sits and *weeps* sometimes, poor thing.'

'The breakfast porridge is salted with Hester's tears.'

'It's all for the best, of course.'

'Well, it would be, wouldn't it?'

A sudden silence. Maia's words, sharply sarcastic, echoed in the crowded room.

Richard said politely, 'You disagree, Maia?'

'Of course not.' Maia smiled a small, tight smile, and sprinkled salt on her vegetables. 'It all works out terribly well, doesn't it? Some well-off woman's spared the trouble of giving birth, Hester's saved from selling herself to feed her little by-blow, and the Summerhayeses have help with their housework. And a clear conscience.'

Hugh touched Maia's arm. 'Darling—'

Again, that small, snapping movement, as though his touch burned her. Maia said, 'A girl to scrub the kitchen floor, *and* a glow of self-satisfaction. Not a bad bargain. Perhaps I too should recruit my staff from a Salvation Army home for fallen women.'

There was a silence. Persia continued to make polite conversation to Philip Shaw; the Warburtons, glancing briefly at Maia and then tactfully turning away, continued to talk to Daisy about Spain. Was it only she, wondered Robin, who saw the dangerous light in Maia's eyes, and who sensed the coiled, destructive anger behind the cynical phrases? Was it only she who saw the pain on Hugh's face?

'You accuse us of hypocrisy, Maia,' said Richard gently. 'You may have a point—'

'*Pa*.' Robin swung round to Maia. Her voice was scornful. 'You're just salving your own conscience, aren't you, Maia?'

Maia cradled her wine-glass between her long, white fingers. She smiled nastily. 'Do explain, Robin.'

'How many of Merchants' staff did you lay off during the Slump?'

She heard Hugh say, 'Robin. Please. Not now,' but she was unable to stop. It was as though a dam had opened, and all her anxiety and anger of the past year was pouring out.

'At least we've given Hester a home. At least she hasn't chucked herself in the river—'

'*Robin!*'

She heard the hiss of Maia's indrawn breath. Hugh said, 'For God's sake, Robin – it's Pa's birthday. And Maia is our guest.'

'I have looked after myself for years, thank you, Hugh. I really don't need a nursemaid.'

Almost everyone had stopped eating. Only Merlin continued to spoon carrots and cauliflower onto his plate. Daisy said brightly, 'I'll clear away, then. Everyone's had enough, haven't they?' She began to stack plates, to heap used cutlery onto a tray.

There were two scarlet marks on Maia's cheeks, as though someone had struck her. But her voice, when she spoke, was calm.

'Since you ask, Robin, I laid thirty-five people off during the Slump. If I hadn't, then Merchants, like so many other businesses, might have been forced to close down. And, yes, I did lie awake at night wondering whether I was doing the right thing. But I did what I had to do. I didn't enjoy it, but it was my responsibility.' She laughed, a hollow, unpleasant sound. 'How comfortable, never to have to make those sorts of decisions. How comfortable just to go with the tide, to stand aside, to live the sort of life that lets you avoid all that. To congratulate yourself upon your virtue, while never letting your comfort be remotely threatened.'

There was a long silence. Hugh's face was bleached white, and a tiny muscle in his eyelid twitched frantically. He said slowly, 'Is that what you really think of us, Maia . . . that we are *smug*?'

Maia shrugged, a small, careless raising and lowering of her narrow shoulders. Her eyes were dark and narrowed, lit only by two orange pinpoints of reflected candlelight.

'I want to know. I need to know.' The urgency in Hugh's voice made Robin shudder.

'Do you, Hugh? Are you sure?'

There was, thought Robin, no pity in Maia's voice as she turned to Hugh. No *love*.

'Then I'll tell you. You hold your jumble sales, your bazaars . . . and yet you come home to this.' Maia's gesture took in the crystal glasses, the silver candlesticks, and all the old, good, beloved clutter that Robin had grown up with. 'At least I am honest. I admit that I like nice things. I admit that I will do anything to hold on to what I have got.' She looked across the table to Richard, her eyes defiant. 'Would any of you give up anything you're really fond of to help someone worse off than yourself? Your piano, Richard . . . your car, Hugh? I don't think so.'

'There is a duty to one's family as well, Maia—'

Maia continued as though Richard had not spoken. 'And, naturally, neither of you teaches at some ghastly little board-school in the Fens, where the parents are semi-literate and the children bathe once a year. No – you both teach in a smart private school in Cambridge, where you are surrounded by civilized people, and decent middle-class values. Then you fit the other sort of people – the messy, feckless, grubby people – into what's left over. Because that makes you feel better than people like me.'

The puddings, brought in by Daisy, stood uneaten on the sideboard. The meringues, the fruit pies, the trifle. The fire had almost burnt out.

Maia looked around the table. Again, that awful, destructive smile.

'The Summerhayeses are such great collectors, aren't they? Music . . . paintings . . . people. You acquire people to fill in the little gaps in your lives, just as you acquire the latest novel to fill that tiny empty space on the shelf. You acquired me because I was pretty, and Helen because she was sweet and obliging. And it was probably terribly amusing, wasn't it, that Helen's father was in the church. You thought you could change her, you thought you could make her into your sort of person, but you couldn't, could you? So you showed her a little bit of freedom, and then you let her go back to her prison.'

Robin said angrily, 'That's not true—'

'Isn't it? You do know that Helen's ill, don't you, Robin? Oh – not TB or influenza, nothing that you can cure with a few philanthropic bowls of soup or cups of tea. Something you can't quite put your finger on . . . something that requires a little more effort.'

Daisy said, 'Helen has always been nervous . . . fanciful . . .'

'Of course she has.' Maia's voice was scathing. 'It's so easy to dismiss someone else's misery, isn't it? *Nerves* – such a convenient label. When did you last visit Helen, Robin?'

The cold blue eyes focused on her. Robin forced herself to think. She realized that she could not remember when she had last seen Helen – in the summer, surely, but no, in the summer there had been Joe . . .

'Helen doesn't seem to want my company any more.' Robin could hear the defensiveness in her own voice. 'She never comes to see me.'

Maia flicked open her cigarette case. 'I take it no-one minds . . . we seem to have finished eating . . .' The corners of her mouth curled as she lit her cigarette. Then she said, 'Helen doesn't go to London because Daddy won't let her, and Helen doesn't come here because she used to be madly in love with your darling brother.'

Robin hadn't suspected Maia of such perception. She watched, hypnotized, as Maia exhaled a cloud of smoke.

'Helen, of course, would fall in love with any passable man who said a kind word to her. Daddy's legacy again.'

Hugh rose suddenly, and left the room. Robin heard the front door slam as he walked out of the house.

454

Daisy said hesitantly, 'Maia – you have had a long day ... the drive to London ... Go to Hugh, won't you ... ?'

Maia bent her head. A curtain of black hair fell over her eyes. Then, straightening, she said: 'Have you ever thought, Daisy, how Hugh hates to be constantly protected? That he loathes the way that you and Richard treat him as though he's a child, or an imbecile?'

Daisy gave a small gasp. Richard said, 'You misunderstand us, Maia. And I believe that you misunderstand Hugh.' Robin had rarely heard her father sound so cold.

Daisy whispered, 'We would do anything to make Hugh happy—'

'Really?' Maia stubbed out her cigarette. 'Yet you have kept him here, tied to you, all his adult life. Do you think that has made him happy?'

It was as though, thought Robin, Maia had deliberately set out to destroy everything her family held dear. A systematic attempt to rip apart the rich, complex fabric of their lives, to seek the weakest spot, the most easily wounded. It occurred to Robin only fleetingly to wonder why, because that clipped, merciless voice stirred up anew all her anxiety and longing for Joe, all her fears for Hugh, all her old questioning of Maia's checkered past. Her anxiety tipped over into rage.

'And do you think you can make Hugh happy, Maia? After all, you're an expert, aren't you? It's not your first attempt at married bliss, is it?'

She could see, at last, a new emotion in those blank blue eyes. Caution. Fear, perhaps. She heard her father say, 'Robin. This is not a suitable conversation for the dinner table. Your mother is tired—' but she disregarded him.

'You're making rather a habit of it, don't you think? Marrying men you don't love.'

'We all have our faults, darling.' Maia's voice was low, wary.

'Don't we just.' Now that she had begun to speak, to voice the concerns that had haunted her for a year,

Robin could not stop. The words tumbled out, pernicious, poisonous.

She heard herself say, 'Only my faults don't cause quite as much damage as yours, do they, Maia? After all, we wouldn't want Hugh to end up like Vernon, would we, shoved down a staircase, cracking his head open.'

Robin heard Merlin mutter '*Christ*' and then felt him lay a warning hand on her arm. But she shook him off, and stumbled to her feet. Her napkin slid to the floor, and she heard the crash as her chair fell backwards as she ran out of the room.

Maia could feel them all staring at her as she rose to her feet. Cold, shocked eyes, burning a hole in her skin. In the hallway, she found her coat and bag. Then she let herself out of the house.

She had driven only a little way when she saw him. Hugh stepped into the centre of the road, forcing her to stop. She noticed that his limp, as he hobbled to the car, was pronounced. She thought what an anachronism he was: his old-fashioned dinner suit, his ancient, well-polished leather shoes, his *goodness* was from a different era.

She opened the car door, and he sat in the passenger seat. She began to drive again, her heart pounding with painful force as she headed along the dark, winding roads. They had travelled five miles or so before he spoke, grasping her hand as it lay on the steering-wheel, so that the car swerved and touched the verge.

'Pull in here.'

Maia steered into the lay-by.

'Turn the engine off.'

As the car engine died, the silence returned. At last, Hugh said, 'I don't understand, Maia. I think you should explain to me.'

'About what? About Helen?'

'Don't be ridiculous.' He had never spoken to her so roughly. 'About this evening. About the things that you said.'

She did not reply but, her nerves jangling, fumbled in her bag for her cigarettes.

Hugh said, 'Did you mean it . . . the things you said about my family?'

Maia lit her cigarette, and sat back in her seat, looking not at Hugh, but out of the windscreen. With an effort, she gathered up the remains of her courage. 'Yes,' she said eventually. 'Yes, I did, Hugh.'

'So you dislike Richard . . . Daisy . . . Robin?'

She said consideringly, '*Dislike* is a little too strong. They *bore* me. Just a little. Oh, Richard and Daisy are very sweet and very worthy, of course, so one can tolerate a touch of ennui. But Robin has become an unbearable prig.'

Anger and hurt mingled in his hazel eyes. 'I had no idea you felt like that.'

'No. You assume your superiority, the superiority of the Summerhayes family. Did you know that I always think, when I visit your parents' house, that I should wear my oldest clothes? So that my good things are not spoiled, you understand. The shabby disorder that your parents cultivate was rather amusing, I suppose, when they were younger – the hopeless maids and nothing in quite the right place – but it has become a little wearing. Squalor is squalor, after all.'

Hugh did not speak at first. His nostrils were pinched and white, and his long, bony hands twisted restlessly.

'That was unworthy of you, Maia.'

She turned to him then, her eyes hard and glittering.

'If you cannot accept me for what I am, Hugh, then perhaps we should part.'

She heard his small intake of breath, and saw his eyes suddenly shut, and his hand, in a gesture that had become so familiar to her, sweep back the lock of hair that had fallen over his forehead.

'Is that what you want?'

'Yes. I think it is.'

Maia began to tug at the ring on her finger. As it jammed on her knuckle, she heard the car door open.

'Hugh—'

'I'll walk. Goodbye, Maia.'

She saw him wince as he had to bend his bad leg awkwardly to climb out of the car. Then she watched his retreating figure as he started up the road. The moonlight outlined his tall, rangy body, and his short fair hair.

She did not know how long she sat there. A part of her expected him to turn round, to come back, to give her another chance. But he did not, of course, and when finally she restarted the engine, there were fingers of grey dawn creeping across the hills and her hands, resting on the steering-wheel, were white with cold.

Robin went, as always, to the winter house. Her shoes crunched the thin snow that covered the lawn, and the palm of her hand was seared by the ice on the banister. Wrenching open the door, she fumbled on the shelf for the matches, and lit the candles. There was no wood in the stove or the basket; ice rimed the windowledge and beaded the cobwebs that festooned the walls and table.

Looking around, she could not work out what had happened. It seemed to her that the place that had once been her sanctuary was disintegrating. Mould flowered on the skirting-boards, a legacy of the high spring floods of recent years, and cold air seeped through the gaps in the planking. The winter house seemed smaller, uglier, as though, almost without noticing, she had grown out of it. When she looked at the table and saw the tumbled boxes of stones and shells and feathers, Maia's voice echoed in her ears. *The Summerhayeses are such great collectors, aren't they?* With a great, hiccupping sob, Robin buried her face in her handkerchief.

At last, she heard the door open, and felt something heavy and warm wrapped around her shoulders.

'You're cold, child. You should come back to the house.'

She looked up at her father. 'Maia—'

'Maia has gone.'

458

In the dim light of the winter house, Richard's face looked grey and lined.

'An awful birthday for you, Pa. I am so sorry—' She couldn't finish her sentence.

Richard said gently, 'It's Joe, isn't it? You are worried for Joe.'

Robin nodded, unable at first to speak.

'You are very fond of him, aren't you, Robin?'

She looked up at her father. 'I *love* him. And it has taken me so long to see it. I've been such an *idiot*.'

Richard raised her to her feet, and hugged her. Her face muffled in his sweater, she forced the words out. 'Do you think Maia is right, Pa? That we stand aside . . . take the easiest option? Only I sometimes think . . .'

'You sometimes think what, Robin?'

'That maybe we are pacifists because we are afraid, and not because of anything else.'

She wanted him to reassure her, to convince her that he, at least, had no doubts.

'Not because of principle?'

'Because we cannot bear to lose our friends . . . or our lovers or our sons. So we'd let anything happen to anyone else.' Her voice cracked again. 'The most awful things.'

He said, 'German planes bombing women and children?' and she walked out onto the verandah, her father's jacket clutched round her shoulders.

'I am afraid that we're only pacifists because then we don't have to risk ourselves, or the ones we love.'

Resting her forearms on the balcony, she looked down to the pool. A thin, opaque ice was forming around the edge of the water. All the questions that had haunted her since Joe had left for Spain returned, breathed into new life by Maia's cold, taunting voice. 'I mean, Pa – do you disapprove of all the men who've volunteered for the International Brigades? Do you think that Joe, for instance, is wrong in fighting for Spain?'

Her father shook his head. 'Of course not, Robin. Joe

is doing what he believes to be right. But there are other ways of fighting for a cause.'

'Letters to our MPs? Demonstrations?' She heard, and instantly regretted, the sarcasm in her voice.

There was a long silence. The flurry of clouds that had brought the snow had long since passed, and an orange crescent moon lay on its back in the sooty sky. Richard said slowly, 'I lie awake at night, wondering about it all. Yes, as Maia pointed out, we raise money for Spain, we send food parcels, and none of that touches our comfortable lives . . . And when the cause is so indisputably just . . . I find myself wondering, if I was a young man . . .'

She saw how tired he looked, how old, and felt a pang of guilt and fear. It shook her that her father, too, should question his beliefs. That his words should echo the argument that unreeled much of the time in her head. Her revulsion from violence; her desire to protect the innocent. If the innocent could only be protected by violence, then did that realization, just as much as Maia's cruel, judgemental words, begin to break apart the beliefs that the Summerhayes family had held for years?

She heard the sound of footsteps on the lawn. Daisy was running towards them, her beaded shawl flying behind her.

'Richard . . . I cannot find Hugh. I thought he was in his room, but he is not. I have searched the house and the gardens. Oh, Richard – I am afraid for him.'

Hugh had gone home with Maia, or he had gone for a walk. He would be back in an hour or two, or in the morning. They said all the obvious, reassuring things, yet were not reassured. None of them went to bed. Instead, they sat in the kitchen, looking up at the smallest sound.

Hugh did not come back in an hour or two; neither did he return in the morning. In the afternoon, Merlin and Richard went out, for a walk, they said – Robin, shivering, knew that they intended to search the rivers and ditches. Daisy washed up and swept floors and polished table tops. For the first time it occurred to Robin that Daisy's busyness, the competence that Robin had always found so galling, was just a way of covering up her fears. If you scrubbed the floor hard enough, you stifled your worst dread.

They received Hugh's letter by the late post on Monday morning. Daisy, standing in the hallway, ripped open the envelope. Robin heard her cry of horror.

'Richard. Oh, Richard. It is too dreadful. Hugh has gone to Spain.'

When Susan Randall and the children fell ill, Helen nursed them, staying at the farmhouse overnight, scribbling a brief note to her father telling him that she would return when she was no longer needed by the Randalls.

Noah and the girls shook off the influenza within a week; Mrs Randall and Michael coughed, scarlet-cheeked, throughout the night. Worried, Helen gave one of the village boys a sixpence to cycle to Burwell for Dr Lemon, and waited, twisting a lock of hair around her finger, for the sound of his Bentley on the rutted drove. Michael sat on her lap, wrapped in a blanket, his blond hair damp and matted, his breathing open-mouthed and noisy.

'It's the air in this part of the Fens,' said Dr Lemon, after he had examined both mother and son. 'Too low-lying and damp, you see, Helen. Bad for the lungs.'

She said anxiously, 'Michael hasn't got pneumonia, has he, doctor?' and he shook his head.

'Give him honey and lemon to drink and keep him warm, and he should be fine. He's a strong little chap.'

Helen, bending to kiss Michael's hot face, beamed proudly.

'I'll leave some cough medicine. It's the mother I'm more worried about, to be honest. There could be a touch of TB. Can you tell me where I can find Sam Randall? I'd like to have a word with him.'

She gave him directions to the pigshed, and settled

Michael in his cot. As he was leaving the room, Dr Lemon paused, and said, 'Are you quite well yourself, my dear?'

Helen looked up at him, surprised. 'Very well, doctor.'

'Only you look a bit peaky. Pale. Do you have a cough, Helen?'

She shook her head.

He persisted. 'Have you lost weight?'

She glanced down at herself. 'I really have no idea. A little, perhaps. It wouldn't be a bad thing, would it? I've always been such a lump.'

'Such an unhealthy thing, this modern craze for slimming. Make an appointment at my surgery, won't you, my dear? I'm sure there's nothing to worry about, but it's always best to make certain.'

Helen, irritated, said nothing. She heard Dr Lemon add, 'Well – don't overdo it, that's all,' and then he left the room.

Helen went to the kitchen to make Michael's drink. She couldn't understand Dr Lemon's sudden concern about her health, and she had no intention of consulting him. She had rarely felt better in her life. In spite of a week of broken nights nursing Michael, she felt almost bursting with energy, so that when she had the chance to doze she was unable to do so. Helen squeezed lemons furiously, then took the kettle from the stove and poured hot water on the honey. Her hands shook a little, spilling some water.

Yet when she caught sight of herself in the small, flyblown mirror in the Randalls' hallway, she stood still for a moment, the cup clutched in her hands, shocked. She hardly recognized her own reflection. The pale, taut skin, deeply shadowed around the eyes, the long grooves between nose and mouth. The dirty fair hair, spiralling madly where she had twisted it around her fingers. She looked old, she thought. Old and ill and perhaps a little mad.

Helen put the cup down on the windowsill. Carefully,

she unbuttoned her cardigan, and did it up on the right buttons. Then she ran her comb through her hair and plaited it.

Michael was asleep. Helen sat down beside the cot, watching him. His eyelashes cast small, lacy shadows on his cheeks, and when she bent and kissed both lids a smile flickered across his face. Something Dr Lemon had said echoed in her mind. *It's the mother I'm worried about. A touch of TB perhaps.* If Dr Lemon sent Susan Randall to a sanatorium, then she, Helen, would be able to take Michael home to the vicarage. Helen, her face pressed against the bars of the cot, slept, and was only woken by the shriek of an owl, a great grey ghost, swooping from the roof of the barn.

Joe had crossed the Channel with a handful of other recruits: men with cloth caps and raincoats too thin for the unpleasant autumn weather. He had a passport, unlike his companions who travelled on three-day return tickets provided by Communist Party officials at King Street. They took the boat train from Victoria, arriving at the Gare du Nord in the mid-afternoon. The only French speaker among the little group, Joe steered them towards the Bureaux des Syndicats, the assembly point in Paris for recruits to the International Brigades. He spent the evening looking up old friends, drinking a great deal of red wine, and composing a postcard to Robin. They filed onto the 'Red Train' at the Gare d'Austerlitz the following morning. The station was crowded with cheering people waving banners painted with the slogans *Vive la République*, and *Vive le Front Populaire*. Joe counted over a dozen nationalities among the occupants of the train before he squeezed into a compartment with some Scots from Glasgow and the three men who had travelled with him from London. Then he closed his eyes, and slept most of the way to Perpignan.

They spent a couple of days kicking their heels in Perpignan before buses arrived to drive them over the

Spanish border. At Figueras, they were barracked in a splendid castle, and spent their days wandering round the dull, dreary little town. Joe took a few photographs and made a sketch or two of the darkened bars, the unenticing brothels. He wrote another letter to Robin, doubtful that it would reach her.

They travelled by train to Barcelona in old wooden carriages that rattled all the way to the city. At every station crowds cheered, fisted salutes were upraised and slogans shouted. *No pasaran* – they shall not pass – and *Viva la Brigada Internacional* resounded as the train lurched from station to station, its carriages sweetly scented by the bunches of flowers thrown in by girls. More flags sported the red, yellow and purple of the Republic, and banners shouted their welcome at Barcelona station. A woman flung her arms round Joe's neck and kissed him, and he felt as though he had got it right at last: he was no longer an onlooker, no longer standing aside. He was making history, he was part of the great popular movement that would turn back the poisonous tide of Fascism.

Barcelona was plastered with posters and slogans. The churches were closed and the streets seethed with people. The normal outward signs of the division of class had disappeared – everyone wore overalls or corduroys, workmen's or peasant dress. There were no deferential forms of address, only the ubiquitous 'comrade'. Revolutionary songs echoed in the bars and cafés, and the words of the Internationale rang in his ears as he walked the length of Las Ramblas. Joe made a hundred friends, promising to visit again, to keep in touch, but had forgotten every name by the following morning.

With a searing headache, he entrained again, for Albacete in Murcia, where the old Guardia Civil barracks had become the central training depot of the International Brigades. The barracks were vast and gloomy, the streets of the bleak little town populated by skinny donkeys, bowed old men and ill-fed children. The recruits were issued with uniforms: the corduroy trousers were a foot too long for the stocky little Glaswegians and Irishmen, and nothing fitted the gigantic French stevedore who had befriended Joe in Figueras. Kitted out with a blanket, belt, plate, spoon, mug, knife and bandolier, Joe felt like a badly tied-up parcel. When he moved, things jangled, threatening to throttle him.

At Albacete, the food was dull but adequate. Slightly worse than at school, much better than in the doss-house. He noticed that the undernourished Glaswegians finished every morsel, muttering with pleasure, and that the middle-class recruits grumbled, appalled at the thought that they might have to fight a war on a stomach full of watery stew and pomegranate. The barracks were cold and damp, and they slept on concrete floors, covered with inadequate blankets.

Training consisted of marching in columns and squares, and hours spent darting round the dreary countryside on 'manoeuvres'. They had no ammunition, and the sound of machine-gun fire was simulated by rattles. In the evenings they listened to long, dull political lectures and drank grappa.

He was beginning to think that he had been wrong again, that his ambition to fight Fascism would dissolve in boredom and frustration whilst wielding a stick of wood that was supposed to be a rifle on some muddy Spanish road, when they were told that they were to be driven to the Front the following day.

At first, it reminded Joe of a school Field Day. The purposeful running around to no great effect, the mixture of anticipation and confusion.

They were somewhere not far from Madrid – he had seen no maps – having exchanged the flat plains of Valencia for a hilly, wintry countryside that, when he awoke in the mornings, reminded him fleetingly of Yorkshire. The hills were scarred with sunken roads, covered with olive groves, their twisted branches grey with frost. They advanced slowly, two men at a time, darting from ditch to ditch, hillock to hillock. 'Like frigging Grandma's footsteps,' muttered Ted Green, and Joe grinned.

The sky was blue, the air windless. It was quiet at first, the silence punctuated only by birdsong and the crunch of their footsteps through the undergrowth. Then Joe became aware of a whistling noise in the air above them. 'Hornets?' he asked Ted, and Ted said, 'No, bullets, you daft bugger.' As they moved forward, the bullets struck the ground around them, sending up little clouds of dust. It seemed both unreasonable and exciting to Joe that someone should be shooting at them.

They paused for a while, sheltered in a sunken road, eating the inevitable pomegranates and brewing coffee. The sun had thawed the early morning frost, and for the first time since he had come to Spain, Joe felt almost warm. He lay on his back, staring up at the pale blue sky, relieved to have discarded, if only for a few minutes, the ever-present blankets, plates and bandoliers.

Then someone shouted, 'Planes – take cover!', and everyone rushed for the shelter of the trees. Joe's blanket rolled to the side of the road, his tin mug tumbled back down the incline. The Nationalist aeroplanes shadowed the hillside, and as he watched, puffs of smoke issued from their bellies. 'Junkers eighty-seven,' said David Talbot, a chemist from Manchester, knowledgeably. 'They must be heading for Madrid.'

The planes flew over them; they were in no danger. Joe watched the great silver shapes of the aeroplanes, and heard the distant thud of the bombs. They began to climb the slope again, ducking behind the scrubby bushes and olive trees. More bullets fell around them, scarring the earth, but still he felt no fear. It just did not seem real. 'Keep your frigging head down,' muttered Ted Green, wriggling on his stomach to the edge of a ridge. The now familiar whining noise, kicking up small explosions of dust, and as Joe watched, Ted's elbows seemed to collapse, so that he lay down, his head resting on the backs of his hands.

Joe peered over the ridge. He couldn't make them out at first, and then, when the haze of smoke cleared, he saw the men dotted among the trees and hollows on the other side of the valley. His first sight of the enemy. His heart began to pound.

'There's bloody hundreds of them, Ted.'

Ted did not reply. Joe looked across at him. Ted still lay on his front, his head cradled on the backs of his hands. He seemed to be asleep. Bullets still whined overhead, but now Joe found that he was afraid of them. Worming his way across the undergrowth, he tapped Ted on the shoulder.

'Ted?'

The other men were all looking at him. Ted did not move at all. Carefully, Joe rolled him onto his back. His eyes were open, and there was a small, neat red hole in the centre of his forehead.

Joe searched for a pulse, but knew that he was dead. Ted Green, who had travelled abroad only once before, to fight as a seventeen-year-old in Flanders, who had been a union organizer in the Twenties, and unemployed throughout most of the Thirties, who had lost his wife and only child to scarlet fever, was dead. You can't be dead, Joe wanted to say. I held your head when you were seasick on the ferry, I taught you how to say please and thank you in French and Spanish, and you taught me how to dismantle and clean my rifle. You can't be dead.

They took up positions on the side of a hill, and for the first time since he had been at school, Joe fired a rifle. He had no idea whether his bullet hit anyone, because it was far too risky to look long enough over the parapet to find out. It seemed to Joe that there were a great many more men on the far side of the valley than on their own side.

The following morning they received orders that they were to occupy a small farmhouse to the side of the hill. Weeks later, he dreamt about that farmhouse. It was a scrappy little building, white-walled, set around a courtyard, its occupants long fled for the doubtful safety of Madrid. Joe couldn't see what strategic importance the farmhouse had, but he guessed that was what all wars – especially civil wars – were like. Fighting for small bits of apparently insignificant land, securing anything that offered the least bit of shelter. They crawled on their bellies along the hillside towards the farmhouse, their heads protected by tin helmets from the bullets that had begun with the dawn to fly. 'I've heard they're goin' tae send us a machine gun,' said Jock Byrne optimistically. 'Coverin' fire.'

To get into the farmhouse they had to run across about fifty yards of exposed ground. Sporadic bullets splintered the earth; if you ran just after a burst of fire you had long enough make it to the farmhouse. Inside, Joe had his first glimpse of what war did to ordinary people's lives. The fleeing family had been able to take some of their belongings with them, but not all. The washtub, the iron bedsteads, the broken wine-pots around the courtyard walls all seemed a pathetic reminder of a shattered normality. If he had let his imagination wander, then Joe could have pictured the family sitting at the huge kitchen table, too heavy to be transported to Madrid on the back of a cart. Instead, unsentimental, he helped the others hack up the table with an axe, so that they could build a fire and cook their first decent meal in thirty-six hours.

The first bullet came through the thick glazing of the kitchen window just as Joe was about to eat a mouthful of stew. Glass splintered across the floor. '*Jesus*,' whispered Jock. Joe wished they had kept the table to shelter beneath.

Edging to the window, his hands and knees carefully placed among the fragments of glass, he managed to stand up and look out of the window. What he saw made his mouth go dry, his stomach turn over. The enemy were no longer a distant, vague line across the valley: in the time it had taken them to occupy the farmhouse, the nationalists had swarmed forward. He could see their machine-gun emplacements only a hundred yards or so away.

There was no sign of a Republican machine gun, no sign yet of any reinforcements. He saw, straightening in the shelter of the wall, that the others were all looking at him, expecting something from him. With a sickening jolt to his stomach, he realized that since Ted Green's death he and David Talbot were not only the oldest men in the small group, but also the only ones with any previous experience of handling a gun. None of the others had been to that sort of school. He wanted to explain that he had always loathed Officers' Training Corps, that he and Francis had got out of it whenever they could, that Francis had disrupted most Field Days with some brilliant, destructive notion. But, growing up several years in a few minutes, he knew that he would, of course, say no such thing.

'We'll have to retreat, I think. They're all over the hill to the east of us.'

The Nationalist army was not rumoured to be kind to prisoners, often executing them out of hand. As they gathered up their packs and rifles, machine-gun bullets sprayed into the kitchen. One of the bullets struck Patrick Lynch in the hand. Joe saw him raise his arm, staring at the jagged wound, touching the scarlet blood as if to assure himself that it was real.

When he peered warily out of the window again, any thought that they could remain here during the day and retreat under cover of darkness dissolved. A blast from a machine gun struck the buildings on the far side of the courtyard; seconds later a tongue of flame leapt from the window. Straw, thought Joe. There must have been straw in there, or olive oil, perhaps – something that was easily inflammable.

Jock voiced Joe's thoughts. 'We'll have tae gae back the way we came.'

They headed back to the doorway at the rear of the house, keeping low, avoiding the windows. The firing was incessant and indiscriminate, the thunder of the bullets as they rebounded off walls and floors deafening. One of the ricocheting bullets struck a man in the back of the neck. They could do nothing for him, but left him in the farmhouse, propped against the wall, an expression of surprise printed permanently on his features.

Flames had taken hold of the buildings at the far side of the courtyard. It had begun to drizzle, and Joe could smell the acrid scent of water on burning wood. The rain was not strong enough to put out the flames – if they remained here, then the fire would eventually reach the side of the farmhouse in which they sheltered, driving them out into the open, to be picked off by the nationalists at will.

Just now, they had the shelter of the intact rear wall, and the smoke. Beyond, the trees were thin, leafless, some distance from the ditch that would provide the first real protection. They must run fifty yards exposed to the Nationalist artillery to the west of them. A chicken run. Joe swallowed.

'One at a time, I think,' said David Talbot.

Jock went first. Small and wiry, not much of a target, the bullets sprayed and missed, and he threw himself into the ditch with a whoop of triumph and a cloud of dust. Another of the Scots followed him, his boots kicking up the earth and dead leaves.

'Third time lucky,' said the youngest of the Cockneys who had crossed the Channel with Joe, and darted out of the doorway.

The bullets struck him when he was halfway across the area of open ground. He seemed almost to freeze in mid-air, his body arcing before he collapsed to the ground. His limbs twitched, and then he lay still. None of the rest of the men, watching from the farmhouse door, spoke. Another man, with a cry of desperation or fury – Joe was not sure which – hurled himself out into the open ground. The bullets caught him and he fell, slumped against the gnarled trunk of an olive tree.

He had a choice, thought Joe. He could be shot running across that damned little strip of land, or he could be burned alive, or he could be taken prisoner and executed. On the whole, he thought he would prefer to be shot.

'I'll have a go—' he began, but his words were interrupted by deafening clatter.

'A machine gun—'

'They've taken the bloody hill!'

'Don't be an idiot, Patrick, it's one of ours.'

Joe ran out of the doorway.

He reached the first tree, and threw himself to the ground. He could feel the fast movement of air as the bullets flew over him. He wanted to lie there for ever, his face against the bare earth. But he forced himself, all his muscles juddering with exhaustion and fear, to run for the next tree. The Republican machine gun rattled somewhere not far away, temporarily silencing the Nationalist one.

He had mentally divided the run into three sections, from tree to tree. He had covered two, there was only one to go. The most exposed section, on the highest ground. Joe took a deep breath and ran faster than he had ever run in his entire life. Bullets whined, certain to hit him, but then the ground suddenly gave way beneath his feet as he tumbled headlong into a trench, his lungs screaming for air.

Chapter Sixteen

In the training depot of the British Battalion at Madrigueras, near Albacete, Hugh Summerhayes slept on a damp palliasse, with a damp pillow, under damp blankets. It was the most noticeable quality of Spain, he thought, the dampness. The blankets, the walls, the floors, were all wet, chill, flowering with fungus. Outside, it rained constantly, a fine, cold, spiky rain that seeped around collars and cuffs, penetrating every layer of clothing. Throughout the day, they drilled and exercised in the rain; at night, when they returned to the barracks, there were never enough fires to dry their clothes. Hugh had two changes of uniform, and both were always damp. He had caught a cold on his first day in Madrigueras, and could not shake it off.

He thought it was the weather that prevented his shellshock returning. It had haunted him, travelling from England to Spain, the fear that he would make a fool of himself, jumping at loud noises, or shaking when they pressed a rifle in his hands. His preoccupation with the cold and the damp seemed to keep all that away. He didn't have nightmares about trench warfare, or Flanders. All that seemed a very long time ago. His worst dream was of lying on an ice floe, his feet in freezing water, fish nibbling his toes.

Besides, he had the boy to worry about. Hugh had met Eddie Fletcher on the Channel ferry. Eddie, sweeping his hair back from a pale forehead that was still pitted with acne, had announced that he was nineteen, and a docker, and that he was going to Spain to fight Fascism. Hugh suspected that he was seventeen and unemployed, but he said nothing, allowing the boy his dignity. In the evenings, when the rest of the men drank and smoked and played cards, Eddie scribbled stories. Once, he shyly showed one to Hugh. His spelling was awful, his writing huge and childish, but the beginnings of a gift for structure and pace were just visible.

Hugh showed Eddie how to clean and dismantle his rifle, and how to stow his belongings in his rucksack so that it did not spew its contents over the ground as soon as they began to march. He helped him to roll his blankets, tying them together so that the rain got to them as little as possible. When they were finally allowed an old Maxim gun for training purposes, it was Hugh who demonstrated to the men how to use it. Because he had fought in the Great War eighteen years ago, because he had been a teacher and was used to giving orders, he was assumed to be the leader of the unit. He accepted the role with grace and amused resignation and an awareness of the responsibility it laid upon him.

He received Robin's letter in the New Year. He read it twice before he chuckled aloud, causing the man on the bench beside him to look at him enquiringly.

'It's from my sister,' explained Hugh. 'She's in Spain, apparently.'

He glanced at the address at the head of Robin's letter. Robin was in Madrid, working in a hospital. She had traced him to Madrigueras, where the British volunteers trained. Hugh read her letter carefully, and wrote a reply. Then he blew his nose, and stifled the cough that itched at his throat, signed his name at the bottom of the page, and limped over to the mess room to find someone to give his letter to.

In October, the armies of the rebel Nationalist Generals Franco and Mola, fortified by assistance from Italy and Germany, had headed towards Madrid. The troops of the German Condor Legion arrived in Spain in November, keen to test their new weapons and new strategies. The Republican government left Madrid for the comparative safety of Valencia, and at much the same time the first battalions of the International Brigades – a mixture of Germans, French, British, Italian and Polish volunteers – arrived in the capital, and were greeted with an explosion of joy and relief. Nationalist soldiers advanced from the south and west of the city; Nationalist planes bombed the working-class areas, pounding the buildings to dust, forcing the people to take shelter in Underground stations and cellars. The ordinary workmen and women of the city, armed with whatever weapons they could find, took to the streets, and by the end of November, the rebel armies had been beaten back. The bombing and shelling continued, however, spiteful and intermittent, but failing to dampen the spirits of the Madrileños.

Robin had arrived in Spain at the end of December with the British Medical Aid unit headed by Dr Mackenzie. On the afternoon of the day that Daisy had received Hugh's letter, Robin and Merlin had travelled to London, to the Communist Party headquarters in King Street. There, she had been almost relieved to discover that it was too late, that Hugh had left for Paris, that he might already have entrained for the Spanish border. Relieved because she could hardly bear to inflict on Hugh the humiliation of using his ill-health as a reason for his early discharge.

She still shuddered when she recalled what Hugh's departure for Spain had done to her parents. They had looked old, suddenly, beaten and frightened and hopeless. All the competence that Robin had always felt unequal to had utterly gone. For the first time that Robin could remember it had been she who had comforted them, she who had soothed and made tea and begun to plan. It had been jarring, in the middle of all that despair and confusion, to discover how much her parents needed her. She hated Maia not only for her betrayal of Hugh, but also for what she had done to Daisy and Richard.

She had parted from Merlin at Liverpool Street station, a plan hatching in her mind as she walked back to her room. That evening she had called on Neil Mackenzie, begging him to take her to Spain with his Medical Aid group. He had agreed, and Robin had found herself, eventually, in Spain, trying to trace Hugh and Joe in the muddle that was the Spanish Civil War. Stationed temporarily at a base hospital in Madrid, Robin had been told that they would be posted nearer to the Front when the situation demanded it.

The splendid houses and hotels in the wealthy districts of the city contrasted with the heaps of rubble that littered the poorer parts. In the hospital they treated both soldiers and civilians. When she first saw the terrible wounds inflicted on children by bombs and shells she had to swallow her distress, telling herself fiercely that she would be of no use to anyone if she could not see for tears. Because she had only First Aid training, she was the lowest of the low within the hospital. She emptied bedpans, made beds, polished floors until they gleamed, and scrubbed instruments. Her hands became red and raw, her feet always ached. Occasionally she was allowed to help bathe or dress a patient, or to feed a man who had lost the use of his hands. Whenever she made a mistake, the terrifying Scots sister who had accompanied them on the journey from England always seemed to see her. Asleep at night, Robin heard Sister Maxwell's icy 'Summerhayes!' in her dreams. When one of the other nurses told her that there was a lull just now, and that things would soon get busier, she found it hard to believe her. She simply could not imagine fitting any more into a day.

Within the space of a few short weeks, she had to get used to a great many things. To sharing a room with three other nurses, to living her life in the sort of public arena she had so disliked at school. To carrying out orders without question. These things she slowly grew accustomed to. She would never grow accustomed to the sight of a child with only a stump where its leg had once been, or to the sound of a grown man crying for his mother.

As soon as she had arrived in Spain, she had begun to look for Hugh, making enquiries of doctors and nurses at the hospital, of patients wounded at the Front, and of the organizers and administrators sent by the Medical Aid organization in London. She had discovered that Hugh was still at the training depot at Madrigueras, so she had quickly scrawled a note to him, posting it the previous week. In the pocket of her apron lay the letter that she had received that morning, and had not yet had time to open. She knew that it was from Hugh.

Sister Maxwell was glaring at her as she made up a bed with clean linen. Robin tucked in the starched sheets with hospital corners of geometric precision. When at last it was time for her ten minute break, Robin rushed to the rest room, kicked off her shoes and placed the kettle on the gas ring. Then she ripped open the envelope, and began to read. Reaching the end of the letter, she let out a hiss of exasperation. The only other nurse in the rest room, a tall girl called Juliet Hawley, said, 'Bad news?'

Robin shook her head. 'No. It's my brother at last. He's at Madrigueras, but he says that he's leaving for the Front any day.'

She sat down on a chair by the window, looking out at the playground of the school that the hospital had requisitioned. The playground was empty of children; an ambulance was being cleaned and restocked, ready to return to the Front, and a couple of nurses were standing in the rain, talking. Hugh's letter was crumpled into a little ball in the palm of her hand; Robin smoothed out the paper, folding it carefully. She did not fear the bombs that fell within a few hundred yards, sometimes, of the hospital; and the thought of working in a unit closer to the Front did not frighten her. But she feared for Hugh and Joe constantly, a terrible, gnawing, uncontrollable fear, a forlorn dread that never left her.

The ten minutes was over. Robin folded Hugh's letter and tucked it in her pocket. She knew, at least, that Hugh was alive. Of Joe, she had heard nothing.

Walking back from the bus stop, Helen always passed Adam Hayhoe's cottage. Often she paused for a few moments to pull weeds from his front garden, or to take away the odd piece of litter that had blown onto the doorstep. That afternoon, in the act of unclasping the front gate, she heard singing.

' "As I walked out one midsummer morning, to view the fields and to take the air . . ." '

Helen's heart began to pound. Dropping her baskets at the roadside, she ran to the front door.

'Adam? Adam – is that you?'

The singing stopped and the door opened. 'Adam,' she said delightedly. 'How good that you have come home.'

Smiling at her, he touched his cap. 'Afternoon, Miss Helen.'

'*Adam* – I told you.'

'I beg your pardon, Helen. Just habit.' His apology did not cancel out his smile.

She noticed that he was wearing his coat and cap. A little of her happiness began to dissolve.

'You're not leaving yet, are you?'

He shook his head. 'I'm just going to the Randalls'. This place has been empty so long the cold's got into its bones. Susan Randall said she'd give me a bed for the night.' He glanced at Helen. 'Walk over with me, won't you, Helen? There's so much I'd like to tell you about. Two and a half years is a long time. And I'd like the company.'

'Two and a half years . . .' she said slowly. She hadn't realized that it had been so long since Adam Hayhoe had left Thorpe Fen. Often, nowadays, she lost track of time, the weeks and the months muddling themselves indistinguishably together.

'You haven't changed a bit, Adam. I have, I know. I've grown so *old*.'

'Old? No.' His face was serious. She was glad that he did not say, as her father would have said, *You're just a girl, Helen*.

'You're as bonny as ever. You look tired, though. Such a hard task, running that great house, doing all the cleaning and that in the church.'

'Oh – that. Anyone could do it. And I have the maid to help at home, and Mrs Readman does all the heavy work at church. I'm not even very good at it. Last week I forgot to order oil, and we had to eat our dinner in the dark.'

He said, 'Will you walk with me?' and she nodded, and headed back down the path.

Although it was only mid-afternoon, the light had already begun to fade. Helen, looking at the low-roofed thatched cottages, shivered.

'Are you cold, love?'

The endearment warmed her. She shook her head. 'No. It's not that. It's the houses – the windows are all black. I imagine things behind them.'

Eyes watching her, voices whispering behind palmed hands. Sometimes the eyes were not human, and the language that the voices whispered was unrecognizable.

Adam said gently, 'When I was a lad and afraid of the dark, and too feared to run out to the privy, my ma told me to imagine there was an elephant standing just outside the door. I'd only seen an elephant in a storybook, of course – a silly great creature with flapping ears and water squirting out of its trunk. You couldn't possibly be afraid of that. I used to look around for this bright, glittery, daft thing whenever I ran out of the back door. Then I wasn't afraid.'

She felt his hand enclose round her elbow, guiding her along the rutted path. 'You must imagine an elephant behind the windows, Helen. Or something else that makes you laugh.'

'Hens. I shall think of our hens. No-one could be afraid of a hen.' She felt herself shake with a laughter that verged on the edge of hysteria, and she made an effort to control herself.

'Tell me what you have been doing, Adam. Have you found work?'

'It was difficult at first – terrible hard. I slept in a ditch, or behind a hedge many nights those first few months. Not that I mind *that* – I've done so often enough before, wandering round the countryside when I was a young man. But an empty belly's harder to get used to. Anyway – I thought I'd better hurry up and get some work before I looked a regular tramp, so I put on my best clothes and went knocking on doors. Offering to mend windows, repair fences – anything.'

They were walking along the narrow track by the field. Adam gave Helen his hand to help her over the stile.

'I had a stroke of luck, though. I worked for a gentleman who'd a couple of nice chairs badly in need of repair. I offered to do 'em for him – I had to twist his arm a bit, tell him plain that I was a good craftsman – but he let me have a go at last. I did a nice job – matched the carving exactly. Then he put me in touch with a lady who had a little shop in Brighton.'

'Brighton!' said Helen. 'That's miles away.'

'It's a nice enough place. Noisy, though. I'd been there before, years ago, just before I was sent out to the Front. Bathed in the sea.'

'I should love to see the sea. Tell me about it, Adam. Tell me what it looks like.'

Standing at the edge of the field, he paused for a moment. The sky had darkened, so that the brightest stars could be seen, and shadows crept along the black ridges of the field.

Adam said slowly, 'It's never the same colour twice. Blue or green or grey, but never quite the same from one day to the next. And the sound of the waves on the stones is like the wind in the reed-beds. And it's so great and strong it makes you feel small. But that's not such a bad feeling.'

On her own, she would never had stood here, the wide expanse of field to one side of her, endless marsh and ditch and reed-bed to the other. She knew what Adam meant: *it's so great and strong it makes you feel small.* Usually, that frightened her.

'It sounds beautiful, Adam.' As the wind picked up, her words were only just audible. They began to walk again.

'Anyway – this lady – Mrs Whittingham's her name – was looking for a carpenter to do some special pieces for her. A couple of matching cabinets, to take some Chinese vases. Horrid things they were, a nasty dark red and black. Mrs Whittingham let me use the back of her shop to make them up, and when they were finished, she sent me off to her brother in London. He owns a workshop. I did a few pieces for him, too.' In the dim light, Helen saw Adam smile. 'I had to talk to the customers, find out exactly what they wanted. Funny characters, some of 'em – there was a lady with a Siamese cat – carried it round with her all day, tucked under her arm like a shopping basket. And a gentleman who wore a dressing-gown whatever time of day I called on him. Fancy thing, mind you – shiny stuff with dragons sewn on, but still, I never saw him in a proper suit of clothes. And he had one of those natty little eyeglasses.' Adam shook his head. 'And the things they have! The jewels, the knick-knacks, the fancy pictures . . . Don't know how they stand it. Everything cluttered up. I like a bit of space, myself. Couldn't abide worrying about all those things.'

Helen could see the lights of the Randalls' farmhouse at the end of the path.

'Are you still working for the gentleman in London, then, Adam?'

Again, he shook his head. 'I've been travelling around

again, doing a bit here and there. I'd some work in Peterborough, so I thought I'd come home, see how the old place is getting on.' He turned to face Helen. 'I don't want to work for nobody, Helen. I want to be my own man. I'll not be at anyone's beck and call ever again. It'll take a while, but I'm going to have a little workshop of my own, you'll see.'

In the February of 1937, the rebel Nationalist army launched a massive assault through the Jarama valley, with the aim of taking the Madrid–Valencia highway, and thus cutting off the capital. The Jarama river lay to the south-east of Madrid, a countryside of hills and valleys and ridges planted with olive groves and vineyards.

By the time he left Albacete for the Front, Hugh had realized that he had a touch of bronchitis. He had had bronchitis every winter since he was eighteen: Ma fussed, but he always pulled through. It just meant a couple of weeks with his chest rattling like a kettle drum, and a few bad nights when the fever made him dream.

One of the chaps suggested he went to the hospital until he recovered, but he did not, because of Eddie Fletcher. Eddie had latched on to Hugh, needing Hugh's quiet reassurance to calm his fears, and Hugh's gentle prompts to get him through the day. He just wasn't the sort of lad made to be a soldier, and had Eddie been a pupil at the school that he had taught at in Cambridge, Hugh would have fudged up some sort of reason to excuse the boy from OTC and games.

But this was war, and Eddie, like Hugh, had made an open-ended commitment to fight with the Spanish Republican army. When they clambered into the lorries that would take them to the Front, Eddie looked white, pinched, afraid. 'I've saved the last of the chocolate,' said Hugh, holding out a hand to help the boy into the truck. Hugh, coughing painfully, remembered that he had been only a year or so older than Eddie Fletcher when he had gone to Flanders. Now he could hardly

481

recall the mixture of excitement and fear and impatience with which he had set sail for France. He felt a flutter of apprehension that what he was about to endure would bring it all back – the nightmares, the day visions, the sense of unending, everlasting terror – and then he knew, looking around the truck, that he would be all right. He would not break down because they depended on him. He would not break down because he had known Maia, and she had loved him for a while, and that had changed him.

He allowed himself, as the lorry rattled through the night and most of the men dozed off, to think about Maia. He did not, on long, long reflection, believe that she despised him or his family. She had said those terrible things because there was a seam of destructiveness in Maia that Hugh recognized to be the legacy of her past. She had not in the end wished to marry him, but he could not resent her for that because he had never thought himself worthy of her. Maia had a cold fire, a sense of purpose, a drive that Hugh had always found hypnotic. She possessed in raw abundance all the light and energy that he had lost, years ago, on the fields of Flanders. He had not, since he had been eighteen, had anything much in the way of conviction, other than a constant, niggling feeling that there were too many injustices in the world. Maia had the clarity of vision that had been taken from him, and beside her he had always felt insubstantial, a shadow. She had needed him for a while, and now she did not need him, something that seemed to Hugh neither surprising nor reprehensible. He had been hurt, of course, terribly hurt, but he knew that the time that he had spent with her had been a privilege, not a right.

He took the photograph from his inside pocket, and looked at it. Next to him, he heard Eddie say, 'Is that your girl?'

'This is my sister—' Hugh pointed to Robin '—and that's Maia. She's a friend. A dear friend.' Richard Summerhayes had taken the photograph years ago:

Robin and Maia, standing outside the winter house, himself and Joe to either side.

Eddie, breathing adenoidally, said, 'She's a corker.'

Hugh smiled and put the snapshot back in his pocket. Then, closing his eyes, sitting upright so as not to provoke his cough, he tried to sleep.

With the dawn came the wind blowing ice-cold into the open-backed lorry. When Hugh coughed, one side of his chest hurt. He pressed his fisted hand against the pain, telling himself that it was nothing, just a stitch. The clouds, blocking the rising sun, made the valley of the Jarama a grey, pearly hollow. He had been through worse than this, Hugh reminded himself. At Arras, he had walked for what seemed like an eternity, half carrying, half dragging a wounded schoolfriend, not realizing until he reached the dressing-station that his friend was dead. A memory that he had never before confronted, but now, oddly, had lost the power to terrorize him. Hugh glanced at Eddie. 'Almost there, old chap,' he said encouragingly. He could see, distantly, the smear of silver that was the River Jarama, gleaming as sunlight peered briefly from behind the clouds.

When they arrived at the Front and took up their positions, they dug a trench. Frost still gleamed on the olive groves that lined the hillside. In the brief lull between the digging of the trenches and the enemy's resumption of fire, Hugh rested and lit his pipe. The pain in his chest was not alleviated, though. The movement of his ribs as he took breath hurt him, and beads of sweat gathered on his forehead and on his upper lip. It occurred to Hugh that this was not a stitch, that he was ill, really ill, and he felt a surge of annoyance that his feebleness should threaten to blight this, his first attempt to do something worthwhile with his life. Then there was a rattle of machine-gun fire from the far side of the valley, like the drum-roll at the beginning of an overture, and it started.

Adam stayed in Thorpe Fen for a week. Once, he and Helen took Michael for a walk in his pram, rattling over the frosted mud, pushing back the hood so that Michael could reach, laughing, for willow catkins. Helen pretended to herself that she and Adam and Michael were a family, out for their Sunday walk. She almost confided in Adam her hope that she might one day be able to adopt Michael, but in the end she did not. The Randalls were, after all, Adam's oldest friends, and to seem to take pleasure in Susan Randall's ill-health must repel him.

In the village, she avoided Adam's company. She still felt that she was being watched and whispered about. Whispers that would, if allowed to grow, find their way to her father. The eyes of the watchers were critical and destructive. Yet she washed her long hair, combing out the tangles, and sponged and ironed her best dress, and darned the holes in her stockings.

On the day of his leaving, Helen walked to Adam's cottage at nine o'clock in the morning. Dressed in his greatcoat and cap, he was closing the front door, his rucksack on the step beside him.

Helen said, 'I'm coming with you to the station, Adam.'

He looked round at her. She showed him her basket.

'I told Daddy that I was going to do the shopping a day early, so that I could spring clean the drawing-room tomorrow.' Helen smiled, delighted at her own cunning.

They walked together down the drove. The bus stop was outside the row of tumbledown cottages that stood in the lowest-lying part of the village. Only the end cottage was now inhabitable. The sedge that covered the roofs of all four had darkened, collapsing in great discoloured hanks from the cottage that had once belonged to Jack Titchmarsh. Cobwebs curtained the little crooked windows, and the door of Jack's cottage was now wedged permanently open, a whorl of leaves, turned to lace skeletons by the damp, carpeting the floor. Patches of clunch had peeled from the walls to the grass, revealing wooden slats like fragile bones beneath. When Helen reached out a hand and touched the wall, her

484

fingertips were blackened by the mould that crept across the wet plaster.

'Squire's letting it all go to pot.' Adam, glancing at the cottages, looked angry.

'You must come back before another two years are out, Adam. Else Thorpe Fen will have sunk into the marsh, and there'll be only the spire of the church sticking up from the peat.'

She had meant it as a joke, but it sounded like a lament. Helen's voice echoed sadly against the derelict walls. When she looked along the drove she saw the bus coming towards them.

They arrived early at Ely station; the train was not due for another quarter of an hour. Adam suggested a cup of tea, and they went into the little café. When he had bought the tea and buns, he sat down in the seat opposite her, and said, 'Helen – I will be back. I promise.'

Stirring sugar into her tea, she tried to smile.

'And not two years this time, neither. Things are getting better for me – I should be able to start putting some money by very soon.'

The café was deserted apart from the woman serving behind the counter.

'Sometimes I feel so frightened—' said Helen suddenly. She had not meant to speak, and her hand flew to her mouth, silencing herself.

When he said, 'Frightened of what, love?' she could hear the concern in his voice.

'I don't know.' She gave a little laugh. 'Silly, isn't it?'

Adam did not immediately reply. Instead, he took her clenched hand in his, his fingers curling round hers, loosening them. 'Tell me, Helen.' He frowned, struggling to understand. 'Is it the house . . . the rectory? Such a big place – there must be so many empty rooms—'

She shook her head, thinking of her attic, where she felt safe. 'I don't mind that. It's where I've always lived, after all.'

'Then . . . your father . . . ?'

She stared at him for a moment, and then laughed

485

again. 'Daddy? How could I be afraid of Daddy?' Yet she thought, for the first time, that she was not speaking the truth. *Honour thy father and mother*, the commandment said. Nothing about love. It occurred to her, alarmingly, that what she now felt for her father was nothing more than a mixture of fear and distaste and duty. She could not remember whether she had always felt like that.

There was a rumbling and roaring as the train pulled into the station. Adam rose to his feet and swung his rucksack onto his back. Outside, standing on the platform, they were enveloped by a cloud of smoke and steam. It blurred his figure, cutting him off from her. It's like this, she wanted to say. There is something between me and other people, keeping me away from them, erasing me. But then she felt his hands rest on her shoulders, and his lips touch her cheek. She did not pull away, but gave a small moan of pain and longing, turning to him so that momentarily his mouth brushed against hers.

Then he was gone. The train heaved and clattered out of the station, a great dragon, belching smoke. Helen stood on the platform until even the tiny pinpoint of black and white had melted into the distance, and then she walked away, her basket cradled against her chest.

Each day, Hugh fought two battles – the public one, against the vast forces of the Nationalist army, and his own private battle, the old war against his failing health. When his fever rose, it was hard, sometimes, to separate in his mind the two struggles. He did not know which he feared more: a bullet breaking through skin and bone, or the fluid that had begun to gather in his lungs, threatening to drown him. After a few days in which he had seen around a quarter of his men cut down, the fever began to produce hallucinations, small twistings of reality that sent him back, fleeing through the years, to what he had seen in 1918. He sank back against the rear wall of the trench, closing his eyes, wondering whether

486

he even wished to continue the unequal struggle for breath. Then someone called out, 'Eddie!' and Hugh looked up in time to see the boy standing up, head and shoulders above the parapet, aiming his rifle. He saw the bullet strike the boy in the shoulder, so that Eddie's frail body recoiled and his knees buckled.

Hugh crawled over to him, opening his jacket. Eddie said, 'I thought if I stood up I'd get a good crack at them,' and then he began to cry. 'Will I die?'

Hugh shook his head. 'Of course not.' Yet he was not sure whether the bullet had struck the boy's lung.

He patched up the wound and made Eddie as comfortable as he could. He searched up and down the trench for the Medical Officer but could not find him; they were, he knew, in the middle of a slaughterhouse. He sat Eddie up and gave him water to drink, and put aside his own rifle, knowing that for him, as well as the boy, the battle of Jarama was over. When dusk came, and the Moors, with their brown faces and black cloaks, began to dart across the valley, rifles in hand, Hugh knew that he must get Eddie to a hospital. Blood was still seeping from the bullet hole, and Eddie's breathing, like his own, was laboured and short. Hugh set off back down the far side of the hill, the boy's arm slung around his shoulder.

He searched for a First Aid station or ambulance, but could find neither. He seemed to be in the middle of a partial retreat. Afraid of becoming caught up in the chaos of men and equipment, he headed away from the battleground. With Eddie propped against him, Hugh walked for miles, losing his sense of direction. The darkness became complete as clouds covered the moon and the stars. From time to time, he murmured comfortingly to Eddie, but the pain in his own chest had become almost unendurable. The warmth of the fever had retreated, replaced by a bitter cold that made him shiver violently. Hugh knew that he could not continue much longer, that he had failed the boy, and failed himself.

He no longer heard the guns. They had been silenced

by the night, or he had walked a long way from the battlefield. He did not think he had ever felt so alone. When a black shape loomed out of the darkness, Hugh struck a match and saw that they had reached a small stone hut. The roof was thatched, the doorway gaped. He helped Eddie inside. There was straw on the floor, and fragments of charcoal, the remains of a fire. A shepherd's hut, Hugh guessed. It seemed sensible to stay there for the rest of the night, and in the morning, when it was light, he would make another attempt to find medical help.

Hugh made Eddie as comfortable as possible, heaping up the straw and laying the boy on it, covering him with his own greatcoat. Soon, Eddie slept. Hugh sat on the dirt floor, staring out of the doorway. He had begun to feel hot again, great waves of heat that washed over his body. The pain had spread, flowering over his entire chest, forcing him to take air in small, painful gasps. He guessed that he had pneumonia.

At last he slept. He dreamt that he was rowing Maia on the river behind Blackmere farmhouse. It was warm and sunny, and the banks were starred with golden kingcups. Dragonflies darted in the hazy air, their bodies jewelled with gold, sapphire and emerald. A kingfisher perched, its plumage dazzling, on a branch. Maia, her eyes the same bright light blue as the kingfisher's wing, was smiling.

But his oar caught a stone and the boat overturned, casting them both into the river. There was a different country under the still surface of the water, all shimmering shadows, the riverbed studded with shells, ribboned with waving weeds. He tried to catch Maia's hand to help her, but she eluded him, always just out of his reach. Water filled his lungs, and he struggled for breath, his entire body screaming for air. To cough was agony. When Hugh awoke, he could hear the boy's breathing, quick and tortuous. After a while he dozed intermittently, jarred frequently into consciousness by terrible dreams.

At last, he opened his eyes and saw through the doorway the grey, frosty outline of the hills. He lay quite still, caught by the beauty of the dawn, taking pleasure in the silence. Then he turned and looked at the boy, and saw that Eddie lay motionless and that the patch of scarlet on his tunic had darkened to crimson. Rising, he touched the boy's face, and found that it was cold.

Hugh knew that he, like Eddie, would die. Anger flared in him when he thought of the life that he had been denied. He had never married, had never fathered children, he had never travelled except to go to war. He had lived a second-hand sort of life, finding passion and adventure mostly in books and music, admiring involvement, yet shrinking from it. And now even this shadowy existence was to be taken from him.

The cold had invaded him, numbing his feet and hands, but he struggled in his pocket to find a paper and a pencil. His hand fisted around the pencil as he tried to write. He wanted to tell whoever found them what had happened, about the waste of it all, the heroism and the ignominy, but in the end he just wrote 'So cold.' The letters were huge and misshapen. Then he lay, his head cushioned by straw, looking out of the doorway. Tiny snowflakes were falling, floating in the still air. In the distance, the sun lit the valley, bands of light searing through the mist. The mist and the distance erased all trace of war. Hugh thought he had never seen anything so beautiful, and he resented bitterly that he should leave all this. His lungs bubbled, forcing him to claw desperately for every breath. Fear seized him, squeezing tears from his lids.

Then he realized that he was standing on the verandah of the winter house. Maia and Robin were swimming in the pool, Helen was sitting beside him. He could hear laughter and birdsong. Maia called, 'Are you coming in, Hugh darling?' and he smiled and stepped forward and felt the warm, welcoming water embrace him.

*   *   *

When fighting broke out in the Jarama valley, the medical unit of which Robin was a part left Madrid for the Front. Scouting around, they found a disused villa to the south-east of the city. Once a Spanish aristocrat's country home, it was huge and elegant and decayed, festooned with spiders' webs, the gleaming patina of its marble floors and rosewood furniture softened by a grey velvet blanket of dust. They chose the villa for its spacious, high-ceilinged rooms, and for its precious single tap of cold running water.

They worked through the night scrubbing floors, washing walls, throwing oil paintings and ornaments into outbuildings and attics. They filled the rooms with beds and cots, and set up operating theatres and a reception area to sort out the wounded. In the early hours of the morning, the field ambulances began to arrive. Eighty men on the first day, one hundred and twenty on the second, over two hundred on the third. No-one slept. In the imposing entrance hall of the villa, with its gilding and its carved balusters, the wounded were sorted into three categories. Those who must be treated urgently, those who could safely be sent to the base hospital in Madrid, and those for whom nothing could be done other than the alleviation of their pain.

Robin was no longer just a bed-maker and bed-pan scrubber. Almost overwhelmed by the sheer numbers of wounded, all the old hierarchies of the hospital at Madrid faded, became unimportant. She took temperatures, staunched bleeding, replaced bloodsoaked bandages, and cut the torn clothes from the men as they lay on their stretchers, murmuring to them gently in whatever language she thought they might understand. One night she found herself in the operating theatre, holding a torch so that the surgeon could continue to do his work when the generator failed. She taught herself to carry on working despite the Nationalist bombs that were aimed at the hospital, even when the entire building shook and powder hissed from the plaster cornices of the grand reception rooms. Because they seemed to be short of everything, she had to tear sheets into strips for bandages, and arrange benches and chairs into makeshift beds. Wounded men crowded every inch of the villa; reception rooms and passageways once peopled only by the ghosts of proud Spanish noblemen were crammed with wounded militiamen, in beds, on stretchers, on the floor.

They did not sleep, because there was no time to sleep. The surgeons operated for an uninterrupted thirty-six hours; in the early hours of the following morning, Sister Maxwell found Dr Mackenzie curled up asleep in bed with a dead man. As the days went on and the battle continued to rage, Robin lost track of day and night. Glancing at her watch, she could not work out whether it was five o'clock in the afternoon, or five o'clock in the morning. Walking to a window, moving aside a curtain, she was almost surprised to find that the sun still shone. Late at night, after working a fourteen hour shift, she would begin to scrub and sterilize instruments needed for the next shift, only a few short hours away. Once, washing out bandages in the sink, she realized that she had dozed, standing there, her arms up to the elbows in boiling water. Her skin was red and inflamed, and she had no idea how long she had slept.

In every ambulance arriving at the mobile hospital from the forward casualty posts, Robin dreaded that she would find Hugh or Joe. She had to steel herself momentarily before glancing at each new face. As her exhaustion mounted, she glimpsed them sometimes, her brother and her lover, seeing their features printed briefly on the faces of strangers. Some of the Spaniards were only boys. Cradling them in her arms as they died, she knew that she had not been mistaken, that war was an abomination, unambiguously evil.

Since Madrid, and the losses they had endured, Joe's unit had become part of the British Battalion of the fifteenth International Brigade.

Even his previous experience of fighting near Madrid

had not prepared Joe for the battle of Jarama. The noise of it, the relentless pounding of guns and aeroplanes. The bombs that pitted the hillside with great hollow craters, the shells that vomited their gouts of flame into the smoky air. The smell of cordite and burning flesh, and the cries of the wounded. Even when the guns fell temporarily silent, Joe could still hear them, echoing inside his skull. The pale earth was pulverized to a muddy clay: at night, the mud froze. They ate, slept, lived in the shallow trench.

They watched German Junkers, the swastikas on their tails clearly visible, and Russian Chatos battle it out in the air. On land, though they fought tenaciously, they failed to stem the steady advance of the Nationalist army to the banks of the river. If the nationalists captured the highway, then Madrid would be lost. Cut off from the units to either side of them, they wondered whether those units still existed, or whether they had retreated, or had been pounded to pieces by shells, leaving them alone, exposed on the side of the hill. In the absence of any other means of communication, they sent out runners, taking it in turns to reconnoitre to left and right. They all felt permanently hungry, thirsty and exhausted. And frightened. The continual fear, which jarred his nerves and made his sleep anything but restful, took Joe by surprise. He had always assumed that you got used to fear, that it diminished in time. Nationalist troops had crossed the River Jarama. To Joe, the valley had become a scene from hell.

Carrying a message to the American Abraham Lincoln Battalion, he stumbled across a wounded man lying in a ditch. When he saw the gaping abdominal injury, Joe wanted to vomit. Flies crawled over the unrecognizable mess of blood and tissue, feeding from the open wound. Worse, the man's eyes were open as he muttered in Spanish for water. It appalled Joe that this man was dying in such a hideous, degrading fashion; it appalled him even more that he knew that he was dying. Joe held his water-bottle to the Spaniard's dry, cracked lips, and cushioned the man's head with his own shirt, knowing all the while the futility of whatever he did. He found himself saying to the militiaman, 'I'll get someone to help you,' and running away, knowing that he was leaving the man to die. He seemed to search around for hours in the chaos behind the lines before at last he found stretcher-bearers, and by that time his sense of direction had gone, lost in the smoke and the noise, and he was unconvinced that he had sent the stretcher-bearers in the right direction. His muscles juddered with exhaustion, and he was overwhelmed by guilt and an awareness of his own failure.

Maia had a note from Léon Cornu, inviting her to dine with him in London. Intrigued (it was only six months since they had last met), she met him in their usual restaurant. After he had kissed her on both cheeks, after they had ordered food and Léon had chosen and tasted the wine, she said, 'Tell me, Léon. You are as much a creature of habit as I. This is all very unexpected.'

The waiter filled their glasses.

'I have a proposition to make to you, ma chère Maia.'

She said nothing, just looked at him.

'A *business* proposition,' he added smoothly. 'Do you remember I told you that I was looking for an outlet in New York?'

Of course she remembered. That day was imprinted for ever on her mind. The lunch with Léon Cornu had been followed by her appointment with the Harley Street doctor. *In my professional opinion, Mrs Merchant . . .*

'Maia – are you well?'

She forced herself quickly back to the present, and managed to smile and say, 'Quite well, thank you, Léon. New York, you said . . . ?'

'I spent six weeks there in spring. I found a most promising premises on Fifth Avenue.'

Maia frowned. 'Fifth Avenue? A *shop*? I thought you were looking for a small factory.'

'Both.' He shrugged. 'The shopkeeper adds a third to

my price and pockets it as profit. As I'm sure you are aware, madame.' His eyes twinkled.

She said, understanding him, 'And you would prefer . . . ?'

'That the profit end up in *my* pocket, of course. *Enfin*, as I said, I have found a splendid premises on Fifth Avenue. Not too big, not too small. Too big to sell just lingerie, but not large enough for dull things—' he made a dismissive gesture '—like furniture or electric lamps.'

As the waiter served the hors d'oeuvre, Maia studied Léon Cornu curiously, but did not yet speak.

He added, 'I thought . . . lingerie and costumery and a small, select *parfumerie*, perhaps.'

'Léon – why are you telling me all this?'

'To ask you to join my enterprise, of course, Maia.'

She gasped, 'Join you? Léon – how could I?'

'It is simple.' He ground salt over his devilled kidneys. 'You get on an aeroplane and you fly across the Atlantic. So simple.'

Maia's fork had not yet touched her food. Her eyes narrowed. 'As a co-owner . . . or a store manager?'

'Both, I hope. Alone, I would struggle to raise sufficient capital for such a venture. I would run the factory, and you would run the store. We could work very well together, don't you agree?'

Maia put down her fork, her food uneaten. Just for a moment the vision of climbing onto an aeroplane and flying away, so far away that none of her memories, none of her past, could touch her, left her almost breathless.

She shook her head. 'I can't, Léon. Merchants—'

'You have a capable manager, do you not, madame?'

'Liam?'

'Who would not, I suspect, be averse to more responsibility, more money. You need not *sell* Merchants, Maia. You could retain your ownership of Merchants while setting up and running our shop in New York.'

'Yes.' She still found it difficult to think clearly, but

494

she could see that it was possible. She said thoughtfully, 'Dresses and lingerie, you said?'

'And perfume.'

'And cosmetics. Such an enormous growth area, Léon. Such profits.'

The waiter returned, clearing away Maia's uneaten hors d'oeuvre. Laughter crinkled the corners of Léon Cornu's handsome face.

'So you are not irretrievably wedded to Cambridge then, my dear Mrs Merchant?'

She paused, thinking. 'No. No, I'm not. But Merchants . . .' Merchants was more difficult. She had made Merchants into her own.

'It is natural that you are attached to Merchants. Merchants is your baby. But babies grow up, Maia.'

She recalled her early years. 'I fought such *battles*, Léon.'

'Of course. And now you are content to sit back . . . to rest upon your laurels . . . ?'

'Certainly not!' She glared at him angrily. 'Oh. You're teasing me.' She managed to smile.

'Just a little.' He refilled their wine-glasses. 'Think about my suggestion, won't you, madame? I'll be in touch.'

Later, leaving the restaurant, she began to see clearly the advantages of Léon Cornu's proposal. She could make a new start. A new start in a city where she would be judged not on her background, and not on the sort of class-ridden gossip that had almost destroyed her reputation, but on her talent. The realization that she could, in spite of everything, shake off the past, was intoxicating.

At Liverpool Street station Maia bought herself a copy of *The Times*, and found herself a window seat in a first class carriage. There, she opened the newspaper and saw the photograph. A bombed village in Spain, where splintered, charred buildings protruded from a desolated landscape like rows of blackened teeth in an old man's gums.

Maia's euphoria evaporated. 'Oh *Hugh*,' she whispered aloud, unable to bear that he should witness such things.

When she slept, Robin saw the faces of the men she had nursed during the day. Men who had died in her arms, men who had died screaming in agony or weeping for their mothers. Waking, sweat streaming down her face, her heart pounding, she sat in the early morning light, her knees hunched up to her chin. 'Do pack it in, Summerhayes,' muttered Juliet Hawley, in the next bed, and she knew that she had cried aloud. Sitting there, still shaking, she could find no comfort in thinking of happier times. The past was Hugh and Joe, whose destinies were now bound up in this tortured country, and Helen and Maia. She had long ago grown away from Helen, and for Maia she could feel only a bitter, betrayed loathing.

Robin had the first news of Hugh from an English Brigader brought in with a head wound. Philip Bretton was twenty-two, and had graduated from Cambridge in the summer of 1936. Both his eyes were bandaged, so it was Robin's task to feed him. When she spilt a single drop of soup onto the blanket, Sister Maxwell, despite a ward of fifty patients, roared '*Summerhayes!*', and Philip said:

'We had a chap of that name in our unit.'

Robin's hand, in the act of lifting the spoon to Philip's lips, paused.

'A decent fellow. Older than most – he was a teacher, I think.'

Robin struggled to keep calm. '*Hugh* Summerhayes?'

'Yes.' The part of Philip's face that was not bandaged was white beneath the tan. His hand crept tentatively across the blanket towards Robin. 'Do you know him?'

'Hugh's my brother.' She took his thin, tanned fingers, as much for her comfort as for his.

'He was ill. Since Albacete, really. He said it was just a cold, but it was worse than that.'

Robin said, 'You'd better eat your dinner, Philip,' and, forcing her hand not to tremble, held a spoonful of soup to his lips. Just then, she was glad that he could not see her face.

He couldn't eat much, though. After a few mouthfuls he shook his head, and turned aside. She thought that he was asleep, but then he said, 'Hugh was looking after a young chap. That was why he wouldn't go to the hospital. Didn't want to leave him. Can't remember the boy's name . . .' Philip's voice wasn't much more than a whisper.

'Eddie Fletcher?'

'That's right. Anyway, Eddie was wounded at the Jarama – shot through the shoulder. Hugh went off with him to try and find a doctor. A couple of weeks ago, I think, though I've rather lost track.'

Very gently, she stroked Philip Bretton's cheek. 'You're tired, Philip. Go to sleep. The doctor will give you something for the pain.'

At first, she almost hoped. She patched what Philip Bretton had told her together with what she learned from other sources. Hugh's unit had been part of one of the first battalions sent to the Jarama front. Most of his battalion were dead, or had been taken prisoner. She discovered that the piece of land on which Hugh had fought had a nickname: Suicide Hill.

Whenever she had ten minutes to herself, Robin searched frantically through lists of names, or badgered the Medical Aid secretary to make enquiries for her at other hospitals. Yet she discovered nothing, no trace of either Hugh or Eddie Fletcher. A bleak, black feeling crept up on her. Working, seeing each day the appalling wounds of the men who had fought at the Jarama front, horror grew in her that her gentle brother should have witnessed this. She could not eat, could not sleep. When she thought of Hugh, her stomach squeezed nauseatingly. She realized, as she worked, and as time passed and still she heard nothing, that Hugh was dead. He was not strong enough to have survived this slaughter. But it was not logic that made her so sure that she had failed to save him. She could not have explained to anyone her conviction that Hugh was dead; they would have attributed her awareness of a yawning absence in her life to superstition, or to exhaustion. In bed at night, she wept for Hugh, silencing her tears so as not to disturb the other nurses. She received a letter from Daisy, begging for news, but did not reply.

When, at last, she received official notification of Hugh's death, her grief was leavened by a fragment of relief. Hugh had not died in battle – he had died of pneumonia, a more gentle death. A few days later, walking with a friend in the garden behind the villa on her first afternoon off in more than a month, Robin saw the tightly curled blossom on the trees, and the bulbs pushing their pale green shoots through the soil. Juliet Hawley had brought a flask and a rug; they sat in the woodland beyond the terrace, and drank the awful, gritty coffee. 'Ghastly,' said Juliet, making a face. She glanced at her watch. 'We'd better dash, or Maxwell will cut us up into tiny pieces.'

They walked quickly back to the hospital. Juliet told Robin about her boyfriend, who owned a garage in Bicester. Robin only half listened. As they reached the hospital, she saw the man standing on the terrace, looking out towards them, his forearms resting on the stone balustrade. Battered beret, khaki jacket, just like all the other militiamen. But this one was different: she knew his ragged black hair, his long, dark eyes, and his tanned, muscular body. She screamed, '*Joe!*', and began to run up the steps. Turning, he held his arms out to her and caught her in them, tightly enfolding her. When, at last, he let her go, she looked desperately at his face, his hands, his arms, touching him, trying to convince herself that Joe, unlike all those other young men, was still whole. Joe was scratched and dirty and bruised, and there were great hollows around his eyes and under his cheekbones. Nothing worse. Yet she knew, looking at him, that he, too, had changed.

He had a couple of hours, he explained. Officially he hadn't leave to be here, but things were quiet at the Front today. He'd discovered that Robin was in Spain through a militiaman in his unit, who'd been treated at the hospital where she worked.

'Why did you come, Robin? Why did you come?'

She said simply, 'Because of Hugh.' Her eyes ached with unshed tears as she said her brother's name.

'*Hugh?*'

'Hugh joined the International Brigades. Maia jilted him, you see. I came to Spain to look for him, to see if I could persuade him to come home.'

'And . . . ?'

She shook her head. 'He wouldn't, Joe. I tried, but he wouldn't. He was like that, you see.' Tears spilled over her lids as she tried to smile. 'He'd do anything for anybody – he was the kindest person in the world, I think – but if he really felt strongly about something, then you couldn't budge him.'

She saw Joe's expression alter as he began to understand what she was telling him.

'Hugh is dead?'

Robin nodded. 'A few weeks ago. He died of pneumonia, they think. Some Americans in the Abraham Lincoln Battalion found him in a shepherd's hut in the mountains.' She wiped her face on the back of her sleeve. 'They buried him up there. And they gave me his things.'

A few letters, a photograph, and a scrawled scrap of paper. She had not been able to read what Hugh had written on the piece of paper. She took the photograph from her pocket, where she always kept it, and showed it to Joe. Tears still trailed from her eyes, dripping from the end of her nose onto her starched white apron. When she thought of Maia, the depth of her hatred made her catch her breath. She was not used to hating.

Curled in Joe's arms, her head on his chest, Robin saw the pale March sunlight caress the lichen-covered balustrade, and she drew Joe close to her, as though she could shelter him with her body, as though only she could keep him safe.

Chapter Seventeen

Helen was alone in Thorpe Fen church. Oblong shafts of sunlight sifted through the stained glass, and made shimmering coloured squares on the stone floor. She had arranged in the vases branches of delicate apple blossom and the creamy white curds of lilac. The perfume of the lilac almost overpowered the scent of the beeswax that she had used to polish the pews. Putting aside her tin of polish and her secateurs, Helen sat down on the pew, closed her eyes and pressed her hands together.

That morning she had received a letter from Daisy Summerhayes telling her that Hugh had died in Spain. Helen sat in silence for a few moments, trying to pray. The words would not come, though. They seemed leaden, heavy, fluttering back to earth long before they could ascend to God. Abandoning prayer, she thought instead about Hugh, relieved that she could recall him now with an equanimity and affection that was untainted by shame. Hugh had been her friend – he had loved her as a friend – and now he was dead. Fleetingly, she wondered whether she had played a part in his death. She had discouraged Maia from marrying him, and Maia had broken her engagement, and Hugh had left for Spain. Yet it seemed to Helen that there was an inevitability about his death, as though the road for Hugh had been mapped out a long time ago, and he had simply wandered from the path for a little while.

Opening her eyes, she saw the window dedicated to

the men of Thorpe Fen who had died in the Great War. The khaki-capped soldier, improbably serene, backed by angels, and the list of names carved on the stone beneath it: Dockerills and Titchmarshes and Hayhoes and Reads. A part of Hugh, Helen knew, had died a very long time ago, on a battlefield in Flanders. Spain had merely completed a destiny that he had begun many years before. Helen tried to imagine Hugh's suffering, and failed. That world – the men's world of soldiers and fighting and glorious death – was unknown to her. It excluded her, and it mocked the triviality of her own unhappiness at the same time as shutting her out. War decided the fate of nations, but permitted women only to watch from its sidelines – nursing, like Robin, or weeping, like Daisy Summerhayes. War took from women the people they most loved – their husbands, their brothers, their sons. The Great War had slaughtered a generation of young men – when Helen looked for a second time at the memorial stone, she could remember, like fleeting ghosts, those boys who had gone to war. Harry Titchmarsh and Ben Dockerill and the Read twins. Men who should now have been living in Thorpe Fen, farming their land, watching their own sons grow.

Guiltily, Helen realized that she had for a moment almost forgotten Hugh. Yet again she tried to pray for the repose of his soul. Her muttered words echoed in the great stone building, and were thrown back at her by the ancient walls. She looked around her, searching desperately for the spiritual comfort she had once found so easily. Reciting to herself the words of the Nunc Dimittis, she found no solace. Opening her hymnal at random, her gaze fell on the first verse of her father's favourite hymn. *Onward Christian soldiers, marching as to war* . . . The words reinforced her desolation. She could imagine Robin, in her own way, marching to war, or Maia, but not herself. Not fat, stupid Helen Ferguson, who'd only ever been any good at keeping house or cuddling babies.

Her eyes were open now, fixed on the jewelled cross that stood on the altar. She could feel the black unhappiness of the previous year returning, hovering just at the edge of her consciousness. Her prayers became more fervent, tinged with desperation. If God shut her out from His love, then what had she left? Standing, she walked to the altar and touched the cross, seeking reassurance. Then, realizing what she had done, she sank back, horrified at herself, glancing quickly round the church.

She was still alone. There was no-one, nothing in the church. It was only an old building full of musty books and monuments to the dead. Suddenly desperate to leave, she gathered up her belongings and walked out of the church and back to the rectory. That too was empty. Helen went upstairs to her bedroom. There she began to weep for Hugh, great heavy tears that she was unable to stem.

In the valley of the Jarama, the two armies had reached a stalemate, the Nationalists pushing back the Republican battle lines a mere ten miles. Madrid, for the time being, was safe. The sense of triumph and relief amongst the Republican lines was tempered by exhaustion and by an awareness of the terrible losses suffered. More than forty thousand men had died in three weeks of fierce fighting, including almost half the six hundred members of the British Battalion, and over a quarter of the American Abraham Lincoln Battalion.

In March, the Republican army won a victory at Guadalajara, thirty miles to the north-east of Madrid. The Garibaldi Battalion of the International Brigades, made up of Italians who had fled Mussolini's regime, helped beat off the attack of regular Italian troops fighting for the Nationalist army. Then, at the end of April, came the news of the fate of Guernica. Guernica was a small town in the Basque country, in northern Spain. On 26 April, on market-day, the German Condor Legion bombed Guernica, destroying the centre of the town, machine-gunning those citizens who tried to escape the inferno.

Although the casualties were now brought in in threes and fours instead of tens and twenties, the mobile hospital was still busy. Months of working in the hospital had changed Robin: to be efficient, tidy and organized was now natural to her. Even her bedroom in the villa adjacent to the hospital was tidy, the contents of her drawers and case folded with an unfamiliar neatness.

Most of the time, she thought about Hugh. While she fed and washed the patients, while she cleaned and tidied the ward, when she had a few blessed moments to herself, she thought about Hugh. It would have been easier, perhaps, if there had been a funeral, a body, something to mourn, instead of just emptiness and absence. Her greatest comfort was to talk to Philip Bretton, who had known Hugh in the days before his death. The surgeon had removed the bullet from Philip's head, and though he had not regained his sight, he had at least survived the operation to lie out on the verandah in the warm spring sunlight.

She had written to her parents, breaking the news. She had not been able to find the right words, her letter had seemed to her stilted and cold. She spoke to no-one about Hugh except Philip and, briefly, Neil Mackenzie. A part of her raged in disbelief and anger that she should lose him like this, that he should die alone, so far from his family, but she kept that part of her closed away, unable to share it with anyone. To speak of him would be to unleash her grief. She would not permit herself that luxury, there was so much work to do.

Helen was washing dishes in the kitchen when she heard the knock on the scullery door. Drying her hands quickly on her apron, she peered through the window.

'Adam!'

Adam Hayhoe's large frame filled the rickety

504

doorway. When Helen beckoned him into the house, he had to bend his head to avoid the scullery's low roof.

'I told you it wouldn't be so long this time. I picked these for you, Helen.'

'They're lovely, Adam.' She buried her nose in the posy of violets, breathing in their scent. 'Sit down, I'll make some tea. No – not here—' she glanced at the scuffed, cluttered kitchen table '—come through to the drawing-room.'

Helen took the best china from the dresser – delicate little translucent cups, rimmed with gold – and covered the tray with a lace mat. In the drawing-room, she poured tea and offered cakes while Adam told her about the months that had passed since he had last returned to Thorpe Fen. He made her laugh, telling her about the funny little shops he made things for, and his rich, eccentric customers. When he described the places he had seen, the cities and the country towns, Helen pictured them in her mind, feeling for the first time in years a resurgence of her old longing to travel.

After a while Adam said, 'And you, Helen?'

'Me?' She couldn't remember a single thing that had happened since he had last come back to Thorpe Fen. The weeks seemed muddled and blank. 'I haven't done anything.' Helen looked down at herself, noticing her stained apron, her laddered stocking. 'I look so awful . . .'

'No you don't.' Crossing the room, Adam took her hand, raising her from her seat. 'You look beautiful.'

She felt his lips touch first the crown of her head, then her forehead. She stood still, a part of her waiting for him to do what Maurice Page had done: to demand, to hurt, to humiliate. But instead he drew her to him, cradling her head against his chest, stroking her hair, asking no more of her than she wanted to give. 'Dear Helen,' he said softly, and she gave a small gasp of delight, and closed her eyes. She could feel his warm skin through the thin fabric of his shirt, and the strength of his arms as they encircled her. She marvelled that a man

505

who was so big, so strong, could be so gentle. She could remember herself as a child, watching him work, seeing his square, muscular hands coax delicate shapes from a block of wood.

'Adam,' she said, enjoying just saying his name. She touched his familiar, beloved face with her hand. She could not believe that she had ever thought him plain.

'My love—'

She caught the whispered endearment, and saw the delight in his eyes that mirrored her own. And then she heard the footsteps in the corridor. Before she could pull away from Adam, the door opened.

Julius Ferguson paused on the threshold, his hand still clutching the door-handle, staring, his eyes distended, at Adam Hayhoe. 'How dare you, sir!' Drunk with rage, his words slurred. 'How dare you touch my daughter!'

Helen's entire body stiffened, but Adam did not immediately relinquish her. As Julius Ferguson stepped forward, Helen, for one long, awful moment, thought that her father might physically force them apart. Pulling away from Adam, she moved towards her father, as Adam's hands slipped from her shoulders to hang empty at his sides.

She said quickly, 'Daddy—'

'Be quiet, Helen! And you, you lout – get out of my house!'

Adam had drawn back only a little way. Though his face had paled, his voice was level. 'I mean Helen no harm, Mr Ferguson. No harm at all.'

A rope of swollen veins pulsed in Julius Ferguson's forehead. 'And how dare you speak of my daughter in such a familiar way!'

'Daddy – please—' Helen's voice was a cry of pain. But her father pushed her aside as though he hardly saw her, placing himself between her and Adam.

'Get out of my house, or I shall send for the police.'

'There's no need for that, sir,' said Adam firmly. 'And no call to be rough with Helen, neither.'

'You have the temerity to tell *me* how to treat my own daughter—'

Julius Ferguson took another pace towards Adam. Helen cried out, 'No, Adam!', and seized her father's arm, trying to force him to listen to her.

The expression in his eyes when he turned to look at her chilled and silenced her. She recognized his cold disregard of the pain he caused her, overlaid by a complacent awareness of his own power.

'Go to your room, Helen.'

'You don't have to go, Helen.' Adam's voice was gentle, and his gaze sought hers. 'Nothing improper has happened between Helen and me, Mr Ferguson,' he added proudly. 'I would never hurt Helen. She knows that.'

'I said, go to your room, Helen!' Julius Ferguson's voice, now harsh and fractured, stabbed at her, forcing her into her old habits of obedience. 'I shall speak to you later.'

Helen ran out of the room then, and stood shaking, her knuckles pressed against her front teeth, in the corridor outside the closed drawing-room door.

'If anyone is to be punished, it should be me.' Adam's voice had faded as Helen had closed the door behind her, but she could still make out his words. 'But I tell you again, rector, I mean no harm to Helen. My intentions towards her are—'

Her father's voice next, interrupting Adam, his words still thick with anger. 'Your *intentions*! You can have no intentions towards my daughter, sir! Helen is a child! A child whom I must protect from men like you!'

'Helen is a grown woman, Mr Ferguson.'

'You forget yourself, Hayhoe. And you forget your station in life.'

'My station in life does not shame me, sir. Wasn't Our Lord also a carpenter?'

Helen, still standing in the corridor, heard the hiss of her father's indrawn breath. His next words were like hammer-blows, battering down the coffin-nails of her isolation.

'You are impertinent, Hayhoe! How dare you speak to me like that in my own house! How dare you even think that someone like you might be worthy of my daughter! You will never come to this house again. You will not write to my daughter, nor try to speak to her. Do you understand?'

Helen did not wait to hear Adam's reply. She knew, as she ran from the closed door, that it would be just the same, that Adam would leave her, as all the others had left her. Her sobs echoed in the vast, empty house. She stumbled upstairs to her bedroom, her face washed with tears, knowing that she had lost him. Wedging a chair against the door so that her father could not come into her room, she collapsed onto the bed, rocking herself, and heard the crunch of Adam's boots on the gravel as he left the house. She knew that he would not come back. She, after all, had pushed him away; she had failed to defend him against her father's anger.

Helen wondered whether, if you lived as solitary a life as she did, you eventually began to fade away, becoming at last only half a person. Whether, in order to exist, you needed to be seen by other people, to be spoken to by other people, like a mirror reflecting rays of light. Whether without that necessary reflection you would become like a will o'the wisp, half-seen, wandering at twilight on the edges of the marsh.

Adam called on the Randalls the next day. Recently his hard work had begun to see a result. Half a dozen furniture shops scattered around England now regularly commissioned pieces from him: tables and chairs and beds and chests of drawers, beautifully constructed of fine, close-grained wood. As he gained confidence he had begun to add his own individual touches – a curling chair-arm, a trim of fine trellis-work across the top of a dresser, or a painted panel. Travelling, he had seen how the world beyond Thorpe Fen had changed since last he had gone out into it, and had realized that in this different world a carpenter need not hide the fact that he loved the rector's daughter.

Adam had opened a savings account in a bank, to put by the money he earned. He needed his workshop, and a few rooms attached, before he could ask Helen Ferguson to marry him. He wanted to take her away from Thorpe Fen here, now, but he knew that he must wait. He could not expect a sensitive, well-brought-up girl like Helen to share the peripatetic life he led. Adam thought of the succession of dreary boarding houses and cheap hotels in which he passed his nights. Occasionally, he still slept behind hedges, if he found himself stranded in the countryside overnight. He did not mind that, he was always content in the open air, but he would not inflict that sort of existence on Helen. The need to find a permanent place in which to live and work had become urgent.

The scene with the rector the previous day had shaken him badly, but had not altered his intention to make Helen his wife. He remembered his reply to the accusation that Julius Ferguson had flung at him. 'I don't reckon I am worthy of Helen, sir. That's why I left Thorpe Fen. But I'll work day and night – week in, week out – to make myself worthy.' A resolve that had only doubled in the twenty-four hours that had passed since he had left the Fergusons'. He had walked out of the rectory by the front door, not the tradesmen's entrance. A deliberate choice, and he had sensed that had not Julius Ferguson been twenty years his senior, then, man of God or not, he would have resorted to physical violence.

After dinner, when Samuel snored in his armchair, Susan Randall took Adam into the kitchen. She washed, he dried.

'We're leaving the village, you know, Adam. As soon as we can sell the farm.'

Adam nodded. 'I had a word with Sam. He said times had been hard.' He thought, looking at Susan's gaunt, tired face, that the move could not come soon enough.

'It's a wrench, see – I've lived here all my life – but we just can't make it pay any more. And I haven't been too good – doctor said the air's bad for me. Sam's sister's husband died last Christmas, and left her with a hundred acres up Lincoln way. Good land. It'll make sense for us to move up there and help out.'

He said reassuringly, 'I'm sure it's the best thing, Sue.'

'Only—' she rinsed a glass '—I'm worried about Helen.'

He took the glass from her. 'Helen?'

'She's so fond of little Michael. Don't break that glass, Adam Hayhoe – it's one of my best set.'

'Sorry.' Carefully, he dried the glass, and placed it on the table. He had always guessed Julius Ferguson to be a cold, possessive father, but yesterday he had sensed something much more insidious. A cloying web of self-serving and distorted love trapped Helen; a patient man, Adam was nevertheless seized by an urgent longing to free her.

He knew that he must wait a little longer, though. He said uneasily, 'Have you told her you're going?'

Susan Randall nodded. 'A fortnight past. But I don't think she believed me.' Her faded, pretty face creased in a frown. 'I can't get through to her sometimes. It's as if she only listens to what she wants to hear.'

'If she's as fond of Michael as you say she is, then it's only reasonable that it'll take her a while to get used to the idea of parting from him. She'll come round, I'm sure.'

He dried the rest of the crockery in silence. When Susan, spreading the wet cloths on the stove, filled the kettle to make a cup of tea, Adam said suddenly, 'Write to me, won't you, Sue, if you're worried about Helen? I move around a bit, but I'll leave you some addresses.'

* * *

After the quarrel between her father and Adam Hayhoe, Helen had expected her father to show his disapproval of her by withdrawing his affection. She could remember many instances in her childhood when, after some minor transgression, her father had treated her with coldness, rebuffing all her fumbling attempts at apology.

Instead, he was affectionate and attentive. He took her to Cambridge to buy dress material, and even attended a film with her in Ely. Choosing material in Merchants, Helen felt hot, confused and distracted. She could not remember which colours were her favourites. The green, surely – but when she held up the apple-green cotton to the mirror she saw how sallow and ill it made her look. Her father suggested the white. *White always suits a young girl best.* Helen bought a length of white dimity, and some muslin to line it. Cutting it out, tacking the pieces together, she felt troubled, but could not work out why.

When she had finished the dress, she tried it on and showed it to her father. He was in his study, working on his sermon.

'You look very pretty, my dear, very pretty.' She could see the approval in his eyes. 'I shall dress for dinner tonight. One should not let the old customs be neglected.'

That evening, Julius Ferguson opened a bottle of sherry, and lit the candelabra in the dining-room. Pouring Helen a glass, he said, 'I don't approve of alcohol for young girls, of course, but you have not had many treats lately, have you, Chickie?'

It was hot; the French doors were open, and moths gathered around the candles. Helen, sipping her sweet sherry, watched them singe their wingtips on the candleflames.

They dined on stewed pork followed by treacle pudding. Ivy cooked the same weekly menu, regardless of the season. Julius Ferguson told Helen little anecdotes about his early life with his parents in India. 'Such a strange country. I intended to return there, to do missionary work, but after dear Florence's death . . . The climate in India is so unhealthy for children. I was sent to board in England at the age of six.'

Helen said curiously, 'Did you mind, Daddy?'

'Mind? What a strange question. I really can't remember.'

She gave up listening, and let her gaze focus on the faded wallpaper and on the shadowy aureoles cast by the oil lamps on the wall. At intervals she smiled and nodded her head. She thought that she was like a wooden puppet, someone invisible pulling her strings.

After dinner, they walked in the garden. The heat persisted into the twilight. The lilies were in flower, their gaping white throats peppered with dusty pollen. Helen could smell their heavy, sweet scent. 'Florence's favourite flower,' said Julius Ferguson, and snapped off a bloom. Sap oozed from the broken stem. 'For you, my dear.' Helen tucked it into her hair.

He asked her to play the piano to him. She played 'Just a Song at Twilight' and 'Sweet and Low'. Then he opened the yellowed, faded copy of 'When you were Sweet Sixteen', and placed it on the music stand. 'Florence's favourite,' he said again. When Helen looked up at the framed photograph of her mother on top of the piano, she saw that Florence, like herself, was wearing a white dress and had a white flower tucked behind her ear. Not a puppet, not a will o'the wisp, thought Helen. She had become a ghost.

In May, given leave from the Front at last, Joe hitched a ride in a lorry to within half a mile of the hospital in which Robin worked. In the afternoon, when Robin's shift had finished, they walked in the gardens of the villa. Carp dozed in the circular pool, and fountains, silent and lichen covered, cast shadows on the still green water. The dusty rose garden was overlooked by crumbling statues of plump cherubs. They picnicked on bread and ham and olives, and took photographs with Joe's camera.

'Almost like old times,' Joe said happily. 'A bottle of wine ...'

'Some decent food.'

'We need music.'

'One of the nurses has a gramophone.' Robin ran back to the house, returning ten minutes later with an old wind-up gramophone.

They played 'Anything Goes' over and over again, dancing through the narrow grass paths that wound around the parterres. For a short time Robin was aware of nothing but the sun and the scent of the roses, and the warmth of Joe's arms around her. When at last the gramophone began to run out and the song slowed and the soprano turned into a bass, they collapsed to the ground, laughing.

She lay propped on her elbow beside him, looking down at him. 'Oh Joe,' she said softly, and gently brushed a lock of black hair back from his forehead.

'What?' His eyes were crinkled up because of the sun.

She smiled. 'I love you. That's all.'

He pulled her down to him, his mouth finding hers. After a while, he said:

'Just before I left England, I saw you and Francis together.'

Her eyes widened. 'You didn't say.'

'I know. Stupid, wasn't it?' His words were flippant, but she recognized pain in his eyes. 'I thought—'

She put her hand over his mouth, silencing him. 'It doesn't matter, Joe.'

Gently, he lifted away her hand. 'It does. I was a fool. I thought that you were still in love with Francis. I thought – oh, that you had to be *certain* of love. But you can't be, can you? It's not like that. It's a gamble, and if you overplay your hand . . . well, at least you've had the guts to try.'

She said, 'I'm not a gamble, my love. I'm a safe bet,' and then she bent her head and kissed him again. Then she lay, her eyes half-closed, her head on his chest, as the sun blurred, shooting rainbow rays across the sky. She knew from the sound of his breathing that Joe was asleep. When she looked up at him, she saw how thin he was: the hollows at his neck and shoulders, and the way the bones seemed to push through the skin of his elbows. It caught at her, making tears sting her eyes. The record still revolved on the turntable, but only very slowly, the words hardly audible. Then the needle lost its track and skated across the surface of the disc, and there was silence.

Later that evening they walked through the garden, to the glade of cork-oaks and junipers that lay to the back of the villa. A river ran through the wood. Standing beside it, in the close green privacy of the woodland, she laid her palms to either side of Joe's face, and began to kiss him. At first he put his arms around her, holding her to him, but then she felt him draw back.

'No.'

'Joe . . .' She stroked his hair.

'I'm crawling with lice. Tried to get rid of the bastards yesterday, but I don't seem to have succeeded.'

She said, 'I'm very good at getting rid of lice,' and began to unbutton his shirt. 'I've had a great deal of practice.' She eased his shirt from his back, dropping it on the sandy bank of the river. Then she unbuckled his belt. She heard him groan, and then she gave him a small shove, so that he fell backwards into the river.

As he shook the water droplets from his head, she dived into the river, cleanly cutting the cold water, and then she swam towards him and he took her in his arms. They sank beneath the surface of the water, and saw only the dim green light of the sun before they emerged a few seconds later, breathless with delight.

In the Randalls' parlour, Helen watched Michael open the parcel she had just given him. His small fat hands ripped the tissue paper, and he laughed when he found the ball nestling in the blue cloth. Running out into the garden, he began to roll the ball along the path.

Susan Randall picked up the sailor suit he had let fall

to the floor. 'It's lovely, Helen. You are so clever. Such beautiful embroidery.' Folding it carefully, she replaced the suit in the tissue paper. Then she said hesitantly, 'Helen. I was glad that you came today.'

Through the open door, Helen watched the little boy playing in the garden. Mrs Randall sat down beside her, and laid her thin, bony hand on Helen's.

'Do you remember that I told you that we were trying to sell the farm? Well, we've found a buyer at last. An artist, of all things. He says he's going to set up weaving shops and potteries in the outhouses. I can't imagine our old pigshed being used for making pots, can you?'

Helen smiled briefly. Michael was weaving between the herb-beds, the new ball clutched in his hand. The late afternoon sun cast long purple shadows on the garden path.

'So we're flitting tomorrow, see, Helen. No point waiting around. The furniture's being sold with the house, and Sam's already packing up the van.'

She saw that she had Helen's attention at last. Helen turned to her.

'You're going to live with your sister-in-law?'

'That's right. Near Lincoln.'

The look of excitement and anticipation in Helen's eyes surprised Mrs Randall.

'And Michael?'

'Michael?' Slightly confused, Susan Randall glanced outside to where her younger son was pulling up nasturtiums and nibbling the petals. 'Michael will settle in easy enough. It'll be a good house for him – nice big garden, and no nasty narrow stairs like this place. I'm more worried about Lizzie. She'll hate to change schools.'

Helen was staring at her. She said, 'You're taking Michael with you? To Lincoln?'

'Of course.' As Mrs Randall looked at Helen, some of the unease with which she had approached the conversation began to return.

'I thought . . .' Helen rose from her seat, and went to the doorway, looking out into the garden. 'I thought there might not be room for two families in your sister-in-law's house . . . and you haven't been well . . .'

'Sarah and Bill never had children. Sarah'll love to have the little ones around. And it'll do me the world of good to have someone to share the work with. I'll be back on my feet in no time.'

Helen's face was very pale; she was twisting a lock of hair around her finger. Susan Randall went to her side and hugged her.

'You'll come and stay with us, won't you, dear? Lincoln's not far away. And Michael will love to see you.'

That evening, Helen made a bonfire. A straggling thing of old leaves and twigs and scraps of wood, it burned easily in the midsummer heat. Blue smoke plumed up into the sky as she fed it.

Her mother's mementoes and journal. Her own dolls and teddy-bear. The poems that she had written years ago, when she was a girl, that she had spoken about to Geoffrey Lemon. Geoffrey was married with two children now. The letters that Robin and Maia had written to her. Robin was in Spain, and Helen had hidden in her attic room the last time Maia had called. It had been a Black Day, and she had known, glancing in her mirror, that Maia would guess there was something wrong with her.

The white dress that she had worn for her first confirmation. A snapshot of little Thomas Sewell. Dropping it into the flames, she watched the child's face curl and crumple in the heat. Hugh's scarf, that he had once left hanging on a hook in the rectory hallway, and she had guiltily taken and treasured. Someone had told her that Hugh was dead, but she could not remember who. These days, things muddled up in her mind. All her water-colours and stories and sketches. Dropping the paper onto the bonfire, Helen saw the flames suddenly seize them, and watched the grey, lacy ashes float up through the trees.

The bunch of wild violets that Adam Hayhoe had once given her, that she had pressed under her Bible. The flowers were brown and brittle, and they crumbled as she fed them to the flames. Her father had sent Adam away, just as he had sent all the others away. Then she threw onto the fire the contents of her bottom drawer. The tablecloths, the pillowslips, the hand towels and lavender bags. All the things that she had collected since she was a young girl, for her first home. She knew now that she would never marry, that she would never have a home or a child of her own. The scalloped embroidery singed, the dried lavender blackened and spat. It was almost dark. Helen stood by the bonfire for a long time watching the orange sparks, all that remained of her hopes, drifting upwards through the hot, oppressive air.

She did not sleep at all that night, but knelt at her window, looking out to the moonlit garden and the village and the fields beyond. The pinks and the phlox were grey and crepuscular, and when the dawn came and long strands of golden light painted the Fens, she saw how empty it all was, and how lonely. Early in the morning, she rose and dressed and went down to the kitchen. She was behind with her parish work; Helen took out the great box of letters and stationery, and began to write. When she read her letters through they did not seem to make a great deal of sense, but she stamped and addressed the envelopes nevertheless. Percy sat on her lap for a while, purring, and then scratched at the door, asking to be let out. When Ivy arrived at half past six, moaning about her feet and crouching in front of the stove, match and kindling in hand, Helen began to help her make breakfast. Porridge and bacon and eggs and tea and toast. She drank a cup of tea, and tore a slice of toast into tiny pieces. Filling the sink with water for washing-up, she looked down and saw her reflection. Drops of water trailed from her wet hand and fell into the glassy surface, and her image fractured into a thousand shifting fragments.

It was market-day in Ely. Sitting down at the table,

Helen tried to make a list. She asked her father for some housekeeping money and, standing in front of the mirror, carefully placed her hat on top of her uncombed hair. She knew that something was happening to her, something dreadful and uncontrollable, a shattering of the spirit akin to the shattering of her reflection when the drops of water had fallen into the sink. But she did not know what to do about it. She did not know how to glue the pieces back together.

On the bus, travelling from Thorpe Fen to Ely, she sang to herself. Old hymns, mostly, and the madrigals that she had sung with the Summerhayeses. She noticed that some of the other passengers were staring at her, so she smiled at them brightly, but they looked away. The bus rattled along the narrow, dusty droves. Fields and streams and bog were to either side of the drove, as far as the eye could see. The emptiness, the openness of it all made the breath catch in Helen's throat and her ribcage tighten.

In Ely, she wandered around for a while, basket in hand. She had left her list on the kitchen table, and she could not remember what she was supposed to buy. It was very hot, and she felt, after her sleepless night, terribly tired. She thought that the cathedral might be cooler, so she went inside and sat down on one of the pews. But the high roof, the great, daunting windows sparkling with coloured glass, cut her off from the God she had once thought she had known. Everything seemed so vast, so dark. The choirboys were rehearsing, and the thin, high voices pierced through her, making her head ache. A man in a cassock was conducting them. Helen sat back in the pew, her half-closed eyes blurred. For a moment she thought that she was watching her father. Another man, walking down the aisle, looked at her and tutted, and she realized that she had left her hat on the bus, and that she had forgotten to put on her stockings. The cathedral echoed with men's voices, disapproving, ordering, demanding. Unsteadily, Helen walked back out into the sunlight.

She found herself in a small, unfamiliar alleyway lined with little terraced houses. Washing was drying in the sun, and a baby howled in a pram parked on the pavement. Helen walked up to the pram and peered in. The baby was very tiny, red-faced, its mouth an angry red O. Helen looked around for its mother, but could see no-one. When she picked up the baby from his pram, she could feel that his nappy was damp, and see the dried milk stains on his ragged blue gown. Holding him against her shoulder, she patted his back, and his crying lessened. She closed her eyes, delighting in the warm softness of his little body. Just like Thomas, just like Michael. There was no canopy on the pram, and she thought that some of his redness and distress was due to the sun. The pram was old and battered, the single sheet torn and discoloured. Soon Helen felt only the small, hiccupping movement of the baby's body as he drifted off to sleep.

'Michael,' she whispered, and kissed him, very gently, on the top of his downy head. Then she began to walk back down the alleyway, the baby still cradled against her breast.

Chapter Eighteen

Of the comrades Joe had fought with at the Jarama, only David Talbot remained. He had seen his friends shot, shelled and blown to pieces, yet had himself suffered only a few scratches and burns. With each passing day, he sensed that his luck must run out.

Not that he had come through his nine months in Spain unscathed. He knew that something was breaking inside him, a result of all that he had seen, all that he had endured. He could recognize in himself the physical symptoms of exhaustion – loss of weight and appetite, the awful, griping stomach pains – but there was more to it than that. He had lost hope. Since May, when the Republican factions had fallen out amongst themselves and had fought each other in Barcelona, all Joe's fears for Spain had crystallized, becoming a certainty. He knew, with bitter conviction, that the Republic could not win. Even the aid that the Soviet Union had given was compromised by Stalin's fear that the democracies would show their disapproval by allying with the dictatorships against Soviet Russia. The great democracies feared Communism, apparently, more than they feared Fascism. Disorganized and divided, its pleas for help ignored, Spain would fall to Fascism. A last bulwark would crumble, permitting the inrush of a darker future.

All Joe cared about now was to survive. His idealism, his illusions had been shot to pieces, and lay buried in the stony Spanish soil with the comrades that he had lost. All he strove for was not to lose his limbs, nor his sight, nor his balls. To get through each day, watching his back, not attempting any heroics, doing what was required of him, no more. Joe maintained the Maxim guns with fanatical zeal, obsessed by the fear that they would break down when they were most needed. When he had tobacco, he smoked constantly, his nails bitten to the quick. He shored up the trenches and did his turn on patrol and could feel, sometimes, the sting of the bullet that waited for him.

Adam signed the rental agreement at midday, and then spent the remainder of the day cleaning out his new workshop. It was on the outskirts of Richmond, not far from the river, a practical distance from the smart shops in the centre of London. The rooms above the workshop were small and attractive, and there was a scrap of garden behind the house. He had worked day and night in order to scrape up the deposit for the house, driven by the recollection of Helen's tortured face, driven also by a fear for her that he was unable precisely to define. Adam reckoned that if he worked flat out it would take him a couple of days to make the house habitable. Then he would go home to Thorpe Fen and persuade Helen Ferguson to marry him. The letter that he had sent to her a week ago told her about the house and about his plans for their future. He had received no reply yet – he had, in fact, received no replies to any of the letters he had written to her. Disturbed, he guessed that the old rector was intercepting his notes.

Adam worked until late in the evening, and then he went back to his lodgings. There was a letter waiting for him on the sideboard; he did not recognize the handwriting on the envelope. He read the single sheet of paper as he ate his dinner. By the time he had finished reading, he knew that he must not delay, that he must return to Thorpe Fen the very next day.

* * *

The summer sales, Maia thought, were like a battle-ground. At the end of the day, she and Liam collapsed exhausted in her office. Maia took a bottle of Scotch and a couple of glasses from the cabinet; Liam, sitting in an armchair, his feet resting on the edge of her desk, read the sports fixtures in the local paper.

Maia poured out the whisky. 'I thought those two ladies were going to fight over the china.'

Liam flicked open his cigarette case, and offered it to her. 'A duel to the death. Handbags at dawn.'

Maia giggled, and leant forward so that Liam could light her cigarette. She read the headline in the news-paper: *Kidnapped baby still missing*. The baby had been taken from Ely, of all places. Nothing happened in Ely.

She passed Liam a glass. 'Just a little one. I know you won't want to be late home. How is Roisin?'

Liam glowed with fatherly pride. 'She is the darlingest girl. Takes after her mother, thank God, though she's blue-eyed.' He smiled at Maia. 'You must come and see her. On Sunday, perhaps?'

'I'd be delighted to, Liam. I really would.' She shuf-fled papers on her desk. Then she said, 'Liam. There's something I'd like to discuss with you.'

At home, Maia worked through the evening, the wire-less murmuring in the background as she checked Merchants' takings against those of previous summer sales. Because of the heat she had had a table set up on the terrace, where she could look out to the garden as she worked and see the slow fading with the twi-light. Once, she put aside her reading glasses and thought of Hugh, who had proposed to her out here. *There'll be plenty more summers*, Hugh had said, but for Hugh there would be no more. Hugh had died in Spain, and sometimes, late at night, after she had a drink or two, Maia sensed his presence and thought that if only she looked back quickly enough, she would glimpse him. Yet Hugh's ghost, unlike Vernon's, was a benevolent one. He haunted her kindly, affectionately, and she knew that when in time he left her she would miss him.

The telephone rang at half past nine the following morning. Maia, standing in the hallway, drummed her fingers impatiently on the table as the receiver whirred and clicked. Someone was trying to call her from a public telephone box.

'Mrs Merchant? Am I speaking to Mrs Merchant?'

She didn't recognize the voice. She said, 'This is Maia Merchant. Who is calling, please?'

'Julius Ferguson.'

There was a long pause, accompanied by more clattering as the caller pushed various buttons.

'Helen's father?'

'Yes, Mrs Merchant.' He sounded irritable, ill at ease with the unfamiliar telephone.

Maia's impatience turned suddenly to concern. 'Is Helen unwell?'

'No. Yes. I really don't know. Is she with you, madam? Is she in Cambridge?'

Maia frowned, bewildered. 'Helen? Here? Of course not—'

'Only she has not been home for two days. I thought perhaps . . .' His voice trailed off, and the awkward silence lengthened. 'I cannot think where she could have gone.'

Maia said, 'She is with the Summerhayeses, perhaps. She's very fond of Richard and Daisy.'

'I bicycled to Blackmere Farm yesterday evening, Mrs Merchant. Mrs Summerhayes has not seen her.' For the first time Maia could detect anxiety, not displeasure, in the dim, crackling words.

She said, 'Mr Ferguson—', but the line whirred and rattled and fell suddenly silent. 'Mr Ferguson,' repeated Maia loudly, into the mouthpiece, but there was no reply.

She stood still for a moment, trying to think what to do. Then she sent her maid for her silk scarf and sunglasses, and ran out to her car. She drove very fast out of Cambridge and through the Fens, noticing, as she drove, the terrible isolation of the place, the narrow, dusty roads, the marshes with their whining haze of mosquitoes, and the lolling, cracked little cottages. In the heat, the sky seemed to have lowered, threatening to crush the earth.

As she headed into the village, the wheels of her car skirling up clouds of dust, she saw the man walking out of the rectory garden, closing the gate behind him. She recognized Adam Hayhoe from countless village fêtes. Maia rammed her foot on the brake, the car screeched to a halt, and she leaned out of the window.

'Mr Hayhoe?'

He nodded, touching his cap.

'Is Helen . . . ?' she began, and felt a rush of worry and disappointment when she saw that his eyes only reflected her own concern.

'Helen's not at home, Mrs Merchant. No-one's seen her since Tuesday morning.' Adam's voice was grim.

'Dear God.' Maia opened the door and climbed out of the car. 'Her father telephoned me earlier.'

'Two days!' Adam's eyes were dark with anger. 'He waited two days before he did anything! Because he was afraid of what people might think . . .'

She stared at him, racking her brain to think where Helen might have gone. 'The doctor, perhaps . . . Helen's friendly with his family . . .'

Adam shook his head. 'I've tried him, Mrs Merchant. Drove over this morning in the grocer's van. The Lemons haven't seen her.' He ran a hand through his greying dark hair. 'And I went and had a word with the police. They said they'd look into it, but of course they're all running around after that missing baby. Seemed to think Helen'd likely gone off with some young man or other.'

Maia whispered, 'She didn't seem well, recently. She has been so unhappy. I am afraid . . .'

Adam's eyes were bleak. 'I'll find her if I have to search every dike, every ditch myself.'

Maia shivered. Then, trying to think rationally, she

524

said, 'I don't think Helen would just run away, you see, Mr Hayhoe. She was afraid of the countryside. She preferred to be indoors.' And a memory of the little room in the attic came into her mind. The bookcases filled with romantic novels, the oil stove, the cradle.

Adam Hayhoe took an envelope from his pocket. 'I got this yesterday,' he explained. 'That's why I came home. It's from Susan Randall.'

'The mother of the little boy that Helen was fond of?'

'They've left the village, Mrs Merchant. Susan thought Helen took it bad.'

Maia stared at him. Something was coming together in her mind, parts of a jigsaw that she could not quite resolve. Then the pieces slotted, and she was seized by a horrible certainty. The newspaper headline, the attic, the cradle. 'Oh God,' said Maia suddenly. 'Oh God.'

She began to run to the rectory, throwing open the gate, trampling the flowers that had wilted with the heat. She knew that Adam was behind her, she could hear his boots on the gravel. Seizing the door-knocker, she beat it loudly against the wood until the maid opened the door. Then, without explanation, she ran inside and up the stairs and along the corridors.

She had only been here once before, but she remembered the way. Maia ran up the attic stairs and moved aside the trapdoor and emerged, head and shoulders first, in darkness. Her high-heeled sandles jammed in the rafters as she stumbled blindly through the tangle of boxes and old furniture and ancient, mothballed clothes.

Then she pushed open the door to the little room at the end of the attic. The light hurt her eyes. She heard Helen say, 'Maia. How nice,' as she looked down and saw the baby sleeping in the cradle.

On the night before his unit marched to Brunete, Joe wrote to Robin. Then he took the ring he had bought in England from the bottom of his rucksack, wrapped it up in a scrap of cloth and placed it in the envelope along with his note. He had written:

*I meant to give you this in England, but somehow
the time never seemed to be right. Such a foolish
reason, and now I can feel the sand running
through my fingers. We seem to have had so little
time, don't we? When I think of the years that I
have known you, it reminds me of one of those
awful dances where you keep on having to change
partner. I wish it would stop. I would like to be
still. I am afraid, Robin. I have diarrhoea and lice
and trench-foot and all the least romantic ailments
you can think of. The fear is the worst thing,
though. But I'll feel better if I know that you have
this. The ring is a token, just a small token of what
I feel for you. I love you so much, Robin. Whatever
happens, you must always remember that.*

That night, he ducked behind the lines, searching for
a First Aid post, hoping to give the letter to someone who
knew Robin. They marched the next morning to the
triangle of villages – Brunete, Villaneuva del Pardillo,
and Villaneuva de la Cañada – that commanded the road
to Madrid. The Republican government planned to try
to push back the Nationalist army from Madrid so that
the fascists would no longer be able to bombard the city
with their artillery. It was the first major Republican
offensive of the war, and it returned the British Battalion
to the slaughter and chaos of the battle of Jarama.

When he had the time and the capacity to think, Joe
knew that what he witnessed at Brunete confirmed
his worst fears. The Republican army was
outnumbered and, worse, outarmed. German planes –
Messerschmitts – flew low overhead, mocking the
republicans' attempts to shoot them down with rifle fire.
Lines of command broke down, leaving the units lead-
erless and confused. The chaos seemed to Joe to be a
vision of hell, a hideous labyrinth in which there were
no rules, and death was a random, meaningless visitor.
When, in the confusion of intense fighting, Joe realized

that the Republican army was shelling its own troops, he raised his fist to the heavens, his fury a parody of the anti-Fascist salute.

The stench of death was exacerbated by the terrible heat; the long, dangerous nights were made worse by an intense dry cold. In the small islands of tranquillity between furious onslaughts of fighting, it occurred to Joe that he was ill. Whatever he ate he inevitably threw up a half hour later. He had hollows between his ribs, and the constant griping stomach pains had become a greater preoccupation than his fear of death. He wondered whether he had dysentery and knew that he should get to a hospital, but it seemed wrong, somehow, to leave the guns and his comrades. Besides, he had lost the ability to take independent action; he survived from moment to moment, carrying out orders, manning the gun, the noise and the terrible things he saw filling his head, erasing all capacity for thought. He had become an automaton, an inefficient machine that knew only about killing. The things that he had once held dear – his photography, his love of the countryside and music – seemed to belong to another person's life. Time itself had become distorted, so that an hour crouched in a trench became an aeon, so that the ten days of battle telescoped together and became one single long, nightmarish day.

The initial surprise of the first offensive could not be maintained. Republican advantage turned, as always, into gritty, stubborn defence, then into the sort of desperate heroism that staved off retreat but did not bring victory. The end, when it came for Joe, was a muddle. Nationalist aeroplanes were flying overhead, their undercarriages almost touching the tree-tops, taking pot-shots at Republican soldiers. Joe's guts had been particularly bad that day, and his head pounded in rhythm with the guns. David Talbot, firing the Maxim as Joe fed it shells, looked at him.

'If you're going to throw up, then for God's sake don't do it here. Frank Murray can take over for a while.'

Joe scrambled out of the trench, and began to worm

his way over the ridge, rifle in hand. He could hear the low rumbling of an aeroplane, but he did not care, all he wanted was to be sick in peace.

The force of the bomb, dropped only fifty yards behind him, shook the earth. His entire body reverberated with the impact. When he rose unsteadily to his feet, his vision had blackened. It cleared only slowly until, looking back, he saw the crater where the Maxim machine gun had been. He began to walk in no particular direction. His right shoulder, and the whole of the right side of his body was sticky with a warm wetness. Looking down at his right hand, he watched with fascination the blood that trailed from his fingertips.

He walked on a little further, stumbling in the tussocky grass. And then, overhead, he glimpsed the bright orange arc of the trench-mortar as it split into a thousand deadly fragments around him. As he sank to his knees something struck the side of his head, a terrible, intolerable pain, so that when the blackness came, in his last instant of consciousness he welcomed it.

The bell rang every morning at a quarter past six. Then chapel, then breakfast, then bedmaking. At a quarter to eight the working day began. Helen worked in the laundry. It was a big, dark building, with long tables and benches. The tables and benches had to be scrubbed daily, the floor cleaned until the stone flags were white. The laundry smelt of hot soapy water and washing-soda, and the walls ran with condensation.

The women weren't allowed to talk in the laundry. Helen didn't mind that, and though her hands and arms were red and raw from the hot water, she didn't mind the work either. Although she wasn't as quick as some of the girls, she was conscientious and painstaking. The silence and the monotony of the work suited her jangling, troubled mind. Though some things upset her – the baskets full of baby clothes that they had to wash for the orphanage, the dog-collared chaplain who lectured the women on their sins every morning – she managed, on the whole, to keep at bay her Black Days.

Some of the other women mimicked her for the way that she spoke. One called her 'Duchess', laughing at the way she crooked her little finger while drinking her mug of tea. The nickname stuck. A red-haired woman spat at her in the corridor, and once, in the laundry, she felt sharp fingers pinching the flesh of her arm and twisting it until the tears ran down her face. 'That's for stealing that poor woman's baby,' a voice whispered. 'Bitch. They'll send you to the nuthouse.' Slowly, Helen began to realize that she had done something very dreadful. She couldn't remember much of it because great patches of time were missing. She could remember walking home from the Randalls', and she could remember the bus ride into Ely. She could remember the cathedral, and the boys singing. She could remember finding the baby in the pram, and she realized now that although she had thought that the baby was Michael Randall, he had in fact been another woman's child. He had been much younger than Michael, and fair, not dark. She could remember buying powdered milk and bottles in the chemist, and napkins, vests and gowns in the drapers. She could remember that she had caught a different bus home than her usual one, and that she had been careful to alight a couple of miles from Thorpe Fen. Then she had walked through the fields, the baby in her arms, sneaking into the vicarage through the kitchen garden. The maid had gone home for her lunch, and Daddy had been in his study. Helen had been very, very quiet. Of the two days she had spent with Michael – no, not Michael – the baby had, she had discovered later, been called Albert, Albert Chapman – she remembered nothing at all.

She remembered Adam and Maia coming to her room. Maia had taken the baby, Adam had helped her out of the attic. Climbing down the stairs, Helen had begun to scream when she had understood that they were taking Michael from her. When her father had remonstrated with her she had lunged at him, beating her fists on his chest, scratching his face.

She could not remember anything about the police station. She remembered being driven in a van to this place, and having to undress, exchanging her own clothes for the rough dress and apron that she now wore. Tentatively, she had asked one of the warders whether she was in a boarding school or a hospital, and the wardress had laughed and told her that she was a card, and that this was a women's prison. She could remember clearly being left alone in the cell, and realizing the awful emptiness of her arms. She had wanted to die. She had not left her cell that day; the wardress had come, shaking and scolding her, but had eventually left her alone, heaped in a corner, her knees hunched to her chin, her fisted hands pressed against her face.

On the whole, she didn't mind the prison. Some of the girls were nice, and some were unpleasant, but most of the time they left her alone. The wardresses sometimes shouted, which Helen didn't like, but the one who had called her a card was quite kind and brought her old magazines and knitting wool. She was too tired to read the magazines, but she knitted, slowly and painstakingly, a pair of mittens for the kind wardress.

Very few men came to the prison. Only the chaplain (Helen put her fingers in her ears during his sermons), and the doctor. She submitted to his brief examination with her eyes closed, humming to herself to block out the sound of his voice. Another man asked her all sorts of questions about the day she had taken the baby. She thought he might be a policeman, or a lawyer. On visiting day, Maia explained to her that she was sending a different sort of doctor to see her – a lady doctor. The lady doctor was called Dr Schneider, and had grey hair and glasses and a strange accent. She tried to make Helen talk about the baby, but she couldn't, it just made her cry. Instead, she found herself telling Dr Schneider about all sorts of other things. About silly little things like the house she had made in the box tree when she had been a little girl, or the meadow with the orchids behind Thorpe Fen church. Sad things, like her mother's diary, and awful things, like her date with Maurice Page. And then things she had never told anyone before. Bathing in the tin bath in her bedroom, and looking up to see her father, his face distorted by the shadows cast through the narrow gap between door and jamb. Kissing her father good night, and fearing, when he drew her to him and hugged her, that she would suffocate.

At the start of the battle of Brunete, Robin had driven west with Dr Mackenzie and two of the orderlies to find another site for their hospital. They requisitioned a farm, scrubbing out the low white buildings, sending details of their position to the trucks and ambulances waiting at the Jarama front. On 6 July, the casualties began to come in.

It was, she thought, even worse than at the Jarama. The same dreadful routine of receiving and sorting the wounded, of patching and bandaging and stitching, and holding a lamp when Dr Mackenzie picked, with painstaking care, the fragments of shrapnel from a young, ruined body. The same feelings of despair at the futility of it, overlaid all the time by a terrible, haunting fear. She had lost Hugh, and at every moment she dreaded hearing that she had lost Joe.

She thought that if she tried not to think of Joe then perhaps, just perhaps, he would be spared. Perhaps whatever malevolent god it was that watched her would let her be, tricked into thinking she didn't care. Seized by a grim superstition, she shut out all images of both Joe and Hugh, and let herself think only of her work. When the stretcher-bearer delivered to her Joe's letter, she thrust it into her pocket, lacking the courage to read it. Later, alone, she ripped open the envelope, and the ring, wrapped in its scrap of khaki, fell out. She was gripped by a panicking, awful certainty that Joe had tempted fate, that he had made himself noticeable. Robin did not put the ring on her finger, but threaded it on a length of string, hanging it around her neck, tucked beneath her uniform, so that it could not be seen. When, the following day, she looked up from dressing a wound and saw Neil Mackenzie standing in the doorway of the ward, his eyes searching until they came to rest on her, she wanted to run away, to hide, so that she did not have to know.

Maia met Adam in a public house on the banks of the Cam.

'A drink, Mrs Merchant?'

'I would like a gin and tonic, if you please, Mr Hayhoe. An utterly enormous gin and tonic.'

Maia sat in the garden, while Adam bought the drinks. Punts glided up the river, hardly breaking the still surface of the water. When Adam returned, Maia picked up the glass that he placed in front of her, and drank.

'I spoke to Mr Hadley-Gore this afternoon.'

'And . . . ?'

She could see the anxiety in his eyes. Over this last, awful week she had come to like and respect Adam Hayhoe. She said flatly, 'And he was not encouraging.'

Maia offered her cigarette case to Adam, who shook his head. She had driven to London and back that day to speak to the lawyer she had engaged to represent Helen. The very famous, very expensive lawyer.

'Mr Hadley-Gore visited Helen in that ghastly prison yesterday. He told me that he does not think she will be able to cope with a trial. Apparently she was in tears through most of the interview.' Maia flicked some ash onto the grass. 'The baby was neglected at home, you see, Adam, and Helen cared for it very well over the two days she was in the attic. So he'd hoped to show Helen as some sort of benefactor . . . a do-gooder . . . the rector's daughter doing her bit for the feckless poor. But if she breaks down at the trial . . .' Maia shook her head. The day had upset her, and the long hot drive had made every muscle in her body ache. 'And it won't help that her father refuses to speak up for her.'

Adam grimaced. 'I tried to talk to him, but he wouldn't let me in the house.'

'Alec Hadley-Gore wrote to him. Apparently, Mr Ferguson's greatest concern is the shame that Helen has brought on her family. On her father, in other words.' Maia's voice was caustic. 'So much for Christian charity. Despicable man.' She swallowed the rest of her gin.

Adam said gently, 'You're doing everything you can, Mrs Merchant.'

'It's not enough,' she said bleakly. 'Helen has been in that dreadful place for a week now. Both of us know what it would do to her if she were to spend *years* there. And . . .'

She could not finish. She could not tell Adam Hayhoe, who loved Helen, what Alec Hadley-Gore had explained to her that afternoon. That, if convicted, Helen might not be returned to prison, but could be sent to a mental institution instead. Maia, lighting a second cigarette from the stub of the last, rose and went to the far end of the garden, where it looked out to the river. Instead of the silvery, heat-hazed Cam she saw rows of iron beds, barred windows, and the bare tables and benches of an institution. She knew that she could not let Helen go to a place like that. Maia tried to relax her mind, to search for the sort of solution she had always before been able to find for the most intractable of problems.

At length, she realized that Adam Hayhoe was standing next to her. She said slowly, 'The name of the baby, Adam. What was the name of the baby?'

Mrs Chapman's house was just as awful as Maia had imagined it would be. A rack of stained grey nappies – baby Albert's, presumably – dripped on a clothes horse, and though it was mid-afternoon, bowls encrusted with congealed porridge cluttered the table. There was a smell of sour milk and soapy steam and rotting vegetables.

Mrs Chapman's three runny-nosed daughters gawped at Maia.

'If you're from that nosey parker Committee,' said

Mrs Chapman, as she stirred a saucepan full of something grey and unpleasant, 'I haven't seen hide nor hair of the idle so-and-so for three months.'

Maia said calmly, 'I'm not from the Public Assistance Committee, Mrs Chapman. My name is Mrs Merchant. I'm a friend of Helen Ferguson.'

The wooden spoon stilled. 'Bit of a nerve, then, coming here.' The voice was sarcastic, but Maia noticed the fleeting gleam of interest in the round dark eyes.

'I thought we should talk, Mrs Chapman.' She glanced at the three little girls. 'Alone, if that's convenient.'

'Beryl . . . Ruby . . . Pearl . . . get on outside. And you'll see the back of my hand if you're back before tea.'

The three little girls ran out into the drizzle. Mrs Chapman, looking at Maia, said, 'Not that there's anything to talk about.'

'Oh, there is.' Maia took her cigarette case and lighter out of her bag. 'There's a great deal to talk about. Cigarette, Mrs Chapman?'

Maia lit both cigarettes. Then she said, 'I called on you to suggest that you go to the police and tell them you've decided to drop the charges against Helen.'

She heard the hiss of the other woman's indrawn breath. But again, briefly, that flicker of calculation. Sarah Chapman folded her arms in front of her.

'And why, tell me, should I do that? After I went through such a nightmare when I thought I'd lost my little pet.'

The little pet was back in his dirty pram in the street. Maia could hear his yells.

The outraged voice continued. 'Only a mother could know what I went through.' Scornful eyes surveyed Maia, in her navy blue costume. 'Have you little ones of your own, Mrs Merchant?'

Maia said coolly, 'I have a department store in Cambridge. I have a large house, and the latest model of motor-car. I holiday abroad whenever I please, and I have two wardrobes full of clothes. I wear nothing that's

534

more than six months old. Except my furs, of course. Furs age so well.'

Her gaze, as she spoke, focused on Sarah Chapman. If she had discussed this course of action with the lawyer she had engaged to represent Helen, then Maia knew that he would have forbidden her to pursue it. Bribery, and perverting the course of justice.

She saw the dark eyes narrow, and knew, with an inward sigh of relief, that she was understood.

'Nothing could make up for what I've been through,' said Mrs Chapman meaningfully, stubbing her cigarette out on top of the stove.

'I'll speak plainly, Mrs Chapman. Nothing will be gained from Helen going to prison – or to a mental institution. That is what will happen to her if this case goes to court. You do see, don't you, that neither Helen – nor I – nor you – would gain anything from that.'

'It wouldn't bother me in the least if the silly bitch goes to prison. Caused me a lot of trouble, she did. Had the police and the cruelty people round here, asking all sorts of questions.'

Maia smiled. 'Of course I understand that you should be compensated for the distress you suffered, Mrs Chapman.'

The baby was still bawling. As Sarah Chapman watched Maia, the expression in her eyes altered from wariness to contempt. 'You're all the same, aren't you? Think you can buy your way out of trouble. People like you think that anything can be bought, don't you?'

Through the years, Vernon's voice still echoed. *Come, Maia – you'd sell yourself for a few jewels and a wardrobe of clothes.* She too had been bought.

Maia shrugged. 'Can't it?'

With the mixture of pride and greed and intelligence that she recognized in the other woman's face, Maia acknowledged an affinity. She chose her words carefully.

'I'm merely looking for a solution that suits both of us. Come, Mrs Chapman – you're a practical woman, aren't you?'

The brown eyes narrowed again. 'It'll take more than a pound or two, I can tell you.'

Maia's heart began to beat faster. This was the part she always enjoyed; when she knew that the bargain was made, and that the terms must be hammered out, and her own advantage secured.

'I thought,' said Maia, 'twenty pounds.'

'Twenty pounds!' Sarah Chapman spat her contempt. 'If you've a big house and a car and all the rest of it like you say you have, Mrs Merchant, then you can do better than that. I may be hard up, but I'm no fool.'

'Thirty, then.'

'Oh no.' Mrs Chapman began to wipe ineffectually around the table-top with a handful of her dirty apron. 'I want to get out of this dump. That'll take more than thirty pounds.'

Maia acknowledged that this shoddy creature knew exactly what she wanted. Just as she did. Sarah Chapman, like herself, enjoyed breaking rules.

'You do understand that we must be discreet, don't you? That if you suddenly became a great deal better off, questions might be asked. Questions that would be awkward to both of us.'

There was a pause. 'A weekly sum, then. That'd do nicely.'

'Three pounds per week for two years,' said Maia crisply.

'Five. For five years.'

Maia shook her head. She thought with distaste that she would be tied to this woman and to this squalor for as short a time as possible. She made as if to leave the house.

As her fingers touched the door handle, she heard the voice behind her say, 'Three years, then.'

She felt a great wash of relief. Her mouth was almost too dry to speak.

'Yes. That's reasonable. I am content with that. I will arrange for the money to be paid to you as soon as you have informed the police that you wish to drop all charges against Helen.'

Mrs Chapman said dubiously, 'They won't like it.'

'Of course they won't.' Maia, glancing back, smiled. 'But you're a resourceful woman. You'll think of something. And do bear in mind, Mrs Chapman, that you must keep our little bargain strictly to ourselves. After all, you will be as compromised as I.'

She left the house. Out in the street, walking back to her car, her knees shook slightly. She had just successfully completed, Maia thought, the most important bargain of her life.

After Neil Mackenzie had told Robin that a German plane had bombed the machine-gun post that Joe and another Brigader had manned, he had explained to her that the bomb had made a direct hit, and that Joe had been buried out at Brunete, in the trenches. Robin had known what he had meant, though: that there hadn't been enough left of Joe to bury.

Dr Mackenzie wanted her to take some time off, but she refused. She had work to do. She carried out her duties on the ward with quick, waspish efficiency. Her eyes dared them to criticize her, or to sympathize with her. She held on to this, her work, because it was all she had left.

Loud noises made her jump, and at night she woke frequently from appalling dreams, so that even the few hours' sleep allotted to her were broken. She could not eat, and the weight fell off her. Because she was thin, she was always cold. In the evening, when she went to her camp bed in the stables and sat, her coat wrapped around her nightdress, she took Joe's letter from her writing-case and read it over and over again.

I wish it would stop. I would like to be still. I am afraid, Robin.

Waking very early each morning, she would remember with a physical shock that made her heart squeeze and her entire body judder, that Joe was dead.

The continual return to a realization that was unbearable persisted throughout the days. If she forgot even for a second, then she had to endure all over again the overwhelming onslaught of grief. Along with the grief was the terrible anger. Joe, who had been young and kind and gifted was dead. Lesser men – ordinary men, talentless men – had survived when he had died. Sometimes she felt that if she could just twist aside from time, just see things through a slightly different aspect, then she would discover that she had been mistaken, and that Joe, with whom she had intended to spend the rest of her life, would still be there. She told herself, *It will be better when I am used to it*, but could not imagine herself ever becoming used to it.

She received a letter from her mother telling her about Helen. When she read it, she felt nothing. That Helen had been imprisoned for abducting a baby seemed only a fitting part of a world that had become random and cruel. Daisy had written, *So you see, Maia was right. We neglected Helen, didn't we? None of us had any idea that she was in so distressed a state that she would do such a dreadful thing*. She could almost hear the bitterness in her mother's voice, crossing the immense distance that lay between them. *We let ourselves become self-satisfied, Richard and I. It is a terrible thing, to realize that.*

The kind wardress tapped on Helen's shoulder as she was feeding pillowcases through the mangle.

'The Governor wants to see you, Ferguson.'

Drying her hands on her apron, Helen followed the wardress through a series of passageways and locked doors. The Governor, a stout woman with her iron-grey hair in a bun, looked up when Helen came in.

'Your clothes, Ferguson.' She pointed to a brown paper parcel on the table. 'You may change in the medical room next door.'

Helen, confused, stared at the parcel. She remembered

what the other prisoner had said. *They'll send you to the nuthouse.* She began to tremble.

'Well, what are you waiting for, Ferguson? Don't you want to go home?'

Helen whispered, 'Go home?'

'The charges against you have been dropped,' said the Governor briskly, and returned to her paperwork.

In the medical room, dazed, she put on the dress and cardigan in which she had arrived in prison. The kind wardress escorted her to the gates, and said, 'Be a good girl now, Ferguson. We don't want to see you back again,' and she was left standing in a strange street, her small bundle of possessions under her arm.

Then a familiar voice called out her name. Helen looked up.

'Maia?' she said. 'Oh, Maia.' And, running towards her, began to cry.

In the hospital, Helen began to feel better. They left her alone mostly, in a little room with yellow sprigged wall-paper and flowery curtains. Dr Schneider came and talked to her every now and then, but mostly she just lay there, looking out of the window to the fields of butter-cups that lay beyond. She hadn't realized she was so tired. Gradually, the jangling in her mind calmed. She realized that she had not been able to think clearly for a very long time. Lying there, the past began to fall into place. Since she had sat on the verandah of Robin's winter house and said, *I'd like a little house of my own. And children, of course*, so many things had gone wrong. She had lost first Geoffrey and then Hugh; she had tried to break away from her father's imprisoning love, and had failed.

At first, she refused to see anyone except Maia. Then one day the nurse gave a parcel to her.

'A gentleman brought this for you, Helen.'

She unwrapped the tissue paper. Nestled inside it was

a box, three inches square, inlaid with pictures made of coloured wood.

'He's waiting outside. Can I show him in?'

Slowly, Helen nodded.

Tall and broad-shouldered, Adam filled the room. He said, 'It's so good to see you, love. So good,' and she beckoned him to sit down on the chair by the bed.

'This is lovely, Adam.' She held up the box.

'There's a place for rings and trinkets.' Adam opened the box. It was lined inside with crimson velvet. 'The pictures in the panels are of things that remind me of you. There's your cat, see.' He pointed to the tiny black cat, inlaid into a side of the box. 'Old Percy. I've got him down in London with me now. Still tries to chase the birds, but he's past it now, poor old fellow. And there's a rose. Do you remember when you pinned one of my roses to your hat, Helen?' He turned the box again. 'And a dancing shoe.'

'We've never danced together, Adam.'

He shook his head. 'Oh, we did, love. Years ago, at the harvest supper.'

Helen lay back on the pillows and thought very hard. Then she murmured:

'I arise from dreams of thee
In the first sweet sleep of night
When the winds are breathing low
And the stars are shining bright.'

A tear trailed slowly down her cheek. She whispered, 'Oh Adam – what you must think of me!' Covering her eyes with her hands, she was overcome with shame at what she had done. She was haunted by the realization of how that mother must have felt when she had discovered the empty pram.

She heard Adam say, 'What do I think of you? Well, I'll tell you, Helen. I think that you're the finest girl I've ever known. I always have done.'

Helen turned away, her eyes tightly closed. 'I'm tired, Adam. I think I shall sleep.' She heard him tiptoe out of the room, and she dozed, clutching the box in her hand.

Days passed. It seemed to Helen quite impossible that she should ever even begin to join up the scattered threads of her life, as Dr Schneider suggested. With Dr Schneider's help she had peeled away so many layers that she was not sure whether there was anything left to rejoin. She was unable to read, unable to knit; sitting at the window, looking out at the field, she felt as empty as a shelled husk. When the nurse suggested she dress and sit out on the verandah, it took her shaking, unsteady fingers an age to do up her buttons and tie her laces. Outside, she saw to her surprise that the leaves on the trees had begun to brown a little at the edges, that the grass had the pale ochre tinge of late summer.

Dr Schneider met her outside on the balcony. 'Shall we walk, Helen? There's a very pretty path through the wood.'

They walked along the cinder track that led between the trees. Helen's short hair, cut in the prison, was blown by the breeze about her face.

'It is beautiful, is it not?'

Helen turned slowly around, looking at the distant fields with their haze of yellow buttercups, at the river, and the smooth brown fish that darted between the shimmering weed, and at the great trees above her, whose crowns of dark green leaves almost touched the sky.

'Yes,' she said slowly. 'Yes, I suppose that it is.'

Dr Schneider encouraged her to begin to draw and sew again. Maia visited, elegant in cream silk. Helen was surprised to find herself laughing aloud at some of the stories Maia told her. She began to feel hungry once more, and to sleep properly at night. She walked to the shop in the nearby village and bought herself a magazine and a bar of chocolate. Washing her hair, she used her sewing scissors to tidy her ragged locks into a neat blond bob.

While she was sitting out on the verandah, sketching the view, a shadow fell across her drawing-paper.

Looking around, Helen smiled when she saw Adam. He bent and kissed her cheek, and gave her a bunch of Michaelmas daisies.

'They are lovely. I do miss my garden.'

He drew up a wicker chair and sat beside her. 'There's a garden at the place I'm renting in Richmond. Just a little patch, mind.' Leaning forward, Adam took her hand. 'The house is for us, Helen. For us to share.'

Her heart had begun to beat rather fast.

'I didn't mean to ask you yet. I meant to wait until you were truly well. Only I've waited so many years that I can't seem to wait any longer. Will you marry me, Helen?'

She turned away from him. The sketchpad slid from her lap to the paving stones. Unable to speak, she just shook her head. She heard his sigh, and hated herself.

'Is it because of what I am? It's different in London, Helen – it's not like at Thorpe Fen. People don't care so much what sort of place you were born in.'

She whispered, 'It's nothing to do with that.'

There was a silence. She knew that he was waiting for her to explain, but how could she begin to explain to Adam Hayhoe that she had had to begin again, like a piece of paper that has been rubbed clean of all pencil marks? How could she begin to explain that there was nothing left of the old Helen, that he was proposing marriage to a woman who was little more than an empty shell, a random twist of bone and skin and flesh?

She heard the wicker chair scrape on the stone as Adam rose to his feet. Looking up, she glimpsed the hurt on his face. She said wildly, 'I don't know what I want, Adam. I just don't know.' She touched his arm. 'Don't hate me, Adam, please. I couldn't bear that.'

After he had gone, she went back to her room. She couldn't draw any more, and her knitting lay unfinished on the table. There was a terrible hurt inside her, as though her heart itself was sore. She sat by the window, trying to work it all out. Was it possible that she had always looked in the wrong direction? That love had been there all the time? That her romantic yearnings for Geoffrey, for Hugh, for Maurice Page, had been delusions, false fire, wisps of bright vapour in the marshes?

When Dr Schneider knocked on the door Helen, glancing at the clock, saw that an hour had passed.

'You did not come to lunch, Helen.'

'I wasn't hungry.'

'Has something upset you?'

She shook her head silently, wanting to be left alone, but Dr Schneider persisted.

'Has your unhappiness something to do with the gentleman who called?'

'He proposed to me,' she said angrily, 'if you must know.'

'And . . . ?'

'And I turned him down.'

'Ah. Well, that is your right, Helen. You have the right to choose who you will marry.'

'I *want* to marry Adam!' Furious, she thumped the table with her clenched fist.

There was a short silence. Then Dr Schneider said gently, 'Yet you turned him down. You must have had a reason for turning him down, Helen.'

She had to struggle to put the reason into words. 'He doesn't understand. He doesn't understand that I am *nothing*. I wasn't anything much before, but I'm even less now. He still thinks of me as sweet little Helen. Dutiful and obedient. A good daughter. A regular churchgoer.' She could hear the bitterness in her voice.

'Are you sure that is what Mr Hayhoe believes you to be?'

Her anger suddenly left her. 'Oh . . . I don't know. I don't know anything any more. That's the trouble. I know nothing and I have done nothing.'

Dr Schneider took both Helen's hands in hers. 'Then change that, Helen. You have the power to change it. You must decide what you want to do, and then you must do it. It doesn't matter what you do as long as you feel it is right for you.'

Eventually Robin realized that the staff at the mobile hospital were giving her the easiest jobs and the lightest duties. The realization was humiliating; fleetingly she thought of protesting, but her anger died stillborn, stifled by an apathy that had become habitual to her. Dully, she acknowledged that she had become clumsy and incompetent, that the other nurses quietly cleared up her messier mistakes, and made her frequent cups of tea, and covered for her if she was late back from her lunch break. Their silent sympathy forced her to question her usefulness, but could not touch the great well of grief inside her. It did not seem reasonable to Robin that she should share with these men and women, who were every bit as exhausted and battle-weary as herself, the depth of her misery. What she had lost divided her from them. She could not bear their kindness, she hid from it, retreating to the quiet kitchen garden at the back of the farmhouse at the end of each day, guessing how kindness could break through the fragile protective armour in which she had clothed herself.

Sitting in the courtyard among the dusty peppers and garlic shoots, she heard footsteps behind her and turned round to see Dr Mackenzie.

He came to stand beside her. 'I'm leaving next week – it's the end of my tour of duty. I want you to come back to England with me.'

'I can't.' Her voice was rough with disuse. 'People need me here.'

'And people need you at home. Your parents, for instance, Robin. Your friends.' He reached out to take her hand, but she moved back, unable to bear any human contact. He said firmly, 'You have a future, though you may not believe it at the moment. You must go back and pick up the pieces. You must comfort your parents for the loss of your brother, and you must take up the place that's held for you at the Royal Free.

You've done your bit, Robin. This is the last time I shall tell you what to do, I promise. Come home.'

After he left, she sat there alone, watching the sun go down. In her mind's eye she could picture the pondweed gleaming green beneath the surface of the river at Blackmere Farm, and smell the bitter, salty scent of balsam and watercress. Rubbing her aching head, Robin could not understand the intense longing that had welled up inside her, the first real feeling she had experienced since Joe's death. Bewildered, she wrapped her arms around herself, looking at the mountains, but thinking of home.

Helen stood on the station platform. Dr Schneider had lent her money and had explained to her how to read a railway timetable. Now, her small suitcase gripped in one hand, the box Adam had made her clutched like a talisman in the other, she waited for the London train.

It screamed into the station in a great cloud of smoke. Helen opened the door and climbed into the carriage. She had expected to feel nervous and afraid, but she did not. Instead, she felt only excitement and anticipation. She had never been to London, and the thought that she might see all the great things she had only read about was almost unbearably delightful.

She had decided to leave the hospital only the previous evening. She had suddenly realized that if you were a blank piece of paper, then you must begin, eventually, to draw on it. She wanted to draw all sorts of things. Places and people, and all the things she had never done. She wanted to go the ballet, and to watch a football match. To holiday at the seaside and to see the mountains of Scotland. To ride on an escalator in a department store, and to have her hair permed. To watch the sun set, alone, and to see the sun rise while sleeping in the arms of the man she loved. And eventually she would draw children on her empty piece of paper, her own children. But that could wait for a while, for there were so many other things she must do first.

The train drew away from the platform. As it travelled along the line, Helen saw the slow build-up of village to town, town to city as she approached London. She thought that there was a name that she must write on her slate. Helen imagined her own hand, drawing with beautiful curling loops and intricate gilding the name *Adam*.

Chapter Nineteen

In her absence, the verandah of the winter house had collapsed, its fractured balcony tumbled and askew, bleached like bones. Treading through the tangle of nettles and brambles at the back of the winter house, Robin scratched a rotting plank with her nail, and saw the powdery wood crumble and trail to the undergrowth in a fine stream of brown dust.

The pool was a dank basin of desiccated weed, a small circlet of dark water lingering at the deepest part of the hollow. Mosquitoes kissed the surface of the water, and eels writhed in its sullen depths. There was a sour smell of decayed and rotting vegetation. Robin climbed up the narrow steps. The planks were whitened at their ends by the sun, protruding over the dried-up pond, finding nothing to cling on to.

Ivy snaked along the walls of the hut once more, sealing the door and windows. When she tore the ivy away, tiny hairlike tendrils adhered to the wood. Pushing open the door, Robin glimpsed the jagged patches of blue that could be seen through the roof. Broken tiles scattered the floor, and there was a bird's nest on top of the wood-burning stove. She remembered the day they had come to Blackmere. Hugh had stood beside her in the winter house, and she had said, *I'd like it to be mine, Hugh. In the summer we shall have a boat. We shall sail for ever.* She stood motionless, listening to the awful gulping sound of her breathing. This was the worst thing, she thought. That she could never tell when it was going to happen. Several large tears gathered at her lids and trailed down her cheeks.

Robin wiped the tears on the back of her hand when she heard Daisy's footsteps on the verandah. She had come home expecting, despite everything, to find Blackmere Farm unchanged. And yet Hugh's death had, of course, altered so much, damaging Richard's health, and sapping Daisy of her bright vitality. Bills had not been paid, repairs to the house had not been carried out. Neither of her parents looked as though they had slept or eaten properly for months. She had dismissed the latest maid, an idle, careless girl, recalling with a shudder Maia's mockery of the Summerhayeses' servants. She had cleaned and tidied the house herself, had called the doctor for her father, and found a builder to mend the roof, and had cooked hot food and laid fires in the grates. She had put her own losses aside while she sorted out the sad muddle of her parents' lives. She had witnessed Richard's frail silence, and Daisy's constant veering between unconvincing cheerfulness and overwhelming grief with an aching heart.

She opened the door of the winter house to her mother. Daisy looked round the little room.

'Ugh – it was always so spidery. I used to wonder how you could bear it, Robin.'

Robin smiled. 'I never minded that sort of thing.'

Daisy's thin, brown-freckled hand trailed over the broken shells, the damp-discoloured books.

'Did I tell you about the memorial service we had for Hugh, darling? It was in the church – there was no other suitable place. A rather lovely building. So peaceful. So many people came . . . from Hugh's school . . . from the village . . . I hadn't realized how many people loved him.' Daisy's voice faltered, and then brightened. 'Anyway, I met an old woman who knew the family who lived at Blackmere Farm before we bought it. She remembered the lady who lived here.'

'In the winter house?'

Daisy nodded. 'She was a consumptive, as we thought. She lived here day and night, winter and summer. Can you imagine, Robin? She had three daughters, and the youngest was only ten when she fell ill. She promised herself that she would live until they were all safely married.'

Robin looked out of the window, to the dried up pond and the shallow river beyond, to the fields and the horizon, and the vast cloud-streaked sky.

'And did she?'

When she looked back, she saw the expression on Daisy's face.

'I could bear *that* . . . I could bear to go first. But this – to lose both my boys – after I tried so hard for poor Hugh—' Daisy's face was contorted in pain. Reaching out a hand she drew her daughter to her, hugging her tightly.

Outside, a blackbird sang in the willows. After Daisy had returned to the farmhouse, Robin went back to the verandah, and began to pull away at the pieces of rotten wood, throwing them into the dried up pond. They tumbled into the shallow basin to protrude at random angles from the cracked grey silt. There was a drumming sound: dark circles pitted the mud as the rain started to fall.

Sunlight softened the outline of mill and chimney and lightened the rows of smoke-blackened terraces. At Elliot Hall the housekeeper had directed Robin to the mill. Now she waited in the lobby, almost deafened by the hammering of the looms in the adjacent weaving shed.

A man pushed his way through the wide double doors. Short, stocky, thinning grey hair, fleshy face. Robin searched in his features for Joe, but could not find him.

'Mr Elliot?'

'Aye.' He shouted over the noise of the machinery. 'Who's asking for me?'

'My name's Robin Summerhayes.'

He seized her hand and shook it. 'You wrote me a letter about the lad.'

Robin nodded. 'I thought I'd come and see you. Do you mind?'

John Elliot's answer was to take his coat and hat from the peg, and open the door. 'Don't hang about in this racket then, lass,' he bawled. 'You'd best come to my office.'

She followed him across the cobbled courtyard to a small brick building. John Elliot's office was cluttered and dusty, yellowing sheafs of paper piled on the filing-cabinets. He said apologetically, 'I don't use the place much. I'd rather do the paperwork at home these days.' He pulled out a chair for Robin. 'Sit thee down, lass, and Sally can get us tea.'

When she had her tea, she took the photographs out of her bag. 'I thought you might like to see these.' She slid them across the desk. 'We took them in Spain.'

Robin watched Joe's father thumb slowly through the snapshots, peering intently through his reading glasses. The two of them, in the garden of the Spanish villa. They had danced between the flower-beds, and the air had been heavy with the scent of roses.

Joe's father took off his spectacles, folded them, and replaced them in their case. His eyes glittered. 'I can't imagine our Joe a soldier. Didn't seem cut out for it.'

She said sadly, 'I don't think he was. He hated it at the end. He went to Spain because he believed so strongly that was the right thing to do.'

'Aye.' John Elliot rose and went to the window. 'He always had a lot of daft ideas in his head.'

His back was to her, but she saw him raise his hand to his eyes. She said softly, 'You should be proud of Joe, Mr Elliot.' Then she rose and placed her hand on his arm, looking out of the window to the streets and high purple hills beyond.

'Aye. And I am.' He blew his nose loudly. 'You were a friend of his, you say, Miss Summerhayes?'

'Yes.'

'A good friend?'

'A very good friend.'

'Joe always played things close to the chest . . . never talked about owt to his dad.'

She said simply, 'We loved each other.'

'Ah.' The syllable sounded like a sigh. 'Would you have married him, lass?'

She didn't even need to think. 'Yes. Yes, I would.'

'It's a devil.' John Elliot blew his nose again. 'A devil.'

There was another silence. When eventually he spoke again his voice was taut with pain.

'But who will I give all this to?' His gesture took in the mill, the houses, the village itself. 'Why did I spend my days getting all this . . . ?' And he stopped, silenced, his head bowed.

Robin caught the train to Ipswich, and then took the branch line to the coast. The waves were trimmed with a fringe of white foam, and the salty wind stung her eyes as she walked along the sand.

She glimpsed the outline of Long Ferry Hall as she had seen it first years before, fine lacework against an empty sky. Then the turrets and the crenellations, and the two wings, like arms embracing the courtyard. A letter from Charis Fortune had told her that Francis had gone abroad: Charis had had postcards from Marseilles, from Tangiers, from Marrakesh. And then, for a long time, nothing. Robin imagined Francis wandering steadily further into the desert, a bottle in one hand, a cigarette in the other, becoming lost.

A lorry was parked on the paving-stones. As Robin approached the front gates a man's voice called out, 'You can't go in there, love!'

She looked around, and shouted to the head poking from the cab of the lorry, 'Why not?'

'Private property, love.' A man swung out of the cab and crossed the paving-stones towards her.

'I'm a friend of—' she paused for a moment, searching for Vivien's latest surname '— a friend of Mrs Farr.'

'Mrs Farr doesn't live here any more. Sold the house lock, stock and barrel. Funny old place, mind you. Lots of little rooms where you don't expect them.'

'Do you know where Mrs Farr is living now?'

'Not a clue, love.'

'Do you think—' hesitantly, she glanced at him '—do you think that I could have a look inside the house? Just a quick look.'

He shook his head regretfully. 'More than my job's worth. It's to be a government place, see.' He tapped his nose. 'Hush-hush. Boffins in white coats.'

'Oh.' She felt defeated.

He began to walk back to his lorry. He called back, 'Something to do with the next war, I think.'

'War?' she said. 'What war?', but he did not reply.

She stood there for a moment, shut out by the gates, and then she began to walk back to the station. Only once did she look back and see, silhouetted against a darkening sky, the little belvedere on the roof. The dying rays of the sun silvered the old stone, so that the roof and columns looked as though they were encrusted with a thin layer of snow.

Robin's rooms had been let in her absence, but the writer of detective stories had moved out of Joe's flat. She had dreaded this homecoming even more than she had dreaded seeing her parents, but she found, unlocking the door and looking round, that its familiarity was a comfort to her. An important part of her life had died with Joe, but here, at last, she could reassure herself that those years had really happened. She had not found Joe at Hawksden, and nor had she been allowed to remind herself of those long-ago, entrancing days the three of them had spent together at Long Ferry. But here in the flat, sitting on the battered sofa with Joe's old summer jacket wrapped around her shoulders, she could mourn him properly. She dusted the rooms, sweeping away all evidence of the empty months. When the kettle was boiling and she had lit the gas fire, she could almost hear his quick feet running up the stairs, almost see his face as he opened the door and smiled at her.

Often, she talked to him. In the evening, coming home tired after her first week studying medicine – *An awful day, Joe – I had to dissect a lung, and I dropped it on the floor. Then the Tube was so crowded and I forgot to buy any food, so there's only these biscuits. They'll do, won't they?* In the morning, getting ready for lectures – *Coat, bag and books. D'you think it'll rain? Yes, I'll take an umbrella. Oh – and my hat – thank you Joe.* She knew that if anyone heard her they would think that she was mad, but she did not care. Some days were better than others. On the good days, the exhausting disbelief in his death that had taunted her in Spain muted to a kinder pleasure in his continuing presence. On bad days, her voice echoed against empty walls.

She bought newspapers, but could do no more than glance at the headlines. At night, she dreamed of the mobile hospital. Sights she had thought she had forgotten came back to her, like a reel of film replaying. She knew that Republican Spain would fall, and that there would, inevitably, be another war. She thought bitterly that in a few years it would all begin again. She would help clear up the mess. That was what people like her did.

She received the letter from Helen a month after she started at the Royal Free. Enclosed with it was an invitation to Helen and Adam's wedding. Placing it on the mantelpiece Robin began mentally to compose her note of refusal. Then she read the letter.

Do you remember that we promised to celebrate together the great events of a woman's life? We celebrated Maia's wedding, and you getting your first job, Robin, but I never celebrated anything. Well, now at last I have something to celebrate. I am to marry my beloved Adam, and we are to travel to Scotland for our honeymoon. It will be a quiet wedding – I know that you must miss Hugh and Joe terribly, but it would mean so much to me for the three of us to be together again. Please come.

It rained on the day of Helen's wedding. Robin's mind drifted as Helen and Adam made their vows. Restless, disinterested, her gaze scanned the guests. Adam's cousins and aunts, each one tall and dark and heavyset, like Adam. Dr and Mrs Lemon, uncomfortable in their wedding clothes. And herself and Maia. When she looked at Maia she felt an habitual, empty sort of hatred.

Outside the small church, the rain made the rice swell and stick and the confetti painted coloured spots on Helen's cream straw hat and cobalt blue suit. Rain battering against his face, Adam took Helen in his arms and kissed her. Someone took photographs and then they all caught a bus, dripping and laughing in their finery, back to the Hayhoes' house. 'I haven't been in a bus for *years*,' said Maia, and Robin ran her finger through the condensation on the window, so that water droplets trickled down the glass.

Helen had prepared a cold luncheon. The house was small and pretty, a Victorian artisan's cottage which Adam had filled with good furniture and Helen had decorated with floral curtains and cushions. Robin, watching the Hayhoes, thought that they had the sort of easy intimacy that some married couples take years to acquire. They finished each other's sentences, and anticipated each other's needs. Adam's eyes followed Helen wherever she went, and he had the slightly dazed look of a man who couldn't believe his luck. After they had eaten, Dr Lemon proposed toasts to the bride and groom, and Adam made a short speech.

A taxi arrived to take the newlyweds to the railway station. More rice and confetti, and when Helen threw her bouquet out of the taxi window, Robin caught it. Some awful automatic reflex left over from netball practice at school, she supposed, quickly passing the posy of rosebuds and stephanotis to the youngest Hayhoe cousin.

Maia said, 'Weddings are so ghastly, aren't they? Even the ones when one actually likes the people who are getting married.'

Robin did not reply.

'I thought I would leave.' Maia squinted at her watch. 'The worst of it's over, and I'd rather not help with the washing-up. I'd like you to come with me.'

Robin said stiffly, 'I'm going back into London. Not to Cambridge.'

'I'm not driving to Cambridge. I've a journey to make. And I need to talk to you, Robin.'

'I don't want to talk to you, Maia.' Her voice was taut with barely suppressed anger and bitterness. 'In fact, I'd really prefer never to see you again.'

'There are things I should explain.'

There was, improbably, a pleading look in Maia's beautiful eyes. Robin felt a mixture of weariness and anger.

'I only came here for Helen's sake. Because that ridiculous promise we made years ago seemed to mean so much to her.'

Maia smiled sadly. 'None of us got what we wanted, did we?'

'I felt I owed her,' added Robin irritably. Rain was trailing down the back of her neck, between her blouse and jacket collar. 'Whereas I don't owe you a thing, Maia.' She began to walk back to the house to find her bag and gloves.

From behind her, she heard Maia say, 'I want to explain to you why I couldn't marry Hugh.'

She stood quite still, her arms clutched round herself. Then she turned slowly back.

'Don't you think it's a little late for that?' When she saw the small narrowing of Maia's pale eyes, Robin knew that her words had stung. 'Besides, I thought you explained things quite well a year ago.'

'I want to tell you the truth. I never told Hugh the truth. Please. You've nothing planned, have you?'

Robin thought of the empty flat that she must return to, the remains of yesterday's shepherd's pie that she would heat up for her tea. Her anger dissolved. 'No. Nothing planned,' she said sadly.

Maia drove west out of London. For the first half-hour or so neither woman spoke. The busy roads and crowded houses of London were exchanged for the rolling hills and pretty villages of Berkshire. Robin sat hunched up in the passenger seat, staring out of the side window at the rain streaming down the pane. Her brief flare of anger with Maia had gone, replaced by a cold resentful dislike. When she looked across she saw that the old Maia had returned: cool, unruffled, beautiful. She was seized by an impulse to disrupt that self-control.

'Very well, then. Truth-telling. Let's start at the beginning, shall we, Maia? Tell me about Vernon.'

Maia's eyes were focused on the road ahead; her fingers loosely gripped the steering-wheel. The wheels of the low-slung sports car threw up curls of brown water from the puddles at the side of the road.

'After my father killed himself, I had to find a husband. I couldn't think of another way of living the sort of life I wanted to live. So I chose to marry Vernon. I didn't love him, Robin, and he didn't love me. We were both mistaken in what we thought we were getting. Vernon thought that because I was young, I would do what I was told . . . and I – I thought that once I had the house, the jewellery, the clothes I would be happy. We were both wrong.'

Robin said stiffly, 'I know this – I guessed it. You didn't drive me all this way to tell me this, did you, Maia?'

Maia went on as though she hadn't spoken. 'Vernon hated women. Not just me – all women. He thought that all women were calculating and underhand and deceitful. He thought that to be with a woman degraded him, and yet he had a need of that degradation. He had his first experience of physical love in the War, with a prostitute. I suppose that coloured everything that came afterwards.'

Robin, listening, shivered. Maia's tone was cool and detached, as though she was describing something that had happened to someone else. Yet she remembered meeting Maia in the garden of her splendid house all those years ago, one half of her face still beautiful, the other a grotesque caricature of beauty.

'He used to hit me, Robin. I thought at first that it was to make me do what he wanted me to do, but then I realized that it was because he enjoyed it. It gave him some sort of pleasure. And he raped me. Again, because he enjoyed it. I don't think he enjoyed sex without that element of coercion. Some of the things he made me do I still cannot bear to think about. The humiliation . . . the degradation . . . I felt so *powerless*.' Maia changed down a gear to accommodate the winding road. 'Anyway, I thought I could put up with it, but then I realized that I couldn't. I began to feel so ill – so sick and tired. I knew I couldn't bear it any longer, so I went to see you in London, but you had gone away. When I got back to Cambridge, I found out that I was late for Merchants' staff party. I knew that Vernon would punish me.'

Rain lashed against the windscreen of the car. Almost in spite of herself, Robin found that she had to know.

'So you killed him?'

Maia laughed. 'Dear Robin. Always so forthright.' She steered the car to the side of the road, slowed to a halt, and pulled on the handbrake. Then she reached into her bag and took out her cigarette case and lighter. When she had lit her cigarette, she said, 'I've thought about it over and over again. I almost managed to convince myself that it was an accident. That he slipped on the stairs because he was drunk, or I stumbled against

557

him because I was frightened, and he lost his balance. But I know that none of those things are true.' Her eyes lidded, and she said dreamily, 'Such a little thing, in a way, to reach out and push. He might have fallen anyway. If he hadn't been drunk I wouldn't have been able to do it. He was a strong man, you see, and I've always been slight.' Maia glanced at Robin. 'But I did do it. I saw my chance of freedom, and I took it. I knew that no-one would ever be able to prove anything. I gave him a shove and I watched him fall, and I can honestly tell you, Robin, that I felt nothing but relief.' Maia's eyes had closed, she leaned back in her seat. 'Such a little thing,' she said again.

There was a silence. Robin could hear only the pattering of the rain on the leather hood of the car. At last she said slowly, 'If you'd explained, Hugh might have understood.'

'So he might. It's hard to know.' Opening her eyes, Maia wound down her window and dropped her cigarette end into the mud.

'So you haven't explained a thing.'

'I haven't finished yet.' Maia started up the car again. 'We're almost there. Only a few more miles.'

They had crossed the Hampshire border, and were threading through a maze of narrow, winding roads and lush beechwoods. The wind blew the wet, coppery leaves from the branches; they stuck to the windscreen of the car.

They passed two lodges, facing each other beside wide wrought-iron gates. Robin could see in the distance a large Georgian house. More woodland, the tree-tops shadowing the road so that they formed a tunnel. Through the ranks of beech and elder, Robin glimpsed a house. Weatherboarding clung to the brickwork, dormer windows peered through the tiled roof. Maia braked.

'It used to be a gamekeeper's cottage.' She brought the car to a halt on the verge outside the gates. 'I bought it a few years ago. The family who own the estate were selling off the odd acre to pay taxes.' She climbed out of the car, and opened the gate. Robin followed after her, stiff from the long drive.

The narrow gravel path was enclosed by beech hedges, the front garden faced by laurel. Maia said, 'They will be inside because of the weather,' and rapped her knuckles on the front door.

A grey-haired woman, wrapped in a floral apron, opened it. 'Mrs Merchant!' She smiled, and stood aside to let Maia and Robin in. 'We were beginning to worry . . . such terrible weather.'

'I was held up, Mrs Fowler. This is a friend of mine, Miss Summerhayes. Robin, let me introduce you to Mrs Fowler.'

They shook hands and murmured pleasantries, but Robin, standing in the narrow hallway, noticed that Maia was looking around, searching for something.

Or someone. 'She's in the kitchen,' said Mrs Fowler. 'We're making cakes for tea.'

Maia smiled, and beckoned Robin to follow her. The rooms of the cottage were small and cosy, the furniture battered and comfortable. Maia opened the kitchen door.

A small girl was standing at the table. She was about six or seven years old, Robin guessed. Wrapped up in an apron, her hands were white with flour. When she caught sight of Maia, she began to smile. Making a strange whooping noise, she loped unsteadily across the room, and flung herself in Maia's arms.

A pretty little girl. Black hair, a gap-toothed grin and pale blue eyes, just like Maia's. Such uncommon eyes, such a rare colour.

Robin glanced quickly from Maia to the child, making connections, understanding suddenly almost everything.

'She's your daughter,' said Robin. It was a statement, not a question.

Maia, still hugging the little girl, smiled, and spoke

into the child's ear, 'Maria – look in Mummy's bag.' She tapped her leather handbag.

Maria slid out of her arms and crouched on the floor, struggling one-handedly with the clasp of the bag. Maia, careless of her stockings, knelt down on the stone flags and unclasped the handbag for her.

'Maria is seven years old.' Maia glanced up at Robin. 'And, yes, she is my daughter.'

Maria drew out of the handbag a small parcel. She made the whooping sound again as she held it up triumphantly to Maia.

'Yes, darling. Clever girl.'

Robin watched as the child ripped open the wrapping paper. A bag of sweets, a hair-ribbon, and a packet of colouring pencils tumbled out onto the floor. Robin felt dazed and winded, as though the breath had been knocked from her lungs.

'I'll make some tea, shall I, Mrs Merchant?' asked Mrs Fowler. 'And Maria and I shall finish the cakes. There's a fire lit in the drawing-room.'

In the drawing-room Maia raked the coals with the poker, and beckoned Robin to sit down. Then she said, 'You've noticed, I suppose, that Maria isn't quite like other little girls of her age.'

Robin thought of the child's unsteady lope across the floor to her mother, her struggle to open the handbag with one hand.

'She has some paralysis in the left side of her body, doesn't she? And—' she looked at Maia, and felt for the first time in years, pity for her '—and she doesn't speak.'

'Maria's hearing is very poor. She can hear a plate being dropped on the floor, but she cannot hear me say her name. She doesn't speak at all.'

'She's a lovely little girl, Maia,' said Robin gently.

'Oh, I know. I didn't think so at first, mind you. I was so angry when I realized that I was pregnant with Vernon's child. I thought of it as his revenge. Tormenting me even from the grave.'

Outside, the wind had picked up, hurling raindrops against the panes. The coals in the fireplaces glowed warm and red.

'I realized I was pregnant about the time of the inquest. I'd been feeling sick and exhausted for ages, but it hadn't occurred to me that it might be because I was expecting a baby. I've never been terribly regular, so I didn't take any notice of *that*. I was quite ignorant, you see, Robin.' Maia smiled. 'I'd always thought of myself as sophisticated, but I was really quite ignorant.'

There was a knock at the door, and Mrs Fowler came in with a tray of tea and biscuits. When she had gone, Maia added, 'As soon as I realized the truth, I decided to get rid of it. The idea of being pregnant was bad enough – the idea of being pregnant with *his* child was intolerable. So, as soon as the inquest was over, I went to London and bought some pills. "For All Female Ailments" – you know the sort of thing.'

'They don't work. I've seen half a dozen women at the clinic who've tried them, and then resorted to a knitting needle or carbolic soap.'

Maia shuddered. 'I couldn't do that – I'm too squeamish. Well, when the wretched pills didn't work, I got the address of a doctor. It wasn't easy – I didn't dare ask anyone I knew because they'd be bound to be suspicious. After all, I was supposed to be a grieving widow, wasn't I? Eventually I plucked up the courage to ask the chambermaid of the hotel where I was staying – I said it was for a friend of mine, though I don't expect she believed me. So I went to a horrid little doctor in a dire little house. He had clammy hands and shiny patches at the elbows of his suit. He refused to do it – he told me that I was too far gone.'

Maia poured out two cups of tea, and passed one to Robin. 'I'd been planning to go the Continent anyway, and I suppose I thought that if I just ignored it, it might go away. To be honest, I hoped that I might miscarry – that if I rattled around Europe like a madwoman it might budge. Then, when I realized that I was actually going to have to give birth to the wretched thing, I thought that I'd find a discreet clinic in Switzerland, and pay some placid Hausfrau to adopt the creature. Only it didn't work out like that.'

Robin took a mouthful of tea, and began to feel warm again for the first time that day. She noticed how the words poured from Maia, as though she was almost relieved to be sharing her secrets at last.

Maia brushed back her hair from her face. All the customary flippancy had gone from her voice. 'I'd bought myself a car – I thought it the most terrific fun. I drove around France – on my own, mostly – and then I decided to go to Spain. I thought the baby couldn't possibly come yet – even I knew they took nine months, and I didn't think I could possibly be as far gone as that. I felt quite well, then, and it didn't even really show. Dresses were still loose then, thank goodness, and I always wore corsets. I suppose I just looked a little plump. Anyway, I went into labour when I was driving across Spain. I was in the middle of nowhere, absolutely the middle of nowhere, and this awful pain started. I thought I was dying – and that was just at the beginning. I couldn't believe that women were expected to endure such agony, and I certainly couldn't believe that some of them *chose* to go through it more than once.' She looked up at Robin.

'First babies are usually the worst. And I've been told that you do forget.'

Maia shook her head. 'I haven't forgotten. I remember every moment of it. Anyway, I was in a dreadful little village, utterly incapable of getting anywhere civilized, so they took me to a nunnery. The nuns seemed to be expected to nurse the sick.'

'It's the tradition there. At the mobile hospital where I worked we trained some local girls, because most of the nuns, of course, nursed the Nationalists.'

Maia put aside her teacup. 'They were kind enough. I didn't understand a word they said, though. One of them spoke a little French, but I was too ill to remember

562

much of my French. I was in labour for two days.' She smiled, but her eyes were dark with remembered pain. 'My one comfort, the whole way through, was that I was certain the baby must be born dead.'

Robin whispered, 'But she wasn't.'

'No. Half-dead, the poor little thing. They christened her immediately – they called her Maria because they were convinced that in a few hours she'd be with the Mother of God. I was terribly ill – I had a fever. I bled and bled, and for days I didn't know where I was or what was going on. After about a fortnight, when I was beginning to be well again, I discovered that the baby was alive and that they'd found her a wet-nurse. They brought her to me. I remember that I took one look at the awful, drooling little thing, and then I just yelled at them to take her away. Vernon again, I thought – he was laughing at me. He had waited until I thought I was free, and then he'd left me with a monster.'

Maia took a deep breath. 'I thought I'd be able to leave her at the nunnery. I thought there'd be an orphanage or something. But they didn't want to take in a foreigner's sick child – or I couldn't make them understand what I wanted them to do.'

'So you brought her back to England?'

'Eventually. I drove away with the baby and the wet-nurse – can you imagine it, Robin, me, driving across Spain with a screaming baby – she seemed to scream most of the time – and a peasant girl who didn't speak a word of English?'

Robin smiled. 'Not really.'

'The journey was not one I care to remember. When I reached the coast of France I paid off the girl, and caught the Channel ferry. I'd bought some bottles and things in Boulogne, and I'd booked a private cabin on the boat. I didn't have a clue about babies. I had to ask one of the stewardesses how to make up the bottle and change a nappy. But the funny thing was—' Maia's brows contracted '—she was all right on the boat. She slept most of the way. Perhaps the motion of the waves rocked her to sleep. And when she was awake, she was nicer. She smiled at me. I'd never seen her smile before. I didn't think she could.'

'It takes a few weeks for a baby to learn to smile.' From the kitchen, Robin could hear the child laughing. 'And if she was ill after birth – and premature – it would probably take a while longer.'

'Anyway, as soon as I got to England I drove round Kent, looking for a place to leave her. I found somewhere quite easily – an orphanage near Maidstone. Then I went back to France for a while to recover my own health, and to work out what to do next. I thought I was free, you see. I knew that I wanted to run Merchants – I'd known that for ages. I made a plan of what I was going to do, and in September I sailed back to England.'

'And Maria?'

The room had darkened. Maia's face was shadowed. 'I didn't go back to the orphanage straight away. I was working so hard at Merchants . . . and to be honest I was still trying to pretend she didn't exist. But then one day I was visiting a supplier in Kent, and I thought I'd pop into the orphanage and pay the bill. They took me up to the room where they kept her. It was awful, Robin, you just can't imagine. They'd put all the handicapped babies together. Rows of iron cots. No toys – nothing to look at. Her bottle was propped up in the cot, they changed her in the cot. I don't think anyone ever held her. When I questioned the nurse, she told me that it was a waste of time doing anything for these babies other than feeding and bathing them.'

Robin recalled little Mary Lewis in the scullery in the terraced house. Crouched in her basket like a dog. Dr Mackenzie had told her that the child had been better off with her family than in an institution, but she had not then believed him.

Maia had begun to speak again. 'She'd even forgotten how to smile. She had awful sores on her body, and I didn't think she'd grown as much as she ought. I had to leave her there for a couple of weeks while I made arrangements, but I felt so guilty, walking away from her. And angry that I should feel guilty. After all, I hadn't wanted her in the first place. I'd enough on my plate trying to run Merchants. Anyway, I thought a private foster home would be the answer – a girl I knew who travelled a lot had sent her son to one. But it wasn't easy to find anyone who'd take on a child like Maria. I advertised through an agency – they interviewed dozens of women. Most of them only wanted the money, of course. Then they found me Annie Fowler and I knew straight away that she was the right person for Maria. I bought this cottage, and took Maria out of the orphanage and drove her down here. And do you know, almost as soon as she was away from that awful place, she began to look better?' Maia smiled at the memory. 'I drove down every now and then so that I could see that everything was all right. I thought that once I was certain that she was being decently cared for, I'd be able to stop visiting. Forget all about her again. But somehow I couldn't.'

There was a silence. Rain still trailed down the windowpanes, and a delicious scent of baking cake wafted through the house.

'So you brought me here,' said Robin slowly, 'to tell me that you couldn't marry Hugh because he would have found out about Maria?'

'More or less.'

'Because you thought that he might condemn you for not acknowledging your baby?'

'Something like that. I certainly didn't see how he could condone it.'

'He might have understood,' she said again. Though, remembering Hugh, whose honesty and simplicity had shone through him, she was uncertain.

'Rather a lot to ask, don't you think? "Oh, and by the way, Hugh, you don't mind that I murdered my husband and had his baby secretly, do you?"' Maia did not smile. 'Don't you think, Robin, that something like that would

565

have condemned our marriage from the start? That wrongdoing in the past has a way of tainting both the present and the future?'

There was a silence. Robin's fingers pleated the folds of her skirt.

'And besides, he might have pitied me. I couldn't have borne that.' Maia's expression was bleak. 'Anyway, Hugh wanted children.'

'He was good with children. He managed to get the dullest boys through their Oxbridge entrance.' Robin glanced at Maia. 'But you couldn't face going through that again after what happened with Maria?'

'Just the thought of it appalled me. Childbirth was such a . . . a *violation*. I suppose it might have been different . . . in a private clinic . . . with experienced doctors. Although I've been told that I'm too thin.' Maia grimaced, glancing down at herself. 'I don't have good childbearing hips. But no, there was more than that.' She rose from her seat and went to stand at the window. Robin heard her take a deep breath.

'On the day of your father's sixty-fifth birthday I went to London, to Harley Street, to consult a specialist about Maria. Annie Fowler had brought her up to an hotel the previous night – I met them at the hotel and drove them to the clinic. You see, I'd never consulted a doctor to find out whether Maria's condition was hereditary. I couldn't face it, I suppose. And as I'd never liked and didn't want children, I didn't think I needed to. I'd always thought . . .' Maia's voice trailed away.

'You'd always thought what, Maia?'

'That Maria is the way she is because of something in *me*. Because of what I was . . . because of what Vernon had done to me. And when I started seeing Vernon, after he had died . . . well, that just confirmed it. Madness, you see. And my father must have been mad, too, mustn't he, to take his own life.' She laughed, a hollow, dreadful sound. 'Three generations, Robin. Can you imagine what other horrors I might have brought into the world? Can you imagine what monstrous sons I might have presented to poor Hugh?'

Maia was silent for a moment, and then she added, 'I can remember every word the specialist said to me. "*In my professional opinion, Mrs Merchant, you cannot be sure that another child would not be similarly blighted.*" Well, I can't say that I was surprised. It was one of the reasons – one of the many, many reasons – that I always said that I'd never marry again.'

She turned back to Robin. 'You do see that I couldn't do that to Hugh? You do see, don't you? I'd been trying to break off the engagement for months anyway. I just couldn't find a way of doing it. I realized that I was going to have to make him hate me. So I did. It worked. Too well, far too well.' Her voice was taut with pain as she whispered, 'I had no idea that Hugh would go to Spain, Robin. None at all.'

The long silence was broken by the sound of the door opening. The little girl limped in, her good hand carefully gripping a plate bearing two small iced cakes.

At last, Maia spoke again. 'I'm leaving England soon, Robin. A friend of mine has asked me to go into business with him in New York. It'll give me a new start. I don't think I can bear to stay in this country much longer. There's nothing left for me here. I'm going to take Maria and Mrs Fowler with me, and find a house for the three of us. No more secrets. I am so tired of secrets.'

When Maia swung Maria up in her arms and kissed her, Robin knew that she had been wrong about one thing. Maia was capable of loving someone, after all.

People told Robin that time healed, but she was unconvinced. You just became more used to it, that was all. You stopped expecting the footsteps on the stairs to be Joe's, you stopped thinking, walking in the Fens, that the man leaning on the gate, smoking his pipe, was Hugh. Sometimes she even regretted the passing of those small, painful moments. They had made the people she loved live a little longer.

Christmas was the worst time. Herself, her parents, Merlin and Persia, trying to make the house in the Fens look busy. Richard and Daisy talked in a desultory fashion of moving back to London, but Robin suspected that they would never leave Blackmere Farm. She would never grow used to the change in her parents – to Daisy's need for her, or to Richard's old, tired face. To being their only child. Sometimes their love for her weighed her down.

She visited Helen in Richmond, and wrote to Maia in America. She knew that they had grown apart. Only sometimes did she glimpse the ties that still bound them, that were more, perhaps, than just a shared past, shared secrets.

Her work was hard; frequently she studied until midnight. She did not, like one of the other women on her course, faint at the sight of the corpse she was to dissect, and neither was she now upset by the occasional jibes of male students, or the neglect of some male professors. She worked with the dogged perseverance that she had come to realize was her greatest asset. She knew that when the time came, she would specialize in paediatrics. Maia's damaged child, and all those other children – children she had nursed in Spain and at the clinic, and poor little Mary Lewis in her basket – still haunted her. Reading book after book in the hospital library, Robin thought it more probable that Maria's handicaps were due to her premature, difficult birth than to an hereditary condition. She kept her convictions to herself, but felt, just for a moment, a flicker of her old passion. Women still died giving birth in insanitary conditions; babies were still unnecessarily damaged by incompetent midwives and doctors. If she no longer felt that she could change the world, she thought that she could perhaps improve her own little bit of it.

At the end of February it snowed, great white flakes that blistered the smoke-grey sky. She had felt restless all day, unable to settle to anything. Sleeping little the previous night, dreaming of Joe, she had woken with the tears cold on her lashes. On Wednesday afternoons, most of the other medical students pounded round a hockey field. An unattractive prospect – pleading a cold, Robin sloped away. Unable to face returning to the empty flat, she slipped into a cinema and bought a ticket. The film, already halfway through, was a complicated story about a factory girl and the son of a mill owner, made even more complicated by the factory girl's flashy twin sister. Robin yawned and dozed and wriggled in her seat.

She woke up a little when the newsreel began. Something about King George and Queen Mary, then a rather dull item on sugar beet farming in East Anglia. Then – and Robin straightened, flicking her fringe out of her eyes – a film of an exchange of prisoners in Spain. They looked, somehow, so familiar, those men. The corduroy trousers and jackets, the navy blue overalls. The thin, defeated faces, trying even now to smile. One of them gave the clenched fist salute, and Robin wanted to weep. Then the tall, thin, dark prisoner turned and look straight at the camera.

'*Joe!*' she cried aloud, and her hands slammed against her mouth. Most of the people in the row in front of her turned and shushed her, but she didn't even hear them. Standing up, gripping the back of the seat in front of her, she stared at the screen, her heart pounding.

The newsreel finished, and was replaced by a cartoon. Gazing at the inane, mouthing creatures, she wanted to shout to the projectionist, to demand him to turn back the reel. Someone grabbed her sleeve, telling her to sit down, and she stumbled back into her seat, her legs refusing to bear her any longer. After only a short while her elation died. She had made a mistake, she told herself. She had thought that she had seen Joe so often since she had left Spain – a black-haired man striding along Oxford Street, his jacket out at the elbows – a voice in the queue in Woolworths. Each time she had been mistaken. She sank down, a dark despair washing over her. Yet she did not leave the cinema – instead, she sat through the cartoon and a short film about Canada and the factory girl's romance all over again. By the time the newsreel began for the second time she had gnawed her fingernails to the quick. She looked up, hardly able to focus, and saw him again. There was a mark on the side of his head that she thought was a scar. She refused to let herself cry for joy because then she would not see him clearly.

She sat through the entire programme two more times. Each time it was the same: as soon as she saw him she was certain, but the moment his features disappeared from the screen her doubts returned. When she left the cinema and went out into the night, snowflakes kissed her skin. Skipping a lecture, she returned to the cinema the following afternoon. By the time she had sat through the programme four more times, she was convinced that Joe was alive.

Joe made his own way across France. The Quaker organization that had overseen the exchange of prisoners provided him with a small amount of money and a ticket for the boat train. He had evaded their offers of an escort because he needed to be by himself.

He travelled slowly, resting frequently. The headaches that he had suffered for months after he had been injured had gone, thank God, but his right arm still hurt. A Quaker doctor had checked his health before sending him across the border, and Joe had sensed the reality behind the encouraging noises. He knew, though, that he had been lucky not to lose his arm. Just as he had been lucky not to die of the head wound, and lucky not to be shot by his Nationalist guards. It was just that he did not feel particularly lucky. Only terribly tired.

On the train to Paris, a young man, looking at him curiously, asked him whether he had fought in Spain. Joe shook his head, and looked resolutely out of the window. Conversation died, and the young man shrugged his shoulders impatiently and returned to his newspaper.

For what he knew would be the last time, he thought through the events of the last eight months. The shrapnel that had wounded him at Brunete; then, waking from unconsciousness God knows how many days later to find himself in a Spanish hospital. A blur of pain and sickness and unfamiliar voices and faces. They had put him in an ambulance, and he remembered how it had lurched over the rough ground. They had been ferrying him to the American hospital in Madrid, but the ambulance had lost its way and strayed into Nationalist-held territory, and both the driver and his stretcher-bearers and the four casualties inside the ambulance had been taken prisoner. They had made him walk for a while, stumbling blindly across the stony earth, and then they had thrown him into a lorry. He had ended up in a Nationalist gaol along with a dozen other members of the International Brigades.

He said a final mental goodbye to the men with whom he had been imprisoned. To the men who had died of sickness or injury, and to those who had been taken out of their cells and shot. To those who had died refusing to change sides and fight for Fascism, and to those who had died because they had looked the wrong way, or said the wrong thing. He examined all those things one last time, and then he put them away, knowing that he could bear to see them no longer. He would talk to no-one about Spain, not even to Robin.

On the ferry, he stood on the deck, letting the fine spray wash over him. For eight months now he had doubted that he had a future; he had become accustomed to that uncertainty, and found himself unable to plan. Just for a moment he felt a surge of anger that he had lost what had once been precious to him. He had some movement in his right hand but not enough, he knew, for the delicate manipulation of lenses and dials, or for the meticulous work of developing film. He experienced a brief, bitter grief, and then both that and the anger left him. All that had gone before his imprisonment seemed tinged with unreality – a game, almost, that he had fleetingly played. He could not return to what he had been before. He knew, picturing it in his mind's eye, that he would not be able to bear the noise and bustle of London. He would begin to get well again when there was silence and hills. He found himself longing, as he never had before, for the village where he had been born. He thought that he probably would end up doing what he had tried to avoid all along – helping his father to run the mill. It seemed as good as anything else. His need to be in the centre of things had vanished, and would never return. He would be content to be on the margins, watching.

The Quaker administrator, checking her lists, had told him that Robin had left Spain the previous September. He needed the hills and the cold fresh air, but most of all he needed Robin. When he closed his eyes and thought that he might hold her in his arms in less than a day, tears mingled with the salt spray on his face.

Robin could not concentrate on her work, and could not sleep at night. She expected Joe every moment of the day. Each morning, when she left the flat, she scribbled a note explaining where she was. She left the door unlocked, knowing that he would have no key.

On 12 March, German troops marched into Austria. The fear that once Robin had believed only she felt could be glimpsed in the eyes of every passer-by. The tension was almost tangible, and she knew that people's refusal to talk about the situation in Europe was due now to apprehension, and not to complacency. Yet the newspaper headlines had ceased to frighten her. She was waiting for Joe – she existed each day in an agonizing, euphoric limbo – and yet a small part of her had found peace, and was quietly convinced that together she and Joe would be able to endure whatever the future brought.

On her way back to the Tube she saw the aeroplanes

flying overhead, painting the London sky with arcs and whorls of white. She stood for a moment watching them, and then she walked into the station and bought her ticket. The carriage of the underground train was half empty; a few tired housewives drooped over string bags of shopping, a couple of schoolboys swapped cigarette cards. Usually Robin studied the day's lecture notes as she travelled. Today, she could not.

The train rattled into a station. Only four more stops to go. Each day, her impatience to reach her home increased. On the adjacent line another train pulled in.

She saw him then. Sitting almost opposite her in the second train, his elbow on the back of the seat, his hand propping up his head. Joe turned and looked slowly through both windows at her. She saw the angry red mark of the scar on his temple, and the pallor of his skin. And the smile that suddenly lit his face. Robin's hands pressed flat against the glass as though she could reach through it and touch him.

Then she ran towards the door and across the platform and up the stairs. At the end of the corridor, Joe held out his arms to her.

THE END

THE SECRET YEARS
by Judith Lennox

During that last, shimmeringly hot summer of 1914, four young people played with seeming innocence in the gardens of Drakesden Abbey. Nicholas and Lally were the children of the great house, set in the bleak and magical Fen country and the home of the Blythe family for generations; Thomasine was the unconventional niece of two genteel maiden aunts in the village. And Daniel – Daniel was the son of the local blacksmith, a fiercely independent, ambitious boy who longed to break away from the stifling confines of his East Anglian upbringing. As the drums of war sounded in the distance, the Firedrake, a mysterious and ancient Blythe family heirloom disappeared, setting off a chain of events which they were powerless to control.

The Great War changed everything, and both Nicholas and Daniel returned from the front damaged by their experiences. Thomasine, freed from the narrow disciplines of her childhood, and enjoying the new hedonism which the twenties brought, thought that she could escape from the ties of childhood which bound her to both Nicholas and Daniel. But the passions and enmities of their shared youth had intensified in the passing years, and Nicholas, Thomasine, Lally and Daniel all had to experience tragedy and betrayal before the Firedrake made its reappearance and, with it, a new hope for the future.

0 552 14331 6